BREAKING ROSALIND

GIGI STYX

AUTHOR'S NOTE

This dark romance book romanticizes psychopathic behavior for entertainment. If you're offended by Stockholm syndrome and prolonged scenes of torture at the hands of a deranged maniac who's always one step ahead of the heroine, do not continue reading.

TRIGGER WARNINGS

This is a dark romance that includes dub-con, graphic depictions of torture and violence, and sexually explicit scenes. If any of this content is triggering for you, please do not read this book.

Abduction
Adoption
Anal sex
Assassination
Baby oil
Blackmail
Bondage
Branding
Breath play
Candle play
Castration
Cavity searches
Chastity
Child abuse (backstory)
Cock slapping
Cutting
Degradation
Dismemberment
Drugging
Dubious consent
Evisceration
Extreme edging
Face sitting
Female genital stitching
Forced arousal
Forced pregnancy (backstory)
Gags
Gore
Grooming (backstory)
Gun play

Hate sex
Hebephilia
Humiliation
Inappropriate use of a 12-inch barrel antique pistol
Inappropriate use of surgical equipment
Kidnapping
Knife play
Leroi slander
Mass murder
Matricide
Medical play
Memory of animal cruelty (not by the main characters)
Mind games
Mummification (not auto erotic)
Murder
Mutilation
Patricide
Pet play
Primal kink
PTSD
Revenge
Scars
Sensory deprivation
Stockholm syndrome
Suspension
Russian roulette
Teenage pregnancy (backstory)
Temperature play
Torture
Toys
Tracker insertion
Unnecessary surgery
Veganism slander
Verbal denigration
Workplace sexual harassment

Reader discretion is advised. If you find any of these topics distressing, please proceed with caution or consider choosing a different book. Your mental health matters.

For all the girls who want the villain to fuck them like a psycho.

PROLOGUE

ROSALIND

Infiltrate the mansion.

Abduct a four-year-old girl.

Kill anyone in my way. Even if it's Mom.

The average eighteen-year-old shouldn't be so proficient in weapons, but nothing about my life has been normal since Mom married a predator. My stepfather is one of the Galliano brothers, a crime family infamous for drug and human trafficking.

I didn't choose this world, but after years of being the victim, I'm ready to become the villain.

Sunlight beats down on my back like a disapproving parent as I creep around the garden's perimeter. A tall fence blocks my view of its interior, and the roses climbing on them release floral bursts that mingle with the scent of fear.

At the first sound of Miranda's soft giggle, my heart pounds hard enough to burst.

She's close.

Crouching low, I inch my way through a gap in the hedge I made earlier. I keep my footsteps light over the soft grass and hold my breath. No amount of training can stop the leaves from rustling against my bulletproof jacket.

The noise can't be helped. The mansion's security system has four blind spots, and only one of them gets me close to Miranda without alerting the guards.

I catch a glimpse of her crouched in front of a pond, her brown hair styled into a cascade of ringlets so stiff they remain still in the breeze. They've dressed her in a frilly pink gown with a tutu skirt that barely covers her underwear, paired with rhinestone sandals that shimmer in the sunlight like diamonds.

My nostrils flare, and my hands curl into fists.

This is how they clothe her in between my scheduled visits?

They thought they could banish me to boarding school and do whatever they pleased with Miranda. I'm not the weak, sniveling child they can banish. Thanks to their neglect, I made connections. Got trained. Now, I'm back for Miranda.

"Miri?" I whisper.

She turns her head to the left.

"Behind you," I say.

Straightening, she turns around. The moment our gazes lock, my heart melts, and my chest fills with warmth. Photos could never capture her sparkling eyes or dimpled cheeks. She's the most beautiful child in the world.

"Rosa?" she asks.

I give her an eager nod. "That's right."

Her deep blue eyes widen. "What are you doing here?"

"Come to me, and I'll tell you." I reach out a hand and beckon her into the blind spot.

Miranda glances to the right, where Mom sits on a bench at the edge of the pond, her face buried in a tablet. Hatred sears my veins, and my fingers itch to claw out her eyes. What kind of mental gymnastics must go through her mind each morning when she sees this little girl, or is she still so blinded by all the wealth?

I hold my breath, praying to anyone who will listen that she doesn't look our way.

Moments pass, and Miranda still hasn't moved. Anxiety coils through my insides like a constrictor and squeezes tight. If I step into the garden and pick her up, I won't just alert Mom. Every security guard working for my corrupt stepfather will be on us in seconds with guns drawn.

"Hey," I say, my voice rising with desperation. "I brought you a gift."

Miranda tilts her head, her rounded features sparking with interest. "What is it?"

I reach into my cargo pocket and pull out a box. "Here. Another unicorn."

She moves closer, her steps tentative. I keep my features light and even to mask my inner turmoil. Frustration roils through my gut and my breath turns shallow.

What lies have Matteo and Mom spewed to make a four-year-old girl so wary?

She reaches for the box, just as Mom's sharp voice says, "Miriam, come away."

My jaw clenches.

Her name is Miranda.

Mom shoots up from the bench, dropping the tablet. My heart plummets into my stomach, bringing up a wave of panic.

Time has run out, and so have my chances for a peaceful abduction. I burst out of the bushes and scoop Miranda into my arms.

Eyes widening, Mom reaches into her pocket and produces a pistol.

Shit.

"Drop my daughter!" She points the gun at my head.

"Your daughter?"

Forcing Miranda's face into my chest, I draw my weapon and shoot her between the eyes, releasing over four years of resentment.

Despite my use of a silencer, Miranda screams, breaking my moment of relief. Mom falls to the ground just as sirens blare from the mansion, filling the air with the chaos. Alarm explodes through my insides, and I disappear into the bushes, clinging onto the wailing child.

"Hold tight, Miri."

"Put me down!" she cries. "You're hurting me!"

My heart shatters into jagged pieces. When she's old enough to understand, I'll explain that this is for her own good. With me as her parent, she can have a normal life.

For now, I'll withstand her hatred.

I run alongside the hedges, my breath coming in ragged gasps. The sirens grow louder, as do Miranda's cries. There's no way we're getting out of here unnoticed, but I've spent four years planning for every possible scenario.

An armored car pulls up, its engines still running. I fling open the back door and jump into the seat, still clinging onto Miranda.

"What took you so long?" Britt's blonde head whips to the side.

"Drive." I pull the door shut.

The central locking system whirs into place, and the car hurtles down the tree-lined drive that runs between Matteo's mansion and the neighbors.

Miranda's tiny fists pound on my shoulders as she screams for help, and I hold her close. "It's okay, Miri," I murmur. "Everything's going to be alright. I'm here to protect you."

Britt slams on the brakes, making Miranda and me lurch forward.

"Fuck!" she screams.

My head snaps up to the windshield, where an SUV blocks the road ahead. When I turn to the back window, another car closes in on us from behind.

"We're trapped," she snarls.

"Miri, listen carefully." I stare into her huge, blue eyes, trying to convey the intensity of the situation. "Those men are going to shoot at us. Hide behind the seat, so you don't get hurt."

Her bottom lip trembles. For a brief second, I wonder if she'll try to break free again, but she nods.

I release my grip on Miranda, and she ducks down, staying close to the floor. My pulse has never beaten so hard or fast, but I've already prepared for a blockade. As I reach for a helmet, the SUV's back door opens, and a man steps out. It's Matteo.

Seeing him is a punch to the gut. Shock seizes my chest in a clawed grip, stealing my air. My blood chills, and goosebumps spread across my skin. I timed this attack to avoid my stepfather. He was supposed to be away on business.

Bitter memories flood my mind, threatening to drown me in a

whirlpool of betrayal and pain. I struggle for breath, my pulse quickening, my feet rooting to the tarmac.

"What are you doing?" Britt yells from the front seat. "Get rid of them."

My best friend's voice jolts me back to reality. I snap on the helmet, reach for the grenade launcher beneath the front passenger seat, and throw open the door. "Watch Miri."

Stepping out, I sling the weapon on my shoulder. One of the men flanking Matteo fires a shot that hits me square on the chest. My armor absorbs the impact of the shot, pain exploding through my rib cage. I rock backward and manage to catch myself before I fall.

"Don't shoot," Matteo yells. "They've got my daughter."

My lip curls, and prickly heat flares across my chest. That's the first time my stepfather has admitted to being Miranda's father. He raises his palms in a gesture to surrender, but nothing this bastard could say or do will stop me from taking my baby.

Aiming at Matteo and his goons, I pull the trigger. A grenade flies out and explodes with a deafening roar, sending out an explosion of shrapnel and fire. A rain of bullets hit me in the back as I dive into the back seat.

Britt accelerates, and the car lurches through the wreckage. Triumph fills my chest as we speed away toward the airport. This unauthorized side quest will get us into trouble when we return to HQ, but this was the whole reason why I trained for four years to become an assassin.

My recruiter at the Moirai said I would become strong enough to take out any target... And he was right. Because of him, I'm able to take back my daughter.

I turn to where Miranda crouches and pull her onto my lap and check her for injuries. "Are you okay, baby girl?"

"What was that?" she asks through hiccupping sobs.

I bury my face in her ringlets and sigh. "You're finally coming home."

ONE

ROSALIND

People think an assassin's life is glamorous, but it's full of indignities. Nobody talks about the grueling torture training, tedious escape techniques, or the stomach-churning process of building a resistance to alcohol, drugs, and poisons.

I've crawled through alligator-infested sewers, rifled through rotting guts to find a microchip, and once, I fucked a decrepit old billionaire into a sex-induced heart attack.

Of all the demeaning shit I've endured for the job, none has been worse than being rejected by a man I never wanted.

Leroi slams me against his living room wall. It smells freshly painted, and the sofas look brand new. I make a note that something messy must have happened since my last visit. When he presses the barrel of a gun into my temple, I'm forced to stop spying and look up into eyes that burn with hatred.

I despise older men, even if our age difference is only six years, yet I play the part of a woman desperately in love. Arching my back, I push my breasts into his broad chest and wrap a leg around his ass, trying to get him aroused.

My horny act worked fine enough with Leroi until now. It's

never failed on a red-blooded man, except that Leroi acts like his heart pumps cryogenic fluid. His personality is equally frigid. I've never once seen this bastard crack a smile.

He flashes his teeth. "First, I told you never to come here uninvited."

The sneer in his voice makes me want to stab him with my emergency syringe, but I need to keep up the act. Leroi is the key to gaining access to the real targets—his cousins, Benito and Cesare Montesano, mafia princes with million-dollar bounties on their heads, protected by an army of loyal henchmen.

Roman, their older brother and leader, is on death row. The client wants to leave his demise to the electric chair.

"Leroi," I whine. "Please."

He slides the gun's barrel down the side of my face in a mockery of a caress. "Then I told you never to return."

"But I need you," I whisper.

His gun slides over my bottom lip, smearing my red lipstick. "Now I'm thinking the only way to make you listen is with a bullet."

Anyone acting so thirsty for a man deserves to be shot. Leroi has told me to fuck off in a dozen humiliating ways, but I have a mission.

I slip my hand between our bodies, trying to reach for his cock, but he snatches my wrist with a punishing grip. Sweat breaks out across my brow. Seduction training wasn't part of my academy's curriculum, and I'm naturally inclined to despise men. My boss knows I'm no honey trap, but he always sets me up to fail.

Shit. If I can't maintain this man's interest, then I'll never get invited to the Montesano mansion and I'll never reach my targets.

Movement at the far end of the living room snatches my attention. I glance over his shoulder and lock gazes with a tiny blonde who can't be much older than Miranda.

Bile rises to the back of my throat. Leroi must be like Matteo, dating age-appropriate women in public, but privately, favoring the young. I'm tempted to stick Leroi with the syringe, but I'm already in enough trouble with the Moirai.

Instead, I spew some bullshit so heinous that Leroi just laughs. He hurls me out of his apartment, and I make a mental note to myself: Men with lumps of coal instead of hearts don't react well to the news of fake pregnancies.

I hang around outside his closed door for several minutes, wondering how the hell to salvage my mission. Maybe I could arrange the blonde's unfortunate disappearance?

No way. I'm a murderer, not a monster. Monsters leave their victims alive to wallow in trauma and pain.

With a sigh, I hobble down the hallway toward the elevator. Fuck Leroi and his humongous dick. That soulless bastard made me break my fake Louboutins.

———

At this time of the morning, most of the rush hour traffic has died down, leaving the streets relatively quiet. I hobble past office blocks, apartment buildings, and the occasional cafe, daring anyone to ogle me in my slutty red dress.

When a black van slows in my periphery, every fine hair on the back of my neck stands on end. This vehicle can only belong to the Moirai Group, New Alderney's largest firm of assassins, and my employer of fourteen years.

The vehicle makes a right turn at the next intersection and stops in my path, making my steps falter.

Shit.

I'm supposed to be in bed with Leroi, pursuing pillow talk, not pounding the pavement.

There are only so many times I can bullshit my way out of this failing mission, and I've already exceeded my quota.

As I approach the van, a side door slides open, revealing my recruiter and handler. In the almost fifteen years I've known him, Gunther has been perpetually thirty-five. He flashes me a grin of ice-white teeth, his pale blue eyes glittering with suppressed annoyance.

I step into the van, take a seat, and try not to sigh.

"What progress are you making with infiltrating the Montesano stronghold?" he demands.

"Leroi only communicates with his cousins at the nightclub or via text," I reply.

"So, what's he messaging them?"

My jaw tightens. It's this level of intrusiveness that wrecked my progress with Leroi. After catching me snooping through his texts, he choked me to the brink of unconsciousness. The only thing that saved my life was humping his leg until I climaxed.

That was enough to convince him I manipulated him into breath play by fucking with his phone. He kicked me out for topping from the bottom, and I left with my life.

"He's deleting those messages now," I lie with a shrug.

Gunther's eyes narrow, an impressive feat considering all the Botox. "Is he getting suspicious?"

"Not of me." I smooth down my mahogany hair. "Leroi is completely infatuated."

He turns his gaze to a laptop, and some of the tension in my shoulders melts. "Keep working on him," he mutters. "He might be helpful with a potential job that's paying multiple seven figures."

I perk up. "Who do I need to kill?"

Gunther chuckles, the sound mocking and harsh. "Nice try, but you're still demoted."

"This makes no sense. I'm the closest we've ever gotten to the Montesano—"

"The last time we trusted you on a large-scale mission, you damaged two-hundred grand's worth of assets on a side quest."

My jaw clenches. He wouldn't understand, even if I explained why I went to rescue my daughter. Gunther would only use his knowledge of Miranda as a weapon to get me under his control.

"Didn't you make mistakes when you were eighteen, or are you too elderly to remember that far back?" I ask.

His amusement fades, leaving his face a tight mask. "Don't tell me you're falling for Leroi Montesano."

"I prefer men in their twenties."

"Some say you don't prefer men at all," he mutters.

No amount of nips or tucks or fillers can compensate for

Gunther's antiquated views. No amount of time can make this decrepit old bastard forget I once rejected his advances.

He and others from the Moirai think I'm in a relationship with Britt because she helped on my side quest to save Miranda and doesn't shun me like everyone else, but we're just good friends. She's the only person in the Moirai who isn't a backstabber.

I'm not looking for any form of romantic relationship—I fuck enough assholes as part of my job. Besides, if I didn't want Gunther ten years ago when he didn't look half as gruesome, I sure as hell won't want him now.

My gaze wanders to the laptop. "We both know I can complete this job. Authorize me to take out the brothers directly—"

"Denied." He leans back in his seat.

"Why?"

"The client wants a swift execution with no chance of retaliation, which means simultaneous assassinations and no loose ends."

Pursing my lips, I exhale my frustration in an outward breath. Gunther has already demoted me to an analyst. If I tell him the truth about losing my connection with Leroi, I may as well dig my own grave.

"Leroi isn't taking anyone into the Montesano estate. Let me hook up with one of the brothers."

"Impossible," he says. "The oldest is safely behind bars, and the middle brother hasn't shown an interest in anyone since his broken engagement."

I rub the back of my neck and sigh. "You're just reciting information I gave you."

Gunther double-clicks a recent photo I took of Cesare the last time I spotted him at the Phoenix nightclub. "And of course, the youngest is so protected, he only gets to fuck the help."

Cesare Montesano is classically handsome with sharp blue eyes and a Roman nose but hides his masculine beauty with piercings, floppy hair that he ties back, and tattoos.

At twenty-four, he's four years younger than me. Bestowed with two parents, siblings, cousins, and a spectacular mansion at the top of Alderney Hill, he's had a dream life. While I was creating cadavers, he was dissecting them at Beaumont Central Medical School. And when he dropped out, his family handed him a nightclub with an attached restaurant.

I shake my head. What a waste of gifts.

The picture disappears, bringing my attention back to Gunther. "So you see, the only way into the family is through a trusted relative."

I reach for the laptop and open another file. "Or there's the bodyguard, Gilberto Agostini. He drives into the club with the brothers. He's at their house every day, is a natural flirt, and has a closer relationship to the family than Leroi."

Gunther slams the laptop lid shut. "You're not authorized to approach him."

"Why not?"

"Because another operative is working on him." Before I can call him out on his bullshit, he rises off his seat and flings open the door, letting in the scent of a freshly mowed lawn. "On the subject of family... How's your sister?"

My stomach plummets, and I glance past Gunther's smug features to what's beyond the van's exit. We're at the gates of Tourgis Academy.

He's threatening Miranda.

Who is, of course, *not* my little sister.

I don't correct his mistake. Only three other people know Miranda's true parentage. I shot one between the eyes and took care of the second with a grenade launcher. Britt is the third, and I trust her with my life.

"She'll be fourteen now," Gunther says, his voice carrying a hint of nostalgia.

I maintain a poker face, using all my training to appear detached. This is exactly why I've kept Miranda at a distance. Gunther will exploit any vulnerability to keep me under his control.

"Same age you were when I recruited you from your academy."

Dread crushes my chest like a boulder. Gunther's message is

loud and clear. If I don't find a way to infiltrate the Montesano mansion, he'll come for Miranda.

TWO

CESARE

Medical school never taught me how to bring someone back from waterboarding. Maybe I would have stuck around if they'd taught us how to revive them from lethal torture.

I kneel beside Ricky Ferraro's unmoving form and pull the wet cloth off his face. The snitch's scraggly face is as still as death, and his lips have turned blue. The hose I used to drown him lies at my side, still pumping out a steady stream of cold water across the bathroom floor.

"You still with me, Rickyboy?" I slide my fingers beneath his jaw, but there's no pulse.

Shit.

My gaze darts around the tiled space, part of me expecting someone to barge in and demand to know what the hell I'm doing with a wet corpse. Thank fuck everyone's too excited with my brother's release from prison to poke their nose in my business.

Another One Bites The Dust by Queen pumps in from the dance floor, giving me an idea. It's about 100 beats per minute, the perfect tempo for cardiopulmonary resuscitation.

Interlocking my fingers, I position my hands on his chest and begin compressions in time with the music.

"One, two, three, four. Another one bites the dust," I chant alongside Freddy. "One, two, three, four. Come on, you dead cunt."

I pause for a few beats and stare down at his pallid face, expecting him to jerk or cough or show some sign of life. He doesn't.

My eyes narrow. If I gave a shit about Ricky, I would pinch his nose shut, tilt back his head, and blow oxygen into his lungs, but there's no fucking way I'm locking lips with that slimy motherfucker.

When I deliver a precordial thump to his sternum, Ricky doesn't so much as twitch.

"Don't you dare check out on me now," I snarl. "I haven't finished waterboarding you yet."

The door opens, letting in a blast of music and a scream. I raise my head and lock eyes with our new bartender, Tania.

"Close the door," I snarl.

Tania rushes toward us, letting the door swing shut. I curl my lip, not bothering to hide my contempt. How typical of her to assume I want her company.

"Oh my god," she screeches. "Is he okay?"

She stands in the stream of hose water, staring down at the unresponsive man tied to an upturned chair.

"What do you think?" I ask, my voice flat.

"Did you—" Her eyes widen.

Rising to my feet, I wait for her to put together all the pieces. Despite the two-inch long lashes and bubblegum-pink hair, Tania isn't stupid. She studies biomedical sciences at Alderney State University. When I interviewed her for the job, she was intelligent enough to suck my cock to perfection.

"Did I what?" I ask.

"You killed him." She pats down her apron and extracts a phone.

"What are you doing?" I ask, my lips curling into a smile.

"Calling 911."

I spring into action, my fingers curling around her neck.

"Cesare—"

"The Phoenix is under new management." I slam her against the wooden door, making her features twist with agony. "Now that my brother is out of prison, everyone who fucks with the Montesano family will end up like this dead motherfucker, or worse."

Her phone falls to the ground and slides across the stream of water.

"Please," she rasps, her hands trying to pull my fingers off her throat.

"Please what, Tania?" I say with a grin and tighten my grip around her neck. "Use your words."

Her face turns a shade of red that clashes with the pink hair and matching brows. Tears run down her cheeks as she chokes, streaming in rivulets of black mascara.

She moves her lips but can't make any sounds. It isn't until she falls limp that I realize she's fainted.

"Shit." I release her neck, letting her crumple to the floor like a marionette with its strings cut.

The door opens again. Gil lumbers in, filling the bathroom with his massive frame. Light bounces off his shaved head as his gaze bounces from Ricky's dead and bound body to Tania's.

Gil once took a bullet for Dad, which elevated him to the family's golden enforcer. When Dad died and my brother, Roman, got locked up, Gil became his right hand. He's like another older brother and is loyal as fuck. But at times like this, he's a nuisance.

Lips tightening, he steps inside and fixes me with a glare. "Is she dead?"

"You think I'd kill a girl in my own nightclub?"

"Cesare," Gil growls.

"She passed out," I mutter.

With a grunt, he walks across the bathroom and turns off the hose. "Get changed out of those wet clothes and go join Roman in the VIP section."

"You're no longer in charge," I say. "Roman's out of prison and—"

"There's a dead body, a living witness, and a homicide detective walking around the club looking for an excuse to send Roman back to death row," he snarls. "Put on something dry, let me clean up this mess, and go take a walk in front of some fucking cameras."

My jaw clenches. A man gets one little drug problem, and he's forever treated like a kid incapable of creating his own alibi.

———

About an hour later, I sit behind the desk, watching the club from a wall of screens broadcasting various locations around the building.

I wanted to catch up with Roman, considering today is his first taste of freedom, but he's too busy stalking the daughter of the man who framed him for murder. He stands on the edge of the dance floor, watching a group of women performing synchronized movements.

My cousin, Leroi, sits in the VIP section with a petite woman who's the opposite of his usual tall brunettes. Like Roman, Leroi is nine years older than me, but has worked as a hitman for two decades.

Leroi is a fucking hero and the reason my big brother is free. Earlier in the week, Leroi massacred every cocksucker connected to Roman's conviction and found a bunch of computer files that proved his innocence.

And what was my part in this daring mission?

Gil blocked me from leaving the club the entire night, saying Leroi didn't need my help. When the cops visited the next day asking where I was the night of the mass murder, Gil replayed video footage and lined up over thirty people to give me an alibi.

Roman rises off his seat and hugs Leroi, which is something my big brother didn't do when I met him moments after he was released. Old memories resurface of how it felt to be excluded by my brothers and their friends for being too little.

When I was young, the nine-year age gap was as wide as Lake Alderney. Now that I'm twenty-four, it's just as vast. Part of it is because we're so different. The other part is a secret I want to forget.

Leaning back, I clench my fists. "Fuckers," I mutter under my breath. "Nothing ever changes."

I imagined the day of Roman's release differently, with the family celebrating his freedom at home around the dining table like old times. Instead, I'm on the outskirts in my own club, watching Roman strengthen old bonds.

My gaze wanders to the screen covering the entrance, where a familiar-looking woman strolls in, wearing a little black dress that showcases her long legs and barely covers her pert tits.

Stifling a groan, I kick myself for lusting after Leroi's clingy ex. She's the hottest woman who ever stepped into the Phoenix, yet she chose my cousin, not me. Because Leroi is a man in his fucking prime, in control of his fucking life, and isn't protected by an army of armed babysitters.

I shouldn't want her, yet she never fails to steal my attention. Besides belonging to someone else, she's a nightmare.

Last time she was here, she threw a drink over a waitress who flirted with Leroi. Now, she stalks his apartment like he's the only man in New Alderney with a functioning dick.

I rise from my seat and jog around the desk to get a front-row seat of Leroi's showdown with that crazy bitch. After my cousin puts her in her place, she's going to need a cock to cry on.

THREE

This is turning out to be my worst mission. Gunther has never once mentioned Miranda, but then, I've always exceeded his expectations. Until now. The look in his eyes yesterday put me on red alert. I'm already researching affordable ways to send her to school out of state.

All I want is to keep my daughter safe and have a real relationship with her instead of the sporadic visits I barely manage because of my job. She's fourteen already, and I have four years before she goes to college. All my plans are turning to shit because I can't gather the information Gunther needs to execute a hit on the brothers.

This mess is all because of Leroi Montesano. Unlike most targets, who are easy to manipulate, his heart is encased in an armored tank. I doubt he even loves himself.

I stride past the club's coat check and through the double doors that lead to the dance floor. Bass music pounds through my bones, reminding me to at least act like I'm here to have fun.

Plastering on a smile, I walk through the club in time with the beat and roll my shoulders to the melody. The attention I attract is immediate, because in this black body con dress and red stilettos, I look down to fuck.

If Leroi is here tonight, he'll be sitting in the VIP section, exchanging words with the middle Montesano brother, Benito. I wasn't lying to Gunther when I told him this was how they communicate. It's almost impossible to eavesdrop on someone within a cacophony of conversations and loud music.

As I pass the dance floor, I catch my first glimpse of the oldest brother, and my steps falter. The alert I set up on the Montesano family informed me that Roman had been released from prison, but I didn't expect him to be at the club so soon.

Roman stands at the edge of the VIP section, dressed in a black suit, looking like he spent his entire time behind bars lifting weights. He's talking to Benito, and they're staring at a group of women making synchronized movements like they're in an aerobics class.

I reach the cordoned-off area, and Benito's features flicker with recognition. He's seen me here dozens of times with Leroi, so he steps aside to let me in. My heart skips a beat the way it always does when I'm close to a target.

Attacking the Montesano brothers in their own club without backup or bulletproof armor would be suicide. Most of the people inside are connected to the family and would strike back with lethal force.

I find Leroi sitting in a leather armchair, nursing a tumbler of liquor. As soon as our gazes meet, his eyes narrow. I pull back my shoulders, stick out my chest, and force myself not to cringe.

He rises out of his seat and towers over me, even though I stand five-eleven in my heels. The hatred in his eyes burns through what's left of my self-respect, but I power through.

"Hey," I say with a broad smile and attempt to spew an apology.

Before I can even finish speaking, Leroi cuts me off with an insult. Powered by the threat hanging over Miranda, I let his harsh words slide over my head and raise a hand to cup his cheek.

Leroi snatches my wrist, spins me around and holds me in a painful arm lock. I grind my ass into his crotch and moan, trying to get him aroused. His deep snarl sends a shiver down my spine that settles in my pussy.

"How many times do I need to tell you to fuck off?" he growls, his hot breath fanning my ear. "It's almost like you're begging for death."

My heart races, and adrenaline surges through my veins. The muscles of my core constrict, and all sensation travels to my clit.

Torture training has fucked up my fight-or-flight responses. Whenever I'm in the presence of a dominant man who doesn't want me dead, my body automatically prepares me to fuck.

"Please, Leroi," I beg with a groan. "You're the only man who can make me come."

This always worked on him before. Or it did until he moved in that little blonde. Now, he's fixated on her. Tossing me aside, he strides out of the VIP section toward the group of women his cousins were watching on the dance floor. My heart plummets to my stomach, which churns with mounting dread.

I can't lose Leroi. Especially not after Gunther's threat to recruit Miranda. I need to say something—anything to get back his attention.

As I teeter after him on my heels, a set of strong arms encircle my waist. That's when I inhale the mingled scents of earth and smoke. Annoyance prickles my skin and I ready myself to break this guy's ribs.

"Fuck off," I snap, my head whipping aside. "Let go—"

I lock gazes with Cesare, the youngest Montesano brother, and my breath catches. The shock must register on my face because he smirks.

He's even more handsome up close, with a golden complexion, sanpaku eyes, sculpted cheekbones, and a chiseled jaw. His facial piercings are gone, so there's nothing impairing the sharp angles of his face or his raw sex appeal.

What should be intimidating is softened by messy strands of raven-black hair that beg to be tamed. The playful glimmer in his pale irises scream mischief.

"Why would a beautiful woman like you harass a man who's moved onto someone else?" he growls in my ear.

My pulse quickens. I have one of my targets within my grasp. Why the fuck am I bothering with Leroi? If I can get Cesare to take me home, I could gather intel on the Montesano estate and get Gunther off my back.

I run through everything I know about Cesare. He's the baby of the family. Always at his mother's side until she left. Since he dropped out of medical school, he's been surrounded by bodyguards, which is why he only ever fucks his employees. I wonder if that will ease off, now that the oldest brother is out of prison.

My mind runs through tactics. Which persona would work best on Leroi's cousin? Simpering only works until the cum has cooled. Bitter experience has taught me that these types of men love the chase. They're just like cats. Making things too easy for them will get you dropped like a broken toy.

If I'm going to get Cesare to fuck me, then I'll have to make him sweat.

"Hey." He squeezes me around the middle. "I'm talking to you."

"Men who know how to please a woman are hard to find," I say over the sound of the music. "Let go of me. I want a screaming orgasm, not a few lackluster pumps."

Cesare flashes his teeth. "I could make you scream."

"You wish," I say with a grin. "My pussy aches for a man who knows what he's doing. Not some kid."

His smile falters, and I know I've struck a chord. There's almost a decade's age difference between Roman and Cesare. As the youngest brother, he's probably had enough of being treated like a child.

"Younger men have shorter refractory periods," he says.

"What does that even mean?" I reply with what I hope is a ditsy smile.

His chest inflates. It's a sign that he enjoys my attention or loves being the source of information. Either way, he's giving me plenty to manipulate. "A short refractory period means I can fuck you all night before I'm spent."

My gaze drops to his full lips. "Promises, promises."

His eyes darken. "Think I'm lying?"

"Men will say anything to get their dick wet."

All traces of amusement vanish. "If it's a screaming orgasm you want, I'm your man."

"Prove it." I lick my lips.

He frowns. "Prove what?"

"Let's see what you're working with." I run my hands down his chest.

His pectoral muscles tighten beneath my touch, telling me he's eager to impress. I trail my fingers down his tight abs and stop at his waistband.

"Why did you stop?" He wraps his hand around my wrist.

"I'm looking for something more filling." My gaze wanders to the dance floor, where there's no sign of Leroi.

Cesare leans in close and brushes his lips against my earlobe. "Come with me."

My heart soars. "Where to?"

His grip around my wrist tightens, and he marches me through the VIP section toward an exit secured by a hulking guard. When he opens the door for Cesare and steps aside, I have to bite the inside of my cheek to hold back my triumph.

I saunter alongside Cesare in my stilettos, making sure to stumble. Magazines say that men love women in heels because they make a woman arch her spine and give the illusion of longer legs.

Experience says otherwise.

Fourteen years of working as an assassin has taught me that men love heels because they make a woman vulnerable. Hell, any sign of weakness works on carnivorous men like catnip. The quickest way to catch a predator at night is to walk in a zigzag and stumble. They'll crawl out of the shadows like hungry hyenas.

Cesare holds me steady with an arm around my waist. "Careful sweetheart."

He's no different from all the others. Instead of exploiting a physical weakness, he's taking advantage of a mental vulnerabil-ity. Cesare acts like he's saving his cousin from a deranged sex addict, when, in reality, he wants that lustful attention turned to himself.

My lips curl into a smile.

This predator is about to become my prey.

FOUR

CESARE

I tighten my grip around the crazy bitch's waist, pulling her body flush against mine, and walk her through the hallway that leads to my office. Normally, I wouldn't encroach on Leroi's territory, but I wanted her the moment she first stepped into the club.

By the time I was ready to make a move, she was fucking him in the alley. Now that he no longer wants her, she's fair game.

"What's your name, sweetheart?"

She places a hand on my chest. "Do you even give a fuck?"

"No, but mine is Cesare."

"And why would I care?"

"Because you're going to be screaming it later."

She huffs a laugh. "Out of frustration?"

My eyes narrow. She has a smart mouth for a clingy little stalker. It's a good thing I have something to keep it full.

"No, sweetheart," I say. "I'm going to fuck you so hard that you'll think my name is *Oh God, Too Big,* or *Jesus Christ.* I want to make sure you know it's Cesare."

The sound of her giggle makes my chest inflate, and I slide the hand on her waist down to her ass.

"Is your cock even big enough to back up that arrogance?" she asks.

"More than you can handle."

We reach the door to my office, and I push it open. The room is bathed in chandelier light, illuminating a vast leather desk that overlooks a wall of screens. Each screen looks out across different parts of the club.

A mahogany bar that spans the entire back wall, showcasing shelves of crystal decanters and bottles of some of the rarest liquor in existence. It's a sight that has most women gasping with awe, but this one just tightens her lips with indifference.

I walk her to the desk. "Not impressed with the decor?"

"Let me put it this way," she says with a shrug. "I've seen bigger and better."

"Then allow me to show you something that will impress."

She turns to me, her eyes sparkling, her red lips curving into a knowing smile. "What's that, then?"

"Get on your knees and find out."

A laugh bursts from her lips. It's a full belly one that makes her double over with her arms around her middle. Her shoulders quake with mirth, and she cackles until she can hardly breathe.

My stomach drops, and irritation spreads across my skin like a rash. All traces of arousal drain from my deflating cock.

This bitch has no idea who she's mocking.

"What's so funny?" I say, holding back a growl.

Straightening, she gazes up at me, her eyes shining with amusement. Eyes I want to see bulging when I choke her until her last breath.

"This was your big chance to prove you could measure up to Leroi, and what do you do?" She snickers, the corners of her eyes crinkling. "Order me on my knees to suck your cock."

I flash my teeth. "What's wrong with that?"

"Nothing if you're a little boy playing in his daddy's office." Her gaze wanders around the room, taking in the leather furniture and looking anywhere but at me.

My annoyance quickly simmers into the beginnings of rage. Women don't laugh at me, they kneel and crawl and obey.

My heart pounds so hard that its echoes reach my eardrums. This annoying cunt is about to give me pulsatile tinnitus. Before I know it, my hands are around her throat, and I'm pinning her to the desk.

"What did you say?" I snarl through clenched teeth.

Her eyes glaze, and her back arches off its leather surface. "Oooh," she says, her voice breathy, and she runs her fingers over the back of my hand. "Now, this is a promising start."

I glare down at the crazy bitch. Why isn't she scared? Hours ago, when I slammed Tania against the door, she clawed at my hand and cried, yet this woman beneath me doesn't show the slightest bit of fear.

"You like that?" I say through clenched teeth.

She squeezes my hand, showing me to hold harder and cut off her air. "Hell yes."

"Open your fucking legs," I growl.

She parts her thighs.

"Wider."

She obeys.

My cock stirs, and I reward her by tightening my grip around her throat. "Are you wet for me, baby?"

She laughs again. "You haven't done anything to impress me yet."

I curl my lip, wanting to hit her where it hurts. "You're a fucking pain in the ass. It's no wonder Leroi replaced you with someone better."

When her eyes flash, and her amusement morphs into anger, I know I've dropped the right insult.

"Better?" she spits. "How about younger?"

"You afraid of getting old?" I ask, my voice mocking.

Her laugh sounds bitter. "Leroi takes up with a girl who doesn't look old enough to drink alcohol and that's all you can think to say?"

It takes every effort not to flinch at the affront to the family honor. She doesn't get to slander Leroi just because she got dumped. Leroi doesn't deserve to be disparaged. Bullshit like that can ruin a man's life.

Jaw clenching, I lean close to her face and snarl, "My cousin doesn't fuck kids."

Too many emotions flitter across her features for me to process. I'm no expert on the minds of women. The last one I got close to abandoned us at our lowest, so how the hell could I interpret their mannerisms?

I should end this now. Cut my losses before she ruins my night. Grab this annoying cunt by the hair and throw her back inside the club. Better still, toss her into the alleyway with my foot in her ass and make sure she never returns.

Her fingers slide down to my erection, breaking me out of my thoughts.

"How about you stop fixating on Leroi and show me what you've got?" she says.

My eyes narrow. I can't resist a challenge. Especially not one where I can put her in her place.

"With pleasure," I reply with a sneer.

She gives me a sharp nod. "Make me scream your name."

I reach between her legs, and my fingers brush against the crotch of her panties. I slide the fabric to the side, exposing her pussy, and am pleasantly surprised to find it's slick.

"Wet for me, already?" I ask.

"Hardly," she replies with a snort.

I can't help but grin. She's defensive, obviously still stinging from Leroi's rejection. I can handle her prickly attitude if it gets me what I want.

My fingers explore her swollen clit. I rub circles around it, expecting a gasp or even a moan. Instead, she pinches her lips and rolls her eyes.

Fuck this bitch. She's getting on my last nerve.

With a snarl, I rip off her panties and slap her pussy. Her eyes widen, and she sucks in a breath.

"You like that?" I deliver another slap.

She bites down on her bottom lip and groans. "Not particularly."

Triumph fills my chest, and arousal fills my cock. It looks like she doesn't want to admit that she's into pain. I can work with this. I can't remember the last time I had a real masochist.

My hand descends on her pussy again, this time with an extra sting.

She moans, her eyes fluttering closed.

I lean over her and grin. "You're just a dirty girl who needs to be punished."

She jerks her head to the side. "You wish."

I chuckle. "Actually, I don't give a fuck. You're going to spread those legs wider for me so I can whip your pussy, and you're going to love it."

"Whatever."

To my surprise, she raises her heels to the desk's surface and holds her knees open. Her pussy is bare and completely soaked, each delicious fold glistening with her juices.

Arousal floods my cock so quickly the edges of my vision turn black. By the time I steady myself, my mouth waters with the need for more of that sweet, wet cunt.

I curl my fingers and resist the urge to taste. This mouthy bitch doesn't deserve my tongue.

It's rare to find a woman who truly enjoys pain. Many pretend they do to impress me or appear edgy, but they balk the moment I take them to the playroom. This one looks like the real deal.

It's a pity she's so aggravating.

I unbuckle my belt, yank it out from my pants, and slap the leather against my palm.

Her fingers tighten around her trembling thighs. "Are you going to tease me to death all evening or give me what I want?"

Without even thinking about it, I swing the belt down her pussy with a crack. She flinches, her knees jerking, and hisses through her teeth.

My cock surges, urging me to give her another. "Tell me you love this."

I deliver another strike that makes her squeeze her eyes shut and gasp.

"Oh, God," she says with a moan.

"I already told you," I sneer. "My name is Cesare."

"Christ."

The muscles in my jaw tighten, and I exhale through flared nostrils. Fury and frustration coil through my guts, threatening to strike. I'm not surprised Leroi rejected her for someone more agreeable. No woman I've ever met has had such power to aggravate a man as much as she excites.

She bucks her hips and whimpers, begging for another strike of the belt, but my cock has other plans.

I want to fuck her so hard that her teeth rattle. Pound into her with the full force of my strength until she prays to me for mercy.

Most of all, I want her helpless beneath me and humbled. But for that, I'll need restraints.

I toss the belt aside and pull her off the desk. "Come with me."

"Where?"

"We're going to my playroom."

FIVE

ROSALIND

Cesare marches me to his Lamborghini, and I shut the fuck up, not wanting to ruin this once-in-a-lifetime opportunity to infiltrate the Montesano stronghold.

Tonight isn't about murder. Gunther has only authorized me to gather intel, so killing Cesare won't get me paid. The firm doesn't explain why each target needs to be killed, and we're not paid to ask questions.

If I take out Cesare without permission, I'm looking at another fine, which will add to the mountain of debt I already owe the firm. The worst-case scenario involves Miranda getting hurt. And we'd lose the chance to kill the other two brothers when the Montesanos tightened their security. That's why I'll scope out their home for weaknesses and return with backup.

Cesare drives us in his dickmobile through the hairpin turns of Alderney Hills with one hand on the steering wheel. The other works its way up and down on my thigh, while he makes all kinds of filthy promises.

I squirm in the leather seat, buck my hips, make the right noises, and keep my temper in check. This would be hot if he wasn't so reckless. The visibility here is terrible, with tall evergreens blocking our view, yet he barrels through these treacherous roads notorious for their fatal collisions.

My training as an assassin meant withstanding most forms of torture, but witnessing Cesare risk our lives within this beautiful feat of engineering for sex is pushing my limits.

When we reach tall electric gates guarded by a small army of armored guards, some of the tension eases. The Montesano mansion is the perfect fortress, sitting at the top of a hill and surrounded by impenetrable walls and a dense forest.

I hold my features in a mask of indifference as one of the guard peers in through the open window and stares at me through narrowed eyes. When he allows us entry, all traces of anxiety and annoyance give way to a thrill of success.

My heart pounds the way it usually does when I'm close to achieving a goal. I inhale a deep breath to slow down my pulse.

Cesare navigates the last stretch of tree-lined roads toward a white mansion lit up like the Pantheon. I'm no expert on architecture, but I know enough to recognize the classical Roman influences in the stone columns that make up its grand entrance.

I study the building, taking in every detail, including the double doors that make up its entrance, its tall windows, the guards marching through the dark, and the pathways.

As I commit the security measures to memory, Cesare's fingers slide up to my wet pussy, making my breath catch.

"Still horny, baby?" he asks, his voice dripping with arrogance.

My nipples tighten. I bite down on my bottom lip, not wanting to give him the satisfaction of a moan.

"Not particularly," I mutter.

He snickers, his fingers thrumming my clit. "Liar."

I release a shuddering exhale, excited only at the prospect of gathering intel on the Montesano brothers. The bonus I get from this job might make a dent in my debt to the firm for all the equipment I damaged when I rescued Miranda.

When we drive past the mansion's double doors with no sign of slowing, my heart plummets into my lap. My plan won't work if I can't explore their residence.

"What's wrong?" I murmur. "Changed your mind about showing me your playroom?"

He turns to me with a wide grin. "Eager?"

I scoff. "This isn't the first time a man has promised a red room of pain that's turned out to be a mattress on the floor lit up by a colored lightbulb."

The smile fades, as do all traces of smugness. "After tonight, I'm going to ruin you for other men."

"We'll see about that," I mutter with a suppressed smirk.

Cesare stops the car at the other side of the mansion where the walls are covered in ivy. Up ahead is a manicured lawn that's mostly dark, leading to an illuminated swimming pool. Behind it stands a much smaller structure built of the same white stone as the mansion.

When he opens the door, I pull on my handle, only to find it locked. A mocking laugh lodges in my throat. Did he think I would try to escape? He struts around the front, his lips curling into a satisfied grin, and finally allows me to exit.

As I step out into a juniper scented garden, he clamps a hand around my bicep as though I'm his prisoner.

He leans in, his breath hot against my neck, and whispers, "You're not going anywhere, love."

I roll my eyes. Does he act like this with all the impressionable young women he meets at the club?

What a creep.

Cesare frog-marches me down a path that leads to the pool house, and I turn around, casting the mansion a wistful glance. That's where I need to be, sneaking through the hallways where the brothers will be at their most vulnerable.

My mind races through different scenarios. I could drug Cesare and sneak into the house through a service entrance or a window. That would help me explore the hallways and find the brothers' bedrooms. After uploading some draft schematics along with pictures and footage, I'll return to Cesare, act like he's the god of sex, and continue gaining his trust until the right time to strike.

There's so much to explore, including the grounds. Surely one of the huge trees bordering the electrified wall can provide my colleagues an opening? I'll forward the information to Gunther and ask for permission to perform the assassination.

Maybe then I can earn my way out of debt.

"…Make you beg." Cesare's voice drifts back to my thoughts.

I turn to him and frown. "What?"

He lifts a brow, his lips tightening. "I said, I'm going to cuff you to the bondage chair and make you beg."

"Beg for more, I hope?" I ask.

Eyes hardening, he clenches his jaw as though I've just hurled the most heinous of insults. "Of course."

I turn my gaze to the moon reflecting on the swimming pool, wishing I didn't have to be so antagonistic. Part of it is out of rebellion for enduring so much rejection from his cousin, the other part is an ingrained habit.

Once I've formed a persona on a job, it's difficult to break out of it until my target is dead. That, and my default mode with men is bitchy. After a lifetime of bullshit and abuse, it's impossible to empathize with creatures driven by ego, power, and their dicks.

At the end of the pool, we continue past the tall pillars of its veranda toward arched windows standing six-and-a-half-feet tall. Cesare opens the glass door to let me into a neutral-colored living space with stone floors, beige sofas, and a kitchen.

"Why are you taking me to your pool house?" I ask, my brows rising.

Grip tightening, he jostles me past the table and through a door, into a room of white walls and littered with black BDSM furniture.

My jaw drops. Not because of all the equipment hanging off racks, but because the space is unpretentious. Almost clinical. Most men would paint the walls red or black or purple, but this playroom is tasteful. It's not at all what I expect from Cesare Montesano.

He releases my arm and stands by the door, letting me walk around. There's a metal cage the size of a barrel, barely large enough to contain an average-height woman, and a leather platform with vertical bars that point toward the ceiling for securing the submissive's legs. I run my hand along a bondage chair with outstretched armrests and splayed leg rests as I take in the room.

Black-framed photos hang on the wall, featuring Cesare subduing a naked woman wearing a leather hood. My brows rise.

Beneath all the tattoos, designer clothes, and edginess is an insecure boy, desperate to impress.

Shaking off that thought, I run through my plan. I'll tire out Cesare with sex, wait until he's drowsy to inject him with a powerful sedative, then comb the grounds and the mansion for weak spots. After forwarding everything I record to Gunther, I'll ask for authorization to complete the mission.

Gunther knows I can do it. This won't be the first time a lone assassin has slaughtered an entire mafia family.

"See something you like?" he asks.

"Yeah." I turn around and fix him with a wide grin. "But I didn't come here for the aesthetics. You promised to make me scream."

SIX

CESARE

My inner therapist asks if fucking a woman obsessed with Leroi will compensate me for not being able to free Roman from death row, but I tell that bastard to go to hell. This sexy, smart-mouthed brat is hot and horny for me. Not for him.

I grab her by the throat and grin. "You can start by taking off those clothes and get on your knees."

Her eyes glimmer with mischief. "What happened to introducing me to all your toys?"

"Keep sassing me like that and you'll find out the hard way."

She grabs my dick and grins. "Looks like you're already there, but let's see if you can keep up."

Nostrils flaring, I grab her wrist and back her against the wall. She's stubborn and trying to be brave, but her pulse racing against my fingers tells me this is just a front. I'm going to enjoy breaking her spirit.

"Rule number one," I growl. "You will call me sir or master. Bad girls who fail rule number one get edged all night and sent home with unsatisfied pussies."

Her breath catches. "Is that supposed to scare me?"

"Don't test me, love."

"What's the second rule?" she asks

"You will submit to my demands." I bring my face down to

hers. Our lips are so close we breathe the same air. "No matter how dark or depraved, you will obey me without question."

"And if I don't?" she asks with a smirk.

"Then you'll find out how inventive I am with my punishments."

"We'll see," she replies. "Anything else?"

A muscle in my jaw ticks. She's too bold and full of defiance. If words won't get through to her, then maybe a demonstration of my abilities will earn me some respect. Releasing her wrist and neck, I step back and give her space.

"Take off your dress, then get on your knees and crawl to the breeding bench."

Her head swivels around the room, and her gaze stops at the leather bench with stirrups. I wait for her eyes to widen, her face to pale, or for her throat to tighten, but she shimmies out of her dress like she crawls through dungeons every day.

What the fuck? I'm not complaining, but I thought she'd be more resistant after all that sass. My gaze drops to a juicy pair of tits that defy gravity, a trim waist, and long, toned legs I can't wait to see encased in leather.

After kicking the dress to the side, she gets down on her hands and knees, then crawls across the floor. Her tits sway with the movement and I lick my lips, already imagining them adorned with clamps.

As she passes, I catch glimpses of the moisture gathered in her pussy, it drips down her inner thighs. The sight of her so aroused makes my cock surge, and I stifle a groan. It's so rare to find a woman who genuinely loves this kind of sex. Something about her says she won't need a safe word.

Following her to the bench, I grab a handful of her hair and jerk her head backward to force eye contact.

She gazes up at me through wide hazel eyes, her lips parting with a gasp. My insides flare with victory. That's more like it.

"Climb onto the leather surface and lie on your back."

She obeys without comment or hesitation, making me raise my brows. No balking, no breathing, no barbs? Does it matter if she's doing everything I want? Maybe all she needs is a firm hand to make her submit.

"Good girl." I nod my approval. "Now spread your legs and show me that wet pussy."

Her eyes glint, but she parts her thighs. I walk around the other end of the bench to attach her ankles to the cuffs and get a front row view of her glistening folds.

Ignoring the rush of sensation to my cock, I lift her leg and fasten the leather strap around one ankle and then the other. As I slide her wrists into another set of restraints, her breath quickens, and she closes her eyes.

When I'm done, I step back to admire my work. Her dark hair fans out over the leather, framing long lashes resting on high cheekbones. A flush spreads across her creamy skin and her pouty lips redden. Her perfect breasts move with each of her ragged breaths, making her look beautifully vulnerable.

"How does it feel to be completely at my mercy?" I ask.

She stares up at me, her pupils dilating, her breaths quickening. My heart pounds with anticipation as I pinch her nipples so hard she whimpers.

"You like pain?" I ask.

She nods.

I slap her breast, making her moan. "Where's that smart mouth now?" I murmur. "You just crave a man who can put you in your place."

She nods again, her pretty lips parting but making no sound.

"Why are you suddenly mute?" I ask. "Are you afraid of what I might do to you now that you're helpless?"

She shakes her head. "No."

I grin. "You should be."

She trembles, her eyes once again fluttering shut. I walk around to where her legs are spread, but the sight of her juices soaking the leather beneath her pussy makes me lightheaded.

"Fuck," I growl. "You're soaked."

"Please," she whispers.

"Please what, love?" I ask. "Use your words."

"Please.... I can't wait much longer. Just fuck me, sir."

I sway on my feet, my hands gripping the leg restraints for balance. This is too easy. A few minutes ago, she was a bold bitch and now she's begging.

Seriously, what the hell made the difference? The undressing, the crawling, or the bondage? Her easy submission is almost disappointing. I was looking forward to using the toys, teasing that sweet pussy and denying her pleasure until her spirit broke, but she's already desperate and dripping and begging.

"Master," she says, her voice hoarse. "I need your cock."

Fuck.

Confusion dissolves, replaced by a lust so intense my skin breaks out in a sweat. I've been hard for this woman for at least an hour—scratch that, for weeks. Ever since she sashayed into the Phoenix, looking like the most alluring femme fatale, I've wanted her to be mine.

I slide my hand down her belly, feeling her muscles quiver beneath my touch. The heat of her skin seeps into my fingers, and I part her folds to reach her swollen clit.

"Is this what you want, love?" I ask. "For me to fill your cunt with my cock?"

She bucks her hips. "Please, sir. Let me come."

My cock pushes painfully against my zipper, wanting to give her exactly what she craves. Any lingering feelings of disappointment vanish as my ears fill with her pants and moans.

I ease open my fly, and my erection springs free. She raises her head, her eyes widening with a gasp.

"So big," she moans. "Give it to me, Master. Now."

Arousal surges. There's only so much a man can resist. After tearing open a condom and sheathing my cock, I thrust so deep inside her she howls.

Her inner muscles clamp around my shaft with an unusually tight grip, and her tits jiggle with each thrust.

The glassy look in her eyes vanishes, replaced with something knowing. "Let's see how long you last... *Master*."

The way she says it implies that she's left out the silent 'bater.'

"Bitch," I say through clenched teeth. "Was all that submission an act?"

She licks her lips. "I got tired of waiting. Now, hurry up and give me some Montesano cock."

My nostrils flare. Did she just call me Leroi's replacement?

Infuriating doesn't begin to describe this bitch. I wrap a hand around her throat and squeeze.

"Are you even a fucking sub?"

"You tell me." She bucks her hips, meeting me stroke for stroke. "Now, show me what you've got. I'll be taking notes."

Darkness clouds the edges of my vision, and I clench my teeth. She's testing my manhood, pushing my limits, judging my performance. In a minute, she'll compare me with Leroi just to get under my skin.

I should pull out, remove her restraints, and end this scene. I should toss her out through the gates and leave her to walk home naked. Her mind games are too adversarial, too antagonistic, and too aggravating, but her tight pussy is too addictive.

She moans, clearing my mind of all thoughts. I fuck her harder, faster, deeper, but her eyes still glint with challenge.

"Is that all you've got?" she asks.

Madness consumes my psyche, crowding out what's left of my sanity. I tighten my grip around her neck and pound into her with so much force that the bench groans. The throat beneath my fingers convulses, trying to take in air, and her mouth opens and closes with choking breaths.

Her eyes widen with alarm. "Ces—"

Whatever she's about to say next is cut off by another violent thrust that makes her eyes roll to the back of her head.

"Where's that smart mouth now?" I growl.

The muscles of her pussy tighten in response, as though trying to asphyxiate my cock in revenge. She milks me hard enough to draw the cum from my balls, and I drive into her faster, harder, my gaze boring into her bulging eyes.

She writhes beneath me, struggling to breathe, each desperate gasp filling every fiber of my being with power. The last vestiges of my common sense warn me she's about to reach her limit. If I continue choking her, she'll lose consciousness.

Her lips move but make no sound, as though trying to beg for mercy or restraint, and the defiance in her eyes morphs into alarm.

"That's right," I say through gritted teeth. "Now, come around this Montesano cock."

Her pussy spasms on command, sending me hurtling over the edge. I pound into her through my own spurts of pleasure and rip my hand away from her throat.

She gasps through her climax, and I collapse against her prone form, panting hard, our frantic breaths mingling to form a cacophony of satisfaction. My darkness ebbs back into the shadows, leaving behind an overwhelming sense of bliss.

Nothing could prepare me for the intensity of hate sex. That all-consuming sensation of possessing and dominating this woman is a high that hits better than any drug. If I had Rosalind, maybe I would never have gotten addicted.

The feel of her sweet cunt still twitching around my cock is hot beyond measure.

"I fucking knew it," I say through panting breaths, my chest roaring with triumph. "Knew I'd have you begging and screaming at my command. You just needed the right man to push your buttons, baby, and I'm about to make you cry for more."

"Nice try," she murmurs. "But I'd rate that effort a six out of ten."

SEVEN

ROSALIND

Sex with Cesare was a solid nine out of ten, and I only struck off a point because he let me goad him into skipping the foreplay. His cock must be studded or pierced because the way it rubbed against my g-spot should make it a weapon of mass destruction.

I'm still drunk from a cocktail of endorphins and euphoria when Cesare laughs. It's the mocking, maniacal mirth of a madman who's just unraveled a mystery.

My eyes, which were half-lidded, snap open.

"What?" I ask through panting breaths.

"I've got to say," he pauses, mid-chuckle, to look me up and down. "Your pussy is a nine, but your attitude is a one. That averages out at—"

"A five?" I spit.

He withdraws, pulls off the condom, and tucks himself back into his pants. As though answering my question is too much of an effort, he unbuckles my ankle restraints and releases my legs before moving onto the leather straps around each wrist, freeing each without a word.

Chest heaving, I push off the leather bench, glaring a hot beam of anger into his broad back. Wasn't he supposed to be an easier target than Leroi? Or was he only easier to manipulate because he only wanted to bust a nut?

"I'm readjusting my score," I say.

He walks to the other side of the playroom to a trash can where he deposits the used condom.

My eyes narrow. He was supposed to be insecure and eager to prove himself, but maybe that was only lust. Or I've pushed him so far that he's given up. Either way, I'm losing him. But if he orders me to leave, I can take the scenic route around the grounds and gather information on their defenses.

"Get dressed," he says, not even bothering to make eye contact. "I'll drive you to the gates where someone will take you home."

My stomach drops.

Shit.

If I don't turn around this situation, then I fucked him for nothing. I rise off the leather bench and walk over to where he stands at a table of supplies and opens a box of latex gloves.

"Why did my pussy only get a nine out of ten?" I ask.

He snaps on the gloves, grabs a pack of disinfectant wipes, pulls one out and strides back to the bench. I spin around, my mouth gaping open as he cleans the leather surface as though getting it ready for the next woman.

"Damn," I mutter. "At least Leroi gave me aftercare and snacks."

He straightens, his shoulders squaring. The veins in his neck swell beneath his skin, and I smirk.

Looks like I've finally gotten through to this asshole.

When he turns back to meet my gaze, his features are pinched. "You're still naked."

I fold my arms across my chest. "You're not sending me away without at least a snack."

His eyes shutter, and I raise my brows with defiance, daring him to lash out. There's a method to my madness. I need Cesare to invite me to stay over or at least fuck me until he falls into an exhausted sleep.

Right now, I can't afford to inspire his indifference, so I'm aiming for his hatred. Men like him, who like to dominate women, wouldn't be able to resist pounding me into submission once more with their cocks. It's just a matter of holding their interest until it's time to strike.

"Will you shut the fuck up if I give you a drink?" he asks.

I offer him an eager nod.

Cesare turns back to the bench, wipes down the restraints, and then strides out through the door. Some of the tension in my chest eases at the prospect of prolonging my stay.

I rush to my purse, pull out a bottle of OPA, and pop it open before following him into the pool house's living room. Oxypentanol renders a target unconscious faster than GHB. Its effects last up to thirty-six hours, but can be reversed with an antidote.

Cesare walks past the dining table and sofas, too self-absorbed to notice what I'm doing, and pauses in front of a kitchenette.

By the time I reach him at the counter, he's opened a cabinet full of bottles. All I need to do is appeal to his nature as an asshole to render him unconscious.

"Give me your strongest vodka," I say, resting my head on his shoulder.

Shrugging me off, he pours me a generous amount into a tumbler, returns the bottle, and strides back across the room. Any other time, I would balk at his shitty manners, but I take the opportunity to gulp down the liquor and top up the glass with OPA.

"Cesare?" I ask.

He pauses halfway to the playroom without turning back to meet my gaze.

I raise my chin. "If my pussy is a nine, then my other holes are elevens."

No reaction.

"I'm not just saying that. Leroi once said I was a fifteen when he was silencing me with his cock down my throat."

He snorts. "Is that right?"

"So, he speaks," I mutter.

Finally, he turns, his cold gaze flickering up and down my naked body. It's a cold assessment that makes my fingers tighten around the glass.

When my tongue swipes over my bottom lip, his gaze sharpens, and my skin prickles under his scrutiny. Moments pass, and the tension builds until my ears ring.

No man in history has ever turned down a blow job, but it looks like Cesare might be the first. I don't think I've ever met anyone so mercurial. He was so eager before, and now he's acting indifferent.

It's maddening he's got me desperate and trying to impress. Mirroring my own tactics.

"Okay, I'll put on my dress and let myself out." I hook my thumb toward the glass doors.

"Get on your knees, then," he says, his words glacial. "Let's see if your mouth is good for something other than talking shit."

I raise my tumbler. "Hold my fucking drink. I'm going to need something in thirty seconds to wash away the foul taste."

He snatches the glass and knocks back its contents. Triumph punches through my chest, but it's too early to celebrate my victory. The formula I gave him is colorless, odorless, and so bland it would have picked up the taste of vodka. But there's a slim chance he'll see through my ruse and raise the alarm.

When he doesn't grimace, I drop to my knees and force down a grin.

I unzip Cesare's pants and pull out his cock. Even half hard, his shaft is long and thick with prominent veins. He's just as huge as Leroi, but that's not what makes my breath catch. His bulbous tip is pierced with four silver beads attached to thick barbells.

Feigning disinterest, I ask, "What kind of piercing is that?"

"A magic cross," he replies with a smirk.

"Oh," I murmur. "That's why you felt so different."

He slides his fingers through my hair, making my scalp tingle. "I thought it was only worth a six?"

"Different isn't always better." I lick my lips, my pussy already throbbing.

"That was the most intense fuck you've ever had," he snarls. "Don't deny it. I felt how your cunt pulsed around my cock."

I scoff. "That was barely a tremor. I've had better climaxes with my pinky."

His fingers in my hair tighten, delivering a sharp pain that heightens my arousal. He jerks my head back, so I'm forced to look into his eyes.

"Are you going to continue to give me sass, or will you demonstrate those cock-sucking skills?"

I snatch his shaft, making him hiss through his teeth. The OPA should already be working its magic by now, but Cesare must be resistant. Lucky for us both, he's my most attractive target and best fuck.

It's almost a pity he'll have to die.

Swirling my tongue around his head, I flick the piercings, and his body tenses. He's salty and sweet, with a hint of bitterness from the condom's spermicide. But I've tasted far worse.

The fingers tangling in my hair loosen a little, allowing me more room to maneuver, yet he still guides the movement of my head.

With my free hand, I ease his pants further down and roll his balls, which are surprisingly smooth.

Cesare groans, and I let him bob my head up and down his shaft. The piercings slide back and forth against my tongue and the roof of my mouth, making my pussy throb.

"Eyes on me," he says.

When I look up, his pupils are tiny pinpricks, bringing out the pale flecks in his blue irises. It's a sign that the drug is taking effect, but I need him pliable and drowsy before he comes in my mouth and kicks me out.

I increase the suction, eager to raise his heart rate to accelerate the drug. His breathing turns ragged, and his hips jerk.

"Good girl," he rumbles. "So much better when you can't talk back."

"Go fuck yourself," I mutter around his cock.

He chuckles, the sound rich and deep. "Use your words."

"I said—"

His fingers tighten around my hair, making my breath catch. Then he flashes his teeth and growls, "I'm gonna fuck your throat."

Before I know it, he's thrusting into my mouth and down my windpipe. My eyes water, and I breathe hard, trying not to choke.

Part of my training as an assassin was getting rid of my gag reflex so I could stay focused when a target loses control. Staying alert, I increase the suction, ready to catch him when he falls.

Soon, his thrusts slow and become more erratic. When his fingers loosen their grip, I know he's fallen under the drug's influence.

Taking him deeper, I close my throat around his crown, and he climaxes with a guttural groan, flooding my mouth with salty fluid. His knees buckle and my hands shoot out to break his fall, and he collapses into my arms.

His cock slips from my lips, and I lay him on the floor, making sure he's still breathing. Then I grab his wrists and drag him through the pool house's lounge and into the playroom.

It's time to change into something more suitable to infiltrate the mansion and search the grounds.

EIGHT

CESARE

Fuck. My. Head.

My cranial nerves throb in sync with my heartbeat, pain spreading down my spinal cord. Every drop of moisture has vacated my throat and mouth, leaving me parched. Even my kidneys ache with dehydration.

Did I get wasted last night?

No.

I've been clean for three years, with no access to anything stronger than alcohol, and almost never get drunk.

So why does it feel like I have the world's worst hangover?

With a groan, I roll to the other side of the mattress, only to tumble onto the tile floor. Agony radiates across my back from the impact, making me wince.

"Since when do I sleep on the wrong side of the bed?" I mutter.

I inhale a deep breath, still too fucked up to consider shifting my carcass. Mingled within the scents of antiseptic and leather is something sweet and floral with a hint of citrus.

Is that magnolia?

Bitter memories rise to the surface, and I force them back to the recesses of my mind. It's been fifty-eight months since she left, thirty-four since she died, and thirteen since I destroyed the estate's magnolia trees.

No. This must be an olfactory hallucination brought on by a migraine... or a more ominous pathological process.

I clutch my head.

Stop this, Cesare.

You're falling into a hypochondriacal spiral.

Despite the searing agony, I manage to crack open an eye, only for the morning light to sear my retina.

"What the fuck?"

I sit upright, blinking over and over to adjust my gaze. Eventually, my vision clears, and I find myself in the playroom.

That explains the leather scent, but since when do I fall asleep in the place where I fuck?

I squeeze my eyes shut, trying to concentrate through the pounding headache. What happened yesterday?

Roman got released from prison, and we fucked up some traitors, what else?

My chest tightens, and I gasp for breath, my vision tunneling as my body floods with adrenaline. I'm losing control, and on the tail end of a full-blown panic attack. I haven't had a blackout in eighteen months.

A cold sweat breaks out across my brow. Is this another relapse?

Shit.

Shit.

SHIT.

They're going to lock me up again and force me to go cold turkey. Or maybe this time, they'll send me to an institution. There will be doctors, blood tests.

If they get their hands on my DNA...

My insides twist with nausea. I scramble to my feet and stumble to the bathroom, but the door jams. Before I can jiggle its knob, my stomach revolts, and I bolt out of the bedroom, across the living area and go straight to the kitchen sink, where I dry heave.

Through the spasms and convulsions, my hindbrain screams

that something is amiss. If I had drunk so much alcohol to warrant this blistering hangover and blackout, then where's all the liquid?

What the fuck happened after the waterboarding?

My stomach riots, but I hold on to that thought. I got changed and looked through the monitors. Roman was going to hook up with that woman and then there was Cousin Leroi...

I turn on the tap, stick my mouth under the spray, and wash out the taste of bile.

Leroi walked in with a tiny woman in a gold dress, and then his stalker arrived...

Realization hits me in the solar plexus, my head snaps up, and I stare at the kitchen tiles. Last night, I rushed out to the club to see fireworks and ended up spanking the bunny boiler's pussy on my desk.

My dick throbs at the memory. I didn't just spank that bare pussy. I whipped it with my belt, and she loved every minute.

A distant scream pierces through my musings. I shut off the water to hear a woman shouting. My stomach drops. I brought the stalker home to tie her up and...

And what?

The next scream has me running out the French doors. I pause at the pool, my heart palpitating, and cast my gaze across the lawn.

It's like looking through a haze. My perceptions are distorted, but I'm not hallucinating. It's like standing on the edge of a dreamscape, only it looks like the estate is in a state of emergency.

Guards rush toward the mansion, and my sympathetic nervous system kicks me in the gut. Montesano men don't kill innocent women. Especially not their cousin's exes.

I run toward the gathering crowd, wondering what the hell I did last night and why I can't remember. Did I choke her to death? Did I get so fucked up that I hung her by the entrails?

Black fog creeps along my periphery and thins across my vision to form a thin haze. Memories assault my psyche in a blinding rush. Her, crawling on her hands and knees. Her, lying strapped to the bench with my hands around her throat as she struggles for air.

And then...

And then...

I run into a hard body, which flinches.

"Hey," a deep voice snarls. "Oh, it's you." He chuckles. "Didn't see you there."

My vision clears and I lock gazes with Gil. He's grinning, which must be a sign that what he's looking at can't be so bad.

He flicks his head up toward the tower. "Take a look."

I tilt my head. A half-naked woman stands on a balcony ledge, wearing torn sheets around her crotch and breasts. Her hair is a mass of wild curls that stand out in all directions.

Relief courses through my veins, melting away the tension. I stumble forward, barely catching myself on Gil's arm.

That's not her.

Leroi's stalker's hair was straight. And she had much larger breasts.

"You okay, Cesare?" Gil asks with a frown.

"Fine," I rasp.

He leans in close, his nostrils twitching the way he does when he's trying to sniff me for traces of alcohol. "You sure?"

I step back. "Yeah."

"Gil," says a sharp voice from behind us.

I whirl around and lock gazes with my brother, Benito, the one with the Ivy League law degree and a stick up his ass. He's dressed in a three-piece suit and wearing spectacles with plain glass lenses.

He looks past me as though I don't exist. "I need you in a car out front to take Roman to the gates. The police are on the other side, wanting answers."

I scowl. "For what?"

Benito tilts his head toward the hysterical spectacle on the balcony. "There's a warrant out for her arrest. Multiple witnesses, including a detective, saw her disappearing last night with Roman."

With a nod, Gil bolts around the side of the house.

"How can I help?" I ask, still not sure if this is a lucid dream.

Benito's features pinch. "Stay out of the way and keep that woman you brought home in your playroom."

My stomach drops to the paving stones, and a chill rushes down my spine. Any offense I might take about being called a nuisance vanishes. Benito knows. The guards at the gate would have told him if she had left, which means she's somewhere on the grounds.

But in what state?

I can't let this become a repeat of the situation with my pet rabbit.

After shooting me a disapproving glower, Benito storms away, his shoulders bunching. I watch him disappear around the corner before rushing back toward the pool house, determined to find what's left of that woman.

I hope to fuck she's still alive.

By the time I trudge across the lawn and back to the pool house, my legs are dragging like they're made of lead and my arms hang heavily at my sides like clubs. I try sifting through my memories once more to dredge up what might have happened to the woman, but it's blank.

The morning sun scorches my skin like a crackling fire, making sweat trickle into my eyes. My vision blurs, and I stumble forward, light-headed and dizzy from the heat. I'm clinging onto consciousness, on the brink of passing out.

This is no ordinary hangover. This is the work of narcotics.

All the symptoms point toward a date rape drug: fatigue, headache, nausea, dizziness, and memory loss.

Leroi's stalker must have drugged me with something potent, but when? Was it during a struggle? Is she dead? I'm still coming down from a sedative, which means I wouldn't have had the time or capacity to hide a body.

So, where the hell did she go?

I shuffle alongside the pool, which reflects bright sunlight that sears my eyes until I squint. Grimacing, I run through the possibilities based on personal experience and what I learned on the job and in medical school.

It can't be GHB. That only lasts a few hours. I've taken that shit before with no lingering aftereffects. Roofies? I shake my head. Rohypnol would make me groggy, like I've just come out of sedation, not make me feel like the walking dead.

What the fuck did that woman do, and why? To make Leroi jealous? If she wanted a rebound fuck, all she needed to do was ask, but drugging me is a step too far.

I shove open the door and step into the air-conditioned pool house. Cool air hits my skin, and I inhale a deep breath to calm my churning stomach. I glance around for signs of the woman, but all I find is a single empty tumbler on the coffee table.

Is that how she administered the substance? There are dozens of less obvious ways to drug someone. Surely, I would have noticed something?

I pick up the glass and sniff, but it only smells of vodka. Not that it matters. Most date rape drugs are odorless. The sound of the shower coming from my bedroom makes me lumber inside. Earlier, when I wanted to hurl my guts, the bathroom was locked. Has she been in there the entire time?

My instincts tell me to wait and see what she does next. I stumble to the bed and lie back as though I'm still unconscious from the drug.

Eventually, the shower turns off, the door opens, and soft footsteps pad across the tiled floor. My pulse thuds in my eardrums, its beats heavy and sluggish.

Closing my eyes, I leave a thin line of vision to observe her moving into my periphery. She calls my name, but I remain still to reel her in.

The mattress dips as she climbs onto the bed, and there's no spike in my heart rate, no surge of adrenaline. The drugs have dulled my reactions, but I'm aware of what's happening.

She leans over me, filling my nostrils with the scent of sweet magnolia, and all I can think of is another woman who was equally treacherous. With the proficiency of a trained medic, Leroi's stalker examines my pulse and pupil, confirming that she not only administered a drug, but one she expected would keep me incapacitated for a few more hours.

My blood boils, and my empty stomach roils with bitter rancor. What will she do next?

It takes every effort not to flinch when she brushes the hair off my face, and my breath catches when she kisses my forehead.

I study her through my lashes. The morning sun shines through her mahogany strands, coloring her flyaways a vibrant shade of burnt orange. I have no fucking clue why my mind focuses on her beauty, but when light glints on the tip of a needle, my hand shoots out to snatch her wrist.

NINE

ROSALIND

It took hours to scour the grounds, and I have the information the firm needs, but the sun is rising too quickly. Thank fuck the pool house backs onto woodland because that's the only thing standing between me and getting caught.

I lie flat within the undergrowth, my heart pounding loud enough to drown out the woman's screams. Every few minutes, an armed guard lumbers close enough to my hiding place to shoot the back of my head, but they're all focused on the commotion.

My phone's reception up here is spotty at best, and these files are taking an eternity to upload. Gunther keeps sending me texts, requiring more footage, more pictures, more ways to penetrate the Montesano stronghold.

At times like this, I wish I had entered a less nerve-wracking profession, like venom-milking, landmine-removing, or stunts. But without the Moirai's resources or training, I'd never have been able to take back Miranda. She makes the bullshit I endure worthwhile.

I told Gunther I was here with Leroi because I wasn't authorized to approach Cesare, but the OPA isn't infallible. A small percentage of people are resistant to the drug and can wake up after a few hours without the antidote.

Gunther knows that some people who ingest it inhale their

own vomit and choke, but that's a risk he's willing to take because it's a natural death.

Eventually, the screaming stops, and the small crowd at the side of the house disperses. Most of the men saunter in the direction of the driveway, where I'm sure there's some other spectacle.

My phone's progress bar has been stuck at 92% for what feels like an hour. I could leave the handset here to continue uploading, but I still haven't paid off the firm for all the equipment I destroyed the time I took Miranda.

"Hurry the fuck up," I whisper to my phone.

Sunlight filters through the thick canopy and warms my back, making me break out into a sweat. It was dark when I put Cesare to bed, and dark when I prowled around the mansion, recording all the doors, windows, and vulnerabilities.

The sun was barely rising when I walked around the grounds, taking in the electrified and barbed wire fencing that top the estate's tall walls. Now all that hard work is about to be ruined because the cellphone towers can't quite reach the summit of Alderney Hill.

I crawl on my belly toward the back of the pool house, hoping the connection there is better. An ultra-rich mafia household should be able to arrange a reliable connection, right?

My phone buzzes with a message from Gunther.

Files received. Permission granted to return to Leroi and administer the antidote.

Finally!

I text back about Cesare:

Do I have permission to proceed with T3?

He replies with:

Permission denied.

I grind my teeth. Killing even one Montesano brother wouldn't just pay off the amount I owe the firm. I'd have enough money to quit the Moirai and get a normal job that allows me to see Miranda every day. We could form a connection, be a real family, and maybe start building better memories.

We could cook together in our own kitchen without the threat of the firm breathing down my neck. Hell, I'd even welcome something as simple as spending weekends lazing around. I want eye contact, conversations, the chance to make her smile.

All of that could be possible with enough money, but Gunther wants to keep me indebted. That way, he can send me out on menial missions and torture me in perpetuity for refusing his sexual advances.

If I leave the firm with an outstanding balance, I won't just die. Gunther might also take Miranda.

At this rate, I'll work for the Moirai Group until the day I expire.

"Asshole."

I crawl through the shrubbery, making my way back to the pool house. The bathroom window I left open is still ajar, and I climb in without a sound.

After stripping off the catsuit, I spread it on the bath and dissolve it with solvent. Then I turn on the shower to wash away the evidence. Once the black liquid disappears down the drain, I climb into the tub and let the hot water soak my hair and skin.

I take one last look around the bathroom before unlocking the door and stepping into the playroom where I left Cesare. He's sprawled on his front, in a different position, but that's not unusual. Targets who are resistant to drugs sometimes move around as they take effect, but oxypentanol always prevails.

"Cesare?"

I slide onto the bed and check his pulse. It's steady. I pull back his eyelid and inspect his pupil. It's small, but that's normal for someone under the effect of a powerful depressant.

A sigh slips from my lips, and I brush the hair off his face. If I'm lucky, Cesare will order me an Uber, and that will be the last I see of him or his cousin.

Last night was the best sex of my life. There's a darkness to Cesare that calls to mine that I can't resist. Leroi was an empty chasm—composed and captivating, but cold. Cesare's eyes are like fire, drawing me in with their intensity until I'm consumed by his flames.

In another life, I might want to pursue a relationship with Cesare. He's exciting and not as jaded as most men, but his days are numbered. Gunther will pass all the intel I gathered on the mansion's security to the team of assassins he favors.

It's only a matter of time before a small squad breaches their defenses and eliminates the Montesano brothers. The next time I see Cesare, it will be as a minuscule percentage of my share of the bounty on an electronic paycheck.

My job is done, and it's time to go.

Leaning over him, I place a kiss on his forehead before reaching into my bag to extract the antidote. His jugular vein pulses beneath my fingertips, and I ready the pre-filled syringe.

Before the needle touches his skin, a hand grabs my wrist.

Cesare glares up at me, his eyes flashing. "Now, what the fuck is a girl like you doing with a syringe full of poison?"

TEN

CESARE

She stares down at me, her eyes widening, her features freezing with shock. My fingers tighten around her wrist with a grip that would make any other woman wince, but she doesn't even flinch.

"Answer my question," I say through clenched teeth.

Her response is a lightning-fast punch to the side of my head that turns my vision black. Pain explodes through my skull like dynamite, sending up an attack of nausea.

My grip on her wrist loosens, and she yanks her arm free. By the time I open my eyes, the playroom is out of focus and a blurred figure is sprinting toward the door.

"Bitch!"

I scramble off the bed and give chase, but my steps are uneven while she's already in the next room. My heart thuds, but my adrenal glands are too fatigued to pump out the necessary fuel to power my movements.

Pushing through the sluggishness, I force my heavy limbs into pursuit. I reach the French doors, but she's already halfway past the pool. Naked, she races straight ahead, with a curtain of dark hair flying at her back.

I stumble after her, my head pounding with each heavy step. At this rate, she'll escape. Someone else will catch her and tell my big brothers that I can't even manage a woman. Benito will tell Roman I screw up all the time, and they'll strip me of all responsibilities.

Up ahead, I spot two gardeners approaching the shrubs that border the patio.

"Get her," I roar.

Their gazes snap in our direction, and the men exchange glances before dropping their tools and rushing toward her. The woman darts into the bushes, but the gardeners cut her off at the other side.

"Come here, sweetheart," one of them says, his voice lecherous.

I grind my teeth and hold back a possessive rage. If one of them so much as touches her...

She bursts back through the plants and charges at me, her eyes blazing.

My nostrils flare. Bitch thinks because she drugged me, she can just barrel past.

"Come here," I snarl, my arms opening wide.

The woman doesn't slow, and I ready myself to snatch her as she tries to dodge. We're heartbeats away from touching, and it takes every effort not to focus on her bouncing tits.

At the last second, she veers left. My hand snaps out and clamps around her arm, and I yank her off balance toward the pool. She crashes into my chest, and we tumble into the water with a loud splash.

Holding my breath, I cling to her naked body, and she thrashes and struggles to break free, but I hold tight. As we sink to the bottom, her body goes rigid, seeming paralyzed with fear. My feet reach the floor, and I push off, propelling us to the surface.

We break through the water, and she gasps for air, sounding like she's in the throes of a full-blown panic attack.

"Let go of me, asshole," she screams.

"I ought to drown you for that stunt you tried to pull with the poison."

"It wasn't—"

"Don't lie to me," I snarl.

"Need any help, sir?" One of the gardeners asks.

"If she tries to run, shoot her kneecaps." I walk the woman to the shallow end and force her up the ladder.

Both men extract their guns and point them at her trembling tits.

"Don't get distracted by her body," I growl, wanting to tell them she's an assassin, but I stop myself from elaborating.

Word would only spread around the estate, then my brothers and Gil would take over the interrogation. I want to handle this myself without getting the usual lectures.

She climbs up the ladder, her toned muscles glistening in the sunlight. Any other time, I would drink in every inch of her physical perfection, but I'm still stinging from the attempted murder.

I climb out after her and snatch one of the gardener's guns and wave it toward the French doors.

"Get inside," I snap.

She hesitates for a tense moment, her gaze darting from me to the other men as though calculating her next move. Her features are tense but not frightened, proving to me that she must be a professional.

"Try to run, and I'll shoot you in the spine."

Her eyes harden, and she sets her jaw. Without another word, she walks toward the French doors. I follow behind her, training my gun on her back, ready to fire if she decides to fight.

This little assassin is about to learn the hard way that she's fucked with the wrong Montesano brother.

ELEVEN

ROSALIND

My heart thumps painfully against my ribs. I'm still reeling from Cesare restraining me underwater, and now I'm getting traumatic flashbacks. The chlorinated water turns briny as I remember Gunther's uncanny face reviving me with his lips. No one will ever stop me from thinking he drowned me in the Atlantic Ocean as an excuse to give me mouth to mouth.

What the fuck is wrong with Cesare? I injected him with enough oxypentanol to keep him unconscious for thirty-six hours, yet he's standing behind me with a gun. He's either a freak of nature or he's so accustomed to sedatives that his body has built up a resistance.

I shove aside my speculations. Cesare already thinks I tried to inject him with poison and probably won't believe me if I tell him it was an antidote.

The only way I can handle this situation is by playing things cool. No matter how he managed to overcome the OPA, he's still vulnerable from its side effects. If I can separate him from the gardeners, then it's only a matter of time before I can knock him out and escape.

Stepping into the pool house, I glance over my shoulder. Cesare walks in after me, dripping water everywhere and holding me hostage with his gun. The other men still hover by the shrubs, watching us through the French window, so I continue through to the playroom.

I scan the racks of BDSM toys, searching for something to use as a weapon. There's a thick leather bullwhip I could fashion into a noose, but using it would require getting too close.

"That's far enough," Cesare rasps.

"Are you even going to let me explain?" I turn to meet his bloodshot eyes.

He laughs, the sound manic. "No need," he says, his breath heavy from exertion. "But you will tell me your client."

I frown. "What do you mean?"

"Cut the bullshit. You're an assassin." When I shake my head, he adds, "Everything makes sense now, from why you stalked my cousin to how easily you spread your legs. You were sent here to kill me, and you failed."

The accusation doesn't even make my heart rate blip. I've weaseled my way out of worse situations. Instead, I snort.

"You're insignificant. This was all about making Leroi jealous."

He flinches, his features hardening, and I know I've struck a nerve. Cesare Montesano isn't just the youngest of the three brothers. He's also the misfit. Roman and Benito are more like their cousin, Leroi: cold-blooded, calculating, composed. Cesare is impulsive and hot-headed, with his emotions running too close to the surface.

It's easier to see the chips in his armor, and one of them is how he compares himself to his older male relatives.

"You're lying," he says, his voice dangerous and low. Then he points his gun at my thigh. "Tell me who sent you or I'll lodge this bullet in your femur."

My heart skips several beats. He means every word, but his eyes are so unfocused and glassy that his aim is likely to be off. If his bullet tears through my femoral artery, I'm dead.

"Alright." I raise both hands. "I'll talk."

He nods, his chest still rising and falling with labored breaths. His skin is pallid and still drenched from the water. Swaying on his feet, he stares at me through a dreamlike haze. How the hell is he functioning when he looks on the verge of collapsing?

"Just let me dry off," I say.

"So you can run away again?" He flips off the gun's safety with a sharp click. "Talk."

The sound triggers hundreds of hours of training in how to disarm an assailant. Adrenaline surges through my veins, and I lunge forward.

Cesare's eyes widen, and he steps back. "What are you—"

My fingers close around his wrist and twist. The gun points to the ceiling and fires, making my ears ring. A rain of plaster and dust falls over our heads, clogging my throat.

Tightening my grip, I wrench on Cesare's arm, making him double over with a roar. "Crazy bitch!"

One swift elbow strike to his ribs makes him drop the weapon, but he kicks it to the side.

"Shit." My last hope of an easy victory skitters across the tiled floor and under the bed.

Cesare hurls his weight against me, and we both tumble to the floor. Even under the influence of OPA, the power difference is overwhelming. He's bigger, stronger, and heavier, but I have one significant advantage: I'm in complete control of my senses.

Twisting, I deliver a knee to his balls that makes him howl. I scramble to my hands and knees in the direction of the gun, but Cesare grabs my ankle and drags me back.

"Who sent you?" He crawls on my back, his fingers closing in around my throat.

He pins me to the hard floor, forcing out all the air from my lungs. I twist and turn and buck, trying to break free from his grip, but there's no escaping his superior body mass.

Sweat breaks out across my brow as I struggle beneath his weight. No matter how I wriggle, he keeps moving to anchor me into place. When his erection pokes into my ass cheek, I take that as my prompt to switch tactics.

"Are you trying to kill me or show me a good time?" I ask, making my voice husky. "Because newsflash: choking makes me wet."

He chuckles, the sound harsh. "I'm going to enjoy your slow death."

"Fuck, Cesare," I moan. "Do a girl a favor and let her die with your huge cock in her pussy."

His breath hitches. His grip loosens for the fraction of a second I need for an opening. Throwing my head back, I slam it into his nose.

"Fuck!" Cesare flinches back with a roar, and I twist free.

Heart pounding, I launch myself across the room toward the bed. He's right behind me, his body heat scalding my back. Just as my fingers close in around the gun, his fist lands on the side of my head. Pain flashes through my skull like lightning, and the room spins.

"Drop the gun," he bellows.

Fuck that. I need to stay conscious, get the fuck out of here, and survive another day for the sake of my girl.

I turn around, readying the pistol, but a second punch knocks me to the ground. My fingers loosen, the gun falls to the floor with a clatter, and I go limp.

———

Heavy, labored breaths pull me back into awareness. The intense throbbing on the side of my head tells me that only minutes have passed since Cesare knocked me out. I hold still with my eyes closed, feigning unconsciousness to bide time.

My body is upright, and I'm sitting on a leather surface with my arms and legs splayed. This must be the bondage chair I noticed last night.

Peeking through my lashes, I find Cesare sitting on the bed with the contents of my purse spread out across the mattress. I cringe at the sight of the handgun, syringes, knives, vials of liquid, and compressed fabrics, but my stomach plummets when he's scrolling through my phone.

He must have bypassed its security by scanning my retina. Everything inside it, from the contacts to the photos, has been carefully curated to protect my identity. But it's not foolproof. A determined investigator could break through the encryption and reveal anything incriminating.

"What are you doing?" I rasp.

"What's this icon?" He holds up the handset.

"Which one?" I ask, already knowing he's found the Moirai Group's app.

He strides over, his eyes flashing, and holds the screen up to my face. "This one," he hisses and points at the icon of the spinning wheel. "Why is it protected with a password?"

"It's an e-reader containing the complete works of Homer." The lie rolls off my tongue with practiced ease. "And the password exists, so no one scrolls around and messes with my bookmarks."

He sways on his feet, his gaze still unfocussed. "What is it?"

My heart pounds. There are three passwords. The first will open the Moirai app, the second will delete it and send the firm an SOS with GPS coordinates, and the third will wipe the data and open a text file of The Odyssey with annotations.

There's no point in aggravating Cesare by making him delete the app. Gunther already knows my location, and the firm can't yet magic a method to penetrate the Montesano stronghold.

"Minus sign, six hundred," I say, giving him the third.

He taps in the passcode, his breath still labored, and curls his lip. "Huh?" He blinks once, twice, three times, before shoving the screen back in my face. "What the fuck is this?"

"Ancient literature," I reply.

"Bullshit." He backhands me across the face, making my head snap to the side. "No more lies."

My eyes narrow, and I clamp my lips shut. I've been trained to withstand harsh interrogation tactics. Cesare will get frustrated or bored before I break.

He flashes his teeth. "Now, tell me exactly who the fuck you are, where you came from, and who sent you, or I'll introduce you to my scalpel."

TWELVE

CESARE

The edges of my vision turn black from a cocktail of adrenaline, drugs, and extortion. I want to sleep off the toxins running through my veins, but I can't do a thing until I get the truth.

Standing back, I glare down at my little captive. The restraints force her chest forward and her arms wide apart. Her legs are spread wide, displaying her waxed pussy.

I grit my teeth. How the fuck can something so alluring be so treacherous?

"Stay silent," I hiss. "I dare you, because I'm itching to rip out each secret until you scream for death."

She sucks in a deep breath and stares up at me through hazel eyes.

"My name is Rosalind," she says, her voice calm. "And I was sent here to gather information."

"Go on," I reply.

"The New Alderney Times is doing an exposé on organized crime within Beaumont city, and it's my job to find dirt on the Montesano—"

"No," I snap. "You're not a fucking reporter."

"Call them. My boss is Gunther Hoffmann, managing editor at the Times. He'll tell you everything. Use my phone."

I scoff. "I'll speak to your handler after proving you wrong."

"Then go online and find his number," she says. "Call the fucking switchboard. I'm telling the truth."

Lip curling with disgust, I stalk across the playroom to the bed, where I left her phone and search online for the newspaper's phone number. One glance over my shoulder tells me that Rosalind is checking her restraints, but I already tightened the cuffs and adjusted the buckles out of reach.

The phone rings, and a receptionist answers. I ask for Mr. Hoffman, and she places me on hold. Music pipes through the speakers, making me roll my eyes. No matter what this bitch says, I know she's no reporter.

"Did you reach him?" she asks.

I ignore her.

"Hoffman speaking," says a gruff voice.

"Did you send a reporter to investigate the Montesano family?"

"Who is this?" he barks.

"Answer the fucking question."

He hesitates. "Is Rosalind alright?"

I glance over my shoulder at the naked woman and frown. "She's alive. Let me ask you another question. Is it newspaper policy for your reporters to drug their subjects?"

Hoffman falls silent for so long that I wonder if he's still on the line. Then he sighs. "Of course, not. That's strictly against our newspaper's code of conduct. Where is Rosalind? Let me send a car to take her back to the office for disciplinary action."

All this line of bullshit has done is confirm that her firm has covered its bases and provided their assassins with great cover stories. Unconvinced, I hang up and walk to the other side of the playroom, where I load a trolley with a tray of surgical tools and push them toward my little captive, who stiffens.

"Did you speak to Gunther?" she asks, her voice guarded.

I nod. "He wants to send a car to whisk you back to the office."

Swallowing hard, she glances down at the trolley. "What happens now?"

"Most firms of assassins are small boutiques, run by a single coordinator." I hold up a knife and make a show of examining its blade. "Only one is influential enough to infiltrate the New Alderney Times."

Her breath quickens. "What are you talking about?"

My cousin, Leroi, is probably the best assassin in New Alderney. When we were discussing ways to save my big brother from the electric chair, he talked us through our options.

We needed to assassinate a whole host of corrupt officials who had been bribed to convict Roman for a crime he didn't commit, all while making sure nothing led back to us. Once they were dead, we had to wipe out the family of the man who framed him for murder.

Leroi said there was only one firm large enough to take on the job, but paying for a job of that scale would leave a money trail connecting back to us. That firm is rumored to have its own academy and branches all over the world.

"You work for the Moirai Group." I hold the blade to her throat. "If the next word I hear from you is bullshit, I will slice open every major blood vessel and bathe your delectable body in crimson."

She shivers, her gaze sweeping down my crumpled black shirt to the erection straining through my pants.

"You promised me a scalpel," she says, her voice breathy. It's a pathetic attempt to employ reverse psychology.

"I lied. As did your handler."

"So, what now?" she arches her back, and my gaze drops to her breasts.

I run the flat of the blade down her cheek, and stare into the most intricately colored hazel irises. They're a dark green that borders on gray with pale striations lit up by a stardust of amber. Her fear is masked by a spark of defiance that draws me closer.

"It would be a shame to ruin such a pretty face," I say with a grin. "I'll leave that until last."

She shivers. "Anything I can do to change your mind?"

I drag the knife down her jawline and press its tip into her neck. She barely flinches from the sting, further confirming my suspicions that she's a trained assassin, but the sight of her blood is too intoxicating to resist.

Leaning in, I swipe up the crimson trail with my tongue. "Delicious."

When her breath quickens, I draw back to find her nipples tightening and her clit swelling. Heat shoots straight to my cock. There's no faking that level of arousal.

She releases a nervous chuckle. "What is this, death by a thousand cuts?"

My little captive is so bold, so brave, so brilliantly suited to my tastes. "Oh, sweetheart. You're my perfect toy."

"Wh-what do you mean?" she asks.

"Assassins like you are untraceable. I can take my time, breaking you with no fear of being reported to the police."

"Wait," she says. "Aren't you going to interrogate—"

I lean forward and silence her with a kiss. She parts her lips to protest, but I slip my tongue into her mouth. She tastes sweet—a tantalizing cocktail of fear and desire. I feast on her mouth, savoring the feel of her lips and teeth and tongue.

When I pull away, she's thrashing against her restraints. "Cesare," she says through panting breaths. "Don't you have questions?"

"Just one."

I stride to the other side of the playroom, toward the shelves where I keep my most prized toys. The one I'm looking for sits inside a metal box.

Flipping it open, I extract an antique revolver with a wooden grip and a twelve-inch barrel.

"Hey, Rosalind?" I say.

"What?"

"Have you ever played pussy roulette?"

THIRTEEN

ROSALIND

It's time to step up from my training with the Moirai Group. A full-fledged psychopath like Cesare won't just stop at waterboarding, electric shocks, sleep deprivation, starvation, or even sensory deprivation. He's planning on playing out every sick torture fantasy imaginable.

There's no telling what kind of damage a gun will have if he fires it into my uterus, or how many organs it will tear through before it reaches my heart. I can't die and leave Miranda all alone.

What if Gunther decides to recruit her into the Moirai? She couldn't handle the rigorous training. What if she falls prey to a different breed of predator like her father?

"What do you want to know?" I rasp.

Cesare holds out a palm. "We'll get to the questioning later."

"I'm authorized to release—"

Slap!

My head jerks to the side with the force of his blow.

"Answer my other question first." He waves the pistol.

"What? Have I heard of pussy roulette?"

He nods, his eyes shining with sick pleasure.

"No," I reply. "But I think the name of the game speaks for itself."

Cesare grins, his gaze dropping to my exposed pussy, and my

fight or flight urges me into action. I twist my arms, trying to loosen the leather restraints, but they're still too tight.

"Here are the rules," he says. "I will spin the cylinder of this revolver and load one of its chambers with a bullet. Then I will stick its barrel deep into your cunt. Each time you fail to answer a question to my satisfaction, I will pull the trigger. Got it?"

"Or you could just ask me and I'll—"

Slap!

My nostrils flare. This sadistic bastard doesn't give a shit about gathering information. I need to switch tactics.

"Got it?" he says with more bite.

"Got it," I say through clenched teeth. "May I say something before we begin?"

"Speak."

"At least sterilize the fucking gun."

He chuckles and taps my cheek with its barrel. "Oh, my sweet Rosalind. What makes you think you'll live long enough to succumb to an infection?"

I squeeze my eyes shut. It was worth a try.

"But if you insist."

My eyes snap open, and I watch Cesare walk to the other side of the playroom, where he sets the gun down on the counter and reaches for a transparent box.

He turns to flash me a grin. "While I'm here, I may as well clean the bullet."

Whistling a tune I don't recognize, he snaps on a pair of gloves and extracts a pack of sterile wipes. It takes everything I have to force my gaze away from the transfixing spectacle.

I focus all my attention on freeing my right hand and tuck my thumb into the gap between my little and ring fingers. Once my palm is compressed, I jerk the arm downward.

The leather strap strains and creaks, freeing me about an inch. I grit my teeth and try again with a harder tug. My skin scrapes against the rough material, but I manage to wiggle out my hand up to the first knuckles.

A squeaky wheel brings my attention back to the other side of the room. Cesare pushes a trolley carrying a small first aid box, the revolver, a bullet, a ring gag, and a scalpel.

"Shall we begin?" he asks, his eyes dancing.

Shivers skitter across every inch of skin, but I hold my body still. While he's kneeling between my legs, I can free my hand, maybe grab the blade and stab him in the throat.

Cesare picks up the scalpel. "First, I need to mark you as mine."

"You do that with all your victims?" I mutter.

"Only the ones I want to keep alive."

That should make me shudder, but it gives me hope. Cesare steps between my spread legs and grabs one of my breasts.

"You have the most fantastic tits." He gives it a hard squeeze, and I shiver.

With surgical precision, he brings the blade to the skin and presses. Sharp pain slices through my nerves, and my breath catches. I hold still as he carves the letter C, and my brain releases a rush of endorphins that heats my cheeks and lights up every pleasure center.

His gaze rises to meet mine. "No screaming?"

"I've had worse."

The manic smile falters, and he dabs at the blood with a cotton swab.

While he carves a smaller M inside the C, I work on trying to free my right hand.

"You like pain," he says, his voice breathy as he cleans up more blood.

"What makes you think that?" I ask.

"Dilated pupils, accelerated breathing, increased heart rate, erect nipples." He brushes a thumb over my peak, making me shiver. "But the most obvious sign that you're enjoying this is your swollen clit and the mess you're making of my leather."

"Complaining?" I ask.

He draws back, his gaze fixed on my pussy. "Not at all. It just means I don't need to lubricate the gun."

My stomach plummets. I might enjoy a bit of pain, but nothing as extreme as a bullet ripping through my internal organs. "Cesare, let's make a deal. I'll let you do anything—"

"No!" He stabs the scalpel into the side of my thigh, his eyes wild.

I flinch at the pain, my jaw clicking shut.

Cesare yanks out the scalpel, releasing a burst of agony, places it back on the trolley, and picks up the ring gag.

"Don't think you can provoke me into killing you quickly." He wedges the ring between my lips. "You're my pet, now. I want you to last."

I clench my teeth, not wanting to submit, but he grabs my cheeks with both hands and squeezes hard.

"Open, or I'll break your teeth and you won't be so pretty," he snarls.

My hands twist within the restraints, trying to free the widest part around the knuckles. I can't yet break out, but I wrestle against Cesare's hold anyway, trying to buy more time.

His other hand closes in around my throat and he squeezes. I open my jaws, letting him shove the ring between my teeth, and he fastens the straps around my head.

"You can scream and cry all you want, but first, you're going to answer some questions." He flashes me a manic grin.

My pulse races. Sweat breaks out across my hairline and trickles down my brow. This is insane. How am I supposed to answer his questions around a gag?

Every fiber of my being screams at me to gouge his eyes, and I make one last desperate tug at my arm.

The force of my movement jangles the buckle, and Cesare's gaze travels to my right arm.

"What's that?" he asks.

I rip my hand out of the leather restraint and swing at his face. He sidesteps, his laughter mocking.

"Clever little pet," he says with a sneer. "I'm going to enjoy breaking your spirit."

I tell him to go fuck himself, but I can't even form words with my mouth forced open.

Cesare snatches my wrist and slams it against the chair's wooden crosspiece, eliciting an explosion of pain. This time, when he buckles me back in, it's tight enough to grind my wrist bones.

Shit.

He tightens the left restraint before wiping away the blood

from the scalpel wound on my thigh and then covering it with a flesh-colored bandage.

The stupid gag won't even let me grind my teeth, so I release my frustration in a scream.

"Blink once for yes and two for no." He brandishes the revolver. "Is that understood?"

I blink twice.

"Good girl."

"Asshole," I say, the words garbled.

"I'm going to enjoy this, too." He picks up a bullet and smirks.

My breath comes in shallow gasps as I'm forced to watch him slide the bullet into the chamber before spinning it with an audible click.

I can do this.

I can survive this psychopath.

There's a one in six chance that the gun will fire. That's almost seventeen percent. Lower, considering I plan on answering every single question with something plausible.

My throat tightens. How ironic that he plans to kill me by shooting into the organ that produced the only worthwhile thing in my life. I picture Miranda as a newborn, my heart squeezing. Whatever happens, I need to survive... For her.

Cesare kneels between my spread thighs and stares at my pussy. "You've gotten even wetter."

I blink twice, trying to deny my arousal, but when he brushes the cool metal over my clit, every nerve ending across my back and inner thighs tingles, and I shiver.

"Liar," he says, his voice thickening with arousal. "You love the danger."

He slides the barrel up and down my folds, making an obscene wet sound. I shake my head, my breath coming in heavy pants.

Cesare chuckles. "You were made for pain."

When he positions the gun at my entrance, I squeeze my eyes shut, and when he pushes the barrel into my passage, I moan.

His breathing quickens, synchronizing with mine as he fucks me with the twelve-inch barrel. I clamp around the cold metal, my insides quivering.

This is sick, this is twisted. I should be working on breaking free, but Cesare has fastened the restraints so tightly that all I can do now is play along until I find another opening.

I buck my hips and give in to the sensations as he presses the pad of his thumb on my swollen clit. Pleasure builds and builds until all sense of survival gives way to the urge to climax. Just as the ecstasy sharpens, he shoves the barrel against my cervix.

"Are you an assassin, yes or no?"

I blink once for yes.

He nods.

"Do you and your handler work alone?"

As much as I want to lie to protect the Moirai Group, I can't. No two-person operation has the clout to infiltrate the New Alderney Times.

I blink twice.

"Do you work for a family?"

I blink twice.

He pulls the trigger with a click.

The gun doesn't fire, but my adrenaline spikes, and my entire body goes rigid with shock. In that terrifying moment, I could have died without seeing my baby again. I thrash in my restraints, screaming out a protest.

"I was telling the truth, asshole," I yell, but can't form the words.

He gazes up at me and grins. "I already know you work for a specialized firm of assassins. I was asking about the client."

Shit.

"Now, let's start again, pet," he says. "I'm going to run through some names. You're going to confirm who wants me dead so badly that they're prepared to pay an assassin."

Molten fury burns through my chest, but my veins fill with cold fear. I can't win with this tricky bastard. He's determined to trip me up with ambiguous questions so he can pull that trigger.

The door behind us opens, and Benito Montesano strolls in, staring into his phone. "Leroi texted to say—" His jaw drops. "What the fuck?"

Cesare yanks out the revolver, springs to his feet, stands in front of me, presumably to hide my nudity. What can I say? He's a gentleman and a ghoul.

"Brother," Benito says, his voice low. "What were you doing with that gun?"

"Let's discuss this outside."

Benito disappears behind the door, leaving me alone with my racing heart.

"Stay here." Cesare shoves the revolver's glistening tip between my eyes.

"As if I could even move," I mumble through the gag, rattling the buckles of my restraints.

He grins, but his eyes are glacial. "Don't even think about it, pet. If you make me catch you again, the next round of torture won't be so pleasurable."

I let my arms fall limp, flash my eyes, and let out a garbled, "I'll be good."

Cesare strides to the door with the revolver, and I hold still until the door swings shut. My mind races for a way to escape this mad house before he returns.

The next wrong move won't just cost me my life. Cesare will keep me alive and use my body to fulfill his every sick and twisted fantasy before he grants me a painful and humiliating death.

FOURTEEN

CESARE

I jostle Benito out of the pool house, not wanting him anywhere near my Rosalind. My brother hasn't gotten laid since he was dumped by his fiancée. He acts like he hates women, but Rosalind is hot enough to tempt even a eunuch.

We move in silence until we step out into the pool area. Benito directs me to the narrow path that leads through the bushes that surround the building's posterior, and points at the security camera.

"Leroi told me everything. Did you know she snuck out through the bathroom window to search around the grounds?"

"You saw her on camera?" I ask.

"No. I saw the window open, and the shrubbery move, but there was no sign of the woman."

"What are you saying?"

"Whoever she works for must have supplied her with an advanced form of anti-surveillance clothing. Have you found out the name of her firm?"

"We were getting there before you interrupted," I reply.

Benito's lips tighten. "How the hell did you bring an assassin of that caliber into our home?"

I flinch, my blood heating with resentment, already sick of the double standards. Sometimes, I wonder if they know my secret because I've always been the family scapegoat.

Every mistake I make is amplified until it becomes the original sin. The rest of them can screw up and get the benefit of the doubt.

"Did you ask Leroi the same question?" I growl.

He doesn't reply because the answer is obvious. Benito wouldn't dare question Leroi or ask why our cousin, the trained assassin, couldn't recognize a colleague in disguise.

"Rosalind was Leroi's fuck buddy for months until he discarded her and found someone else. Was it wrong to assume he'd already checked her out and made sure she was harmless?"

Benito's pinched expression fades, replaced by something less judgmental, but there's still no sign of an apology.

I fold my arms across my chest. "So, it's okay when Leroi fucks up, but I get called out for doing the same?"

"What have you found out?" he asks.

"Still working on her," I say with a smirk. "She has a high tolerance to pain, so I've had to get creative."

"You've had her for long enough. What's taking so long?"

Annoyance simmers beneath my skin, itching to explode in a hot rush of fury. Benito is an asshole whose only vice is being condescending. Instead of fucking away his troubles like any normal man, he lives to be a perfectionist and a critic. He belittles everyone yet can't even see his own shortcomings.

Shoulders squaring, I close the gap between us and glare into his arrogant face. "She drugged me with something that made me black out on and off. Part of that time, I was wandering around the grounds, off my head on her sedative."

Benito frowns.

"You remember seeing me under the balcony, right?"

He gives me a hesitant nod.

"I was drugged, incoherent, and with no memories of the night before and you didn't notice I needed help?"

He runs his fingers through his hair and sighs. "I had my hands full. The police were at the gates with a warrant to arrest the woman who was trying to throw herself off the tower."

"We all make mistakes, brother. Part of being a better man is acknowledging your own fuckups." I clap him on the shoulder.

He pulls away, his features morphing back into their usual stern self-righteousness. "Roman wants you to move your... equipment to the basement."

"Why?" I snap.

"He needs to turn the pool house into an art studio."

My jaw clenches and I curl my fists. "I've used that space for years."

"Roman's special guest needs it," Benito says with a huff. "And she's more important to us than a woman you're going to kill."

I can't argue with that. Roman has the dirty job of romancing that crazy balcony woman out of hundreds of millions of dollars' worth of her late father's assets. Rosalind's interrogation can take place anywhere.

"When do you need us out?" I ask.

"The removal boys will come down in ten minutes to reinstall your furniture in the basement."

"Fine," I growl. "Anything else?"

"Find out who hired her, and how she hid from the cameras. Keep us updated."

Benito turns on his heel and walks across the lawn. I glare at his back, wondering if he thinks I'm just tormenting her for my own pleasure. Admittedly, I enjoy watching Rosalind squirm, but I wanted to get the answers in my own time.

Instead of walking around the front of the pool house, I continue around its perimeter to the back. My gaze follows the security camera, which swivels with my movement. I climb in through the bathroom window and land in a low crouch, trying to retrace the steps Rosalind made while sneaking about and gathering intel. She'll expect me to walk in through the door, and I want to observe her from another angle.

A female voice sounds from the other room, making my breath catch. Did she break free and remove the gag? I hurry to the door and crack it open.

The voice doesn't belong to Rosalind, but Roman's woman

from the balcony. I'm pretty sure her name was Emberly. She's frozen in the middle of the room, staring at Rosalind, horrified.

Chuckling, I take off my shirt and roll my shoulders. It's time to give her a little show. I step out, my gaze raking up and down her body. She's tall and wiry, with unruly curls, huge green eyes and without Rosalind's impressive tits.

"Have you come to play?" I ask with a raised brow.

Her eyes widen, and she stammers, her voice raising an octave with each incoherent word. I advance on her with a grin, making her skitter backward. As soon as she turns her back, I roar with laughter.

Poor Roman. The only thing wild about that woman is her hair. And maybe her temper. For once in my twenty-four years of life, I have the more exciting toy.

Rosalind releases an incoherent tirade.

I turn back to where she's splayed out on the chair. "Don't worry, pet. Nothing could ever captivate both my heart and my cock as completely as the way you take my revolver."

Her features twist into a rictus of fury. I close the distance between us and stick my fingers through the ring gag and down her throat. Rosalind chokes, her eyes watering.

"We don't have much time, so I'll make this quick. Are you ready to answer my questions?"

Nodding, she loosens a tear.

She must have noticed I didn't spin the revolver's barrel, increasing her odds of being eviscerated in the next round of pussy roulette. No assassin, no matter how well trained, can survive a bullet tearing through her internal organs.

I pull my fingers out of her mouth and trace the wet trail with my tongue. Rosalind tries to jerk away, but I hold her steady by the neck.

"When I remove your gag, all I want to hear from you is the truth. Is that understood?"

She nods.

"Alright." I reach behind her head, unbuckle the leather straps, and slip the ring from behind her teeth.

Rosalind breathes hard, her features tight, her pretty hazel eyes burning with fiery hatred. "What do you want to know?"

"What's the name of your firm?"

She swallows. "The Moirai Group."

"And your client?"

"Capello."

"Which one?"

"I don't know," she rasps.

"How many of us were you sent to kill?"

She hesitates.

"What?" I snap.

"None. I was supposed to gather information on you via Leroi," she says, her gaze dropping to the floor. "When he stopped responding to me and you came along—"

"And you decided to take advantage of the opportunity?" I say through clenched teeth.

She shrugs.

"What kind of information?" I ask.

"Hidden entrances, security systems, and any weaknesses we can exploit."

"Why?"

"They didn't say," she mutters. "I just gather the intel."

"How did you remain undetected by the cameras?"

"A catsuit made of a fabric that disrupts infrared and thermal imaging. Before you ask, I dissolved it in the bath."

Frustration wells in my gut, and I exhale through flared nostrils. We could have passed on the fabric to our meth team for analysis. "What about the drug?"

"I slipped oxypentanol in the vodka. It's a formula developed by the firm's research and development team," she replies in a monotone. "I have a question for you. How did you wake up without the antidote?"

"What can I say, pet? I have a fantastic anatomy."

Her gaze drops down to the erection straining through my pants. "I've had bigger."

"And then Leroi moved onto someone less aggravating."

She scowls, her lips pursing, mirroring my own displeasure. I leave her stewing in her own insecurities and walk to the section where I keep the restraints. After selecting handcuffs, leg irons, and a waist chain, I return to where she's still trying to burn me to ash with the force of her glare.

"I'm going to release you for transportation. If you're a good girl and behave yourself when I attach these restraints, I'll grant you one request. Though I'm hoping you'll be bad."

"What happens if I don't cooperate?" she asks.

"I'll make you wish you'd lost that game of pussy roulette."

She shudders. "Fine. I won't resist."

I position myself between her spread legs and unbuckle the first wrist cuff. Rosalind's arm flops down to her thighs, a dead weight from being elevated for so long.

She groans with relief, the sound going straight to my aching cock.

"Good girl." I move to the next cuff and release her arm, which also falls to her side.

As I turn to reach for a handcuff, a fist hits my balls with the intensity of a miniature freight train. Pain explodes through my groin. My knees buckle, and I drop to my floor, clutching my screaming testicles.

"Fuck!" I roar.

She leaps off the bondage chair, grabs my discarded shirt, and races out of the playroom.

Breathing hard through the agony, I make a count of three before rising to my feet and giving chase.

Rosalind is going to be my most exhilarating prey.

FIFTEEN

ROSALIND

I burst through the French doors and into the outdoors. Up ahead is the pool and the sun-drenched lawn that stretches up to the mansion. On either side of me are the newly pruned bushes that surround the pool house.

Darting to the right, I duck beneath the shrub and crawl toward the back of the building. My arms feel like rubber and my fingers are less nimble than sausages. The only part of my body that seems to be functional are my legs.

All I need is a few minutes to find a place to hide.

When Cesare charges in one direction, I'll launch myself in the other and keep evading him until I find a way to escape.

Twigs and stones scrape my hands and knees as I crawl around the pool house, and branches scratch my skin. My heart pounds hard enough to make every limb tremble, and my traitorous pussy throbs, seeming to think we're playing hide and seek.

She's forgotten how Cesare fired a pistol into us and now only remembers all the pleasure. She's under the impression that he's determined to give us lots of intense orgasms.

Thank fuck I'm ruled by my survival instincts, which can recognize a deranged predator.

Heavy footsteps pound across the nearby stone tiles, coming

to an abrupt stop. He's looking around, trying to work out where I've gone.

"Rosalind!" he bellows. "You better run fast because when I catch you, those holes are going to hurt."

My stomach lurches. I crawl faster through the bushes and round the corner of the pool house. Sunlight filters through the foliage, its warmth on my back a beacon guiding me to safety. I clutch the shirt in one hand, ready to wear it the moment I find somewhere to hide.

When Cesare's footsteps thunder in another direction and eventually fade, I poke my head out of the greenery. The space behind the pool house is mostly forest land with plenty of potential hiding spots. Straightening, I sprint toward the trees bordering the estate. Leaves rustle overhead, and twigs snap underfoot as I speed through the evergreens, searching for the perfect spot.

My breath comes in ragged gasps, and my heart clambers like a mouse fleeing a feral tomcat. My gaze lands on a tree with branches low and sturdy enough for me to reach. Clenching Cesare's shirt between my teeth, I launch myself up the trunk.

Rough bark scrapes over the sensitive skin of my belly and inner thighs, but it's nothing compared to what I need to escape. Hoisting my upper body up to a thick branch, I swing up my right leg to get a foothold.

Just as I'm about to raise my leg to join it, a rough hand grabs my ankle and yanks me down with a powerful tug.

Cold shock barrels through my chest, and my lungs release a scream.

My body slams into strong arms that wrap around my torso like an iron vise, trapping me against a broad chest. Cesare stares down at me, his eyes wild and manic, his features twisted into a sinister grin.

"Going somewhere, pet?"

Dread plummets in my stomach like a stone, hurtling my psyche into a pit of terror. I elbow him in the gut, but it only makes him tighten his grip and cackle.

His hot breath scorches the side of my neck as he growls, "Tag. You're it."

"This isn't a fucking game," I say from between clenched teeth.

He snaps a handcuff around my wrist, making my panic spike. I slam a fist into the side of his head, but he snatches my other arm and secures it with the cuff.

His thick erection grinds against my ass, making my pussy clench. He bites down on my earlobe hard enough to make me whimper.

"Why are you so eager to leave? We were having so much fun."

His fingers close in around my nipples, twisting and pinching them until I squirm. I can't tell who's the bigger psycho. Him for carving his name into my skin and chasing me across the woods, or my pussy for getting so desperately aroused.

My survival instincts rear to the surface, screaming with alarm. This is life or death, not foreplay. At this rate, there's no way I'm getting out of this alive.

I need to stay calm. Remember my fucking training. I have to picture Cesare as a cold-hearted mercenary and not a man capable of giving me the most intense orgasms.

Planting one foot into the ground, I sweep my leg behind his ankle, drop my weight, using his momentum to force him onto his spine.

Cesare crashes on his back with a thud, releasing a spray of leaf litter. I jump to my feet, grab the shirt, and loop it around his neck as a garrote.

He gazes up at me, his eyes glinting. "Don't fight it, pet," he says, his voice low and menacing. "This is happening, whether you like it or not."

I pull the shirt tight, cutting off his air. "Think again."

Gasping, he claws at the fabric, trying desperately to pry it off his windpipe, but I yank it even tighter and shove a foot against his sternum for leverage.

"Breath play?" he croaks, his smile twisting.

"What the hell is wrong with you?" I snarl and keep up the pressure.

His eyes bulge, his face reddens, and he struggles for air. "That's enough now."

I huff an incredulous laugh. "You think I'm going to stop?"

"No... but." He wheezes, uttering through ragged breaths. "I. Can't. Let. You. Escape."

I lean backward, increasing the pressure of the garrote, until he sputters, and his eyes roll to the back of his head. Now's the ideal chance to choke Cesare to death, but Gunther wants the Montesano brothers to die in a single strike.

Leaving the other two alive will only make them extra vigilant. Worse, they might recruit another crew of assassins to take out both me and the client.

When Cesare slumps, I release one end of the garrote and allow him to drop to the ground. His tattooed chest rises and falls with shallow breaths, showing he's alive.

I crawl around his prone form and snap on the leg irons, locking them in place before I stumble to my feet. Sweat-dampened hair sticks to my skin, and I raise both hands over my face to wipe my eyes.

He grabs my ankle, lurching me off my feet. I drop to my side and groan.

"Why can't you just stay down?" I snap.

"Because. You're. Not. Leaving," he replies through hacking coughs and drags himself up my legs. "I marked you. You're mine."

"My body isn't yours to claim."

"The fuck it isn't."

He can't take me back. I can't fall back into his clutches. I need to survive for Miranda. I launch a kick at his head, making it snap backward, but he's determined not to let me escape. My hands scramble through the ground, rifling through twigs and debris until my fingers close around a stone the size of my fist.

With every ounce of my strength, I slam it into the side of his head.

Cesare's features twist into a scowl and he grips tighter. "Bitch. Your punishment is about to get worse."

"Get fucked." I hit him again and again until he finally releases me and falls atop my legs like a dead weight.

I shove him off me with a grunt and scramble to my feet, still winded from the struggle. The forest spins around me like a carousel, and I need to hold my bound arms steady for balance.

A large vehicle rumbles in the distance and stops at a parking spot, giving me a potential means of escape. I glare down at the handcuffs and study their mechanism. If I had enough time, I'd use an instrument to pick the lock so I could secure them around Cesare's wrists, but the vehicle door opens and heavy footsteps approach.

I need to hide Cesare. Now.

Bending, I grab his bound feet and drag his unconscious body into the undergrowth. The handcuffs dig into my wrists as I tug him over the rough terrain.

Once I'm satisfied he's hidden, I crouch beside him and join my forearms. The least efficient way to escape handcuffs involves attacking its weakest link: the chain.

I make tight circles with my wrists, turning the metal links until they tangle and lock. Once they're secure, I twist, breaking a link in the chain with a snap.

My hands fall free, and I cry out with relief. Adrenaline continues to flood my system because I'm still not safe. After taking off Cesare's belt, I stumble to my feet, walk out of the bushes and pick up his shirt.

An escape plan takes form in the back of my mind as I sprint toward the vehicle, jumping over tree roots and dodging low-hanging branches.

If I can't hide in its undercarriage, then I'll hotwire its engine and ram it through the gates.

Whatever it takes to escape this madhouse.

When Cesare awakens, he'll have a sore head and a bruised ego. With any luck, I'll be long gone and gathering intel for another job, miles away from that maniac.

The only time I want to hear from him is as a name written on my paycheck.

SIXTEEN

CESARE

I stand in front of Roman in Dad's old study, still feeling off my game from the effects of the sedative. My head pounds from the blow with a blunt object, my throat burns from that bitch's garrote, one side of my face is encrusted with dirt, and my hair is tangled with twigs.

Her little stunt bought her a few hours head start, and by the time I combed the grounds to find her, she was gone.

We don't know if she escaped with the men who moved my playroom to the basement or is still on the grounds, biding her time for the right moment to slit our throats.

Roman sits behind his desk, his fingers steepled, features etched with fury. Leroi just left after imparting bad news. One of the people he was supposed to have killed resurfaced at the club last night and will cause the family a shitload of trouble. And the crazy woman from the balcony is smashing up her new room.

Everything's turning to shit, and I'm taking the brunt of Roman's displeasure.

"Explain to me how you got your ass handed to you by a woman half your size," he says, his voice dangerously low.

"She's an assassin with the Moirai," I reply.

His brows rise. "Did she tell you that?"

"I worked that out by myself, but yeah, she confirmed it." I tell Roman about Gunther, who I reached through the New Alderney Times switchboard, but he's stone-faced by my deductive capabilities.

Benito probably already poured poison in his ear, which is why he's so unimpressed.

He stares up at me through eyes as dark as Dad's, and I hold his gaze, despite the way my insides want to squirm.

This is worse than failing to become a surgeon. Worse than being locked in a room and having to go cold turkey.

"You led an enemy through our gates," Roman snarls, completing that thought.

"I didn't know—"

"You could have fucked her in the Phoenix or taken her to one of your playrooms across the street," he barks.

He's right. I should have known better. Something about Rosalind drew me in. Maybe because I saw her with Leroi so often. Maybe because she acted so unimpressed. She wove her web like a black widow spider, and I fell right into her trap.

There's no running away from the fact that I've fucked up.

"Did you get the name of her client?" Roman asks, his voice pulling me out of my thoughts.

"Capello."

"Which one?"

I shake my head. "She didn't know."

"And you didn't press her?"

"That was the plan until your removal men showed up to dismantle my playroom. While I was transporting her to the house, she escaped."

Roman slams his fists on the table, his eyes blazing. "Stop trying to shift the blame and fix this mess."

"Fine. I'll call her boss at the Times—"

"Rosalind's little sister came to Leroi's apartment, demanding her whereabouts." He slides a piece of paper across the desk. "Leroi says she was wearing a Tourgis Academy sweatshirt. You're going to use the sister as bait to lure Rosalind back."

"I'll drive down there now."

"Get cleaned up before you pick up the girl, and don't screw up this second chance."

He doesn't need to tell me twice.

———

An hour later, I'm sitting in my Lamborghini outside Tourgis Academy's grand entrance. It reminds me of an old British manor house with its climbing ivy, impressive outbuildings, and manicured gardens. The campus is surrounded by ten-foot-high iron gates that create the illusion of exclusivity, privilege, and safety.

Rosalind and I have unfinished business, and I'm not just talking about the missing information. Thanks to her, Leroi and my brothers think I'm a bumbling fool.

She's an enigma in a beautiful little nutshell. I want to crack her open and spill her secrets. I want to watch her break. I want to taste her fear, dine on her desperation. I want her at my feet, crying tears of blood, begging for another chance to suck my cock.

Arousal shoots straight to my groin as I imagine the possibilities.

The phone rings, ruining my fantasy. But it's not Rosalind calling me for a rematch, it's Roman.

"What?" I say.

"Are you in place?"

"Right outside the gates," I reply.

"And you've made contact with the girl?"

"We're still texting. She thinks I'm taking her to big sis."

Roman pauses for a heartbeat. "Don't mess this up."

My muscles tighten and my gut roils with frustration. Everyone talks as though Rosalind is a bratty sub I'm not man enough to control, when she's actually a trained assassin skilled enough to fool even Leroi.

"I'll take care of it," I snarl.

"No excuses. We're counting on you." He hangs up before I can utter another word in my defense.

"Fuck." I slam my fists on the steering wheel. "Fucking bitch."

My phone buzzes with a text from Rosalind's sister:

They just let me out of detention. Be down in a minute.

I pull down the mirror and check my reflection. My eyes are

still a little bloodshot from Rosalind's cocktail of drugs, and I'm probably still concussed, but I've looked worse.

Beyond the gates, a set of doors open, letting out a group of kids in white shirts and black blazers. The boys wear pants and the girls wear plaid miniskirts that barely reach their knees.

My lip curls. How can Rosalind approve of this for her little sister? Whoever designed this uniform needs to be on some sort of register.

As the small group filters out of the gates, one of the boys pulls on the arm of a girl with the same heart-shaped face as Rosalind's. Only she's sweeter looking and likely infinitely less infuriating. Her eyes widen, looking almost too big for the rest of her features.

The girl yanks her arm out of the boy's grip, making me chuckle. She's just as feisty as her sister. When the boy slams her against the iron railings and sticks his hand up the girl's skirt, I'm out of my car in an instant.

"Hey," I yell. "What the fuck do you think you're doing?"

The boy turns around, his mouth gaping open with shock. He takes one look at my scowl and backs away with both hands raised. "Hey, man. We were just talking."

"Since when did boys talk to girls like that?" I ask, my voice low.

The boy's face pales. "I-I was just kidding around. It wasn't that deep. I was just trying to be funny."

I grab him by the collar and slam his head against the iron railing. "Then you won't mind telling me your name."

He gulps. "T-Toby."

"Toby what?"

"Who are you?" He squeezes his eyes shut.

"His name's Toby Nesbitt," the girl says, her voice sharp with an edge of viciousness. "He's a senior at our school, and he's a bully and a dick."

I grab little Toby by the throat. "Stay away from this girl. Don't touch her, don't talk to her, don't look at her, don't even think about her unless you want to lose your teeth. Got that?"

Toby swallows hard. "Yes, sir."

"Now, apologize to Miranda."

His gaze darts in her direction. "I-I-I'm sorry. It won't happen again."

I turn to the girl. "Anything you want to tell him, love?"

Her face tightens. "Yeah. Stop talking about me, Toby. Or I'll break your nose."

The boy nods.

"You heard the lady." I shake him hard enough to make his teeth rattle. "Now, scram."

Toby scampers away, not turning back until he joins a group of kids at the other end of the road.

The girl turns to me and beams, her eyes sparkling. "Thanks for coming to my rescue. Are you Cesare?"

"That's right." I give her my most charming smile. "Rosalind lost her phone, so she asked me to tell you not to worry."

Her shoulders sag with relief. "That's great. She missed an important meeting at school and didn't call or text. I was so worried. She's never late for anything. I was about to call the cops."

I chuckle. "Want me to take you to her?"

Her gaze wanders to the Lamborghini. "Is that your car?"

I nod. "Want a ride?"

She glances at the small group of kids still lingering on the street and bites her lip. "How do I know you're not a stranger?"

Clever girl. I'm proud of her caution. I reach into the pocket of my leather jacket and pull out a scrap of paper. "Recognize this?"

She glances down at it, her brows furrowing. "I left that with her boyfriend, Leroi."

"Ex," I mutter. "They broke up. I'm her new man."

Her gaze flicks up to meet mine. "Really?"

I reach into my pocket, pull out my phone, and scroll to the photos app. "Recognize this guy?" I show her a selfie I took of Benito and Leroi the night before the Capello massacre. "That's me with my cousin."

Her breath catches. "You and Leroi are related?"

I nod. "You went to Leroi's apartment this morning, looking for your sister. He was telling the truth when he said she wasn't there. She was with me."

Miranda stares up into my eyes, scrutinizing my features for the truth. I gaze back, having nothing to hide.

"I might be the rebound guy, but I've liked Rosalind for months. She brightens my evening every time she comes to my club."

Her jaw drops, and her cheeks turn pink. "You own the Phoenix?"

"Want a tour?" I ask.

"Let's go!" She jogs to the Lamborghini.

Chuckling, I open the passenger side door, letting her scamper inside. Once we're both settled in, I turn the key, and the engine rumbles.

Miranda bounces in her seat, her gaze taking in the illuminated dashboard and leather interior. Gasping, she says, "This is so cool!"

My chest inflates with pride. "Buckle up, sweetheart, it's going to be a wild ride."

Miranda squeals and fastens her seatbelt. "I'm ready."

As I pull out of the parking spot and drive past the gawking kids, she turns to meet their stares and gives them the middle finger.

Snickering, I activate the central locking and turn up the music.

What a cute kid.

It's almost a pity that I plan on breaking her sister.

SEVENTEEN

ROSALIND

Hours later, I hobble into Moirai HQ. My ears ring, I'm covered in soot, reeking of exhaust fumes, and tracking black footprints across its pristine white interior. Somewhere in the recesses of my memory, I'm sure I've forgotten something, but my mind is too frazzled to care.

My entire body is fucked... literally, but I had to get away from Cesare.

The medics rush me to the infirmary, where I'm forced to decontaminate before anyone will assess my injuries. After a bio scan that determines I'm not carrying tracking devices, I'm put on a cocktail of intravenous painkillers, antibiotics, and nutrients to replenish my energy.

A team of physicians surround my cot, healing the cuts, bruises, and the burns inflicted from stowing away in the truck's undercarriage.

I'll need to return in a few days after the initials Cesare carved into my breast heal, so they can complete the tissue regeneration and laser resurfacing to remove the scars.

The Chief Medical Officer, Dr. Daniel, approaches with a tablet. "You have a mild concussion, two broken ribs, and multiple lacerations. We're going to keep you under observation for forty-eight hours."

"Can I at least leave the infirmary?"

He snaps a bracelet around my wrist. "Certainly. Any change to your vital signs and the monitor will summon you back to the medical wing."

"Thanks." I rise off the cot.

"One more thing, Rosalind. Gunther hasn't approved the charge of your treatment to his budget, so I'm going to add it to your tab."

My stomach plummets into the hard floor, bringing up a wave of nausea. It's taken ten years to make a dent in the amount I owe the firm for the damaged equipment. I can't add to those debts.

"B-But I completed my mission," I stammer. "All the information Gunther wanted is—"

"Take it up with your supervisor." Dr. Daniel raises a hand.

My jaw tightens. "Don't worry. I will."

Minutes later, I walk through the maze of hallways that lead to Gunther's office. A few other operatives cast me wary glances as I stride past, but I'm too furious to meet their gazes.

Gunther is determined to keep me in debt bondage. If he'd authorized me to kill Cesare, all my expenses would be paid, plus I'd get a six-figure bonus to help pay off my debts.

I reach his door, where a team of my colleagues stream out, each of them giving me a double take.

"What?" I snap.

They smirk, like I'm a joke. I came first in all the theoretical exams and graduated at the top of our class. I was the first among us to get a solo mission, while they were all supporting other assassins or stuck in HQ gathering intel.

A decade later, I'm doing their grunt work while they're the ones getting all the accolades. All because of one side quest. Even if I knew going after Miranda would turn me into the Moirai Group's indentured servant, I would still do it again. That doesn't mean I should remain demoted until I die.

"Rosalind." Britany grabs my arm and pulls me to one side. "They said you got promoted and moved overseas."

I glance into Gunther's office, where he's deep in conversation with Axel, a tall blond asshole who always looks stunning in a black tactical suit that leaves little to the imagination.

My throat tightens, and my veins burn with resentment. I haven't seen him since the Paris job, where we spent four months pretending to be a couple to get close to the target. When he failed the mission and ended up tortured to the brink of death, I rushed in with explosives to kill his target and dragged Axel's broken body from the wreckage.

The bastard promised to transfer his bonus, but when we reached HQ, he changed his story. I thought he was different, but he was just one of the many people who pretended to like me until I was no longer of use.

I tear my gaze away from the backstabber. "Gunther said what?"

She drags me down the hallway, rounds a corner, and glances over her shoulder to make sure no one is looking. "He said," she repeats in a lower voice. "That you went to the branch in Zurich to take a senior position."

"That's bullshit," I hiss.

We duck into a stockroom lined with vending machines. I walk to the retina reader and lean into its blue light for a scan.

"First of all, I'm still on the Montesano job. Second, I got caught by the younger brother."

Her breath catches. "Is that why you're wearing a monitor and robe? Are you hurt?"

"Just a few cuts and scrapes." I walk to the first machine and press a finger on the scanner to request a replacement phone. "One of them called the New Alderney Times to confirm my ID. Gunther knew I got caught, which must be why he told everyone I'd been transferred."

She claps a hand over her mouth, her eyes going wide. "Does that mean everyone else who got promoted overseas is captured or dead?"

"Probably," I mutter. "It's not like he sent a rescue team."

"Fuck." She leans against the wall, her gaze going distant.

Britt is no stranger to the firm's double dealing. She was fined for helping me rescue Miranda, except she's made enough kills to pay off her debt.

I took the blame for our little side quest and told Gunther I'd forced her to come along, so I got the brunt of the punishment. As much as I wanted to cover Britt's fine, I couldn't. Gunther relegated me to an indefinite ban from high-paying jobs and the humiliation of assisting remedial assassins.

The worst part is that I can't quit until my balance reaches zero.

The display on the machine reads: *Handset activated. Do you wish to deactivate previous handsets?*

I tap YES on the screen and the display reads: *Handset deactivated.*

A brand-new phone drops down the chute. I pick it up and slide it into my pocket.

Then I order a general-purpose field kit containing a catsuit, hexylpentose and oxypentanol in vials and disposable syringes, plus a silenced pistol, and a knife.

After collecting my new supplies, the display reads: Balance -303,877.65. That's not my bank balance. It's how much I owe the firm.

"Fucking crooks," I mutter.

Britt appears at my side and winces. "Let me transfer some funds to your account."

"No." I place a hand on her shoulder. "You've already given me the biggest gift ever. I won't drag you into any more of my problems."

Her gaze softens as she takes in my meaning. "Are you sure? I don't mind."

"I'll speak to Gunther. He owes me for trying to cover up my capture."

She gives me a hesitant nod, not believing that speaking with Gunther will make a difference. No matter how often I tell him to remove my demotion, he always finds an excuse to refuse. All because I continue to refuse his advances. Now, I finally have a way to call the man out on his bullshit.

"What are you doing for dinner?" she asks.

"Having it with you?"

She chuckles. "Text me when you're ready."

Gunther's office is at the other side of a boardroom where he holds weekly briefings for each project our section has on its roster. Twelve assassins report directly to him, and I'm technically the thirteenth because I'm stuck as an analyst.

Analysts are recruits who have survived the Moirai Academy's deadly curriculum. Most are between eighteen and twenty-one. At the grand old age of twenty-eight, I'm not just a relic but a cautionary tale.

Because of Gunther's mistreatment, only a handful of assassins speak to me directly. Most whisper about me when I'm in earshot, warning others not to screw up in their assignments in case they end up indebted, like Rosalind.

I pass the boardroom table and open the door, not bothering to knock. Gunther leans back in his desk chair, his face illuminated by a lamp. His brows rise the tiniest fraction, showing both his surprise and the effects of his Botox.

He grins. "Rosalind, take a seat."

"I'll stand." I fold my arms across my chest. "What's this I hear about you telling everyone I got promoted overseas? Is that the standard excuse you give when operatives get captured and you leave them for dead?"

His smile melts. "How did you escape?"

"Does it matter? What I want to know is why I'm over three hundred thousand in debt? Why didn't you approve my medical expenses?"

Shifting uncomfortably in his seat, he clears his throat, his gaze darting to the door. "I didn't think you would escape the Montesano brothers."

"Why wouldn't I when I saved Axel from an impossible situation and completed the mission he failed?"

Gunther's shoulders rise, and his gaze drops to his desk. "Axel's report says otherwise."

"Can you blame him for lying when you've kept a skilled assassin in debt for a decade? He probably thought you'd fine him too for his failure. Now, it turns out that every promotion is actually a cover up for someone we won't rescue, and—"

"Enough." He waves his hand. "Tell me what you want."

"You're going to write off my debts."

He huffs. "Impossible. HQ will decapitate me for making fraudulent transactions."

"Then revisit all the money I didn't get for contributing to a kill, starting with Axel. Claw back my bonuses, take me off probation, and give me an assignment."

Jaw tightening, he screws his eyes shut and inhales through flared nostrils. "I don't have the authority—"

I slam a palm on his desk, making him flinch. "You're just punishing me for rejecting you when I was a new recruit."

"And you're just going to skip over stealing an armored car, a grenade launcher, guns, and ammunition?" he asks with a sneer.

"Which I would have paid off in a few kills if I hadn't been demoted," I snarl.

He sighs, exhausted from having this conversation every time we meet. For the first time, he can't lord his power over me and smirk because I finally have some dirt that will stick.

If the assassins knew the true death rate, everyone who's already built up a nest egg would leave. Gunther wouldn't be able to recruit enough impressionable young people to make up for the mass exodus, and the smaller firms that value their employees would get all the work.

"Fine," he growls. "As of today, you are restored to your former rank."

"What about my debts?"

A muscle in his jaw flexes. "You can pay them off with future bonuses."

"And all the past bonuses I should have earned?"

"Claw those back yourself by convincing your colleagues to do the right thing." He folds his arms across his chest.

My stomach sinks. Thanks to Gunther's machinations, that's never going to happen. "I need you to sign off my medical bills and the costs of replacing everything I lost while gathering information on the Montesano mansion."

"Fine."

"And I get the next paid assignment. No more analyst bullshit."

"Yes, yes." He waves me away. "Now, get out of my sight."

I turn on my heel and walk out of his office, my heart rising back to the center of my chest. Gunther was telling the truth about not having the authority to write off my debt, but it always pays to start a negotiation with an impossibly high demand.

It will take a few more missions to put me in the black, but once I've built up a small nest egg, I can finally quit the Moirai Group and live like a normal human being.

I might even be able to build a relationship with Miranda.

She's moved from screaming every time I visited her at school to indifference to cold politeness. Even though she doesn't remember that terrible afternoon, part of her is still affected from seeing me kill her guardians.

I want to tell her why I did it, but she's only fourteen. Far too young to know anything about the circumstances of her birth.

My phone buzzes as I step out into the hallway to message Britt. It's a text from a number not in my contacts. When I open it, it's a photo of Miranda with her wrists bound and her head in a reverse bear trap.

Terror seizes my chest as my phone floods with more and more gruesome images, ending with the message:

> Come alone to the alley beside the Phoenix at midnight or little Miranda will die. In agony.

EIGHTEEN

CESARE

Contrary to popular belief, nightclubs aren't closed during the day. While we wait for patrons to arrive, employees busy themselves cleaning, stocking the bar, and supplying local dealers with meth. There's even an outlet at the back where we supply overpriced booze to people who order online.

I guide Miranda through the Phoenix's front doors and give her a moment to soak in her surroundings. She steps into the foyer, admiring the mirrored walls and velvet curtains with wide-eyed fascination. She tilts her head to gaze up at the crystal chandeliers used to illuminate the space and can't help but release a tiny gasp.

"You own the whole building?" she asks, her voice breathy.

"Yeah, along with a few others," I reply with a chuckle.

She pauses to place her palms on the unoccupied coat check desk, her head swiveling in all directions. "This is so cool."

"You haven't even seen the club yet." I wrap an arm around her shoulders and guide her toward the double doors. "You've never been to a nightclub?"

She shakes her head.

"Come on, let me show you around."

I take her on a brief tour, showing her the DJ booth, the private function rooms, and my office, where she marvels at the wall of surveillance screens. I even play one of her favorite songs she can prance about on the dance floor. As we walk around, people acknowledge me and are careful not to glance at my underage companion.

As we take a seat in the VIP section, she glances at the bar and asks, "Can I have a cocktail?"

"Anything you want, love."

I wave over Tania, the pink-haired bartender who walked in on me giving Ricky CPR.

She flounces over, her lips downturned, her eyes burning with resentment. "What can I get you?"

"Two Shirley Temples," I say.

Her gaze slides to Miranda in her school uniform before she turns back to me. "Is this a joke?"

I flash my teeth. "Just get us the drinks."

Rolling her eyes, she returns to the bar, most likely muttering curses. I turn to glare at her back. Stupid bitch is making me look bad in front of my guest. If she's still sore about being choked, then she should have quit.

"What's wrong with her?" Miranda asks, her gaze following Tania's retreating figure.

"Bad day?" I reply with a shrug. "So, what kind of jewelry does your sister like?"

Her mouth forms a perfect O. "Are you going to buy her a ring?"

"Something like that." I smirk, picturing Rosalind squirming on my dungeon floor, with nipple rings adorning those glorious tits. "What do you think of diamonds?"

Miranda launches into a monologue about her own likes and dislikes, without once mentioning her sister. Concealing a frown, I question if they're as close as Leroi implied.

Tania returns with two vibrant mocktails and slams mine on the table with a vicious smirk. Liquid splashes across the surface, barely missing my pants leg. "I spat in that."

Miranda recoils, her features contorting with disgust. Blood rushes through my ears, and my pulse pounds in sync with my mounting rage. Tania is no idiot. She's acting up to provoke a violent reaction, hoping Miranda will see my darker side and run for her life.

"You're fired," I snarl, my hands balling into fists.

Tania's jaw drops. "What?"

"Get out."

"B-But Cesare—"

"Now," I say through clenched teeth.

Tania's face pales, her chest rising and falling. She reaches for one of the Shirley Temple glasses, but I snatch her wrist and pull her down so she can hear my warning.

"Don't even think about throwing a drink in my face," I growl, making her whimper. "Now, apologize to my guest, pack your things, and leave."

I glance at Miranda, who sits frozen, her eyes wide. Fuck knows what's racing through the little girl's mind, but if this run-in with Tania makes Miranda think less of me, the pink-haired bitch will have more things to worry about than being fired.

"Cesare, you can't do this," Tania cries.

Bruno lumbers over. "Problems, boss?"

"This bartender needs to be shown the door." I release Tania's wrist.

Bruno grabs her arm and drags her away, leaving Miranda gaping.

My heart sinks, and my chest tightens at the thought of her reaction. I was having so much fun with the girl, letting her think I was safe to be around. I turn to her, my brows pinching and stare at her shocked profile.

"Are you alright, love?" I ask.

She whirls on me, her eyes sparkling. "That was so cool. You were like..." Her features turn serious, and she lowers her voice. "You're fired."

A weight lifts off my chest, and the muscles squeezing my heart loosen so quickly that I chuckle. "Glad you approve."

"She deserved it." Miranda glances at her drink and grimaces.

"We can forget about those. Are you hungry?" I ask.

"Why?"

"Because my karaoke bar makes the best wagyu burgers."

Miranda grins. "I'm starving. Let's go!"

———

If Miranda wasn't the spitting image of Rosalind, I would swear they weren't related. The girl has told me all about her love of K-pop, J-pop, K-dramas, and anime, but she hasn't once asked about her sister. It's almost as though she's trying to avoid the topic.

My manager, Allegra, takes us to a private room, and I let Miranda order anything from the menu. For every alcoholic drink she selects, I substitute it for something without the liquor. Miranda sings a few songs as we wait for our orders, and I can't help but grin at the way she dances with her hands.

She makes me wish I had carefree younger siblings to spoil and protect instead of two older brothers and Gil who treat me like I'm a screwup.

Our burgers arrive, along with a fuckload of sides Miranda wanted to try. I can't help but chuckle as she chatters nonstop about the amount of fun she's having. Her excitement is contagious.

"So, you have a nightclub, a karaoke bar. What else?"

I rub my chin. "Our family owns all the stores on this block."

She leans into me and whispers, "Including Wonderland?"

"What do you know about Wonderland?" I ask with a scowl.

"Only that it sells adult stuff."

"Adult stuff." I raise a brow.

"You know, handcuffs, masks, whips. Will you take me for a tour?" she asks, her eyes twinkling.

I shake my head. "No way. Rosalind would have my balls."

She giggles. "She would."

"So, what's she like as a big sister?" I ask.

Miranda's smile fades, taking all traces of exuberance with it, leaving her empty and distant.

"What's wrong, love?" I ask.

She hesitates, her tiny jaw flexing as though she's trying to compose a difficult essay. "Rosa never has time for me," she replies, her words measured. "And she would never let me eat food like this."

"Like what?" I glance at the banquet of burgers, fries, sides, and milkshakes.

"Junk food. If she isn't disappearing for weeks or months, then she's eating vegan health food. All she cares about is homework, exercise, and routines."

"I'm sure Rosalind means well."

Miranda scowls. "Maybe."

"Do you live with your parents?" I ask.

"They're dead."

"Oh." My brows rise. "Were you close?"

"We were until they died," she mutters.

"Car accident?"

"My mom got shot in the head, and my dad died in an explosion."

Frowning, I study her blank features. She talks about their deaths in a monotone, making me wonder if she's still dealing with the trauma. If Rosalind also witnessed their deaths, maybe that's the reason she became an assassin.

"I'm sorry. How old were you at the time?" I ask.

"Four."

"And it's been you and your sister ever since?"

Miranda takes a large bite from her burger, seeming reluctant to answer. The poor kid. I was eighteen when Dad died and twenty-two when I heard about Mom's death. Old resentment rises to the surface, and my stomach twists into painful knots. She would still be alive if she hadn't left. The food lingering on my tongue sours, and I toss my burger back onto its plate.

I pick up the remote. "Want to watch a movie?"

"Only if it's horror. I'm not allowed to watch anything violent."

A smirk tugs at my lips. "Have you seen *Saw*?"

"Do you have it?" She bounces on her seat.

"It's my fucking favorite."

After switching channels, I order us more drinks and start the movie. Miranda scoots closer, already trembling.

My gaze drops to where she's tucked beneath my arm. "I thought you liked horror."

"But I also like being scared," she replies with a smirk.

A laugh escapes my lips, and I squeeze her shoulder. "If it gets too much, we'll turn it off."

"It won't."

"Let's see how brave you are, then."

We spend the rest of the evening watching the movie and laughing when Miranda flinches at the jump scares. It's the most fun I've had since that hellish week when Dad died, Roman got arrested, and Mom left us for Tommy Galliano.

I clench my fists, my mood souring at the mere thought of the Galliano brothers. The door opens, pushing me out of my thoughts. Allegra arrives to clear our plates and gives me the side-eye.

We used to fuck until I realized she was faking her interest in bondage and tried to downgrade us to vanilla. Ignoring her attempts to capture my attention, I order us chocolate brownies and ice cream for dessert.

I don't react when Allegra returns with the dessert and brushes the back of my hand with her fingers. She will never compare to my Rosalind. Rosalind is my pet, my plaything, my pretty new pastime. I don't need movies or music when I can break her apart, piece by beautiful piece.

Miranda sets upon her sweet treats like she hasn't just eaten burgers and every side on the menu. "This is awesome," she says through her mouthful. "I've never had brownies with white chocolate."

"Hey, do you like pranks?" I ask during a lull.

"What sort of prank?"

"Something that will get her attention."

Her eyes widen. "Sure."

"I have a replica of the reverse bear trap in my office. Do you want to play a little trick on your sister?"

NINETEEN

ROSALIND

Cesare Montesano has Miranda.

An onslaught of images flood my screen, each one more harrowing than the last.

My breath freezes, and my heart pounds hard enough to crack my ribs. My brow breaks out in a cold sweat and my palms become slick. Last time I was this terrified was before the c-section, when the doctor explained he would cut me open to extract my baby.

I stride to the nearest locker room, change into a tactical suit and requisition guns and knives and portable explosives. If Cesare wants me to meet him outside the Phoenix, then he's either torturing her inside or in one of the many downtown Montesano businesses.

The only question is which one?

I call his number, but it goes straight to voicemail.

"Cesare," I hiss into the speaker. "What the fuck are you doing to my sister? If you hurt her, I won't just make you suffer. I won't just kill your brothers. I will take days making them scream."

After kitting up, I jog to the exit that leads to the stairs, but my wrist cuff sets off the alarms.

Security staff at the door block my path. Their supervisor, a burly blond man with the same cold blue eyes as Axel, takes my wrist.

"You're not cleared to leave the building, operative," he says.

"This is an emergency," I reply, my voice tight with anxiety.

He waves a scanner over my wrist cuff and reads out the results. "Dr. Daniel wants you confined to HQ. If you want to leave, take it up with him."

"There's no time." I shove past the guard, only for two more to grab my arms and hold me in place. "Let go of me."

The supervisor sneers. "Keep your composure, operative, or you will be subdued."

My stomach lurches and the full implication of his words hits me like a punch to the solar plexus. If I get violent, I'll spend the next thirty-six hours under the influence of oxypentanol. That's time I can't afford to waste.

I glare at him and the guards holding me back. "Fine," I say, trying to hold back a scream. "Let go of me and I'll speak to the doctor."

The moment the guards release me, I take off in a sprint toward the infirmary, my pulse pounding in my ears. My academy training prepared me for being captured by an enemy, but I never thought an enemy would come after my daughter.

Screams echo through the hallways as I reach the infirmary, but it's nothing compared to the terror screaming through my heart. Cesare is the worst kind of psychopath. Everything to him is some kind of sexual game.

Painful knots form in my gut, making me whimper. He already has Miranda's head in a bear trap. What else is he doing to my little girl?

I find Dr. Daniel in the infirmary tending to an operative covered in blisters and burns. My throat clogs with the overwhelming stench of chemicals, but I force myself to keep going.

A medic steps in my path. "This section is closed to—"

I shove him aside and keep going. "Doctor. You need to give me clearance to leave the premises."

Dr. Daniel turns to me with a frown. "You're out of medical garments and putting yourself at risk of infection."

"Clearance." I hold up my wrist cuff. "It's a matter of life and death."

He frowns and is about to say something when a hand lands on my shoulder.

"Rosalind, what's this I hear about you attacking the door staff?"

I whirl around and lock gazes with Gunther, my hackles rising. This is the same bastard who made sure to inform me he knew Miranda studied at the Tourgis Academy and implied he would do something to her if I failed my mission.

But can I afford not to tell him? Gunther might be the only person who can make the doctor lift my restrictions on leaving.

"Cesare Montesano has my sister."

His eyes widen. "What does he want?"

"Me in exchange for her."

"Any ideas where he's holding her?"

"Not sure. He wants me to meet him in the alley beside the Phoenix nightclub."

"Then she can't be too far away," he says with a decisive nod. "Stay here. I'll send a rescue team—"

"Like you did with me?" I interrupt.

Face paling at the prospect of anyone learning his secret, his gaze darts around the infirmary, his features slackening with a combination of panic and paranoia. The nearest person to us is Dr. Daniel, who is too busy dealing with a patient's chemical burns to overhear my barb.

Gunther's features harden. "Threatening me won't save your sister. I've already given into your demands."

"It was a fair question. Don't expect me to swallow that bull-shit about non-existent rescue teams," I say from between clenched teeth.

"How the hell did the Montesano brothers get hold of your sister? Did you bring her up during the interrogation?"

"Of course not," I snap. "Leroi Montesano must have had me followed."

He shakes his head, his features pinching with disapproval. "Sloppy."

Guilt tightens my chest, even though I know this line of

conversation is a distraction. He wants to make me squirm in revenge for holding the firm's double dealing over his head. It's just like the squabbles we used to have about my demotion, which usually escalated until time ran out or he threatened me with disciplinary action.

"Dr. Daniel won't give me clearance to leave HQ," I say. "Can you override it?"

Gunther spreads his arms wide. "The Chief Medical Officer outranks a section supervisor. You'll have to convince him."

I turn back to where I last saw the doctor tending to the patient, but he's already gone.

Fuck.

Gunther leans against the wall with his arms folded over his chest. I don't need to look at him to see his beady eyes soaking in my panic. He's a creep who enjoys making me suffer. No amount of torture or humiliation will ever satisfy his unending need to compensate for his bruised ego.

When I can't find Dr. Daniel, I grab the nearest medic by the throat. "Where's your boss?"

His eyes widen. "What are you doing? Let go."

"Call the CMO."

He swallows hard. "He's probably gone to the dispensary."

I release the medic, storm past Gunther, and head to the room at the end of the infirmary. My supervisor follows at a distance, but I'm too riled up to pay him any attention.

The entrance to the dispensary is locked. Since I don't have the clearance to enter, I bang on it until Dr. Daniel steps out.

"What is it now?" he asks with a frown.

"Give me clearance to leave HQ. One of my targets has abducted a family member."

His lips pinch, and his brow furrows into a frown. "Your injuries—"

"Don't mean a thing if my sister is harmed."

I pause, take a deep breath, and force myself to stay composed. Gunther hovers close, soaking in my torment. If I become any more agitated, one of them will put me on suspension. I need to think like an assassin, not an asshole. An idea slots into place, and I square my shoulders. It's time to hint at an indecent proposal.

"Dr. Daniel, if you let me go, I will submit to any medical procedure and any amount of bedrest." My throat tightens, and I say in a much lower voice. "I'll do anything you want."

His gaze travels down my tactical suit and turns assessing. A shudder runs down my spine, and I hold back a surge of revulsion. I have fucked much worse men for much less.

After what feels like an eternity, the doctor gives me a slow nod. "Alright. You have my clearance to leave, but you will return afterward for a full medical examination. Then you will... *submit* to a prolonged bed rest."

"Yes," I rasp, the tension around my chest loosening. "Thank you, sir."

He pulls out a device, taps a few buttons, and my wrist cuff lights up.

"Aren't you going to take it off?" I ask.

"No. This is to keep a record of your vital signs after you leave."

In other words, he wants to keep tabs on me in case I return to HQ and renege on our deal. He won't just be able to track my location. With one command, he can order me confined to the building until I fulfill my end of the bargain.

I'm too grateful to the slimy bastard to care. Without sparing Gunther a glance, I turn on my heel and jog out of the infirmary.

Now, more than ever, I resent the maze of hallways that make up our headquarters. I pick up my phone and check it for messages from Cesare, but there's nothing.

I try not to think of what that could mean. Try not to picture my precious little Miranda tied to a bondage chair and subjected to the worst kind of torture, but it's impossible. Cold-blooded men don't care about the virtue of innocent girls. I was eleven when Matteo married Mom and started making advances.

Memories of everything Cesare did to me rise to the surface, making me shiver. I sold myself to the Moirai for the strength to protect Miranda. Now, she's in unimaginable danger. How the hell will she cope with such horrific trauma?

"Rosalind?"

Britt jogs to my side. "What happened to dinner? You were supposed to text when you finished with Gunther."

"The Montesanos have Miranda," I reply, my voice low.

Her features drop. "You sure?"

"Cesare sent photos." I hand her my phone.

Without breaking her stride, Britt scrolls through the pictures, her breath catching. "What are we going to do?"

We.

My heart fills to bursting. Britt is the only person who stuck by my side during my decade of probation, even to her own detriment. This is why I love her so much. She's ready to sacrifice her reputation on another rogue mission to save Miranda.

"He wants me back, so I'll do the swap."

She nods. "I'll be on a rooftop with a sniper—"

"No." I grab her arm. "The client was very specific. He wants all three Montesano brothers killed at the same time, or he won't pay."

"But this is Miranda," she says in a much lower voice.

"If Gunther put me in ten years of purgatory for the misuse of company assets, what do you think he'll do if we screw up a paying mission?"

She stays silent because we both know the answer. It won't be just Gunther on our backs, but the entire group's leadership, including international HQ. They won't just kill us slowly, they'll take Miranda.

As we approach the exit, the guards from earlier straighten, expecting more trouble. Their leader's gaze drops to my wrist cuff, which would have been removed if Dr. Daniel had an ounce of integrity and wasn't such a creep.

When the cuff doesn't set off the alarm, the guards let us out into the bank of elevators that lead to the ground level.

Britt bows her head during the ride up. She's probably thinking of a way to rescue Miranda without killing Cesare or getting me captured.

I stare at her profile, my throat tightening. "Don't."

"What?" she asks.

"Whatever you're thinking won't work because it's not the same as last time. Last time, we had the element of surprise.

Cesare knows I'm coming, and he suspects I won't arrive without backup."

"But we can still—"

"No." My voice is firm. "We are not taking any chances with Miranda."

Britt looks away, her lips pursed.

"Britt?"

"Fine. I won't touch Cesare," she says with a weary sigh.

"But you'll be at the other side of the alley, ready to grab Miranda, bundle her into a vehicle, and speed her to a safe location."

"And leave you behind," she says, her voice flat.

"It's the only way," I reply. "I'll handle Cesare."

"What about his brothers?" she asks. "Or their mafia militia? Will you handle them too?"

I stare at the numbers increasing on the elevator display, not wanting to conjure up the image of what she's implying.

No amount of torture or degradation is too much to keep Miranda safe. I wouldn't just sacrifice my body to save my little girl, I would sacrifice my soul.

The elevator doors open, and we step out into the final vestibule before we reach the outside world. It's a white space with vents between the tiles known to blow poison to incapacitate intruders.

My gaze flicks to a ceiling equipped with motion sensors, cameras, and small openings for automatic weapons. What a pity the leaders of such a well-designed firm consider their employees to be disposable.

The doors open, and we step out into the ground floor parking lot, where Britt walks us to an SUV.

"Let me handle Cesare," I repeat for emphasis. "I need you to focus on making sure Miranda is safe."

Tremors vibrate down my spine. This is what it feels like to be the fictional hero who sacrifices themself to save the world. For once, I'm not the villain. I'm a mother who will go to any lengths to save her child.

I can only hope that I survive.

TWENTY

CESARE

I stand by the door with the reverse bear trap. Its rusty-looking jaws wrap around the lower half of the face with a spring that loops around the top of the head. Although made of foam and painted in acrylic paint, it's a realistic replica, down to the levers and bolts and screws.

Miranda gazes up at me through eyes too sparkling and bright for an innocent girl in the presence of a predator. She removed her blazer and tie when the food arrived and now sits with the first two buttons of her shirt loose, her sleeves rolled up, and her hair tied back in a messy bun.

I offer her a genuine smile. "Are you ready to prank your sister, love?"

She falls back on the couch with a giggle that thaws my icy heart. Kids are so much more expressive than adults. Every emotion plays on their faces. She's so easy to read and a hundred times more likable than her sister.

"Okay, but we need blood." She grabs a bottle of ketchup, squeezes some on her fingers, and smears it over her hairline.

My brows rise, and my smile widens. "I'm impressed by your commitment, but that won't be necessary."

"What are you waiting for?" she says. "Put me in the trap."

Chuckling, I place the replica over her head and adjust the straps around the back of her neck. "Can you breathe?"

Her shoulders droop. "I thought it would be heavier."

"Disappointed?"

"It isn't even made of metal."

"You don't think I would put you in a real trap?" I ask with a frown.

She huffs. "Rosa's going to know it's fake."

"She won't."

"How do you know?"

"Because a server wore it last Halloween to pose with the customers, and it looked real enough in the photos."

Satisfied with that, Miranda holds still while I pour fake blood at strategic points beneath the trap's jaws and the straps that touch her skin.

"Now tie my wrists," she says.

"What?"

"So it looks like I can't escape or fight back," she says, as though the answer is obvious.

My brows pinch, but I smooth out the expression. I don't hurt innocent people, especially those I like. But when she grabs her school tie and shoves it in my hand, I can't help but oblige.

I wrap it tightly around her wrists, secure it with a knot, and step back. "That should do it. Can you cry on demand, or will you need help?"

"No, I can do it," she replies from behind the trap.

I walk to the dimmer switch and adjust the lighting to create the right atmosphere. Sinister and dark with enough illumination to bring out the tears and blood streaming down Miranda's face.

"Ready, love?" I raise the camera.

She takes a deep breath and contorts her features into a look of anguish and pain.

I take a few pictures, but when the fat tears roll down her cheeks and turn black from her mascara, I switch to video.

Clever little girl.

Miranda's chest rises and falls with wracking sobs, as though she really is in pain. I adjust the zoom to capture the perfect shot, then I gesture with my arm like a conductor, urging her to push her performance to the next level.

"Please stop," she cries. "It hurts."

"I haven't even started," I growl for the camera.

Miranda screams, and the sound is like a concerto. She writhes and thrashes on the seat, her wrists straining against the fabric.

The scene would be heart-wrenching if I didn't know it was staged.

"Cut," I say.

She flops back to the sofa in a peal of giggles. "Let me do the editing. Rosa's going to freak!"

———

Half an hour later, after taking some more gruesome-looking photos, I send the first of many messages to Rosalind and wait.

Miranda scrolls on a burner phone, alternating between learning the steps of a viral dance and gorging herself on a selection of desserts from the menu.

Her phone rings, and I take it to the door, leaving her alone in the room. The two men I ordered to stand in the hallway and keep her inside acknowledge my presence with nods.

I continue down the corridor into Allegra's empty office and answer, "Hello, Miranda's a little tied up right now. How may I be of assistance?"

"You fucking bastard," she hisses. "If you hurt her—"

"That's no way to speak to the man holding little Miranda's life in the balance," I drawl. "And such a sweet young thing."

She stifles a sob. "What do you want?"

"You. On your knees. Naked. Begging. Bleeding. Is that too much for a man to ask?"

"If you hurt her, I'll flay the skin off your tiny penis and force it down your throat."

I chuckle. "You and I both know it's big." In a much firmer voice, I add, "Be aware who I'll punish for your next insult."

She breathes hard, and the sound goes straight to my cock. This is exactly where Rosalind belongs—at my mercy.

"Just..." she exhales a shuddering breath. "Just please take her out of that awful trap. Her life is hard enough without you adding to her trauma."

My brow furrows. Trauma?

"I'm coming, alright? I'll be at the alley beside your club. Please... I'll do anything you want. Just release her."

I hang up, my triumph over Rosalind turning sour at the reminder that little Miranda lost her parents at the tender age of four. Earlier, I tried to delve for more details, but she fell silent.

When I return to the room, Miranda is drinking a milkshake topped with whipped cream, nuts and a chocolate-coated wafer.

"Having a good time, love?" I ask.

She gives me an eager nod. "Was that Rosa?"

I lower myself in the seat beside her. "Yeah. She was pretty scared."

She scoffs. "I would have liked to hear that."

"Can I ask you a serious question?" I pause, watching her freeze mid sip. "How would you describe your relationship with Rosalind?"

Miranda's face pinches.

"What is it?"

She shakes her head.

"Does she hurt you?" I ask.

"Nothing like that," Miranda mutters. "I just hate her."

"Why?"

She glances away. "You won't understand, because you're her boyfriend. It's obvious how much you love my sister."

Any other time, my jaw would drop and my eyes would bulge out of my head at that foul accusation, but I keep my poker face.

"Is that what you think?" I ask.

"Why else would you try so hard to impress me?" She raises her straw to her lips.

I hold back the laugh bubbling up in my chest. What little Miranda sees is the extent of my determination to recapture her sister. But if love means wanting to choke a woman until the light leaves her eyes and fuck her until she bleeds, then consider me smitten.

Miranda's phone buzzes with a text from Rosalind:

Ten minutes away.

Turning back to Miranda, I offer her what I hope is a gentle smile. "Drink up, love. I have a hot date with your sister."

TWENTY-ONE

ROSALIND

I lean forward in the front seat of the car, my stomach twisting into painful knots. If this traffic doesn't clear, then everything I sacrificed for Miranda will go to ruin. I didn't save her from one predator so she could end up in the clutches of another.

Britt reaches across and squeezes my shoulder. "I don't like this plan."

"What choice do I have?" I ask, my voice tight.

"But exchanging yourself for him—"

"Britt." I clench my teeth. "Please."

She sighs. "Alright, alright. The moment I get Miranda, I'll exit the alley and drive straight to you-know-where. The part of the plan I'm struggling with is where you say you'll join us, but won't tell me how you'll escape."

"Don't worry about me. I'll find an opening."

"The Montesano brothers will be prepared for you this time," she says. "That's why your best chance of coming out of this alive is if I follow—"

My throat tightens. I turn to glare at my best friend. "Drop it. I'm not risking the most precious people in my life."

Britt stares straight ahead, her jaw tense. She's the firm's best getaway driver and could probably extract me out of the alley with Miranda, but she's already done too much for us. I won't risk her life.

She's going to take Miranda straight to the out-of-state apartment we've set up as a place to escape the Moirai. The academy has been compromised. Both Cesare and Gunther know about it, so we'll have to keep her out of sight until I can find a new boarding school.

"Fine," she replies with a sigh. "At least make sure you're equipped for an escape."

I gulp. "He'll search me."

"Not everywhere." She reaches across to the glove box, revealing a black container resembling a glasses case.

I take it out and snap it open to find a selection of syringes. "What are these?"

"The latest in microscopic trackers. It's in the beta phase and hasn't been fully tested in the field. Slip one beneath some scar tissue. If he's that observant, he won't notice the needle prick or any minor swelling. I'll be able to track your location to an accuracy of three feet."

My breath hitches, and for the first time since obtaining those tortuous images from Cesare, I feel hope.

Thanks to Dr. Daniel and his team's laser skin resurfacing techniques, my scars are very few and none of them are raised. I wait until we reach a stoplight before opening my jumpsuit and injecting the tracker into my belly button.

"Good choice," Britt says. "He'll suspect you'll sneak in weapons and trackers, so you'll need some decoys."

"Already ahead of you."

After dabbing the liquid with a swab, I place the syringe back in the container. Then my gaze lands on a round object the size of a penny.

"Can I use that?" I ask.

Britt flashes me a grin. "As a distraction? Sure."

Over the next ten minutes, I work on creating several decoys, including a small cache of drug canisters I place in a latex condom and slip into my vagina.

Any other time, Britt would snort and joke about my hiding places, but she's seen the photos. Cesare Montesano is the kind of monster that would threaten an innocent girl with a contraption that could rip open her head.

"If the consequences for killing him without authorization weren't so dire, that bastard would already be dead," I mutter.

"Some clients are so picky." Britt rounds the corner to the high street. "They don't realize how difficult it is to get all three targets into the same location to execute a triple hit."

"Did he authorize collateral damage?" I ask.

"No," she says, her voice dripping with contempt. "He wants the lackeys intact."

All the stores are closed at this time of the evening, and it's too early for the party crowd to fill the streets. Up ahead, the Phoenix Nightclub is lit up in neon, its entrance devoid of guards.

Britt parks on the other side of the road. "We're here. You ready?"

I force in a deep breath. "Check the tracker."

She glances down at her smartwatch and swipes at the screen. "It's active. You're good to go."

Gulping, I send a text to Cesare to let him know I'm close.

Cesare texts back:

Meet us in the alley. Alone.

"No, fucking way," I mutter.

"What?"

"He wants me to go alone."

Her gaze hardens. "But not on foot. Let's swap places, and I'll slip out of sight."

"And as soon as Miranda gets into the car—"

"I'll reverse out and won't stop driving until I'm one thousand percent certain we're not being followed."

Warm gratitude floods my heart and spreads across my chest. "Thank you," I say, my words choked. "I couldn't ask for a better friend."

"Just promise me you'll find a way out," she says, staring straight ahead.

She's still annoyed I didn't take up her offer to get us both out of the alley. If we were dealing with any other hostage, I would take the risk, but Miranda is untrained, untested, and untainted by the world of crime and death.

After shuffling to switch places, I take the steering wheel and continue down the road. Sweat beads across my brow, and my heart pounds hard enough to rattle my bones.

"I haven't been this nervous since the last time I had to rescue her," I say.

"If things get desperate, say the word and I'll burn those abductors to ashes," Britt replies from where she's tucked between the dashboard and the front passenger seat.

A shaky laugh escapes my chest, and I make a right turn. "Then all three of us will be on the run."

There's a truck parked ahead of us, blocking one end of the dim alley. The only source of illumination comes from a faint light above the nightclub's side exit.

My fingers grip the steering wheel as I wait for movement, but after a minute, I pick up my phone and send a message:

I'm here.

Seconds later, a police car rolls in behind us, its headlights filling the alley with light.

"Shit," I hiss.

"What?" she whispers.

"We're blocked on both sides."

"Don't worry about it."

My stomach lurches. I'm already picturing how I had to use a rocket launcher to escape the last time we were blocked in. Ten years of being relegated to analyst work flashes before my eyes, and I shudder.

It's not like we have any other choice.

The truck's back door rolls up, revealing a figure in black armor and a helmet standing with his arm around Miranda's narrow shoulders. My heart skips as though someone has infused me with a thousand volts of electricity.

Her academy uniform is in disarray, its white shirt marred with red stains. She looks more bewildered than hurt, her wrists bound with her school tie, and her eyes darting from side to side. Despite being subjected to torture, I don't see any visible injuries, but the worst of her trauma will be on the inside.

The man in armor leans his head to her ear and says something that makes her nod. He turns his attention to me and beckons with a gloved hand.

"Remember to get the hell out," I whisper.

"Go," Britt whispers back.

I open the car door and walk through the alley on shaky legs, fixing my gaze on Miranda. My hands curl into fists. What the hell did Cesare do to my little girl? Her shoulders are tight, and her entire body trembles as she takes quick, shallow breaths. She holds her features in a tight mask as though trying to contain her emotions.

As I approach, the man kicks down a set of steps and stands aside with Miranda tucked tightly beneath his arm.

"Climb up," he orders, his voice muffled through the helmet.

"Let her down, first."

He barks a laugh, his free hand hovering over the gun on his belt. "I call the shots. Move."

My jaw tightens. That little act of rebellion almost got Miranda hurt. With a deep breath, I climb the steps and enter the truck.

"Are you alright, Miri?" I ask.

Her features flicker with the strangest expression before the man releases her from his grip, and she jumps down and bolts.

I whirl around, trying to check that she's safe, but the man yanks me further into the truck, and the doors slam shut.

"Let go of me—"

A needle stabs into the side of my neck, making me flinch. I elbow the man in his armor, making him slam my body against the wall.

"Welcome back, pet," the voice says through the helmet. "We're going to have so much fun together. This time, there will be no escape."

TWENTY-TWO

CESARE

I stand behind my little assassin, waiting for her next move, and taking nothing to chance with my prey. My breath hisses through my helmet, filling my eardrums with the sound of my anticipation. Every inch of my body thrums with excitement, from my head to my steel-toed boots.

Rosalind turns around, clutching the injection point on her neck, her features twisted with delicious contempt.

Every instinct wants to revel in the way her eyes burn with liquid fire, but it's too early to celebrate. A professional like her won't easily succumb to the muscle relaxant.

"What was that?" she asks.

"See what it's like to be drugged? Not pleasant, is it, pet?"

"Tell me," she says through clenched teeth.

I grin, resisting the urge to gloat. Rosalind is not to be under-estimated, even when trapped. She is my most dangerous prey, my most enjoyable challenge.

Tires screech from outside the truck, followed by the sound of a collision. On instinct, my gaze snaps toward the doors. Rosalind charges, knocking me off balance. I stumble backward, my helmet crashing against the wall of the truck.

She lurches for the doors on her hands and knees, her fingers scrambling at a lever to fling the doors open. Her breaths come in ragged gasps, mingling with the groan and creak of metal.

I stand over her, my head cocked. "Going somewhere, pet?"

She ignores my question, focusing only on getting away. What an intriguing little assassin. She could have used that opening to slip a weapon between my helmet and collar to deliver a fatal blow. But that weak shove only bought her a few seconds to escape.

Sirens wail outside, punctuated by the crunch of metal, and then gunshots. It sounds like Rosalind didn't come alone. Benito will nag if anything happens to the cops we have on our payroll. An engine revs, followed by an even louder crash as a vehicle slams into the back of our truck.

The door rolls open, revealing her SUV. Two figures sit within its darkened front seat—Miranda and Rosalind's dour-faced accomplice.

Still blocking the other end of the alley behind them, Officers Rizzo and Barzelli exit a squad car that's crushed like a concertina. Both cops shoot at the SUV, even though it's obviously bulletproof.

Rosalind's accomplice opens her door and steps out with a pistol. She's a bulky blonde with hard features and startling blue eyes.

"Let go of her," she yells.

I scoop Rosalind off the floor and hold her to my chest like a shield. Her friend adjusts the aim of her weapon to my helmet.

"I'll give you a count of three to reconsider," I shout. "Or Rosalind will lose a kidney. One."

"Go," Rosalind croaks. "You promised."

Her friend's gaze bounces from Rosalind to the confused girl in the SUV's front seat. The corner of my mouth lifts into a smile. It looks like the friend was supposed to escape with Miranda, but ignored those orders to stage a daring rescue.

"Let her go, you sick bastard!" the blonde hisses through gritted teeth.

"Two," I say with a grin.

"Britt, please." Rosalind's voice breaks.

Britt's eyes flicker with uncertainty, torn between her loyalty to Rosalind and her mission to protect Miranda. I tighten my grip on Rosalind, making her groan.

Sirens grow louder, echoing through the narrow alleyway, alerting us all that the officers on our payroll have called for backup.

Desperation flashes through the friend's eyes before she retreats into her SUV. I toss Rosalind into the back, where she crumples like a broken doll.

I lock gazes with little Miranda, who stares at me through wide eyes, looking betrayed as hell. My heart aches at having to burst her bubble. Once she pieces everything together, the poor girl will realize she's been duped.

As I grab the door to pull it closed, the accomplice fires two shots into my bulletproof armor. Dull pain radiates from the point of impact, but it's nothing more than a nuisance. Ignoring her, I slam down the door and pound on the wall three times, signaling the driver to move.

As the truck rolls forward out the other end of the alley, I advance on my prey.

"I told you to come alone, but you disobeyed. That was very naughty. You're racking up the punishments quickly, pet."

Rosalind shrinks back, her features twisted. She knows she's trapped, but I want to see her flounder. I want to see the panic in her eyes when she realizes all hope is lost and she has once again become my toy.

"Don't act like you weren't already planning something sick," she says through clenched teeth.

I incline my head. "That's true, but I also planned to let you come. Now, I'll enjoy watching you squirm."

"As if you don't already. What was in that syringe?"

"Why? So you can take an antidote?"

If contempt was a flamethrower, the hatred burning in her eyes would reduce me to ashes. I step toward her, wanting to feel the heat of her passion.

Rosalind's chest rises and falls with rapid breaths. She shuffles to the corner, pressing both palms on the walls, trying to use them as leverage to stand.

It looks like the muscle relaxant is finally working, but I'm not taking any chances. There's a reason she needs to know which drug I injected into her, and it isn't about an antidote.

She could be fishing for information on which symptoms to mimic because she's immune to its effects. Then, when I drop my guard and remove my armor, she'll attack.

"Fool me once, little Rosalind," I sing, "But you won't fool me twice."

"What did you do to Miranda?" she asks, her words slurring.

"Nothing she didn't enjoy," I reply with a chuckle.

Anguish twists her face, her eyes welling with tears. "I will fucking kill you," she grinds out. "I will tear out your cock by the root and feed it to you, piece by piece."

"Have you done that before?" I ask, my voice breathy.

"Come here and find out."

I approach her, my cock hardening as though volunteering to become the tribute of her sadistic fantasies. Rosalind might be loathsome, but there's no denying that every twisted part of me finds her captivating.

She kicks out, aiming for my crotch, but the muscle relaxant is already taking hold, rendering her movements futile. I grab her ankle and drag her onto her back.

"Oh, Rosalind," I say, reaching for the zip-ties. "If you want to suck my cock down to the root, then it's all yours."

Her eyes widen, and she kicks out with her free foot. "Don't twist my words, asshole."

Holding her still, I fasten zip-ties around her ankle and secure it to a loop of metal at the end of a spreader bar. Rosalind squirms and screeches, her free leg continuing its futile effort to push me away. Each kick weakens under the effect of the drug.

Rosalind's defiance fuels my predator instincts, and I almost wish I hadn't injected her with so much muscle relaxant. Her resistance is exhilarating. Breaking her is the ultimate challenge. I make a mental note to even the odds next time to give her more of a fighting chance.

As I grab another set of zip-ties, her boot flies up to my helmet, connecting with a resounding thud. Laughing, I snatch her other ankle.

"So keen," I croon.

"Fuck you!" she screams, her voice going straight to my aching cock.

"Now, now. I know the sexual tension between us is unbearable, but you'll just have to wait."

Not wanting to waste any more time, I attach her other ankle to the metal loop at the other end of the bar.

Rosalind trembles. I can't tell if that's out of fear or from the vibrations coming from the engine. The muscle relaxant will only affect the somatic nervous system, causing temporary paralysis while keeping her senses intact. The drugs won't interfere with her body's fear response.

Confident that she's completely under the influence, I pull off my helmet and lean over her with my lips grazing the shell of her ear.

"This would be so much more satisfying in my dungeon, but no matter." My tongue flickers on her skin, tasting the barest traces of salt. "You're mine now, Rosalind, every delicious inch."

She shudders, but my armor is far too thick to enjoy the full extent of her terror.

"I... Will..." She swallows.

"What's that, pet?" I bite down on her earlobe, making her hiss. "You'll kill me?"

She grunts.

"You can try. In fact, I dare you to carry out those threats. But I will break you into beautiful little fragments, and you will enjoy every agonizing second."

TWENTY-THREE

ROSALIND

My heart hurls itself at its cage, desperate to break free. It's one of the few parts of my body capable of movement, since the rest of me is paralyzed.

At first, I thought it was a sedative, but when my limbs stopped cooperating, my terror spiked. The academy trained us to withstand torture, immobilization, and the two combined.

No straight-thinking interrogator would add such a strong incapacitating agent to the mix. My tongue is sluggish, and my lips refuse to move. Cesare isn't interested in me answering questions. He revels in my helplessness. He delights in my terror. He wants a toy who can withstand his brand of torture and still find pleasure in the pain.

I refuse to give into this sadistic bastard. My body might be paralyzed, but my mind is still sharp. I will gather every ounce of strength I have left and wait for the moment to strike.

He releases his teeth from my earlobe and sits back on his heels to admire his handiwork. A dim, overhead light casts his features in shadow, accentuating their sharp angles. Such masculine beauty is wasted on this psychopath. At the first chance, I'll rip through that facade and uncover the true monster.

"You're wearing far too many clothes, little pet," he says, his eyes gleaming with amused malice.

If I could form coherent words, I'd tell him to go screw himself, but he'd only take that as an invitation.

He reaches into a side pocket and extracts an oversized knife. It's curved with a tip that tapers to a sharp point. The cutting edge is smooth, while its spine is as jagged as alligator teeth.

Light bounces off its blade as he tilts it to the side, exposing its flat.

"Say hello to Lucrezia," he says with a sharp grin.

My throat tightens. Of course, he's named his knife.

He slices the blade up the fabric of my jumpsuit, the cold metal sliding up the side of my calf and against my inner thigh. It's so slow and sensual that I swear he's peeling off its top layer. My lungs spasm, pushing out a moan.

"You like that?" he says, his voice whispery with excitement.

I want to call him a sick fuck, but I can't even form the syllables.

As the knife makes its slow ascent toward my pussy, my breath quickens, and the pulse between my legs pounds hard enough to burst my eardrums.

"You're wondering if I'll lose control and slice your labia into sashimi," he murmurs.

My adrenaline spikes. That image hadn't crossed my mind until he opened his perverted mouth. Cesare won't cut me there, will he? He might have dropped out of medical school, but he should know the dangers of lacerating women in the wrong places.

When he sets down his knife to trace his fingers over the elastic of my panties' leg opening, my fear morphs into arousal.

"You're so beautiful when you can't speak or fight back." His lashes are lowered, with his gaze fixed between my spread legs.

He circles my clit with the pad of his thumb, making it swell. "Did you want to know what happens to the female genitals during sexual arousal?"

"No." I try to say, but it sounds like a moan.

"Vasocongestion. It's when the vessels in the pelvic area dilate, allowing more blood to flow into the clitoris, labia, and vaginal walls. This contributes to sensitivity, lubrication, and readiness for my cock. But do you also know what else?"

I know I want to stab this man in the throat.

He continues rubbing my clit with maddening precision, each glide of that hateful thumb infusing me with shocks of ecstasy.

"One slip of the knife could be fatal," he says.

Shivers run down my spine. Cesare had better kill me before this drug wears off. If anyone's genitals end up as sashimi, it'll be his.

He continues caressing me with those infernal strokes, his full lips parting to reveal a peek of his tongue. The muscles of my pussy tighten in anticipation as he leans closer, his hot breath warming my skin.

Just when I think he's going to push the cotton fabric to one side and expose my pussy, he picks up the knife and moves its blade past my zipper, slicing the fabric up to the waist.

Relief escapes my lungs, but only for the few moments it takes for him to remove my boots, socks, and the rest of my pants and toss the scraps into a corner.

He looms over me, straddling my hips and brandishing his gleaming knife. With precise cuts, he slices through the upper half of my jumpsuit, each slash grazing my flesh and drawing panicked gasps but no blood.

The fabric falls away in tatters, exposing my skin. Dread pounds through my veins, seizing my heart in its cold grip. This wouldn't be so terrifying if I could scream or cower or flinch. Cesare has me completely at his mercy, bound and unable to resist.

Despite the fear coursing through my nervous system, the assassin in me notes that he expresses his madness with control and grace. It's almost as though he's practiced undressing women with sharp objects.

In moments, I'm stripped to my regulation sports bra and panties, and lying several feet away from my shredded clothes.

"Better," he says, his gaze roving my skin. "But there are more places where a clever little assassin like you could be hiding weapons or tracking devices."

All the air escapes my lungs.

Cesare cuts through the middle of my sports bra, exposing my breasts. My pulse quickens as his gaze drops to my nipples, and he squeezes both between his fingers.

Sparks of pleasure zip across my skin and settle around my needy clit. Thank fuck I didn't stick the tracker there. His digits slide down toward my belly button, causing my stomach to coil with anxiety.

GPS devices emit electromagnetic signals that are easy to detect with the right equipment. If Cesare is as well-versed in electronics as he is in the human body, I'm screwed.

The air thickens, and tension builds until the weight of my dread is crushing my lungs. The sensation eases when he glides past the hidden tracker and stops at the waistband of my panties.

He brings his face so close to mine that we're breathing the same air. "I'm going to perform a full-cavity search to make sure you're not bringing in any contraband." He smirks. "Although in your case, it would be cuntraband."

Fury heats my blood, carrying hot rage to the outer layers of my skin. One day, it will be Cesare lying helpless beneath me. I'll pay him back for every moment of this humiliation.

He slices through my panties, brings them to his nostrils, and takes a deep sniff. "Delicious, but I want more."

Panting harder than a feral tomcat, he grabs the spreader bar and lifts my feet toward the ceiling. He stands up and secures the metal pole to a set of hooks hanging from above. When he releases them, I'm hanging mostly upside down with my legs spread, my head and shoulders sliding on the floor.

Cesare stares down between my legs, making my cheeks heat. The academy never taught me how to cope with this level of humiliation.

"Too low," he mutters and yanks down a pulley that causes the spreader bar to raise my exposed pussy level with his crotch. "Now, let's see what you're hiding here."

He snaps on a pair of latex gloves. "I was going to make an excuse about why I didn't bring any lube, but it looks like you've produced plenty."

Fuck this bastard.

He slides his fingers over my slit, creating obscene wet sounds that make me want to clench my teeth. This is insane. My body shouldn't be so desperately aroused. Yet when his digits slip into the first inch of my pussy and move in slow, deliberate strokes, the pleasure electrifies every nerve ending, instilling me with shockwaves.

My muscles clench around the cylinder I hid in my vagina. I want to squeeze my eyes shut and squirm, but I'm frozen. Frozen to do nothing but wait for the inevitable.

"So tight," he groans, his fingers still teasing my entrance and refusing to go further.

He knows exactly where I've hidden my stash, but he's drawing out the torment.

"You look good enough to eat." He leans close and inhales a deep, noisy sniff. "And your scent is mouthwatering."

A pained groan escapes my lips.

"Tell me what you want." He leans down and fixes me with a smirk.

I send him my most venomous glare. This bastard knows precisely what he's doing. He's getting me exactly where he wants, begging for his tongue.

Frustration builds low in my belly. If I'm going to die tonight or at some point soon after, then he'd better make it pleasant. By now, Britt would have escaped the cops or whoever else is on their tail, and she'll take Miranda somewhere Cesare and Gunther will never guess.

His fingers reach down past the cylinder and feel around until he touches a spot that makes my body flinch. The movement is involuntary, as is the explosion of ecstasy.

"Do you want me to continue rubbing your g-spot?" he asks, his voice so deep that all the fine hairs on my body stand on end. "Do you want me to make you come hard enough to shake the walls of the truck?"

I want to tell him to get real, but the way he's stroking over that spot has my eyes rolling to the back of my head. My entire body is a raw nerve, every inch of my flesh overcome with the urgent need for release.

Sweat breaks out across my skin and rapid breaths billow in and out of my lungs. I don't know what game he's playing or how he intends to win. Hell, I'd give in if it meant he would continue what he's doing with that finger.

He slides another digit into my pussy and scissors them open, stretching me further. Pleasure mingles with pain, and I can't help but moan.

Please... I want to say. *Please, never stop.*

His fingers close in around the latex sheath, and he pulls out the cylinder containing my decoys.

"How disappointing," he says, his voice frigid.

The heat I felt earlier disappears, replaced with the cold, harsh reality that I'm stuck in a truck with a psychopath.

"Now that you've lubricated my fingers, I'll search the other cavity."

My breath catches, and I send every ounce of concentration to my fingertips. If I can make one of them twitch, I might be able to move when the time is right.

Cesare's thick fingers press down on my anus, which is so relaxed that it barely offers any resistance. The stretch is incredible, mingling pleasure, pain, arousal and panic. My body gives into the sensations as he enters me to the hilt with those long fingers, which move in and out with a rhythm that matches the beat of my racing heart.

"I own you," he growls. "Every delectable inch. Every hole is mine to plunder. Mine to fill."

My breath shallows. I'm still so aroused from all that pressure on my g-spot that, for a moment, a tiny part of me wants to agree.

I focus on my fingers, my toes, my watering eyes, trying to get something to move. If Cesare continues this sweet torment, I might lose what's left of my mind.

TWENTY-FOUR

CESARE

I gaze down at Rosalind's slumbering form. She's beautiful when she's not running that smart mouth, with plump lips the shade of damsons, thick lashes, high cheekbones, and a pert nose.

Her mahogany hair spills across the leather platform like dried blood with tresses curling toward her perfect breasts and nipples that look like they've been dipped in Chianti.

Last night, the muscle relaxant wore off a lot faster than expected, and she broke out of the zip-ties and freed her ankle from the spreader bar. She was about to liberate the other when I injected her with a sedative.

I kept her drugged and bound for the rest of the journey back to Alderney Hill and into the estate. Now, she's in the new play-room, where my furniture was moved into a basement room beneath the mansion.

Escaping won't be easy, and locating her will be near impossi-ble. An intruder would have to find our wine cellar, work out which of the barrels is a hidden entrance, and then navigate a maze of hallways protected by biometric security doors.

Rosalind is trapped.

Leaning close, I inhale her sweet scent and scowl. Why must she smell like magnolias? The earthy combination of citrus and rose never fails to heat my blood to anger.

My fingertips trail down the pulse point on her neck, feeling its steady beat. I study the patch of skin on the side of her breast where I carved my initials, finding it only raised and reddened. Rosalind must have healed the incision in the brief time we spent apart, using an advanced form of medical technology I'm eager to learn.

"What secrets do you hold, pet?" I ask her unconscious form. I can't wait to unravel her, piece by delicious piece.

I grin, my chest inflating with satisfaction. This powerful little creature is mine. Mine to possess, mine to break, mine to shape into my perfect toy. Rosalind will appease my darkest desires and succumb to my every whim. I will wear down her spirit, turn her into my blank slate, and build her up to fulfill every depraved fantasy.

After attaching each of her fingers in a steel hand trap and securing her wrists with rigid handcuffs, I check my phone, which hasn't stopped buzzing with alerts since I arrived.

It's a text from the burner phone I gave Miranda:

> What was that about?

> Cesare, what's happening?

> Where did you take my sister?

> Why were the police shooting at our car?

> Cesare?

My heart sinks, and my lips tighten. If Rosalind had come alone as I had ordered, I would have returned Miranda to Tourgis Academy unaware and un-traumatized. With a sigh, I tap out a message.

> It's not what it looks like. Your sister's friend ruined what should have been a romantic surprise by ramming into a police car.

Dots appear on the screen.

Britt said I was in danger.

My brow furrows, and I type:

From who?

She types back:

You. She says you want to hurt us both.

My lip curls. This Britt character needs to watch her mouth.

Did I hurt you?

She replies:

No. I had the best time.

I respond with:

Maybe Britt feels neglected because Rosalind
wants to spend time with her new boyfriend.

Miranda sends me an animated gif of a laughing skull. I take that as a good sign until she writes:

Can I speak to my sister?

Shit. Why am I working so hard to appease a little kid, when I have everything I want? Her older sister, naked, bound, and under my control. Part of me still thinks I owe her something because I haven't felt so entertained in forever.

Ignoring my common sense, I carry Rosalind to the bed. After covering her perfect tits with a sheet, I take a picture of her and type out:

Sorry, love. Rosalind can't talk right now. She's
sleeping.

The dots reappear, and I wait for Miranda's response, but it doesn't come. I stare at my screen with a peculiar mixture of relief and disappointment. Relief that Miranda has stopped digging for the truth, and disappointment that she's accepted such a flimsy excuse.

Next time I see Miranda, I'll chastise her about being so trusting. She jumped into a stranger's car without checking my credentials. I could have been a predator, a pervert, or a psychopath. If my intentions toward her had been nefarious, she could have gotten hurt.

I wait a few minutes for her to respond, but when there's only silence, I climb out of bed, carry Rosalind back to the bench, and secure her to its leather surface with a series of straps.

With each finger encased in metal splints, there's no way for her to escape.

The door opens, and Benito steps in, his features pinched as though he smells something sour. "You've retrieved the assassin."

I snatch a sheet, cover up her nudity, and snarl, "What do you want?"

"There's been an incident," Benito says with a delicate sniff. "Dominic attacked Roman's special guest."

My breath catches, and my eyes widen with disbelief. Who would want to hurt the crazy balcony woman? Nobody knows how important she is to our family's future, except Sofia, our housekeeper, and the three of us brothers. Everyone else thinks she's just a woman Roman picked up from the club.

"Why?" I ask.

"That's what we're about to discover," he says. "Roman needs you to drag his carcass out of the pool house and into an interrogation room."

I fold my arms, my gaze sweeping down his three-piece-suit. "Why don't you do it?"

"Roman wants me to go to Tourgis Academy to pick up Dominic's daughter." My jaw drops, and I'm about to protest when he raises a finger. "Before you claim to be the pied piper of taking girls hostage, we need someone capable of sweet-talking the headmistress."

My lips tighten. "Tell me what you really think, brother."

"Rolling up at the school gates and demanding Dominic's daughter will only get you arrested."

"Alright, then. Why doesn't Roman drag Dominic to the interrogation room himself?"

"Because he's busy calming down a hysterical woman who is one psychotic break away from realizing she's a hostage we intend to kill," Benito says with a sigh.

My jaw tightens. That's a lot of talking to disguise the fact that he could have dragged Dominic to the interrogation room instead of walking past it to ask me to do the job.

"The longer he's left unguarded, the more likely his accomplice will put a bullet through his head to stop him from talking," Benito adds.

"Fine," I growl and usher him out of the playroom.

Ten minutes later, I'm entering the French doors of my former sanctuary. Dominic lies unconscious on the pool house's floor, sullying its stone tiles with blood. His face is a mass of cuts, bruises, and exposed bone, but the rest of his body appears to be untouched.

"What the fuck happened to you?"

I crouch down beside him, studying his battered face with a mix of curiosity and disgust. Roman must have lost his mind defending his special guest because there's no artistry to Dominic's wounds.

My ears prick at the sound of feminine crying, mingled with Roman's hushed words of comfort. I turn to the door that used to lead to my inner sanctum and scowl.

There's probably a reason my brother didn't lock this woman in the basement and torture her into signing over our stolen property. Benito must have convinced him to carry out some unnecessary and convoluted scheme.

I won't interfere, but I'm intrigued.

Rising to my feet, I walk around an easel, finding a male figure sketched in faint charcoal with an oversized dick. I snort, wondering if Roman posed naked.

When movement sounds from the door, I walk back to the unconscious man, hook my arms beneath his pits, and drag him out through the door.

At the distinct squeaking of a trolley wheel, I release my quarry and straighten.

Sofia pushes a cart laden with covered bowls, plates, and silverware. Her eyes widen at the sight of Dominic's battered face.

"Do I need to be worried?" she asks, her lips thinning.

"Not until I find out if he has any accomplices. Benito says he attacked her." I nod in the direction of the pool house.

Her jaw hardens, and she glares down at Dominic with so much hatred that I raise my brows. "I knew that one was no good. I made him gnocchi yesterday, and he let it go to waste."

"A travesty," I mutter. "Don't worry. I'll punish him for wasting your fine cooking."

Her features tighten, and she glances around as though checking that the coast is clear. My insides twist with unease. The only time she gets like that is when talking about my secret.

"He's been calling the house, threatening to speak with Roman," she says, her voice hushed. "If you keep ignoring him—"

"I'll take care of it," I say.

Sofia purses her lips, knowing full well I won't speak to that bastard. She's about to launch into one of her lectures when I place a hand on her shoulder.

"Trust me. He won't live long enough to tell Benito or Roman the truth."

TWENTY-FIVE

The first thing I think of when I awaken is Miranda. If Britt managed to escape, my daughter will be safe and stashed away where no one will ever threaten her safety.

I still don't know what that twisted bastard did to my little girl. Her face was free of cuts or bruises, but who knows what damage he's done to her psyche?

A ghost of a headache pounds at my temples. It's the kind of pain that would slice through my nerves if it wasn't muffled by drugs.

He must have administered painkillers after sticking me with that second needle. But why?

Keeping my eyes closed, I slow my breathing and assess the state of my body before alerting anyone that I'm conscious.

The air is mostly stale with hints of chemicals and leather, and there's a weak fan blowing cool air against my skin. It tightens into goosebumps, telling me I'm still naked.

I turn my attention to my extremities. Each finger is attached to something rigid and metallic. From the way the digits stretch taut within their restraints, I'm guessing it's the BDSM version of a splint.

Heavy leather straps encase the rest of my body, starting with

"

one holding my neck, another across my shoulders, and more at strategic points along my torso and legs.

The pressure of the restraints is a constant reminder that Cesare has adapted. Any chances of him underrating my abilities are slim, considering I'm completely immobilized.

"I know you're awake," says that loathsome voice. "Your blood pressure just spiked."

That's when I realize one of the bands around my upper arm is a cuff to measure my BP. It was bad enough that he strung me up in a meat van and forced me to get aroused enough to lubricate his cavity searches. Now, the sick bastard is monitoring my vital signs.

He threads his fingers through my hair and twists, and my eyes snap open.

Cesare looms over me in a dimly lit room, illuminated by a flickering lightbulb. I have no doubt it's there for dramatic effect.

Piercing blue eyes shine down on me like beacons of malice, contrasting with the shadows cast by his angular features. He looks disheveled, with his jaw covered in stubble and wavy strands of hair framing his face like tendrils of darkness.

Shivers run down my spine, and every fine hair on my body stands on end. I meet his gaze with indifference, refusing to show any signs of weakness.

"What did you do to Miranda?" I ask through clenched teeth.

He yanks my hair, jerking my head to the side. "I'm the one who asks the questions."

I swallow.

"What did you do while I was unconscious?" he asks.

"Remember that chance you had to interrogate me, and you wasted it by sticking a gag in my mouth?"

He sucks in his cheeks, his features twisting into a smirk. "Annoying as ever." After releasing his grip on my hair, he walks toward a table at the other side of the room. "Lucrezia will convince you to talk."

I seize the opportunity to take in my surroundings. We're in a replica of the pool house's playroom, with all the BDSM furniture. There's no sign of a window and the lack of circulating air suggests we're in a basement.

Six feet behind the table I'm strapped on is a security door with a biometric scanner. My only way out is to overpower Cesare and escape using his fingerprints or retina scan.

He returns with the curved knife and runs the flat edge over my breasts. "Lucrezia is aching to try Lingchi."

"Death by a thousand cuts," I say, forcing my voice to remain even. "That's unoriginal, even for you."

His grin falters, and I know I've struck a nerve.

"You carved your initials into my side boob, and I got that fixed. Take a look if you don't believe me."

His gaze doesn't flicker, telling me he already tore off the bandage and examined the healing wound.

"You misunderstand me," he says through clenched teeth. "Lucrezia wants to cut you piece by piece until all that's left is a torso I can fuck."

The weight of his words sink into my bones, leaving behind a sickening chill. Tension fills the playroom, and the air becomes too thick to enter my lungs. I know the difference between a promise and a threat. I also understand Cesare's brand of predator.

He enjoys the thrill of the chase and toying with his squirming prey. I need to convince him he'll lose interest the moment he starts chopping off body parts

"How will you hunt me if I don't have limbs?" My voice wavers, betraying a hint of anxiety.

I won't rest until I find out what he did to Miranda. I can't escape if I don't persuade Caesar to allow me to remain intact. Fretting over her fate will have to wait until I can secure my survival.

"There are places I can slice that won't affect your ability to run... Much."

"Labia sashimi is old news," I say with a shaky chuckle, "But you have my full consent to eat my pussy."

His eyes flash, and he bares his teeth. "That kind of attitude will get you killed."

"I could say the same to you," I reply.

He grabs my throat, sending tingles of anticipation down my spine. A surge of heat settles between my bound legs, igniting the flames of my arousal. His gaze bores into mine as he leans in so close that our noses touch.

"Have you forgotten," I rasp. "Breath play is my kink?"

"One of these days, I'll squeeze too hard."

"That will be a good day to die." I raise my head a fraction to bring our lips together.

He flinches, his lips twisting with contempt.

"I've been trained to withstand torture," I say. "All these implements on your racks are nothing but foreplay. If you want what's in my head, you'll tell me what you did to Miranda."

His eyes narrow. "You first."

"Fine," I say with a sigh. "After you drank the oxypentanol, I snuck out through the bathroom window and walked around the grounds. Now, tell me what I need to know."

"Not good enough," he snarls.

"I took photos."

"Of?"

"Windows, doors, gates, boundary walls, barbed wire, electric fence. I scoured the perimeter of the grounds, gathering anything I could find to paint a complete picture of your security."

His eyes narrow. "Why?"

"I already answered your question. Now it's time to answer mine."

He glares down at me, his chest rising and falling with rapid breaths. I hold his stare for a few heartbeats, letting him know I'm not scared.

Feigning boredom, I let my gaze travel down to the massive skull tattooed between his pectoral muscles. Huge wings border it on either side that stretch across to his shoulders.

Each arm is adorned with sleeves of tattooed skulls. The left is more ornate, mingling with crowns and jewels and roses, while the right reminds me of the piled bones in the catacombs beneath Beaumont City.

"See something you like?" he asks with a sneer.

"I'm not playing this game." I look him dead in the eye.

He scowls, but there's no snappy reply.

"How do I know you're not holding Miranda in another room?"

"She left with your friend," he snarls.

"Tell me exactly what happened yesterday," I say. "With proof."

A muscle in his jaw flexes, and the veins on his temples bulge. I hold my features into a tight mask, not giving him a single opening. The drugs have worn off, and my head is clear. I need to know what he did.

"Fine," he growls. "I picked her up outside her academy and told her I was your boyfriend. She took one look at my dazzling smile and jumped in my car."

I shake my head. "She wouldn't be so reckless. How the hell did you find her, anyway?"

"When you didn't come home, Miranda went looking for you at Leroi's apartment."

"How—"

"You were sloppy. Somehow, she found his address."

My mind races. I've been assigned to the Montesano case for months, using that time to hook up with their cousin, Leroi. I mentioned I was dating a man with that name, but gave no specifics.

"She didn't believe me at first, but when I showed her a photo of me and my cousin at the club, she was convinced I would take her to meet you."

Dread pools in my gut. "And where did you go?"

"I showed her the Phoenix, gave her something to eat, and we watched a movie."

My jaw drops.

"Then you groomed her into letting you put her into one of your contraptions," I say.

His body tenses, his shoulders rigid as though he's taken offense. I don't understand why, considering he stooped low enough to abduct a fourteen-year-old child from school.

"You want to speak to Miranda?" he asks, his lip curling with contempt.

I hesitate, wondering if this is a trick. If Britt got away, then Cesare won't be able to contact my daughter. Since I have nothing else to lose, I give him a nod.

"Then tell me the purpose of those photos," he says. "I want specifics. Who is coming to attack and when? How many? Tell me everything, and you can ask Miranda yourself what I did."

Adrenaline surges through my system, making my heart thrash like a caged beast. I don't have that information, but I can speculate. Even if I did, there's no guarantee he'll keep me alive long enough to escape.

This is a dangerous gamble, but I'm not without leverage. "I'll tell you everything you want to know," I say, my voice steady despite the fear pulsating through my veins. "But first, you need to prove that Miranda is safe."

His knife flies toward my face, its blade lodging into the cushioned table. I clench my teeth, my sinuses filling with the scent of fear and blood.

"Do you think you can make demands?" he snarls, his eyes burning with the flames of his fury. "You're in no position to negotiate."

"Prove to me that Miranda is safe." I enunciate every word, my courage rising with each frantic heartbeat.

Cesare turns on his heel and disappears through the door.

Something tells me it was a mistake to call his bluff.

TWENTY-SIX

CESARE

Hours after walking out on Rosalind, I'm cooped up in the back of a truck within a war zone lower down on Alderney Hill, reconsidering every life choice that's relegated me to being the family errand boy.

If the Capello family hadn't orchestrated Dad's heart attack and framed Roman, I would be still in medical school, slicing open cadavers.

If I hadn't let Mom talk me into becoming a surgeon, I would be out there with my brothers, fighting through a small army of soldiers for a chance to kill Capello's son.

If the Capello twins hadn't framed me for slaughtering my pet when we were kids, then Mom wouldn't have thought I was a burgeoning psychopath. She also wouldn't have fought so desperately to keep me away from the family business. When she told me I was different from my big brothers, that was an understatement.

My vendetta against the Capello family is just as burning as Benito's, yet Roman has demoted me to the triage truck to assist Dr. Brunelli with casualties.

I snap on a pair of gloves and turn to my patient. Joe sits shirtless on a folding chair, his arm dripping with blood. The balding bastard stares up at me like I'm his executioner.

Gunshots resound outside, mingled with the sound of explosions. Every few minutes, something knocks into the triage truck, making its walls vibrate. It's an insulated trailer, converted into an operating room and a space for first aid.

"Where's Dr. Brunelli?" Joe asks.

"Operating on a man with a chest wound," I say.

Joe shifts in his seat. "I'll wait for him."

"Scared of me?" I ask.

He gulps, his gaze darting everywhere except mine. "You're the…"

My jaw tightens, and I wait for him to say I'm the screwup, the addict, the psycho baby brother everyone's forced to tolerate. I stare him down, daring him to repeat any of the shit I've overheard.

"Well, you're the torturer," he mumbles.

"Who's your only chance of fixing you up. Unless you'd like to continue bleeding out? You ever had your blood pressure taken?"

His brow furrows. "Of course."

"That bullet is dangerously close to your brachial artery, the same vessel those cuffs use to measure your BP. If it bursts, you're dead."

Joe's eyes widen, and he glances down at his arm. "You sure?"

I step back. "Let's wait and see. I've seen men die from strangulation, water torture, being burned alive on a bonfire, but this will be the first time I watch someone bleed to death from being a scared little bitch."

He finally meets my gaze. "Alright."

I turn to a tray of surgical instruments, itching to pick up the scalpel and start cutting. Any other time, I would relish this chance to perform surgery. Today, it's at the bottom of a long list. I want to be the one who guts Samson Capello, and if I can't kill him, then I'd much rather be breaking Rosalind.

"You going to give me a painkiller, Cesare?" Joe's voice trembles.

"If you hadn't wasted the last ten minutes crying for Dr. Brunelli, you would have already been prepped and anesthetized," I say, barely able to conceal my annoyance. "Now, there's a line of men needing my attention, and we don't have that luxury."

Joe trembles, his forehead covered in a sheen of sweat. The pleasant scent of antiseptic is now overpowered by the stench of his anxiety.

I pick up the scrub brush, grab his arm, and clean the wound with a sterile solution. Joe winces, his body tensing, his lips parting with a groan. I'm not normally an asshole to my patients, but Joe was one of the bastards who talked shit about me when I was going through withdrawal.

"Flinch, and my scalpel will slip. If I nick that artery…"

"Oh, god," Joe moans.

"Correct. Right now, I am the only thing that stands between you leaving this truck alive and serving my father in heaven."

"Like the father, the son, and the holy ghost?" he asks, his voice wavering.

"Enzo Montesano, asshole."

I hold the scalpel against Joe's skin and make my first incision. The layers of flesh part beneath my blade, revealing red tissue. Blood bubbles up, filling my senses with its rich, coppery scent.

Joe's pained whimpers fade into the background of my exhilaration as I part more layers with calm precision and expose the lodged bullet.

I take the forceps, maneuver them into the wound, and grip the bullet. Joe's muscles tense as I extract the metal and deposit it on the sterile tray with a clink.

"There," I say. "That wasn't so bad."

He exhales, his body slumping with relief.

I pick up a needle and thread. "After I've closed the wound, you can go back to the battle."

Joe's breath quickens. "Can't I get a bandage instead of stitches?"

"Sure, if you want to risk infecting your open wound, sepsis, bleeding out, and dying," I reply. "But if you'd rather have a clean, neat scar as a souvenir of surviving the battle of Alderney Hill, you'll shut the fuck up and take my needle like a good boy."

Joe's eyes flash, his nostrils flaring, but he clamps his mouth shut and nods.

"Smart choice," I mutter.

I hold the wound together and pierce his flesh with the needle, leaving a trail of fine thread. Joe winces, but doesn't make a sound. He holds still, gripping the edge of the table as though it's the only thing keeping him on this side of the veil. Lucky for him, I take pride in my work.

After the final stitch, I secure the thread with a knot and step back to admire the perfectly closed wound. The edges of his skin align perfectly, promising a minimal scar.

Joe exhales, his body relaxing against the fold-up chair. "Thanks, Cesare."

Nodding, I apply a sterile bandage over the wound and slip off my gloves. "Remember this the next time you and your pals want to call me a liability or a weak link."

He pales, his features falling slack. "Uh... Yeah. Sorry about that. Nobody meant any harm. We all talk about each other to blow off steam. To cope with all the stress."

"Get the fuck out and call in the next patient." I flick my head toward the back door and dispose of the gloves.

With another mumbled apology, Joe snatches up his clothes and stumbles out, not even bothering to dress. As I clear up the sterile tray and discard the used supplies, a large hand clamps on my shoulder.

"Well done, son."

I turn around to meet Dr. Brunelli's smiling eyes. We used to call our family physician Dr. Mario because his mustache looked just like the video game character, only thicker and bushier. It's now streaked with gray, but his blue eyes still hold the same friendly twinkle.

"It was just a bullet wound," I mutter.

He chuckles, the sound rich and deep. "You still have a talent for surgery, but your bedside manner could use a little work."

I shift on my feet, my gaze dropping to the floor, already knowing what will come next.

"Isn't it time you returned to medical school?" he asks. "Twenty-four is still young—"

"No."

"Last time we talked about this, you were waiting for Roman to be released from death row. What's changed?"

"I can't leave the family when Samson Capello is still out there, paying assassins to scout the grounds for an opening," I reply.

"It's only a matter of time before the final Capello dies. Then you'll need a purpose."

The message behind his words hits like a punch to the gut. I'm not a necessary member of the Montesano family. I don't fit in.

Roman is the leader, who's been running our operation from prison since Dad died. Benito is the diplomat who rubs shoulders with the dignitaries too afraid to be seen with Roman. I'm the black sheep they keep in the background.

Even Mom thought the same when she caught me with a sliced-open rabbit and assumed I was a psychopath. Nobody believed me when I told her I'd found my pet murdered, but she, Dad, and Dr. Brunelli decided between them that I should be a surgeon, so I wouldn't become a serial killer.

He sighs. "Cesare."

"This morning, Roman beat Dominic half to death because Samson Capello paid him a million dollars to kill his special guest," I say.

He nods. "I treated Emberly today. She's recovering nicely in the pool house."

"I can't leave my brothers to be outnumbered. We still don't know if Dominic had any accomplices."

Dr. Brunelli cups the side of my neck, his touch firm and warm. "Your brothers are strong, capable men who can handle themselves."

Before I can look too deeply into what he's implying, the doors burst open. The two of us part, just as Roman steps in, dragging a man in body armor.

It's cousin Leroi, looking feverish, pale, and a hair's breadth away from death.

TWENTY-SEVEN

CESARE

My jaw drops. I step backward, my calves bumping into the chair.

What the fuck happened to Leroi?

Our cousin grimaces, his face drenched in sweat. He's clinging to the same tiny woman he brought to the Phoenix, only she's no longer wearing a sparkly gold dress.

Her face is pale. Too pale for the deep coffee shade of her hair, more aligned with her huge, cornflower blue irises. Our gazes lock, and the expression crossing her features borders on terror.

"Bring him here." Dr. Brunelli flings open the door to his operating room, letting Roman sling Leroi onto the unoccupied cot.

"I'm fine," Leroi grits out between clenched teeth.

The doctor scoffs. "Is that why you're hemorrhaging from the stomach?"

Leroi tries to rise, his body trembling with fatigue and pain. He reaches out for his little girlfriend, but Roman pushes him down.

The doctor attaches restraints. If I had to guess, it looks like the wound Leroi sustained earlier has made him disorientated and delirious. He's losing blood at an alarming rate and is too far gone to realize he needs urgent help.

"Fuck," Leroi roars and tries to break free.

"Stay still and let the doctor do his job," my brother says, his stern voice hiding his unease. He holds Leroi in place until the last of the straps are secured around his body.

"Thanks, Roman." Dr. Brunelli glances at the girl, then at me. "Leave the operating room, please, and check the young lady for injuries."

When the girl remains rooted in place, I move behind her and reach for her shoulder to guide her out. She spins, brandishing a scalpel.

Before it reaches my throat, I snatch her wrist and hold her in an arm lock. Nice try, but after getting blindsided by Rosalind, it's best to assume that any woman involved with Leroi is going to be a handful.

Leroi continues to struggle against his restraints, grunting and cursing until his words become an incoherent blur.

"Easy, love," I say, my voice soothing. "Leroi is safe with Dr. Brunelli. He's been with the family since before we were even born."

She stares up at me, her eyes wide with terror.

Earlier, Roman interrupted my time with Rosalind to explain that Samson Capello had taken Leroi's girl hostage at a mansion lower down on Alderney Hill. It looks like spending time with that sick bastard has left her traumatized and stab happy.

"I'm Cesare." I flick my head behind us toward the three struggling men. "Roman's youngest brother."

She stiffens, her face paling.

I'm an ally. Why is she scared of me?

"What's your name?" I ask.

"None of your business," she snaps, her voice trembling.

"Fucking sedate him," Roman growls in the background, holding down Leroi's head as it thrashes.

"Already one step ahead of you," the doctor replies.

"Alright, Miss None-of-your-business, it's time to go." Still gripping her by the wrist, I usher the girl out of the chaotic operating room, giving her hand a gentle squeeze.

Her scalpel drops to the floor with a satisfying clink, and I guide her to the fold-up seat.

While I appreciate a pretty woman with a blade, the one she holds is already stained with blood. Besides, if anyone's going to slash me across the face, I want it to be Rosalind.

I pick up the dirty scalpel and toss it in the sharps' disposal bin, just as Leroi's girl reaches into the sterile tray to steal a fresh blade.

She has the same delicate stature as Miranda. At first glance, they could easily be the same age. This one is older, despite looking so innocent. The difference is in their eyes. Miranda is all brightness and sweetness and light. Leroi's girl has a darkness that might exceed even mine.

"Are you hurt?" I ask.

She shakes her head.

My gaze wanders to a nick on the side of her neck. I gesture in its direction and ask, "What's that all about?"

She covers the wound.

"Do you want to talk about it?"

She shakes her head, her fingers tightening around the scalpel.

"Alright, then." I raise my palms, letting her know I don't mean any harm.

The girl is skittish, wearing men's clothes that are at least twelve sizes too big. Something really fucked up must have gone down at Capello's hideout, which is why she's refusing medical attention. Every man in that family was the worst kind of sexual deviant.

I swallow hard, my mind scrambling for the best choice of words. "If what happened up there went deeper than the cut to your neck, I know a female doctor who can prescribe Plan B and test for infections."

"No," she says, her voice soft. "No, thank you. But Samson's still alive and he needs medical attention."

My nostrils flare. "What?"

"Leroi shot him in the stomach. He's bleeding out."

"And?"

"You need to save his life."

"The fuck I do." I turn to the door. "Where is he? If Leroi can't kill that bastard, then I'll finish him off."

The girl appears in front of me in an instant and holds her scalpel to my throat. I glare down into her ferocious little scowl.

In the blink of an eye, I could overpower this little waif, disarm her, and make her howl loudly enough to rouse Leroi from his sedation. But she belongs to my cousin, the hero who murdered the entire Capello family and found vital evidence to get Roman released from death row.

I can't repay Leroi by hurting his woman, even if she's starting the fight.

"Are you really trying to make me heal Samson Capello at knifepoint?" I ask.

She nods.

A laugh escapes my lips. It's bitter, brittle, and brimming with bile. "When I was young, that cold-hearted bastard and his psycho twin killed my pets and presented me with their dead bodies. They made it look like I was the psychopath."

"Then why do you want him to die so quickly?" she asks, her words flat.

My eyes narrow. Is this sweet-looking girl a kindred spirit? Based on the scalpel pointed to my throat, I'd say she isn't trying to protect Samson.

"Wait," I say, keeping my voice steady. "You want Sam to be healed so you can torture him slowly?"

She nods again.

My shoulders sag with relief. "Why didn't you tell me that before, love?"

"I thought that was obvious," she says.

"How about we make a deal? You put down the scalpel and let me operate on Samson. You can even watch and I'll teach you a few things about human anatomy. In exchange, I swear to help him survive long enough for you to get your revenge."

"How do I know you won't double-cross me and kill Samson?" she asks.

"Because his family was responsible for the downfall of mine," I say. "Because Samson and his brother murdered my pet. Because Samson stole my brother's fiancée and left him with a stick up his ass. Because Samson ordered a hit on a woman staying under our roof. Because after everything we all suffered, keeping Samson alive so he can endure more torture is my chance to get a measure of revenge."

She studies me for several moments before withdrawing the scalpel. "Alright then, but if you try to kill Samson—"

"Then you have my permission to stab me wherever the fuck you want. I won't even fight back."

The corners of her lips twitch. "Seraphine."

"What's that, love?"

"My name. It's Seraphine."

I offer her my widest smile. Not the polite one I show the outside world, but the true one reserved for those who share my darkest desires. "Seraphine, my girl, that's a fitting name for a dark angel."

She grins, revealing pearly white teeth, the expression sunny and sweet and savage. I can't help but wonder if cousin Leroi knows he's attracted a woman even more sinister than an assassin. But then again, he's a hitman.

Maybe his preferences veer toward femme fatales and lethal little ladies.

TWENTY-EIGHT

ROSALIND

Maybe my timing is off, but it feels like an entire day has passed since Cesare walked out, leaving me in the dark. My body is crying out for food, my head is pounding, and my throat spasms with the need for liquid.

These symptoms will pass. They always did during captivity training.

There's absolutely no escape with my fingers held taut within metal splints. I'm stuck here until I can convince Cesare I would be a more interesting hostage if left unbound.

Nobody is coming to my rescue. Gunther will continue telling everyone I've been promoted overseas. He doesn't want me spreading the word that the firm is covering up the fact that it deems us expendable.

Britt might know my exact location, but she'll never get past all the guards. Even if she did, there are biometric security measures, and the impossible task of sneaking me out undetected.

No matter how much time passes, or how much I try to keep my mind distracted, my thoughts drift to Miranda. Is she safe? Is she traumatized? Is she alone?

Britt was supposed to go to the train station to pick up a bag from the lockers and escort Miranda to an apartment out of state. I need to find out if Cesare had them followed.

Hunger gnaws my stomach once more, making me sigh. Cesare will arrive when he thinks I'm at my most desperate and he'll expect me to exchange information for sustenance.

He'll be disappointed.

I close my eyes and let my thoughts float into the ether to clear my mind. Just as I'm drifting into a deep state of meditation, the locking mechanism whirs to life, and the heavy metal door creaks open.

My pulse races in anticipation. I keep my eyes closed as heavy footsteps approach, but nothing can stop my senses from filling with the sweet aroma of hot chocolate.

Saliva floods my mouth, anticipating something to soothe my dry throat. I swallow over and over, refusing to succumb to temptation.

"Sorry to have kept you, love," Cesare says, his voice light. "It's been a busy day, and the night was a war zone. I brought you something to eat."

Annoyance prickles my skin. The bastard sounds like he's talking to a pet. I crack open an eye to find him looming over me, holding a tray containing a bowl of fruit, yogurt, a steaming cup of hot chocolate, and a bottle of water.

The flickering lightbulb illuminates the ends of his disheveled hair, which falls loose in cascades of dark waves. My jaw tightens. Such extreme masculine beauty is wasted on the wicked.

"Fuck your food," I rasp, my voice cracked. "What did you do to Miranda?"

His nostrils flare. "Why are you so antagonizing?"

"Because men who interfere with underage girls don't deserve any respect."

"Even if you're completely at their mercy?" he asks, his lip curling.

I look him full in the face. "Let's be real here. You're going to torture me for information, use my body to satisfy every sick fantasy, and eventually let me die. Am I right?"

"Depends on if you're worth keeping alive," he replies.

"You might have trapped my body, but I won't give you what you want."

He flashes his teeth. "And what do you think that is?"

"Information, entertainment, a sense of twisted fulfillment," I reply, my voice dripping with venom. "Whatever I do, the result will be the same. I may as well die without giving you the satisfaction."

"You want to know what I did with little Miranda?" he asks, his voice menacing and low.

Goosebumps prickle across my skin, and every fine hair on my body stands on end. I tighten my stomach, hold my features in a grim mask, and resolve not to show this sick fuck and ounce of my pain.

"Answer me," he growls.

I give him a stiff nod.

"Then I'll lay down some ground rules. You get to speak to her for five minutes. If she asks where you are, tell her I've taken you to the Grimaldi Hotel in New York. You will not send any coded messages to her or your friend."

My jaw drops. I was expecting him to tell me what he did to Miranda, or at least show me the rest of his video clips or security footage. Besides, Britt was supposed to have disposed of Miranda's phone, so she'd be impossible to track.

"How do you have her number?" I ask, my voice tight.

"She and I got on extremely well," he purrs in a tone that makes my stomach lurch.

I grind my molars, trying not to react to the innuendo. He wants me weeping, flinching, cursing out his name. This type of man loves to see a woman crumble.

"Are you going to keep boring me with preamble or let me speak to Miranda?" I ask.

Annoyance flickers over his features, but he regains control, sets the tray down on my stomach, and slips a hand into his pocket.

"After the five-minute conversation is over, you will tell me everything about your firm's plot against my family, or Lucrezia and I will start cutting body parts."

"Fine," I rasp.

He plucks the bottle off the tray and twists open its cap with a crack. Slipping his hand under my head, he lifts it up and brings the bottle to my mouth.

"Drink," he says.

I rear back, but the hand at the base of my skull holds me in place.

"Why?" I ask.

"Little Miranda can't think I'm not keeping you fed and watered," he replies, as if the answer is obvious. "We don't want her worried or upset."

I glance at his features, finding no trace of his usual malice or smirk. If I hadn't witnessed this sadistic fuck firsthand, I would think he was serious about protecting Miranda's innocence.

"Open." He shoves the mouth of the bottle into my closed lips.

With a sigh, I obey and allow him to pour the water onto my tongue. Cool liquid trickles down my throat, soothing the parched membranes. I swallow over and over, feeling it slide down my esophagus and into my empty stomach.

I don't know his intentions or what kind of game he's playing with Miranda. This isn't the first time someone has manipulated me using my little girl, but it will be the last.

Cesare only needs to drop his guard for a second and he's dead.

Once he's satisfied that I've had enough to drink, he pulls back the bottle and sets it back on the tray. His hateful eyes bore into mine, searching my features for signs of weakness.

I glare back, channeling my deepest hatred.

"Ready, pet?" He raises his phone.

"Yes," I reply, my voice clearer.

His eyes leave mine for the few seconds it takes for him to dial, and my heart pounds hard enough to make my ribs throb. The seconds feel like an eternity as I wait for the person on the other end to answer.

My mind runs through a scenario where Cesare's men captured Britt and Miranda and they're being held at a facility. That everything I sacrificed in the fourteen years since I ran away from home has landed us in the same situation I escaped—under the control of a perverted sadist.

"Cesare?" Miranda's voice bursts through the speakerphone, brimming with an unusual excitement.

"Hello, love," he says with a grin. "Your sister has finally recovered from her hangover and wants to say hello."

Miranda's sweet giggle drifts through the speaker, and my chest tightens with a twisted sense of jealousy. I can't remember the last time I made her laugh, or if I ever did. My stomach twists at the thought of this monster bringing her joy when I struggle to even make her smile.

I stare at the phone, not daring to meet Cesare's gaze.

"She's so lame," Miranda says. "Let me speak to her."

"Miri?" I ask, trying to hold back a swell of relief.

If she sounds so carefree, then maybe she isn't hurt? Abuse isn't that simple, though. There were times Matteo made me feel beautiful, special, wanted.

"How's New York?"

"Great," I reply, my voice strained.

"Did you know Britt is holding me captive in a tiny apartment? I'm missing a test while you're on a shopping trip with your amazing new boyfriend."

Her complaints accelerate. She misses her friends, her freedom, and she's missing a week of detention for misdemeanors she won't reveal.

My heart races as she speaks, and I struggle to process her words through a haze of frustration, longing, rage and relief. She has no idea that this supposedly amazing boyfriend of mine has me trapped in the BDSM boudoir from hell.

"Slow down, baby," I say, forcing my voice to stay even. "You're speaking too fast."

"Ugh, don't call me that," she says with a huff.

I dare not reprimand her. Keeping my voice even, I ask, "What happened the night you met Cesare?"

"When he picked me up from the academy?"

"Yes."

"We went to the Phoenix," she replies, her words speeding up with excitement, completely oblivious to my rising panic. "Did you ever see his office? It's got leather seats and an entire wall of security screens. He let me try the DJ booth, and we ordered cocktails, but the waitress spat in them, so we went to his restaurant next door and sang karaoke! Then we had the best burgers ever with meat from Japan and the milkshakes were so—"

"Miri," I say, my voice rising with restrained hysteria. "Did he hurt you?"

Another pause, and my insides twist at the thought of that monster hurting my little girl. Bile rises to my throat, and I swallow back the mounting dread.

Miranda bursts into a peal of giggles. "It was a prop."

"What?"

"After we watched Saw, we wanted to play a prank. That bear trap thing was a prop."

My stomach lurches. "But did he touch you?"

"Like what?"

"Miri," I say, my voice strained. "What did I tell you about older men?"

"Ew, no!" I can almost hear her wrinkle her nose. "I would never try to hook up with your boyfriend. All he ever talked about was you."

Despite her reassurance, my gaze drifts to Cesare's face, who glares down at me with sick satisfaction. I swallow hard, trying to keep my attention on the phone.

"He's a hundred times better than Leroi."

"You met him?" I ask.

"When you weren't at your apartment, I searched through your tablet and found his address."

Nausea grips me by the throat. Leroi really told his psycho cousin I had a sister.

"Were you wearing your academy uniform?" I ask, already knowing the answer.

"How did you know?" She only hesitates for a beat before continuing. "Leroi's too grumpy and old. I approve of your new man. He's perfect. Can I talk to him now?"

Cesare taps a button on the phone to take it off the speaker, his smile widening as he brings it to his ear. He turns his back on me and walks to the door, deep in conversation with Miranda.

My gaze bores into his broad back, and my mind reels with confusion. She likes him. They had fun together and established some kind of friendship. She doesn't know that beneath that handsome facade is a crazed maniac who enjoys torturing women.

Panic lances through my heart when he places his palm on the biometric reader and disappears behind the door. All the effort I spent protecting her from predators has only brought us under the control of an even greater monster.

Matteo never stuck a gun in my vagina and pulled the trigger, yet Cesare would have done worse if I hadn't escaped.

What the hell is he doing to my daughter?

TWENTY-NINE

CESARE

I walk into the hallway, leaving Rosalind to stew. She thinks I've corrupted her baby sister. Maybe I went too far, letting the girl watch that gory movie, but I made sure to cover her eyes when the scenes got too graphic.

The little feast I gave her was probably the first time she could eat whatever she wanted, and I made sure the chefs used the best ingredients. Wagyu beef, organic vegetables, and freshly prepared desserts. Only the finest for the little sister of my pet.

Rosalind belongs to me. By extension, so does Miranda. Except I plan to be the protective older sibling she never had. That starts with bringing her back to New Alderney to complete her education.

"Can you talk sense into my sister?"

"What's up?" I ask.

"I wasn't exaggerating when I said Britt left me alone in an apartment."

"Where is it?"

She hesitates. "I can check the map app."

"Do it."

A few seconds later, my phone buzzes and I glance at the screen, finding an address on the border of Delaware and New

Jersey. My stomach dips at the prospect of entering Galliano territory, but I shake off the feeling of dread.

"Got it," I say. "Is the door locked?"

"Yeah," she replies.

"How many floors up?"

"Five," she says.

"And no fire escape?"

"No."

"Are you hungry, hurt, or in any immediate harm?"

"I'm fine. Just bored and lonely."

"Alright." I exhale, releasing lungfuls of frustration. "Let me send you some money. Use it to keep yourself entertained. I'll work on locating which apartment unit you're in and get you as soon as I can."

"Thank you," she says, her voice softening with relief.

Her gratitude fills my heart with a mix of warmth and pride. So, this is what it feels like to be a protector. The big brother I never had.

"Don't mention it, love," I say.

After ending the call with Miranda, I forward her a screenshot of an untraceable credit card she can use to buy whatever she wants online. I send Dr. Brunelli a text to forward a letter to the Tourgis Academy, excusing Miranda for her absence.

The door leading from the wine cellar clicks open, and I whirl around. Benito steps in clad in bulletproof armor, a reminder that he was allowed to participate in last night's battle, while I was relegated to triage.

"What did you learn?" he asks.

"I'm about to find out," I answer.

His lips tighten. "What's taking so long? Leroi's little stalker can't be that difficult to crack."

"You forget something, big brother. Everything we saw in that club was an act. Rosalind is a trained assassin pretending to be a simpering submissive."

His features pinch, as though I'm making excuses. "Let me speak with her."

"And say what?" I snap. "Talk, or I'll wrap you in so much red tape you'll be struggling to breathe. Diplomacy won't work with a woman of her caliber, neither will clever threats. She doesn't give a shit."

"And torture?"

"Pain gets her hot. It's like foreplay." The corner of my lips lift into a smirk.

Eyes narrowing, he closes the distance between us and squares his shoulders. "Don't get too attached. Do whatever is necessary to uncover the threat and eliminate her."

"Don't you have a contract to scrutinize or an official to schmooze?" I ask in a low growl. "Stop micromanaging and leave me to do what I do best."

His phone pings with an alert, diverting his attention. "You have until tonight."

He turns on his heel and heads toward the door without another word. My brow pinches. This isn't like Benito. He usually nags until he's made his point.

"You late for an appointment to remove that slide rule from your ass?" I ask.

He doesn't even flinch.

Resisting the urge to taunt him further, I watch my brother leave. I would have gotten some answers already if he hadn't come to interrupt my progress.

The door clicks shut, and I return to the playroom. Rosalind lies on the leather table with her eyes squeezed shut, her features forced into an expression of calm.

But I'm not fooled.

My line of communication with her little sister gives me more leverage over her than the threat of Lucrezia. I stand over her, my fingers tracing the soft skin of her arm.

"You've had five minutes with Miranda. Now, it's time to speak."

"What do you want to know?" she asks.

"When will the assassins strike? Where? How many? Which methods? Tell me everything."

She swallows. "When I returned to HQ, they'd just finished discussing the intel I sent."

My anger surges at the reminder of how she tricked me into knocking back a drug that rendered me unconscious for hours.

This wretched little bitch had the whole night and half the morning to detail every weakness in our security.

"Continue," I say.

"I just told you. I wasn't at the meeting."

"Then speculate," I say through clenched teeth.

"It'll be a triple hit, which will require a trio of assassins striking in quick succession. It's too risky a job to allow one person to shoot all three."

I nod. "Any back up?"

"One per assassin."

"Their role? Will they be armed?"

"To help them move in and out of the locations without being detected. They'll come with vehicles, explosives, any kind of tech to aid their escape."

I lean in closer, studying her features for signs of deception, but she's unnervingly stoic. "When will they strike?"

"At the first opening."

"Which is?"

She inhales a deep breath. "Triple hits are difficult. They'll wait for the next time all three of you are together."

I stare down at Rosalind, waiting for her to elaborate. Silence stretches out across the playroom, broken only by the pounding of my pulse.

When Roman was on death row, we looked into multiple ways to get him released. I wanted to fly a helicopter into the prison when he was out for exercise, but Benito and Leroi said it wouldn't work. Alderney State Penitentiary is too well guarded, with high towers manned by marksmen.

All escape scenarios ended with the same result. The authorities storming our stronghold, and Roman spending the rest of his life on the run.

He was innocent, with an iron-clad alibi for the night that woman was murdered, but Frederic Capello had so much dirt on the judge and everyone connected to the case that he buried the truth beneath corruption and lies.

Our only chance of freeing Roman was to attack the threat at its source. First, we needed to take out the officials keeping him behind bars. Next, we needed to kill Frederic Capello, his brothers, his cousins, his lieutenants, his bastard sons. Every motherfucker capable of striking back needed to die.

Roman had to wait a year and a fucking half for the right moment for Leroi to wipe out the entire Capello family. That's why I believe Rosalind when she says a triple hit is difficult. If one of us survives the assassination, we wouldn't stop until everyone involved was dead.

"Tell me about the holes you found in our security," I say.

She looks me dead in the eye. "None."

"Bullshit."

"The perimeter of your estate is surrounded by twelve-foot-tall walls coated in anti-climb paint. Those can still be scaled, and maybe someone could get past the barbed wire and electrified fencing, though I'm sure your guards will notice any glitches in the current."

That's true, but I refuse to give her any recognition. "Continue."

"A five-minute search of the County Clerk's office shows that every plot of land surrounding yours is owned by a real estate company that once belonged to your father."

Frederic Capello embezzled Dad out of his entire portfolio, his casino, and a whole host of other assets Roman is working hard to retrieve.

"And?" I say through clenched teeth.

"Each time the firm sent an analyst to scope out the land, they never returned."

The corners of my lips twitch. Our guards might gossip like a bunch of assholes, but they're competent, mostly loyal, and leave no fucking traces.

"So, how will they get to us?"

"Same way I got to you," she says, her eyes hardening into flint.

Her words cut through the air like throwing stars, each lodging into my chest. Cold seeps into my heart as I piece together her meaning. I'm the weakest link. The trojan fucking cat carrying enemies disguised as quarry within its jaws.

My breath quickens, and culpability wraps its icy fingers around my throat. I should walk away, report everything I've learned back to Benito and Roman, then put a bullet in her skull. Finish this hateful little assassin before she fills my mind with more poison.

Fury pounds through my eardrums, drowning out my self-restraint. Through clenched teeth, I hiss out the words, "What the fuck does that mean?"

"Every system, no matter how well designed, has its weaknesses," she says, her eyes searching my soul. "Your cousin was supposed to be my way in through the Montesano gates. He never so much as introduced me to any of his friends."

She pauses, letting the words trickle through the cracks in my defense, letting my fury simmer to a dangerous boil until my ears ring. My hand finds Lucrezia, and my fingers tighten around her hilt.

Every reprimand my brothers and Gil ever made rises to the surface, to mingle with her taunts. I'm useless. A liability. I caved into her trickery within minutes while Leroi stayed strong for months.

"But you brought me straight into the heart of your estate with the promise of kinky sex," she says, her lip curling. "I didn't even need to inject you with drugs. The promise of a blowjob combined with rudimentary reverse psychology got you swallowing an entire vial of oxypentanol."

Rosalind gazes up at me, her eyes smoldering with defiance. She's daring me to lash out in a fit of rage and make a mistake she'll exploit. To give her an opening so she can escape.

Rosalind thinks I would succumb to her transparent taunting. My blood simmers at her manipulation, and my heart rages at her insinuation that I'm a burden to the family. I grind my teeth, forcing in ragged breaths to maintain my cool.

"Months of letting Leroi fuck me resulted in nothing. He was too much of a professional to drop his guard. You, on the other hand, were so easy to manipulate—"

My free hand wraps around her throat, making her gasp. The tray I left on her stomach falls to the floor with a clatter, but I pay it no mind.

I tighten my grip, my fingers digging into her soft flesh, wanting to squeeze out all her lies. Wanting to stop her from looking so fucking smug. Rosalind's eyes blaze with a flicker of triumph that confirms my suspicions.

"How can I believe a word you say, when it's all designed to anger me into violence?" I snarl, holding back the force of my fury. "You want me to trip up, and I won't give you the satisfaction."

When her features even out into that cold mask, I know she's hiding her disappointment.

I step back and release my grip around her throat.

"Next time you try to incite me to anger, it won't be you I punish."

Her breath hitches as she catches the implication that I'll hurt Miranda, but I'm past giving a shit. I walk toward the sink for a mop and bucket to clear up the mess.

This is the last time I'll allow Rosalind to slither under my skin.

THIRTY

ROSALIND

My heart pounds loudly enough to burst my eardrums, and I'm breathing hard, still shaken by the force of Cesare's rage. Maybe taunting him about his weaknesses was a step too far. Instead of inciting him to get angry enough to make a mistake, I made him self-reflect.

Shit. This over-emotional psycho is evolving.

The sound of running water turns my attention to the right-hand corner of the room, where Cesare fills a bucket. Of course, he cleans his own dungeon. Any sane person would balk at the sight of a woman being held against his will.

Do his brothers know I'm here? Does Leroi? The answer to both questions is probably yes, considering it was Leroi who passed on information about Miranda.

Miranda.

I squeeze my eyes shut and exhale my pent-up tension. Britt moved her to the safety of our secret hideout. It's only a matter of time before she takes my girl overseas, where any of my enemies can't reach, including Cesare and Gunther.

Now that I haven't returned to work, Gunther will probably sniff around Tourgis Academy for Miranda. He'll work out a way to send me a warning to keep the firm's secrets or make her pay the price.

Britt is smart. She knows how to hide Miranda. At least that's what I thought. How the hell is Miranda still in contact with Cesare? Britt should have confiscated her phone.

Cesare approaches the bondage table, his menacing presence breaking me out of my thoughts. Without another word, he picks up the pieces of broken plates and sets them on the tray.

My stomach growls, and I shift uncomfortably within the leather restraints, wondering if he'll make me eat the spilled yogurt.

The mingled scents of dairy and ripe fruit invade my senses and flood my mouth with saliva. I swallow, my insides rioting for food. I know it won't last. Every time we went through survival training, it would take seventy-two hours for the hunger pangs to disappear. After that, fasting is a breeze.

He moves the tray to the door, picks up the mop and dips it in the bucket. In moments, the delicious scent is overtaken by the sharp tang of cleaning solution. Cesare cleans the mess in silence, his methodical movements almost meditative.

I follow his actions with a strange mix of fear and fascination, wondering how he'll break the silence and how he'll punish me for my defiance.

My fingers try to curl within the splits, but the leather bites into my skin, securing each digit to the metal exoskeleton. There's no room for escape with each strap so rigid and thick with zero give.

Giving up on the futile effort, I study Cesare's features, but all I find is a mask of concentration. Is he replaying my last rant? Is he recalibrating his approach to break my spirit? The silence between us thickens until it takes on a solid form and pushes down on my chest.

Stop this.

In a captivity situation, the hostage must balance introspection with awareness. The hostage must never maintain a psychological dependence on the captor or risk forming an emotional bond.

I turn my thoughts inward, recalling an old academy lecture on the survival rule of three:

Operatives can survive three minutes without air, three hours in extreme heat or cold, three days without water, and three weeks without food. My heart sinks. If I can't manipulate Cesare into slipping up, then I need to find another way to break free.

It's me who needs to evolve. I need to cast aside the dry lectures and study Cesare for new weaknesses and test different approaches to gain his trust.

"Tell me the name of your client again," his sharp voice slices through the silence.

"Capello." I turn to meet his gaze, but he's focusing his attention on squeezing the mop head.

"Which one?"

"Frederic is dead, so the contract would have died with him," I say.

"Then who?"

My throat tightens. Gunther never once told me the name of our client. I had to overhear it through conversations with the assassins he deemed worthy of highly paid missions.

Cesare glances up, his eyes narrowing, his fingers gripping the mop so tightly his knuckles turn white. "Don't test me," he says through clenched teeth. "Don't even think of holding back or making any demands."

The threat hangs in the silence like a sword, or perhaps the inappropriately named Lucrezia. Everything from the coldness in his eyes to the sneer on his lips suggests that if I don't answer, he'll make me wish for death.

My survival instincts force me to improvise.

"One of his relatives who didn't die in the massacre must have contacted the firm to carry out the hit," I say.

Cesare's mask cracks, and he throws his head back with a cackle so maniacal that the fine hairs at the nape of my neck stand on end.

What the fuck did I just say to set him off? This man keeps me off balance with his unpredictable reactions. His laughter echoes off the walls, making every molecule in the air tremble.

I inhale a sharp breath through my teeth, my muscles tensing. "Did I say something funny?"

The laughter ceases, and he regains control of his features and turns to me, his eyes glinting with malicious triumph.

"We captured Samson last night," he says. "He's being tortured to death."

"Oh." I exhale, releasing only a fraction of my tension. Gunther didn't tell me Frederic Capello's older son had survived the massacre. I just assumed our client was a more distant relative.

This changes everything.

Cesare no longer has a reason to continue his interrogation. The Moirai Group will keep the Capello deposit, since there are no survivors left to pay the final invoice for the triple assassination, and I can return to work.

He raises his brows, prompting me to speak.

My tongue darts out to lick my dry lips. "As soon as the firm knows Samson is dead, they'll call off the hit."

He closes the distance between us, still gripping that infernal mop. Water drips from its sodden fibers, leaving a puddle at his feet. I remain still, forcing myself not to shrink, as my mind puzzles through the most tactful way to phrase my request.

"If every member of the Capello family is dead and can't start any new contracts, then you and your brothers are no longer targets," I say.

"Correct." He rocks forward on the balls of his feet, his eyes dancing with delight.

"The Moirai Group knows I'm here," I add. "Someone will demand my release."

"The way your boss did when I called his number?"

My throat constricts, my lungs tightening with the ache of betrayal. Cesare has a point. Gunther sure as hell didn't dispatch a crack team of operatives to extract me from the Montesano stronghold. he probably didn't even send that fucking Uber.

"That's different. It's a new set of circumstances if the client dies. If you continue keeping me here—"

"You became my property the moment you poisoned my drink."

"Technically, it was the drink you poured for me."

"Which you made me down with reverse psychology."

"Let me go, Cesare," I say. "The Moirai Group is ruthless to those who hold their operatives captive."

"Don't fight it, pet."

He grips my chin so tightly that I swear I can feel every fingerprint, and glares into my eyes with an intensity that sets my blood on fire.

"You stopped belonging to that firm the moment you took my mark." He speaks so matter-of-factly, it's as though there's a reality where humans are property.

"Let me go," I snarl.

He flashes me a grin. "You're mine. There isn't a single place where you could hide from me because I will always find you, my pretty pet."

I spit in his face.

The hand holding my chin hostage whips out like a cobra and delivers a slap so hard that my head snaps to the side. Stinging pain radiates across my cheek, and my sinuses fill with the scent of blood.

Clenching my teeth, I hold back a barrage of insults. This crazy bastard and his antics have eroded my common sense and made me forget my professional training. Stupid acts of defiance will only get me maimed. I need to stay focused on finding an opening for escape.

He wipes the spit with his fingers and places them in his mouth. Groaning, he savors each digit as though feasting on nectar.

I stare at his tongue, the pulse between my legs pounding hard with a cocktail of terror and another sensation I refuse to name.

Cesare leans so close that his face becomes a blur. His scent is earthy, smoky, intoxicating. It clouds my thoughts and dulls my senses. I hold my breath, waiting for him to strike.

"Bad pets who don't accept their place earn punishments," he growls through panting breaths. "And you're about to receive a lesson in obedience."

THIRTY-ONE

ROSALIND

Shivers break out across my skin and down my back. I can't catch a fucking break. I want to close my eyes, turn my head, and shut out all traces of this insane bastard, but he's looming so close that I can't even block him out.

"How did you escape?" he growls.

"What?"

"When you knocked me out and left me in the bushes to die. How. Did. You. Get. Past. The. Guards?"

"That blow wasn't fatal," I say, trying to keep my voice from trembling. "It was only meant to—"

"Answer my fucking question."

I gulp. Telling him will only help close breaches in his security, but staying silent is equally dangerous.

"One of the men talked about driving into town to run an errand," I lie. "I hid in the back seat of his car and stayed silent until he was distracted."

"Who?"

"I didn't catch his name," I say.

He draws back, his nostrils flaring, his gaze assessing. "If this is bullshit..."

"Why would I lie?"

"Everything about you is fake," he says with a sneer. "I used to watch you fawn over my cousin at the club like an eager sub, but that was just a ploy to gather information on me."

I remain silent, letting the accusation hang over my chest like the door of an iron maiden. Every moment with Leroi was an affront to my psyche. He's cold, calculating, controlled, and conceals his emotions deep within a heart of ice. Not to mention the age gap. I despise older men.

"Answer me." Cesare's voice cracks like a whip.

"What's the question?" I snap back.

"What about you is even real?"

My lips clamp shut.

He grabs my throat. "If you want food, then you'll earn it."

"Fuck your food," I yell. "I told you everything about getting the firm to call off the hit. I even explained how I escaped. You don't get to crack me open and expect me to spill out my life story."

Tensing, I steel myself for his hand to tighten around my neck, but he releases his grip, turning his attention to the puddle and cleans up the water with his mop.

My temples throb in time with the pounding of my pulse, and I watch him return the mop and bucket to the sink, then wash his hands with the precision of a surgeon. Cesare Montesano is so mercurial one would think he had multiple personalities. That, or he regulates his emotions like a ther-mometer.

After drying his hands with a paper towel and tossing it in one of his color-coded waste containers, he walks to a table beneath shelves of plastic boxes.

I bite down on the inside of my cheek to sharpen my senses. Do I stay silent and wait for his next move, or do I try to appeal to his last shred of sanity? Unlike his cousin, Cesare isn't a man of stone with veins filled with ice. He's tempestuous, hot-blooded, and impulsive. I need to learn to navigate the nuances of his temperament.

"Do your brothers know you're withholding information that could call off the hit?" I ask.

As if not hearing a word I say, he opens the box and extracts an AAA battery. After putting it back into place, he selects another container and pulls out a little black toy about the size of a lipstick.

My jaw tenses and the pulse between my thighs quickens.

The dirty fucker.

"You can't keep me here as your plaything," I say. "Even if you don't care about my firm's retaliation, think of mine."

Calmly, he sets the items on a trolley, along with a metal box and a bunch of medical supplies, then wheels them over to my side.

"Cesare Montesano," I say through clenched teeth. "What the fuck do you think you're doing?"

"Choking doesn't work on you," he says. "It only gets you wet. Pain doesn't work either. And I can't starve you into submission, so I need to get creative."

"With a vibrator?" I laugh. "You do understand the effect they have on women?"

Ignoring me, he walks around the end of the table, where he pushes down a lever and the lower half of it collapses. My legs fall at a ninety-degree angle, making me stifle a gasp.

The only thing I found tolerable about Leroi was that he was also a pleasure dom. Before I ruined our arrangement by snooping around his apartment, he would make me orgasm repeatedly until I would cry for mercy. I doubt Cesare will be so giving.

He loosens the straps around my knees, forcing them apart and exposing my pussy to his scrutinous gaze. If my ankles weren't so tightly restrained, I would kick him in the face.

"What are you doing?" I say through clenched teeth. "I don't consent to sex."

He scoffs. "I wouldn't fuck you if my cock was on fire and your cunt was the only wet surface."

I huff a laugh. "You're only saying that to get the upper hand."

"Which of us is strapped to a bondage table and is about to earn themselves a gag?" he asks.

"Which of us is still bitter about being beaten up by a girl?"

He slaps my inner thigh, the sting shooting straight to my clit. I exhale a shuddering breath, trying not to moan.

"Fine words for the bitch who can't get enough of me. You're soaked."

A flush rises to my cheeks, and prickly heat spreads down my neck and over my chest. I squirm within my restraints under the weight of his stare.

"As if you're not rock hard," I snap, trying to pass on a measure of my shame.

"I am, pet, but that's because I have you completely at my mercy."

"You're sick."

"That's an understatement."

My stomach lurches, and a bout of fear rushes between my spread legs. I grind my teeth, wishing my body had a more appropriate response to a dangerous situation with a man I despise.

"All this toying with me is so unnecessary," I say through clenched teeth. "Don't you have a drug empire to run?"

"Sure, but first, I have a pussy I need to spank."

The slap hits with a resounding sting that has me arching my back and cursing my stupid mistake. I should have found another way to infiltrate the Montesano stronghold instead of having a one-night stand with this lunatic.

He slips on a pair of disposable gloves, tears open an antiseptic wipe and swipes my pussy with it, cooling my heated flesh. I'm panting, trembling, curling my toes at the intense cold.

"What is this?" I rasp. "Temperature play?"

"Not yet."

He opens another wipe and concentrates his efforts on my labia. The muscles of my pussy clench with need, wanting him to stop teasing and fill me with one of his fingers.

Just as I'm about to say something disparaging, he sets down the wipe and pulls on my inner lip. My mouth clamps shut, and I fall silent.

"Such a pretty little pussy," he says, his voice a reverent whisper, each syllable breathy with admiration. "And it's all mine."

I try to raise my head, but the band over my brow keeps me firmly in place. "Not yours," I say through panting breaths. "It's—"

A sharp pain lances through my labia as he pierces the delicate skin. My brain is so scrambled that the sensation registers as pleasure, and I let out a strangled cry.

Sparks of ecstasy travel through every nerve in my body like strings of dynamite, making my muscles stiffen, and my back arch even higher. I'm about to inhale when he pierces the other labia and makes me howl.

"Good girl," he croons. "You're taking your stitches so well."

"What the fuck?" I scream in a strange mix of anger and arousal.

"Almost done," he says and pierces me again with the needle.

I collapse against the leather table, my legs trembling as I work through a deluge of sensations. Pain. Pleasure. Panic. The needle moves in and out of my tender flesh, repeating the motion until my mind finally pieces together a mental image.

"Did you..." My throat spasms. "Did you just stitch up my labia?"

"You said you don't consent to sex."

He stands back and admires his handiwork with a fond grin, and another emotion slides into place.

Outrage.

"What the fuck is that?" I ask through clenched teeth.

"I sewed your pussy shut. No one will ever fuck you without your consent. Not even me."

"Am I supposed to thank you for being a gentleman?" I screech. "Because a decent human being would set me free, not resort to female genital mutilation."

With a non-committal hum, he inspects the stitches. "Clean it every day with a saline solution," he says with the air of a medic delivering a prescription. "Avoid aggravating the area while it's healing."

"Alright." I roll my eyes. "Remove these fucking splits off my hands and I'll take good care of it."

By it, I mean Cesare.

He shakes his head, his fingers sliding close to my opening and gathering my fluids. "You're dripping, absolutely soaked. Even though you're bitching about it, you love being my pet."

I close my eyes, trying to shut out his nonsensical tirade. How do I explain to a man who doesn't want to listen that my body went through years of this kind of training and found its own way to process pain? Cesare would probably interpret that as an invitation to play.

He runs the pad of his finger over my swollen clit, sending a jolt of pleasure that shatters my thoughts. My breath catches, and my thighs jerk within their restraints.

"I love how you're so sexually responsive. My perfect little toy."

"Cesare," I say through clenched teeth. "You can't keep me—"

He pinches a nipple between his fingers, cutting off my words.

"You're mine, little pet. Mine. I can do this all day long. Keep you on the edge until you break and spill your secrets. The sooner you realize this, the sooner I'll allow you to come."

Sweat breaks out across my skin. I need to kill Cesare before he destroys what's left of my sanity.

THIRTY-TWO

CESARE

All the blood has rushed from my head and has gone straight to my cock. The sight of Rosalind sweating and squirming has me so hard that the edges of my vision are going black.

I didn't sew her entire labia shut, only the labia minora. And I didn't touch her clitoral hood. The stitches will dissolve after a week, leaving her perfectly intact. But she'll think twice the next time she calls me a rapist.

Sliding my finger over her swollen clit, I flick my gaze to the monitors. They're beside the bondage table in case I get carried away and allow her to climax.

Her resting BP is usually well below the average of 120/80, but now it's reached 153/96, telling me she's past the excitement phases of the human sexual response cycle and veering toward the end of the plateau phase.

Based on her heart rate of 145 beats per minute, she's on the brink of orgasm. That, and the way her face contorts. She clenches her teeth and glares up at me with a mix of desperation and defiance.

The room temperature rises several degrees, matching the heat radiating from her delectable body. Tension crackles against my skin, electrifying and hot. Her need for release is palpable, like a vessel about to rupture.

I lean into her, my lips grazing her ear. "Whose pussy is this?"

"Mine."

The alarm I programmed into the monitor shrieks. I withdraw my finger and smirk. "Wrong answer, pet."

Rosalind shoots me a glower of such intense hatred that my balls draw up into my abdomen, and I nearly come in my pants.

"Gone limp already?" she asks through panting breaths.

I chuckle. "Reverse psychology won't work this time, pet. I know all your tricks."

Her eyes narrow, the fire in their hazel depths burning with malice. I release her nipple and step away from the table, giving her a moment to recover.

"What's the point of all this?" she asks, her chest rising and falling with rapid breaths, making those perfect tits quiver. "You're childish."

I smirk at the insult, already accustomed to her brand of bullshit. Rosalind isn't just a sexual masochist, she's a master of psychological warfare. She uses words as weapons, but her tactics only work once. I've never met anyone who completely holds my interest. The alarm continues to ring, telling me she's still dangerously close to climaxing. Any physical stimulation, even a slap, might push her over the edge.

My fingers twitch to touch her, but I curl my hands into fists.

"I hate you," she snarls.

"That's just stage one of Stockholm syndrome," I say with an approving nod. "You'll soon move into the next."

"You're insane." Her hysterical laugh goes straight to my cock.

"You'll grow to crave it. By the time I've finished with you, your pussy will purr for me."

She purses her lips, looking like she's gathering enough saliva to spit.

I clutch her cheeks. "Every time you spit at me, I will extract a tooth." When her eyes flash, I add, "Go on, test me. I double dare you."

Her blood pressure spikes. Only this time, I don't think it's out of arousal. I hold her stare as her pupils constrict to pinpoints, and she jerks her head to the side.

"Dirty little assassin likes to be threatened," I say with a chuckle.

"You're wrong," she snaps.

"Let me cool you down." I walk to the refrigerator at the end of the playroom, my back warming with the heat of her glare, open its ice box, and extract a cube.

By the time I return to her side, her blood pressure is down to 140/90. Still elevated, but likely due to the stress of not knowing what's about to happen.

I walk around to her spread legs and notice one of the stitches has already broken. My brow furrows. I should take better care of my pet.

After sliding on a pair of gloves, I wipe up her lubrication with gauze and dab at the stitches with an antiseptic solution. Rosalind flinches as the cold liquid makes contact with her skin, but she doesn't complain.

The blood vessels in her clit are engorged, turning it an intense shade of red. I rub the ice cube on her swollen bud, tracing its smooth contours. Rosalind tenses, her breath hitching. The therapeutic cooling should alleviate the burning heat of her desire and bring down her BP and heart rate out of the plateau phase.

The ice melts, dripping onto her labia, and her entire body quivers. When I blow a stream of air on her clit, she moans.

"That's one part of you that will always tell the truth," I murmur between her spread legs.

"It's just as deluded as you," she snaps, her hips jerking.

I grab her thigh. "Stop squirming. You'll aggravate your stitches."

"Whose fault would that be, asshole? I didn't ask you to sew up my labia."

Picking up a lighter, I flick its flint wheel and ignite a few sparks before bringing up a flame. "If you can't stay still like a good pet, then I'll have to cauterize your cunt."

Her blood pressure spikes, and she sucks in a sharp breath. "You wouldn't."

I hold the flame to her inner thigh, making it quiver. "What do you think?"

"You're disturbed."

"Careful now," I say, my voice laced with authority. "You can act as cold as you want, but your body wants to surrender."

"Oh, and I suppose if you tickle me and I laugh, that means I find you funny? Get real," she says through panting breaths.

I place the ice cube on the dish, pick up a candle, and light its wick. Its glow fills the room, casting a warm glow on Rosalind's porcelain skin. Holding the candle a foot above her inner thigh, I drip wax onto her skin.

Each droplet lands on her flesh with a soft splash, creating a pool of heat that makes her legs jerk. I move the candle closer to her pussy, letting the wax continue to drip.

Her body tenses. Her breath comes in ragged gasps. Her clit seems to expand in anticipation of the impending heat, so I cool it down with the ice.

"Fuck," she groans. "What is wrong with you, Cesare Montesano? I already told you everything I know."

"You've exhausted your usefulness as an informant," I say, my breath quickening. "The only reason I'm keeping you alive is because you make such an interesting pet."

Her hips buck, bringing the wax even closer to her pussy, and she moans. "Don't you have anything better to do, like selling drugs?"

"You're the only narcotic I need. You and the way you squirm under my touch."

She raises her head, pulling the restraint over her brow taut. "If I ever get control of that candle, I'm going to stick it up your ass."

Chuckling, I drizzle wax to her outer lips. "All you need to do is ask."

"Isn't this supposed to be an interrogation? Ask me a fucking question. Want to know what happened between me and Leroi? I'll answer."

"No thanks," I lie with a smirk. "But you can tell me how you became an assassin."

"A-Alright," she says. "But you have to let me come."

"You drive a hard bargain."

"Yeah, I'm sure it's hard."

Snickering, I blow out the candle and set it on the tray. When I pick up a small vibrator and twist its dial, its motor hums to life.

"No," she says.

My brows pinch. "No, what?"

"If you're going to make me come, use your fucking tongue."

THIRTY-THREE

CESARE

I had to walk away, and not just because I needed to report back to my brothers with Rosalind's intel.

My pet has a way of taking control of a situation. She wants to call the shots, even though it's her who's naked, horny, strapped to a torture device, and aching for release.

It's what I admire and despise about her most—that inner kernel of strength I can't penetrate. Nothing I do, say, or make her endure can break through that shell, but that won't stop me from trying.

I limp through the basement's darkened corridors, my cock so hard it hurts. Arousal courses through my veins, hot and thick and furious, powered by the challenge of breaking Rosalind.

Where does she find the determination to endure? I shoved a gun up her cunt and pulled the trigger, yet she fought with every shred of strength to escape, only to return without hesitation the moment I took her sister.

Rosalind is unlike any woman I've ever met, and I'm eager to explore her limits. What will I find when she's broken? A sniveling little creature, begging for mercy or a raging warrior?

Women don't have balls of steel. They cry and simper and flee at the first moment of trouble.

Just like Mom.

Mom didn't even wait for Dad's body to cool before she married Tommy Galliano. She jumped from one powerful man to another without a backward glance and left Roman to rot on death row to enjoy a life of luxury and power in New Jersey.

By the time I exit into the wine cellar, my erection has vanished, leaving me tasting the bile of Mom's betrayal. I ascend the stairs and walk down the bright marble hallways, passing staff members who acknowledge my presence with nods.

I reach the door of Roman's study, where he and Benito are already deep in conversation. Pausing, I strain my ears, trying to catch any hint of my name, but all I hear are muffled voices. Benito's tone carries a hint of concern, while Roman sounds frustrated.

My lips tighten. With so much going on in the business, why would I think they're badmouthing me? Probably my guilty conscience.

Opening the door, I step inside to find them both sitting on the sofas at the far end of the room. They each cast me glances before turning back to a laptop.

"What's going on?" I ask.

"Tell you later," Roman rumbles. "Now that you're here, tell us what you got from the assassin."

Benito navigates to an app on the laptop and calls a contact. Moments later, Leroi appears on the screen. He's shirtless and sitting up in bed with his abs wrapped in bandages.

"How's the wound?" Roman asks.

Leroi grins. "Healing."

Benito shifts in his seat. "Cesare is here." He turns to me. "What did you find out from the assassin?"

"Hi Cesare," says a soft voice.

Seraphine sits on the bed beside Leroi, wearing a blood-stained robe. Her hair is now a mid-brown compared to the rich espresso from the night before.

I flash her a grin. "You taking care of my cousin?"

She leans on Leroi's arm and nods.

"What did Rosalind say?" Benito asks.

Standing between the two sofas, I deliver a full report,

starting with how she arrived in the alley with an accomplice who escaped with her sister.

"Her accomplice crushed Rizzo and Barzelli's squad car," Roman mutters.

I raise a shoulder. "My plan worked, and I've made sure Rosalind won't ever escape. She says the only way to cancel the hit Samson placed on us is if he calls it off himself or the firm gets evidence of his death."

"Oh." Seraphine places a hand over her mouth, her blue eyes widening.

"What?" I ask.

"Samson's dead. I just electrocuted him in the bath."

Leroi gazes down at her as though she's said something cute.

"Shit," Benito mutters.

"What does the firm want?" Roman asks. "A death certificate?"

"Seraphine severed his head," Leroi says. "Would that work?"

Roman leans forward in his seat, rests his forearms on his thighs, and frowns. "I need to send that head to the Di Marco Law Group."

Leroi raises a brow. "So they know he's no longer in line for the inheritance?"

"Yeah." Roman turns to me. "Take a leakproof container down to the cottage beneath the sycamore tree and deliver the head to Joseph Di Marco."

"I killed him," Leroi says.

"Then Cesare will send it to whoever's in charge," Roman growls.

I scowl. "Why not Gil?"

My big brother raises his brows. I square my shoulders and meet his gaze. He's only been out of prison for just over a week. That doesn't give him the right to act like he's Dad.

"Cesare," he says, his voice low. "Benito just led a series of raids to gain back control of the meth lab, the warehouse by the dock, and the crew of the Bella Lucia."

I flinch at the mention of Mom's name. One quick glance at my other brother tells me he's no longer affected by her absence. Benito has a way of dismissing anything he deems as irrelevant.

"You forgot about my arrangement with the Salentino sisters at the Newtown Crematorium," Benito adds.

Without missing a beat, Roman adds, "And he's also liaising with insiders at the casino for when we get it back."

My back stiffens, and I cast another glance at Benito, whose gaze is glacial. He doesn't need to say the words because I hear them loud and clear. Benito takes on so much work because he thinks I'm weak and can't handle the weight of being a Montesano.

"You could have asked me for help," I mutter.

"Possibly, but there was no margin for error," Benito drawls.

Resentment burns across my chest and surges through my temples. My nostrils flare, and I clench my jaw. He's doing it again. Telling me I'm a screwup. A man makes one mistake when he's younger and everyone thinks he can't handle responsibility.

"Enough," Roman says before I can muster up a reply. His gaze hardens, making him look exactly like Dad. "That head is the only thing standing between us taking back control of the family business and being taken down by assassins. You are the only person I can rely on to make sure it arrives at the Di Marco Law group."

I swallow hard, my heart pounding at the gravity of his trust.

"Fine," I mutter. "I'll pick it up."

"Bring it here first, so we can tell the Moirai to end the contract."

"Sure thing, Roman." I turn to Benito. "And I'm going to need to use the jet this evening."

"No," Benito says.

"Why not?"

"Someone from Tommy Galliano's side called, asking for a meeting."

Terror punches me in the heart. Alarm spikes, and my pulse ratchets up to eleven. This is a message from the Galliano brothers. If I don't comply with their demands, they'll expose my secret and force my hand. I force my face into a mask of composure, trying to hold back the rising panic.

My chest tightens, each breath coming harder and harder with the crushing weight of dread. Benito already thinks I'm a waste of space, and it won't take him long to infect Roman. They'll both stop tolerating me the moment they discover the truth.

I grit my teeth and ask, "What does Galliano want?"

"It's probably about the meth lab," Roman mutters. "Capello didn't abduct our scientists. It was that scaly bastard."

All the breath leaves my lungs in a desperate exhale, but it's too early to feel relief. The business discussion could just be a ruse to deliver a blow to my already crumbling reputation.

"I want you in the club tonight, watching the monitors for suspicious activity." Roman raises a finger. "Before you complain, Benito will be at the door, making sure Galliano doesn't storm the entrance with his men."

My gaze flicks to the laptop screen, where Leroi has already fallen asleep. His girlfriend sits beside him, her attention riveted to her phone.

"Hey, Seraphine," I say, making her glance into the camera. "Be with you in twenty minutes."

I walk out, my stomach roiling with trepidation. Miranda will need to wait another day for me to rescue her from captivity. But if tonight goes badly, I may not even have a future.

THIRTY-FOUR

ROSALIND

Just when I tried to get a semblance of control over my captivity, he left.

Now all I have for company is the scent of antiseptic and the constant beep of those loathsome monitors.

Shit.

Hours pass. I can't exactly keep track of the time in this windowless room, but my stomach has stopped growling with hunger. My body's survival mechanisms have kicked in, suppressing the constant ache for food.

My mind is clearer, and I can refocus my efforts on escape. I try to flex my fingers, but the thick leather bindings holding them to the metal splint restrict their movement.

If I'm ever going to get out of this contraption, it will be with Cesare's permission. As much as I despise the thought, he's got me completely at his mercy.

Footsteps approach, and my pulse spikes. I force my breaths to slow so the monitors won't betray my agitation. Too late. The door swings open, revealing the bastard himself, clad in his usual black shirt and pants and holding a steaming bowl of something that smells divine.

"Time to eat, pet," he says.

A growl rips through my stomach as though his words have

summoned back my hunger. I tighten my jaw, wishing it would shut the fuck up, but saliva floods my mouth at the mingled scents of honey, warm milk, and cinnamon.

He chuckles and looms over me with a bowl. "Who's a hungry girl?"

"Not me," I say through clenched teeth.

"You need to eat."

I jerk my head to the side. If I take even a mouthful of food, then he's won. He'll erode my mind in a cycle of hunger and desperation and use that weakness to extract information about the firm that could get Miranda hurt.

He grabs my chin and turns my face to meet his gaze, but I squeeze my eyes shut, refusing to give him any kind of satisfaction.

"Look at me." His grip tightens. "Open your fucking eyes and eat."

The sweet, tantalizing aroma intensifies, and he smears something warm and thick and gooey on my lips. It takes every ounce of willpower not to lick them clean. When he tries forcing his coated fingers between my lips, I clench my teeth.

Air crackles against my bare skin as though his anger has charged the room with electric sparks. My muscles stiffen with the force of my determination. I won't give that bastard an inch.

"Stubborn little thing," he says, his hot breath warming my cheek. "But I have ways of making you eat."

I hold my breath, waiting for him to pry open my jaws, but he releases my chin and steps away. The bowl lands on a table with a clink, and his footsteps retreat to the other side of the room.

My heart thrums a steady beat. The only reason it isn't racing is the concentrated effort I've put into slowing my pulse. If he wants to beat me into submission, I'm ready, because that shit won't work.

At the approaching squeak of a wheel, I crack open an eye to find him pushing a trolley. On its surface is a surgical tray filled with metal instruments, and a transparent tube I've seen on IVs, only thicker.

I huff a laugh, but it carries no mirth. "Is that a feeding tube?"

"This is a gastronomy tube," he replies with a sneer.

"You're not sticking that down my throat, and don't even think of sliding it into my nostril."

He continues toward me, his eyes flashing. I clench my jaw, meeting his glower with a glare just as hateful. The flickering lightbulb illuminates him from the back, turning the edges of his hair a vibrant shade of mahogany.

Cesare looks like a horror movie villain, a younger, hotter version of the type that eats livers with fava beans and Chianti.

A shudder runs down my spine and settles between my legs. When he picks up a sponge with a pair of forceps and runs its wet surface over a spot on my stomach, my adrenaline spikes.

"What the hell are you doing?" I rasp.

"Cleaning the surgical site."

"What for?" I hiss.

He sets the sponge back on the tray. "To insert the G-tube into your stomach. By the way, you look stupid with your lips covered in rice pudding."

On instinct, I snap, "As if I give a fuck."

Realization dawns on me like a bucket of mop water to the face, making my breath hitch. This crazy bastard is going to perform major surgery on my body just because I refuse to eat.

He picks up a scalpel, looks me dead in the eye, and says, "I won't bother with the anesthetic since you enjoy pain."

Scenarios rip through my mind like the shutters of a silent movie. Him feeding me with a tube through the stomach, then sewing my mouth shut for sass, then amputating each limb in response to some perceived slight.

He's already stitched my labia to seal my pussy shut. By the time he's finished with me, I'll be eyeless, limbless, and in no position to escape. All because I refused to eat the rice pudding.

"Fuck!" I scream. "Give me the food."

Huffing out a laugh, he sets down the scalpel, picks up the bowl, and dips his fingers into the creamy dessert.

"Go on." His sticky digits hover over my mouth.

Every instinct screams at me to jerk away, snap or scream or spit.

"Bite my fingers, and I'll extract your teeth," he says with a chilling calmness that tightens my nipples and makes my clit throb.

I part my lips and allow his fingers to slide onto my tongue. The sweet, creamy rice pudding fills my senses, making each nerve ending sing with rapture. As someone who eats vegan to maintain optimal health, this is the most delicious thing I've eaten in over a decade.

"Good girl," he says. "You're taking it so well."

My throat bobs, and the backs of my eyes sting with humiliation. I hate this man with every fiber of my being. I want to tear him to shreds.

He scoops up more rice pudding with his fingers, offering them to me like a sweet sacrament. The heat of his stare burns into my skin, but I refuse to give him the satisfaction of knowing that he's won this twisted game of dominance.

"I had a pet once," he says, sounding wistful. "She got pregnant and died."

Swallowing hard, I picture another woman held hostage in this room, her belly swollen with Cesare's spawn. I don't need to imagine being forced into motherhood against my will. That agony is already seared into my memory.

"What happened to her?" I rasp.

He takes a deep breath, his Adam's apple bobbing as if he is suppressing a flood of feelings. My heart skips a beat. Did she die in childbirth, get gunned down while trying to escape, or did he kill her in a violent rage?

"Cesare?" I rasp.

"Her belly was sliced open, and the babies also died."

His voice falters with the detached regret someone might use for talking about a long-lost animal companion and not an innocent woman he abducted, impregnated, and probably subjected to a botched c-section.

What the hell is wrong with this man? I knew he was unhinged, but this revelation only fills me with more dread. My mind spins in gruesome scenarios, each more horrifying than the last. His family won't let him get away with keeping a woman captive. Not when his older brother just got out of prison for a murder. Right?

Right?

The next finger full of pudding tastes sour, but I force myself to endure for the chance of escape. I can't risk any more modifications to my body or the threat of getting infected and too weak to run.

"Cesare," I whisper, "Please tell me about your last pet."

He pauses, his shoulders sagging as if weighted down by the loss of the poor, innocent woman he tortured to death. "She was beautiful. Light brown eyes like yours and soft brown fur."

My throat tightens. "Fur?"

"She was my best friend," he continues, his voice softening. "She'd hop out of her cage and nuzzle my hand, looking up at me with those trusting eyes. When I let her out to play in the yard, she'd always run back to me, nudging my leg for attention."

I stare up at him, my breath quickening. So, he's comparing me to an animal? "Was she a hamster?"

"Rabbit," he rasps. "And more than just a pet. She was my companion, my confidant, my comfort. Stroking her while she sat on my lap was the closest thing I had to heaven."

Swallowing the rest of the pudding, I scan his face for insights into his humanity. His eyes are glassy, detached, as if he really is pining for a long dead rabbit.

"Who killed her?" I rasp.

His eyes flash. "It wasn't me."

I flinch at the intensity of his protest. "Okay, then who?"

"My brother's friends cut her open. They wanted to see what was inside."

The rice pudding churns in my stomach, and I suck in a sharp breath.

"She was still warm when I found her, with her entrails and the babies scattered on the grass. I tried to piece them back together, but it was hopeless." His voice breaks.

"What happened next?" I whisper.

"My mom found me covered in blood, trying to bring my dead rabbit to life, and she screamed." His jaw tightens. "Said I was in danger of becoming a psychopath."

"Oh." I gulp. "I'm sorry."

His sticky fingers graze over my breasts, and he leans in close. "That's why I plan on taking good care of you."

I squeeze my eyes shut, feeling his hot breath against my skin. So, this is his villain origin story. He probably sees himself as a tragic hero, forced to become a dark protector.

"Cesare, I'm not a rabbit."

His lips graze my cheek. "You're far more precious to me than a ball of fur. That's why I plan to break you open, pry out all of your secrets, and rebuild you into a creature of my own making."

My jaw tightens. His mother was right. He is a psychopath. If I allow these mind games to continue, I'm in danger of becoming exactly what he wants.

THIRTY-FIVE

CESARE

Hours later, I lean forward on the desk, staring at the wall of monitors broadcasting different angles of the Phoenix. Music filters in through the walls, making the office seem more isolated.

I miss my pretty little pet. I could have played with her, but Benito kept blowing up my phone about tonight's meeting. Roman wants to delay starting a war with the Galliano brothers, while I need them both to die with my secret.

What a pity Roman assigned Benito to watch the front door. He probably knows I would have shot the Galliano envoy, whatever the consequences, but not for the reason he thinks.

Fuck. I wish Rosalind was here, bound and kneeling beneath the desk between my spread legs. Nothing beats hate fellatio. She could glare daggers at me while she swallowed down my cock to the root. Every time her teeth grazed my shaft, I would wonder if she would bite.

My gaze drops to the camera I set up in the underground playroom, where Rosalind lies within her binds. She's sleeping, based on the app monitoring her vital signs. When she awakens, her blood sugar will dip, and she'll be plagued once more with hunger pangs.

An alert pops up on my screen. It's a photo from Miranda of a pizza she's warmed up from the freezer and a large tub of ice cream.

I glance at the time. 10:34 PM. My stomach grumbles, reminding me I should have eaten more than Sofia's rice pudding.

Miranda asks when I'm going to fetch her, but I can't answer. I'd planned on flying out earlier today, but I had to pick up Samson's head, chat with Leroi and Seraphine, take the head to Roman and wait for him to finish talking with Rosalind's boss, then deliver the head to the Di Marco Law Group, so they could release Frederic Capello's assets to Roman's special guest.

I don't want to make Miranda promises I can't keep.

My gaze wanders back to a monitor, where Roman and Gil sit in the club's VIP section, waiting for the Galliano envoy. When Gil rises off his seat, I stiffen in mine, only to slump as he approaches some blonde.

Gil steers her toward the front of the club, looking as though he plans to throw her out through the front door. Instead, he opens the side door leading to the cloakroom and bends her over a table.

"Look at that!" I say with a laugh.

When Gil isn't up my ass being Roman's second set of eyes, he's a helpful motherfucker. Always willing to scoop up a clingy woman I'm tired of fucking.

That's what I did with Leroi. The moment I was sure he no longer wanted Rosalind, I snapped her up before anyone else could shoot their shot. Except I won't discard her.

Rosalind is mine until she perishes.

On the next screen, a pink-haired woman walks into the frame, where the camera points at our security guard, Bruno, standing in the alley, smoking a joint. It's Tania, the former bartender who caught me waterboarding Ricky Ferraro and later spat in Miranda's cocktail.

My eyes narrow as she gets on her knees and pulls down Bruno's zipper. I snort. "Is she trying to get back her job?"

As her head bobs up and down over his shaft, a masked figure steps into the frame, holding a gun. He shoots Bruno, then punches Tania unconscious, leaving her lying in the man's blood.

I jump to my feet. "What the fuck?"

The figure turns to the camera, pulls off his ski mask, and waves. It takes a moment to process that manic grin. Then it hits like a punch to the gut, leaving me winded.

Matty Fucking Galliano.

My heart races. Every vein in my body surges with adrenaline and rage.

Shit. Shit. Shit.

He can't be here, outside the building, where my brothers can see him. They'll want to know why the fuck he's grinning like a lunatic into our security camera with Bruno's blood staining his boots.

They'll ask what kind of message he's trying to send, and he'll tell them every filthy secret I've been desperate to hide.

I rush to the security console, turn off the camera pointing at the alley, and delete the past five minutes of footage.

After grabbing my gun, I sprint out of the office and through the hallway, knocking down employees as I hurry past.

"Boss?" asks one of our security guards from behind.

"Stay away from the exit," I bark.

By the time I reach the door and push it open, both Bruno and the unconscious girl are gone, and there's no trace of Matty. I inhale sharply, my nostrils filling with the faint stench of garbage and urine.

My heart pounds and I glance up and down the empty alley. That was no hallucination. I know what I saw.

When I glance down at my feet, the ground is wet. I'm about to check that it's blood when someone steps out from behind the dumpster, casting a long shadow.

This is the first time I've seen Matty Galliano in the flesh. His silver hair sweeps off his face in loose curls that fall inches beneath his ears. His long nose dominates his face, overshadowing beady eyes and a mouth as sharp as a razor.

Today, he wears a black leather duster with white gloves and a matching turtleneck that stretches inches beneath his chin as though he's allergic to fresh air.

The air crackles with tension as he approaches, each step

calculated and deliberate. If he thinks he's a predator, then he's found the wrong prey. I'd sooner stick a knife in his windpipe.

"Looking for me, son?" Matty Galliano's gravelly voice sets my teeth on edge.

"Don't call me that," I snarl.

He flashes me a smile, the corners of his eyes crinkling with false warmth. "Scared of the truth?"

Bile rises to my throat, making me want to spit. My blood boils at the sight of this man, another reminder of Mom's infidelity.

"Don't tell me you're the Galliano envoy," I say, my lip curling with disgust.

He flicks his head toward the club. "Tommy's in there, talking to Roman."

My throat thickens. Both Galliano brothers crossed into New Alderney.

"What the fuck do you want? I'm under orders to shoot any Galliano sympathizers."

"Is that any way to speak to your father?" he asks with a smirk.

"You're not—"

"You've been ignoring my calls," he snarls, his words as hard as his eyes. "I tolerated this bullshit because I had an heir, but my children and wife were staying overnight at Cousin Freddy's sixtieth."

It doesn't take a genius to work out that Leroi killed Matty Galliano's family along with the Capellos. Now, this twisted old bastard thinks he can harass me into replacing his dead offspring.

"What do you think I am? Your spare?"

His smile drops. "You're my last chance, son."

"My father is Enzo Montesano. Not you," I grit out.

"You have my mother's eyes," he says as if I hadn't spoken, "The Galliano build, even the same hair."

"No," I rasp.

"You're my son, Cesare. Tommy had a vasectomy after having his sons, and I'm the only other man who fucked your mother around the time of your conception."

I breathe hard to control my rising anger, but when his words sink in, I turn off the gun's safety with a click. "Shut your filthy mouth."

Galliano raises his pistol. "Don't do this, son."

"Get fucked."

"Just hear me out. Tommy went to a lot of trouble to organize a meeting with Roman. He could be walking into an ambush just to give me a chance for us to talk."

"Then say what you want and leave," I snap.

He nods. "We want you to join our ranks."

I laugh, the sound manic. "Why the fuck would I leave my brothers for a pair of crooks who stole our meth lab?"

"Because we're your blood." He pats his chest. "You ever wonder why you don't have your brothers' bulky build or dark brown eyes? It's because you're a Galliano, not a Montesano."

"I take after my mother," I say through clenched teeth.

"Look again. You're the spitting image of my son when he was your age."

There's no reply to that statement because it's the truth. I've seen family photos online and there's no denying the resemblance. Five years ago, Mom left a note beneath my pillow, explaining the truth of my parentage and urging me to leave my brothers behind and join the Galliano family before they learned the truth.

"Roman has been out of the game for too long," Matty says. "He's weak, just like his father, Enzo. Tommy is expanding our territory to New Alderney. The Montesano family is a sinking ship, and I'm offering you a lifeline."

I stare down the barrel of Galliano's gun, wondering which one of us is faster on the trigger.

"Don't think of shooting, Cesare," he says. "I have four other guns trained on your head. You have twenty-four hours to give me an answer."

"The answer is no."

"Twenty-four hours," he bites out. "I will not take no for an answer."

A fist of anguish tightens my chest at the implication that he will force my hand by telling Roman and Benito my secret. The

Galliano brothers don't just lead the biggest crime family in New Jersey. They're close associates and beloved cousins of Frederic Capello.

My brothers must never discover I'm related to any of these bastards.

THIRTY-SIX

ROSALIND

I stare up at the flickering lightbulb, my eyes streaming with tears.

The chastity belt strapped to my hips has a device that vibrates just enough to stimulate my clit, but not enough so I can climax. No matter how much I try to grind against it, every time I reach a certain level of arousal, it's programmed to shut off and leave me frustrated.

I can't sleep. I can't think. I can't even breathe. This relentless cycle of pleasure and denial is breaking me faster than any conventional form of torture.

Sweat coats my skin and soaks the table's leather surface. My tongue is swollen and dry. My throat is raw from gasping for air, and the worst part of this predicament is that my captor has left me alone.

Wires stretch from the monitors to the toy. Every time my blood pressure reaches a certain threshold, and it finally feels like I'm close to release, the toy deactivates. When my BP drops, the vibrations restart, increasing their intensity, until I'm back to the edge.

Cesare Montesano is a menace. This bullshit should be banned by the Geneva convention or Mafia code of conduct.

The door swings open, and the man himself enters, clad in a

black silk shirt that skims his muscular chest and hugs his broad shoulders. It's unbuttoned to the sternum, revealing tantalizing glimpses of his tattooed olive skin.

My teeth grind. This torture has me so desperate and horny that I'm starting to find him attractive.

He stops at the doorway without his usual smirk. The dim, flickering light makes his features more angular and accentuates the sharpness of his cheekbones and the cruel curves of his mouth. If I gave a damn, I'd say he looked bothered.

His gaze sweeps over my trembling body as though he's taking inventory of a possession. I force my muscles to still as he traces every counter, every inch of my exposed flesh.

It's been over a decade since I last felt so vulnerable. I swore to myself this would never happen again, yet here I am under another man's control. Angry heat rushes to the surface of my skin, making my nipples tingle. I clench my teeth, not wanting to show him any weakness.

Cesare's features harden. "You pissed on my floor."

"I'll shit on it if you don't set me free," I snap.

He storms to the corner of the room and picks up the mop, bucket, and a huge plastic bottle. I break out in a fresh sweat, wondering if this is the start of a new sadistic game.

Without another word, he opens the bottle and pours its contents on the floor, filling the air with the citrus scent of cleaning fluid. After returning the container to the sink, he mops the floor clean.

"You would save so much time if you acted like a normal psychopath and gave me a bucket," I rasp

"Tell me about Leroi," he says, his tone flat.

"I thought you weren't interested in me sexually," I reply. "Something about not wanting to stick your cock in me if it was on fire?"

He finally meets my gaze. "Do you want to get untied or not?"

My heart skips a beat. "Turn off the fucking vibrator," I say through clenched teeth. "Please."

He walks around the table and unplugs the toy. At the sudden absence of vibrations, my muscles relax, and I can finally exhale.

"Talk," he says, the word soft.

Cesare really is in a strange mood. Maybe he and his brothers negotiated with the firm and they've demanded my release? My mind is so scrambled that it's giving way to false hope.

I swallow, my tongue darting out to lick my dry lips. "Leroi was my target. Based on our surveillance, he was the most probable way to access the Montesano estate."

He stares down at me with an intensity that makes my skin prickle. It's like he's searching my features for any signs of deception. I hold his gaze, refusing to break under the weight of his scrutiny.

"We knew he went to the Phoenix to speak to either Benito or you, so that's where I was assigned," I add.

He nods. "You were wearing a white, strapless dress."

My breath catches. How on earth does he even remember? "I don't remember seeing you that night."

"I was watching the monitors," he replies. "What did you say when you sat beside him in the VIP section?"

The corners of my mouth pinch into a grimace. "I asked if he fucked as hard as he looked."

"What did he reply?" Cesare asks.

"Leroi told me to get lost," I mutter. "It looked like he was waiting for someone. I told him I'd look elsewhere else for a dom who had what it took to tame a bratty sub and then ground against some other guy on the dance floor.

"What happened after Leroi spoke to Benito?"

I pause, unsure if he really recalls that evening or if he searched for it in the club's surveillance footage. "He grabbed my wrist, took me into the alley, fucked me against the wall, and walked away without a word."

Cesare's eyes narrow, and a muscle in his jaw flexes. "He didn't even bother to ask for your name?" he snarls through clenched teeth. "Was it so good that you went back for seconds?"

I huff a laugh.

"What?" he snaps.

"It was my job. I had to get close to Leroi to gather information about you and your brothers."

Silence hangs in the air like a guillotine as Cesare glares down at me like I'm a piece of shit. I force my breath to even, not wanting him to see the stress in my vital signs.

Cesare doesn't strike me as a man who would judge a woman for having a one-night stand, but he might be envious of his older, more experienced cousin.

As an only child who spent the first eleven years of my life in a boarding school, my knowledge of family dynamics is only theoretical, but I think Cesare might have some sibling rivalry. Our intel stated Leroi lived in Enzo Montesano's estate until he was ten.

The door swings open, making my head snap toward the exit. Roman Montesano steps in, wearing a burgundy robe and a face like a thunderstorm.

His gaze locks with mine for the brief moment it takes for Cesare to rush forward and usher his older brother out into the hallway.

When the door slams shut, I close my eyes, strain my ears, and try to eavesdrop.

"What happened last night?" Even though Roman's voice is muffled, I can still sense his tone is urgent.

Cesare hesitates for a beat before whispering, "What are you talking about?"

"Tania was found dead in the dumpster."

For a moment, I think they've walked away, until Roman adds, "The staff say you were last seen rushing out to the exit that leads out to the alley."

My breath shallows as I lean as far toward the door as my bindings will allow. If I remember the intel correctly, Tania was a university student who worked at the Phoenix as a bartender.

Roman's voice drifts back into my consciousness. "You turned off the security camera and erased five minutes of footage."

"One of Galliano's men was out in the alley," Cesare says. "I deleted the footage so I could kill him without witnesses."

"Is that why you went without backup?"

Cesare doesn't reply.

"This looks suspicious," Roman says, his voice heavy with accusation.

"I didn't kill her," Cesare snarls.

"Gil says last time he saw Tania, you were choking her against the bathroom wall because she saw you waterboarding Ricky Ferraro."

"But I let her go," he says.

"Then four other employees said you came in days later and fired Tania while you were drinking with an underaged girl in an academy uniform."

My jaw drops.

Are they talking about Miranda?

THIRTY-SEVEN

CESARE

I should have killed Matty Galliano the moment I stepped out into the alleyway and damned the consequences. Now, Roman is glaring at me like I'm the type of serial killer that targets women.

Galliano must have killed Tania while I was rushing out to meet him and dragged her body behind that dumpster. In a panic, I turned off the only cameras that could prove my innocence.

"I'm going to ask you a question, little brother," Roman says, his voice heavy with suspicion and tinged with disgust. "And I want a straight answer."

My throat tightens and sweat breaks out across my brow. This is it. The moment he realizes I'm not a Montesano but a product of Galliano scum.

"Did you kill Tania?" he asks.

"No." I meet his accusation with an unwavering gaze

He studies me for several heartbeats, searching for signs of deceit. The basement hallway closes in around us like the walls of a coffin, suffocating me with its oppressive weight.

"I didn't do it. I swear," I say, and want to cringe.

"How many men have you interrogated who have said the same?" Roman asks, his gaze boring into mine. "You're hiding something, and I want to know what."

Five years on death row has exaggerated the differences in our physiques. In the world of boxing, Roman would be a heavyweight, and I would be a middleweight. I'm 6'2", while my brothers are both 6'4". Even Benito the pencil pusher outweighs me by at least twenty pounds.

That bastard, Galliano, was right. I have the Galliano eyes, the Galliano physique, the Galliano hair, and even the Galliano propensity for violence.

Roman places a hand on my shoulder. "Are you back on drugs?"

"No." I shake my head. "And I'm not hiding anything."

He gives me one of those slow nods that says he doesn't believe a word I've said, but is too nice to call me a liar.

"What are you still doing with Leroi's little assassin?"

"Rosalind is mine," I snap.

"Why is she still alive?" he asks with more bite.

"I've secured her properly this time. She won't escape."

Roman breaks eye contact and sighs. He would have gotten daily reports from Gil on the time they made me go cold turkey. I can tell he's disappointed that his brother was once an addict. I can tell he's thinking I'm a weak link.

"That Moirai asshole using the New Alderney Times as a front called me back about Capello's death," Roman murmurs.

"What did he say?"

"It was noted."

"And the contract on our lives?"

"Bastard hung up," he mutters.

I flick my head toward the closed door. "Rosalind's clients only pay in full after the kill. If they die before then, the Moirai keep their deposits and don't fulfill the contract."

"They had better not," Roman growls.

"I can always double check with her."

He nods. "Do it."

"Sure thing, Roman."

My brother steps back, his shoulders hunched. I stay rooted on the spot, waiting for him to reach the end of the hallway before moving, but he pauses.

"If you didn't kill Tania, who did?"

"Someone from Galliano's side, wanting to start trouble," I say.

"Who did you see in the alley?"

"Just Tania, sucking off one of our security guys."

"Bruno said he was shot at from behind."

My eyes widen. "He survived?"

"The bullet grazed his skull, leaving a flesh wound. He blacked out for an hour, then raised the alarm."

"And that's how they found Tania?" I ask, my voice breathy.

Roman advances toward me, eyes blazing, his shoulders expanding to take up the entire hallway.

My heart races, and I swallow hard, trying to stem my resentment toward Galliano. He must have known I would hide all evidence of our conversation and used that opportunity to murder the woman everyone knew I'd been fucking.

That bastard is so desperate to have me at his side that he would frame me for murder.

"Would you like some advice, baby brother?" Roman snarls.

"What?"

"Take it from a man who got locked up for the murder of a woman he didn't know, was miles away from when she died, and never even fucked." He pauses, and the tension in the hallway thickens like coagulated blood. "This does not look good."

I nod.

"Is there anything you want to share?" he asks, his tone sharp enough to cut throats.

The question hangs in the air like a noose.

Sidestepping, I ask, "Where's Tania?"

His lips tighten, mirroring Dad's disapproval. "Gil put her in a freezer with Ricky Ferraro." His brows rise. "The informant you killed."

"Don't say it like you didn't waterboard him first," I snap. "And I didn't kill Tania."

He raises a finger, giving me another of Dad's expressions. "Stay the fuck out of trouble. I got enough police attention from our special guest."

I nod.

Roman finally breaks eye contact, but I don't allow myself to deflate because I know he's not finished.

"There's a welcome-home party tomorrow night. Benito's inviting all the movers and shakers in Beaumont City, and he'll be onstage, welcoming me back. I want you up there to show a united front."

I flinch. "Is that the only reason?"

He places both hands on my shoulders. "Can you handle that, Cesare?"

"If you're asking if I'm still using—"

"I'm asking if you can get onstage and say a few words," he says, his voice softening. He cups my cheek the way he used to when I was little and gives me a reassuring big-brother smile.

Prickly heat creeps across my skin, and I feel like the annoying little kid who used to trail after Benito and the Capello twins, begging for scraps of attention.

Shrinking with reflected embarrassment, I glance away and mutter, "I'm twenty-four, not eighteen."

He chuckles, the sound warm and rich. "Time went still when I was inside. In my mind, you'll always be my kid brother."

I shift on my feet and squirm, not knowing what the fuck to say. Sometimes, it's hard to relate to Roman because he's nearly ten years older. He was always this mythical older brother who barely had time to notice me when I was growing up. It's strange to see him outside of prison, and his presence is both unfamiliar and overwhelming.

"You were drugged without your consent," he rumbles. "That's got to have a lingering effect. You remember that time when Mom ate tiramisu laced with Marsala wine?"

The reminder of her alcoholic relapse rips open the fissures in my heart, making it bleed with sorrow and resentment. Pain spreads across my chest and thickens my throat, making my words come out choked.

"I'm not a drunk and I'm no longer an addict," I say.

He nods, the corners of his eyes crinkling. "No, you're not, and I'm proud of you for staying clean." He pats my cheek. "Keep it that way."

This time, when Roman steps back, he continues to the end

of the hallway and out through the door. I slump against the wall, my mind spinning in all directions.

Roman's brotherly concern was him dangling the carrot. If I screw up one more time, it will be the stick. But if he discovers my secret, will it be the gun instead?

How much do I really know about my oldest brother? If given the chance, he would wipe out every Galliano in existence.

Matty Galliano is determined to create a rift between me and my brothers. He's already making them suspect me of murder. How much longer until he tells them the truth?

I need to track down that bastard and his older sibling and kill them both before they succeed.

THIRTY-EIGHT

ROSALIND

I push against the leather restraints, too freaked out by what I heard.

Cesare didn't answer Roman's question about what he saw when he stepped into the alley. From the way Roman spoke, it sounds like he even thinks his brother is guilty.

Shit.

I knew Cesare was a murderer, and I knew he was a psychopath. But is he the type of man who would kill a lover, dump her body in the alley beside his own club, and conceal the truth from his brother?

This torture must be screwing with my mind because I don't know what to think.

And how does Miranda fit into this sordid mess?

I squeeze my eyes shut, trying to cut through my hunger, my thirst, my lingering arousal, my complete and utter confusion.

She doesn't.

Miranda didn't witness the waterboarding. That was the dead woman, Tania. Miranda was only there when Cesare fired her in front of the staff. Miranda was also in the safe house when Cesare may or may not have murdered Tania in the alleyway.

The door swings open, and I even out my features. There's no point in antagonizing Cesare by mentioning what I overheard, otherwise he'll upgrade his method of torture to something I can't abide. If he ever noticed how I stiffened in the swimming pool, then he'd drag me out of the basement and drown away the last vestiges of my sanity.

He wouldn't risk giving me the chance to escape. Most likely, he'd put me in sensory deprivation.

His footsteps approach, and the fine hairs on the back of my neck stand on end. Eavesdropping on that conversation has made me think of my own survival. What's Cesare's end game?

It's always the same with the predatory type of psychopath. He'll lose interest after he breaks my spirit and turns me into an obedient pet, then I'll die.

"Want to come?" he asks.

"Who doesn't?" I reply through clenched teeth.

"Look at me."

I crack open an eye.

All traces of mania have left his expression, leaving him looking somber. This is probably some kind of lull because he's realized he isn't invincible.

"Are you sure the hit is canceled?" he asks, his voice deceptively calm.

I gulp. "You should know I can't give you guarantees."

"Explain."

"Unexpected events like Roman's release from death row will cause waves. If he's innocent like the papers say, then whoever framed him might want to finish the job the state of New Alderney failed to execute."

He scowls. "So, the information you gave me is useless. What's the point of keeping you alive?"

My adrenaline spikes, and the monitors go apeshit. I grind my teeth and force in a deep breath to slow my pulse. "I can't control who wants you dead."

"Give me something," he growls through clenched teeth.

"Okay." I lick my lips, my heart fluttering with nerves, wishing I could think straight. "Don't be at the same place at the same time. That makes you too much of a tempting target. If you do, then wear bulletproof vests."

"How does that help protect our heads?" he asks with a sneer.

"It's company policy not to damage the face so the corpse will be recognizable."

"And you get paid." Every word drips with venom.

His eyes bore into mine, his features hardening with judgment and scorn. He acts like my line of work is lower than his.

Forcing back the sting of his judgment, I hold his gaze. Cesare Montesano wouldn't know how it feels to be powerless, outcast, and desperate to save a child from a life of abuse.

"It must be nice to be pampered with no responsibilities apart from keeping yourself alive," I say. "Assassins make clean kills and don't drag out people's pain by torturing them or peddling drugs."

He flashes his teeth. "You think you're better than me?"

"Murder is just business," I say.

His lip curls. "Anything else you want to share?"

"Have you ever thought of being less of an asshole? That could slash the number of people who want you dead."

A sadistic cackle pierces my eardrums and makes my skin crawl with dread. What the hell possessed me to provoke this maniac and goad him to subject me to further horrors?

When he walks to the sink to wash his hands, my stomach plummets, and I imagine him sewing my mouth shut.

My heart pounds as he returns to the end of the table and stands between my spread legs.

"Still want to come?" he asks.

I stiffen.

This has to be a trick.

He unbuckles the chastity belt and rubs the pad of his finger over my swollen clit. Sparks of pleasure skitter across my sex, and the muscles of my pussy tighten with need.

I've wanted to come for hours, if not days.

"Are you... are you serious?" I choke out. "Because if this is another of your games—"

"No game."

As he makes gentle circles over my needy clit, a part of me wants to sob with relief. This is a hundred times more intimate than the chastity belt's vibrator, and I'm so sensitive that I feel every ridge of his skin.

His slow strokes detonate tiny sparks along my nerves,

burning slowly toward what's going to be an explosive climax. If he even allows me to come.

Arousal makes my heart pound, and the muscles of my pussy clench and release in sync with Cesare's finger. I glance at the monitors and shiver as my blood pressure and heart rate climb. No matter how slowly I force myself to breathe, I can't control my body's response.

Inhale. Stay calm. Exhale. Don't spike. Inhale. Exhale.

Shit.

The numbers climb toward the dreaded threshold. I hold my breath, close my eyes, and try to stem the rising tide of arousal, but it's no use. The alarms blare, making my ears ring with the shrill sound of my body's betrayal.

Cesare's finger slows to a halt.

Emotions flood my psyche, causing my internal walls to tremble under the weight of fury, fear, and frustration. My eyes sting with unshed tears, and it takes every ounce of strength to keep them from spilling.

"Eyes on me."

My eyes snap open, loosening two tears.

"Hump it," he says, his grin widening with malice.

"What?" I rasp.

"If you're that desperate to come, then take what you need."

I hesitate, my eyes wide, my heartbeat pounding against my eardrums. "Is this a test?" I ask, trying not to stumble over my words. "Some kind of joke?"

His gaze softens. "Go on, pet."

I should close my eyes, turn my head, and refuse to play his sick games. But hunger, thirst, and hours of sexual torture have changed the chemistry of my blood. My hormones rage at me to take what's offered and clear my head with an orgasm, so I can think through my escape.

My survival instincts wonder what happens if I give Cesare everything he wants and he gets bored? Will I end up like Tania, dead and discarded?

"Want a shower?" he asks.

I clench my jaw. There's no fucking way he'll ever unbuckle these restraints. I'll say yes, and he'll drench me with the sprinklers. Or a hose. Or he'll stick my head in a bath.

Shit. I should stop imagining the worst.

"If you want me to take you to the bathroom, then you'll come on my finger like a good pet," he growls.

My resolve crumbles, and I buck my hips within the restraints, rubbing my aching clit against his finger. It feels so good that my throat loosens a whimper.

"Tell me how much you love this," he says.

"Get fucked," I reply through clenched teeth.

"Watch your mouth." He slaps my thigh, and the sting goes straight to my clit. "If you don't want me to pull my hand away, then you'll beg me for more."

Gritting my teeth, I force back a moan. "I love it."

"Louder."

"I said I fucking love it," I snap, my hips jerking.

"Tell me more."

"Your finger is so thick," I say through clenched teeth. "I love rubbing myself against it."

He flashes me a grin, his eyes dancing. "What else?"

I've fucked men to perform kills or to gather intel, but none of them have ever forced me to say something so degrading. Humiliation burns through my body like an inferno, electrifying my nerves with an endorphin rush.

My senses become agitated, alive, alert, and my pleasure receptors sing. I'm trembling with anticipation, my breaths coming in short bursts, desperate to chase these intense sensations. Even if I wanted this to end, my hips can't stop writhing.

What the fuck is this crazy bastard doing to my psyche?

He's fine-tuning my kinks, transforming me from someone who enjoys pain into the truest form of masochist.

"Dirty little pet," he says with a cruel chuckle. "So horny, so wet. Humping my finger like a bitch in heat."

I grit my teeth and grind out, "Don't. Fucking. Stop."

He reaches over and delivers a sharp slap to my breast, sending another jolt of pleasure to my clit. Quivering, I moan, my nipples aching for his cruel fingers. I want him to pinch and twist them. To make me scream.

"Fuck," he groans. "You're dripping. Streaming for me. Shaking like a fucking slut."

I squeeze my eyes shut, loosening tears that roll down the sides of my face and mingle with my sweat. The last vestiges of my self-respect scream at me to get a grip, but my hips won't stop chasing the pleasure.

It's intoxicating.

"You should see your cunt," he says, the words taunting. "It's fucking pulsing."

"F-Fuck you," I snarl through gritted teeth.

"Is that what you want, pretty pet?" His voice drops to a low growl that makes my fine hairs stand alert. "You want me to remove your stitches?"

Yes. God, yes.

I need him to fill me with that massive cock. I need him to pound into my pussy like a beast. I need him to fuck me with all his might.

"Fuck no!" I yell, the denial tearing me apart.

He pulls his hand away and steps back, leaving me alone in the horror of my own lust.

"Time for a shower," he says with a smirk.

THIRTY-NINE

ROSALIND

If I thought my heart was pounding before, it's now hurling itself against my ribcage. I can't stifle my fight-or-flight response. I can't control my arousal. My throat is parched, and the small amount of rice pudding from earlier has reset my hunger response. Worst of all, he's gotten me aroused to the edge of insanity.

With the alarms on my vital signs filling the room with sound, Cesare would have to be comatose not to notice I plan to escape.

"Don't stress," he whispers, his voice a sinister purr. "Even if you used those combat skills, you'll never get through our biometric security."

"Want to bet?" I ask through clenched teeth. "There are enough scalpels here to pluck out your eyes. I'd even cut off your hand."

His laugh grates on my last nerve. "Does my pet have a fetish for dismemberment?"

Shivers run down my spine. Why the fuck am I giving this sick bastard ideas? I glance down at the huge tent in his pants and grimace.

"I prefer castration."

His grin falters, providing me with a petty sense of satisfaction.

"Do you want this shower or not?" he asks with a sneer.

I raise my shoulders. "Ready whenever you are."

Cesare unbuckles the thick leather belt around my chest and waist first, followed by the one holding down my hips. I lie still and wait for the best moment to strike.

He releases the restraint on my neck, and adrenaline surges to my limbs. As he moves between my spread thighs, I consider my chances of kicking him in the balls.

No. That's stupid.

He'd tie me up again and do something worse than sew my labia shut. I need to exercise restraint, at least until he releases my arms.

The splints holding my fingers straight could make a weapon. Each digit is attached to a thick metal plate that runs between my knuckles and wrist, which will add weight to my back-handed punches.

"I know what you're thinking." He crouches between my legs, delivering soft kisses to my inner thighs.

Each press of his lips sends sparks to my already tormented clit. He strokes the sensitive skin there with feather-light touches that make my pussy twitch.

"Right now, I'm thinking about a shower," I say.

"Liar," he says, his voice light. "You're going to knee me in the balls until I double over and then rush to the door."

"You missed the step where I pluck out your eye," I reply with a nervous laugh. "How far will I get when your home is so full of staff?"

"It won't be the first time you've escaped."

"Still sore about that?" I ask.

"Of course not." He releases the strap on my left leg, followed by my right.

He pauses as though waiting for me to deliver the kick to his groin, but I remain still.

Not yet...

He walks to my left arm and attaches a metal cuff before releasing the leather restraint.

"What are you doing?" I hiss.

"Pets like you don't break easily." He walks out of range,

holding a chain attached to the metal cuff. "I'll keep you chained like a dog until you learn to be my good girl."

I grind my teeth, fighting back the urge to snap, knowing that any rebellion will sabotage my chances of escape. Instead, I focus on how to convince him to release my fingers.

Cesare circles the table and clasps another cuff around my right wrist, then forces my arms together with a thick chain. When he links them with a padlock, my heart sinks.

"Isn't that a little excessive?" I ask, my voice trembling with restrained fury. "One would think you were scared of a girl."

His strong arm wraps around my shoulders, and he helps me to sit up. My back aches from lying on a hard surface for so long, and I grimace.

"You're a skilled assassin with a track record of deceiving even the best of men."

My eyes narrow. He must be talking about Leroi. Before I can use that knowledge to my advantage, he helps me off the table and onto my feet.

Dizziness slaps me across the senses, leaving me seeing spots. Even if I wanted to kick his ass, my legs wouldn't cooperate. They're unsteady from a mix of inactivity and low blood sugar.

The sick bastard has left me uncoordinated and weak.

"Easy now, pet," he says, like I'm a skittish colt.

With one hand at the small of my back and the other holding my bound wrists, he leads me to the sink.

My lip curls. I fucking knew this shower was a scam.

He presses down on a lever between the taps, and the tiled panel behind it swings open to reveal a white bathroom. Strobe lights blink to life, burning my retinas.

"You people have thought of everything," I mutter.

"This playroom used to be a long-term prison," he says. "My dad installed the bathrooms because he couldn't stand the stench of the captives."

After marching me through the tiled chamber, he stops beneath the shower, and he raises my bound arms to a set of wall-mounted hooks. I struggle against the chains, my body shaking with the effort.

"Is that what I am now?" I spit. "A long-term prisoner?"

"Once you're broken in, you'll be allowed to sleep in my bed and eat with the family." He runs a hand down my back, leaving a trail of heat.

"No amount of torture will turn me into your willing plaything," I snarl.

With a smirk, he takes off his shirt, leaving me glaring at the toned muscles and tattooed skin of his chest. My gaze lingers on the lines and dips of his torso, taking in his defined six pack.

Cesare Montesano is perfect. At least physically. It's a shame nature wasted all that physical beauty on a creature so morally depraved.

He unbuckles his belt, pulls down his zipper, and eases down his pants. My breath hitches as he frees his huge, pierced cock, which drips with a bead of precum.

All the moisture leaves my throat, and fresh lust kicks me in the cunt. Heat shoots down to my core, and my pussy grows wetter, coating my inner thighs with arousal.

Squirming on my feet, I squeeze my legs together, trying to create a little friction, but I'm so desensitized from all that teasing that it's futile.

His gaze sweeps down to my pussy and back up to my eyes. Then he flashes me a cocky grin that makes me want to knock out his perfect, white teeth.

"See something you like, pet?"

"Nothing at all," I snap.

After toeing off his shoes and kicking them to the corner of the bathroom, he returns to my side and twists a knob on the wall. Two huge shower heads release cascades of water. Warmth pours down onto my head, erasing the grime from days of captivity.

Wetness clings to Cesare's naked body, making him look even more tantalizing.

"Sure about that?" He pushes on a dispenser, fills his palm with soap, and moves around my back. His large hands stroke my breasts, stoking the flames of my lust. "I can't get enough of you."

"You're deluded." I flinch away from his touch.

"And you're in denial," he replies, his fingers trailing down my belly. "Open your legs."

"What for?"

"I want to make you come."

"No," I snap.

He chuckles. "No?"

Water pours down on our heads, the sound of it muffling his heavy panting. As his fingers travel downward, I hold my breath, hoping they won't linger, but they reach that tiny groove in my skin that can't be fixed with laser resurfacing.

Clenching my teeth, I force myself not to shudder as he rubs back and forth along the fourteen-year-old scar, making my heart lurch. He's going to ask about it, and I need a distraction. Now.

"What's that?" he asks.

I blurt the only thing that comes to mind. "You know, Leroi might have been a cold-blooded bastard, but he never left me unsatisfied or bored."

With a snarl, he snatches back his hand and shoves me against the wall, his eyes burning with a fury that borders on insanity. Then he grabs my throat and cuts off my air.

The hot water zaps away some of the tension, but I can still feel the intensity of his glower. I raise my chin, meeting his gaze, refusing to be cowed. I can handle the physical torture and even being choked. For Miranda's sake and mine, the last thing I need is for this maniac to learn how I got that scar.

"Are you comparing me to my cousin?"

"Difficult not to, considering he was the last man I fucked," I rasp.

"He has a new woman," he hisses. "So, don't talk about him unless you want the gag."

My lips tighten, and I breathe hard through my flared nostrils. "Don't forget," I say through choked breaths. "You're the one who approached me, knowing my history."

"Do you want to come or not?" he snarls, his fingers tightening around my neck.

"I'm getting sick of this game," I say.

"Yes or no."

I clench my eyes shut. "Yes."

He reaches between our bodies and rubs my clit with firm strokes. My hips buck, and I tremble under his touch.

"Forget about him. You're with me now," he growls.

The heat from the water and the steam have me dizzy and disoriented, but not nearly so delirious as to agree to his ownership. I shake my head, focusing only on the sensations.

"These are my tits." He releases my neck only to pinch my nipple, triggering a burst of pain.

Shivering against the onslaught, I part my thighs. His fingers quicken their pace on my throbbing clit, eliciting desperate moans.

"If you stop, I swear on everything that's holy that I'll bite a chunk out of your face," I growl.

"I won't," he says, his thick cock pressing against my belly.

"Free my hands," I say, my voice urgent. "We can do this together."

His laughter echoes off the bathroom walls. "Not a fucking chance."

"Bastard." I yank at my restraints, making the metal clank.

"Such a foul-mouthed little toy," he growls into my ear, sending shivers down my spine. "You need to learn to respect your master."

"You're deluded."

"I control your pleasure," he snarls and punctuates the statement with a squeeze. "I control your pain. I control whether you eat or sleep or shit. That's the very definition of a master. Now, beg for that orgasm."

When he eases off the pressure, I lose my instinct to rebel.

"Please," I say, my voice breaking. "Let me come, please."

He resumes his touch, only faster and with more pressure. The sensations overwhelm my system, and the entire bathroom fades away. My breath hitches, and my body arches toward release.

With my eyes closed, I can pretend that the man dominating me is someone other than Cesare Montesano. He'd be tall, dark-haired, and muscular, with tattoos and a devilish grin. And exactly my age, if not younger.

Shit.

Did I just describe the asshole breathing down my neck?

"Such an eager little pet," he growls, his hips rolling, his erection grinding against my belly. "Come for me. I want to hear your pleasure."

My body keeps teetering over the precipice but never falls, as though its new default state to pleasure is being edged. I move my hips against his fingers, trying to increase the friction, but it's impossible.

So, this is what they call a ruined orgasm.

"Come on," he says, his voice deep and seductive. "Let go. Let yourself fall."

"I can't," I say through clenched teeth. "That stupid chastity belt—"

"Come for your master." He pinches my nipple hard. "Now."

Every orgasm he denied me hits like a thunderstorm, striking me with bolts of lightning. My body convulses and jerks under the onslaught, my muscles spasming with each charge of electricity.

The weight of all the pleasure makes my knees buckle, and I drop toward the floor, but Cesare wraps an arm round about my waist, and holds me to his chest.

He strokes my clit throughout the climax, prolonging its intensity, until it feels like I'm being consumed. I cry out, unable to hold back.

"Good girl," he croons. "See how you're coming at my command? Your brain is releasing floods of oxytocin, that will create an unbreakable bond."

I collapse against his chest. "One day, I will stick a knife in your heart and leave you bleeding to death."

He strokes my hair. "That's the spirit. The more you fight me, the harder you'll fall."

"I won't."

Laughing, he pulls me closer. "We'll see, pet. We'll see."

Rage-filled tears spill down my cheeks and mingle with the hot spray. One day, he'll drop his guard, and I'll strike.

It's only a matter of time.

FORTY

Roman just made his grand entrance with his date to a thunderous applause. Now, Benito and I are standing at his back staring at a sea of guests while he makes a speech.

Tuning out talk of his goals for improving New Alderney's justice system, I go over my lines. My goals have never been as lofty as my brothers' plans to expand the family empire. All I've ever wanted since Dad died was to pull our family together. Roman's return from death row brought us back together, but Matty Galliano has the power to split us apart.

I push my thoughts away from that bastard and focus on what I want to say. Roman only asked for a few words, but I want this gathering of friends, family, and powerful players to know the Montesano brothers have a bond that extends beyond blood.

Just as I'm working out how to phrase it, a gunshot rings out, and Roman hits the ground.

Chaos erupts in the ballroom as staff and guests rush toward the exits. More gunshots ring in my ears, mingling with the screams and shouts and shattering glass. Benito crouches at my side, with his gun in hand, providing cover for Roman's fallen body. I move in front of them both with my pistol trained on the stampede.

My blood boils and betrayal pounds at my heart with both fists.

Rosalind lied.

She said the Moirai would cancel the hit on us once we gave them evidence of Samson's death. Some bastard shot at Roman anyway.

There should be two more shooters plus their backup, but what do I know? If Rosalind bullshitted about us being safe from assassins, then she probably also fabricated everything she told me about the way they organize their missions.

I need to focus on taking out the shooters and stop thinking about the traitorous bitch I left chained to the shower.

My gaze scans the crowd, on high alert for any suspicious figures. Emberly, Roman's special guest, runs toward the side exit with a young waiter. Before I can react, I catch a glimpse of a still figure in the corner aiming a pistol.

In the split second I take to identify him as a threat, I've already shot him through the eyes.

"Cesare," Benito yells. "Don't shoot into the crowd."

I turn the gun into the crowd and fire at every fucker standing still or not moving in the right direction.

By the time I look around for Roman's woman again, she's already disappeared. Shit. Big brother is going to be pissed, but our lives are worth more than her ill-gotten fortune.

There's a bottleneck at the doors, where the escaping guests are being funneled out by security. A gray-haired man in a purple tuxedo breaks out from the crowd. Since he reminds me of Tommy and Matty Galliano, I shoot him in the kneecap. When he clutches his wound without firing back, I finally allow Benito's warning to register.

It should be me tending to our big brother.

"Cover my back," I snarl at Benito with my eyes trained on the crowd. "Let me check on Roman."

The asshole doesn't move from Roman's side. I can't tell if it's out of shock or if Benito thinks he's better than me at first aid.

I don't have time to ponder on that when another man in a tuxedo bursts out of the crowd with a gun. His first shot goes wide as he's jostled, but I don't give him a chance to fire a second.

When a bullet lands in his neck, he falls backward and gets swallowed up by the throng.

"Cesare, will you stop fucking shooting?" Benito roars.

"Then you take over," I yell over the chaos.

When Gil and Tony burst through the crowd, each holding weapons, a part of me relaxes. Gil presses his fingers to his ears, looking like he's in communication with our people watching the security cameras.

I look beyond the pair with my gun still trained on the stragglers in case one of them tries to shoot our men in the back.

A dark-haired woman in a black dress emerges from the crowd with her hand in her purse, using their larger bodies as cover. She has the same athletic frame and precise movements as Rosalind, but twice the audacity.

She's trying to complete the mission.

Our two men run shoulder to shoulder toward us with their weapons drawn, oblivious to the little viper.

"Tony," I yell. "Behind you."

The bald man spins around. Instead of shooting the woman, he charges at her like a linebacker and knocks her onto her back. Gil glances over his shoulder to find Tony punching her into unconsciousness. Seeing that his friend is fine, he continues toward where we're crouched on the stage.

That's two shooters down. If what Rosalind said was the truth, there's at least one left. I glance around, my blood roaring in my ears. They could be anyone. Anywhere.

Gil mounts the stage and speaks to my brothers. Movement out of the corner of my eye tells me that Roman survived the hit. There's no time for relief because we still haven't identified the other assassins.

My pulse pounds in my eardrums as I scan the emptying ballroom. Somewhere on the edge of my awareness and mingled in the panicked screams, Roman yells something about his missing guest.

Gil mutters something about finding the man who shot Roman, but that's irrelevant. There wasn't one gunman but an entire team of assassins.

Benito grabs my shoulder, snapping me out of my thoughts. "Emberly is gone."

"Forget her," I snap. "We need to find the Moirai—"

"Leave that to the others." He pulls me up to standing. "We can't let Emberly escape."

I love my brothers, but their priorities are fucked. Instead of working together to track down the assassins, they want to hunt down the crazy balcony woman to swindle her out of a stolen inheritance.

Roman runs in the direction the woman left, while Benito takes another exit. I don't give a shit about getting back the casino and all the other bullshit Emberly's father stole from Dad, so I jog toward where Tony is dragging the female assassin toward the body of the man I shot.

As I walk off the stage and down its steps, the phone in my jacket buzzes. I pull it out of my pocket, finding multiple notifications from the surveillance app. My adrenaline spikes, and I open up the camera feed.

The bathroom is empty.

While the Moirai was shooting my brother, Rosalind slithered out of her chains and escaped.

My jaw clenches. All this time, she must have been in contact with her firm, waiting for the right moment to stab me in the back.

If she's somewhere on the grounds, I will find her.

When I do, I will hit her where it hurts.

FORTY-ONE

ROSALIND

Cesare didn't even have the decency to leave my chains long enough for me to sit on the floor. If he had, then I could have reached the sink and worked out a way to escape the bathroom.

Only one thing is better than being in the dungeon, and that's the lack of flickering light.

The bastard secured my chains to a pipe and heavy-weight hooks. No matter how much I throw my weight backward, it's no use. I'll be in this bathroom for hours, maybe even days, until Cesare decides to play his sick games.

Leaning my head against the tiled wall, I strike the wall with the metal hand-split, trying to at least free one finger. When that doesn't work, I chew at the thick cuff around my wrists, which might as well be shoe leather. These shackles aren't BDSM gear. They're the type of heavy-weight restraints that belong to a government agency.

I won't give up trying. It's just a matter of time before I find the chain's weakest link.

The clanking of metal breaks me out of my thoughts. It's coming from the playroom, sounding like someone is trying to find their way in. Stiffening, I glance toward the door.

This can't be Cesare. He had no trouble pushing the lever that turned the wall behind the sink into a door. His brothers would also know about the secret entrance, so it's probably a lackey, coming to interfere with what he thinks is a helpless woman.

Or Gunther finally staged a rescue party?

I shake off that thought. My handler probably wants me dead.

My heart pounds with two-parts trepidation and one-part anticipation. What have I got to lose by calling out?

Nothing.

Even if it's a Montesano employee, he doesn't know about the sink.

"Hello?" I call out.

The banging stops. "Rosa?" asks a familiar female voice. "Can you hear me?"

My heart skips several beats. "Britt?"

"How do I get inside?"

I blurt out an explanation. A second later, my best friend bursts through the door, dressed like a waiter.

My jaw drops. Britt must have followed the tracker I injected into my belly button. I glance at a metal cylinder hanging around her neck. It's an encryption override module, which explains how she bypassed the biometric security.

Eyes widening, she takes in my naked form. "Are you hurt?"

I give her a nod and try not to squirm. Explaining why Cesare left my body unmarked might be more humiliating than suffering all his bullshit.

"How on earth did you get past all the guards?" I ask.

Britt rushes to my side with a set of bolt cutters and surveys the chains, the hooks, and the wrist cuffs.

She snips the padlock holding my hands in the metal split, and the leather comes loose. "I ducked out before the shooting."

"Shooting?" I free my hands with my teeth and toss the splint on the floor while she crouches to snap my ankle restraints.

As we both slip into catsuits made of material to render us invisible to security cameras, Britt explains that the Moirai sent a team of assassins to infiltrate Roman's welcome-home party as waiters and guests.

I frown, wondering if it's a good idea to replicate the method another assassin used to take down the Capello family. There's no time to question it when she presses an energy bar to my lips and cracks open a small bottle of water.

"Are you alright?" she asks.

"Yeah." I down the entire contents while chewing. "Let's go."

We race out of the bathroom, through the playroom, and out of the door. My steps are unsteady and my gut churns with nausea at the sudden influx of sustenance, but I push through, not wanting to waste Britt's deadly risk.

She didn't just break through the Montesano family's security. She abandoned her mission. If Gunther discovers Britt jeopardized a lucrative triple assassination for me, she's dead.

We continue down the corridor, through another security door, and into a wider hallway lined with doors and cameras. I shiver at the reminder that this is where the Montesano family keeps their prisoners.

The faint noise of yelling and gunshots is my only source of comfort, knowing that anyone watching the security cameras will be too preoccupied with the assassinations notice if our catsuits don't keep us completely invisible.

Britt turns to me, her features hardened with determination. "It will be chaos upstairs. There are hundreds of guests trying to escape the shooting. We can't go back the way I came."

"Alright," I rasp. "Then let's go in the opposite direction. If there isn't another exit, we can find a hiding place."

Britt rushes ahead down the hallway, passing the underground prison cells, and stops at another door. Her encryption override module lets it open with a click, and we continue down a darkened stairwell that leads to another door.

It shuts behind us, encasing us in darkness. From the musty air and the faint hint of damp, I can already tell that this lower part of the basement isn't as well maintained as the place where they keep their captives.

Britt presses a plastic item into my hands that I immediately recognize as night-vision goggles. I slip them on over my head and allow my vision to adjust.

We're inside a huge chamber spanning at least a thousand square feet. Metal tubing snakes along the walls, connecting massive vats. Stacks of wooden barrels reach toward the high ceiling, reminding me a little of the library at my old academy.

"What in the prohibition?" Britt whispers. "This has to be an old-fashioned distillery."

"The Montesanos were the founding mob family in New Alderney," I whisper back as we navigate the maze-like pathways. "I had no idea they brewed underneath their mansion, but it means there has to be a back door where they smuggled out the booze."

She grunts her agreement.

For the next several minutes, we examine the walls for any signs of another door, a hatch, or a chute. There's no way Cesare's great grandfather allowed his henchmen to carry barrels of illegal alcohol through the house or out the gates. If we're lucky, we'll find a disused tunnel leading to a point lower down on Alderney Hill.

The water and energy bar kick in, infusing my body with renewed strength. Escaping the Montesano stronghold is the opportunity I need to be free of the Moirai. Gunther will assume I'm dead, and I'll be free to join Miranda in our out-of-state hideout.

With any luck, the other assassins took out all three brothers, so there'll be no-one to come after us for revenge.

Britt coughs, breaking me out of my thoughts. "Found something."

"What is it?" I rush around a stack of barrels to her side.

She stands in front of a wooden panel covered in dust and cobwebs and reaches for a small crowbar. "Let's give it a try."

My heart flips. It's tall and wide enough to fit a barrel. Even if the exit below is blocked, we'll find a way out. I hold my breath as Britt wedges the crowbar into the crack and tries to pry it open. The wood creaks and groans, and the wooden panel gives way, revealing a metal door with a cross-shaped keyhole.

"Shit," I mutter.

"No problem." Britt reaches into her backpack.

Heavy footsteps resound down the stairs, filling the chamber with a thunderous echo. Every fine hair on the back of my neck stands on end.

"Rosalind!" Cesare bellows.

Terror grips me by the throat, and my stomach sinks like a concrete block. How did that crazy bastard survive the shooting?

I turn to where Britt is picking the lock, my heart pounding hard enough to break through the metal door.

"Focus on opening the hatch." I rifle through her backpack and extract a gun. "I'll handle him."

"What are you doing?" she hisses. "Stay hidden."

If Britt found this hatch, then so will Cesare. I can't allow us both to get caught.

"One of us has to be free to take care of Miranda," I whisper. "Besides, you're the tech whizz. I'm the better marksman."

"I swore to pay you back." Her voice breaks. "I owe you my life."

"And I told you we were even. Then take care of Miri. And get rid of her phone because she's in contact with that maniac."

She's about to protest when I step away, leaving her to continue picking the locks. Britt has done enough for Miranda and me already. There's no way she could handle this psychopath's brand of torture.

"Rosalind," Cesare growls.

I creep along a stack of barrels and peek out to find his shadowy figure disappearing behind a large crate. He holds his phone with one hand, using it as a flashlight, and in the other he grips a gun.

Silence stretches across the abandoned distillery, broken only by the defining thud of my pulse. I wait for Britt to open the door, while dreading the reappearance of Cesare.

If the triple hit failed, then it means the assassins have either abandoned their mission or are dead. I no longer need to fear Gunther's retaliation if I kill Cesare. His death is the only thing standing between me and my freedom.

"Rosa," Britt whispers, just as Cesare jumps out from behind a nearby stack of barrels.

On instinct, I shoot him square in the chest. He stumbles and lands on a rack of bottles before shooting upward.

As I'm about to turn around to join, a heavy weight slams on my head and everything goes black.

FORTY-TWO

CESARE

The bullet hits my protective undershirt, saving me from a deadly shot but none of the pain. The impact explodes across my chest, and I stumble backward into an iron rack.

My blood boils. Cold venom fills my veins. Everything I learned about Stockholm syndrome is bullshit. My own pet tried to put a bullet through my heart.

I shoot at a high rack, smashing through its frame. Just as Rosalind tries to make her escape, a barrel falls from the top, knocking her out cold.

My phone drops to the floor with the flashlight facing the ceiling, lighting up a dour-faced blonde. She hesitates for the second I need to land a shot in her chest and falls back behind the stack of barrels.

That's the bitch who locked up Miranda.

I stalk toward her with my gun leveled. The distillery fills with her heavy footsteps and breathy whimpers as she tries to slither away.

When I reach Rosalind, I kick away her gun, tear off her goggles, and turn off my phone's flashlight. She's unconscious, but I'm not taking any chances.

My priority is the accomplice. I want to know how she bypassed the biometric security, tracked down my pet, and discovered the location of great-grandfather Paolo's distillery.

An intrusive thought whispers that he's not my ancestor, but I tell it to get fucked. Nature doesn't mean shit. I was nurtured to be a Montesano.

Rounding the corner, I find the blonde stumbling along the wall of barrels with a hand over her chest. The other clutches at the racking system, trying to keep herself upright.

"Tell me how you bypassed our security in exchange for a quick death," I say.

"Fuck you." She darts to the side and disappears into a hatch.

"Shit!" I chase after her, finding her vanishing down a chute.

How the hell did I not know about this extra breach in our security?

I fire round after round into the chute, determined to kill her before she can escape and move Miranda. Seconds later, a heavy thud tells me she's reached a barrier at the bottom.

If she survived the gunshots, I doubt she'll have the strength to break out of the tunnel. I slip the gun in my pocket, pull out my phone and fire a text outlining the situation to our head of security. He'll find a way to extract the blonde and dispose of her carcass before it causes a stink.

Gil calls back, and I answer in one ring. "We've found the shooter," he says. "The gate staff held back everyone who came without ID and we're still hunting down runaways. I can't find Roman, so you'll need to question the assassin."

"Where are you holding the suspects?" I walk back to where Rosalind lies on the floor, unmoving.

"There's six guys holding them at gunpoint in the ground floor storage room."

"Fine." I scoop her up and arrange her over my shoulder. "Increase the guard. I'm bringing over my little assassin."

Minutes later, I walk into a room where a group of guards have their weapons trained at a huddled mass of guests and waiting staff, each bound with zip-ties. One of the armed men is Joe, whose bullet wound I healed.

After depositing Rosalind on the floor, I turn to him. "Make sure this one doesn't escape."

He nods. "Sure thing, boss."

I lean in close and whisper, "Watch her carefully. Note who makes eye contact with her or starts any kind of conversation. She's a known assassin."

Joe frowns, casting her another glance. Nothing about her face or delectable body says she's deadly, but that's Rosalind's superpower. She will lure you in with her extreme beauty and strike at the most unexpected moment.

"Cesare." Gil appears at the door. "Over here."

I follow Gil out through the hallway into another room, where four men hold guns to a naked man who's crouched on all fours. He's athletic and blond, looking exactly what I would expect of a trained assassin.

"Is he talking?" I ask.

"No." One of the guards kicks the man in the ribs and he doesn't even flinch.

That's all the confirmation I need to know he's a member of the Moirai. It looks like all these assassins have a high tolerance for pain.

———

After returning to double-check that Rosalind is still unconscious, I secure the shooter with zip-ties and a mild paralyzing agent, then transport him down to a basement interrogation room.

It's empty, save for an adjustable table and the trolley containing my tools. The shooter's eyes stay closed as I set him up for questioning, but the moment I jab him in the shoulder with the scalpel, he flinches.

The man glares up at me through blue eyes that grate on my nerves. The shade reminds me too much of Matty Galliano.

"Let's not waste time with denials," I say. "The surveillance footage caught you shooting at my brother, and you took down two guards before you reached the wall. You're an assassin."

His jaw flexes.

I tap the tiny tattoo on his hip. "And I know you're from the Moirai."

His nostrils flare. "You find that out from Rosalind?"

"You know her?"

He huffs a laugh. "You could say that."

My eyes narrow, and I take another look at his features. Some might call this bastard handsome, if you like clean-cut, Scandinavian Ken dolls.

Rosalind would never take a second look at this asshole. She likes her men, dark, dangerous, edgy. She likes a man strong enough to challenge her brattiness. She likes a man like me.

Or does she?

I thought Stockholm syndrome was kicking in before she stabbed me in the back. Maybe all that flirtation and banter was just a ploy to make me lower my guard. I was sure only I could make her wet.

My eyes narrow. Before I can stop myself, I ask, "What does that mean?"

"Rosalind and I had a great time together in Paris. Four months of good food, good wine, and good fucking."

My nostrils flare. "Is that right?"

He smirks. "Best time ever."

"Let me ask you something." I walk around the interrogation table, keeping my eyes trained on the bastard's face. "Does every assassin from the Moirai Group work from the same playbook?"

He remains still.

"Or do you memorize the same dossier on your targets and their weaknesses?"

He takes several deep breaths, each one measured and controlled. I don't need an electrocardiogram to tell he's trying to calm his racing heart.

I press the scalpel into his eye socket. "Answer my question."

"Yes," he hisses.

"Yes, what?" I reply.

"We keep a file on each target, including a psychological profile of their habits, weaknesses."

"What does the Moirai say about me?" I ask with a sneer.

"Your choice of sexual partners is limited to your employees," he says through ragged breaths. "Is that because you can only get it up with women under your control? Is that what you did with Rosalind?"

Is this asshole trying to goad me into flying into a rage and giving him a quick death?

"What else?" I ask, my voice tight.

"You have a drug problem. It's why you dropped out of medical school."

I clench my teeth. That bullshit is in the past. "Anything else?"

"The reason you've never had a girlfriend is because the only woman you ever loved was your mother."

"Where did you learn that?"

He raises a shoulder. "The file."

"Whose file?"

"The one Rosalind kept when she gathered intel on your family."

Betrayal floods my senses, stinging my sinuses and filling my senses with the scent of blood. Did she overhear that bullshit from Leroi or the shit-talking guards?

"According to the files, you're the Montesano family's weakest link," he says with a dry chuckle. "Roman was unreachable on death row. Benito was unreachable because of his impeccable conduct. You, on the other hand, would stick your dick in anything under the right circumstances."

"And what would those be?"

He huffs a laugh. "Not too bright, I see."

"Interesting," I say, my voice sounding far away.

"What?"

"The distraction technique," I reply. "All you assassins use the same tactics. Do you even have an ounce of personal flair, or are you running through a checklist?"

His jaw clicks shut.

"Here's what's going to happen," I say. "You're going to stop talking about Rosalind and making her punishment worse."

He flinches. "She's alive?"

My lip curls into a smile. "What did your intel say I would do to her?"

When he doesn't speak, my smile turns into a cheshire grin. "What's wrong, shooter? Cat got your tongue?"

I wait several heartbeats for him to say something taunting, but he remains silent.

"Are you working out that the information you memorized might be wrong? That I'm not a hot-headed, drug-addicted manic who will kill you for speaking out?"

His Adam's apple bobs up and down.

"That would be partially right," I murmur.

He stares into my eyes, his pupils dilating. I nod, recognizing the rush of adrenaline that comes with the fight-or-flight response to anxiety. This asshole is realizing that he can't goad me into cutting his throat.

"You shot my brother. Then you had the nerve to brag about fucking my pet. I'm sick of hearing your voice, so I'm going to make sure you can't speak."

He sucks in a sharp breath.

"That's right." I trail the scalpel down to the edge of his mouth. "I'm going to take your tongue."

FORTY-THREE

ROSALIND

A sharp kick in the ribs jolts me out of unconsciousness. Each breath feels like razor blades tearing through one side of my chest, and I wonder if I've cracked a rib. I force myself to stay still, even as my heart thrashes against its cage like a trapped animal.

Did Britt escape?

Last thing I remember, she'd opened the hatch. She wouldn't want to leave without me, but she also wouldn't let herself get caught. I shot Cesare in the chest, giving her the opening she needed to jump into the chute.

I crack open an eye and peer through my lashes, finding myself lying on the floor of a room crammed with men and women stripped down to their underwear.

Eight guards stand around us holding automatic weapons, and I shiver. This is a peculiar change to waking up alone in Cesare's dungeon, but not unwelcome.

A large hand lands in my hair and pulls me up to sit. "Get up."

The bastard manhandling me is a stranger with malevolent green eyes and a scar down his cheek. I'm sure he's one of the men I saw a few days ago at the gates, but it doesn't matter. Even though my ankles, arms, and wrists are bound with zip-ties, I have full use of my fingers.

All I need is a distraction, and I'll get the fuck out.

Feigning wooziness, I let my eyes roll in their sockets and scan the room for exits. There's a door on the right, which possibly leads to a hallway, but reaching it means taking out the guards. Behind me is a window secured with iron bars.

This is the downstairs storeroom. I recognize it from the time I walked around the Montesano mansion, capturing footage for Gunther.

"Is she awake?" asks a man I don't recognize.

"Does it matter?" the one holding me upright asks back.

They both snicker.

My jaw clenches, and I wonder what the hell happened between that barrel falling on my head and now. The man releases my hair, and I fall back to the stone floor with a grunt.

I use my ruse of helplessness to scan my body for injuries. The pain in my ribs has already faded, giving me a clue there probably isn't a fracture.

"Leave her alone," says a female voice hoarse with tears.

"Friend of yours?" a male voice asks with a sneer.

"No, but there's no need to kick a helpless woman."

The man chuckles. "This bitch is an assassin. People like her are the reason you're all being held in this room."

The woman defending me falls quiet.

He returns, and all the fine hairs on the back of my neck stand on end. The air shifts as he pulls back his leg for another kick.

"Wait," I rasp. "I'm awake."

"Thought so." He steps back, allowing me to shuffle up to sitting.

Blinking away the remnants of my headache, I take a better look at my fellow captives sitting on the floor, recognizing at least four other operatives from the Moirai. None of them makes eye contact, and none of them are Britt.

That has to be a good sign.

"Are you alright?" asks a bleached blonde, whose pink bra strains under her augmented breasts. Her cheeks are streaked with mascara-blackened tears.

"Yeah." My brows furrow. "Why are we all here?"

"You should know." The man grabs the hood of my catsuit.

"Everyone in this room either came to the boss's party without ID, or the name they gave doesn't check out. Point out the assassins, and we'll let the innocent people go home."

My stomach plummets to the stone floor, and my lips form a denial. I clench my teeth, already knowing that lies at this stage are futile. The Montesano family already knows I work for the Moirai.

"Talk, bitch." He gives my head a hard shake.

Every operative in the room lowers their heads. Throughout my ten years of being demoted, each one of them has derided me with ridicule, snide remarks, or direct insults. At least two have taken credit for my work, swindling me out of bonuses that could have paid off my debt.

I don't owe any of them my loyalty.

A guard points his gun to the blonde. "Maybe you're defending your colleague?"

"Don't be stupid," I snap.

He swings the barrel of his weapon at me. "What did you say?"

"A trained assassin wouldn't identify themselves by rushing to my defense. She's obviously a civilian."

He flashes his teeth. "How do I know you're telling the truth?"

"Does she look like a trained killer to you?"

The man glances at the blonde, scowls, and lowers his weapon. He doesn't speak, not wanting to admit he's wrong.

"Why are you being so mean?" says a voice beside me that grates on my nerves.

I turn to find Greta hiccupping with tears. The assassin's red hair is styled in a messy chignon with tendrils that barely conceal her black eye.

Greta graduated from the academy the same year as Britt and me. During the graduation run, when we had to compete for a paying job in the Moirai, she shoved Britt down a hole that led to the Beaumont City catacombs and left her there for dead. I saved Britt, making me lose the top spot and a hundred-thousand-dollar bonus that would have paid for Miranda's education.

Glancing down at my lap, I force back a wave of resentment.

Greta is always quick to take advantage of an opportunity. She never fails to discredit my contributions to her missions. If it wasn't for her continued sabotage, Gunther might even have reconsidered my demotion.

"What are you trying to say?" the man asks. "That you're an escort like her?"

Greta hiccups. "I'm a reporter. Just call my boss at the New Alderney Times—"

"Shut the fuck up," he snaps.

My shoulders tighten. Greta doesn't realize she just identified herself as one of the assassins. I glance around, trying to make eye contact with the others I recognize, but they avoid my gaze.

I grind my teeth. What are they doing? All five of us working together could break through our zip-ties, disarm the guards, and drive a vehicle through the gates. We even practiced situations like this at the academy.

"Four-two-seven-five," I mutter the code under my breath, my gaze wandering around the room.

Branson, a dark-haired operative from the year below, offers me a subtle nod. I glance at Greta, who stares at me through wide eyes before blinking YES in morse code.

Over the next few minutes, I capture the attention of the other operatives, and each of them confirms they will execute the attack sequence. Greta even messages the name of their client, GALLIANO.

Heart pounding in anticipation of a fight, I twist within my restraints, trying to find the right angle to break free.

"What are you doing?" The scarred guard from earlier rushes at me with the gun.

"What does it look like, asshole?" I break my wrist free of the zip-ties, snatch his weapon, and shoot him in the thigh.

With a roar, he drops to his knees.

"Get her," someone yells.

The rush of movement I expect from Branson, Greta, and the others doesn't materialize. Instead, the Montesano goons surge forward, while my colleagues remain as stiff as tin soldiers. I swing the pistol toward the nearest guard. Before I can even think about firing, my ears ring with the sound of gunfire and my arm burns with white-hot pain.

Agony radiates across my shoulder and down to my spasming fingers. A massive body slams into my side and knocks me on the stone tiles with a painful thud.

I raise my free arm to fight back, when a guard unleashes a barrage of punches that leave me seeing stars and gasping for breath.

"Bitch," he bellows as the room spins.

The last thing I think about as my eyes roll to the back of my head isn't my failure, or even if Britt made it to Miranda. It's my colleagues' cowardice and utter betrayal.

They agreed to fight with me and escape. Instead, they set me up as a scapegoat. Even in a life-or-death situation, these bastards never change.

From this moment on, I will take any chance I get to save myself and to throw the Moirai under the bus.

FORTY-FOUR

CESARE

I'm not cold-blooded like my brothers and Leroi. My anger runs hot.

Think of it like a clock. At twelve, I'm neutral. Three, annoyed. Six, furious. Nine, incandescent with rage. It rises until about eleven, then once it heads back to twelve, my head clears, and I regain control.

That's when I'm capable of the cruelest and most calculated acts of violence.

When I was younger, Dr. Brunelli told Mom it was a dissociative state, saying that my mind disconnected to deal with intense anger. That was his explanation for why I supposedly killed the rabbit and tore out her unborn kits.

They were all wrong.

And not because I would never hurt anything I deemed innocent and cute.

Sometimes, a man gets pushed too far.

These days, a man can't enjoy his pet without some other bastard trying to spoil his happiness.

I straighten my surgical gloves and turn back to the shooter. He was extremely talkative while I was preparing him for surgery, told me his name and spilled a slew of facts about his mission, but I was beyond the mood for mercy.

Axel thrashes within his restraints on the leather operating table, his mouth wedged open with two steel cheek retractors that I attached to his head brace.

His mouth is packed with cotton gauze to soak up the blood. If I gave enough of a shit, I would crack open the box containing the suction wand. Since I don't, I'll have to rely on my leather apron to keep me clean.

"Tell me more about how you fucked Rosalind in Paris," I say, my voice coming from afar. "Tell me again how you made her come all over your cock."

Axel's eyes widen, and he tries to shake his head within their restraints. As I shift the table, adjusting his position to a more upright angle, his breathing becomes loud and strained.

A strangled noise echoes from his throat, sounding almost like an apology. He's already proven himself mentally weak and can't hide his emotions like my pretty little pet.

My lip curls. "Next time someone tells you to shut up or they'll cut out your tongue, don't call their bluff."

At the first sight of my new Bard-Parker No. 4 scalpel, he screams.

"Enough of that," I snap. "It's too late for explanations."

I grab his tongue with the forceps, pulling it taut. With my free hand, I make the first incision along the floor of Axel's mouth. My blade slices through the tissue, releasing a pool of blood which gets soaked up in the sterile gauze.

Carefully avoiding the major arteries, I cut the sides of Axel's tongue, replacing the soaked gauze to maintain a clear field of vision.

Blood runs down the sides of Axel's mouth, down his chest, and into the leather.

"This isn't working," I mutter. "You're bleeding too much."

After pulling out the gauze, I pick up a kitchen torch and grimace. "This was all I could get at short notice."

Axel doesn't reply because he's lost consciousness. I make a mental note to see if I can acquire a drug to keep prisoners awake during torture.

Frowning, I cauterize the wounds and continue slicing through the organ, releasing heat and the stench of burning flesh.

Sweat beads on my brow as I seal the major arteries and coagulate the blood.

Once I've freed his tongue, I place it on the tray and focus on suturing the wound. Even though the torch has taken care of the bleeding, I need to minimize the risk of any postoperative infections.

"You still with me, Axel?" I ask.

He remains silent. If I had to guess, he's experiencing vaso-vagal syncope or neurogenic shock—both conditions strongly associated with pain.

I wipe the blood off his chest with antiseptic wipes, clean up the tongue, and attach it to his shoulder with staples.

Axel's eyes snap open.

"Welcome back," I say with my widest grin. "The fun has only just begun. Before you tell me what I need to know about the shooting, you're going to answer a few questions about my pet."

He groans, his eyes streaming with tears.

I give him an encouraging nod. "Don't worry. I've worked through my issues. This time, I'm prepared to listen. One blink means yes and two means no."

———

The entire night passes, as does most of the morning, and I still haven't had the chance to deal with my pet. She's more formidable than I anticipated. It's as though she is immune to the psychological effects of Stockholm syndrome. Her shooting me in the chest is the clearest sign that I need to change tactics.

Roman comes in to conduct his own interrogation and maims my shooter, so I have to call on our family physician to repair the damage.

Cardiac surgery is more complicated than a glossectomy and isn't something I can learn on YouTube. Besides, this shit-talking assassin needs to survive long enough to teach Rosalind a lesson.

The LED lamps above us shine down on the man's chest, while casting the rest of the basement in shadow. I hand the surgical stapler to Dr. Brunelli. He hasn't spoken a word to me since he entered the room and found the man with a gunshot wound to the chest.

I can tell he's pissed by the way his brow pinches. His thick mustache twitches behind the mask as though he's muttering under his breath.

After closing the chest wound, he says, "Explain to me the point of performing surgery on a man already marked for death."

My lips tighten behind my mask and I bristle. "I didn't shoot him. It was Roman."

The old man gives me a familiar narrow-eyed look, just like he used to when I was a child. He thinks I'm lying. If anything goes wrong with the family, it's always my fault.

"Ask Roman if you don't believe me." I flick my head toward the unconscious man. "Better still, ask him."

"You going to tell me Roman also removed his tongue and attached it to his shoulder?" he asks.

I shrug. "He was talking shit."

With a weary sigh, Dr. Brunelli pulls off his gloves. "Have you thought about what we talked about?"

"How can I return to medical school when there's a contract on our lives?" I ask. "The assassins already shot Roman. They won't stop coming after us until they're dead."

The doctor frowns but doesn't speak. I already know what he's thinking. It's not difficult, considering he and Mom concocted the plan to make me a surgeon to stop me from becoming a serial killer.

I pull off my gloves and toss them in the medical waste bin. "Before you accuse me of making up excuses, let me remind you that I never wanted to be a doctor."

"Yet you have enough surgical supplies to equip a clinic," he says.

"Can't a man have a hobby?" Rolling my shoulders, I shrug off my gown and head toward the exit.

"You're not staying to finish?" he asks.

"I left my pet unconscious upstairs." I wave a palm over the security scanner, and the door unlocks with a soft click.

When I step out and ascend the stairs, Sofia ambushes me

with a trolley of panzerotti that fills the hallway with the scent of melted cheese and garlic.

My brow furrows. Last night she was so relaxed and happy in her black gown with her hair nicely styled and make-up. Now, she's tense, the lines on her face looking harsher after witnessing Roman's recent brush with death.

Roman's welcome home party was supposed to mark the end of our family's run of bad luck. Galliano and the Moirai assassins ruined Sofia's joy.

"You okay?" I ask.

Her gaze roves up and down my leather apron, her lips tightening with disapproval. "You're too skinny. You should eat more."

"There." I grab a pastry, take a huge bite, and offer her a smile that makes her eyes soften.

She gives me a pat on the cheek before wheeling the trolley toward the surveillance room, where I imagine everyone is still scouring how the hell the Moirai Group could get past our security.

I continue to the room where I left my treacherous pet. Four naked people sit huddled together, trying not to make eye contact with the six armed men.

As though outcast from her group, Rosalind lies unmoving on her side, bound with an excessive amount of zip-ties.

Adrenaline surges through my arteries, making my eyes bulge. My heart pounds hard enough to trigger a myocardial rupture. When I carried her upstairs, she was only mildly concussed. Now, her beautiful face is marred with a contusion around her eye and a laceration on her lip.

This isn't the work of a barrel falling on her head. Someone punched her in the face. Some filthy bastard damaged my pet.

"Rosalind," I say, my words hardening. "Who did this to you?"

FORTY-FIVE

ROSALIND

I sit up, but my skull ignites with white-hot agony, and I collapse onto my side. That sets off an explosion of pain across my shoulder, which pales compared to the shattering of my illusions. Each jagged fragment slices through my heart like shards of glass.

After four years of intense training and a decade working in the field, I finally understand the truth about the Moirai Group. The time I spent in the academy was just an indoctrination into a death cult.

It's easy to skulk about in the shadows with a gun. Even easier to slip poison in a person's drink or hide in a remote location to detonate bombs. We do this for the promise of power, wealth, and strength, yet all of us joined when we were too young to understand we'd sold our souls.

I thought assassins were the underworld elites.

We're not. We are cowards.

I believed the Moirai Group operated on teamwork, but it's survival of the fittest. The only authentic person there is Britt. Everyone else only cares about themselves, even if it means setting up their colleagues to die.

That's why when Roman Montesano came in earlier, I cooperated with him through nods and silent gestures. Ingratiating myself to him is my only chance of surviving to see Miranda.

He might be the only man capable of saving me from Cesare, who probably wants to make me die slowly for shooting him in the chest.

Someone clears their throat, making me flinch.

"You looking at me?" a man growls.

This is the other reason I'm lying on my side with my eyes shut. The guards are getting bored and are trying to pick fights. After forcing the entire room of hostages to strip, they soon weeded out the Moirai from our little tattoos. The blonde woman from earlier was allowed out with the others, leaving the Montesano lackeys with us assassins.

Someone threads his fingers into my hair and yanks me off the stone floor. "I was talking to you."

Get fucked.

That's what I want to say, but I won't risk getting any more injuries.

"Joe," another voice hisses.

The man holding me releases my hair, and I fall on my side with a painful thud. Someone needs to remind Joe that beating up an injured woman doesn't make him a badass. It just makes him pathetic.

Joe's lumbering footsteps retreat just as another set approaches. This tread is lighter, and the person walks with power, purpose, and poise. My head throbs in sync with my shoulder wound, and I swallow hard.

It's Cesare. He's finally returned for his revenge.

What he asks next makes my breath still.

When nobody replies to his question, he bellows, "Who. Did. This. To. Her?"

My heart tries to break free from my chest and skid across the floor tiles. Cesare must be furious that someone ruined his revenge. He sure as hell doesn't care if I get hurt.

"She tried to escape," a male voice blurts. "She broke through the zip-ties, grabbed a gun and shot Marcello—"

"So, you smashed in her face?" Cesare growls.

The sound of a gunshot makes me flinch. I crack open an eye to find the scarred man clutching his arm. Cesare turns a slow circle, dressed only in a pair of black pants and a leather apron, waving his pistol.

"Who else touched her?" he yells.

My heart jumps to the back of my throat, pounding harder and harder while my mind scrambles for an explanation. He just shot one of his own men. An employee who was protecting the interests of his family.

What the hell is Cesare doing?

"Answer me," he yells. "Or I'll shoot every motherfucker in this room."

The men all speak at once, each trying to escape punishment by blaming their colleagues. My breath quickens as Cesare points his gun from one to the other, his demeanor becoming increasingly manic.

Now would be an excellent chance to execute escape sequence two-eight-three, which enhances discord among the enemy.

There's no point even entertaining that thought because I'm not loyal to the Moirai. I need to focus on my own survival. My eventual escape.

Another gunshot has my eyes snapping open. A huge man wrestles Cesare from behind, holding his shooting arm toward the ceiling. It's the family's most trusted bodyguard, Gilberto Agostini, also known as Gil.

Gil's muscles bulge through his suit jacket as he grapples with Cesare, but the smaller man's strength is almost inhuman. The pistol fires again, bringing down a rain of plaster.

Flinching, I curl inward, only to aggravate the gunshot on my shoulder.

"Cesare Montesano," yells a shrill voice from the doorway, "What on earth are you doing? You will bring chaos to the family!"

I turn toward the exit, where a black-haired woman walks in, holding a pistol. I don't recognize her face from any of the profiles, but she's dressed like a housekeeper.

Cesare stops fighting Gil, who steps back and releases his shooting arm. I hold my breath, waiting for Cesare to use this opening to attack one of his men, but he slips his gun back into the waistband of his pants.

"Better," the woman says.

I close my eyes again, needing more time to process. Cesare flew into a rage because I got hit, even though I fired on one of his men while trying to escape. Even though I shot him square in the chest.

It can only mean one thing:

He doesn't want anyone to get in the way of his revenge, which is going to be epic. Last time, I tricked him into drinking oxypentanol, and he punished me for days then abducted Miranda when I escaped.

A heavy weight rolls around my empty stomach, making my guts tighten and churn with dread.

What I did to him last night doesn't even compare.

Heartbeats later, Cesare walks to my side and scoops me off the floor. The bullet wound in my shoulder flares, making me hiss through my teeth.

"What is it, pet?" he asks and clutches me to his chest.

"Gunshot," I rasp.

His entire body stiffens, and he turns back to the man clutching his arm.

"Did you shoot my pet?" Cesare says, his voice so danger-ously low that all the fine hairs on the back of my neck stand on end.

"Boss." One of the men holds up a palm. "You've got to understand—"

Gil stands between them with his arms folded over his chest. Next to him is the housekeeper, who adds herself to the human shield.

"Take the girl and leave," Gil says. "Unless you want me to tell Roman that you're siding with an assassin."

Cesare flinches, looking like he might shoot Gil. I still don't understand what the fuck is going on in his twisted mind, but I need to stop this a potential gunfight.

I raise a hand to his shoulder, capturing his attention. "Can we go?"

He gazes down at me, his face a mask of rage. I haven't seen him this angry since he realized I was an assassin. My muscles tighten as I wait for him to lash out, but he stalks out of the room, carrying me out like I'm his quarry.

He walks in silence through a pale hallway of marble floors. Armed men and staff part ways for him, their murmured greetings filled with fear and respect. Nobody seems surprised he's dressed like a BDSM executioner and carrying a semi-conscious woman.

Tremors reverberate through his body, a physical manifestation of his pent-up rage. The hand beneath my thigh tightens in a way that makes me think he's making sure I can't escape.

How the hell do I manage his temper? He's exactly the kind of psycho who would keep me by his side forever by removing body parts.

I'd better talk fast before he threatens to amputate my legs.

When his fingers twist around my hair and yank back my head, I finally look him full in the face. His skin is flushed, with every vein around his temples bulging with the force of his fury.

He glares down at me, his teeth bared, his eyes shining with madness. He's still fuming because the housekeeper and Gil interrupted his violent tirade. In a minute, I'll be locked in a basement dungeon with him and his instruments of torture.

"Cesare?" I whisper, trying to muster up words of reason.

"Don't speak," he growls through gritted teeth. The muscles in his jaw clench tight as he fights to contain a hurricane.

My jaw clicks shut.

I slide a hand up his bare arm, trying to soothe his temper, but that earns me a sharp tug of my hair that fills my scalp with lightning bolts of pain.

"No one gets to hurt you," he says through clenched teeth.

A breath catches as I wait for him to voice the unspoken part of that sentence. His eyes are fixed on mine, the intensity of his gaze leaving every inch of my skin tightening with goosebumps.

The air crackles with electricity, and tension mounts as he breathes through flared nostrils, seeming to build and build. Now that we're alone, the target of that fury will be me.

He steps into a stairwell, letting the door behind him swing shut and muffle the activity from the hallway. A moment later, the light flickers off, encasing us in the dark.

As he descends the steps, he finally completes his sentence, "No one gets to hurt you but me."

Shivers run down my spine as he confirms my worst fears.

I'm about to face the repercussions of the assassination attempt on his brother, as well as my failed attempt to escape.

And there isn't a thing I can do about it while I'm injured.

FORTY-SIX

ROSALIND

Cesare carries me through a maze of hallways separated by security doors. Any other time, I would wonder if this underground labyrinth extended beyond the grounds, but I'm far too concerned about facing the consequences of my escape attempt.

The air thickens as we pass entrance after entrance of what might be cells. Finally, he stops at a door that opens into a stark white infirmary.

With an unusual amount of care, Cesare lays me on a cold, metal gurney and secures belts of woven nylon around my chest and waist. Once again, I feel like a prisoner, only this time, the environment is sterile.

Unforgiving lights glare down at me from the ceiling, making me squint. Another restraint tightens around my thighs and as he attaches the final one around my ankles, I sink against the cold metal with defeat.

"Is that really necessary?" I whisper.

Straightening, he fixes me with a glare so chilling that my teeth chatter. I clench my jaw, forcing back a surge of terror. This isn't like me at all. I'm usually so stoic and able to withstand anything.

But this is personal. I might have come here to aid an assassination, but Cesare thinks I'm a pet.

A pet that needs punishing.

Shoulders trembling, he glares down at me and raises a pair of shears. The blades are angled and bent, with a serrated edge and rounded point.

My throat tightens. "What are you doing?"

Without another word, he lifts the edge of my catsuit and snips the sleeve, reminding me of how paramedics cut away the clothing of their patients during emergencies.

Cool metal slides against my skin, making it pebble with every snip. My heart pounds. My stomach roils. My fingers clench in anticipation of an assault.

The air hits the exposed wound, making me wince. I glance down at my shoulder, finding it soaked with blood, and cringe at the sight of the gunshot wound. The bullet still lies embedded within a dark, glistening mass of flesh.

Cesare continues cutting my clothes past the injury and up to my neck, where the catsuit falls loose, revealing my breast. I close my eyes, once again exposed.

"You're going to be alright, pet," he says.

My stomach plummets. He's so calm, it's almost sinister.

With gloved hands that still tremble with rage, he probes the edges of the wound. I tighten my fists, trying to hold myself together as sensations oscillate between stinging, throbbing, and white-hot agony.

Suspense mounts, and the tension builds so high my body surges with adrenaline and my lizard brain screams with primal fear. Any second now, he'll plunge his finger into the wound to twist the bullet. That will be stage one of my punishment. If I lose consciousness, he'll slap me awake, only to repeat the torment.

Instead of doing the obvious, he pulls back his fingers and strides across the infirmary. I stare at the muscles rippling on his back as he opens a cabinet, revealing organized rows of boxes, bottles, and vials.

He grabs a vial and a sharp needle, then fills the syringe with an ominous liquid. I stiffen, my eyes widening. The cabinet door clicks shut, and he stalks back to my side, his eyes glinting.

"What's that?" I whisper.

His brows rise. "It's not me who drugs people in secret. When

I stick a woman with a needle, she knows exactly what I'm doing."

My gaze drops to the bead of clear liquid glistening at the tip of the needle. Some psychopaths keep their captives compliant with sedatives. Others get their captives addicted to class A drugs.

Panic mounts. It's not heroin. Heroin isn't clear but brown. Maybe it's something equally devastating, like crack cocaine.

"Relax," he mutters, "It's only local anesthetic to numb the pain while I work on your shoulder."

The laugh that bursts out of my chest is shrill. "You'd dull my pain?"

"When I give you pain, it will be for my pleasure. Never from another man's wound."

Shudders course through my spine and settle into the marrow of my bones. I thought Cesare Montesano was crazy before. That knowledge hits differently as I come to terms with the fact that I'm unconditionally and irrevocably in the clutches of a psychopath.

"Take a deep breath, pet," he says, his voice soft.

As if hypnotized, I inhale, and the needle pierces my arm. Cool liquid seeps into my veins, spreading a sense of numbness that makes my shoulder sag with relief.

Cesare sets down the needle and strokes my hair as though I'm a beloved pet he's nursing back to health. I dart a glance up at him through my lashes to find his face still etched with hatred. It's like he can't decide if he wants to heal me or kill me.

Correction. He's healing me, bringing me back to peak condition, if only so I can feel the full force of his vengeance.

Shit.

The worst part about this situation is that I don't want to resist, at least until I feel better.

I lie still as he inspects the wound with his gloved fingers, which have stopped trembling. He's gone into physician mode.

The infirmary blurs into insignificance, and my entire world concentrates on this insane mafia prince who believes a few years of medical qualifies him for surgery.

His movements are deliberate, each action precise and calculated. I close my eyes, trying to block out the reality of my predicament.

Miranda is safe, even if she's in contact with this maniac. Now that I'm committed to betraying the Moirai, there's nothing holding me back from sharing information about the firm to negotiate my safety and a possible release.

It's just a question of getting in touch with a Montesano brother who isn't quite as insane.

"You're doing so well, pet," he murmurs, breaking me out of my thoughts.

My eyes snap open just in time to see him reaching past a tray of sterile instruments and taking hold of a swab. He cleans the wound with gentle strokes, removing all traces of blood.

Cold seeps into my flesh, making me want to shiver. I keep my breaths deep and slow, even as he reaches for a scalpel.

Now isn't the time to speak or any kind of distraction. I force my body to remain still as he makes incisions around the gunshot wound and then replaces the scalpel for forceps. I don't feel a thing when he extracts the bullet and drops it on a tray with a clink.

I stare straight ahead and tune out the rest of the procedure, not noticing he's finished until his fingers thread through my hair.

"All done," he says, his voice full of warmth and pulls my hair off my face. "Now, I need to tend to your cut lip and the swelling around your eye."

Cesare hums a tune as he cleans the wound with a cool, antiseptic liquid. The tremble returns to his fingers again, and his eyes harden. I don't need to read his mind to know his rage from earlier is rising to the surface.

He applies a numbing gel to my black eye and dabs ointment on my split lip. My chest lightens with the absence of pain. The relief only lasts a moment because he produces another syringe. Panic reaches through my ribs and squeezes my heart and squeezes so hard I stop breathing.

"Rest, little pet," he says as a needle enters the vein on my neck.

"What did you give me?" I say through strangled gasps.

"Just a little sedative. When you wake up, everything will be different."

My eyes flutter closed as the drug takes effect, and I sink into a deep, dreamless sleep.

———

The next time I awaken, I'm sitting upright with my head bowed. A ball gag lodges halfway toward my throat, and every inch of my body is strapped to a wheelchair.

Faint breaths grate along eardrums, along with muffled sobs. I'm probably so fucked in the head that I don't even realize I'm crying.

Cracking my eyes open, I stare down at my lap and let my vision adjust to the dark. Bandages encase both legs, seeming to be attached to the lower part of its frame.

My gaze wanders past my knees and I see... nothing.

Adrenaline kicks me in the heart.

I jerk forward within my restraints and crane my neck, looking past my knees for signs of my calves, my ankles, my feet. They're either bound so tightly to the chair or—

My mind stutters.

He didn't.

He wouldn't.

He couldn't.

He fucking *could*.

Ice courses through my veins, making my senses break out in a panic. I thrash within my restraints, wiggling my toes to check that I still have feet. Sensation travels up my legs, but it could mean anything from tight bondage to the phantom pain after amputation.

Who the fuck knows if what I'm feeling is real?

A groan sounds from somewhere in the room, making my head snap up. Breathing hard, I take in my surroundings. The room I'm in is dark, without even the courtesy of a flickering bulb. Illumination comes from the digital display of a clock that reads 11:59.

11:59? Is that the time or a coded message?

I jerk back and forth, trying to make the contraption move a few inches, only for it to roll forward. The movement triggers a switch that floods the space with light and burns my eyes.

Breathing hard, I blink away the glare, only to find myself in a much larger room. Axel hangs suspended on a wooden X, naked save for a ball gag and a set of bandages around his chest. The other assassins from the Moirai also hang unmoving to his left and right.

Greta stares at me, her face streaked with tears. That muffled sob I heard earlier didn't come from me. It was her.

What. The. Actual. Fuck?

FORTY-SEVEN

CESARE

I lean back in my seat on the Montesano private jet, sipping a congratulatory Shirley Temple. Everything is finally under control. Rosalind should be rousing from sedation to find her fellow assassins pinned to Saint Andrew's crosses, and her wounds will be healing nicely. Best of all, I haven't heard a word from that Galliano scum.

This gives me the time I need to rescue my little princess from her tower.

Miranda stands before me in the private jet, reenacting her rescue, playing all three parts of the people involved.

She swings the imaginary ax at the door. "Stand back, love," she says in a deep voice that's supposed to be mine. "I'm going to set you free."

I chuckle. How can one sister be so much fun while the other is a vicious backstabber?

"Okay," she says in her own voice and skitters back to the sofa.

She switches back to pretending to be me and reaches into the hole I chopped through the door. "You're safe, now, Miranda."

"Did I say that?" I ask with a smirk.

"Are you telling this story, or am I?" She places her hands on her hips.

"Sorry, love." Raising the glass, I gesture at her to continue. "No more interruptions."

Miranda reenacts how some old asshole in the apartment opposite stepped out with a gun and received the butt of my ax in the gut.

I would have swung the blade at his head for pointing a gun at a little girl, but I didn't want to traumatize her with the sight of violence.

She doubles over, mimicking the injured neighbor before falling into a peal of giggles. "You were like something out of a fairy tale."

"Rapunzel?" I ask, my gaze lingering on her long braid.

She tilts her head the way girls do when you've said something silly. "Little Red Riding Hood. You're the wood cutter who freed me from the big bad wolf."

"And this wolf would be the fat bastard?"

"My sister and her stupid friend." Her lips tighten. "Britt called me last night, telling me to destroy my new phone."

A sharp breath hisses through my teeth. Straightening my shoulders, I force my facial muscles to calm. Despite getting shot and my men's attempt to capture the glum bitch, Rosalind's friend managed to escape the distillery.

"Why would she want you to get rid of a handset that hasn't even yet hit the stores?" I ask, feigning innocence.

"Britt says you're dangerous." She flops in the seat next to mine.

I gaze down into gray eyes a little too large for her face. Everything about Miranda is so cute. It's easy to forget she's related to the woman who tried to put a bullet through my heart. I fidget in my seat, my chest tightening with guilt.

Miranda is far too trusting. I'm not the woodcutter in her little fairytale, I'm ten times worse than the wolf.

"There's something I wanted to talk to you about," I say.

"What?" she asks with a dazzling smile.

"You can't run off with strangers, even if they claim to be friends with your sister."

Her brow furrows and she raises a shoulder. "But you're not a stranger. You're Rosalind's new man."

Frustration wells in my gut. How the hell do I keep this girl out of trouble without letting her know she's technically a hostage? Hell, she even forwarded me the exact coordinates of her hideout. Miranda will always be safe with me, but most men aren't so honorable.

"That's not my point," I say. "I could have been anyone."

"But I saw the photo of you and Leroi, so I know you're connected to my sister." She glances around. "Where is she, anyway?"

Strange how she only asks about Rosalind when she wants to change the subject.

"I took her skiing, and she impaled her shoulder on a branch."

"Is she okay?" she asks.

"Just recovering from some minor surgery." I pull out my phone and show her a selfie I took of us while Rosalind was sedated.

"Why is she always asleep in your photos?" she mutters.

"It's the only time I can ever get her to hold still," I reply with a smile. "Other times, she isn't interested in posing with me."

"Is that because you're in the mafia?" Miranda asks.

I flinch. "Where did you hear that?"

"Your brother went viral after a true crime influencer exposed the conspiracy that nearly got him executed. Some of the commenters said he was a mafia kingpin, so I dug deeper."

"And what did you find?" I surreptitiously press the call button to summon the flight attendant.

Miranda rattles off a list of information she gathered online, her voice getting more and more animated. She talks like organized crime is all heists, high jinks and hot car chases, completely unaware that what she's describing is horrifying.

"It sounds like you've been watching too many movies," I mutter.

Before she can ask if any of it is true, the attendant arrives with a tray of drinks.

"Can I get you something?" she asks with a smile.

"Mimosa," Miranda says.

The attendant shoots me a glance.

"And a glass of orange juice," I add.

As soon as the woman returns to place both drinks on the low table, Miranda grabs the champagne flute and takes a sip.

"That's enough for you." I prise the glass from her fingers and down its contents.

"That was mine," she snaps.

"You're not getting drunk on my watch." I set down the flute and hand her the juice. Alcohol isn't really my thing, but I'll snatch a drink from a woman to prove a point.

"Rosa lets me drink all the time," she mutters.

"I doubt that."

"She does."

I reach for my phone. "Let me call her and check."

Miranda launches herself at me and grabs my wrist. "Don't!"

"Thought so," I say with a smirk.

She whacks my arm. "Cesare, what's wrong with you?"

"I take care of what's mine," I say. "And I already see you as a little sister."

Her eyes widen. "Does that mean you're going to propose to Rosa?"

I tilt my head, picturing Rosalind crawling down the aisle with a remote-control toy in her pussy, forcing her to repeat the vows. Warmth fills my chest at the thought of tying her to me in the eyes of the law.

"When the time is right," I say with a nod. "When I'm sure she'll say yes."

"She'll be stupid if she refuses," Miranda says with a huff.

"Rosalind doesn't love me as much as I love her." I say, trying not to smirk. I love torturing my little pet, but if given the chance, she'd cut off my balls and shove them down my throat.

"What's wrong?" she asks.

"Sometimes, I wonder if she even likes me at all."

"Cesare." Her voice breaks.

"It's true," I say with a sigh. "Nothing I do for her is ever good enough."

Miranda pulls me into a tight hug, and something in my chest loosens. No girl or woman has embraced me since the morning Gil walked in to tell us they'd found Dad dead at the club.

Mom held me while I cried, only to turn distant. Days later, Roman got arrested for the murder of a woman he didn't even know, and then Mom abandoned us to marry Tommy Galliano.

That's the trouble with women. They can't be trusted. A man can spend his entire life basking in the warmth of their unconditional love, only to be left in the cold the moment there's a better offer.

I draw back from Miranda's embrace and gaze down into her eyes, they shine with kindness, compassion, and care. It's hard to believe she and Rosalind even share the same blood.

"Rosa is ruthless, but I think her heart's in the right place," she murmurs.

"What do you mean?" I ask, my brows pinching.

She dips her head.

"Miranda?"

Tears land on her jeans, staining the worn denim with glistening spots. My breath catches, and my heart thumps with dread. I lift her chin, making our eyes meet.

"What is it, love?"

"You promise not to tell the cops?" She wipes her face with the backs of her hands.

My stomach tightens. I don't want to believe it's true, but I have to ask, "Did Rosalind hurt you?"

She shakes her head. "Remember when I told you my parents were dead?"

I'll never forget the matter-of-fact way she described her father dying in an explosion and her mother getting shot in the head. Keeping my face in a neutral mask, I nod.

"Rosa came to the house one day when I was little and killed them both."

My jaw drops, even though I shouldn't be shocked. Rosalind is an assassin, and the Moirai recruits them young. I wouldn't be surprised if the last stage of the training was to murder their parents.

"What happened, love?" I ask.

Miranda tells a tale of being abducted as a child by her older sister after witnessing the gruesome deaths of loving parents. I listen, stunned as she explains how Rosalind left her to rot for years in a boarding school, cutting her off from her former life.

I thought my childhood was shitty, but at least I had parents, siblings, and a home. All Miranda had was trauma.

As soon as the wheels touch the ground, I release our seatbelts and reach for Miranda. She jumps into my arms, her tiny frame trembling against mine. I hold on to her tightly, wanting to shield her from the pain of her memories. My heart races with anger and my blood boils with the need to throttle Rosalind for allowing a young child to witness such horror.

"No one will ever hurt you as long as I'm alive," I murmur into her soft hair.

"What if you break up with Rosa?" she asks, her voice trembling.

Even though her question cuts deep, my answer is immediate. "Not even then," I say, meaning every word. "I'll always think of you as a little sister."

We hug for several moments, and I savor this moment of closeness. Eventually, she pulls back and gazes up at me with glistening eyes and a smile.

"Ready to return to the academy?" I ask.

She grimaces. "I'm going to have so much detention."

"Our family physician already wrote you a sick note for the time you missed. He accused the academy of giving you a stomach bug."

"Really?" she asks with a sunny smile.

"If any staff members give you shit for any reason, text me."

"Because you're going to…" She jumps out of her seat and shadow boxes.

"That's right."

Chuckling, I take her hand and we walk through the plane to the exit. When the doors open with a swoosh of warm air, the morning sun floods in, making my eyes sting. I shield them with one hand and blink away the glare to find a black limo waiting on the tarmac.

The door opens, letting out a smirking Matty Galliano.

FORTY-EIGHT

CESARE

How the fuck did that bastard know I took the jet? I didn't tell anyone I was leaving town. Someone at the airport must be Galliano's spy.

He strides toward us, his grin broadening as he takes in the sight of Miranda.

Fury kicks me in the gut. That scaly bastard murdered Tania because he thought we were connected. I won't let him get his claws on Miranda.

Stepping in front of her, I guide her back toward the attendant. "Wait inside."

"Why?" she asks. "I thought you were taking me back to the academy."

"Now," I bark.

With a muffled yelp, she disappears back into the plane. I turn to the attendant, my teeth flashing. "Did you tell anyone I was on the jet?"

Her eyes widen. "No, Mr. Montesano."

"Take the girl into the bedroom and keep her out of sight until I return. Fuck this up, and I'll carve out your liver. Is that understood?"

Terror crosses her features, but she manages to nod. I make a note to extract her organs if I find out she's the one who called Galliano.

The grinning bastard approaches the jet's steps, raising his gloved hands like he's Marcel Fucking Marceau begging for the chance to mime being shot down in a rain of bullets. As I reach for my weapon, the doors of the limo open, letting out four armed men, each training a gun at my chest.

I lower my hands. Matty Galliano might want me to cross over to his side voluntarily, but he and his brother aren't known for their patience. I've lost count of the number of times I've hung up on him, left his texts unread, or told him to fuck himself, yet he keeps coming back.

"Cesare," he says, his voice bursting with pride. "I'm so happy to see you in the sun."

My skin crawls, and I resist the urge to shudder. If I'm the big bad wolf, then Matty Galliano and his brother, Tommy, are snakes. The man slithering toward the steps wears a python-skin pea coat, complete with raised scales. It's buttoned up, revealing only the white turtleneck that rides up to his chin.

I glare down into his artificially colored face, wondering what the quartet of armed men think of their boss's thick makeup.

"You've grown up to be so handsome," Galliano adds, his voice choked.

My lip curls. "If creepy compliments are your love language, is it any surprise I keep ignoring your calls?"

He gazes up at me like I'm the eighth wonder of the world. It's the same expression Miranda makes when she's fangirling, only not as cute. I can take adulation from women. In fact, I welcome it, but not from this decrepit old man.

"Family is more important to me than life itself, and I..." He inhales a shuddering breath. "Don't shut me out, Cesare. You're the only child I have left."

I grind my teeth, resisting the urge to snap back. It takes every ounce of self-control to hold back from filling this creature with bullets.

"Did you get my message?" he asks.

"The dead girl in the alley?"

"She spat in your drink." His voice grates on my last nerve. "I had to teach her some respect."

An incredulous laugh builds up in my gut. This man is a compulsive liar and a comedian. "You chose her because we fucked, and you killed her to create a rift between me and my bothers."

He raises a finger and smirks, "Half-brothers."

"If what you told me is correct, they're now my only siblings."

When his smile fades, I know my jab has pierced his heart. It's been nearly three weeks since Leroi killed Galliano's kids, and he's desperate to find a replacement.

He reached out several times when they were alive, but never to this extent. Bastard is turning into a stalker.

"Will you consider my offer?" he asks.

"After you sent the Moirai to kill us?" I spit.

He flinches as though slapped. "Not you," he says, his voice breaking. "Never you. The assassins were only supposed to take out Benito and Roman."

Anger simmers in my gut like liquid bubbling in a still. I want to charge down the steps and tighten that turtleneck around his throat. I want to squeeze the life out of him until his eyes bulge out of his painted skull. I want to stomp that face until all that's left of him is gore.

If I got close, his men would barrel me into that limo, and I'd never see the light of day again. Annoyance kicks me in the balls. Since when did I become the fucking damsel?

"The shooter confessed to having three targets, not two," I say.

His features darken. "I'm going to have words with my brother."

I scoff. "Looks like Tommy wants all three Montesano brothers dead."

His nostrils flare, but he remains silent. Tommy Galliano was right to commission the triple hit. There's no way in hell I would ever turn away from my family. We may not have the same father, but we share loyalty, history, and blood.

"Leave it with me, son," Matty says and shuffles toward the limousine.

My fingers twitch to shoot him in the spine, but I force back the urge to start a gunfight and focus on his retreat.

I glare at the leather pants, which lead down to a pair of green cowboy boots, unable to tell if his awkward movements are because of a skin condition or because he's wearing the hide of at least three different animals.

Meanwhile, his goons continue to train their guns on me, and my breath stills as the driver skitters out and holds open the door. At this moment, I can almost understand why Rosalind killed her own parents. If her father was anything like this despicable creature, I would also blow him to pieces.

Galliano is about to reach the door when he pauses. "Who was that pretty little girl?"

My fury reaches a boiling point. I hiss through my teeth, trying to force back the explosion. Reacting would only make Miranda a target. A target of a psychopath determined to do anything to create a rift between my brothers and me, including murdering innocent women.

Holding my silence, I school my features into a mask of boredom.

"My men and I are having one of our special parties on Friday," he says, his eyes twinkling. "It's an intimate gathering of like-minded gents who enjoy sushi off the bodies of young women. After dinner, they serve as our dessert."

My jaw clenches.

He nods toward the plane. "How old is she? Thirteen, fourteen? She's exactly my type."

Blood pounds through my ears, and they begin to ring. I can't tell if he's goading me or if he genuinely thinks I would be interested in someone as young as Miranda. Either way, I can't let anything slip.

"Call off the Moirai," I say.

He flashes me a familiar-looking grin. It's the too-wide smile everyone says makes me look like a psychopath. Seeing it on Matty Galliano makes me think they have a point.

"Come to the party and I'll think about it," he says before scooting into the limo.

Breathing hard, I wait at the top of the stairs for his car to disappear behind a hangar. He may not have said it out loud, but he just threatened an innocent girl.

I turn back into the plane, where the pilot stands outside the cockpit, clutching a wheeled suitcase.

"Take me to Braye Airport," I snarl.

He rears back before regaining his composure. "But sir, we're not clear for departure. We've got to refuel."

"Then refuel and get us out of here."

The pilot gulps before giving me a curt nod and disappearing into the cockpit, leaving me alone with my seething rage.

Moving to another airport reduces the chance of being followed by Galliano. It also gives me time to think. He only caught a glimpse of Miranda. He won't know her face, her name, or where she lives. Hopefully, he'll think I'm a sick bastard like him, who treats young girls as disposable.

Once I've carried out my next phase of revenge on Rosalind, I'll return Miranda to her school with a stern warning not to leave its grounds until the Galliano brothers are dead.

FORTY-NINE

ROSALIND

I twist and thrash within the wheelchair, my body aching to break free of the suffocating bandages. The metal frame beneath me creaks and groans under the strain, waking some of the other assassins, who fill the dudgeon with muffled cries.

They're asking me to rescue them, the way I burst through a window in Paris when Axel botched his mission. The way I once had to shoot a target in the back because Greta had been overpowered. The way I saved nearly all of them in the ten years I served as backup to less skilled operatives.

I strain against my restraints, even though the bandages cut deeper into my skin with each futile attempt.

If I wasn't gagged, I would scream with frustration. We could have worked together upstairs, broken through the zip-ties, overpowered those guards and escaped.

Now...

Now, I don't know what the hell will be our fate. Cesare set up this dungeon to look like one of Miranda's horror movies. Everyone is trying to fight their bonds, except Axel, who looks like he's barely clinging onto life.

That tender moment in the basement infirmary was bullshit. Cesare was only pissed because someone else got to damage his toy. The moment he considers me healed, he will resume his sick games.

When the other operatives stop struggling and stare at a point over my shoulder, I turn my head as far as the bandages allow. Two pieces of fabric on either side of my face restrict my vision like blinkers, so I can't see what's made them freeze.

But I sure as hell can guess.

I rock back and forth, needing to loosen something, anything. Sweat breaks out across my skin and soaks into the bandages, and my wound throbs in time with my thrashing heart.

"Don't strain yourself, pet." His large hands clamp on my shoulders, holding me still.

The warmth of his hands sears through the bandages, making me scream through my gag. Releasing me, he walks around my chair to look me full in the face.

"How have you been?" he asks, his voice echoing through the chamber.

I glance over his shoulder at the other operatives. Four of them watch with rapt attention. Axel just hangs his head.

Cesare grabs my chin. "Look at me and answer my question."

"Fuck you," I yell through the gag. With the ball pressing down on my tongue, the words only sound guttural.

He tilts his head, his eyes glinting with malice. "What's that, pet? Use your words."

I didn't think I could despise anyone more than my stepfather, but Cesare is getting close. He snaps on a pair of gloves, peels back the bandages from my face and inspects my bruises.

"Much better." He unscrews a jar, releasing the sharp scent of menthol.

I glance down to find it's some sort of ointment. Even though I know it's beneficial, I shake my head from side to side, not that Cesare will even give me the choice to refuse treatment.

"None of that," he says, as though speaking to a rebellious child. "This will help with your bruises. In a few days, no one will ever be able to tell that those men damaged your face."

That's the problem. I don't want to look untouched, because that's when Cesare will resume the torture. Only this time, it won't be orgasm denial. He'll probably remove something vital so I can never escape.

An icy burn spreads across my skin as he applies the ointment. I try to shrink away from his touch, but he holds my face.

"There," he says, his voice soft and sinister. "That wasn't so bad?"

He doesn't wait for my reply. Instead, he screws the jar shut and strides past the wheelchair, into the space between me and the other assassins hung on the X-shaped crosses.

"Welcome to the last weeks or months of your lives," he says. "You're here because each of you has been identified as members of the Moirai."

All of them shake their heads, save for Axel, whose looks like it might roll off his shoulders.

Cesare chuckles. "It's too late for denials. You all have the same spinning wheel tattoo on your hip. What is it, the wheel of fate?"

Branson's gaze snaps to me, his eyes shining with accusation. He was one of my colleagues who snickered when I was about to enter Gunther's office after escaping captivity.

Cesare spins around, his gaze narrowing. "Are you flirting with another of your boyfriends?"

I flinch. Branson? Is he fucking joking? Scowling, I shake my head.

He nods, seeming satisfied.

"Each of you will spend quality time with me, explaining the workings of the Moirai. I want to know the names of your leaders, their locations, and where to find your headquarters. I want the name of the person with the power to cancel contracts. Most importantly, I want the location of your client."

My breath shallows. We've all been taught never to speak out against the firm. Britt once joked that operatives without loved ones they can threaten get chips embedded under their skin or was it minor explosives? It sounded outlandish at the time but now it doesn't seem so far-fetched.

"Who will volunteer?" Cesare asks.

Everyone holds still. Nobody would dare betray the firm. At least not in front of witnesses.

He turns to me, his gaze sharpening. "How about you, pet?"

Swallowing around my gag, I glance around at the hanging operatives. As much as I want to nod, I also need to think about the future.

Miranda might be safely tucked away in that apartment, but she only has a month's worth of frozen groceries. If Britt is injured, or didn't survive, my poor girl could be trapped. That's why I need to cooperate with the Montesano brothers.

But Gunther might stage a rescue for six captive operatives. If Brittany survived, she could lead another team directly to this room. In that case, agreeing so readily to betray the firm will have deadly consequences.

I still my features, neither nodding nor shaking my head. After staring at Cesare for a few heartbeats, I lower my lashes, hoping he'll see that as a yes.

"Why did you shoot me in the chest?" he asks, his voice hoarse.

I stare into his sternum, trying to tune out a potential rant.

"Look at me, or I'll kill your boyfriend," he snaps.

I raise my lashes, my brow furrowing, which only makes Cesare's jaws tighten.

"Do you love him?" he asks, his nostrils flaring.

My gaze darts to Branson, and I shake my head.

"Not that one." Cesare strides over to where Axel hangs with his head bowed. "This tongueless bastard you fucked in Paris."

Eyes widening, I choke on the gag, which only makes Cesare laugh. The harsh sound echoes through the room, and every muscle in my bandaged body tenses.

"So, he was right. You're together."

I shake my head again, wondering what the hell possessed Axel to taunt this maniac about the time we had sex. Gunther would have told the team I was his hostage. Was it a misguided attempt to derail the interrogation from the attempt on Roman's life?

And what the hell does he mean by tongueless?

Cesare rushes at me with his teeth bared. "Do. Not. Lie. To. Me."

He reaches beneath the bandage wrapped around my hair

and pulls out enough strands to make me wince. Before I can recover from the sharp pain, he twists the hairs to form a string.

"Have you ever heard of hair tourniquet syndrome?" he asks.

He's so casual about it. I stiffen, wondering what the fuck he's planning.

"No? It's when a strand of hair wraps around a body part so tightly that it cuts off the circulation," Cesare says with a nod.

My throat spasms.

"It can be quite painful. Imagine that body part turning red, then purple, then black because I wove your hair into a tiny noose."

Shudders ripple across my flesh, and I squeeze my eyes shut. That sadistic bastard wants to remove my toes so I can't escape.

"Look at me when I'm about to remove your boyfriend's cock," Cesare barks.

My eyes snap open to find him standing before Axel, winding my hair around the base of his penis. The blond man twitches within his bindings, too weak to put up a fight.

A noisy breath whistles through my nostrils, and I sputter around the gag. Is he serious? Of course he is, and I wouldn't be surprised if Cesare removed Axel's tongue.

He winds my hair tighter, tighter, tighter around Axel's penis until he convulses. I think he's having a fit or some kind of seizure. Cesare either doesn't notice or doesn't care because he's too busy glaring at me with those cruel eyes.

"Let's try this again, shall we?" he asks. "If you don't agree to give me the answers I want, I'll use the tourniquet to amputate your clit."

FIFTY

CESARE

I would never harm Rosalind. But all this talk of that blond bastard filling Rosalind with his rancid cock is fucking with my head. His words echo through my mind, creating a vivid image of my naked pet covered in sushi and splayed on a table, being devoured by three male assassins.

I need to calm the fuck down.

Every encounter with Galliano leaves me unsettled. That last one has me unhinged. He all but threatened Miranda. I had to fly her to a different airport and then drive around town to make sure we weren't being followed before I sent her back to school.

Galliano didn't get a good enough look at her, but I couldn't take any chances. Until that asshole is dead, I'll have to meet her in secret.

One thing's for sure. I need to change tactics with my pet. And that starts with focusing my aggression on any bastard who's enjoyed her tight little cunt.

My fingers tighten on the hair tourniquet I wrapped around the root of that blond bastard's cock. These things are rare and usually take hours to cut off circulation and days to erode tissue.

Since I don't have the luxury of time, I position my body to block Rosalind's view and accelerate the process with a strand of cheese wire.

Blondie convulses, presumably because he knows he's about to be separated from his cock. I pull the tourniquet taut around his shaft, letting the cheese wire sink into his flesh.

Stepping back, I keep my gaze fixed on Rosalind, who stares ahead as though unmoved. Of course, she's unaffected. She's a cold-hearted witch who murdered her parents in front of her baby sister.

Warm liquid drips on my fingers, and the room fills with the metallic scent of his blood. I pull tighter, feeling his body shudder violently beneath my grip.

Muffled cries echo off the walls, filling the chamber with the mingled sounds of despair. The other assassins probably expect to be next in line for the removal of body parts. I can't even revel in their fear because all my attention is on Rosalind's glower.

"Look at what you've brought upon your boyfriend," I say. "This is the price for your betrayal."

She breathes hard, seeming affronted at the accusation.

This is taking too long. His cock is still hanging by twisted strands of flesh. Tired of waiting for the tourniquet. I pull out Lucrezia from the back of my pocket and slice her blade through Blondie's shaft.

I hold the appendage high, reveling in the assassins' muffled cries. Rosalind's gaze doesn't waver, and she only sucks in a breath. No shrieks, no tears, no grief.

I advance on her, my fingers tightening around Blondie's shaft. Every instinct screams at me to shake her until her teeth rattle, wring her neck, and squeeze out the information I need, starting with the reason she lied.

Rosalind convinced us we were safe from the Moirai. That's the entire reason my brothers arranged the welcome-back party, only for her to summon her minions to kill Roman.

When I drop the severed appendage on her lap, she doesn't even flinch.

"Ready to talk, pet?" I ask, still out of breath from a burst of adrenaline.

She glares at me, still defiant.

I unravel the rest of the bandages around her head and

unbuckle the gag, leaving it to fall onto her lap. She splutters and coughs, breathing hard in sympathy for her fallen man.

"Why are you doing this?" she asks, her voice hoarse.

"Thirsty, pet?"

When she doesn't answer, I walk to the table at the back of the room and pick up a bottle of water. After cracking it open, I return to give her a few sips. My gaze wanders to the saline IV I inserted to keep her hydrated during my out-of-town trip. Dr. Brunelli would have come in a few times to keep her and the others topped up, but her bag is now empty because of the detour.

I stroke her hair as she finishes the water, lean into her and whisper into her ear, "How can something so beautiful be so treacherous?"

"Take me away from here," she whispers back.

I draw back with a frown. "Are you ashamed to be seen with me, pet?"

Her lips tighten, which I take as a yes.

"What's wrong?" I snap. "Still pining for that cockless bastard?"

She jerks her head to the side.

Fuck this.

With a swift kick, I release the lock on the chair's wheel lock and push her and Blondie's severed penis out of the room and into the darkened hallway. The door swings shut, and groans resound from the chamber as the lack of movement encases the other assassins in the dark.

I crouch in front of her chair and gaze into her hazel eyes. Eyes the same shape as Miranda's, but which burn with golden flames.

"Talk to me, pet."

"I didn't know there was another hit," she rasps.

My fingers close in around her bandaged thighs, and I squeeze them so tightly she grimaces.

"You're intelligent, powerful, ruthless. A seducer of men," I murmur, my gaze falling to her lips. "A high-ranking assassin like you manipulates the world around you. You could have escaped, yet you stayed in position to coordinate your subordinates to carry out your mission."

"No," she says.

I dig my fingers into her skin, making her gasp. "Then how did you direct Britt past secret entrances, through the maze of underground hallways, and into the hidden bathroom?"

"I didn't."

"Rosalind."

Her eyes widen at the use of her name. Good.

"Help me help you."

Her brow furrows. "What do you mean?"

"I want to protect you more than anything, but all the facts point to you being the master assassin. I searched you for trackers, yet you found a way to communicate with your underlings."

"Cesare, I'm not—"

"Give me something, so I can save you!"

She flinches, squeezes her eyes shut, and shudders. Rosalind is a skillful actress. I almost believe she's frightened, frustrated, even frantic. I'm so enthralled with her performance that I'll do anything to make her mine.

With a shuddering sigh, she says, "You have six hostages—"

"Five," I reply with a smirk. "Your boyfriend shot my brother and just lost his cock. I doubt he'll survive the night."

"You have five hostages," she says, not the least bit disturbed about the impending death of her lover. "Why don't you use that as leverage against the Moirai?"

Loosening my grip on her thighs, I lean back and consider her proposal. It's a smart strategy. But knowing Rosalind, there has to be a catch.

"That's not a bad idea. Now, tell me how you coordinated your escape and the triple hit."

"I didn't," she says with a sigh.

"Give me something else, or I'll kill blondie boy."

"Call Gunther at the Times," she says through clenched teeth. "Tell him everything. He might listen."

"How do I know it isn't a coded message?"

She rears back. "What?"

"You're the mistress of manipulation. How can I trust anything you say?"

Her face tightens, and she swallows hard. She almost looks

the picture of innocence, an older version of the girl I want to protect. I shake off that thought and remember the pain of her firing that gun into my bullet-proof undershirt.

"Work with me," I growl. "The stakes are higher. I need something. Anything to keep you alive."

She licks her lips and hesitates, as though conjuring up another lie. "I'm not as powerful as you think," she says, her eyes glistening. "All those people in there outrank me."

I laugh at the blatant bullshit. "How do you explain being the only assassin who never stops trying to escape? Or how you found an escape hatch no one has used for generations?"

"Desperation," she snarls. "And luck. Have you ever thought that I might have a lot to lose?"

"Says the heartless viper who murdered her own parents."

Her eyes widen.

I curl my lip. "Do you think Miranda forgot?"

"When did she—"

"Some firms have initiation rituals. Did you do that for the Moirai? Kill your mother and father and earn the right to join their ranks?"

Her lips tremble, and tears gather in the corners of her eyes. "She remembers?"

"How the fuck could anyone forget something so heinous?" I snarl. "The poor girl told me on the flight back to Beaumont City."

"Wait. You took her?" Rosalind asks, her eyes widening.

"Yeah, she's back at school with a doctor's note, so she can sit the test you made her miss."

"Oh, god." She bows her head and sobs. "No."

My lip curls. "You can't uproot a child from her family home, then dump her in boarding school, rip her out again, and imprison her in a shitty little apartment."

Her head snaps up, and she glares up at me and wails, "You don't know what you've done."

"Tell me," I say. "Work with me."

She clams up.

Frustration wells in my gut. I thought this change in tactics would make her talkative, but there's a limit to her loquacity.

"Think about Miranda for once. She needs your loyalty, not the Moirai."

I wheel Rosalind away, making a mental note to get in touch with her boss. We might be able to use the hostages to our advantage.

Rosalind's shoulders shake with silent sobs, confirming part of my message is soaking through her thick skull. I'll leave her to stew for a few hours and ask her specific questions about the Moirai.

In the meantime, I'll text Miranda and check that she's settled back to school.

FIFTY-ONE

ROSALIND

I don't know what kind of game Cesare thinks he's playing, but he wants me to sell out my colleagues.

He's changed the dressing on my bullet wound, given me food, water, and a blanket, followed by a shoulder massage. The Cesare I know would rant about me shooting him in the chest, accuse me of masterminding the attempt on his brother's life, and escalate the torture.

I once said he was evolving, but this is ridiculous.

His fingers feel like heaven across my touch-starved body, and I'm melting under his ministrations.

That's how I know at least one part of me is slipping into Stockholm syndrome. After resisting him for so long, I'm beginning to rely on this wretched bastard for external stimulation.

Cesare's presence is pulling me out of the prison of my mind.

He threads his fingers through my hair, infusing my scalp with explosions of pleasure. "Feeling better, pet?"

"Why are you doing this?" I ask.

"You need to be at your best when you're helping me with those Moirai bastards," he murmurs in my ear, sending sparks across my skin.

I shiver, trying to force back my body's response. This is just a facade. A switch up in his psychopathy to throw me off balance.

What he doesn't realize is that I'd already decided to turn against the Moirai until he brought Miranda back. She's now back at the Academy, where she's exposed to Gunther.

I can't even feel relief at no longer being the target of his sadism. He's gotten Miranda confiding in him, sharing her darkest secrets. All I can think is that he's going to corrupt my little girl. He'll manipulate Miranda's resentment toward me to gain her trust and then carry out my worst fear.

I sacrificed everything to protect my daughter. If I don't stop him, that psychopath will turn her into his plaything.

Miranda won't even see it coming, even though I warned her about older men and the process of grooming. It will be just like what happened to me.

Cesare will fill the emotional gap left by a neglectful mother. He'll be her confidante and her protector, the only person in the world she'll feel who truly sees her heart.

He'll shower her with love, recognition, and praise. He'll give her everything she's every yearned for—the things I've failed to provide. She'll be enchanted, just like I was with Matteo.

Before she knows it, Cesare will become her tormentor.

There's only one way to protect her: gather the information he wants and use that knowledge as leverage to earn our freedom. Freedom from him. Freedom from the Montesano family. Freedom from the Moirai.

"What do you think of me, pet?"

"You're a monster." The words slip from my lips.

"What else do you think about me?"

"You're dangerous."

My prey instincts scream at me to be silent, but my mouth won't stop forming words.

"You find me attractive?"

"If the devil took human form, he wouldn't be as handsome as you."

He grins.

"Do you like fucking me?"

"God, yes."

My gaze drops to the IV tube running from beneath the bandage around my hand and toward the liquid-filled bag hanging from a drip. I can't read the word on its label, but it sure as hell isn't saline.

Cesare brushes a strand of hair off my face. "You've finally noticed the scopolamine?"

A breath catches in my throat. I'm supposed to be immune to truth serums, but then nobody ever administered them to me after days of starvation, torture, sedation, and sensory deprivation.

"Yes," I rasp.

"Do you love me?" he whispers.

My heart pounds against my ribs, a maddening tattoo that echoes the intensity of my terror. Panic swells in my chest, stealing my air and erasing the edges of my sanity.

I grind my teeth, trying to fight through the urge to speak, but it's futile.

"No."

He leans closer, his sharp blue eyes piercing into mine and cutting through the last vestiges of my resistance. They burn with an intensity of fury that makes every fine hair stand on end.

He's acting like I gave him the wrong answer, because somewhere in his twisted psyche, he equates torturing a woman half to death with affection.

Finally, his eyes dim, releasing the pressure on my chest. "Will you help me?"

"Yes," I say, because that's the truth. I will give him information, but it will come at a price.

"Good girl. One more question."

Closing my eyes, I focus on the rhythm of my ragged breaths. With enough concentration, I might be able to beat the drug and work out how to negotiate Miranda's freedom.

"Look at me," he growls.

My eyes snap open. A nasty side effect of scopolamine is that it makes its victim incredibly susceptible to commands.

"Did you mastermind the attack on Roman?"

"No."

Shock registers across his features, and his eyes widen before the mask snaps back into place. Maybe it's finally sinking in that I'm just a pawn trapped in a much larger game.

"The other agents are immune to truth serums. How are they doing it?"

I grind my teeth, wanting to be resistant, wanting to bargain this information for my daughter. Past traumas creep to the forefront of my mind, splintering the edges of my sanity. I see Miranda with her head in a bear trap, her face wet with tears and blood staining the white of her shirt. I see Cesare standing over her, shirtless, and holding that antique pistol.

If I tell him what he wants, then Gunther will hunt Miranda. If I don't, then Miranda loses her innocence. Either way, my little girl is in danger, and I'm too enmeshed in chemical bondage to help her.

When a large hand lands on my shoulder, I don't freeze or even flinch. My body floods with pleasure. Pleasure at whatever diabolical concoction he's added to the truth serum.

"Go on, pet. Tell me what they do to evade my questions."

"If you visualize the lie as the truth before saying it, then your body won't react as if it's a lie."

He nods. "I like this cooperative version of you. Now, tell me how to destroy the Moirai," he says.

Gunther's threat over Miranda's life rings like an alarm bell. My mind scrambles to concoct a distraction, a lie, a piece of misinformation that might keep Miranda safe, but the truth claws at my throat.

Whichever way I go, Miranda will get hurt.

"It's impossible," I rasp.

His eyes narrow. "A woman as brilliant as you would have run through multiple scenarios. Tell me what we can do to take them down?"

Relief escapes my lungs in an outward breath. Cesare's question has just enough nuance for me to side-step. The Montesano family has enough resources to hurt the Moirai, but only an insider can destroy them from within.

I know a man. A powerful man. A man who wants to annihilate the firm. He has connections that span levels within the building even I can't penetrate, but he lacks the Montesano's vast resources. Putting them together would help Cesare and his brothers, but what about Miranda and me?

"It's complicated," I say through ragged breaths.

"Why?"

"The drugs. I can't think straight."

Nodding, he reaches to the IV attached to my arm and twists its valve, stopping the flow of serum. I slump back in the wheelchair under a wave of exhaustion.

"Take a break. You've done so well."

I close my eyes, relaxing under his touch as he encases me in bandages. Let him think he's winning this game of wits. No matter what he does to those operatives, they're weeks away from breaking.

He thinks I'm close to spilling my secrets, but I can tell he's becoming desperate. I cling onto the small win, letting the world drift away. The next time I wake up, I'll be stronger. And I'll negotiate a way out of this for me and my baby.

FIFTY-TWO

CESARE

Rosalind is so close to submitting to me I can taste victory on the tip of my tongue. My brilliant little pet doesn't realize how much information she's spilled. With one piece of information, she's given me exactly what I need to make the other assassins speak.

When she awakens, she'll give me more.

After checking she's still secured to the tilt table, I adjust it a few degrees to maximize her disorientation. With the way I'm switching tactics, it's only a matter of time before I shatter her mind.

When she breaks, I will rebuild her to my exact specifications. Then she'll think of me more as a savior than a psychopath.

I leave the room and walk down to the large interrogation chamber, where I left her underlings. Faint sounds echo from within, making my steps falter. Pausing with my ear pressed to the door's cold metal surface, I hear soft taps. They're rhythmic and staccato, reminding me of Morse code.

Shit. The only thing I know is S.O.S. This sounds like an entire conversation.

I broke their fingers to make sure they couldn't untie themselves and escape, gagged them so they couldn't speak, and encased them in darkness. Those fuckers. The last thing I considered was their ability to plot against us with knocks.

As I enter the chamber, my senses fill with the putrid stench of death. More importantly, the tapping falls silent, confirming my suspicions.

The air is heavy, not with the scent of decay but betrayal. I step past the motion sensor that activates the light, and all four of the assassins turn to gape at their dead colleague still hanging from the middle cross.

Blondie's corpse in the middle has already bypassed livor mortis and has begun to decompose. The blood beneath his cross has already soaked into the concrete floor, leaving a darkened stain.

"You should be more concerned about yourselves," I say.

All four pairs of eyes snap back to meet mine.

"I know you're immune to truth serums. You're also communicating with each other to concoct a believable lie," I say. "So, let's try again. Next person to bullshit me won't just join Axel in death, you'll lose body parts."

———

Hours later, I exit the wine cellar, reeling from four different accounts. Axel was the mastermind who orchestrated the assassination attempt. Britt was supposed to shoot Benito but disappeared on an unauthorized side quest to rescue Rosalind. Rosalind is a prodigy who fell from grace. Rosalind was promoted to a managerial position in another office.

All four assassins swear that they're only support staff, yet Rosalind already told me there would be three shooters, each with an assistant to help them escape.

They all skirt around my most important questions: where are the Galliano brothers hiding and how the fuck do we stop the Moirai?

I don't expect them to know the answer to the first, but they must have ideas about the latter. It's as though their overlords have locked away the secret to defeating them behind a wall of terror.

My footsteps echo through the stairwell, aggravating my throbbing head. Enough time has passed since Rosalind shot me in the chest that my ribs no longer ache, yet I'm still no closer to answers.

The phone in the pocket of my leather apron buzzes with the reminder I'm running late to update my brothers on my lack of progress. When I reach Roman's office, a new portrait of him hangs over his desk.

Whoever painted that thing depicted him as a god, with sunlight chiseling his features and turning the ends of his black hair a deep shade of mahogany. Somehow, the portrait's eyes burn like coals. The artist is probably the crazy balcony woman who's now sleeping in my brother's bed.

"Over here," Roman says.

I tear my gaze away from the painting toward the leather sofas on the room's far left. Roman is dressed like he's about to play a round of tennis in the park, and Benito wears a black three-piece suit with his hair slicked back like Micheal fucking Corleone.

"We missed you at the crematorium this morning," Benito says, his voice etched with disapproval. "And at the casino and the club."

"Allegra's taking care of it," I mutter.

Benito leans back in his armchair. "Aren't you spreading her too thinly?"

"The karaoke bar practically runs itself," I say through clenched teeth. "Besides, she has an assistant manager who can pick up the slack."

"This is Allegra, the coke head?" Roman asks, his gaze bouncing from me to Benito.

I flinch. "You questioning my ability to manage my staff? Or are you trying to tell me former addicts never get a second chance?"

My brothers exchange a glance that suggests they've been bitching about me behind my back. That's how the dynamics of our family have always worked. Dad and his golden boys on one side, with Mom and me on the other. Now that our parents have gone, it's just me being the odd one out.

Benito sighs. "No one is calling you incompetent, Cesare."

"Allegra went to rehab and got clean. Are we going to ignore years of faithful service because she once had a problem?" I ask.

"But didn't you and she have a thing?" Roman asks with a frown.

"Past tense," I snarl, bristling at the insinuation I'm defending an ex. "What we did or didn't do is irrelevant."

"It is when you've got her running two of our businesses."

"I wouldn't have to dump all my work on her if you could get through to that asshole at the Moirai."

"They've agreed to a temporary ceasefire." Benito cuts in. "What's the progress on the interrogations? What have you learned?"

"The assassins are immune to pain, truth serums, and the threat of death." My hands ball into fists. "They're like robots that don't listen to reason and can't be scared into submission."

"Nobody's immune to everything," Roman says.

"True, but wearing down a person's defenses takes time."

"Leroi's ex, what's-her-name, has been with you the longest. Shouldn't she be ready to crack?"

"Rosalind belongs to me," I say through clenched teeth.

"Obviously not, if she won't spill her secrets," Benito mutters under his breath.

I cross the room and stand over my asshole brother. "You got something to say about the way I handle women?"

Benito rises. At six-four, the bastard usually eclipses me by an inch and a quarter. Today it's at least four because he's wearing Cuban heels, and I'm in water-resistant shoes designed to shield my feet from body fluids.

He squares his shoulders in the same defensive posture he always uses when anyone mocks the years of celibacy he's spent pining for his treacherous ex.

"I took back control of the meth lab, cleared the casino of betrayers, and spent the entire night cremating them alive," Benito says, his voice tightening with rage. "And you can't get a single woman to speak."

Raising my chin, I meet Benito's glare. "You're too much of a coward to say you're pissed at us both because you finally have to get your hands dirty."

Benito flashes his teeth because I'm right. He won't dare say a word to Roman, who's been spending all his time romancing that skittish woman. I would have broken her in twenty minutes and gotten her to sign over her entire fortune. If Benito had what it took to even keep a woman, he'd understand that Rosalind was a completely different breed.

"Enough." Roman stands and places his hands on both our shoulders. "We only just got the family together. Let's not tear each other apart."

The door behind us opens, letting in a pair of light footsteps that could only be female. I turn around to find Sofia walking in, holding a wicker picnic basket.

"I packed my special panettone," she says with a soft smile, looking at Roman like he's the second coming.

Hell, sometimes I see him sitting behind Dad's desk and can't believe what I'm seeing. I shuffle on my feet, wondering why I'm squabbling with Benito when we're finally together as a family. I should enjoy this moment while it lasts.

We fall silent as she continues toward us with her basket, filling the room with the aroma of freshly baked bread. Roman releases our shoulders and steps around us to place a kiss on the housekeeper's cheek.

Sofia hands him the woven basket and stands back with a sigh as he strides toward the French doors that open into the garden.

"Where are you going?" I ask, making him pause at the exit.

"I'm taking Emberly to Simon's Pond," Roman says with a grin. "She wants to paint a picture there."

My brows rise. I glance at Benito, waiting for him to protest. Instead, he folds his arms and presses his lips into a tight line. Just as I thought, he's directing his frustration at our big brother to me.

Roman steps out onto the patio. "Family dinner tomorrow night. Bring dates."

Without another word, our eldest brother strides down the path that leads to the pool house, leaving Benito and me staring at his back.

Silence stretches out across Dad's former study, broken only by another of Sofia's happy sighs. She gives my arm a gentle squeeze before padding out of the room and closing the door with a soft click.

"I'm glad he's out of prison, but must he be so fixated with that woman?" Benito mutters from my side.

"You don't know what it's like to be locked up," I murmur, my gaze still fixed on Roman.

My brother turns to stare at the side of my face. "Do you still resent me for making you go cold turkey?"

"No," I reply, my voice tight. "Roman spent all that time on death row, getting his appeals rejected and never knowing if he would escape the electric chair. Who are we to judge if he needs time to toy with that woman before snuffing out her life?"

"You might have a point," Benito mumbles.

My brows rise. "What was that?"

"You heard me," he mutters.

Looking him full in the face, I wait for him to repeat himself, but he huffs. "Focus your attention on Leroi's woman. Find her weakness and go deep."

I bristle. "She's my woman, not Leroi's, and that's easier said than done."

"What? You still can't find what makes a woman tick after fucking your entire female staff?"

"If you knew anything about the fairer sex, you'd understand they're more complicated and twice as treacherous than men."

He walks to the door. "If you can't break her, I can call Leroi."

"Who failed to notice he was fucking another assassin?" I snap. "That barb is growing tired, just like the torch you're carrying for Ginevra DiMarco. Move on, accept that she ditched you for Samson Capello, and maybe you'll stop being so bitter."

Benito pauses at the doorway. "You have forty-eight hours to crack Rosalind open before I unwrap her and drag out her secrets."

My stomach drops. Rosalind is mine. Nobody hurts her except me.

"Brother or not, touch her and you die," I snarl.

Scoffing, he disappears in the hallway, leaving me fuming. Benito won't be gentle, like me. He's so out of practice and holds so much resentment toward women that he's likely to damage my Rosalind beyond repair.

Roman and Leroi would forgive me if I broke Benito's fingers, but they wouldn't if they knew I had Galliano blood.

As his footsteps recede, I resolve to protect Rosalind from a creep like Benito while changing my tactics. Before the deadline is up, I will squeeze out every one of her secrets.

FIFTY-THREE

ROSALIND

I wake up with a jolt that hurls my heartbeat up to the state of panic. Rough hands pull at my bandages, leaving the coverings around my head.

A scream rips through my throat, but it's muffled by the gag. I thrash in the dark, but my limbs are held down by tight bands

This isn't Cesare's gentle touch. This man is angry, anxious, agitated. What the hell have the other assassins said about me?

My empty stomach churns, and my skin breaks out in a cold sweat. What if this isn't even Cesare? Cesare always frees my head first, never my body.

Cool metal slides against my flesh as I'm cut free, making it tighten into goosebumps. The man frees my arm and I lash out, hitting something hard.

He shoves me down onto the hard surface. I jerk my legs, but they're still held down by straps. When I curl my fingers, each digit feels encased in plaster.

The bandages around my head finally loosen, and he rips off the ear coverings, plunging me back into the world of sound.

He's breathing hard and heavy, as though seeing me flounder is exciting. Cesare always wanted to see me break, but the man unwrapping me could be anyone.

I make another muffled scream.

He reaches behind my head to unbuckle the gag and pulls it from my parched lips. I gasp for air, my tongue tasting of leather and rubber.

"Cesare?" I croak, my voice hoarse.

"Calm the fuck down." He tears off the blindfold.

Bright lights burn my eyes, and I blink several times until my vision adjusts. When I see a familiar outline, my chest loosens with relief, which gives way to despair.

It's Cesare, not some other man looking to sexually assault a helpless woman. What's more concerning, is that I'm happy to see him. It means my mind is slipping further into Stockholm syndrome.

If I'm not careful, I'll forget my identity and start seeing him as a savior rather than a captor. I might forget that he's put me through unspeakable amounts of horror and start seeing them as acts of love.

"Stop fighting me, Rosalind," he says.

I flinch at his use of my name. "What's happened?"

"You can't stay tied up like this," he mutters. "Too dangerous."

"What do you mean?" My gaze darts around the darkened room.

"No man gets to touch you but me."

My stomach lurches at the thought that another man could enter this part of the basement and subject me to worse. I stare up at Cesare, my heart sinking at the realization that he's now become my protector.

"I thought these dungeons were secure," I rasp.

"My brother thinks he can do a better job extracting information," he says, sounding urgent. "He's not like me. He hates women. If you don't speak, he won't show you mercy or leave you undamaged."

"B-Brother?" My mind jumps to Roman Montesano, who just spent five years in prison for the brutal murder of a woman.

"Give me something," he says, sounding urgent. "Or I won't be able to keep him away."

The lump in my throat throbs in sync with my rapid heartbeat. I've never seen Cesare look so desperate. He cares for me in his own twisted way. Or at least he cares about being the only man who gets to cause me pain.

I gulp. "What do you want to know?"

"How do we hurt the Moirai?"

My tongue darts out to lick my dry lips, and I buy time to work out how to take advantage of the crack in his facade. If he cares for me, even just a tiny bit, then I will leverage that to escape.

"I can tell, but I want a few things in exchange."

"Name them."

"You'll set me free."

He grabs a handful of my hair and jerks my head to the side. "Never."

"Then you'll help me hide Miranda and leave her the fuck alone," I yell.

He releases my hair, only to grab my chin and force our eyes to meet. "What is this fixation with taking her away from where she's comfortable?" he snarls. "Why are you determined to make that girl miserable?"

My breath quickens. I can't tell him the truth. It would be like handing him a loaded gun. "Why are you so obsessed with my sister?"

"You belong to me," he says with a hint of a smirk. "By extension, so does Miranda. Now, speak."

"They'll hurt her if I do."

"Who?"

"The Moirai," I snap. "My boss practically threatened her life. That's why we moved her to another state, and you've just brought her back to New Alderney, where she's vulnerable."

His brows pinch. "You should have said—"

"When you were drugging me, torturing me, or when you had me gagged?" I scream. "Why would I confide in a grown man with twisted sexual tastes who enjoys spending time with a fourteen-year-old girl?"

He flinches, his nostrils flaring.

"Is that what you think of me?" he says, his voice chilling me to the bone.

"What else am I going to think? Miranda doesn't deserve to be around a man like you."

"Are you going to tell me how to take down the Moirai, or will I hand you over to my brother?"

"Miranda—"

"You don't get to use her as a bargaining chip," he snarls. "Not after making that accusation."

My breath quickens. I don't know if I've made her situation better or worse. "I want to tell you everything, but I need to know she'll be safe."

Ignoring me, he removes the bandages from my feet, then releases the strap on my legs, and lifts me off the table.

He carries me across the room and into a darkened hallway. I'm naked, save for a few scraps of bandages around my crotch and breasts, not to mention the wad of fabric encasing my fingers.

"Cesare?" My voice trembles.

"Since you're so eager to meet my brothers, you can join them for dinner."

"Wait!"

"Do you want the gag?"

"If you hadn't taken Miranda again, I would have given you that information." I whack him on the back with my covered fist.

He spanks my ass, sending a sting across my skin that travels straight to my clit. My jaw clenches at my body's inappropriate response. It's like that part of my anatomy isn't connected to my mind.

At the end of the hallway, he places his palm over a scanner and carries me through a door that opens into a darkened stairwell. As he ascends the steps, I memorize the route in case I ever get an opening.

"Where are you taking me?" My voice echoes off its stone walls.

He answers me with another spank that makes me stifle a groan. After days of sensory deprivation, any touch from this sick bastard ignites my nerves like fireworks.

"You're staying upstairs with me," he says, sounding gruff. "Where you'll be safe."

The declaration makes my spine stiffen. Is Cesare deluded, or does he think he's the lesser of evils compared to his brothers?

"What makes you think I'm safe with you?"

"I take care of my pets." He slaps my ass again, only this time, he rubs slow circles over my heated skin. "Benito isn't interested in making you feel good. He'd cut you into pieces even after you spilled everything. Roman would shoot you between the eyes."

"Cesare?" I whisper, my heart pounding, my words dying on my throat.

My mind is so scrambled, I don't know what to believe. Everything I thought I knew about this man is a blur. The only thought that burns true in my mind is my desire to keep Miranda safe.

He doesn't prompt me to continue and moves through what seems like a labyrinth of hallways and staircases. When we reach a bright stairwell with winding stairs, I wonder if he's taking me up to the tower I noticed when I was taking photos of the grounds.

At the top of the stairs, he asks, "Are you going to be a good girl for me, or will I have to keep you in chains?"

"I'll be good."

"Wrong answer." He smacks my ass again.

I jerk in his grip. "What the fuck was I supposed to say?"

"You're still unbroken. A good pet craves bondage."

"I'm not your anything, Cesare," I spit.

He pushes the door open and steps into a large white bedroom containing an iron four-poster with hooks running along its canopy rail. A huge X joins the posts making up the footboard, reminding me of the crosses he used to hang the other assassins.

Any other time, I would shudder at the thought of being chained to a bed, but this room is above ground, drenched in sunlight, with no lingering basement scent.

And beyond the bed is a set of French doors that lead to a balcony and a tree where I can make an escape.

"This is your bedroom?" I ask as he sets me down on my bare feet.

"It is now."

He clips a chain to a collar I didn't even notice was around my neck and leads me into a spacious marble bathroom with a large tub. It's already full, with steam rising from the water.

My eyes widen. "You want to give me a bath?"

"I already told you," he says, his voice sharp. "You're having dinner with my brothers."

Dinner.

Brothers.

Bath.

Old memories surface of lying still on tables with my naked body covered in sushi for the entertainment of predatory men.

This time, I won't be helpless.

This time, I'm ready to fight back.

FIFTY-FOUR

CESARE

Why must I be obsessed with such a stubborn creature? I can't ever grant her freedom, not even in exchange for information that will destroy the Moirai.

I could feed her some bullshit, but promising her one thing and not delivering it will shatter our progress. I noticed how her breath hitched at the prospect of being handed to my brother. I'm the devil she knows, the devil she has learned to trust.

Rosalind will tell me everything when she breaks. It's only a matter of finding her exact weakness. I'm certain she's resentful of her sister, although I can't understand why. The age gap between them is an entire generation—even bigger than mine and Roman's.

After securing her leash to a bath rail, I unravel the bandages around her chest.

"You've lost weight." I cup her breast.

"Starvation will do that to a person," she snaps.

"The total parenteral nutrition I fed into your IV should have kept you sustained."

She flinches, her lips curling with disgust. "You fed me against my will?"

"I always take care of my property." I say and remove the bandages around her crotch. "Your pussy is as hairless as ever."

"If it's a bush you're looking for, find another pet," she says.

My brow furrows, and I run the pad of my finger along the barely visible scar. "What else did the firm remove beside your hair?"

She steps away from my touch. "Are you going to bathe me like a dog or continue to ask creepy questions?"

I lower her into the bath, chaining her wrists to the hooks I installed at the sides of the tub. She sighs in the warm water. This is the first time I've allowed her to bathe since her latest escape.

Her gaze is fixed on my chest as I pull off my shirt, revealing my abs and pecs. Her gray eyes dilate, confirming that she's enjoying the show. When I unzip my pants and let them fall to the floor tiles, her gaze jumps to my erect cock.

"What are you doing?" she asks, her voice breathy.

"You didn't think I'd allow you to bathe alone." I climb in behind her, and she stiffens.

"Relax, pet," I murmur, my hands sliding over her shoulders. "I'm just here to scrub your back."

"If you released my hands, I'd be able to wash myself."

I unravel the bandages around her left hand. It's a lengthy process because of the splints attached to each finger and the way I taped them together to restrict her movement.

An important part of sensory deprivation most torturers miss is the control of their subject's ability to self-soothe. If Benito hadn't threatened to intervene, I would have kept her in this state until her dependence on me became absolute.

After removing the last of the restraints from her fingers, I move onto the other.

"What's the point of freeing my fingers if you're restraining my wrists?" she mutters.

"You want to wash yourself?" I ask.

"Do you even need to ask?"

"Good pets would appreciate the attention." I squeeze liquid soap in my palm and slather it onto her back, my fingers easing her knotted muscles.

She hisses at the pressure but doesn't resist. Why would she, when her body craves physical touch? Eventually, her muscles melt and her posture relaxes.

"I hate you," she murmurs.

"That's just a few inches away from love."

My hands travel around to her front, where I massage her breasts, my fingers tracing over the skin where I carved my initials. The flesh has completely healed, leaving just a hint of a scar.

Her breath quickens as I roll her nipples between my fingers, and she throws her head back, resting it on my shoulder. "I could never love a monster."

"Because I'm a murderer?" I ask. "Every man I ever killed was in defense of the family, and I sure as hell didn't take out my own parents. Can you say the same?"

She flinches. "You don't know anything about me."

My hands slide over her ribs and down to her belly. "Patricide, matricide, homicide, and slow sororicide."

Her elbow lands in my gut. "I never killed a sister."

"Dying doesn't always result in the loss of life." I slide my fingers over the subtle scar tissue above her pubic bone. "How did you get this? A hysterectomy?"

Her shoulders rise to her ears. "I was getting horny until you started boring me with medical jargon. What kind of mafia prince talks like an encyclopedia?"

"Don't change the subject." I bite her ear.

"Then don't bore me with your pretensions of being a doctor." She moans, her hips lifting to brush her ass over my cock.

"Cheap distraction, pet," I say. "And it's a hobby, not a pretension."

"Whatever." She continues rolling her hips, nestling my cock between her ass cheeks. I wrap an arm around her waist, relishing the feeling of control. I'm not deluded enough to believe Rosalind wants to give me pleasure, but I'll play along.

Her desperate need to evade my question about the scar has given me the exact blueprint to breaking her spirit. It wouldn't surprise me if the Moirai required all its operatives to become sterile. Rosalind might even regret having signed up to be a killing machine instead of the giver of life.

"What an eager little pet," I growl into her ear. "Can't get enough of your master's cock?"

"Shut up," she snaps without breaking rhythm.

She grinds against my shaft with a rhythm that has my heart thundering for more. I slide my fingers between her legs and find her swollen clit, making her breath come in uneven gasps.

I'll drop the subject of her hysterectomy scar, at least until after I've come all over those cheeks.

"Why rub against my shaft when you can ride it?" I ask.

"I thought you stitched my pussy shut."

"You have more than one hole."

"Get fucked," she says with a laugh.

The corners of my lips lift in a smirk. Every day I spend with Rosalind gets me further under her skin. I'm only steps away from conquering her spirit. So, when my fingers leave her clit and wander up her pubic bone, I know she'll give me her ass.

She raises her hips and snarls, "Fine. Hold it steady."

"Like this?" I grip my shaft and position it at her asshole.

There's enough bath oil in the water to make it slippery, but when she slides down onto my cock, her tight heat is almost too much to bear. She throws back her head and her lips part with a moan.

"Fuck," I groan, my breath coming in shallow pants. "I knew you'd feel good, but you take my cock like you were made for me."

"For the love of all things holy, stop talking," she hisses, her hands clenching into fists.

Very few women I know volunteer for anal, let alone without lube. Rosalind's determination to keep me distracted just sealed her fate as my perfect toy.

I remain still, letting her take her sweet time encasing me to the root. Her strong muscles squeeze my cock like they're trying to make it submit. My balls tighten, and sensation travels up my spine, lighting up every pleasure receptor.

"Want to keep me quiet?" I say, my hands gripping her hips. "Then ride this cock until I'm too fucked up to ask questions."

She huffs out a laugh. "Don't make promises you can't keep, asshole."

"Fine words when yours is filled with my shaft," I say with a grin.

She rolls her hips, the movements deliberate and slow,

coaxing every nerve ending back to life. Her inner walls ripple around my shaft in sync with the pounding of my pulse.

The bathwater laps around our bodies as our gasps echo in the steamy room. I suck in a sharp breath, my fingers digging into her hips.

"Just like that," I say, my voice choked. "You're riding my cock so well."

Leaning back against my chest, she moves her arms and jangles her chains. "Release my wrists."

"Not a chance," I reply between gasping breaths.

"I could ride you harder, faster. Make you come deep in my ass with a roar."

These are exactly the words I want to hear from my pet, but without the manipulation. I reach between her legs and circle her clit. "How about you shut the fuck up and ride?"

She quickens her pace, making her strokes long and even. With each movement, she moans and arches her back, pressing harder against my pecs. Hot water splashes over the tub's edge and onto the bathroom floor as our bodies collide.

My climax builds. My grip tightens on her hips as I thrust deeper into her tight heat. I'm so close to coming, but I don't want to leave my pet unsatisfied. I rub her clit with firmer strokes, making her moan.

"Fuck," she cries out, her muscles squeezing my shaft so hard that my eyes roll to the back of my head.

With one final powerful thrust, I come deep in her ass, my body trembling from the intensity. My hips jerk, and jets of cum escape my balls, sending lightning bolts of pleasure through my senses as she collapses against my chest.

My world sharpens with perfect clarity. Rosalind is my perfect pet, and I want no other woman but her. I will use every underhanded method at my disposal to make her mine.

FIFTY-FIVE

ROSALIND

Hours later, I teeter down the marble hallway in a hobble skirt and six-inch heels connected by chains. Even if I wanted to break free from Cesare, I wouldn't get very far because the sick bastard has dressed me up as BDSM barbie.

Of all the humiliating shit I've endured as an assassin, this is possibly the most aggravating, because we're on our way to a family dinner with his brothers and their dates.

Staff side-eye us as we pass them, and nobody comments on my attire. I don't usually give a shit about what others think, but can't one of them at least show a smidgen of concern or even surprise? I'm being held against my will as Cesare's torture slave.

He leans into my side, presses a kiss on my cheek, murmuring in my ear, "I've never seen you look more beautiful."

"Get fucked," I mutter.

"Are you giving me consent to fill your other holes?" he asks, sounding so earnest that I want to gouge out his eye with my stiletto. "Because I can remove the stitches."

"No..." I say through clenched teeth. "Psycho."

When we enter the dining room, the first thing I notice is a replica of *The Last Supper,* but with everyone dressed like extras from *The Godfather*. My jaw would drop, but a curly-haired woman in denim is too busy gaping at my appearance.

I recognize her from the pool house. She walked in when Cesare had me tied to that chair. That was a lifetime ago, when the only threat I had hanging over Miranda's head came from the Moirai.

The woman's wide green eyes scan my boned bodice with sheer fabric that probably exposes my nipples under the light of the chandeliers. Jaw dropping, she turns to Roman Montesano as though urging him to say something, but the eldest brother only scowls.

Benito sits beneath the painting between Gil and his blonde date and an empty space. He raises his head from the screen of his phone, mutters something I can't hear through the blood roaring in my ears, then turns his attention back to his device.

Cesare jostles me into the chair beside the curly-haired woman before taking his seat. The backcombed-blonde sitting opposite who's dressed in a 1980s style dress shoots me a withering glare. I meet her gaze. What's her excuse for dressing like an outdated prom queen?

"Look around," Cesare murmurs into my ear. "You're the most alluring woman in the room and you're all mine."

I stiffen, trying to pretend he doesn't exist, but the toy he placed in my pussy roars to life. Cesare announces to the entire table that this is my last supper, which is bullshit because he's having too much fun making me squirm. I tune out the rest of the conversation, trying my hardest not to react. This entire charade is a power play he set up to demonstrate that I'm completely under his control.

The housekeeper slides into the seat opposite mine, presumably as Benito's date. She gives me a pained grimace, seeming to be the only person in the room who both understands my predicament and vaguely gives a shit. That, or she disapproves of Cesare bringing a hostage to the dinner table.

The curly-haired woman looks perpetually confused. It doesn't help that Roman keeps whispering words of reassurance, and the asshole sitting beside me won't stop stroking my neck.

Delicious scents waft from pasta that's shaped like large grains of rice. Cesare eats like it's his last meal, but I stare at my plate.

Cesare leans into me and whispers. "I freed your hands for a purpose, pet. Don't put this good food to waste."

My nostrils flare. I have to remind myself that breaking my fast with heavy food won't just upset my stomach. It will reset the hunger response and put me further under Cesare's thumb.

The toy in my pussy vibrates with more intensity, and I stifle a moan. Biting down on my bottom lip, I force back my arousal, and my eyes roll to the back of my head. Cesare slips a hand on my thigh. "Come on, pet. Let them hear your pleasure."

I'm on the verge of climaxing when a hand slams on the table, making me flinch. Apparently, the blonde threw an insult at Roman's date, and now she's being asked to leave. Her lips tremble, making my own curl.

Can't she see Roman did her a favor? I would give anything to rise off this seat and walk away without consequences. As if reading my mind, Cesare snakes his arm around my waist and brushes his thumb back and forth against the thin fabric over my skin.

The vibrations speed up. Shivers skitter up and down my spine and settle deep inside my core. Clenching my teeth, I curl my fingers into fists. I do not have a humiliation kink. No toy could ever make me come against my will. But the sensory deprivation has gotten me so touch-starved that Cesare's fingers feel like electricity.

As the blonde takes an eternity to leave her seat, Cesare leans into me, his lips grazing the shell of my ear.

"Eat your fucking pasta," I say through clenched teeth.

"I'd rather eat you," he replies.

Benito's head snaps up, and he glares at his younger brother. I can't tell if Cesare is displaying his ownership of me or taunting Benito for not having a date. Either way, he's using me to provoke his brother.

"Can't you just behave like a normal person for once?" I whisper.

"Is that why you're so obsessed with me, pet?"

"I'm not."

"You haven't touched your food or the wine. Anyone would think you were pining."

"Pining for my freedom," I hiss.

When Roman rises from his seat and escorts his date from the room, Benito sets down his phone. He leans forward in his seat, his brows furrowing.

The housekeeper leaves with a murmured excuse about tiramisu, and the dining room falls into a tense silence, broken only by Cesare's heavy breathing.

He peppers kisses down the column of my neck, each press of his lips infusing my skin with sparks. Shifting in my seat, I glance across the table at Gil, who stares at me through dark eyes.

Benito shakes his head. "I'm not surprised you can't get a word out of the assassin, if that's your method of torture."

As if encouraged by his disapproval, Cesare pulls me onto his lap. His arm clamps around my waist while his hand cups my breast. He nibbles my earlobe, making my eyelids droop.

Gil leans forward, his gaze hooded, while Benito's face is a mask of rage.

"What point are you making with this display?" Benito asks.

"Rosalind is mine," Cesare says. "No one interrogates her but me."

Gil shakes his head and sighs.

"What?" Cesare snaps.

He turns to Benito as though asking for permission to speak.

"Where were you last night?" Benito asks.

"Interrogating assassins. Tending to my pet. Why?"

Benito turns to me. "Is that true?"

"Don't speak to him." Cesare pinches my nipple, making me hiss through my teeth.

Benito's features harden. "Was he with you, Rosalind?"

Cesare rolls my nipple, and I let my eyes flutter shut. The darkness is a welcome distraction from Benito's penetrating gaze. Hours ago, Cesare cut me out of my bandages with an urgency that made me think he was another man. I'm beginning to feel like a bone being fought over by two ruthless dogs.

"Why the fuck are you so invested in my comings and goings?" Cesare asks.

"Allegra was found dead in the parking lot behind the bar," Gil says.

Cesare releases my nipple, his body stiffening. My eyes snap open, and I inhale deeply. I recognize that name from the research I did on the Montesano family. Allegra Reggio manages the bar next door to the Phoenix, one of the few legitimate businesses the family held onto after the death of their father.

Ex-employees I questioned mentioned rumors that Allegra and Cesare were buddies who got high together and fucked, but I never once saw them together.

Benito and Gil glare at us as though they think we both committed the murder. Cesare's arms wrap around my waist, his heart pounding hard enough for us both.

"When did she die?" Cesare rasps.

"Sometime after the bar closed," Gil says. "There's footage of her leaving through the back before someone cut the power."

"Her car was in the parking lot the whole night and when she didn't turn up to work the next day, her assistant manager looked inside," Benito adds.

Cesare's breathing turns ragged. "They found her in the car?"

"How would you know that?" Benito leans forward.

I grind my teeth. Guessing the end of a story isn't evidence of having committed a murder.

"It wasn't me who killed her," Cesare says through clenched teeth. "It was Matty Galliano."

My stomach churns at the mention of that monster's nickname, and I fix my gaze on the table. I thought the explosion had blown off enough body parts to render him harmless, but I suppose Matteo is still capable of murdering a woman in cold blood.

"Why would Galliano target Allegra?" Gil asks.

"Same reason he killed Tania," Cesare says.

"And what's that?" Benito asks.

"Same reason he hired those assassins."

Benito's gaze snaps to meet mine. I gulp, hoping he assumes my discomfort is because of Cesare's mention of the Moirai. If there's war brewing between the Montesanos and the Gallianos, no one can ever know my secret. I must protect Miranda.

Benito rubs his chin. "Explain to me in simple terms why you think Matty Galliano, and not Tommy, wants to kill your former lovers?"

"Isn't it obvious?" Cesare shifts on his seat. "He wants to create a rift between us brothers by framing me for murder."

I hold my features in a neutral mask. That explanation makes no sense. Matteo is the more calculating of the Galliano brothers. He wouldn't sneak into Montesano territory and commit murders on the off chance of causing family discord.

Benito is right. Convoluted, harebrained schemes are more Tommaso's style.

"Was he with you last night?" Benito asks.

My lips part. Every survival instinct tells me to cover up for Cesare, but this might be a chance to negotiate my freedom.

"She was asleep," Cesare says.

Gil sighs. "This doesn't look good."

"Why would I murder Allegra?" Cesare growls.

The large man raises both shoulders. "I mean, you killed Ricky Ferraro…"

"Who sold us out to Capello and Galliano," Cesare yells. "And I was giving him CPR when Tania walked in and interrupted."

"Who died the same moment you turned off the security cameras and rushed into the alley when she was sucking off Bruno."

Gil steeples his thick fingers. "Allegra got a new boyfriend last week. Now, she's dead."

"Bullshit," Cesare says.

Silence stretches out for several tense heartbeats as the two men shoot glares at Cesare and me. The air thickens with tension, pushing down on my lungs until I can barely breathe.

Death is no big deal to an assassin, but the thought that Cesare is murdering his ex-girlfriends is unsettling. He's obsessive, possessive, prone to mood swings. He's capable of anything and is also spending an inappropriate amount of time with my little girl.

My insides twist into painful knots. Would Benito stop Cesare from killing women or would he just help cover up his crimes?

Before I can consider the answer, Benito picks up his phone, makes several taps on its screen, and slides it across the table.

Lying on the back seat of a car is a dark-haired woman. Her naked body is covered in puncture wounds and blood. I recognize the knife embedded in her chest. It's the same one Cesare used to cut me out of my jumpsuit.

Lucrezia.

I try to rise off his lap, but his strong arms pin me to his chest. How the hell would Matteo Galliano know Cesare owned the same zombie knife?

FIFTY-SIX

CESARE

Hours later, I scale the side of the Victorian building, using everything available as hand and footholds. My fingers grip ivy, decorative cornices, and protruding bricks as I keep my gaze on the third-floor window of Miranda's dorm room.

Ignoring the phone buzzing in my back pocket, I continue upward. Matteo won't just stop at my exes. He'll ask around until someone works out that my underage friend is Miranda. I can't allow her to get hurt.

Gil and my brother continued grilling me about the murders and then moved onto asking if I had relapsed. All that talk unsettled Rosalind, so I had to take her upstairs. She tries to be strong, but I could tell from the way she flinched at my touch that she thinks I'm a killer.

Now is the time to fix two looming problems: Rosalind's stubbornness and my concerns for Miranda's safety. I plan on using her twisted relationship with her little sister to break her spirit.

"Are you still watching?" I ask for the benefit of the camera mounted on my head.

I left Rosalind sitting up, gagged, and chained to the bed, watching me live stream my ascent to where I left her sister. If she surrendered her body to save Miranda from the bear trap, then it's time to force her to surrender vital information about the Moirai.

In moments, I reach the window and peer into a darkened dorm room. It's stark, save for a single desk-lamp illuminating a scattered array of textbooks and papers. My lips tighten at the lack of photos, posters, or other paraphernalia that could make this room a home. It's more like a prison.

I tap on the glass, and Miranda emerges from the shadows, dressed in a black turtleneck and a matching hat. She slides open the window and grins.

"What's that?" She points at the camera.

"Never seen a head mount?" I ask.

She shakes her head.

"You going to invite me in, love?" I ask with a grin.

She laughs. "What are you, a vampire?"

"Maybe." I flash my teeth. "Or maybe I'm the big bad wolf."

She steps aside, allowing me to climb in.

"Did you pack a bag?"

She scampers to her narrow bed and retrieves a backpack. "Where are we going?"

I pull off the head mount and turn off the phone's camera app. Rosalind doesn't need to hear the part where I need to keep Miranda safe.

"Do you remember those men at the airport?"

Her smile fades. "The ones who got you spooked?"

I nod. "One of them is very dangerous, and he's trying to get at me through my friends."

"What does that mean?" she asks, her breath quickening. "Has he taken my sister?"

"No. Rosalind is fine."

"Then why are you here?" she asks, her gaze darting toward the door. "I thought you were going to take me to the club?"

"I want to take you home."

She shifts on her feet. "Where's Rosalind?"

"Home," I say. "With me."

"I don't understand. Why didn't she come with you to get me? Why do you need to sneak in through my window when she could call the academy and you could both walk in through the door?"

My jaw clenches. These are all good questions. Questions I

want her to ask a strange man with bad intentions, but now I wish she wasn't so suspicious.

I run a hand through my hair, trying to find the right words. "Rosalind can't climb with her injured shoulder. Before you ask, I snuck out because I didn't know if the man from the airport was watching."

Her breath catches. "He's having you followed?"

"I sure as hell didn't tell him when my plane would be landing, yet he still ambushed us on the runway."

She gazes up at me, her eyes wide. There's so much I want to apologize for, starting with making her a pawn in the game I'm playing with Rosalind. If I had left her alone, then she wouldn't be a potential person of interest to that murderer, Matty Galliano.

"Am I really in danger?" she asks, her voice shrinking.

Dropping to my knees, I gaze up into her glistening eyes. "I can't answer that question, love. All I can do is take you somewhere you'll be safe."

"Your house?"

"It's a fortress up in Alderney Hill, surrounded by twelve-foot-tall walls, topped by electrified fences. All the property around it belongs to my family and is patrolled by armed men. My great-grandfather built the house, and since then, no one has gotten past our small army of guards."

"Not even the police?"

I shake my head. "Not even them. You can stay there with your sister until that man is no longer a threat."

"Are you going to kill him?" she asks.

"Any man who hurts innocent women deserves to die," I say through clenched teeth.

"Alright," she whispers. "I'll come home with you."

———

Half an hour later, we're sitting in Sofia's kitchen. It's a basement room filled with stainless steel ovens, a wall of refrigeration units, and a huge island of cookers. This is where she oversees the preparation of meals for the family, dozens of staff members, and our stores of preserved food in the pantry.

Miranda perches on a stool, gazing up at a ceiling extractor fan the size of a small car. Her stress melted on the journey in the back of a limousine, and now she's ready for a snack.

"You can cook?" she asks.

"I learned from the very best," I say.

"Your mom?"

Shaking my head, I swallow down the lump in my throat that appears at every reminder of how she stabbed us in the back. "No," I rasp and turn my attention to the slab of dark chocolate I'm chopping into small pieces. "Our housekeeper, Sofia, always put me to work if I stayed too long in the kitchen. That's where I picked up my skills."

She glances at the milk warming on the stove. "Can I help?"

"Hold on a second while I get the biscotti."

"What's that?" she asks.

"You'll see."

I walk over to the pantry door and slide it open, revealing shelves upon shelves of pickle jars, preserved fruits, and food preserved in glass jars. I grab a selection of items, including the biscotti, and move onto the second phase of my plan.

After glancing over my shoulder to check that Miranda occupied, I turn on the camera and slip it in my back pocket. Rosalind will hear our voices, but the lack of visuals means she won't know we're only talking about food.

I return to the stove with the snacks.

"Do you think you can handle this, love?" I ask.

She huffs. "You think I'm too young?"

I chuckle. "Well, I didn't say that. It's just that..."

"What?" she snaps.

"You've led a sheltered life. They don't teach you this sort of thing at school."

"I'm fourteen, not four," she says, her voice rising with indignation.

"Alright, then. Take hold of this." I hand her a cast-iron pot.

"It's heavy."

I chuckle. "Of course it is."

"Now, what?"

I continue instructing her on how to prepare the hot chocolate, making sure to give lots of praise. Guilt claws at my chest for using Miranda as a pawn to hurt her older sister, but Rosalind has given me no choice.

The Galliano brothers won't call off the hit on us until they're both dead. Now that they're in hiding or surrounding themselves with armed guards, killing them will be impossible.

Which is why I need Rosalind to tell me how to take down the Moirai.

Miranda completes the hot chocolate and pours it into two steaming cups.

"Blow on it," I say. "Then have a taste."

She does as told, then takes a tiny sip. The moment the sweet chocolate hits her tongue, she moans. "It's so good."

"Told you," I say with a laugh, and dip a piece of biscotti into her cup. "Now, try this."

We continue like this for several minutes until the conversation changes to sleeping arrangements. I turn off the phone, noting that Miranda hasn't asked about her sister. This time, I understand why. The poor kid must feel like Rosalind's captive. I'm probably the only person who's ever given her a taste of freedom.

After settling Miranda into an upstairs guest bedroom, I walk up to the tower room. Noise echoes across the stairwell, making me wonder if I'd overlooked something while tying Rosalind's restraints.

This is the first time since her escape that she hasn't been drugged, and I was too much in a hurry to rescue Miranda to bother with wrapping her in bandages.

My heart pounds as I mount the steps, not knowing if I'm about to walk into a tempest.

When I unlock the door and ease it open, I find the four-poster collapsed into a chaotic pile of torn fabric and metal. Rosalind faces away from me, swinging an iron rod at the French doors. My black shirt hangs off her smaller frame with the sleeves folded over at the wrists.

Thank fuck Sofia swapped out the windows for unbreakable glass after the incident with the madwoman on the balcony. Otherwise, Rosalind would have escaped.

When I push the door open, it creaks, making her spin around. She glares at me through wide eyes, her lips pulled into a snarl. The sight of her in my clothes goes straight to my cock.

"You bastard!" she screams.

My heart pounds. I haven't seen her this excited since our primal scene behind the pool house. Stepping inside, I ready myself for her attack. "Why did you break through your bonds? Is something wrong, pet?"

With a war cry, she charges across the room, brandishing the iron rod. "I'm going to kill you for touching my daughter!"

FIFTY-SEVEN

CESARE

Daughter?

I freeze, the word ringing through my ears and muffling her tirade. The scar above her pubic bone wasn't from a hysterectomy but a cesarean, which means...

An iron bar hits me over the head before I can even form my next thought. Pain explodes across my cranium and my vision fills with a constellation.

The world tilts on its axis, not just because of the blow, but because of the devastating news that Rosalind is Miranda's mother.

But how?

I stagger backward just as she swings the iron bar. Another blow lands across my shoulder, the impact jarring me back to the present. Rosalind is a wild, feral creature, protecting her young. I've got to restrain her before she does any more damage to me or herself.

Adrenaline surges through my veins, momentarily dulling the pain of her next strike. I charge at her, aiming to grab the iron bar, but she sidesteps and swings it again. This time, it connects with my ribs, and I release a strangled grunt.

"Rosalind, stop!" I yell above her barrage of screams.

She's beyond reason, and I can't blame her. Rosalind is reliving every fucked-up thing I did to her and imagining me inflicting it on Miranda. How could she know I would never corrupt a child?

All she sees is the monster who imprisoned her, humiliated her, who enjoyed seeing her suffer.

I raise my arms to block another strike. The iron bar hits my ulna bone with a sharp, tingling sensation. Ignoring the pain flaring across my forearms, I lunge forward, wrap my arms around her waist, and throw us both to the floor. Finally, the iron bar clatters to the ground.

She struggles beneath me, her fists pummeling my chest and face with ruthless precision. The time she's spent in captivity has weakened her punches, but I still take the blows. The pain is nothing compared to the shock of her revelation.

Pinning her down by the shoulders, using my superior body weight keeping her in place. "You want to kill me, pet?"

"I want you dead," she screeches, her eyes ablaze with hatred.

"Then do it," I say between panting breaths. "Give me everything you've got."

She lashes out with renewed vigor, her blows relentless, her insults slicing through the chaos like serrated blades. "Monster, sick bastard. Child molester... Just like *him*."

Him who? I flinch, my lips forming a denial, but I'm silenced by a fist to the mouth. Thank fuck we're in the tower where nobody can hear her slander.

When her punches lose their impact, her hands scrabble for my throat and she squeezes. The pressure is constricting, but I don't resist.

"Let it all out, pet," I say through clenched teeth.

"I'm going to tear off your cock," she yells, her voice shrill.

Her knee connects with my balls. Shock barrels through my insides in a continuum of pain and nausea. All the air leaves my lungs, and for a moment, I can't inhale. As my body goes slack, she rolls me off her and scrambles to her knees.

When she picks up the iron bar again, I groan.

Once again, I underestimated Rosalind's skill. Still reeling from the groin strike, I barely manage to grab her ankle in time to pull her back down to the floor tiles.

She lands beside me with a grunt, and I take advantage of her disorientation to snatch her weapon. I toss it across the room, where it lands against the wall with a clatter.

Rosalind lands a fist at my temple, but I wrap my hand around her throat and squeeze.

Tears stream down her cheeks, and her pretty features contort with more anguish than I saw during the time she spent with me in capacity. Remorse punches me in the heart. I wanted to see her break, but not like this. Never out of maternal anguish.

"If you've gotten her pregnant—"

"Look at me, Rosalind," I command, my voice rough. "It's not what you're thinking. I never touched Miranda."

She screams, the words incoherent. Nothing I say is getting through. She won't listen to the truth. Why would she when the sounds and images I sent were so incriminating? She should want me dead.

Keeping my grip tight around her throat, I move us both across the floor to the dresser, where I keep my supplies.

She thrashes beneath me, her fists pounding against my chest, her nails digging a bloody trail across my forearms. Rosalind's rage is only picking up speed, each attack landing with increased desperation.

When I reach the dresser, I stretch out with my free hand, pull open a drawer, and grope around for something, anything, to knock her out and give me time to think. I don't want to use my fists because she's only just recovered from the bruises from her last attempt to escape.

Finally, my fingers close around a bottle of somnochlorate, a drug similar to chloroform, but more powerful. Rosalind bucks and rears beneath me as I unscrew its cap with my teeth, and I hold my breath to avoid inhaling the potent fumes.

She's too blinded in her rage to even notice the bottle. I tighten my grip around her throat and splash the liquid over her face. As she gasps for air, she inhales the drug, and her punches grow feeble.

Her eyes widen, and she rasps, "No..."

"I'm sorry, pet," I say, meaning every word. "But this is the only way I can make you listen."

"You bastard," she sobs.

I swallow, gazing into her fiery eyes, which still blaze with defiance, even as they grow heavy with the effects of the drug. It's a look that fills my veins with ice, a silent promise of retaliation.

"I know, love," I whisper, my voice barely audible over her heavy breaths. "I know."

With each passing second, her struggles fade until her arms fall to the floor tiles like lead weights. Her eyes glaze over, the flames in her irises fade, and the rest of her body falls limp.

As soon as she's out, I scramble to my feet and pace the room, carefully avoiding the wreckage. In her rage, she smashed the television set I left on the dresser, dismantled the four-poster, and splintered the unbreakable glass windows.

How the fuck can I subdue this enraged mother? More importantly, how the hell can someone as young as Rosalind have given birth to a grown-up child?

I never asked Miranda her age, but she must be at least fourteen.

My gaze drops to Rosalind, where her borrowed shirt has ridden up to her waist, exposing the barely visible scar. I drop to my knees and study the subtle groove. Someone got her pregnant when she was Miranda's age or younger, but who?

Based on the accusations she screamed, I can only conclude it was an older man. No wonder she couldn't stand for it to be touched. It's the embodiment of her trauma.

I scoop her up in my arms and carry her out of the destroyed room, down two flights of stairs, and into the hallway that leads to the family bedrooms. The first rays of sunlight stream in through the windows at the end of the corridor, reminding me that neither of us has slept.

When we reach my room, I place her on my bed and pick up the shackles permanently attached to the metal headboard. Rosalind will be furious when she awakens and will start a fight. I lie beside her, ready with my questions.

I'm not ready to think about why it makes a difference to me that she gave birth to Miranda. When I thought they were sisters, I already knew Rosalind was her only guardian.

Dr. Brunelli would twitch his mustache and tell me I had lingering mother issues from being abandoned when I needed her most. He might even suggest that seeing my rabbit with her kits torn out of her belly has made me put mothers on a pedestal.

No, he wouldn't because he still doesn't believe the Capello twins disemboweled my beloved pet.

As soon as I hear Rosalind's sharp intake of breath, my hand shoots out to clamp over her mouth to muffle a scream.

She glares across the mattress at me. The flames in her eyes have returned and burn hot enough to singe my stubble.

"Calm down, pet. I don't want to hurt you again."

An incessant clanking takes my attention away from her face to the cuffs around her wrist, and my stomach drops. Since I didn't bind her fingers, she's now breaking out of her shackles. I rise off the mattress and straddle her hips. These escape attempts are the reason I immobilized her hands. The woman is unstoppable.

"I want to help you," I say loud enough to cut through her muffled rant. "Just answer my questions. Are you really Miranda's mother?"

Her nostrils flare, indicating that she's listening, even if she keeps twisting the chains instead of answering.

"How?" I ask.

She squeezes her eyes shut, trying to block out my question. The answer to my question was in her tirade when she implied I'd gotten Miranda pregnant.

"Let me guess. You were abused."

She sucks in a sharp breath.

"And your mother either knew at the time or didn't protect you when she discovered the truth, which was why you killed her, too."

Tears leak from the corners of her eyes, but she continues twisting the chains, the muscles in her forearms bulging with exertion.

"Rosalind, who is Miranda's father?"

She jerks her head to the side, as though the thought of the man who raped her as a child is too much to bear.

My breath shallows. Growing up, I didn't have a sister. My cousin, Jennifer, doesn't count because she and Leroi left before I was two. I can't imagine Dad abusing his own daughter, but I know that sort of shit happens in other families.

"Was it a teacher?" When she doesn't respond, I add, "Your parent's friend? Was it your father?"

Her answer is a muffled sob that's like a knife through the heart.

Pieces click together, both from everything I learned from speaking to Rosalind and Miranda, as well as what I know about the Moirai. They recruit their people young, which means she must have given birth before training to become an assassin.

"Miranda told me you came to the house when she was four to kill your parents and take her away. Did you join the Moirai to become strong enough to take back your child?"

She finally nods, her body convulsing with sobs.

I try to think of a girl as young as Miranda being forced to endure abuse, only to get pregnant by her own father. My mind can't even form the image. It's too horrific to even contemplate.

Rosalind finally opens her eyes and glares up at me with a hatred that burns brighter than the entire time she spent in captivity. That's when I understand the source of her strength. Nothing I did to her could ever compare to what she endured as a child.

"I swear to you, I didn't touch Miranda," I say.

The snap of metal resounds in the room as she finally breaks through the first of her chains. Instead of clawing at my eyes, she uses her free hand to work at the shackle around her left wrist.

"She was telling the truth about the prank. I asked Miranda to wear a prop for the first set of photos. All the crying and screaming she did for the camera was an act. That conversation you heard earlier was me teaching her to make hot chocolate. Those noises were because she was eating snacks."

Rosalind jerks her head to meet my eyes.

"It's true," I rasp. "You can ask her yourself. She's across the hallway."

When she stops struggling, I think it's because I've finally reached her with the truth, but she lurches at me with both arms outstretched and wraps her hands around my throat.

"Calm down, pet," I say through choked breaths. "You don't want to look disheveled when I take you to your daughter."

"You're going to let me see her?" she says in disbelief.

"As soon as we agree to a truce," I reply.

FIFTY-EIGHT

Exhaling my emotions in an outward breath, I try to restore a sense of calm. I am wrung out, drained from hearing my backstory laid bare like the answer to some puzzle. Strangely, I believe Cesare hasn't laid a finger on Miranda, but no groomer makes a move after a few encounters.

Fighting him is futile. Days spent away from the gym and a lack of good nutrition has sapped my strength. Cesare's face doesn't even change color with my hands around his throat. Instead, he stares down at me without his usual sadistic glee, the intensity of his gaze ripping me to shreds.

He's serious. In his twisted mind, he believes he hasn't corrupted my little girl, but this maniac doesn't have a bone in his body that isn't sexual. He's probably also some kind of addict.

I glance around, taking in a bathroom on the left, along with the door to what's probably a walk-in closet. We're no longer in the balcony bedroom I trashed but somewhere within the mansion's first floor.

Blown-up photos hang on the wall depicting extreme close-ups of a woman in various stages of agony. I skip past them to find a window beyond the footboard that overlooks a tall willow tree, and the exit on the right.

"Take me to my daughter," I say, through clenched teeth.

He peels my fingers off his throat and brings them to his lips, his demeanor changing from shitty psychopath to chivalrous savior. Each kiss he presses into my knuckles is a slap in the face.

I don't believe for one second that he gives a shit about Miranda. He's probably gearing up to some kind of mother-daughter kink. Maybe he wants to keep us both as pets.

But what exactly are my options?

I'm too diminished to win a fight, and he's got my little girl back in his clutches. He also has the backing of his brothers and a small army of goons. I might have bested him when I was alone and at my peak, but I'm compromised.

Fear and exhaustion have taken their toll, rendering me physically useless. So I'll play along, keep them far apart, and bide my time until we can escape.

It's the only option left for me to save Miranda.

"Truce, first," he says.

My blood simmers at the sound of his voice, but I push down my mounting anger. "Truce?" I snarl. "Why do you suddenly want to cooperate?"

He winces, as if remembering the time I'd offered up all the information he wanted in exchange for my freedom. Back then, he wasn't interested in negotiations. He only wanted my unconditional surrender. My unyielding submission.

"I've grown fond of Miranda." He cringes, seeming to realize his words carry innuendo.

My stomach churns at the thought of him feeling anything toward my daughter. I want to scream, to lash out, to inflict all the anguish searing through my veins. I want Cesare to suffer the anguish of being held captive while the person he loves most in the world is at risk. But all I can say to him is, "Why?"

"We have the same age gap between Roman and me. She's like the little sister I always wanted."

Nausea surges at the nostalgia in his tone, but I force my voice to stay level. "What are your terms?"

"Help me take down the Moirai. In return, I'll keep Miranda safe."

"How do I know we won't end up in one of your basements?" I ask.

His jaw clenches, and his lips flatten against his teeth. "I wouldn't hurt her."

"But you would hurt me?" I ask, every word bleeding anger.

"I hurt an assassin who came after my family," he snarls. "You tricked your way into my house, sent security information to the Moirai and masterminded an attempt on Roman's life."

"I didn't—"

"And while your colleagues or underlings ran around the grounds, using the information you provided them to slip away, you shot me in the chest and allowed Britt to escape."

My heart races as I process the truth in his words. Even I can see his point. Cesare was ready to escort me to the gates before I tricked him into swallowing the oxypentanol. I put his family in danger, and he's doing the same to mine. But that doesn't justify the abduction of an innocent child or make him even remotely trustworthy.

"Help me move Miranda to another boarding school."

"No," he growls, his grip tightening on my wrists. "She stays here."

My heart races, and my ears ring with alarm bells. Flashbacks flicker through the recesses of my mind of Mom trying to send me away to school and Matteo insisting that I stay. I struggle against Cesare's weight, even though I don't have a chance in hell to over-power this monster. I buck my hips, trying to throw him off, but he's a lead weight.

"So you can groom her?" I ask, my voice laced with bitterness.

"So I can keep her safe," he snarls, his malicious eyes boring into mine.

"While you're keeping her safe from the Moirai, who's going to keep her safe from you?"

"You will."

I flinch. "What?"

"If you're so determined to think I'm a predator, then you can stay at my side and scrutinize my every move."

I need to stop this bullshit before he gets suggestive. "You will help me move my daughter to a school out of reach of the Moirai. In exchange, I will tell you everything you need to destroy them."

"Fine." He rises off my hips and sinks beside me on the mattress. "I'll make inquiries."

"Don't bother." I sit up against the headboard, roll the tension off my shoulders, and force back a semblance of composure. "I already did the research. Just give me the money, and I'll take her."

"We'll take Miranda together."

My stomach churns, and I tighten my jaw. Cesare doesn't seem like the type of man to hand a woman a suitcase of cash and expect her to return, and he'd be right. The moment I leave with my little girl, I'm never coming back.

He sits beside me and offers out his hand. "Deal?"

Every instinct screams at me to break his fingers. Fingers that removed my bullet wound. Fingers that brought me to the heights of pleasure and pain. Fingers that slid down my tongue and fed me rice pudding.

Now isn't the time for vengeance or even escape. After Miranda is safe, there'll be plenty of time to act.

But for now, all I can do is take his hand. "Deal."

My gaze drifts from our joined hands to penetrating blue eyes that know all my secrets. He's the only person alive who has seen me cry, has made me beg, and knows what I look like when I climax. When he pulls me into his chest, I lose track of that peculiar thought.

"What are you doing?" I ask, my voice wavering.

"When you make a deal with the devil, you need to seal it with a kiss," he says, his lips descending on mine.

Grinding my teeth, I let him savor this hollow victory. He snakes an arm around my waist and pulls me onto his lap, while he tries to push his tongue between our joined lips.

My fingers find his nipple, and I pinch it with every ounce of strength. He groans, his cock hardening beneath my thighs. Of course, the bastard enjoys receiving pain as much as he enjoys his sadism.

I pull away and wipe the back of my hand over my mouth, trying to rid myself of his taste. "Next time you kiss me, I'll bite off your lip."

"Feisty," he says, his eyes dancing with mirth, his fingers tracing up my bare thighs.

Fury ripples down my spine, and I launch myself off the bed. "Where's Miranda?"

He cocks his head and gazes down at me with a smirk. "You can't see her looking like you've just been fucked."

My brow furrows. I glance down at the shirt to find it gaping open and exposing my breasts. The buttons must have popped during our struggle. "Fine," I say through gritted teeth. "Give me something I can borrow."

———

After Cesare insists I take a shower with him and change into a pair of his silk pajamas, he finally directs me down the hallway. The sun has risen, drenching the ivory walls in light and casting sharp-edged shadows across the marble floor.

He stops us at a door and knocks, his features softening. There's no doubt that Cesare is fond of my daughter, but I don't believe for one second that a violent psychopath could ever form a friendship with an innocent young girl.

"Hello?" Miranda's sweet voice filters through the door, making my throat thicken. "Who is it?"

"It's me," Cesare says, his grating voice transforming into something gentle, even soothing. "Are you decent?"

It's jarring to witness his duplicity. Is this the mask he shows to his victims to lure them into his trap? Memories of Matteo bubble up to the surface, reminding me of how I once saw him as a father figure.

Heart pounding, I grab Cesare's pajama top. "She doesn't know," I hiss through clenched teeth. "And you're not going to tell her."

He gives me a sharp nod, seeming to understand the importance of keeping quiet.

The door swings open, there she is. Miranda appears, drowning in an identical set of black pajamas. She's so bright-eyed and happy that I forget my worries. My heart swells, crushing the nagging concern that she's wearing Cesare's clothes.

"Rosa!" Miranda pulls my arm and yanks me into a room the size of Cesare's that overlooks the gardens and the pool.

Tears prick at my eyes at the sight of my little girl. I still don't know how long we've spent apart.

Her school backpack lies strewn on the marble floor with a silver dress spilling out along with a pair of heels. Where on earth did she get money for new clothes?

My chest tightens. It's probably the same place she got the phone she snuck into the New Jersey apartment. Cesare.

I force my gaze to the desk, finding an array of pastries, along with a silver pot of what smells like hot chocolate. The brown smudges on the insides of an empty cup confirm my suspicions.

None of that matters, though. She's healthy, happy, but is she hurt? My gaze rakes up and down her slender form, searching for any signs of trauma or injury.

Her cheeks are rosy, with her mouth covered in faint traces of chocolate and crumbs. All I see is the vibrancy of her youth, but then I was ecstatic in the early days with Matteo.

"Are you okay, baby?" I place an arm around her shoulders and pull her in for a hug.

"Don't call me that," she says with a nervous chuckle and slips out from my embrace. Her gaze flickers toward Cesare, who stands in the doorway. "It's embarrassing."

The rejection makes my heart sink to my empty stomach. I iron out my features and dismiss the brush off as teenage sensitivity. It's not like I know what it feels like to be a regular fourteen-year-old.

At her age, I was heavily pregnant and locked in a room with only Mom coming in during the day to bring me food. After the c-section, I only spent a few weeks at my boarding school before Gunther recruited me to the Moirai.

Miranda walks to the other side of the desk, using it as a barrier. She feigns interest in the pastries and selects a chocolate croissant. I used to think she was a prickly child until Cesare told me she remembers the day I shot Mom between the eyes and launched a grenade at Matteo, his brother, and their goons.

"How's your shoulder?" she asks.

I clutch my bullet wound and frown, my gaze darting to Cesare. "It's healing."

"It's not like you to be clumsy, even if you were skiing."

"Skiing," I say with a tight smile, still unable to fathom how Cesare explained my injury. "It just happened so fast. What's all this food?"

"Did you know they have room service?" Miranda says. "I couldn't sleep after all that hot chocolate. Then I stayed up thinking about the man from the airport."

"Miri?" I frown.

She flicks her head toward Cesare. "You know…"

"No, I don't."

"The one who's been hurting all of Cesare's friends."

I suck in a sharp breath, my mind making rapid-fire connections. Cesare blamed Allegra's murder on the Galliano family and he said they were also responsible for Tania's. He told his brother and Gil that Matteo was trying to create discord by choosing women connected to Cesare to make it look like he was killing his exes.

My stomach plummets with the realization that Cesare brought Miranda into the mansion because he is afraid she'd become Matteo's next target.

Because Matteo saw Miranda at the airport.

Fuck.

Did he even recognize his daughter?

FIFTY-NINE

CESARE

Rosalind is giving me whiplash.

Less than an hour ago, I walked in on her, thinking she was a cold-hearted bitch who murdered her own parents out of a twisted form of sibling rivalry. Now, I can't stop comparing her to my pet rabbit, who also had her belly ripped open.

A single piece of information has changed everything I know about Rosalind, casting her from the villain to a mother desperate to protect her child.

My heart swells, pushing painfully against my rib cage. Mom was a fully grown woman who couldn't even stay faithful to Dad. Rosalind was just a child when she had Miranda, yet she went to such lengths to ensure her safety, even if it meant becoming an assassin.

Mom cheated on Dad with the Galliano brothers, which was how I was born. The moment he died and Roman got arrested, she left Benito and me for what she probably thought was better prospects.

I can't see Rosalind ever ditching Miranda. She would set fire to the estate and the whole of Beaumont City to save her daughter from getting hurt. Maybe if I wasn't so blinded by her connection to the Moirai, I could have appreciated her sacrifice.

Leaning against the wall, I watch my girls interact. Rosalind tries to give her daughter a hug, but Miranda shrinks away from her touch.

My brows pinch. Miranda finds Rosalind repellent because she thinks she abducted her. In her mind, her older sister killed her parents and then locked her away at a boarding school. From the way Rosalind's shoulders sag, I'm certain she's hurt by the constant rejection.

I drop my gaze to my bare feet and grimace, unable to shake off the regret at the part I played in damaging their relationship.

Rosalind needs to tell Miranda the truth.

Miranda needs to know she has a mother who loves her desperately. A mother who sold her soul to the Moirai and even sacrificed herself at the first sign of danger.

Guilt grips my throat and squeezes tight as I remember Rosalind's attempts to bargain. She wanted help to safeguard Miranda and leave the Moirai. I laughed, not appreciating how betraying her firm would put her daughter in danger.

"Who was he?" Rosalind says, her voice rough.

My head snaps up, and I meet Rosalind's fiery gaze. "Who was who?"

"The man at the airport," she says through gritted teeth. "The man you felt so strongly about that you scaled up the academy wall and stole my sister in the dead of night."

A chill creeps up my spine as I remember her sitting through the part of dinner where I laid out exactly how Matty Galliano was butchering women to make me look like a murder.

"He's..." The words stick in my throat, and I cough, trying to think up a way to soften the blow. "Can we talk about this outside?"

Rosalind's eyes narrow, and she gives me a terse nod. "Fine."

I turn to Miranda and smile. "Get dressed, love. We're going down for breakfast in an hour."

When Miranda beams, it takes every effort not to look at Rosalind's reaction. Everything I know about Miranda tells me she doesn't offer Rosalind many of her genuine smiles.

Dread mounts as we step out into the hallway and walk out of earshot. Galliano's relentless attempts to estrange me from my family are now putting an innocent girl at risk. That bastard needs to die. His brother too.

"Who saw her at the airport?" Rosalind asks.

"Matty Galliano, but only for a second," I mutter.

She curls her fingers into the lapels of my pajama jacket and slams me against the wall. "We're leaving on the first flight out of town."

Indignation rears to the surface, making me flash my teeth, refusing to let Rosalind's behavior go unchecked. She may think being Miranda's mother gives her the upper hand, but she's still my prisoner, still my little plaything.

The only thing holding me back from breaking her spirit is the thought of the sound carrying down the hallway and reaching Miranda.

"Watch your mouth, pet," I snarl. "You're about to get punished."

"Really?" a male voice drawls.

Benito strides out of his room, dressed in a navy pinstripe suit. We must have startled him with our spat because he's forgotten to wear the prescription-free glasses he thinks makes him look respectable.

"It's bad enough that you dredge her up from the basement and bring to the dinner table. Now, you're dressing her in your monogrammed pajamas and allowing her to sass you in our living space?"

My lip curls. "I've just made an important breakthrough on the Moirai."

Benito's gaze flickers toward Rosalind, with a gleam in his eyes that suggests he wants to take over the mission assigned to me and unleash a fresh round of interrogation.

Over my twitching corpse.

He doesn't get to muscle in on my romance with Rosalind or take over my friendship with Miranda. I won't allow him to swoop in, claim the glory, and have Roman congratulate him for taking down the Moirai.

I step between them to block his view.

"Don't you have a casino to run?" I ask. "Or a croupier to stalk?"

His gaze drops to the CM stitched on my pajama pocket. "Unlike you, I don't shit where I eat."

As he turns back to his room, I say to his retreating back. "With that stick up your ass, I'm surprised you even shit."

His shoulders tense, and he pauses in mid-stride. I brace myself for an insult, a barbed comment, or even a withering glower. Instead, he grins.

"What?" I ask.

Benito shakes his head.

"You finally got a girlfriend?"

His smile widens.

"What the hell does that even mean?"

When Benito disappears into his room, I don't bother to follow. This new woman of his is probably either a figment of his imagination or some cam girl he's paying online through a site like *FuckPal*.

"Well?" Rosalind asks from behind. "Are we going to catch a flight?"

"Yeah," I mutter. "Tell me the name of the school and the city."

———

In a mere twenty minutes, Rosalind has gotten dressed, called the Brunswick Academy on Helsing Island, and arranged a meeting with its headmaster for tomorrow afternoon.

She's stunning in the burgundy pants suit I liberated from Roman's closet. It doesn't count as stealing if the clothes are brand new with attached labels. Besides, anyone spending enough time with the crazy balcony woman can tell she prefers wearing denim and paint-splattered aprons.

When she swipes one of my hair ties to secure her long, mahogany hair into a tight bun, not leaving a single wispy strand to frame her face, I can't help picturing her as a strict femdom.

"What are you doing for passports?" I ask.

"Britt agreed to leave our ID in a locker at the airport," she replies, her lips tightening. "You didn't have to shoot her so close to the heart."

I place a hand over my sternum. "Neither did you, but you don't hear me sniping about it."

She cuts me a glare sharp enough to slice throats. "I didn't hear a thing."

"If this is about the sensory deprivation, I did what was necessary to break your spirit."

Her lips purse, then her features twist like she's about to say something before thinking better of it. "What happens afterward?"

I cross the room, closing the distance between us and stand so close to her I smell hints of magnolia. My nostrils flare. No matter how many times I bathed her, I can never get rid of that scent.

"After what?" I ask.

"After we've settled Miranda into her new school, what's next?"

I run my thumb over her high cheekbone. "You'll stay by my side and help me destroy the Moirai."

"And when they're dead, you'll let me free?"

The corner of my lip lifts into a smirk. "Trust me, pet. You're going to want to stay."

Her features form a blank mask to conceal what she's calculating. As soon as she's sure Miranda is safe behind the walls of her new academy, she'll disappear without a trace.

But not until after I'm too dead to pose a threat to her daughter.

SIXTY

ROSALIND

Since Miranda stayed up half the night enjoying hot chocolate and snacks, I refuse Cesare's offer of breakfast and insist we leave the mansion at once. That should reduce the chances of him changing his mind about helping my daughter and stuffing me back in the basement.

Adrenaline surges as we descend the marble staircase and walk through a grand entrance of high ceilings lit by chandeliers. I'm so close to leaving captivity that I can almost taste freedom.

Cesare's hand clenches around mine, his grip punishing. Every instinct screams at me to pull away, to elbow him in the gut. I endure for the sake of Miranda and keep my gaze on the huge double doors that lead to our salvation.

My first step out into the open makes my knees buckle as I'm overwhelmed with the mingled scents of flowers, freshly cut grass, and juniper. Birds twitter, and a breeze rustles through the leaves of the trees surrounding the mansion's courtyard.

Miranda bounds down the stone steps, turns in a circle and gasps. "This place looks even more awesome in daylight."

I offer her a tight smile. The Montesano mansion is one of the most beautiful buildings in New Alderney, with its Roman architecture and the ivy growing across its limestone exterior. But underneath its elegant facade rests an underbelly of horrors I never want her to witness.

An armored car waits in the courtyard, and a driver exits and opens the back door. Without waiting for permission, Miranda steps in. My stomach lurches. I taught her better not to enter strange vehicles.

As I follow her, Cesare grabs my arm and leans in close. "Remember, she thinks we're a happy couple."

"Is that why you're gripping me hard enough to cause bruises?"

"Do you know what happens to ungrateful pets?" he growls, his voice so deep that it rumbles through my bones and makes my skin tingle.

"Is it any worse than the pussy roulette, the initials carved into my skin, or the time you sewed up my labia?" I whisper hiss.

With an annoyed grunt, he releases my arm and follows Miranda into the car.

I squeeze my eyes shut and exhale a long sigh. Nothing good will come from antagonizing Cesare. I know that intellectually, but I've spent years trying to stop blaming myself for not resisting Matteo.

The first time I confided in a counselor about Matteo's inappropriate touching, she promptly reported it to my mother, who slapped me for trying to ruin her marriage. Her reaction emboldened Matteo to invite his lackeys to join his sick games.

At the time, I blamed myself for trusting the wrong person. Years later, I blamed myself for not reporting it to the authorities. When I joined the Moirai, I learned that the Galliano family owned the police and were already getting away with bigger and more heinous crimes. That's why I hatched a plan to save Miranda from what I'd suffered.

Fighting back is my retribution for the years I spent being powerless.

"Come on, Rosa," Miranda's sweet voice pulls me out from my past.

I roll my shoulders, suck in a deep breath, and remind myself to play along with Cesare, at least until I'm sure Miranda is safe.

When I step into the car's interior, they're both sitting on opposite seats, chuckling over an oversized computer tablet. Cesare explains the workings of a karaoke program with technology to improve the singer's voice, and Miranda gazes up at him with enough adoration to make my stomach churn.

I lower myself into the leather seat beside my daughter and observe their interactions, looking out for any signs of impropriety.

"Does it work for any song?" Miranda asks. "How does it know where to put the auto tune?"

"The AI already knows which note goes with which lyric," Cesare replies. "Go on, try it."

Miranda shoots me a nervous glance, as though she thinks I'll disapprove. "I-It's alright. I don't really like singing."

Cesare scoffs. "That's not what you said last week when you sang for two hours straight."

The car's engine purrs to life, and my heart shrinks at the thought that Miranda finds my presence stifling.

"Go on," I say with what I hope is an encouraging smile. "Have fun."

When she hesitates, Cesare selects one of her favorite K-pop songs, pics up a microphone, and presses another in Miranda's hands. The music starts, and as soon as he starts to sing, she joins in.

My smile falters, my chest tightens, and my lungs stop taking in oxygen. Flames flicker in my gut at the sight of Miranda completely at ease with a psychopath when our relationship feels so stilted.

I want to pull her away from Cesare and scream that he's an even worse murderer than me, but I've never seen her so relaxed and happy. When she smiles, even the corners of her eyes crinkle. Anyone looking from the outside would think I was the interloper, and they were the ones connected by blood.

Cesare's gaze meets mine, and he reaches out a hand and pulls me over to his seat and wraps an arm around my waist. "Come on, pet. Don't be shy."

Miranda lets out a genuine laugh that's melodic and full of joy. "Rosa doesn't sing or dance."

"Of course she does." He kisses my cheek, his lips lingering on my skin.

Miranda bounces on her seat and squeals. "Oh, you're so romantic. I hope someone will love me as much as you love my sister!"

"The little bastard has to go through me first," Cesare growls.

"Cesare," I hiss.

"Miranda has heard far worse language." He turns to her and grins. "Haven't you, love?"

She gives him an identical smile, emboldened by his terrible influence. "Sure have. Everyone at my school cusses."

"It's a good thing you're leaving Tourgis Academy, then." I say, immediately cringing at sounding so strict.

I don't mean to be so controlling and overbearing. The absence of a concerned parental figure is what left a gaping hole Matteo was eager to fill. The time I can spend with Miranda is limited, and whenever we're together, I overcompensate.

The song comes to an end and Miranda picks another duet. Cesare kisses the top of my head and joins her for the next song, so I pick up my burner phone and text Britt's burner.

I tap out:

Are you alright, B?

When three dots appear, I exhale the longest sigh of relief.

Holy hell. How did you escape?

We formed a truce.

The tracking info says you're moving down Alderney Hill. Where are you headed?

Airport.

Don't worry. I'll be on a rooftop with a sniper rifle.

My chest tightens, and my stomach churns. There's no way in hell I can afford an academy as exclusive as Brunswick without

Cesare. Even in the unlikely event that Gunther clawed back the Paris job's bonus from Axel, I can't use that money without it being traced.

The only way Miranda will be safe from the Moirai is if they think I'm wasting away in the Montesano dungeon or dead.

I type:

Don't. He's helping Miri.

Three more dots appear, and I hold my breath. The day I saved Britt in the academy's final exam is the day I made my truest friend. I just don't want that loyalty to cost her life.

When the dots disappear, I stare at the screen, wondering if she's decided to ignore my request not to confront Cesare.

"Who are you texting, pet?" he asks, his voice a low growl.

My heart leaps, and my gaze darts to Miranda, but she's too engrossed in the Korean lyrics to notice the threat. Turning to Cesare, I force a smile and reply in a low voice, "Just checking on the friend you shot."

His eyes narrow. "Sure you're not staging another rescue mission?"

"For the people who colluded to paint me as their master-mind?" I reply, unable to hide the full extent of my resentment.

He leans closer, his hot breath tickling my ear, sending shivers down my spine. "I still think you're their boss."

"You have too much faith in my talents." I try to push him away with my shoulder, but it's as futile as moving a statue.

"Silly pet," he murmurs, his lips grazing the shell of my ear and igniting my skin with unwanted tingles. "You're the most beautiful, deadly, and cunning woman I've ever met. I'm obsessed."

"Stop that," I hiss through clenched teeth.

Miranda chooses this moment to stop singing and ask, "So, when's the wedding?"

My jaw drops, and I gaze into her wide, blue eyes, which radiate nothing but innocence and hope. What kind of nonsense has Cesare put into my little girl's head?

"What makes you think I'm getting married?" I ask, my chest tightening.

She turns off the music, sets down the microphone, and places the tablet on her lap. "Cesare already told me about how much he pined for you when you were dating Leroi."

"Leroi?" I say through clenched teeth, remembering Miranda telling me on the phone that she'd gone to visit his apartment.

"That's right." Cesare pats my thigh with a smirk. "Now that Rosalind has finally given me a chance, I'm never letting her go."

Angry heat flushes through my veins, and it takes every effort not to tear that hand off my leg and snap his fingers. The only thing keeping me from lashing out is the thought of Cesare withdrawing his help.

The excitement of this supposed romance makes Miranda fall back in her seat and clap. "How did you propose?"

"He didn't," I blurt before Cesare can spew more bullshit.

His gaze turns to meet mine with the barest flicker of annoyance. Faking a relationship in exchange for Miranda's schooling is one thing, but he forgets that I'm also supplying priceless information to help him destroy the Moirai. He doesn't get to trap me into marriage.

"That's because I was waiting for the perfect moment," Cesare says, sounding sickeningly earnest. "When a man finds the perfect woman, he has to court her right."

My heart drops as the full extent of his plan slaps me in the face. The only thing Cesare loves about me is my pain, and my suffering has become his addiction. He's using my relationship with my daughter to secure an endless supply.

Sure enough, Miranda clasps her cheeks, her gaze bouncing between Cesare and me. Her eyes glisten, as though Cesare is about to make her dreams come true.

My stomach churns at the thought of him doing something idiotic, like getting on one knee. To make sure he doesn't make any grand declarations, I reach down to the hand on my lap and dig my nails into his skin.

"Miranda," he says, his voice rough with emotion. "Since you're Rosalind's only family, I want to ask for your blessing to make her my wife."

SIXTY-ONE

CESARE

Miranda's excited squeal warms my heart, and the tears of joy gathering in her eyes are worth the pain of Rosalind's sharp nails. Her talons dig into my hand hard enough to draw blood, but it's already too late.

"Cesare!" Miranda launches at me and wraps her arms around my neck. "Of course, you have my blessing."

Chuckling, I pat her on the back, my chest filling with warmth. Taking advantage of Rosalind's desperation to protect Miranda is a dick move, but I never claimed to be a saint. Hell, I intend to use every tool at my disposal to keep Rosalind from ever leaving, and that includes her daughter.

Rosalind peels Miranda off my chest, settles her into her seat, and buckles her seat belt. Miranda is too ecstatic at hearing my intention or she's used to Rosalind's overprotectiveness to protest.

"Are you going to propose now?" Miranda asks, her eyes shining with excitement.

"No," Rosalind says, her voice tight.

Miranda clasps her hands. "Say, yes, Rosa. I want Cesare to be my older brother."

I turn back to Rosalind, my lips lifting into a smirk. "Do you want me to propose in the hotel or at a candlelit dinner?"

Rosalind's features harden into the tight mask I've come to

loathe. It's the one that hides her emotions. "We've barely been acquainted for a week."

"It's been two, pet," I say with a wink, "And we're more than acquaintances."

"Besides, Cesare has loved you from afar since you started dating Leroi," Miranda adds with a nod. "That counts for something."

"It doesn't," Rosalind says from between clenched teeth. "Let's discuss this after eighteen months."

I turn to Miranda with my most crestfallen face and shrug. "Well, the lady has spoken. Looks like you'll have to wait a little longer before you can call me big brother."

Miranda's features tighten. "Why are you refusing Cesare? Is it because he's in the mafia?"

Rosalind's head snaps to the side, her eyes sharpening with accusation. "What did you tell her?"

"Nothing," I say.

"I looked up the Phoenix online. It wasn't too difficult to work out that you were dating someone in the mafia." Miranda curls her hands into fists, her pretty features hardening with determination.

Rosalind gulps at her daughter's outburst, and her facade falters enough for me to catch a flicker of fear. The nails digging into my skin pierce deeper, sending a clear warning to back off. As I lift our joined hands, Rosalind releases her grip.

"I don't care what he does, Rosa. Cesare saved me from getting assaulted, and he doesn't deserve your coldness."

Rosalind's face drops. "What happened? Who assaulted you?"

"I chased off the little bastard," I reply.

"You scared the shit out of him," Miranda says with a broad smile, her eyes shining with admiration. "When I got back to the academy, he left a letter under my door, begging for my forgiveness."

Rosalind turns to look at me, her features pained. I know what she's thinking. One good deed doesn't erase days of torture, but she started it by seducing me under false pretenses, not to mention the attempted murder.

"Can't you see that Cesare is your perfect match?" Miranda asks, her voice straining.

"There are things you don't understand," Rosalind replies through clenched teeth.

"Like what?" Miranda snaps. "Don't act like you're too good for Cesare when you're a killer."

Rosalind stiffens.

Even I flinch at the harshness of her delivery.

"Miranda," I say, but the little girl continues.

"You killed Mom and Dad, took me away from the only home I'd ever known, and then locked me away at a crappy boarding school. Sometimes, you go weeks and months without visiting and the moment you get a boyfriend who could make us a happy family, you push him away."

Rosalind closes her eyes, her head bowing. "I'm sorry you saw that."

"But not sorry you killed our parents?" Miranda screams. "Not sorry for giving me nightmares for watching them die?"

My brows pull together. I nudge Rosalind, urging her to explain why she murdered her family, but she doesn't speak. I would have shut the fuck up if I'd predicted this marriage proposal would open Miranda's wounds.

"Don't be too hard on Rosalind," I say, "There's more to her story—"

"Drop it," Rosalind snaps.

"Drop what?" Miranda gazes at me from the other seat, her eyes glistening with tears. "Do you know why she did it?"

I grimace, wishing I'd keep my mouth shut. The last thing I wanted was to traumatize Miranda. "It's not my story to tell."

"Why do you get to know, and I don't?" Her voice breaks.

"Miri, it's complicated," Rosalind says.

As my gaze bounces from mother to daughter, I can't help thinking about how I discovered the truth about my own parentage.

It was the week Dad had died in the Phoenix of that mysterious heart attack, and I left medical school to be with the family. Mom's reaction to his death had been subdued, even for her.

When Gil told Roman that Dad had been with some blonde at the time of his death, she didn't even flinch.

She was withdrawn and absorbed in her phone, the same way Benito gets when he's fixated on his device. At the time, I thought this was a strange reaction to grief until Roman got arrested outside the funeral house.

That night, she drove out of the gates, leaving only a note. It said her marriage to Dad had been a mistake she'd regretted, and she was going to correct that by joining Tommy Galliano.

I found a second letter beneath my pillow, explaining that she had gone to join my biological father. She wanted to warn me in case someone spilled my secret, but added I should join her in New Jersey.

That was it. No further explanation, just a sentence telling me I wasn't Enzo Montesano's son. I called Mom, but her phone had been disconnected. I wanted to leave for New Jersey, but the cops had just charged Roman for murder.

When we got the news of her wedding to Tommy Galliano, I thought he was my father. Mom didn't respond to any of my emails or to the letters I sent to Galliano's mansion. I saw her on that bastard's arm in the society pages, looking happier than she'd ever been with Dad.

She took her reasons for cheating on Dad to the grave, and I was determined to forget about the contents of her note until Matty Galliano sent me a letter, explaining that he was my biological father. Now, that twisted bastard is trying to turn my brothers against me by making me look like a liability and a mad dog.

"I can't believe you," Miranda's sharp voice slices through my thoughts. "I already saw the worst of what you did. Why can't you just tell me why you killed them in cold blood?"

Leaning into Rosalind's side, I murmur, "Tell her."

Rosalind shakes her head.

A lump forms in my throat. It's not my place to tell Miranda, especially when I only have a fraction of the story. I know the pain of having only slivers of the truth and to be haunted by unanswered questions.

Miranda rises off her seat to sit at my other side. "Can't you share what she told you?"

I wrap an arm around her narrow shoulders. "The last couple of weeks have been rough. Just give her time."

While the little girl cries into my chest, I stare at Rosalind's profile. She's so lost in her thoughts that she hasn't noticed Miranda is taking comfort from her captor.

Sighing, I make a solemn vow to protect them both from the machinations of Matty Galliano... and from myself.

SIXTY-TWO

ROSALIND

Blurting the truth to Cesare was a blessing and a curse. He's helping me get Miranda out of state, away from her father and the Moirai, but he's determined to interfere with my most precious relationship.

There wasn't much time to rebuild my bond with Miranda after I rescued her from Mom and Matteo. Gunther was furious that I'd taken company equipment for a side-quest instead of reporting to him after my first mission.

Miranda still saw me as a monster when I enrolled her at school and for years afterward. I'd hoped the memory of that day would fade with time, but she only built up walls.

I knew there was a chance I would be the villain of her story and hoped to abduct her without shedding blood, but so much went wrong, and I had to adapt.

Leaving Miranda behind to get molested by her father wasn't an option, considering her uncle is also a pimp. I couldn't let her fall into the same trap I did and become another sex toy.

Cesare gives Miranda's shoulder an absent pat, but his attention is fixated on me. He wants me to lay my secrets bare and expose the wounds of my past when I can't even utter the words.

Miranda isn't the only one who's built walls around her heart. Mine are a fortress of festering corpses, broken skeletons, and shame. Even if I wanted to talk, my mouth couldn't form the words.

I can't let her know she's the daughter of two monsters. I also can't allow her to know her father never died.

A tense silence falls across the back of the limo that continues as we walk through the airport. I glance around, my senses on high alert. Every face that passes could be a threat, especially if Matteo or his men have followed Cesare.

Miranda walks by my side, staring straight ahead and avoiding eye contact. I wonder what the hell Cesare could have said to her in such a short amount of time to form such a deep attachment. The loudspeakers overhead announce flight departures in a cacophony of languages that drown out those thoughts.

Matteo spent months paying me special attention, remembering the little things that made me feel special. He eroded the boundaries bit by bit until he became my entire world. Years passed before I realized what was happening was abusive, and by then it was already too late.

Up ahead are signs to the airport lockers, one of the many locations where Britt and I left items necessary for escaping the Moirai. I guide Miranda toward them, and Cesare follows, his posture also rigid.

After retrieving the bag containing our IDs, I steer Miranda to the ladies' bathroom and usher her inside.

The door closes behind us, muffling the sounds of the airport.

"I already went earlier," she says, her gaze darting to the door.

I pull her toward the bathroom sinks. "What happened between you and Cesare when I was gone?"

Her brows pull together. "What do you mean?"

"Do you remember what I taught you about grooming?"

She flinches, her features clouding with hurt. "Of course, but Cesare isn't like that."

"You've only met him twice," I reply.

"He's the best thing that ever happened to us, and you're about to mess it up."

"Explain."

"He's fun, and not an unfeeling robot. He's generous and lets me eat whatever I want. He cares more about my happiness and isn't obsessed with how I'm doing at school. When I'm with him, it's like having a cool uncle or a protective big brother, but you're like an overbearing headmistress."

My jaw tightens. Cesare gets to enjoy the luxury of being carefree when he's grown up with loving parents, older brothers, and protective bodyguards. His home is a fortress, and he has enough resources to handle the Moirai. He doesn't lose sleep worrying about Miranda's future when he can solve all his problems with money.

I inhale a deep breath and push down my frustration. Maybe he's right and I need to tell her the truth, but I can't traumatize her immediately before she starts a new school.

If she discovers I'm her mother, she'll want to know her father. One quick search in google later, she'll reach out to that sadistic bastard.

She isn't yet mature enough to handle the truth. I pause for the woman exiting a stall to wash her hands and turn on the hairdryer before turning to face Miranda.

"If I'm unfeeling, it's because I've had to make tough decisions. Decisions you're not ready to understand."

She raises her chin. "Cesare trusted me enough to tell me about the man hurting his friends."

"Men like Cesare are dangerous."

"And so are you," she spits.

I wince, the barb sinking like a dagger because she's right. "You need to understand that everything I've ever done was to keep you safe."

"But not happy." She folds her arms across her chest.

The hand dryer shuts off, plunging us both in silence. I watch the woman walk out of the bathroom before turning back to Miranda.

"The place I took you from wasn't a safe environment," I say, my voice tight. "I didn't want you to grow up the same way I did."

She rolls her eyes before glancing away. "That still doesn't explain why you'd turn down someone as good for you as Cesare."

Because he's despicable. Because he's toxic. Because he's a

terrible influence on my girl. Because he makes me confront a part of me that enjoys pain and degradation.

"Cesare might be fun, but he's also reckless, and he's not above using you as a pawn."

She scoffs. "Do you think I'm stupid?"

My brow furrows. "What are you talking about?"

"He only likes me because I'm your sister and that's okay. He's completely obsessed with you."

I grimace. He's obsessed with keeping me as a plaything. He's obsessed with my threshold for pain. He's obsessed with breaking through my calm exterior and watching me squirm.

"And he's not a groomer," she adds. "Groomers try to convince their victims that they're special or something. Cesare always steers the conversation to you. He isn't even remotely interested in me."

Maybe she has a point. Cesare had suggested homeschooling Miranda, but he didn't object when I wanted to send her to Helsing Island. That's the opposite of what happened to me.

When Mom signed me up for a boarding school, Matteo refused, wanting to keep me close. The only time he agreed to send me away was after the c-section, when I was no longer his type.

None of this matters because Cesare won't live long enough to pose any kind of threat.

A stall door opens, and Britt walks out, making Miranda scowl. "I'm going to wait outside with Cesare."

"Don't." I reach for her shoulder, but she shrugs me off and walks to the door.

"Let me get her." Britt rushes toward Miranda

I grab her wrist. "Let her go."

Britt scowls. "You're not seriously going to leave her alone with that psychopath?"

"She'll be safe for a few minutes," I mutter, my gaze scanning my best friend's thinner form. "Are you on medical leave?"

"Everyone's slacking off while Dr. Daniel's on vacation," she replies with a shrug.

For the first time since leaving captivity, I smile. Not returning to the Moirai means not submitting to the medical procedures I promised Dr. Daniel in exchange for giving me clearance to rescue Miranda.

I pull Britt in for a hug. "It's good to see you, but you can't stay."

"Is the rest of the team still alive?" she asks. "Gunther's telling everyone they got demoted to the catacombs to supervise waste disposal."

"Axel is dead, and the rest are still in a dungeon." I pull back from the hug and place both hands on her shoulders. "Don't return to HQ."

"Something happening?" She cocks her head.

"The Montesano brothers are holding an entire team hostage, and all Gunther has given them in return is a ceasefire."

Her lip curls with disgust. "The firm doesn't give a shit."

"Everyone is disposable," I reply. "It's time for that plan you had to leave and never return."

"What will you do?"

"When Miranda is safe, I'll take care of Cesare."

SIXTY-THREE

CESARE

The last leg of our flight to Helsing Island is strained, and not just because of the turbulence. I don't know what happened between Rosalind and Miranda in the restroom, but the tension between them hangs in the air like a noose.

The more time I spend with them, the more I feel like a piece of shit. Miranda isn't just a replacement for the younger sibling I always wanted, and Rosalind isn't just a beautiful and challenging little toy.

They're people with complicated emotions and a strained connection. Their relationship was already fragile, and my interference only made it worse. Miranda's resentment comes from her believing she's an orphan being controlled by her callous abductor. The poor kid doesn't realize she has a loving mother who sold her soul to keep her safe.

And I can't believe Rosalind's strength.

After everything I did to her, she's still willing to work with me for the sake of her daughter. I know in the pit of my gut that this truce will end with a bullet through my head, which is why I need to convince her I'm more valuable to her alive.

I'm not just saying that out of self-preservation. There's something about seeing a mother trying to protect her child that makes a bastard like me want to do better, be better.

The airport in Helsing Island is so drab and small that threats would stick out like flashing neon signs. That doesn't stop Rosalind and me from walking through the terminal with our head swiveling for any hint of Galliano's goons.

All we find are eco-tourists kitted out in mountain gear and parents escorting teenage kids. According to the posters adorning the terminal's walls, we're in some kind of nature reserve. The entire place is a paradise for hikers and birdwatchers.

By the time we step outside into the cool, damp air, the sun has already dipped behind a distant mountain, painting the sky with streaks of blood. This place feels a world away from Beaumont City.

Miranda keeps her eyes downcast, and her posture slumped. I place a hand on her shoulder and murmur, "This is temporary. We'll pull you out as soon as I've dealt with that man."

Rosalind bristles. It isn't my place to make these promises, but Miranda can't spend her life locked away.

She nods and offers me a tight smile that slices into me like a dagger. Once again, I feel like an asshole for straining their relationship.

We take a cab to the island's north side, passing lush hills to reach a village where every other store either caters to the school or sells souvenirs. I would compare the street to something out of *Harry Potter,* but the school looms from a hill, casting everything in shadow.

Since Rosalind spent the morning ordering Miranda's school supplies online to be delivered to her room, the only thing left for us to do is pick up a uniform and some casual clothes she's going to need for the evenings and weekends.

The woman running the school outfitters ushers Miranda into a changing room and makes Rosalind and me wait in the parents' seats. I don't correct her because the thought of being anything to Miranda warms my heart.

Rosalind sits a chair away from me, but I scoot beside her and lean into her side. "Tell me about the Moirai. What's the threat? How many assassins?"

She shifts further into the wall. "Sixteen full assassins, four team leaders, eighty support staff."

"I thought they were bigger."

"So did I," she mutters. "I also thought there were offices all over the country and overseas. Now, I think that was bullshit."

"What do you mean?"

"Every time someone doesn't return from an assignment, our supervisor says they were promoted or demoted to another office."

"But you think they're dead."

"Or abducted," she says, her tone sharp with accusation.

"That's what he said about you before your escape?" I ask.

She nods. "Britt told me he announced I'd been transferred to Zurich."

My brows rise, and I glare at the side of her face, incredulous that my clever little assassin could allow herself to be hoodwinked. "How the fuck did you people not notice anything until now?"

"Operatives don't just disappear into thin air," she snaps. "They're still available via email, text and on video conferences. They just never physically return to the local HQ."

"AI?"

Her lips tighten, and she stares down at her lap. "The firm has enough material on us to make it seem like we're in another location. It's all just a huge illusion to make us think we're invincible."

"Is that why the asshole in HQ doesn't give a shit about the hostages?"

The door opens, and Miranda appears from the changing room, dressed in an all-gray uniform that's even more dour than what Roman had to wear on death row. And she understandably looks pissed.

"Turn around." Rosalind says. "Is it comfortable?"

Miranda places her hands on her hips. "That's not the point. Look at me."

The woman sniffs. "Our uniform is designed to make all students equal."

Rosalind rises off her seat. "What can we do to make the uniforms look more unique?"

"Individuality within the classroom is discouraged."

"Answer the question," I growl.

The woman flinches. "Each student is permitted hair accessories in the regulation colors, as well as stud earrings in white gold or silver, along with one discreet necklace."

"Pack up the uniform and have them sent to the academy," I say.

When Miranda and the women disappear behind the fitting room door, Rosalind turns to me and hisses, "Did you have to be such an asshole?"

"Yes." I fold my arms across my chest. "Now tell me how the Moirai can survive if its assassins keep dying or getting captured?"

She bristles as though I've insulted her family, then runs her fingers through her hair, seeming to realize her misplaced loyalty.

"There's a whole academy of teenagers waiting to fill in the gaps," she replies, her voice low. "Every time a student graduates, they join as an analyst. Think of them like fully trained apprentices, who provide mission support."

"And they get promoted when one of their superiors either dies on the job or gets transferred?" I make air quotes.

She clears her throat. "That's right."

I rise off my seat and walk to the cash register to settle the bill when Miranda emerges from the fitting room. Afterward, we walk through the village looking for a store that sells more than colorful sweaters knitted from the local wool.

Questions rattle through my mind as they enter the first boutique offering something close to women's fashion. How the hell did Rosalind get sucked into an academy for assassins, and how did the Moirai keep something like that hidden?

My phone buzzes, so I lean against the wall and check who's sending messages. It's a voicemail from an unknown number. Holding my breath, I press play, and hope to fuck it isn't my stalker.

"Cesare, it's Dad," says a voice sounding hoarse with tears.

I grind my teeth, wanting to delete it, but I force myself to listen in case he says anything that might endanger Miranda.

"You didn't call me about the gift I left in your parking lot, so I'm giving you forty-eight hours to call me back or I'll deliver another to your gates."

A sharp breath hisses through my teeth. Fuck the Moirai.

Those assassins can wait. This sick bastard needs to be the first I kill. I replay the voicemail, memorize the number he gave me, and walk out into the street.

The worst part about Galliano's ultimatum is that I can't call him back from Helsing Island, not even from a burner phone, in case he traces my location.

But I also can't allow another of my exes to die.

SIXTY-FOUR

CESARE

Blood roars in my ears as I pound the cobblestone streets, and every instinct screams at me to call Galliano's bluff. But I can't when there's a chance he'll make good on his threats. What if someone is tracking us right now from a rooftop? There's no way to tell if that bastard knows I'm here with Rosalind and Miranda.

The connection in Helsing Island is even spottier than the reception at the top of Alderney Hill. Luckily for me, the store down the street doubles as an Internet cafe with a satellite link.

After paying for an hour, I find a corner, download an e-SIM and dial the number.

He answers in two rings, breathing hard down the phone. "Cesare?"

"I already told my brothers it's you who's killing women," I snarl. "They think you want to frame me the same way Capello framed Roman."

"Thank god," Galliano says, his voice choked. "When you stopped responding to my calls, I lost control. You make me so crazy."

My gut churns with a mix of rage and revulsion. I've only met the man once at the airport, yet he's acting lovestruck.

"This creepy shit ends now," I growl.

"Don't do this to me, son. I've already lost so much," he sobs.

I grind my teeth, wanting to reach through the phone and ring his scaly neck. This man doesn't need a son, he needs a straight-jacket, followed by several sedatives and a shot of strychnine.

"Get this straight. No amount of women you kill will ever make me join your family. All you're doing is inspiring me to make your death more painful," I say through gritted teeth.

"You'd kill your own father?" he croaks.

"My father is dead," I snap. "You're just a sick fuck with an infatuation."

The line falls silent, save for his rasping breath. I can almost imagine the gears turning in his addled head. I should hang up, leave the cafe and return to the boutique. He asked for a phone call, and I complied. But the Galliano brothers never know how to quit.

After a gut-churning silence, he finally speaks. "You can't outrun your blood," he says, his voice barely above a whisper. "It always finds a way back."

The line goes dead, and I collapse against the wall. If his knowledge about my life extended beyond my exes, he would know about Miranda and Rosalind. That he didn't bring them up means they're safe.

I return to the boutique, where the girls are sorting out an array of clothing with the salesclerk. The bell rings as I enter, and Miranda turns to me, her mood lifting.

The soft classical music and soothing scents of lavender and vanilla aroma do little to ease my nerves. But the sight of Miranda striding toward me with a bright smile pushes thoughts of Galliano to the background.

"You came back," she says, her eyes as mournful as an aban-doned puppy.

My chest tightens. Is it my imagination or does Miranda need me as a buffer between her and Rosalind? It's impossible to tell, since I can't imagine what it's like to be in her position. I rub the back of my head and grimace.

"Sorry, love. Problems at work."

Her needy expression melts, giving way to eyes so sparkling that I preen in the light of her admiration.

"Problems at your nightclub?" she asks.

"Something like that," I mutter, not wanting to sour her mood with talk of Galliano. I flick my head to the other side of the boutique, where it looks like Rosalind is trying to reduce the pile of items Miranda chose. "Find anything nice, love?"

She shuffles on her feet, her gaze dropping to the floor. "I'm sorry about my sister."

"What do you mean?"

"She means well, but she can be a bitch."

A bitch.

Rosalind is a mother. A survivor. The only woman who captures my attention so completely. No one, not even Miranda, gets to dismiss her as a bitch.

"Don't talk about her like that," I say, my voice firming. "Life outside school is hard on women, especially those without protection. Rosalind makes more sacrifices for you than you can imagine. If her shell is hard, that's because of everything she's had to endure."

"How hard is investigative journalism?" She claps a hand over her mouth and gazes up at me through wide eyes.

"What?" I ask with a frown.

Miranda's breath quickens as if she's revealed something wrong, and it takes a few seconds to realize she also doesn't know Rosalind's true profession.

"You think she's writing an exposé on the mafia?" I ask with a smile.

Miranda freezes.

"She isn't. I already know about her job at the New Alderney Times and a lot more of her secrets. Just give her a break."

"You're just saying that because you're in love," she says.

"She's beautiful, fierce, and strong," I say with a smile, thinking about how much my pet has endured and how prettily she suffers. "Everything a man like me could ever want in a woman."

She raises her brows. "Even though she acts like you're the dirt beneath her toenails?"

"She's treating me mean to keep me keen," I say with a wink. "Has Rosalind ever raised a hand against you?"

"Of course not."

I nod. "And does she work hard to provide you with everything you need?"

"Yes..." She frowns.

"And when she gives you a hard time, what is that about?"

Miranda glares at her feet and scowls.

"Come on, love." I lift her chin, making our eyes meet. "Think."

"I suppose she wants me to study and be healthy," Miranda mutters. "But she acts like she's my mom."

My stomach flips, and it takes every ounce of effort to maintain a poker face. "Final question."

Miranda nods and gulps.

"Have you ever asked her why she did what she did?"

She turns her head to the side, which tells me the answer is no.

"Rosalind loves you more than you could imagine," I say, my voice low. "She just has a different way of expressing her emotions."

"I suppose she told you?"

"She shows me every day how much you're her priority."

Miranda shuffles on her feet, huffs and puffs and looks so sweet that I can forgive her for almost anything. "Alright," she says. "I won't call her a bitch."

We return to Rosalind's side, where I tell the clerk to wrap up everything Miranda selected and deliver the packages to the academy. Rosalind and Miranda leave with a change of clothes both for tonight and for our meeting with the head mistress in the morning.

After a short cab ride to the mountain, I check into our suite at the Brunswick Hotel under the name Charles Montague. It's more luxurious on the inside compared to its gothic exterior, and the other guests look to be parents visiting their children at the school.

Our suite is a quaint, two-bedroom affair, tucked away at the top of the hotel. There's a living area with a marble fireplace burning in one end surrounded by burgundy sofas that match the tapestries and drapes. On the other side of the room is a discreet kitchenette and dining table for the families who don't want to venture out of the mountain. An entire wall of windows provides a panoramic view of the village.

By now, the sun has set, and the streets below are lit up with warm lights. I stand by the window and lose myself in the scene. Anything right now is a distraction from thinking about that conversation with Galliano.

The man needs to die, but he's too well guarded. Every time I pull a weapon on the bastard, he has at least four men training guns on my head. He's ten steps ahead, with more manpower, more resources, and a ruthlessness that has no limits.

The worst part about this threat is I can't tell my brothers the truth. Matty Galliano was one of the people behind our family's downfall. Benito and Roman might not immediately cast me out, but our relationship would change for the worse the moment they discover I am related to those snakes.

"Oh my god!" Miranda squeals from one of the bedrooms. "This is gorgeous. Let me see yours."

She rushes out of her room and across the lounge into the second door, almost colliding with Rosalind who stands a foot away from the doorway with her shoulders hunched up to her ears.

Snapping out of my reverie, I follow Miranda into the master bedroom, where she's already flitting about, exploring every corner with the enthusiasm of a hummingbird.

The room is tasteful, with a four-poster bed along one wall that's draped in rich, dark velvet. If this were one of our hotels, Dad would want to burn the worn mahogany furniture and replace it with something modern.

"Don't you like it, Rosa?" Miranda asks, her voice giddy.

Rosalind remains in the doorway, still and silent. I glance around to find her eyes burning with the threat of violence. When I turn to see what's making her seethe, the corner of my mouth tugs into a smile.

There's only one bed.

SIXTY-FIVE

ROSALIND

All the tension I've felt since becoming Cesare's prisoner rears to the surface, forming a tight band of resentment around my chest. I had faith that I would escape captivity one way or another and I accepted tolerating him for a while until my daughter was safe.

But what I can't accept are these sleeping arrangements. The four-poster bed belongs in a bodice ripper romance, where the blushing heroine gets ravished by the shirtless scoundrel.

I booked a family suite with three rooms. Three, so we could all have separate beds, but Cesare must have changed my reservation to this two-roomed monstrosity.

He stares at me in my periphery, his gaze burning bright. I can almost see that aggravating face of his arranged into a rakish smile. After everything he's put me through, the wretched bastard thinks he can get some ass.

"Let me light the fireplace," Miranda cries. "That will make the room extra romantic."

I grind my teeth and Cesare chuckles. "Need any help, love?"

"Nope! We have fires in our dorms all the time."

She bounds toward the mantle, kneels at the fireplace, and selects from a pile of logs. Cesare steps closer, his eyes still boring into the side of my face.

He places his large hand on the small of my back, setting my nerves alight. Heat surges through my veins and burns the surface of my skin. I step away, my jaw tightening. All that prolonged time in captivity has trained my body to welcome his touch.

"Where are the matches?" Miranda rises from the other side of the bed, looking from side to side like a little meerkat.

Cesare prowls toward her, and every instinct screams at me to grab his arm, but I don't want to alarm Miranda. He might be a monster, but his affection for my daughter is genuine.

I overheard all the nice things he said about me in the boutique. He could have spilled my secret to make a point to Miranda about the sacrifices I made to keep her safe, but he respected my decision.

Groomers isolate their victims. They don't build bridges between them and their parents. Matteo encouraged Mom to attend girls' trips with his men's wives, leaving us to have daddy-daughter time where he would make me feel like he was the only person who truly cared. The only one who saw me and not some lonely little kid.

Cesare is a different kind of manipulator. His focus isn't on separating me from Miranda. He wants to create a bond between us all. If Miranda sees him as a cool uncle, then I'll be forced to keep him in our life.

He reaches into his back pocket and pulls out a silver lighter, making her eyes light up. Then he turns to me and grins. "Come on, pet. You're missing all the fun."

I shake my head and fold my arms across my chest, leaving them both to work on the fireplace. Miranda takes the lighter and instructs Cesare how to arrange the timber for the best flame with a tone of authority that makes me smile.

They work together like they've known each other for a lifetime, and mirror each other's soft smiles. I stand rooted on the other side of the room, forever the outsider. My throat burns, the backs of my eyes sting, and the tension around my chest tightens until I can barely breathe.

Why is Miranda so at ease with Cesare? She knows he's in the mafia and must assume he's also a killer. Why does he get her smiles and laughter and warmth, and I get reluctant glances and no hugs?

I've never seen her so joyful and radiant. The glow of the fire illuminates their faces, making them appear more like family than me and my own flesh and blood.

Cesare turns to me, his smile flickering the moment he takes in my expression. I jerk my head to the side, not wanting him to revel in my pain. It would be so easy to accuse him of forging a connection to Miranda out of spite, but the joy in his features when he's with her is genuine.

Hell, he doesn't even smile like that when he's with me.

My heart pounds so hard that I can't hear what he says when he leans into her and whispers something in her ear. She pulls back with a frown, which makes him give her an encouraging nod. They sit together for a few more moments, exchanging hushed words, while I stand by the doorway like an intruder.

Miranda stands, smooths down her top, and squares her shoulders. "Good night, Cesare."

"Night, love," he says, his voice filled with affection.

She marches around the mahogany four-poster bed, her eyes focused, and her jaw set. I gulp, my heart racing. Will she acknowledge my presence or sweep past without a word?

Cesare rises from the fireplace and watches her approach me. His presence reminds me that I'm being stupid. If I can endure all manner of humiliation in his captivity, then I can handle a little rejection.

If I want her to speak to me, I need to make the first move.

"Good night," I begin, but she wraps her arms around my neck and pulls me into an embrace.

I suck in a breath, taking in her delicate floral scent. Miranda has never once hugged me back, let alone initiated physical touch. My arms wrap around her petite frame as if she might disappear.

Closing my eyes, I savor the moment. Her heart beats as fast as mine as though she's nervous, perhaps even scared. The last time she welcomed my touch, I turned around and shot Mom between the eyes.

"Good night, Rosa." Her sweet voice melts my heart. "I'm sorry for being ungrateful."

My eyes widen. "No," I blurt. "You're not—"

"I shouldn't have told your new boyfriend our secrets. That was wrong. I could have ruined your relationship."

My mind whirrs. What did she say to Cesare?

She pulls back and gazes up at me, her eyes shining and bright. "One day, when you're ready, will you tell me why?"

My throat thickens. I part my lips but make no sound. How could I ever tell this beautiful little creature she's the product of something so ugly? That for the entire time I was pregnant with her, I wanted to die? I don't even have the words to begin.

"Take your time, Rosa." She squeezes my arm and walks out of the room.

I turn to stare at her retreating back, wondering when on earth she became so mature or so compassionate. She didn't inherit that personality trait from her father and sure as hell didn't get it from me.

Maybe someone at Tourgis Academy taught her how to view the world in shades of gray, but I know that isn't right. It's Cesare and what he said to her at the boutique. I know he views me through a peculiar lens and sees a bunch of qualities that I lack. Thanks to his twisted obsession, she sees me as more than just her evil sister.

As she disappears through the door of her room, Cesare's larger body presses into mine. He wraps his arms around my waist and presses his lips on my temple.

"You were beautiful, pet," he murmurs into my hair. "All that raw emotion when you looked at her. One day, you're going to be like that with me."

My spine stiffens.

Every time I think Cesare Montesano might have a bone of humanity, he proves me wrong.

That asshole is only saying that because he wants me to take care of his boner.

SIXTY-SIX

CESARE

Seeing how desperately Rosalind clings to her daughter has restored my faith in women. Her cheeks are flushed, her eyes glisten with tears, and her beautiful features glow with rapture.

I want that unwavering love for myself, and I'm going to get it.

It's only a matter of time.

I press my nose in Rosalind's hair, inhaling the sweet scent of magnolia. It's a flower I used to associate with maternal betrayal, but now it only reminds me of my pretty pet.

She stiffens in my embrace and adjusts her stance like she's readying herself to toss me over her shoulder. I tighten my grip around her waist and anchor her weight to mine.

"What are you doing?" she hisses.

"Come to bed." I grind my hard cock into her ass, enjoying her sharp intake of breath. It could be surprise, or maybe even a little anger, but I can almost guarantee she's aroused.

"You've got some nerve," she snaps, in a low whisper. "I'd rather sleep in the fireplace than share a bed with you."

"I prefer your skin unmarked, but if that's what it takes—"

She slams an elbow into my ribs, knocking all the air from my lungs. Pain splinters across my chest, and my grip releases for the fraction of a second she needs to break free.

My nostrils flare. "Control yourself or I'll keep you tethered."

"Get fucked." She turns on her heel and storms toward the closed door.

I follow her. "Where are you going?"

"To sleep on the couch."

"How will you explain that to Miranda?" I place both palms on the door and cage her with my arms. "You heard her. She's always wanted a big brother."

Rosalind whirls around, her eyes flashing. "She doesn't know you're a psychopath."

"I don't know about that."

Her eyes narrow. "What do you mean?"

"She said I was perfect for you, the woman who killed her parents."

Rosalind's lips part with a protest, but I add, "She knows I'm a villain because she read about me online. Whatever she found made her think I'm a match for her murderous big sister."

Her ferocious scowl is proof that I've broken through her stoic barrier. "There it is," I say, my voice breathy with awe. "You only show your true emotions with people you love, like Miranda. And me."

"You're delusional." She ducks out from under my arms and walks around the bed to the shag pile rug. "If you insist on keeping me in the room, I'll sleep in front of the fire."

"What if she comes in during the middle of the night?"

"She won't."

"What if she has another nightmare?"

Rosalind turns around, her eyes widening. "What are you talking about?"

"She remembers the day you took her so vividly because it replays in her dreams." I cross the room, closing the distance between us.

Face paling, her body goes rigid, and her eyes search mine. "You're lying."

"I'm only repeating what I heard. Did you ever get her therapy?"

Her posture deflates, and she bows her head, answering with a broken whisper. "I thought…" She shudders. "Miranda was so young. I thought that over time, she would forget."

"Tell her," I say. "If she sees that day as a rescue rather than an abduction…"

"I will." She nods as though trying to convince herself. "Soon."

"Come to bed, pet. Let's put aside our differences until we've settled Miranda into her new school. Afterward, you can go back to wanting me dead."

She huffs a bitter laugh, her gaze flickering between me and the canopied bed. Toeing off my shoes and socks, I keep my features even, and force my lips not to smirk.

My intentions toward Miranda are wholesome. I want her safe, happy, and well-adjusted. It's my intentions toward Rosalind that are far from innocent.

I want to break through the rest of her outer shell and reach her inner core. I want to peel away her armor, layer by silken layer, until she's vulnerable and raw. I want to revel in her submission, her strength. I want to bask in the surrender of her spirit.

Rosalind belongs to me, and I will stop at nothing to make her mine.

Keeping my gaze fixed on hers, I unbutton my shirt, making sure to take my sweet time. She pretends to hate my guts, but she loves my body. Her eyes drop to my exposed chest the way they always do whenever I undress.

She can't help herself. No matter how much she pretends not to be affected, I'm a source of endless fascination. Rosalind can't get enough of my tattoos. She's mesmerized by the way the ink shifts with my movements.

"We're meeting the headmistress first thing tomorrow." I deepen my voice, adding an edge of command. "After that, we'll plot the downfall of the Moirai. That's not something you can do when deprived of sleep."

When her tongue darts out to lick her lips, I bite back a groan. How the hell can one woman be so tempting?

"Alright," she says. "I'll get into bed with you, but there will be no touching."

"I can't make any promises." I unbuckle my belt, and the clink of metal has her gaze dropping to my silk-covered erection.

Her lips tighten with disapproval. "And you're going to wear pajamas."

"I sleep naked," I say with a grin.

Her gaze snaps to meet mine, her scowl barely concealing her arousal. "Keep the boxers."

"Fine." I drop my pants, step out of the puddle of fabric and walk to the mattress.

Rosalind's gaze follows my movements, her breath quickening as I slide beneath the cotton sheets. There's no doubt in my mind that her body wants mine as much as mine craves hers. But she's stubborn, set in her ways. She likely still sees me as an enemy, when I want to be her savior.

She hesitates by the fireplace before she slides off the suit jacket, folding it over the back of a chair, revealing the outline of her beautiful ass. I chuckle. My pet must have gone to the same school of uptightness as Benito, only she makes it look attractive.

"What's so funny?" she asks.

"You're rigid when you're not playing a character," I say.

She unbuttons her pants, letting them slide down her toned thighs. Instead of leaving them pooled at her feet, she picks them up and straightens them out with precision and grace, then drapes them on top of the jacket.

"You can tell all that because I don't leave my clothes on the floor like a slob?" she asks.

The insult evaporates under the heat of my desire. I'm too entranced at the way her silk blouse clings to her full breasts, revealing the outline of her stiff nipples. When I borrowed the outfit from Roman's closet, the crazy balcony woman's bras were several sizes too small.

Rosalind's body is athletic, curvaceous, and powerful. She's the perfect blend of femininity and strength, an exquisite creature I want to break apart and rebuild to my tastes. I lean forward, taking in every movement as she continues her unintentional strip tease.

When she finally pulls the top over her head and exposes those lush breasts, my breath catches. I've seen her naked so many times that the outline of her body is etched in my memory in glorious technicolor, but watching her undress for me is an altogether different form of seduction.

Her skin glows in the fire's amber light, accentuating every dip and contour of her curves. She lets the garment fall on top of the pile of clothes and turns to me with a frown.

"You're staring," she says, her voice sharp with accusation.

"Come on, pet. It's nothing I haven't already licked before."

My voice is thick with desire, and I don't bother to conceal my arousal. Rosalind knows what she's getting into when she slips into this bed. Everything that happens from this moment happens with her consent.

She walks to the other side of the mattress, her gaze dropping to the erection tenting the sheets. "Don't get any dumb ideas."

"Believe me, beautiful, nothing about touching you could ever be stupid."

SIXTY-SEVEN

ROSALIND

Denial is a hell of a drug. It's the reason I'm considering getting into bed with the psychopath who's kept me captive, subjected me to torture, humiliation, and blackmail.

If I deny it hard enough, I can convince myself that I don't want that sculpted body or that huge, pierced cock. His eyes burn hotter than the fire, which makes sense, considering he's the devil.

The embers in the fireplace crackle and pop, casting flickering shadows that dance across his chiseled pecs. With those intricate skull tattoos, his body is a masterpiece.

I should sleep on a chair or the rug or anywhere other than sharing his bed, but there's a sick part of me that responds to Cesare and even craves his touch.

"Scared, pet?" he says, his voice.

"Hardly," I say with a scoff.

"Then don't stand there all night. We have an early start."

The thought of tomorrow's meeting is what gets me pulling back the sheets and sliding into the bed, not the prospect of sex with Cesare. I curl up on my side with my back to the fiend, telling myself I won't make the first move.

I glare into the flames, my heart pounding as the mattress shifts with his weight. He slides closer, enough for his body heat to warm my back, but he doesn't reach out a hand.

The pulse between my thighs quickens, and wetness drenches my pussy. I grind my teeth, hating that I'm getting aroused at the mere promise of his touch.

Tension mounts for several heartbeats, and I curl my hands into fists. The snap and crackle of the fire fades in the echo of the roar of blood between my ears.

Why is he lying there, watching the back of my head? I thought by now, he'd make his move. Grab my throat, pin me onto my front and pound into me from behind.

Or something.

But he's just lying at my back... breathing.

I swallow hard, my throat suddenly dry from all the frustration. What the fuck is he doing? The silence between us is maddening. My breath quickens, my skin tingles, my body thrums with anticipation.

This is psychological torture. There's no way I can fall asleep with the threat of Cesare hanging over my head.

"What the hell are you doing?" I growl.

"Problem, pet?" he asks, his voice so deep I feel its vibrations deep in my core.

I don't need to turn around to know he's smirking. This asshole is enjoying this brand of mental manipulation.

"Get fucked," I snap.

"Is that a request?"

I huff a laugh. "Try it and I'll break your fingers."

"Reverse psychology won't work on me, pet," he says. "If you're horny, you only need to ask."

I snort, because the suggestion is ridiculous. As if I would ever ask that maniac for sexual favors. He'll probably misinterpret any request as an admission that I want to be his pet. Which I don't. I don't want to be his anything.

He rolls away, withdrawing his body heat, and groans.

I twist around and shoot him my most venomous glare. He stares at the ceiling. The light flickering on his chiseled profile makes the bastard look like the god of hate sex.

"What are you doing now?"

"Can't sleep."

"Why the fuck not?"

"Boxers are too tight."

My gaze travels down to the bulge straining under the sheets. Maybe it's a trick of the light, but I'm sure I see the outline of his pierced cock.

"Not my problem." I turn around, the movement aggravating my swollen clit.

When he groans again, my nostrils flare. This new version of Cesare who isn't doing everything he can to make me suffer is keeping me off balance. This gentleman act is infuriating.

"You're so full of shit," I mutter.

"What's that, pet?" he asks.

"I can't fall asleep with you acting so strange," I say. "It's unsettling. And stop calling me pet."

"You belong to me. You and—"

Before he can finish his sentence, I throw a punch. He catches my fist and pins me to the mattress, rolling me onto my back. I strike with my free hand into his throat, but he grabs that too, and holds both of my wrists above my head.

He glares down at me with burning eyes, his lips pulled back in a manic grin. Somehow, in the struggle, he positioned himself between my spread legs. He grinds his silk-covered cock into my clit, sending a bolt of pleasure.

"Little pet wants to play."

Of course. I should have known. Cesare is the predator who only likes moving targets. If I'm not fighting him, he's not interested.

"Let go of me." I buck my hips, trying to throw him off, but the movement only creates delicious friction.

"What are you going to do? Gouge out my eyes?" he asks.

"I will if you keep looking at me, you psycho."

He rolls his hips, grinding that hot erection into my pussy. "You're enjoying this, pet."

I shake my head. "You're delusional."

"And you're in denial." He brings my wrists together and clamps them together with one hand. "You can break out of this hold anytime you want, but you won't because you like me too much."

His infuriating grin glows in the semi-darkness. Squirming

beneath his larger body, I jerk my head to the side to avoid listening to his bullshit. "There's nothing I enjoy about you, asshole."

With his free hand, he grips my throat and cuts off my air, making my heart jolt. I glare up at him with my teeth clenched.

"Your stitches have melted, pet. That sweet little pussy of yours is ready to be fucked."

"How the fuck would you know about that? Did you stuff your cock inside me while I was sedated?"

He scoffs. "Do I look like I can't get a woman?"

"Maybe once but not twice," I snap. "Your ugliness is on the inside."

"What are you saying pet?" he purrs, "That I'm hot?"

"You're a fucking maniac—"

His grip around my throat tightens, cutting off my words as the world swims in a dizzying whirlpool. His eyes gleam with a dangerous mix of fury and amusement.

"Perhaps," he says, his voice silky and dark. "But you're the one rubbing her erect nipples on my chest, while squirming against my cock."

"Fuck you." I snap out a sharp breath, feeling my vision blur and narrow.

The room tilts, and my senses go haywire. His grip around my wrist tightens, feeling like it might leave bruises. Wetness seeps through my panties, adding to the friction against my clit. My body moves against his, chasing the pleasure.

"Fight back, pet," he growls, confirming my suspicions.

Cesare enjoys the hunt. He loves the feel of me struggling against his grip.

"Let go of my wrists, and I'll give you a fight," I say through clenched teeth.

Chuckling, he leans down and clamps his teeth into the juncture of my neck. Electricity shoots through my nerves, transforming pain into pleasure. My hips convulse, grinding my pussy against his hot, thick erection.

"That's it, pet," he murmurs, his lips brushing against my neck. "Rub that needy clit against your master's cock. Show me how much you want it."

A cry rips from my throat, mingling frustration with fury. How the hell did I end up pinned beneath this loathsome creature, my body betraying me for another hit of spine-tingling pleasure?

Denial.

I hate Cesare. I hate how he's slithered under my skin. I hate his unwavering attention. I hate how he's the only man in a lifetime who's ever made me feel alive. I hate that he's charmed my daughter. I hate how he's a psychopath, yet is careful not to cross certain lines of consent.

His psychological warfare is working. He's even got me thinking I crave his touch.

Pleasure ignites my nerves, and I release a guttural moan. His grip around my throat tightens, and my vision turns black. A constellation of stars fills the darkness, dancing, spinning, picking up speed as my lungs fight for air.

Oblivion races on the edges of my senses. My instincts scream at me to free my wrists and end this madness, but I thrash beneath his grip, desperate for release.

Pressure builds behind my clit with an approaching orgasm. I move faster against him, chasing the ecstasy. My movements become more desperate, my body eager to climax before I succumb to the dark.

"Come for me, pet," he growls.

His words set off an explosive orgasm that sends out shockwaves of rapture. Every nerve ending in my body tingles. My senses heightened to the point of pain. I convulse, my mouth opening in a silent scream, my core spasming and clenching and under his command.

The hand around my neck loosens, and I suck in a noisy breath.

"Good girl," he says before shuddering and soaking my belly with spurts of his hot release.

I've heard of hate sex, but hate frottage?

Maybe Cesare's psychological tactics are finally working because I'm no longer hiding from the truth. It pains me to admit how much I want more of his freaky shit.

SIXTY-EIGHT

CESARE

I lie on top of Rosalind and loosen my grip around her throat to gaze into her eyes, heavy-lidded and sensual after her orgasm. They hold a rawness, a beauty I have never fully appreciated until this moment. She's never looked so mesmerizing.

She's glowing from her climax with her cheeks flushed pink, and her lips parted and red. I commit her beauty to memory because this rare vulnerability from her is fleeting. Soon enough, she'll close herself off and retreat behind her usual mask of control.

I can't blame her.

The way I treated her is unforgivable, even if she entered my life as an assassin. I release her throat, caressing her reddened skin, and let my fingers glide down to stroke her collarbones.

When she closes her eyes and turns her head to the side, I get the hint and move out from between her parted legs. I lie beside her, propping myself up on one elbow to study her in the firelight.

Her cold body language speaks volumes. I might have trained her to crave my touch, but she wants nothing to do with me. She remains quiet, her chest rising and falling with each breath. A thin layer of sweat covers her skin, making it glimmer.

I can't tell if she feels hatred or shame, but I've seen how she is with Miranda. I want to make space in her heart for me.

"Rosalind," I murmur, my voice rough. "What I did to you wasn't right. I should never have taken it so far—"

"What part?" she interjects bitterly, her fingers closing around the sheets. "When you shoved a loaded gun up my vagina or when you continually used Miranda as bait?"

I grimace at the thought of Miranda losing the last remaining member of her family just because I wanted to enact a sick fantasy. Back then, I was furious after being outsmarted by a woman I'd dismissed as Leroi's cast off. She was an enemy I wanted to have fun with and before gathering information and killing.

Now, I see her as so much more. I see her strength, her determination, her passion, her love. Rosalind is the woman I want by my side, not against me.

"I regret all of it," I finally answer and brush a strand of hair off her face. "I should have made a deal the moment I had you restrained."

"Instead, you made me a plaything." Her jaw clenches and the muscles around her neck tense as though she's reliving days of being restrained.

"You don't understand."

I reach out to touch her hand, to offer her a little comfort, but she whirls around to meet my gaze, her hazel eyes flashing.

"What makes a man decide to take women as property?"

My lips flatten against my clenched teeth. "You make it sound like I do this every day."

"How do I know you don't? You have an entire basement full of cells and you're holding at least two other women against their will—that I know of."

"If you think I touched them, I didn't. Our family doctor is keeping them under sedation. The only hostage I ever got close to was you."

Her lips purse as though she's insulted that I might think she's jealous. "Answer my question."

"You're the only woman I've ever wanted to keep." I stroke

her hair, trying to emphasize the point. "The only one who's ever held my interest for longer than a few nights."

"Why?"

"Because you're challenging," I say.

"That's why you were going to drive me to the gates after we fucked?"

Hope warms my chest, and I hold back a smile. If she's offended that I tried to kick her out on our first night, that's promising. It means she wants my attention.

"You want the truth?" I ask.

She nods.

"You were an amazing fuck, but you kept getting under my skin with all those insults." I trace my fingers along her jawline.

Her lips twitch, and she tilts her head, giving me better access to her neck.

"Think that's funny?" I ask.

"I can't believe you were so easy to rile up back then," she says. "It's like you've evolved."

"You keep me on my toes," I mutter, wanting to kiss her soft lips.

She closes her eyes again and turns, giving me a delectable view of her back. I scoot behind her and spoon her body. To my surprise, she doesn't flinch. My palm slides over her belly and I rub slow circles over her supple flesh, wondering how it would feel if she ever got pregnant with my child.

I smile at the thought of having a smaller version of Rosalind. A dark-haired little girl with bright hazel eyes who would look to me for protection and guidance. With Rosalind as her mother and me as her doting father, she would never feel abandoned and isolated.

My cock swells at the thought of filling her with so much cum that she bears my child, and I tighten my arm around her waist. My lips find her neck and I gently nuzzle her skin, lost in the thought of owning Rosalind so completely.

She shivers under my touch, but doesn't pull away. "Go the fuck to sleep."

"Promise you'll stay."

"What are you talking about?" She turns her head but doesn't make eye contact.

"You're planning to kill me after I've transferred the funds to the academy."

"No," she says with a bite.

I close my teeth around her earlobe. "Don't lie to me."

She pauses for several moments before exhaling a long sigh. "I was thinking about doing it after we dealt with the Moirai."

"Was?" I ask, my chest lifting with hope.

"You're not worth the effort." She closes her fingers around my arm and shoves it off her waist.

"Because you're warming to me," I say with a smirk.

She huffs. "You wish."

"I really am sorry, Rosalind," I say, meaning every word.

She rolls onto her back and turns to meet my gaze with eyes so pained I draw back to suck in a breath. What I did to her cut deeper than anything she had to endure as part of being an assassin. I think of how she was impregnated by her father and stiffen.

Could I be as bad as that incestuous rapist?

"You can't erase days of torture with money and an apology," she says.

"What can I do?"

She closes her eyes and shakes her head as though the question is far too complex for a simple answer. I study the contours of her face in the flickering light of the fire, marveling at the way her long lashes rest perfectly against her high cheekbones.

I wanted to see what was beneath her beautiful, strong exterior and I found someone I can't let go.

My gut twists with regret. I should have treated her better, given her more respect. Even if she was part of a plot to destroy the family, I should have recognized she was a pawn in a much larger game.

"Give us our freedom," she murmurs.

My heart lurches at the thought of releasing Rosalind and losing her forever. "That's the one thing I can't do, pet. Once I set you free from your employer, you will belong to me."

"Then your apology means nothing." She turns her back to me and faces the fire.

The chill in her voice makes me pull her against my chest.

"One day, you'll come to realize that belonging to me isn't a sentence. You'll be free to do whatever you want. If you don't want to live in the mansion with the family, I'll buy you any kind of home you desire. We can have our own space. Be a family. It's all yours."

"As long as I spend the rest of my life with you?" she grinds out.

"Would that be so bad?"

She shoves me off her and scoots away from me on the mattress. "Go to sleep."

Frustration pounds through my skull, and I release an angry sigh. "Someday, you'll understand that you're not a caged bird, but a phoenix waiting to rise from the ashes, and I'm the man who will set you free."

"Freedom in captivity. Isn't that an oxymoron?"

"You've lived your entire life under someone else's control," I say. "If it wasn't the bastard who got you pregnant, then it was the Moirai."

"What makes you different?"

"Because I won't use and discard you. I want to make you happy. I want to protect you. I want to give you the world."

Turning back, she looks at me. I see a flicker of something beyond the reflection of the flames. Curiosity, perhaps, with the faintest hint of hope.

Silence stretches between us for what feels like an eternity, broken only by the crackle of the fire. Her shoulders rise and fall with each deep breath, but she doesn't respond. She also doesn't turn away.

This is not a rejection.

Maybe, I'm finally getting through.

SIXTY-NINE

ROSALIND

Hours after returning to the Montesano mansion, I'm still on a high from my departure with Miranda. Cesare didn't even have to tell her to give me a hug. She did it all on her own, even though it was brief. The last time she looked at me without resentment or recoiling was before I shot Mom.

That connection, that moment of love, was more effective than Cesare's attempts to tether me to his world.

I watch him from one of the leather armchairs in his black-and-white bedroom. He's standing at the window overlooking the garden, scowling down at his phone. His muscles strain against the fabric of his fitted black shirt, a clear sign of his tension.

His phone has been blowing up with messages since we stepped off the plane. It isn't business, because he hasn't texted back or returned the calls. From the way his features shutter with suppressed rage, I would guess the sender is a former girlfriend.

None of this is my concern, but I can't help but wonder what kind of woman is capable of crawling so deeply under his skin.

"Why won't the Moirai just accept Roman's cash offer?" he asks for the second time.

I take a sip of my water and sigh. "Would you hire a firm of assassins known to accept bribes?"

He scowls but doesn't answer.

"Most of our targets are men and women too powerful for the average criminal to kill without consequences."

"And?"

"In this world, power equals money. If a target can offer us twice what the client paid, then doing business with the Moirai becomes a risk."

He grunts. "They only give half a shit about the hostages."

"If you're saying that because of the ceasefire, you're wrong."

"What's that all about?"

"They only agreed to stop attacking because they're buying time for the next graduation run."

"What does that mean?" He sinks into the arm of my chair and drapes his arm around my shoulder.

"My boss is in charge of the Montesano mission, and he's lost all his key assassins. All the other teams are busy with their own jobs, so he'll have to wait for new recruits."

At his blank look, I set down my glass and explain how the Moirai works. It's something I didn't completely figure out until recently because its practices are shrouded in secrecy and deceit.

"Everyone directly involved with the killing is either an analyst or assassin."

He threads his fingers through my hair. "Got it."

"The Moirai don't take on recruits from the outside world. They recruit runaways and scout potentials from boarding schools outside New Alderney and then take them out of their classes for specialized training."

Cesare scowls. "Let me get this straight. They pluck kids out of schools?"

"That's exactly what I'm saying. They target kids whose parents don't invite them back for breaks because they're the ones who won't be missed."

He slides his fingers out of my hair and strokes my neck. "That's how you joined?"

"Yes." My voice thickens. "But that's not the point. Gunther has a manpower problem that can only be solved after the next round of eighteen-year-olds graduate."

"And when is that?"

"Depending on how many assassins get promoted overseas,

the last Friday of the quarter. And promotions are euphemisms for dying or getting lost on the job."

He stares at my profile for several moments until my skin burns. I sit still, endure his scrutiny, and ready myself to deflect the inevitable question.

"How could your mother not notice you weren't at school?"

"We have a tiny window to take down the Moirai at its weakest," I say, my voice tightening. "Now isn't the time to dredge up ancient history."

He cradles the back of my head and leans close, his lips grazing the shell of my ear. "You're deflecting, pet."

"Leave it." I rise off the seat and walk to the window and stare out across the lawn.

At this time of the afternoon, the setting sun casts long shadows across the manicured lawn. Gardeners tend to the flowerbeds with holsters attached to their overalls. I focus on the workers to take my mind off the past. When that doesn't work, I shift my attention to the stone pathway leading to the swimming pool.

The limestone building is bathed in an orange light that gives it an illusion of warmth. It seems like a lifetime ago since Cesare brought me there for a one-night stand. Beyond the limestone columns and floor-to-ceiling windows are signs of movement. I wonder what they did to the pool house after they moved Cesare's BDSM furniture to the basement.

"Have you ever spoken to anyone about what happened?" His deep voice intrudes on my musings, making my shoulders stiffen.

"Britt knows," I reply. "And we fixed it."

Cesare growls. "That's not what I mean."

"That subject is off limits," I say through clenched teeth.

He rises off the armchair and appears behind me, his body heat warming my back. "You need to talk about it to someone, pet."

"Perhaps, but that person isn't you." I turn around and meet his harsh blue eyes. "I could never open up to the man who held me captive for days and forced me to endure all kinds of torture for his amusement."

His features pinch, but he doesn't speak, because he knows it's the truth. Every time I tried to negotiate, he laughed. He continues staring, his gaze boring into mine, silently urging me to continue.

"I sure as hell won't share the details of my past with a man who will use my trauma as ammunition, because that's what you did each time you took Miranda and waved that knowledge like a red flag."

"She was always safe."

"How was I supposed to know you'd be different with her when all I'd ever seen of you was sadism?"

He glances away, finally seeming to understand. "I told you I'm sorry."

"Yeah, you did." I walk around him and settle back into the armchair. "But trust isn't something that can be bought."

I open a laptop and stare at its screen, trying to create some distance. Cesare seems to think what we did in bed last night was some kind of breakthrough. But very little has changed. I'm still his captive. He still calls me his pet. The only difference is that I've agreed to help him defeat the assassins.

"Back to the subject at hand," I say, my voice sharp. "The Moirai only agreed to the ceasefire because they've run out of manpower to complete the Montesano job."

"So they're just buying time before their new recruits are ready to replace the hostage?" he asks.

"That's right."

"How do we stop the graduation?"

I raise my head and stare up at him with a frown, he looks back, his gaze earnest. "We don't. All the leaders will be at the headquarters, observing the new recruits in a room full of screens, while everyone lower down in the ranks will be supervising graduation. That's the perfect time to attack."

"Where's the HQ?" he asks.

"There's no point in telling you because it's deep underground and protected by advanced security. We're going to send a Trojan horse."

"Okay, and how's that going to work?"

"Call the Moirai and offer to send back the hostages in

exchange for a longer ceasefire. They're going to send a small team to collect them and maybe even take that opportunity to complete the mission."

He scowls. "What part of that is Trojan?"

"Put sacks over your men's upper bodies and send them to the Moirai instead."

"That won't get them past the security."

"No need." I close the laptop. "Your men will take the people sent to collect them by surprise and add them to your group of hostages."

His eyes widen. "That's…"

"Brilliant?" The corner of my lips lift into a smile.

"Fuck." He punches his palm and races to the door. "Let's do this."

Smiling, I rise off the armchair and walk across the room. Gunther is relying on recruiting what's left of his team to replace the hostages, but he's about to lose much more.

If everything goes right, then it won't just be me who is free from the Moirai, but every young person they're about to corrupt.

As I reach the door, it swings shut. I grab the knob, but he's already turning the lock.

"Cesare," I snarl.

"Leave it with me, pet," he says from the other side of the door. "I'll be back later with the results."

I slam my fist on the wood, my molars grinding hard enough to crack the enamel. No matter how many times this bastard tries to be nice, he's still my captor.

Fuck Cesare.

The moment we take down the Moirai, he's screwed.

SEVENTY

CESARE

I run down the hallway, unable to shake off Rosalind's words. She still thinks I'm her captor and maybe she's right.

What she doesn't understand is that she's holding me captive, too. Her regal presence, her strategic mind, and her capacity for unconditional love has captured my heart. I bound down the stairs, passing a maid who drops her tray and curses under her breath. Snickering at her loss of composure, I reach the ground floor, trying to catch Roman before he disappears into the pool house to watch over his crazy balcony woman.

I find him behind his desk, scowling over a pile of contracts. His expression is almost identical to the portrait of him hanging on the wall.

Gil sits on an armchair beside the mahogany bookshelf, watching porn on mute. As I peer over his shoulder, he turns off the screen.

"What were you doing at the airport?" Roman asks.

"Rosalind and I came to a truce. Part of that included taking her out of town on an errand."

My brother raises his brows, wanting me to continue, but I shake my head. I trust him, but shutting the fuck up is the only way to stop a secret from spreading like a rash.

"If you're asking why I didn't use the jet, it's because someone at the airport leaked my movements to Galliano."

He nods. "The sooner those bastards are dead, the better it's going to be for us all. Tell me about this truce."

I repeat Rosalind's plan to trick the Moirai into handing us more hostages. Gil barks a laugh and gets up to gather a group of men, while Roman picks up the phone.

"You sure they're going to believe we'd swap their assassins for more time?" he asks.

"They're suffering from a staff shortage and won't send anyone important," I reply with a shrug. "What have we got to lose?"

"Fine." Roman taps a few commands into his screen. "But I'm coming with you, and we're both wearing armor."

"Let me wake up the hostages. The Moirai will probably want proof that they're still alive."

I leave the study and continue down the hallway to the stairs leading to the wine cellar. When my phone buzzes with a text, I know it's coming from an unknown number. My gut churns with a bitter brew of resentment and regret. Galliano is getting desperate. Now that I've responded to him once, he won't stop badgering me until I put him out of his misery.

After passing through the door disguised as a barrel, I navigate the maze of hallways toward the basement infirmary. My footsteps echo against the stone walls as I pass the empty cells, wondering if I'll ever have the chance to house either of the Galliano brothers. I need to know how they seduced Mom.

Our family has used the space beneath the mansion for all kinds of shit, starting with great-grandfather Paolo's distillery. Dad used to tell us that Alderney Hill was covered in fragrant trees like juniper and balsam fir to disguise the smell of crime. All those juniper berries eventually found their way into the gin.

I shake off that thought. Dwelling on juniper trees will only lead to memories of the magnolia trees I destroyed after Mom's death.

Fuck. Finding out that Rosalind is also a mother has me thinking more about Mom. The two women are nothing alike.

Mom was petite with blonde hair, blue eyes, and a warm smile, while Rosalind is a dark-haired Amazonian warrior.

I shouldn't make comparisons, shouldn't ask myself why Rosalind would kill for Miranda and why Mom left us in the dust, but my brain won't stop obsessing on their differences.

Rosalind is strong, loyal, enduring—everything Mom wasn't. Rosalind walked back into my clutches after I first took Miranda, knowing exactly what she would suffer. No matter what I tried, I couldn't break through her hard shell until she thought her child was under threat.

Mom and I were so close. Our relationship wasn't fractured like Miranda and Rosalind's, so how could Mom leave us so easily? What was so unlovable about me?

I find Dr. Brunelli napping on the cot in the infirmary's corner with a paperback half open on his chest. His mustache twitches under each heavy snore, making me huff a laugh.

"What are you reading?" I ask.

Jerking awake, he sits upright, his glasses slipping down the bridge of his nose. "Cesare, you're back." He blinks as though processing my question before glancing down at his book. "Just an old psychology book."

"How are the hostages?"

"Stable and sedated." His gaze flicks to the wall clock. "It's almost time to replace their IVs."

"Wake them up. Roman's just called their boss, who will want proof they're still alive."

He tilts his head to the side and cracks his neck. "Anything else?"

"Prepare for more."

"How many?"

"Don't know yet, but it can't be more than another ten."

His brows form a deep V. "Do I need to warn you about the dangers of keeping them under long-term sedation?"

"Someone should have warned them about the dangers of trying to assassinate a Montesano."

The smile he gives me is weak and not because he's tired or he thinks I'm corny. Dr. Brunelli knows I'm not a Montesano. He found out while I was going cold turkey. At least that's what he claims, but I wouldn't be surprised if he heard it directly from Mom. He took care of all her pregnancies.

He swings his legs off the cot and lands on the concrete floor with a soft thud. "Leave it with me," he says. "I'll make sure they're alert for any phone calls."

"No painkillers for the broken fingers," I say. "These fuckers are more dangerous than the average foot soldier, especially the women."

Dr. Brunelli chuckles. "I've been dealing with the family's enemies longer than you've been alive. Don't worry about me."

Satisfied that he has the situation under control, I continue back toward the wine cellar, wondering if everyone who works for the Moirai has a story like Rosalind's.

I step out of the cellar and into the stairwell, remembering that all four of the assassins we captured conspired to frame Rosalind for arranging the shooting. Now that my illusions of her being an invincible leader have shattered, I realize they only wanted her to take the fall.

Sofia descends the stairs, her shoulders hunched, and her jacket pulled tightly around her neck.

I stare up at her from the bottom of the stairs, my muscles tensing. "Are you alright?"

She snaps out of her musings and places a trembling hand over her mouth. Her eyes dart around the stairwell like she's searching for threats.

"What's wrong?" I ask.

"I went to St. Anne's Church, you know, the one in the Parisii Cemetery, to put some flowers on my brother's grave," she says through rasping breaths. "His plot is behind the row of weeping willows next to the new rectory."

I nod, already picturing the spot. "What happened?"

"Someone crept up on me from behind. I didn't see his face, but he was wearing a mask."

I picture the masked man who appeared in the Phoenix's video cameras. Matty must have come after Sofia when I wouldn't answer his texts.

I bound up the steps to close the distance and place a hand on her shoulder. "Was he armed?"

"Only with a massive knife." She shudders. "I shot him and didn't stop running until I reached the car."

"When did this happen?"

She stares ahead, trapped in the memory of the attack. "I don't know. Just now. I came straight here to grab some bottles."

Guilt claws its way into my chest and squeezes my heart. I wrap my arms around Sofia's shoulders and pull her into a tight hug. "If I'd known you would be a target, I would have warned you not to leave the gates."

She sighs against my chest. "Benito said the Galliano brothers might go after your women, but I didn't think that included me."

Drawing back, I gaze down into dark brown eyes the same shade as my brothers. "We should have known. You're this family's backbone. When Mom left, it was you who stepped up."

The smile she gives me is strained. "How long will this feud last?"

"I need to find where the hell Matty Galliano is hiding. He keeps popping up in New Alderney, so he must be nearby. I'll do everything I can to destroy him before his next strike."

She nods. "He can't get away with this."

I grip her shoulders. "I'm sorry you got dragged into this mess. When he killed Tania, I thought it was a one-time thing he did because his brother was in the club with Roman. When he killed Allegra, I knew it was a pattern, but there was a more obvious target I needed to protect."

"Don't blame yourself," she says with a soft smile and places a hand on my cheek. "Benito warned me, but I had to lay flowers for my brother's birthday."

"Did you manage to hit him before you got away?"

"I didn't bother looking back. By the time I reached the car, the parking lot was empty." She pats my cheek once more and continues down the stairs.

My anger mounts with each retreating step. I meant to do something about Galliano the moment I was sure Miranda was safe. Now, it's time to act.

I will kill that cold-hearted bastard, no matter the price.

SEVENTY-ONE

ROSALIND

I pace the bedroom, my blood sizzling. How dare that asshole leave me behind in his locked bedroom? I can break the lock, climb out of the window, turn any of the crap he's keeping here into a weapon, but acting against him might jeopardize our plans to destroy the Moirai.

He only locked me in because he thinks he's caged my mind.

Shit.

Bastard knows too much about my weaknesses, which is why he thinks he can trust me not to trash his room or attempt an escape. He's right, of course. I wouldn't do anything to compromise Miranda's safety.

Now is probably a good time to snoop around his room and dig up some dirt on the asshole. If he's careless enough to leave me in his private sanctuary, then he's practically handing me his secrets.

The only difference between this room and his dungeon are the lack of visible toys. I start with his desk, and rummage through the drawers, finding nothing more than pens, notepads, and a key.

On the far left stands a closet-sized cabinet containing crystal glasses and exotic looking bottles, but none of them are liquor. The refrigerator is filled with bottled water and snacks. If I didn't know any better, I would think Cesare was a recovering alcoholic.

The bookshelf beside it holds leather-bound copies of literature by the Marquis de Sade in French. There's also the German edition of Venus in Furs by Leopold Von Sacher-Masoch, along with other classical works of erotica.

I pull out a copy of Story of O and place it on the armchair for future reference. If I'm going to spend the day reading foreign literature, it may as well be something modern.

After finding nothing else of interest, I stroll into the walk-in closet. The walls are black, reflecting his personality, as are the clothes hanging from the open rails.

I stride to a tall cabinet secured by an ebony door to find it locked, which only piques my interest. A moment later, I'm back with the key I found in his desk drawer and slide it into the lock.

The door opens, revealing a four-foot-tall safe on the floor. The space on top of it is a gun rack of automatic weapons along with meticulously labeled boxes of ammunition, but I'm more interested in the shelf above eye level containing leather albums.

My breath quickens. I reach up and pull down the first album. It's heavier than expected and filled with photos of a beautiful blonde woman with cornflower-blue eyes, holding a dark-haired baby. She reminds me a little of Leroi Montesano's newest plaything.

Forcing down a surge of irritation, I turn the pages, finding more pictures of the same woman and boy, chronicling their lives. It's Cesare and his mother, Lucia.

Occasionally, they're joined by other members of the family. I immediately recognize Enzo, the father, and younger versions of Roman, Benito, and their cousins, Jennifer and Leroi.

Cesare and Lucia are always separate from the others as though they're not part of their family but outsiders. I focus more on the photos of the large gatherings, where the pair of them are less relaxed. Cesare's posture is tense, as if he's perpetually on guard, and Lucia's smile is strained.

The last album contains more recent photos of Cesare and his mother on formal occasions like his high school graduation, business launches, and various society weddings. Cesare's smile is always too rigid, and Lucia's eyes are glazed, looking like she's high on drugs.

I replace the album, my mind whirring at the intensity of the mother-son dynamic. The intel I gathered on Lucia Montesano was limited. She remarried within days of her husband's death and then died two years later during routine cosmetic surgery.

Cesare hasn't had any significant relationships. I heard talk of a girlfriend at medical school who also dropped out in their first year, but it didn't seem relevant. Now I wish I'd dug deeper.

The burner phone he gave me buzzes with a text message. I pull it out of my back pocket to find a photo of Miranda, grinning into the camera wearing a pair of diamond stud earrings.

When did she get those?

Another photo pops up on the screen of a wicker hamper filled with chocolate bars and her hand emerges from the corner, giving her bounty a thumbs up.

My jaw drops. "What the hell?"

Then there's a flurry of messages:

Thank U Rosa!

It's followed by a barrage of hearts and smiling face emoji wearing sunglasses.

My shoulders sag. When did Cesare organize these gifts? That amount of junk food will be detrimental to her health, but I can't help but smile at her enthusiasm.

After taking a gun with a few clips, I lock up the cabinet and return to the armchair to exchange messages with Miranda. Thanks to her new stash of chocolate, she's already made friends with the girl next door, who will give her a tour of the school and its grounds.

I chat with Miranda for the rest of her free period, which is something I couldn't do while at the Moirai. When out on the field, I had to focus on the mission. I also couldn't exchange messages with her inside HQ because all communications were monitored.

Fucking Cesare. The moment I start thinking he's still an asshole, he surprises me with something thoughtful. He didn't even try to take credit for the gifts because the notes attached said they were from me. Warmth fills my chest and I continue texting my little girl. It's hard to deny that his presence has brought us closer together.

When Miranda's lessons start, I make a breakfast of some protein bars from the minibar, wash them down with water, and continue my exploration.

Cesare's bathroom has an oval tub that's large enough for two, along with a separate shower with no sign of chains or hooks. By the looks of things, he doesn't bring women into his private space. At least not the ones he likes to torture.

I run myself a bath, making sure to pour lots of lavender oil in the tub, before immersing myself in the warm, soothing water. All the tightness in my muscles melts away, but I don't think that's because of the bath.

Miranda is happy and safe in her new academy. Cesare and I made sure nobody followed us to Helsing Island, and I'm only days away from getting my freedom from the Moirai.

I close my eyes and luxuriate in the bath, letting the water lap against my skin. The space fills with the scent of lavender, adding to my relaxation.

We're a good team. I have the knowledge to take down my employer and Cesare has the resources. We need weapons, manpower, surveillance, and armored trucks, all of which the Montesano family has in abundance.

Some of the tension I've carried since my demotion releases in a long sigh, and I sink further into the warm water. For the first time in years, I can finally envisage a happy future. It's murky because I'm still Cesare's prisoner, but he's the lesser of all the threats hanging over our necks.

About an hour later, the bedroom door unlocks, and he walks into the bathroom. I glance up to find him shirtless, his features held in a scowl.

I sit up. "Something go wrong?"

"Your plan worked perfectly," he mutters. "We got six more hostages."

I wait for him to continue, but he sits at the edge of the tub and runs a hand through his hair.

"Then what's the problem?" I ask.

"Matty Galliano attacked Sofia."

I stiffen, a sharp breath whistling through my teeth as I picture the family's middle-aged housekeeper. "Did she survive?"

He rises, his hands bunching into fists. "She shot him."

My heart pounds, and I hold on to the edge of the tub. "Is he dead?"

"Don't know. She didn't look back."

"Oh."

The bastard is probably still alive because he's a cockroach. He survived the grenade I launched at him the day I took back my daughter. I'm sure he'll survive a bullet.

He punches his palm. "We need to do something about him, now."

I stare at his broad back, my excitement mounting. Gunther kept me on a short leash after I was demoted for wasting company resources. There wasn't enough time to devote to researching the Galliano family or their latest hideouts.

When I was his stepdaughter, Matteo used to split his time between multiple houses, making him difficult to track. If Cesare can help me hunt him down, that will bring me one step closer to securing Miranda's freedom.

"What do you suggest?" I ask.

"I'm going to text him, arrange a meeting, and shoot him between the eyes," Cesare growls.

"That won't work." I rise from the tub.

He whirls around, his eyes narrowing. "How would you know?"

Panic explodes across my chest. The bathroom is suddenly too warm, and the air too thick. Cesare must never know Miranda is the daughter of a man he despises.

Holding my features into a neutral mask, I reply, "High-ranking men like him don't meet enemies without backup, otherwise there would be no need for assassins."

He hesitates, his jaw flexing, as though battling with some kind of decision.

"What?" I ask.

His expression smooths. "How would you like a job with the Montesano family?"

"I'm not leaving one secret society to join another," I mutter, eager for him to return to the subject.

"Help me take out Tommy and Matty Galliano."

My heart skips several beats. The answer is an emphatic yes, but I need to play it cool and leverage this into something advantageous for Miranda and my future.

"I'm already helping you take down the Moirai," I say. "What are you offering in return for the Galliano brothers?"

"Five hundred grand," he replies. "A piece."

I huff a laugh. "You're joking."

"A million."

My pulse quickens, but I paste over my excitement. "That's the going rate for a high-ranking target, but you're asking me to take out the don of New Jersey and his consigliere."

"What do you want, then?" He folds his arms across his chest and glares at me, his chest rising and falling with rapid breaths.

"My freedom," I say, looking him square in the eye. "And two million each."

Cesare falls silent, his jaw working in a slow grind. He's affronted that I suggested leaving, and I can practically see the gears turning in his head.

I would kill the Galliano brothers for free, but even a million dollars would set up a nice college fund for Miranda and buy us a small family home. We don't need anything lavish. I could get a job as a personal trainer or teaching self-defense.

After what feels like an eternity, he gives a single nod. "Deal."

"I'm going to need more than a one-word answer."

He clenches his teeth. "A written contract?"

"Repeat back our deal in your own words."

His cold eyes harden, never wavering from mine, and the veins in his temples pulse. I can only assume it's at the indignity of being asked to recite terms he finds repugnant.

"You will help me kill Tommy and Matty Galliano," he grinds out, each word sounding pained. "In return, I will pay you two million dollars for each and grant you your freedom."

"And Miranda?" I ask.

"Miranda's too," he says through clenched teeth. "Do we have a deal?"

I hold out my hand. "Deal."

His gaze sweeps down my naked body before settling on my proffered hand. "Seal it with a kiss."

I step out of the bath. "Then you're going to kiss a different set of lips."

SEVENTY-TWO

ROSALIND

Cesare's gaze flickers down to my pussy, and his lips widen into a salacious grin. When he looks up, it's with eyes I can only describe as manic.

It's odd how an expression I once found terrifying is now exhilarating, but then I'm no longer mummified or strapped to a torture table. I'm also not weak with hunger or thirst.

I step forward, closing the distance between us, my body dripping water to the marble floor. His grin fades, replaced with a look of raw hunger that borders on predatory.

Well, I have something he can eat.

"On your knees."

His hand whips out and grabs my throat, cutting off my air. Incandescent blue eyes burn into mine, their irises flickering with danger. "I don't take orders."

"Neither do I."

I break free from his grasp, sweeping my leg in a move that sends him crashing to the marble floor. As he lands on his back with a grunt, I straddle his chest.

"Not today, *pet*," I say with a sneer.

His eyes flash, and he bares his teeth, but there's something in his gaze that borders on amusement. He grabs my hips and tries to buck me off, but I dig my fingers into his hair and lean close.

"Are we going to seal this deal or not?" I ask, my voice breathy.

"You drive a hard bargain," he growls, his fingers tightening on my hips.

"Bet that's not the only thing that's hard."

With a smirk, he flicks his head, motioning for me to take what I want. I clamber up his body and straddle his head, putting all the weight on my legs.

Cesare grabs my hips and pulls me onto his face, making us both groan.

The first swipe of this tongue on my slit feels like being struck by lightning. Bolts of ecstasy surge through my system, setting off up every pleasure center. Gasping, I cling onto his hair, making him growl.

His tongue makes back-and-forth strokes over my clit that make my breath come in shallow pants. I want to squeeze my eyes shut and focus on the sensations, but nothing is more satisfying than looking into Cesare's half-lidded eyes.

Deep groans resound from his mouth, sending vibrations through my core. I roll my hips, riding out the pleasure on his face as my pubic bone grinds against his nose.

He says something, but it's muffled.

"What did you say, pet?" I ask with a smirk. "Use your words."

Rolling his eyes, he lifts me off his hip. "Turn around. I want you facing my cock."

I change position so my ass and pussy completely cover his face. When I glance down, I find his cock straining through his pants, looking desperate for release. I reach down and slide my finger over the cloth-covered length, eliciting another deep groan.

Cesare's tongue swirls around my swollen clit, making my thighs tremble. This time, I place all my weight on his face. A sadistic part of me wants him to suffocate or drown in my juices.

"Pull out my cock," he growls.

With a chuckle, I unzip his pants, releasing that thick length. The four studs on his crown gleam in the light, making me want to ride his cock.

"Suck it," he says.

I slap his shaft, making him bob to the side. "You don't deserve my mouth."

Cesare groans, his tongue moving faster. I continue delivering sharp spanks, turning his cock redder, thicker, juicier. Precum flies out of its tip with every blow, making me groan.

Shit. What is it about this twisted psycho that gets me so excited? I should want a saner man who doesn't torture people in his basement, yet there's something about Cesare Montesano I can't resist.

Pressure builds up around my clit, making it feel like it's doubled in sensitivity. I squeeze my eyes shut and pant through the sensations.

As the strokes of his tongue slow, I wrap my fingers around his shaft and squeeze tight. "I swear to everything that's holy, if you leave me hanging, I'll rip off your cock."

Chuckling, he picks up his pace, laving my clit with such delicious strokes that I swear I can feel every ridge of his tongue.

Pleasure builds and builds until it feels like I might explode. I rock back and forth over his face to increase the friction. Finally, he reaches up and pinches one of my nipples, sending a surge of pain that makes me crack.

My orgasm comes in a hot rush, drenching my system with wave after wave of liquid rapture. I jerk and spasm over Cesare's face as I ride through the powerful sensations, but his hands hold my hips in place. His tongue continues moving in slow circles, prolonging the sweet torment until I'm wrung dry.

"Please," he groans around my folds. "Get on my cock."

He doesn't need to ask me twice.

I rise off his face and shuffle down his torso. His huge, veiny cock lies flush against his abs, leaking streams of precum. After turning around to face him, I straddle his hips and hold his shaft at the base.

Cesare's handsome face is smeared with my juices, but he gazes up at me like I'm the goddess of rapture. For a few heartbeats, I don't see the psychopath who abducted Miranda and made my life a living hell, only a tortured hero with a tragic past.

I shake off that image. My hormones are malfunctioning, and

my judgment is clouded with lust. Now isn't the time to sympathize with my former captor.

"Ride me," he growls.

Maybe he did have to ask me twice, after all.

Squeezing my fingers around his cock hard enough to make him hiss through his teeth, I lower myself onto his crown. The metal balls of his piercings slide over my labia, which I swear is more sensitive since the stitches dissolved.

Cesare holds me steady by the hips as I slide down his cock, letting it stretch me open. The piercings rub against a spot inside me that ignite lightning bolts of bliss.

Shivering, I release a moan. When he's fully sheathed, his hands grip my hips hard enough to bruise. "Stay there," he says, his voice breathy with awe. "I just want to look at you. Memorize how your tight cunt squeezes my cock."

I relax my muscles just to piss him off, and he laughs. It's an expression I've only seen on him in the photo album, a full smile that reaches his eyes and radiates pure joy.

When I squeeze around him, he groans. "Fuck, Rosalind. You have the tightest, sweetest pussy."

"I know." I smirk.

"Move," he rasps. "Please."

Raising my hips, I let him feel the slow drag of my walls against his shaft. His hips buck beneath me in protest of the languid pace, but I ignore him and relish in the press of those piercings.

His hard eyes never leave mine, even as his hands explore my belly, my waist, my breasts. As I roll my hips, he rolls my nipples between his fingers.

He's watching me, studying my expressions as I ride his thick cock. This time, I don't mind his fascination because I'm also transfixed by his face.

A sheen of sweat glistens on his forehead, highlighting the angular lines of his brow. Somehow, while lying beneath me on the marble floor, his hair has spilled loose from its fastening and spreads around his head like a dark halo.

I can't tell if he's a devil or a saint, but his cock feels like heaven. My pussy is so sensitive, I feel every ridge, every vein, every contour of his shaft. One of his four piercings rubs back and forth against a spot that ignites sparks of sensation so intense that I squeeze my eyes shut and bite down on my bottom lip.

"Harder, pet," he growls. "This is your final warning."

Ignoring him, I continue at my steady pace. Maybe it's because I've climaxed already and I'm in no hurry for that second orgasm or maybe I want Cesare to know what it feels like to beg for release. Either way, I keep my rhythm slow and torturous and savor the sounds of his desperation.

His fingers leave my nipples and grip my hips again. He bucks into me, sending an explosion of pleasure that radiates from my core, making me gasp.

In a swift movement, he rolls to the side, sending me crashing on the marble tiles. His palm lands on the back of my head as he pins me to the floor.

I'm lying face-down on the marble with my ass in the air, trying to rise, but he presses his elbow between my shoulder blades, keeping me in place.

"Cesare," I snap.

His lips graze the shell of my ear. "I warned you earlier, and told you to fuck me harder," he growls, his voice guttural and deep. He reenters me with a hard thrust that makes me see stars. "Now, I'll show you what that means."

He fucks me at a brutal pace on the bathroom floor, each thrust a hot lash of pleasure.

"Let go of me, you asshole."

He laughs, the sound cruel. "That's not what you were saying a minute ago. I'm not going to stop until you come apart."

I dig my fingers in the cold marble, trying to buck him off with my hips, but that only increases the friction. His piercings rub against my g-spot with disturbing accuracy, making the muscles of my pussy clench and spasm around his thick cock.

"That's right, pet," he growls. "Fight me."

All traces of affection I might have had toward this bastard evaporate. How could I have ever thought a bunch of photos was proof of Cesare's humanity? He must have cast off his soul and locked it in that safe.

The worst part about this is that he makes my nerve endings

sing. Every part of my body comes alive as he fucks me without mercy or restraint. It's like he's worked out the cheat code to my pleasure and wants to unravel me with a precise mix of humiliation, ecstasy, and pain.

I hate the way he makes me lose control, the way he forces me to feel. Most of all, I hate the way this man brings me closer to my heart's desire: a meaningful relationship with my daughter.

He drives into me, the crown of his cock hitting my cervix with punishing force. It's unyielding, it's ruthless, and it's making me moan into the tiles with each brutal assault. His thrusts reduce me into a bundle of raw nerves.

Every inch of my body becomes hypersensitive. As he fucks me harder, even the draft over my skin feels like a caress.

"I hate you," I gasp out. "As soon as I come, I'll kill—"

He silences me with another wave of pleasure that makes my eyes water.

"You're mine, pet," he growls into my ear, his fingers tightening around the back of my neck. "This beautiful body beneath me. Mine. This sweet little cunt squeezing the life out of my cock. Mine. These sounds of pleasure you can't suppress. Mine."

"Not. For. Long," I say from between clenched teeth.

His sharp laugh makes my skin tingle. "This pleasure that brands you, breaks you, burns you from the inside out. That's mine too. And your hatred, I'll swallow it whole. Because you're going to want me after this is over."

Shivers skitter down my spine at his sinister words, making me aware that I'm screwed. Cesare has found a different way to break my spirit, and it's more effective than torture. Humiliation and resentment course through my veins, mingling with the throbbing pleasure.

Even though I'm being fucked ruthlessly on the bathroom floor, there's a part of me standing on the edge of a precipice, teetering toward a chasm of euphoria.

"Come for me, pet." He reaches between my legs and strokes my aching clit with the same forceful rhythm of his thrusts, coaxing another humiliating moan.

"Not. Your. Pet," I say through clenched teeth.

"Now!" he growls.

The words slam into my psyche like a command.

I want to resist, to deny him this victory. But my traitorous body responds with a seismic orgasm that tears through every fiber of my being.

The pleasure is blinding, blurring everything else into insignificance. I'm flying through a haze of ecstasy, my body dissolving into the ether.

Cesare's laughter echoes through an inferno of sensation, and I'm vaguely aware that he's coming. As my orgasm fades, his lips return to my ear.

"You have a deal," he says, his voice penetrating the haze. "But by the time we've killed the Galliano brothers, you'll be so addicted to me you will never want to leave."

My eyes snap open, and I stare sightlessly into the void. Even as my heartbeat slows, there's no denying that was more intense than anything I've ever experienced. Pleasure still echoes deep in my core, a reminder of the power he wields over my body.

If I don't take control of my desires, I'm afraid Cesare might be right.

SEVENTY-THREE

CESARE

The next morning, after my anger has cooled and after Rosalind hate fucks me until my balls ache for mercy, I'm driving her to one of the armories our family owns across town.

It's a huge warehouse, guarded by some of our most hardened men, where we keep the explosives too volatile to keep beneath the estate. We will need this level of destructive power to penetrate the inner sanctum of the Moirai headquarters.

Rosalind is quiet in the passenger seat, pretending to be busy sending texts to Miranda while her eyes are on the passing buildings. The air is thick with tension and no amount of background music can clear the heavy silence.

Last night changed our dynamic. Both for the better and the worse. Galliano's attack on Sofia got me so worked up emotionally that I agreed to her audacious demand for freedom. Now, she thinks we're equals.

Granted, she's strong, intelligent, highly trained, and lethal, but she will forever be my property. My pet. But I agreed to free her if she killed the Galliano brothers. I'm tempted to make the fatal blow myself and keep Rosalind at my side on a technicality.

The industrial estate comes into sight. It's one of the few with a checkpoint of armed guards around its gates. The buildings behind it stand tall against the sickly yellow sunrise. No one could ever suspect it contains enough weapons to level half the city.

As we approach, the guards exit their checkpoint and ready their weapons. I slow down to lower my window, and they wave me inside.

We park outside a door secured with biometric identification technology, and I step out. Rosalind puts her phone away and follows, her gaze roaming over the building.

Curiosity gnaws at my ego about how our armory compares to the Moirai, but I quell that ridiculous thought. Rosalind has already turned her back on her old firm. It's only a matter of time before she realizes she wants to stay with me.

I open the door and usher her into the cold, sterile space carrying the scent of gunpowder and metal. The lights snap on, illuminating rows upon rows of crates stacked toward the ceiling, each one carefully labeled.

We walk around the boxed guns toward the back of the building where we keep the explosives. Gil once compared the inside of our armory to a Home Depot for militias. It's spacious like a home improvement warehouse, but instead of tools and supplies, it is stocked with weapons of all sizes.

I glance over at Rosalind to gauge her reaction, but she remains stoic. Her gaze scans a carton of grenades and moves onto a box of C-4 explosives with an intensity some might find unnerving. Having a ruthless assassin at my command is exhilarating.

"What do you think?" I ask.

She tilts her head. "There isn't nearly enough to penetrate the Moirai's lower levels, but it's a start."

My jaw drops. "How deep is the building?"

"At least ten stories."

"At least?" I ask.

"I'm not authorized to access the lower levels," she says with a shrug. "Which is why we need more explosive power."

"Leave it with me. I can reach out to other families."

"We need an accelerant," she says.

I raise my brows. "What kind?"

"Mercury nitrovolucite."

"Never heard of it. Is it anything like fulminated mercury?" I think about the TV show where the main character throws a crystal of the compound on the floor to trigger an explosion.

Rosalind makes a see-saw motion with her hand. "It's more stable, which makes it easier to transport. If we can introduce mercury nitrovolucite inside the Moirai HQ before we detonate the bombs, it will increase our chances of destroying even the lowest of levels."

I suck in a deep breath, already picturing how Benito will react to us creating a crater in the middle of Beaumont City. "How much collateral damage are we talking?"

"None." She shakes her head for emphasis. "The building is a mile away from its nearest neighbor. There's no chance of anyone getting hurt."

"Fine. Where do we get your mercury nitrovolucite?"

"Do you have any contacts with full-scale industrial laboratories?"

———

An hour later, we're pulling into an office building a block away from Beaumont City's largest shopping mall. Underneath it is where Roman relocated the meth lab he and Benito rescued from the Galliano brothers.

We take an elevator down to the third level basement and continue through an empty underground parking lot and through two sets of security doors into the sterile laboratory.

Rosalind's gasp is audible over the low hum of machinery, and my chest inflates with pride.

"Impressive," she says, her gaze sweeping past a row of industrial-sized rotary evaporators and up to the wide exhaust ducts snaking across the high ceiling.

We continue past tall distillation columns and a room filled with drums toward where a group of cooks clad in white hazmat suits gather around a counter, checking the purity of their latest batch.

At the sound of our footsteps, my former chemistry lecturer, Dr. Cortese, turns around and waves us over with a glove-covered hand.

My stomach drops at how much she's aged since she and her team were abducted. Her hair has turned gray. She's still beautiful, but her wrinkles have deepened.

What the hell happened to her while the Gallianos held her captive?

I hide my shock with a smile. "Dr. Cortese."

She breaks away from the group and pulls me into a tight hug. "It's so good to see you, Cesare."

Resting her head on my chest, she sighs as though I'm a close friend. I return the hug, noting that Dr. Cortese never showed me this level of affection during her time at the university or even after I introduced her to Roman.

She draws back with a sad smile and is about to say something when her son, Christian, barges in with a broad grin. "What brings you here? Did you graduate?"

My gaze bounces from my former teacher to my former classmate. It looks like Christian is trying to protect his mom. "No." I force my features not to grimace at the reminder of why I dropped out of medical school. "The family business became more urgent, so I had to leave."

They both nod, not needing any further explanation. If Dad hadn't died and Roman hadn't been arrested, the Galliano brothers wouldn't have infiltrated the lab and abducted our cooks.

Stepping back, I sweep an arm toward Rosalind. "My associate needs a large quantity of mercury nitrovolucite."

Rosalind steps forward. "I've only made it on a small scale and as part of a chemistry class, but I can provide a detailed formula and instructions."

Christian ushers her to a part of the counter where they hunch over a notebook, leaving me behind with Dr. Cortese. I turn to the older woman and ask, "Is there somewhere we can talk?"

With a nod, she walks toward a wall of steel shelving units, where there's a door leading to a dormitory of bunks. She wanted them installed for nights when someone needs to stay behind to monitor a batch or can't make it home because of a late-night experiment.

Before I can step toward her, she turns around to face me, her blue eyes etched with pain. "I know you want answers, Cesare. Everyone does." Her voice is ragged, barely louder than the clink of glass beakers from the other side of the room. "I just... We had to produce meth for them. They were so forceful."

Guilt forms a knot in my chest. I hadn't even considered asking her why she cooked for the Galliano brothers. Two psychopathic maniacs and an army of armed lackeys is no match for a science lecturer and a handful of college students.

"Nobody blames you. You did what you had to do to stay alive," I murmur, trying to ease some of her tension.

Sighing, she bows her head, her shoulders deflating with relief. "Those men were monsters."

My chest burns with curiosity. I never understood why Mom would sleep with the Galliano brothers while she was married to Dad, let alone leave us to marry Tommy. Dad had his faults, but he wasn't a psychopath who murdered women for sport.

"Did you meet them?" I ask.

She shudders. "Tommy was a regular visitor. He used to complain that the meth was weak and forced us to develop a better blend."

"But yours was 99.6% pure," I say.

"He wanted something stronger, with a bigger kick, and punished us when we failed."

My brows pull together in a deep frown. "What happened?"

Her gaze lowers. For several seconds, it looks like she won't answer, then she sits on one of the bunks and stares at her lap. "He hurt Christian and threatened to spray his brains across the lab if we didn't make this miracle drug."

I curl my hands into fists. Tommy Galliano doesn't know the first thing about chemistry. If he did, he'd understand that perfection is impossible to surpass.

"What did you do?"

"We formulated something new," she mutters. "It wasn't meth. It was more chemically similar to cocaine. We called it benzo."

"Benzo," I repeat, already knowing it's an abbreviation of cocaine's chemical name.

"It was highly addictive, with even worse side effects than any other drug. Tommy forced Christian to try every batch to make sure it wasn't poisoned or subpar."

My breath quickens. "Is he alright?"

"We developed another formula on the side to help Christian cope with the addition and side effects. We called it pellucid because it worked like an antidote."

"Is he still addicted?" I ask.

"No, but it's taken a toll on his mental health."

I shake my head, disgusted at how Galliano could exploit a mother's love and use her son as a guinea pig. "Is there anything I can do to help?"

"Roman is paying for therapy," she replies with a soft sigh, "But if you ever get the chance to kill Tommy, I want to spit on his face as he dies."

"Galliano won't get away with this," I say, meaning every word. "And if he's still alive when I've finished with him, I'll let you make the killing blow."

She raises her head to meet my gaze, her eyes hardening with determination. "That bastard deserves to burn in hell for what he did to my boy."

Christian bursts into the room, his eyes shining. "Mom. Rosalind is a treasure trove of amazing formulas."

Dr. Cortese stands, her features softening, and joins her son. I follow after her, my heart sinking.

Galliano used Christian as a pawn in his power games, just as I used Miranda against Rosalind. Is there any difference between me and my paternal uncle, or am I equally monstrous?

Apologizing to Rosalind wouldn't be enough.

She probably wants my blood.

SEVENTY-FOUR

ROSALIND

After sharing the formula for mercury nitrovolucite and its instructions with the team, Cesare takes me to another set of elevators that lead directly to the shopping mall. It's just before the lunchtime rush, and the place is filling with shoppers, all oblivious they're standing above a secret laboratory.

A fragrant mix of cuisines from the food court fills the air and makes my stomach rumble. My gaze darts toward a vegan café that produces fresh wheatgrass shots.

"Where are we going?" I ask.

"You need new clothes," he says. "I'm taking you to the Dolce Vita boutique."

"Never heard of it."

He flashes me a smile. "The owner is a distant cousin."

We reach a store front with windows adorned with mannequins displaying designer clothes that wouldn't look out of place on a Paris runway. I can only guess that the price of the garments would exceed a month's salary.

"Are we going to a high-end place that needs me to blend in?" I ask.

He turns to me and frowns. "What do you mean?"

"These clothes are very nice, but I only wear them for work when I'm trying to infiltrate upscale events."

"You've got to wear something," he says.

"Follow me."

I take Cesare to another side of the mall to a large store that sells walking boots, outdoor gear, and practical clothing with no frills. The mannequins are dressed in khaki and flannel, with backpacks slung over their shoulders.

He glares at a green fleece jacket and scoffs. "You going camping?"

Leaning into his side, I murmur, "I sure as hell don't want to hunt down the Galliano brothers in a body con dress and heels."

He snorts a laugh. "Get what you want here, but I'm taking you back to the boutique for something that doesn't make you look like a hiker."

I roll my eyes. If the Moirai wasn't monitoring my bank account, I would walk away from him and spend my own money. Since that isn't an option, I endure Cesare's running commentary about my poor taste in fashion.

"Call me a hobo all you want." I hold up a pair of trekking pants to my waist. "But sometimes, a woman just needs to deliver a flying kick."

He snickers. "Point taken, but khaki?"

"I prefer to wear black."

The image of me decked out in black tactical gear must finally register because he shakes his head and grins. "Fine, but we're going back to the boutique."

"After stopping for something to eat," I say.

His eyes narrow. "I'll take you to one of our restaurants."

"Do they sell shots of wheatgrass?"

His lip curls. "Why the fuck would anyone want to drink juiced grass?"

"Don't knock it until you've tried it." I walk toward a row of tactical boots, leaving him cursing under his breath.

After buying two changes of clothes, we stop at the vegan café. It's empty, save for a red-haired woman with freckles, who greets us with a warm smile.

I order two shots of wheatgrass, a spirulina smoothie, and a kale salad. Cesare glares at the menu as if it's personally offensive.

I take pity on him and order a portobello mushroom burger with sweet potato fries.

"First time here?" asks the red-haired assistant.

His lip curls. "And hopefully my last."

She gives me a sympathetic smile and scurries over to the kitchen. I elbow him in the ribs for being an asshole. "You might actually like the burger."

His cold eyes roam over the café's green decor, his lips tightening with disapproval. "We'll see about that."

When he folds his arms across his chest, I see glimpses of the boy in the photo album. Sometimes, it's hard to reconcile this version of Cesare with the creature in the leather butcher's apron who tortured me for days.

The assistant returns with our drinks, and I pull him toward a nearby table.

Cesare takes a sip of his vegan strawberry mylkshake. I wait for him to gag or whine about the lack of cow's milk, but he simply grunts.

"Thinner than I would prefer, but not bad," he says, his tone gruff.

I knock back my shot of wheatgrass, letting the green liquid infuse my body with a surge of energy. Cesare watches, his lips turning downward with thinly veiled disgust.

"Your turn." I slide the second shot across the table.

"Peer pressure won't work on me, pet," he mutters without even sparing the wheatgrass a glance.

His phone buzzes. He pulls it out of his jacket, checks the screen, and scowls.

"Problems?" I ask.

"It's nothing." He shakes his head, his features smoothing. "Are you satisfied that the mercury nitrovolucite will penetrate the Moirai's lower levels?"

"Yes and no," I reply.

"What does that mean?"

"We're going to need someone to place crystals at strategic points along floors three, six, nine, and twelve, to create a domino effect."

He gives me an eager nod. "Britt?"

I shake my head. "She's already left town."

"Then who?"

"There's a man who was in the academy the year above me, who disappeared with half the class during the graduation run."

He leans forward, resting his chin on his steepled fingers. "I thought leaving the Moirai was impossible."

"This guy is special. They say he joined already fully trained and had already completed a hundred missions by the age of fourteen."

"Child assassins?" Cesare shakes his head, his nostrils flaring. "I'm not surprised he left them."

"He's always at the graduation runs, picking off the weakest candidates."

"Killing them?" he asks with a frown.

"Saving them," I reply, my mind dialing back ten years. "Xero appeared at my graduation run when I was trying to pull Britt out of a pitfall trap. Someone tried to kill her, and she broke her ankle."

Cesare nods, his eyes narrowing.

"It was chaos. I was fighting off other candidates while pulling out my friend and then Xero chased them off with a gun."

"But you didn't run?"

"I took advantage of the opening to get my friend," I say with a shrug. "Xero offered to take Britt, but she refused."

His brows rise. "Take her?"

"People who fail the graduation runs end up indebted to the firm for the cost of their education. Her injury would have added to the amount she owed, so he offered Britt a place in his gang."

"Why did she refuse?" Cesare asks.

My emotion surges, gripping me by the throat. I glance to the side, fighting back the urge to cry. Everything about my daughter's conception and birth still hurts, as does the time we were separated. Most nights, I couldn't sleep, not knowing if she was safe, not knowing if Matteo was sharing her with his twisted lackeys.

"What is it?" Cesare asks.

Forcing down the lump in my throat, I meet his gaze. "I told her my plans to take Miranda after I graduated, and she wanted to help. We completed the graduation run and walked through the finish line together."

"Sounds like a good friend," he says, his eyes softening.

"The best." I take a long sip of my spirulina smoothie, barely tasting the creamy concoction.

Cesare picks up his burger and takes a bite, looking contemplative. We eat without speaking, and I appreciate the silence he's giving me to control my emotions.

My recent captivity has left me more sensitive than ever. I don't have the mental bandwidth to rebuild the protective layers I usually keep around my trauma. It's worn down, leaving me vulnerable and exposed.

I pick at my salad, tune in on the soft background music and the hum of the barista's machine, trying to refocus on the subject. Cesare is uncharacteristically patient and eats his mushroom burger without complaint.

"Xero kept in touch with Britt for a few years," I say. "He also has contacts within the Moirai who owe him favors."

"Other assassins?" he asks.

"Support staff." I set down my fork. "Mostly people not directly involved in the hits but janitors, cleaners, and people in tech."

Nodding, he takes another sip of his shake. "So Xero could get the crystals into the Moirai?"

"I can set up a meeting and ask. If he's poaching assassins before they graduate, then he also has a vested interest in taking the firm down."

Cesare wipes his mouth with a napkin. "Are you sure you can trust him?"

"The only other way to get the mercury nitrovolucite where we need it is for me to return to the Moirai."

"Set up the meeting," he growls.

I down the second shot glass. "Then our next step is the Parisii Cemetery, where we'll bribe a guard to pass on a message into the catacombs."

SEVENTY-FIVE

CESARE

Shortly after finishing a surprisingly edible lunch of vegetables, nuts, and fungus, we get a call from Christian, who's having trouble producing the sample batch.

I return Rosalind to the lab where she decides to stay the night to help the team produce the large quantity of mercury nitrovolucite we need to obliterate the Moirai.

Being around large quantities of drugs makes me antsy, even though I haven't had a craving in years. Not wanting to take any chances, I leave Rosalind behind, stopping at the Parisii Cemetery before returning home.

I slip the guard five hundred-dollar bills along with the number of the burner phone I gave Rosalind. This Xero character might be more willing to cooperate with another disgruntled assassin than with a member of the Montesano family.

The text I got earlier was a summons from Roman to attend another family event. Since I'm no longer trying to torture Rosalind, I didn't want to bring her along only for her to be insulted by Benito or to suffer Roman's withering glares.

My brothers only see her as the woman who stalked Leroi, tricked me into ingesting drugs, and then passed on vital information about our security to the Moirai. They don't see the beautiful, courageous woman who's fiercely protective of the people she loves.

After the two of us take down the Galliano brothers and destroy the Moirai, my brothers will have no choice but to show Rosalind some well-deserved respect.

When I get home, Sofia directs me to the movie room. It's one of the few spaces in the house that isn't some shade of cream and ivory, with charcoal walls adorned with black and white photos of our favorite actors.

I follow Sofia to the room's bottom tier, where she deposits a tray of milkshakes on one of the low tables in front of the twelve-seater sofa. One quick glance at the screen tells me they're watching *The Godfather*.

When Roman was on death row, I used to dream about moments like these. Now, all I feel is a sense of impending dread. I glance at Leroi, the only man here who's brought a date.

Little Seraphine curls into his side like a kitten, her bare feet tucked to the side. Leroi's hand rests on her shoulder, his fingers playing with a strand of her hair, which has now faded to a pale blonde. Even my cousin, who only lived with us for ten years, shares more blood with Benito and Roman than me.

More than ever, I feel like the odd one out. It's only a matter of time before those Galliano bastards reveal my secret.

Wincing, Leroi picks up a strawberry shake. I step forward, wanting to ask how his wounds are healing, but I don't want to intrude on the family gathering. Instead, I take a seat on the farthest end of the sofa, keeping my eyes on the screen.

My phone buzzes with a text alert that sends my teeth on edge. I pull it out and glance at the screen, only to find a message from Rosalind telling me they tested a small batch of mercury nitrovolucite and are ready to begin full scale production.

Exhaling a long breath of relief, I turn back to the movie. It's great that we'll soon have the explosives, but I can't help but worry that I haven't heard from Matty Galliano since returning from Helsing Island.

Did Sofia land a fatal blow? It's doubtful. Tommy would be baying for her blood, regardless of whether his deranged brother came at her with a knife. What if they're planning something big?

"Where's your little assassin?" Benito's voice interrupts my thoughts.

My head snaps to the side. "She's helping Dr. Cortese and her team."

Seraphine leans up to whisper something in Leroi's ear that makes him nod and grimace.

"How do you know she's not a Trojan horse?" Roman asks.

"Rosalind is trustworthy," I say from between clenched teeth.

"Because fucking one cousin for months before hooking up with another is the mark of her devotion?" Benito asks, his nostrils flaring. "You were supposed to pump her for intel, not lead her into the lab I clawed back from the Gallianos."

"Benito is right," Roman says. "You need to end her like you did with the shooter."

I shoot out of my seat. "Doesn't my judgment mean anything?"

Benito, Roman, and Leroi stare up at me like I'm *Scarface*, yelling at them to say hello to his little friend.

"You don't know the first thing about Rosalind." I point at Leroi. "How could you not tell she was a trained assassin?"

My cousin winces, and Seraphine places a comforting palm on his chest. I know I'm an asshole, trying to deflect blame. Sometimes, being surrounded by my cousin and big brothers makes me regress.

"Leroi was busy planning and executing the massacre of an entire family." Benito smooths down the lapels of his shirt as though congratulating himself on having won the argument.

"Stop it." Leroi pinches the bridge of his nose, clearly sick of our bullshit.

"Benito, sit down," Roman says.

Glaring at me like I interrupted his movie, Benito lowers himself into his seat. I should tell them that Rosalind is a victim of the Moirai, but that would require details. They all know Miranda exists, but I won't make an innocent girl even more of a target.

"Here's what's going to happen," Roman says over the sound of gunfire. "You will return to Isabella Cortese and put the assassin back into the basement where she belongs. After she's helped you destroy the Moirai, you will kill her."

I grit my teeth. "I'll kill Rosalind after you kill Emberly."

Roman's nostrils flare, but he doesn't answer.

"You've already taken back the casino her father stole from Dad, as well as a bunch of assets. Now it's time to take her back to the tower and throw her off that balcony."

If looks could kill, I'd be soaked in gasoline, trussed up on a bonfire, and torched to cinders by Roman's burning gaze. But I'm past giving a shit.

I point at Benito. "Are you still pining for Ginevra DiMarco, who broke your engagement to be with Samson Capello? The same woman whose father scammed Dad out of nearly a billion dollars' worth of assets?"

Benito flinches, but he recovers in an instant.

Fuck him and his unflappable facade.

"How does it feel to be dumped for a man without a cock?" I ask with a sneer.

Benito charges out of his seat, his hands curling into fists. Veins bulge from his forehead, and I revel in his loss of composure. Seeing him so unhinged is more satisfying than punching him in the face, more exhilarating than a hit of meth.

I raise my fists and ready myself for a fight, but Roman grabs his arm and pulls him back.

"Enough!" Leroi roars. "I didn't go through all this trouble for the three of you to tear at each other's throats."

Benito glowers at me for several seconds before resuming his icy façade, then he returns to his seat and hangs his head. My chest tightens at the reminder of everything Leroi sacrificed to save Roman from death row. He didn't just eliminate the Capello family and Matty Galliano's sons.

The details are murky, but he also rescued Seraphine. The Capello twins kept her in their basement as a plaything. A shudder runs down my spine at the memory of what they did to my rabbit.

Leroi took Seraphine home, even though that made him the target of the Moirai, who blew up his downtown penthouse apartment. Both his mentor and the boy he adopted tried use her as a bargaining chip with Samson Capello, forcing Leroi to kill them to save the girl he swore to protect.

Shit, that's me.

I'm both the bastard who kept a woman in a basement as a pet, and the hero sacrificing it all to save an innocent girl.

Four pairs of eyes stare at me like I'm more riveting than *The Godfather*. I can't meet Seraphine's gaze anymore. I did to Rosalind what the Capello twins did to her. Those bastards are related to the Galliano brothers, which also makes them my distant cousins.

"Cesare," Leroi says. "Are you good?"

I clear my throat. "There's one more thing I need to say."

When nobody speaks, I continue. "What Rosalind did was strictly business, and before anyone asks, she didn't shoot Roman in the chest. That man is dead. I tortured him to the edge of his sanity. Then I made Dr. Brunelli revive him from the brink of death so I could torture him again."

Roman's jaw clenches, but he nods.

"Rosalind isn't the one who brought in six other assassins, that was you." I point at Benito and Roman.

"Us?" Benito growls.

"You two invited a bunch of strangers into our home, knowing that the Galliano brothers were trying to expand into our territory. Before you blame a woman whose information just got us six more hostages and a plan to destroy the Moirai, look at yourselves."

I fold my arms, waiting for one of them to bring up my failures. Instead, I am met with silence. Being the youngest in a family sometimes means being left out or having your opinions dismissed. But that doesn't mean I'm not watching from the outside.

Leroi glances from me to my brothers. "Anyone got anything else to add? No? Then how about we all shut the fuck up and enjoy the movie."

Seraphine turns to me with a warm smile and pats the seat beside hers. We bonded over the triage surgery I performed on Samson Capello to make him medically fit enough to endure another round of torture.

I'm sure she thinks I'm a doctor.

Returning her smile, I lower myself onto the seat. Benito rewinds the movie, even though we've seen it over a hundred times.

If I'm honest, I prefer *Scarface*, but I'm going to enjoy this family moment while it lasts.

SEVENTY-SIX

ROSALIND

With a yawn, I step out of the elevator and into the mall. At this time of the morning, most of the stores are closed and there's no sign of shoppers, but I spot the occasional cleaner.

I stayed up the entire night, working with Christian on the amount of mercury nitrovolucite we're going to need to reach the deepest levels of the Moirai. Large-scale production of chemicals is far trickier than the experiments we conducted at the academy.

Industrial manufacturing introduces a whole new set of variables I hadn't contemplated, and there's no room for error when ingredients are volatile and rare. I'm just so glad I had Christian's expertise.

As I head toward the deserted food court, a door opens and the red-haired woman from yesterday steps out of the vegan café holding an A-frame board advertising the day's specials.

Our eyes meet, and she raises a hand to wave. "Wheatgrass shots again?"

Actually, I was thinking of strong coffee, but wheatgrass is exactly what I need to boost my flagging energy levels. "Make it two with a coconut cappuccino."

She gives me a thumbs up and disappears back into her store just as my phone vibrates. Only two people have this number, but Miranda prefers to text than call.

I accept the call. "Hey."

"Good morning, pet," Cesare drawls, his voice a deep rumble. "I'm pulling into the parking lot."

"Meet me at the café."

He makes a disgruntled sound. "See you there."

I snicker at the thought of him eating another vegan meal. I'll eat meat on missions or if I'm sure it's of the best quality, but my body prefers plant-based substitutes. Besides, after days of not eating, I'm in desperate need of nutrition.

Slipping the phone back into the pocket of my cargo pants, I open the café's door and step inside. My nostrils fill with the mingled scents of baked goods and freshly ground coffee, and I make my way to the counter, where a large cup of coffee awaits.

As the redhead pours wheatgrass into shot glasses, I take a sip of my cappuccino. It's rich and velvety, thanks to the coconut milk, with a hint of caramel. I'm about to ask about the blend she used when I feel the prick of a needle.

On instinct, I drop my coffee and pull out the tiny dart. The ceramic cup smashes on the floor, splashing my ankles with hot coffee. Whirling around, I lock gazes with a large figure at the door, holding a compact sedation device.

"Dr. Daniel?"

It's the Moirai's Chief Medical Officer. He's sporting a new goatee and a deep tan from his recent vacation, but I would recognize that square jaw and gray buzz cut anywhere.

The older man flashes me a smirk.

I reach for something, anything, to use as a weapon, but my arms drop to my sides, and I collapse to my knees.

The woman behind the counter gasps. "Are you alright?"

Dr. Daniel rushes to my side and grabs my arm. "It's alright," he says, his voice exuding authority. "I'm a doctor."

My mouth opens in a scream, but the drug has already taken effect. The room spins and distorts with the colors of the cafe warping into a kaleidoscope of bizarre shapes.

"Should I call 911?" the woman asks, and she sounds so far away.

"No need." The doctor picks me up and scoops me into his arms. "I'll take the young lady to my car and administer first aid."

"B-But can't you do it here?" she asks.

My heart thunders, a booming echo between my ears, drowning out the doctor's reply. I feel him moving at a steady pace, then the movement of his arm as he opens a door, and steps out into a world that has lost all familiarity.

The shopping mall has transformed into a surreal landscape of squares that bend back and forth like palm trees in sync with my quickening pulse.

My eyes roll back as I struggle to focus on the immediate threat. I've been captured by the Moirai. More specifically, by its Chief Medical Officer, who is technically support staff.

But why?

As far as everyone knows, I'm a hostage, like all the others who infiltrated Roman's party. The only person connected to the firm who knows I'm cooperating with the Montesano brothers is Britt, and she's already left the country.

Dr. Daniel breaks into a run that makes my stomach lurch. His arms tighten around my body as he weaves through the disturbing landscape and down what feels like a stairwell.

Nausea grips me by the throat, making me gag. I flap like a rag doll in his arms, my limbs loose and unresponsive. He's combined a muscle relaxant with a hallucinogen to keep me helpless. But for what?

"None of that," he says, his tone admonishing. "Bear with me until we reach the ambulance, and I'll give you an antidote."

Out of spite, I retch against his shirt. The doctor grunts his displeasure but doesn't break stride and continues descending to what looks like an abyss.

Another door opens, followed by another, and he flings me on to a hard surface. My arms splay outward, only to be shoved back to my side by the rise of cold metal railings.

I glance around, unable to make sense of my surroundings. It's a confined space with walls that curl in to form the ceiling of a cocoon. The harsh, sterile scent of hospital-grade disinfectant burns my nostrils as I force in measured breaths, fighting the urge to panic.

The beeps of machinery remind me so much of the room

Cesare held me captive, but that's impossible. We must be in some kind of vehicle.

"Do you know how elated I was to see you leave the Montesano stronghold?" He snaps a belt around my chest. "When you didn't return straight to HQ, I became concerned."

Panic flares in my chest, and my breath quickens. How would he know my movements?

He fastens another restraint around my waist. "The only reason I didn't report your whereabouts was because of our agreement."

My mind goes blank, and I scramble to understand what he means. I know better than to bargain with my superiors in the Moirai. They're all liars...

"Aah," he says, his voice lifting with amusement. "Now, do you remember offering me your submission in exchange for signing your medical release?"

Disgust rolls in my gut as I recall my desperation to leave the Moirai. Cesare had taken Miranda and made me think he would tear her head open with a reverse bear trap.

The doctor's hot fingers trace the contours of my face, infusing my flesh with ripples of revulsion. I would squirm under his touch, but the drugs in my system make it impossible to move.

Another needle pierces my skin, and cold liquid flows into my veins like ice. It's a terrifying contrast to the feverish heat of the digits sliding down my neck.

If that's an antidote, it's not working because I'm still hallucinating. My limbs jerk, making me realize he's only reversed the muscle relaxant.

"Good girl," he croons, his fingers skimming my collarbones before tracing the hollow of my throat. "We're going to get along just fine with the experiments."

I blink once, twice, three times to clear my vision, but it's still a twisting vortex of metal. His face morphs into view with blank features and a grin of piano keys that extend toward his ears.

I can't do this anymore.

I can't endure another moment of torture.

"You spent the night beneath the shopping mall. What was that about?"

"Dr. Daniel?" I rasp. "I couldn't go back to HQ directly. I was being followed—"

He slaps my face so hard my head jerks to the side. "You weren't," he says, all traces of levity gone. "The tracker showed you moving to the airport, where you met another operative before disappearing out of range."

My throat tightens. Whatever device he put in my body didn't track my movements to Helsing Island.

"When you returned to spend the night in the Montesano mansion, while your fellow operatives were still underneath it, so I could only assume you'd struck a deal."

"I was stalling for time. They wanted me to show them the location of the headquarters."

"So you diverted them with disinformation?" he asks.

"It's standard procedure," I reply. "I took him to a warehouse on McCutts Island and said our facility was underground."

He injects something else into my vein that infuses me with searing heat. A rush of nausea clogs my throat as he withdraws the needle.

"Nice try. It's too bad I don't give a damn. By the time I've finished experimenting on you, there'll be nothing left of you to return to HQ."

A sharp breath whistles through my teeth as the word returns to focus. I'm strapped to a gurney in the back of a van with blacked-out windows. Dr. Daniel stands over me, slicing open my shirt with a pair of shears.

I struggle within my restraints. The muscles of my arms straining against the tight bands. He cuts through the center of my sports bra, between the cups, and shoves the fabric aside. Cool air swirls over my breasts, making my nipples tighten.

He chuckles. "Gunther warned me that you were a sexy little thing."

"I'll kill you both."

"How are you going to do that when I plan on preserving your body parts for science?"

The doctor leans in, his lips dangerously close to mine. His warm breath fans against my skin, carrying the scent of acetone.

Cold panic surges through my veins with a burst of adrenaline. I snap my head forward and slam my forehead into his nose with a satisfying crunch.

Blood spurts from his broken nose. He stumbles back with a scream, knocking into another gurney. I've bought myself a little time, but not nearly enough.

As he rights himself, I get a view of an unmoving figure lying on the gurney with their intestines spilling out onto a sterile sheet.

Terror shoots down my spine like a bolt of lightning. My gaze snaps to the victim's pale face.

It's Britt.

Dr. Daniel killed my best friend.

Now, he's advancing toward me, his features twisting into a murderous scowl.

SEVENTY-SEVEN

CESARE

If Rosalind thinks I'm going to endure another vegan breakfast, the joke's going to be on her. Leroi's tough love helped us mend a few bridges, and we all had breakfast together this morning as a family.

I walk toward the cafe with a spring in my step, eager to see my little pet. Things between us might have started out badly, but I can tell her distrust of me is softening.

Rosalind could have used the time we spent apart to extract Miranda from her new academy and walk out of my life forever, but she didn't. For all her protests, she can't ignore our spark. She's drawn to me, just as I am to her. Deep down, she wants me to convince her to stay.

It's only a matter of time before my brothers see her as an asset and welcome her into the family.

As I step into the cafe, I'm hit with the scent of freshly brewed coffee. The woman who served us yesterday stands in front of the counter with a mop, but there's no sign of Rosalind.

She pauses to greet me with a pained smile. "Your girlfriend fainted."

My gaze snaps to a door that leads to an inner room, and I wonder if she's lying down, dazed from being exposed to so many chemicals. "Where is she?"

"A doctor caught her before she fell and took her away." The woman's features fall as she completes her sentence, as though she's realized she's describing an abduction.

"Which way?" I growl, my heart slamming against my ribs like it wants to wring her neck.

She points to the right. "He said his medical bag was in his car."

I'm already bolting out of the store and racing down the hallway toward the parking lot. Stores whizz past in a desperate blur. Matty Galliano must have taken her for one of his sick games. The bastard laid low to make me think he was dead, so I could drop my guard.

Sweat breaks out across my brow as I burst through the exit and tear down the stairwell. I can already predict what I'll find. Rosalind, in the back seat of my car, stabbed to death.

Just like Tania. Just like Allegra. Just like he tried to do to Sofia.

Then there'll be a team of homicide detectives ready to arrest me for her murder. Panic spikes as my feet pound down the concrete steps and dread wraps around my neck like a noose.

I can't allow him to hurt Rosalind. She's only just freed herself from the Moirai and hasn't even connected with her daughter.

Shit. What will I tell Miranda?

I slam open the door to the lot's top level, sprint to the Lamborghini, and fling open the passenger-side door. The front and back seats are empty, untouched. My chest loosens with relief, which only lasts until I hear a scream.

Jerking out of the car, I scan the parking lot to find a black van parked thirty feet away beside another exit. Adrenaline kicks me in the gut, and I lurch forward.

It's Galliano.

Racing toward the van, I pull out my gun. Light streams out from between its back doors, broken by the occasional movement. Fury mounts, roaring like a wildfire in my veins. Blood rushes between my ears. If he's laid a finger on my Rosalind, I won't care how many snipers he's got trained on my head.

I try the door. It's jammed. I shoot at the lock, sending its mechanism flying across the concrete floor. With one hard yank, the door opens.

Inside are two gurneys. Rosalind lies naked on the right with an eviscerated corpse on the left. In the middle, a gray-haired bastard who isn't Galliano whirls around with his pants around his ankles. His erect cock bobs, its reddened crown a moving target.

In the split second it takes to aim the gun, my rage revolves around my mental clock face from nine to twelve and then to one.

Time slows. My mind falls silent as I pull the trigger.

The bullet speeds through the van's interior, piercing his shaft and slicing it clean in half. As the top of his cock flies off in an arc of blood, the man crumples to the floor with a shriek.

Time snaps back to normal. Without realizing it, I've freed Rosalind and I'm now strangling the screaming man with a garrote I've fashioned from the corpse's small intestine. His eyes bulge. His mouth opens and closes like a gasping fish. His blood-soaked hands fumble uselessly at his throat.

"Cesare," Rosalind yells through the haze.

"What?"

"Let go of my best friend's guts."

My gaze darts to the naked figure lying eviscerated on the other gurney. It's Britt. I release her intestines and step out of the pool of blood with my palms raised in surrender.

"Sorry," I mutter. "I didn't know."

Rosalind is naked, save for the scraps of fabric still clinging to her limbs. I scan her body, looking for signs of damage, but see no visible injuries. Not that it makes any difference. Sometimes, the worst injuries are on the inside.

"Don't touch him," she growls. "Dr. Daniel is mine."

A noisy gasp pulls my attention back to the old bastard writhing in a puddle of his own blood. He curls in a ball, clutching his hemorrhaging crotch.

Rosalind grabs the man by the hair and drags him to the floor and onto his knees.

"You groomed me." She delivers each point with a punch. "Manipulated me into thinking I was special. Stole my innocence."

My brows pull into a frown, and I study the man's bleeding face. This can't be Miranda's father. He's supposed to have died in an explosion.

A flash of light pulls my attention back to the parking lot, where cars stream in from its entrance. I glance back at Rosalind who rains blows on Dr. Daniel with ruthless precision. Her words drip with years of resentment and repressed rage, each syllable a punch to the gut.

At this rate, someone will call the police. Getting arrested isn't a big deal, but I don't need the Moirai knowing that Rosalind is no longer my prisoner. After activating the Lamborghini's central locking, I step into the back of the van and secure the door.

By now, the man is no longer recognizable

Rosalind pummels his face with a defibrillator paddle. "I'm not a cum dumpster. I'm not a toilet. I'm not a table or a plate. I'm not a toy. Not a pet. Not a pawn."

The last two statements make me flinch. Is Dr. Daniel a proxy for other abusive men? Men like me?

Any other time, the sight of a beautiful woman splattered in blood would get my cock straining against my zipper, but there's nothing arousing about Rosalind's trauma. I'm one of the bastards who contributed to it, and she's still my captive.

The man hangs limp within her grasp, his body swaying with the force of her blows, which are losing intensity. I step forward with my palms raised, hoping she understands I don't mean her any harm.

"You're getting tired, love," I say, my words soft. "Let me hold him up for you."

She casts me a weary look, as though considering whether to attack. I don't want to fight. Rosalind may have more agility, speed, and fighting experience than me, but I have more raw strength. Strength is what it takes to subdue her, but I don't want her to get any more hurt.

I hold still, waiting for her to decide whether I'm a threat. Instead of lunging at me, she nods, releasing Dr. Daniel to the expanding pool of blood.

Resisting the urge to snap on a pair of gloves, I pick him off the floor and hold him up with my arms hooked beneath his shoulders. Rosalind continues her rant, punctuating her words with blows.

The impact of each strike reverberates through Dr. Daniel's limp body, but it's her words that make me wince. The man she's describing is me.

I abducted her.

I drugged her.

I restrained her.

I cut through her clothes.

I subjected her to sexual torture.

Hell, I'm worse than Dr. Daniel because I went deeper than just her body. I used Rosalind's daughter as a pawn to manipulate her into obedience. The only reason she's hanging around is to secure her freedom from my family's wrath.

The monster she needs to escape is me.

Rosalind pauses mid-punch, crumples to the floor and convulses. Froth bubbles from her lips, and her eyes roll to the back of her head.

I drop the dying man to the floor and trample over his body.

It looks like she's been drugged.

SEVENTY-EIGHT

ROSALIND

I wake up with a gasp, feeling like I've run a marathon. My throat burns, my heart races, my muscles scream with fatigue. Sunlight burns through my eyelids, giving me an idea of the time. It must be around noon or early afternoon, which means I've been unconscious for over five hours.

My eyelids flutter, but they're gummed shut. The last thing I remember was being abducted and under the influence of psychedelic drugs, followed by Dr. Daniel cutting through my clothes and—

Pain slices through my chest, making me gasp. He captured Britt and ripped her body open with his sick experiments. Britt was supposed to have escaped the Moirai and left the country. She had an apartment in a suburb outside Geneva, ready for a new life overseas.

"Rosalind?" Cesare's deep voice cuts through my thoughts.

When I open my eyes again, he hovers above me, clad in a white shirt. I guess his black one probably ruined when he held Dr. Daniel while I pummeled the shit out of his carcass.

We're in a cream-colored room with windows lining its curved walls, providing a stomach-lurching view of the sea.

"Where are we?" I ask.

"The Bella Lucia," he says. "My dad's yacht."

"Is there any way to close the curtains?"

He glances over his shoulder and turns back to me with a frown. "You don't like the ocean?"

Suppressing a shudder, I focus all my attention on his face and reply. "It's not my favorite view."

Cesare straightens, reaches for a remote, and points it at the windows. A soft hum emanates from their direction, but I keep my gaze averted until the room is completely shaded.

He turns back to me, his eyes clouding with concern. "Want to talk about it?"

"Why I don't like the sea?" I ask back. "No."

"I'm asking about what happened this morning. Who is Dr. Daniel?"

"The Moirai's Chief Medical Officer."

He grimaces. "How the fuck did they find you?"

"With a tracker. Is he dead?"

"Alive," he murmurs. "Barely. After stabilizing you, I called for a clean-up crew to take him to one of the cells in the basement. I thought he would be more useful alive than dead."

I nod.

Grief seizes my lungs. "And Britt?"

"My cousins are taking care of her at Newtown Crematorium."

Pain hollows out my chest and travels to the back of my throat, making my eyes burn with tears. I can't believe she's dead. My breath hitches. Pressing my lips together to suppress a sob, I nod.

"Hey," he murmurs, his voice so soft it's barely audible. "I'm sorry. She was a good friend who didn't deserve such a terrible end."

A hysterical laugh bursts from my lips. "What's the difference between Dr. Daniel's experiments and what you do to your enemies in the basement?"

Gritting my teeth, I brace myself for Cesare to grab me by the throat and hiss something defensive. We all justify the heinous shit we do, thinking it makes us better than the other monsters, yet nobody wants to see the reflection in the mirror.

Instead of lashing out, he sits at my bedside and stares at me for several heartbeats. I shift on the mattress, wondering if I've pushed him too far.

"What?" I ask.

"How do you feel?"

I fidget, my mind trying to make sense of his odd behavior. Where are the accusations that I'm back in touch with the Moirai? Where are the demands for information? Keeping my features schooled, I glance toward the door. "I've had worse."

"Rosalind," he says with a sigh. "Do you need an STI panel?"

"No." I shake my head. "You got there before he could..."

I can't even say the word. The tight band of control I have over my emotions is hanging by a thread.

Out of the corner of my eye, I see his shoulders sag with relief. That's when I finally realize something between us has changed. He reaches to take my hand, then seems to think better of it and withdraws.

"When I found him standing there with his cock out, I thought the worst," he says, his voice rough.

I close my eyes and exhale. "There's nothing worse than real-izing someone you care for has suffered an agonizing death. Britt was there for me from the beginning. I've known her since we were fourteen."

"When you joined the Moirai's academy?"

"We were at the same boarding school in New Jersey, when she introduced me to Gunther, who became our boss," I say. "As much as I hate the Moirai, I could never have gotten Miranda out of that house without their training."

We fall silent for several moments, and my mind drifts to Britt's last moments. How long did she spend with that psychotic doctor? Was it hours or days? The last time I saw her at the airport, she wasn't concerned about being followed. Maybe he caught up with her when they were abroad.

"What happened after he took you from the café?" he asks.

"It all happened so fast," I say, my gaze fixed on my lap. "He didn't share my whereabouts with the Moirai. What he wanted to do was purely for his entertainment."

"I'm sorry," he blurts.

My head snaps up, and I meet his piercing gaze. "What are you talking about?"

"For keeping you locked up like that and treating you like a plaything. For using Miranda and you as pawns. For everything."

"You already made things right," I say, not wanting to compound the horror of my captivity with Dr. Daniel by rehashing my time with Cesare.

"You can't forgive me so easily."

My lips tighten. "Sometimes forgiveness is about letting go of trauma so the victim can move forward. This isn't about you, alright?"

He breathes hard, looking like he wants to argue his point further. I'm still reeling from what happened to Britt. I can't cope with his outpouring of guilt.

"As long as you hold up your end of our bargain, we're even," I say.

"And then you'll leave me?"

There's no way in hell I'd answer that loaded question. If I tell him the truth, he'll switch up on me, and I don't have the mental bandwidth to endure that.

I turn to meet his gaze, his eyes flicker with emotion. The tough exterior he wears cracks for just a moment, revealing a rare glimpse of vulnerability. I see so much of the young man in the photo album and have to remind myself he's only twenty-four.

"Are you planning on keeping us against our will?" I ask.

"No," he says, as though the admission hurts. "If you want to go, I won't stop you."

"But you'll do everything you can to convince me to stay?" I ask.

He nods.

"Alright."

"Just... alright?" he asks, his brows knitted.

Scooting to the side, I pull back the sheets. "I mean alright, get under these sheets and make me forget I was nearly sliced open."

His eyes glimmer with hope and maybe a little skepticism. He still doesn't believe I don't want to slice open his throat after everything he's done, but sensory deprivation has made me crave his touch. He's also given me several things I've always desired. A relationship with my daughter, a way out of the Moirai, and his respect.

I reach out a hand and beckon him closer with my fingers. "If you want forgiveness, then you're going to come here and earn it."

SEVENTY-NINE

CESARE

Is this a trick? Is this the moment she rips out my jugular in revenge for keeping her captive?

My gaze drops to Rosalind's deceptively delicate fingers. Every fiber of my being wants to get close to her, but I would be insane to get in bed with a woman capable of killing a man with her bare hands. Especially so soon after she suffered a violent encounter.

I gaze into her face, noticing the subtle flecks of green and gold in her hazel eyes that give them such a mesmerizing depth. They're raw, sad, and shimmer with unshed tears, making every fiber of my being burn with the need to soothe her pain.

My heart doesn't just ache for Rosalind and everything she's suffered. It bleeds.

"Cesare," she says, her voice coaxing. "I won't bite."

"It's not your teeth that's got me worried."

"You think I'm going to lash out?"

"How else will you handle all that pent-up rage?" I ask, trying to lighten the mood.

Her hand drops to the mattress. "You can't train me to crave your touch and then not give it when I'm feeling vulnerable. Take off that shirt and get into this bed."

Guilt twists my gut and gnaws at my insides at the reminder.

It's worse because there's also a part of me that surges with pride in having her need my touch.

Before I know it, I'm toeing off my shoes and sliding off my shirt, eager to comfort her. Rosalind scoots back, giving me space to slip under the sheets.

As soon as I'm in position, she rests her head on my shoulder and curls into my side. My heart swells as she nuzzles closer and slides her palm over my chest. I wrap an arm around her back and hold her close, reveling in the feel of her soft skin.

"Better," she says with a long sigh.

I inhale the scent of her hair, the familiar mix of citrus and magnolia that soothes my senses. It's a unique mix I only associate with my beautiful, dangerous Rosalind.

"This feels so nice," she murmurs into my neck, her breath tickling my skin.

I couldn't agree more, but nice is an understatement.

Holding her close like this, feeling her body relax against mine, it's something I could savor for the rest of my life. But it's a taste of heaven I haven't earned, and Rosalind knows it, too. I squeeze my eyes shut, trying to find the right combination of words to express my regret.

It's not just regret. The more I know about this woman, the more I find to respect. To revere. I saw the mess she made of Dr. Daniel's face. His nose was broken in at least two places. Although she was drugged, restrained, and in the throes of grief, she still fought back like a warrior.

I part my lips to speak, but my mind goes blank. What I did to Rosalind isn't something that can be erased with a simple apology. I would spend every moment in my life trying to make amends, if only she wouldn't leave.

She groans, and the first time I've ever heard her express pain.

"Are you alright, love?" I ask, my fingers threading through her hair.

"Cramps," she says with a moan.

I stiffen, my brows furrowing. "Is that a side effect of the drugs?"

"More like a side effect of missing an appointment for my contraceptive shot."

"How do you normally cope with them?" I place a kiss on her temple, wanting to take away her discomfort.

"The shot," she mutters.

Shit.

"Let me get you something," I say, readying myself to jump out of bed.

Her limbs tighten around me with a punishing grip. "You're not going anywhere."

I exhale a low groan, frustrated that she won't let me help, but grateful that she still wants me close. This is exactly what I wanted. Rosalind wrapped around my little finger, craving my touch. I wanted her to be my perfect plaything, my deadly little pet.

The reminder that I'm one of a list of men who have manipulated her makes my insides churn with a concoction of jealousy and remorse. I want to kill them all for causing her pain. I want to erase every harmful memory and replace them with the three of us as a little family.

"Alright, love," I tell her. "I'll stay."

"I can handle a few cramps, but I'm sick of being threatened or taken or tortured," she says, her voice shattering.

My stomach lurches, and I ready myself to restrain her wrists if it turns into a violent outburst. I deserve all her anger, but not until we've dealt with the Galliano brothers and the Moirai.

"I hear you, love," I murmur, my fingers still twisting through her silken strands. "If you need to work through your anger, we can talk about it, or I can take you back to the dungeons to confront that bastard."

Instead of lashing out or even pushing me away, she relaxes into my embrace and exhales a sigh.

"Rosalind?" I lean down and kiss her forehead, finding that she's fallen asleep.

The sight of her slumbering so peacefully in my arms fills my heart with a mix of desire and dismay. Despite all the harm I caused her, she still trusts me enough to fall asleep in my arms

Deep down, I know none of this is real.

Rosalind and I both understand it's just a by-product of her captivity and a manifestation of Stockholm syndrome. It's like being addicted to drugs and wanting one last hit before going cold turkey.

Losing her is inevitable, and I no longer have the heart to force her to stay. She's no longer the sexy little assassin I wanted to make my toy, but a broken woman with a tragic past.

And a mother.

I reach for the phone I left on the bedside table and send a text to the Chief Stewardess with a list of items Rosalind will need for her cramps. Then I scroll down my list of contacts and send a text to Miranda, who should have a free period after lunch.

She answers in seconds with emojis that makes me smile. We exchange several messages about her classes, new friends, and an upcoming trip to one of Helsing Island's nature reserves.

After obtaining a list of Rosalind's favorite restaurants and dishes from Miranda, I ask her to record a video wishing Rosalind a speedy recovery.

I forward Miranda's suggestions to the stewardess and spend the rest of the afternoon watching Rosalind sleep. It's a little pocket of peace we can both enjoy before returning to the chaos of the outside world.

EIGHTY

ROSALIND

When I wake up again, the cabin is much darker, with no traces of sunlight streaming through the blinds. Cesare hands me my phone, where there's the sweetest message from Miranda, telling me to feel better soon.

I lie on my back playing it over and over, my eyes filling with happy tears and my heart swelling with love. Cesare gazes down at me with a soft smile.

"Did you ask her to record this?" I croak.

He raises a shoulder. "I asked her for ideas on what you like to eat, and she dragged the information out of me about your cramps."

I'm almost certain it's a lie, but I don't push. Cesare has single-handedly built a connection between my daughter and me, something I struggled to manage in a decade. Thanks to him, she sees me as someone worthy of love.

"How are the cramps?" he asks.

"Duller," I reply with a smile.

His gaze travels down my bare chest to the sheets puddled around my middle. "I hoped the heating pad would make a difference. The stewardess brought a range of painkillers, but you should also take magnesium."

I sit up, leaning my back against the headrest, and watch Cesare walk to the dresser where he's lined up a range of pill bottles. His muscles ripple on his back, making the skull tattoos come to life. His hair is untied, forming loose waves that cascade toward his broad shoulders.

Sometimes, that masculine beauty is jarring, although I can't fathom why. If I focus on how good he looks, it hurts.

"Ibuprofen okay? If you want something stronger, I got hold of mefenamic acid, but I have others if you want something different."

Warmth spreads through my heart at this saner, less sadistic version of Cesare who wants to give me choices.

"I've only ever had naproxen, but that was years ago," I reply.

He selects a bottle and brings it over with a glass of water. When my stomach rumbles, he frowns.

"Hungry, love?" he asks.

"I didn't eat at the lab with all those chemicals," I mutter. "If you have a snack bar or some nuts—"

"How would you like zucchini pasta with avocado Alfredo?" he asks as he hands me a glass of water and two pills.

"How did you—" I shake off the question. "Miranda?"

He chuckles. "She told me all about your fixation with raw vegan food. I arranged for the chef of the Raw Kitchen to come over and fix you a meal."

My eyes narrow. "When you say arranged, does that mean abducting her at gunpoint?"

"I bought out the restaurant for the night and paid double her usual rate to come and cook."

"There's no cooking in raw food." I knock back the pills, swallowing them down with the water.

He grins. "That's what she said. She's waiting in the galley for your order."

The warm feeling in my chest turns to a flutter. "That's... Thank you. Can I borrow some clothes?"

His gaze darts to the room's low table, which is covered in piles of boxes. My smile falters at the reminder of the lingerie and leather he forced me to wear to his family dinner, but he takes my hand.

"It's not what you're thinking. The owner of Dolce Vita called earlier to arrange a delivery of the items you ordered."

I straighten. "Oh."

"Would you like a massage before your shower?"

"Don't tell me you hired a professional to massage my knots?"

"Not exactly." His lips tick up in a smirk, and his eyes twinkle with mischief.

My brows rise. "You?"

He nods, all traces of amusement fading into something serious.

I can't handle this kinder version of Cesare who isn't being overbearing or calling me his pet. That was a man I mildly despised, but at least I knew his motives.

Bitter experience has taught me that powerful men are only generous and nice when they want more than you're prepared to give. Kindness is only a trap men use before they unleash their inner monster.

"You've done enough," I mutter, my gaze dropping to my lap.

"Don't fight me. I need this just as much as you."

"Why?" I ask, my voice barely a whisper.

"I don't know how else to say I'm sorry," he replies.

"You've already apologized."

"But it's not enough," he growls. "I have to make things right."

"Cesare," I say with an exasperated sigh. "You're doing enough."

"Then why can't you look me in the eye?"

My gaze snaps up to his face, which is a mask of pain and frustration. He breathes hard, running his fingers through his hair. I've never seen Cesare look so agitated. Not even when I refused to crack under interrogation.

Maybe my past has skewed my instincts. Maybe there's something beautiful seeing the monster before the man. At least this way, the personality switch isn't so jarring.

"You can't undo what happened, and nothing I say will erase the memory of what you did," I say, my voice measured. "I know you're sorry, but the person who needs to do the forgiveness is you."

His brows pull together and draws me closer. "What do you mean?"

"You're punishing yourself, Cesare," I murmur, reaching up to touch his cheek. He leans into the contact, closing his eyes. "This guilt you're feeling isn't about me. This is about you."

"How do you cope as an assassin?" he says.

"I haven't killed as many men as you think," I say with a smile. "And everyone who died at my hands was a terrible human being."

His shoulders sag. "I've never felt bad about hurting anyone who was a threat to the family."

"When did you realize I was different?"

"I should have known it the moment you sacrificed yourself to save Miranda. It didn't register because I'd do the same for my brothers. When I found out you were her mother, it all clicked into place."

"You don't like hurting mothers?" I ask.

"Any woman who brings life into the world and would sacrifice everything to save their child deserves my respect," he says, his voice hoarse.

I pull him down on the mattress beside me, threading my fingers through his hair. He stiffens at first, then he relaxes enough to rest his head on my shoulder. "Thank you."

"For what?" he rasps.

"For saving me from a painful and humiliating death," I reply. "For leaving Dr. Daniel alive enough to be interrogated. For everything you've done to help Miranda and me."

He exhales, his breath warm and ragged.

"This is the part where you say you're welcome," I say.

He chuckles, but the sound carries no mirth. "I should have done more."

"Would it help if I told you I wasn't sorry?"

"What do you mean?" he asks.

"Teaming up with you is the best thing that's happened to me in years." I massage his scalp. His eyes remain shut, but his features finally relax. I add, "You accomplished everything I struggled to do for Miranda without even trying."

"Let me erase that man's touch," he says.

"You don't have to do that," I murmur.

His fingertips brush my thighs, a featherlight touch that sends shivers down my spine. "If any man's touch is going to linger on your skin, it should be mine."

EIGHTY-ONE

ROSALIND

Cesare's fingers travel up my waist, detonating every pleasure center until my skin feels like it's been set alight. I don't want to dwell too deeply on why my body feels so intensely for my former captor so soon after I was abducted by another.

There has to be more to our bond than some twisted psychological connection or a case of better the devil you know. When he scoops me up into his arms, my heart feels safe, protected. Cesare feels like home.

"What are you doing?" I ask, my arms wrapping around his neck.

"Taking you to the spa."

My stomach drops. "We're leaving the cabin?"

"If you're worried about your thalassophobia, I've ordered the crew to pull down all the blinds to the windows."

"I wouldn't call it a phobia," I mutter. "Just an awareness of its dangers."

He carries me across the cabin and out of the door into a hallway of white floors and polished mahogany walls. "Did something happen?"

His question triggers a memory of a long-forgotten academy training exercise, and a shiver runs down my spine. "No."

"Don't want to talk about it, love?" he says, his voice soft.

"Maybe later," I mumble and bury my face in his neck.

He doesn't push for more information. Instead, he cradles me to his chest. "You don't have to be so strong around me," he murmurs. "I know you've been through hell, and I want to take care of you."

His words are a balm on my frayed nerves. As unhinged as Cesare can be, he's one of the few men I've met who want to look beyond the surface. A terrible trait from an interrogator, but wonderful as a boyfriend.

Boyfriend?

I shake off that thought. We're more like enemies who have agreed to a truce. A little voice in my head asks about the fucking, but I focus on the rhythm of Cesare's steps and the thud of his heartbeat against my ear. There's no point in classifying an arrangement that's only temporary.

We continue down a set of stairs, passing blacked out portholes, and I notice the boat isn't rocking.

"Are we still out at sea?" I ask.

"We're moored in St. Anne's Marina," he says. "Does that make a difference?"

"Don't know," I reply with a nervous chuckle.

At the bottom of the stairs, he opens a door, letting out the calming scent of cedar. He steps into the spa, a long space of wooden walls divided by a glass wall.

Cesare carries me down a walkway that separates a glass-fronted sauna and a narrow exercise pool that hums with its own current. At the very end of the spa, he lays me on a stone table beside a condensation-covered wall, which I can only guess leads to a steam room.

This is a hundred times more tasteful than the party yacht Matteo shared with his brother.

As he pulls off my t-shirt, I gaze up at him and smile. "What now?"

He flicks his head toward the ceiling, where a series of recessed shower heads glint in the dim light. "Now, we get you nice and clean."

Before I can ask any more questions, he steps to a small corner console and flips a series of switches. Warm water sprays from the shower heads above, drenching every inch of my body.

A laugh bursts from my chest at the sudden downpour, which washes away an entire layer of tension. I turn to Cesare as he pulls off his boxers, exposing his long, thick erection.

My gaze bounces to the quartet of piercings studding its crown to the bottle he picks off a shelf.

"Magnolia bodywash, okay?"

A breath catches in the back of my throat. "Did Miranda tell you that's my favorite flower?"

He shakes his head. "It's your signature scent."

"Most people can't tell the difference between one flower and the other."

"Our garden used to be full of magnolia trees."

"But not anymore?"

His smile fades. "I removed them."

That's when I remember Magnolia trees featured heavily in the photos of Cesare and his mother. One picture that stands out is of her sitting beneath the sprawling branches, pulling him close to her chest, when he was about five or six.

"Why?" I ask, reaching out to touch his arm.

"She left us without explaining." He returns to the table and pours the liquid soap into his hands. "The only time we got to see her was in the society pages. She loved those trees, but they became a constant reminder that her love for us was all bullshit."

"Did you ever speak to her after she left?"

"A few times," he mutters, his gaze dropping to the magnolia-scented lather building up in his palms. "What she had to say was difficult to hear."

"I'm sorry."

"It's in the past."

He runs his soapy hands over my breasts, his fingers tracing over my curves. His touch is practiced, delicate, and more soothing than I care to admit.

As my muscles melt under his ministrations, I exhale a long sigh, and gaze up to find the pain hidden behind his eyes. I regret digging into old wounds, especially when he was careful not to pry into mine.

His hands glide down my waist, tracing the contours of my hips before sliding down my thighs. His touch is unhurried, as though he's sculpting me out of stone.

I study the intricate design adorning his chest, noting that the skull between his biceps is feminine and surrounded by angel wings. My fingers trace over the tattooed skull wearing a crown on his forearm.

"What do they represent?" I ask.

"Everyone I've lost," he says, his fingers reaching between my thighs. "The skull king is my dad, and then above it is my uncle."

"And the one on your chest?"

He gives me a wry smile. "My grandma. She was an angel."

I want to ask more, but his finger circles my clit, and the question dies in my throat, replaced by a gasp. His pale eyes bore into mine with an intensity that makes my mind scatter.

When he smirks, I know he touched me on purpose so I would shut the fuck up. My thighs part to give him more access to my pussy, and my hips jerk in time to his movements.

"Do you like that, pet?" he asks.

"Don't call me that," I say without heat.

"Tell me to stop, and I will." His fingers pick up their pace.

Biting back a moan, I jerk my head to the side. My fingers curl into fists at the return of the version of Cesare whose balls I want to crush.

He chuckles, the sound deep and low, sending shivers down my spine. "Nobody touches you but me and nobody ties you up but me."

"For a split second, I thought I'd unlocked your inner sensitivity. Now you're back to being insufferable."

His digits move deeper, obliterating my senses and making my arch back off the platform. "If this is suffering, then I'll add that nobody gets to torment you but me."

"Oh fuck," I say through panting breaths.

"I washed off that bastard's touch." He leans down and nips my ear. "Now it's time to mark you as mine."

His fingertips grazed a sensitive spot deep within me that detonates a series of explosions. Pleasure ripples through my body, making my breath catch. My mind spirals, and I lose myself in the intensity of his touch. All the other bullshit melts away as he sets my insides on fire.

I grab his shoulders, trying to anchor myself, my fingernails digging into his biceps. Water continues cascading down on us both, washing away all traces of the liquid soap.

"Are you coming for me, little pet?"

"Not even close," I lie through shallow pants.

He grins that super wide grin that used to make my stomach lurch. Now, that look sends heat shooting through my core.

"Are you sure about that?" he asks, his voice dangerous and low. "Because if you're not satisfied, I can bring out the toys."

I try to clamp my thighs shut around his hand, but that only encourages him to press harder on that spot until I'm writhing beneath him, trying to stifle my strangled gasps.

Satisfaction flickers across his features as he continues tormenting my sensitive walls. I never knew I was capable of multiple orgasms, but he's drawing out every ounce of pleasure until I see stars.

"You're coming at my command like a good little pet," he murmurs, lips brushing against my ear. "

The second orgasm feels like he's plugged me into a socket. Pleasure courses through my system with volts of electricity, making my muscles convulse. Every inch of my skin becomes a raw nerve, and even the water hitting my skin feels like molten caresses. The intensity is almost too much to handle, and I fill the room with screams.

What the hell is this man doing to me?

If I don't take control of him, I'll end up exactly where he wants me—begging and kneeling at his feet for another hit of pleasure.

Another surge of ecstasy overwhelms my circuits, making the thought fizzle away.

Eventually, the sensations fade, and I finally catch my breath. "My body isn't a switch you can turn on and off."

"Want to bet?" His fingers press down on that spot.

My hand whips out, and I grab his cock. "Take your fingers out of my pussy or I'll rip it out by the root."

EIGHTY-TWO

CESARE

Rosalind tugs my shaft, jerking me forward with a surprised grunt. I brace the edges of the stone table with both hands, trying not to crush her smaller body. She pumps my cock like it owes her money, her eyes burning with challenge.

Water cascades down on our heads, making her look like a goddess. I would fall on my knees and worship her temple, but she just threatened to tear off my dick.

"Feeling brave, pet?" I growl.

"Stop calling me that." Her fingers tighten into a grip that has me standing on tiptoes.

"Or what?" I thrust into her clenched fist, pushing back against her control.

This is a dangerous game. I doubt my little assassin has the raw strength to carry out her threat, but she could cause a penile fracture.

"Or edge to the brink of sanity," she replies.

"I'd like to see you try."

She sits up, shoving me backward until my hamstrings hit the second bench. Before I can regain my balance, she climbs on top of me. Her limbs wrap around my neck and waist in a death grip that would make a lesser man shoot his load.

No woman has ever taken the reins like this, but I knew

Rosalind was special the first time I had to wrestle her into submission. She reaches down, holding my cock steady, and lowers her wet pussy onto my crown.

Her movements are slow, and eyes never leave mine as she takes me in, inch by agonizing inch. My cock swells within her tight, wet heat, needing some precious friction. I grab her hips to guide her movements, but her teeth clamp down on my lip with a sharp sting.

"No. I'm in control."

"Fuck," I groan. "Then move."

Once my shaft is fully sheathed in her sweet cunt, she rocks her hips in a gentle rhythm that has my toes curling.

"Come on, pet," I growl. "You're strong enough to ride me until my knees buckle."

"That's not the point."

"Shit."

"You edged me for days."

"Hours," I say.

"It felt like a lot longer." Her inner muscles tighten around my shaft. "You're not even close to coming, yet you can't take being teased for a few seconds."

My eyes narrow at her rebuke, but I don't reply because she's right. I rigged up the vibrating chastity belt to keep building her to the edge, never allowing her any release.

"I'm sorry," I murmur.

"Tell me that again after an hour."

My eyes squeeze shut, and I grit my teeth against the overwhelming pleasure. Having her tight cunt muscles squeeze my cock is the sweetest form of torture.

"Look at me when I'm edging you," she snaps.

Opening my eyes, I stare into her hazel irises that burn like twin orbs of fire. Her long, dark hair lies flat against her face, accentuating her high cheekbones and plump lips.

My breath quickens. It hurts to look at her when she's this beautiful and wrapped around my cock.

"Don't you dare come," she growls, her finger closing in around my nipple and squeezing tight.

"Bitch," I snarl.

She laughs, like I'm the plaything and she's the one in control. "You should see yourself, trying so hard not to come apart." She punctuates that statement with a squeeze of her cunt muscles. "I love seeing you agonized and desperate."

"Declaring your love so soon, pet?" I say through clenched teeth.

"You'll have to work harder than that to even get me to like you," she replies, giving my nipple another painful twist. "But I love seeing you squirm."

"Vixen."

I rock my hips back and forth, trying to create a little friction, but that earns me a slap so hard that my head snaps to the side.

My cock, the confused idiot, jumps at the sting. I clench my teeth and growl.

"No moving," she snaps.

Warm water cascades down her alabaster skin, pooling in her collarbones before coursing down her perfect breasts. Her erect nipples rub against my chest, infusing my veins with molten fire.

Her heated gaze burns into mine and her plum-colored lips curve into a triumphant smirk. She's a predator watching her prey squirming within her trap.

My hips twitch with the need to thrust, but I know better than to break her rules. Not if I ever want to climax again within her tight heat.

Why the fuck do I like seeing her above me, glowing with so much power?

"We don't have all evening," I say with a groan. "Your raw chef is waiting in the galley."

She rolls her eyes. "Nice try, but you still don't get to come."

"Rosalind," I growl.

"Oh, I'm Rosalind, now?" she asks, her voice giddy with amusement. "What happened to vixen? Or pet?"

Frustration builds up around my balls, making me bow my head and groan. This isn't how I pictured things when I started training her to be my plaything. I wanted her jumping on my cock, not this endless tease and denial.

"Bad girl." I give her ass a playful spank, making her pussy muscles spasm around my shaft.

Interesting.

Rosalind's eyes widen. "Don't you dare."

I spank her again, this time earning myself a pretty gasp. She jerks against me, her cunt clenching so tightly around me my knees buckle.

"Fuck," I groan. "Looks like I've found a loophole."

She reaches down, her fingers wrapping around my balls in an unspoken threat. "Try it again, and you'll be screaming falsetto."

My cock jumps at the prospect of getting more of her attention. I bare my teeth, my palms rising in surrender. "Truce?"

"What kind?" she asks.

"Where you let me pound you against the wall and give you that third orgasm."

"And what do you get in return?" Her nails scrape over my chest, making me suck in a sharp breath.

"The pleasure of watching you come undone. Feeling those sweet walls ripple around my shaft, and hearing you cry out my name."

When she shivers, I know her resolve to make me suffer is weakening. Her nails dig deeper into my chest, leaving crimson lines of pain that make my cock throb.

"That's not what I call a hard bargain," she says, her lips curling into a smile.

"Trust me, love. It doesn't get any harder than this."

She throws her head back, releasing peals of laughter that make my heart soar. This is the first time I've ever made her happy without acting as a mother-daughter go-between. The first time she's taken my cock that wasn't a way to derail my thoughts.

It's hard to believe that only hours have passed since she escaped a fate worse than death. How many people could have Rosalind's level of resilience? I can count them on one hand.

"How about a challenge?"

My brows rise. "I'm listening."

"You slip your fingers between us and rub my clit. If you can get my pussy to clench around you hard enough to trigger your own orgasm, then you get to come."

"And if I don't?" I ask.

"Then you spend the rest of the evening unsatisfied," she replies, her eyes glinting.

My nostrils flare. If these games of dominance are what it takes to take her mind off nearly getting mutilated to death by that doctor, then I'll play along.

It's the least I can do to help my vicious little pet.

EIGHTY-THREE

Cesare made me endure hours of edging, yet he's sullen after ten minutes of getting blue balls. It turns out that he needs fiction to climax. After he rubbed my clit to completion, I climbed off his cock, leaving him hard and throbbing.

Now, he's glaring at me over the most delicious dish of zucchini linguini. The chef he hijacked for the day has also made an entire cheesecake from cashew nuts, almonds, and coconut butter.

Cesare picks at his food, still pissed from being left hanging. Seeing him so uncomfortable is healing a part of me I didn't realize was broken. I've trained myself not to be a people pleaser, but this is the first time I've used a man's frustration for entertainment.

"Are you going to eat or just sit there, brooding?" I nod at the pesto-stuffed mushrooms he's left untouched.

He slides the plate across the table. "You have it."

I devour the mushrooms as though I hadn't already demolished my portion. Umami flavors explode on my tongue from the harmonic mix of tamari, garlic, and vegan cheese.

His eyes soften. "You like that?"

"Mmmm." I nod, still too ravenous to speak.

Maybe it's all the days I spent involuntarily fasting, but

nothing hits better than sharing a scrumptious, highly nutritious, organic meal with my former captor.

"How's the spaghetti?" I ask.

He scoffs. "This will never be pasta."

"Alright," I say with a chuckle. "How is the spiralized zucchini?"

"You're enjoying it," he says, his words gruff. "That means I like it, too."

After eating, we leave the yacht with several takeout containers that I insisted on bringing along for a midnight snack. It's time to interrogate Dr. Daniel about how he found me and gather information about the Moirai's lower levels.

A full moon hangs low in the sky, partially shrouded by mist. It's hard to believe I spent an entire day on water without triggering my phobia, but Cesare has a way of commanding every ounce of my attention so that nothing else matters but him.

I'm dressed in a pair of black Balenciaga cargo pants with a matching hoodie that probably cost over a month's salary. The boutique must have altered the garments to my measurements because it fits better than the items I bought from the mall, and the fabric gliding against my skin feels like heaven.

Cesare's gaze lingers over my form as he drives us back to Alderney Hill. The slight tug at the corner of his lips betrays the pleasure he's taking in my more relaxed mood, and his eyes gleam with appreciation.

"Did I ever mention you're the strongest woman I've ever met?" he asks.

"Is that why you're so fixated on owning me?" I ask.

He reaches across the front seat and grabs my hand. His fingers are gentle, comforting, warm. "Not just strong, but beautiful. Sometimes, I look at you and I'm awestruck."

Any other time, I would pull away, not wanting to give Cesare the impression I plan on staying beyond the end of our deal. But his touch is the comfort I need after my harrowing morning.

"It's the training that's impressive," I mutter. "Not me."

"Not true." He pauses at the gates for the guards to let us

through. "You forget that I've met three other Moirai-trained women. None of them compares to you."

My heart sinks at the reminder of Britt. Not so much at the operatives in the basement who allowed me to attack the guards alone, resulting in my getting shot. The moment they colluded with each other to blame me for orchestrating the hit on Roman, I lost any sense of giving a shit about their fates.

He parks outside the mansion's double doors, and we go straight to the basement. I expect my skin to crawl or break out in a sweat considering this is where I was held captive, but Cesare's presence beside me bolsters my strength.

After passing through a series of biometric security protected hallways, Cesare pauses at a door. "You don't have to go inside."

"If you think I'll find the sight of Dr. Daniel triggering—"

"I know you can handle it," he says.

"Then what's the problem?"

"Do you really need that bastard spoiling your good mood?" he asks. "He knows he won't leave this basement alive. He could say anything to break your spirit."

The lining of my stomach flutters with nerves. I meet Cesare's concerned gaze and gulp. "He won't get the chance to taunt me about what he did to Britt."

Cesare nods. "Keep him focused on what you need to know."

I suck in a deep breath, thankful for the reminder. We covered interrogation techniques at the academy, but they skipped the part about handling grief and personal entanglements. Maybe they didn't expect us to form emotional attachments in such a competitive learning environment.

Cesare opens the door, and we step into a dark space. He places a hand on the small of my back as the room brightens with fluorescent lights.

Dr. Daniel hangs upside down on the external spokes of what I can only describe as a giant hamster wheel. He's spattered in blood and naked, save for a black ring at the base of what's left of his penis. The subtle rise and fall of his chest is the only sign that he's alive.

Outrage explodes from my heart, filling my veins with molten fury. I stride up to the man who tortured and mutilated my best friend.

"You don't get to sleep your way out of this." I punch him in the gut.

His body jolts, and the walls echo with a shocked moan.

"Better." Stepping back to get a better view of his face, I turn to Cesare. "Bring his head to eye level."

With a nod, Cesare pushes a lever on the metal contraption, making it rotate with several jerky clanks until Dr. Daniel hangs upright.

He glares at me through bruised and bloodshot eyes. The bridge of his nose bends to one side then the other, from where I slammed my head into his face, and his skin is still speckled with blood.

"You're going to answer some questions," I say, my voice eerily calm. "It's in your best interests to cooperate, or we'll keep you here in agony until you rot."

"The Moirai won't take kindly to you colluding with targets," he rasps.

"How would they react to knowing you're murdering operatives?"

His swollen face splits into a sickening grin. "What makes you think I'm acting without authorization?"

My breath catches, but I keep my face in a neutral mask. "What does that mean?"

"Gunther signed you over to me for medical research the moment you left the building. And when Britt failed to report to her new mission, Gunther gave me her, too."

Blood roars through my ears, and my insides twist with guilt. "What are you saying?"

"No operative leaves the Moirai," he says. "Nobody gets to retire, either."

"So, Gunther wrote her off?"

"She was spreading rumors. Rumors that started when you told her about the promotion plan," he replies, his gaze raking over me with a taunting flicker.

My stomach drops.

The cameras must have picked up the conversation we had

when I escaped Cesare and discovered that Gunther told everyone I'd been promoted overseas.

"You got her killed," he says with a gurgling laugh.

Cesare pushes past me and sticks a metal object into the doctor's gut, making him roar with agony. "Cut the crap," he snarls. "The only people who got her killed were you. You and Gunther."

"S-Stop," Dr. Daniel gasps, his face contorting in pain as he tries to squirm away from what looks to be a prod, but it's firmly embedded in his gut.

I grip his chin. "Answer my questions, or my friend here will infuse you with five-thousand volts of electricity. You might have been trained to endure pain, but no human body can survive cooked organs."

The doctor shudders. I have no idea if Cesare's cattle prod is that strong, but neither does this bastard.

"What do you want to know?" Dr. Daniel asks through gritted teeth.

"Where's the tracker?" I ask.

His gaze drops to my belly. "Inside your cesarean scar."

My jaw clenches. Of course, he would assume the scar wasn't from a hysterectomy. He's the man who administers my birth control shots.

"Are there any more of your trackers in my body?" I ask.

He shakes his head.

"What's its range?" I ask.

"Mainland United States of America," he says.

"What about Canada, Mexico, and all the surrounding islands?" I ask, disguising my question to protect Miranda's location.

He shakes his head. "They don't work, which is why we make sure our operatives wear devices that use satellite GPS and cellular triangulation and Wi-Fi."

Relief loosens my chest, and I exhale. This lines up to what he said earlier about my location vanishing at the airport. The sensation doesn't last long as my thoughts shift to my best friend.

Swallowing back a lump in my throat, I ask, "How did you find Britt?"

"She was sneaking about the lower levels of the mall," he rasps. "I can only assume she was trying to make contact with you."

The words hit like a punch to the gut. She was supposed to leave the country, but must have stayed behind out of worry. When he shot her with a tranquilizer gun, there was no one to rush to her rescue.

Cesare places a hand on the small of my back. I turn to meet pale eyes that shine with worry, and I give him a reassuring nod.

"Who else has access to the GPS trackers?"

"Senior management," he croaks. "Gunther, Henry, Marlena, Major Kline, and the director."

"What's beneath level ten?" I ask.

"Nothing," he says. "Just a data bank."

"The data center is on level eight."

He shakes his head. "You don't understand. Levels eleven to thirteen are where we keep the artificial intelligence servers."

I already guessed that they kept enough data on operatives to create digital avatars of us after our deaths. No one would doubt that an operative moved overseas when they were available for telephone conversation or video chats.

My phone buzzes. I pull it out and check the screen, only to find a message from an unknown caller that says: *Midnight in Paris.*

Looks like Xero wants to meet us tonight at the Parisii Cemetery.

When I nudge Cesare and show him the message, he asks the doctor, "What do you know about Xero?"

The doctor's lip curls. "That terrorist?"

"You know him?"

"He's an anarchist who wants to destroy all kinds of organized crime. If you ever get the chance, kill him."

I roll my eyes at the exaggeration. The only organization Xero wants to destabilize is the Moirai. If we can convince him to let us use his network of contacts, it will only be a matter of time before we catch up with Matteo.

But until then, I'll keep this old bastard alive.

EIGHTY-FOUR

CESARE

The message Rosalind received didn't contain any specifics about where in the cemetery Xero wanted us to meet. After turning that old bastard upside down again, we set off for the Parisii Cemetery.

It's in the Parisii neighborhood, one of the oldest in Beaumont City and surrounded on the east, south, and west by houses and parkland. I drive to the only entrance that appears to be manned and slip the guard a hundred-dollar bill.

He unlocks the gates, and we continue down an unlit driveway flanked by weeping willows whose branches shift in the breeze to reveal glimpses of tall mausoleums.

Rosalind hasn't spoken since our conversation with the doctor. I can tell she blames herself for what happened to Britt, but she should be turning that vitriol to the Moirai.

"What else can you tell me about this man?" I ask.

She rubs her temple. "There are so many rumors. Some say he picks off weaker candidates to join his group of rebels. Others claim he runs a rival organization."

I rub my chin. "Did you believe Dr. Daniel?"

"If Xero wanted to destroy the Moirai, one of his contacts would have poisoned the air supply. Or the water. I think he wants to target its leaders."

"Hmmmm."

"Oh, and another thing. Don't be surprised when you see his face."

"What's wrong with it?"

"His mugshot went viral on social media."

I snort. "What for?"

"Tearing out someone's heart."

A man steps out from behind a tree and stands in the middle of the driveway with his arms folded over his chest. I'm tempted to rev up the engine to teach him a lesson, but that might ruin our chances of finding the Galliano brothers.

I ease off the gas, letting the car come to a stop inches from where he stands. Despite the brightness of the headlights, I still can't see his face.

The man unfolds his arms and points to a path between a row of mausoleums on the left.

Rosalind unfastens her seatbelt and reaches for the door. By the time I turn off the engine and pick up my gun, the man has already disappeared into the shadows.

"What is it with assassins and their secrecy?" I mutter.

The walkway is so dark we have to illuminate our path with our phone's flashlights. At the end is a limestone mausoleum built like a Roman temple, with pillars stretching up to a portico roof.

I only know all this architectural shit because Dad used to boast that great-grandfather Paolo commissioned the mansion to look like a villa he grew up around in Salerno, Italy. Cool story, except I'm not related to Dad or any of his ancestors.

My veins contain tainted blood.

That thought is cut short when the mausoleum door creaks open, revealing a darkened chamber lined with vaults. After stepping inside, we descend a staircase leading to a vaulted corridor that stretches at least fifty feet.

I lean into Rosalind's side and whisper, "Been here before?"

"No, but I know Beaumont City was originally a mining town before they built the catacombs," she replies. "They must have used this space to store the bodies of people who couldn't afford graves."

"Charming,"

We continue in silence to the end of the corridor, where I push open yet another door that leads to a lit room. My nostrils fill with the smell of blood, making them twitch.

I step further inside first, holding a gun to find a man in black, hunched over a stone platform. On it lies a trembling man, his head is covered by a hood. In the corner is a stone sarcophagus containing a squirming figure, wrapped up in chains.

Unlike the man, she's fully clothed, and I'm almost certain the remote control on the bench is operating the sex toy that's making her moan.

"Since when do Moirai assassins pair up with targets?" he asks, still giving us his back.

"I've left," Rosalind says.

He picks up a machete and slams it down on his victim's arm, cleaving it in half. After tossing the limb onto a pile of dismembered body parts, he shifts to position the machete over the man's leg.

"What brings you to my territory?" he asks over the muffled screams.

I place a hand on Rosalind's shoulder, already sick of this bullshit. The shadowy figures and creepy meeting place, followed by the dismemberment, were all set up to make him seem intimidating.

"Cut the theatrics," I drawl. "No one is impressed by this."

He slams the machete down on his victim's leg, separating the lower limb from the rest of his body. The man goes rigid and howls.

"Is this Xero?" I ask Rosalind.

She shrugs. "Maybe?"

He finally turns around, holding the severed leg. Beneath a black hood is a face I doubt even his mother could love. I thought my eyes were pale, but this man's irises belong to an animated corpse. Or a fucking snowman. Beneath the hood are traces of blond hair so pale, it might as well be white.

He probably thinks the two silver rings on his bottom lip make him look edgy, but all I see is a piss-poor attempt to hide a pretty boy. I glance at Rosalind for her reaction, and I'm relieved to find her unimpressed.

"Is this a bad time?" I ask. "Because I hate to interrupt a man while he's satisfying his darker urges."

He laughs, revealing a pierced tongue. "I don't take kindly to men using my territory as a murder ground. Homicides attract cops, and cops attract the press."

"Looks like we have something in common," Rosalind says. "Long time, no see."

So, this is Xero. What a pretentious asshole.

His gaze flicks up and down Rosalind's form. "Looking good. Can't say the same about the company you keep."

"You going to get to the point?" I wave the gun at the pile of severed body parts, which includes a head and a torso.

He tosses the leg onto the pile. "That was a lackey of the man who tried to murder a woman from your household."

I stiffen, remembering how Sofia told us she was attacked at her brother's grave. "Show me his face."

Xero raises a finger. "First, I want to know what you and Rosalind want."

"The man who attacked that woman is targeting everyone associated with me," I say through clenched teeth. "I want to hunt him down before he kills anyone else."

"Then we have something in common," Xero says. "What do you want?"

"His name is Matty Galliano. I want you and your team to locate where he's hiding."

Xero nods. "That won't be a problem. Anything else?"

Rosalind steps forward. "We're planning something big to coincide with the next graduation run. I need your people to smuggle some items into levels eleven through thirteen to take down the entire building."

His eyes widen, and his lips curl into a broad grin.

"Sounds like you're planning a real party." Xero rubs the bloody edge of the machete on his sleeve. "Count me in."

EIGHTY-FIVE

ROSALIND

Dr. Daniel hovers above me in a circle of iron with his limbs outstretched like the Vitruvian Man. Warm droplets of blood drip on my face from his broken nose and severed penis.

I try to thrash within my restraints, but they're like a cocoon, and I can't move my limbs. Then saltwater rises from all directions, threatening to pull me into the sea.

Shit. This is getting worse.

The waves part, and Britt's corpse advances toward me with her arms outstretched. "You killed me," she says in a hopeless monotone. "Because of you, I died the worst possible death."

I open my mouth to scream, but it fills with the doctor's blood. Spitting it out, I yell, "You were supposed to be overseas. If I'd known—"

Cold intestines slap me in the face. I can't turn my head because my hair is welded to the raft.

Waves bob up and down from beneath, keeping me afloat while the doctor hovers down. His iron circle upends my raft, tipping me into the freezing sea. I gasp, but saltwater fills my nostrils and clogs the back of my throat.

Zombie Britt swims up from the darkness, her teeth clenched. Black bubbles rise from her lips as she screams, "You left me to die, now I'm going to leave you to drown."

Hands grip my shoulders and shake me out of my nightmare. My eyes snap open, and I'm lying on my back, staring up at Cesare's concerned face.

The morning sun drifts in through the curtains, adorning the ceiling with streaks of orange. My heart pounds so hard that its reverberations reach my fingertips. My sinuses still sting with the phantom sensation of burning saltwater, and it takes a second to realize I'm awake and haven't jumped into another dream.

"You were screaming," he says, his voice soft. "Was it a nightmare?"

Twin waves of grief and guilt crash over my psyche, threatening to pull me under. I squeeze my eyes shut, loosening tears. "Britt was there, accusing me of leaving her to die."

"It wasn't your fault," he says, his fingers threading through my hair. "Nobody is responsible for what happened to her but that deranged doctor and your boss who signed her death warrant."

"Tell that to my conscience," I mutter.

"You need closure."

I crack open an eye. "Closure?"

He draws back and sits up against the headrest. My gaze skims over the skulls on his chest before I meet his eyes.

"What do you mean?" I ask.

"When you lose someone you love, only two things will help you move on. The first is a funeral, and the second is revenge against the man who killed them."

My breath stills. "Are you talking from experience?"

"We weren't invited to my mother's funeral," he mutters. "And I never had a chance to deal with the man who persuaded her to get a worthless boob job."

"What about the surgeon?"

Cesare bares his teeth. "He tripped and fell on his scalpel. Multiple times."

"But that wasn't enough," I say.

"I won't rest until the Galliano brothers are dead." He turns to me, his eyes softening. "Go downstairs, stab the doctor to avenge Britt, and I'll drive you to the crematorium, where you can say goodbye to her properly with a burial."

Sucking in a breath, I try to push down a swell of emotion threatening to consume my sanity. Dread pools in my gut at the thought of seeing Britt's dead body, and my insides twist into painful knots.

"Maybe later," I mutter.

"Rosalind…"

"It's too soon." I shake my head, trying to sift through my muddled thoughts. "I just can't."

"Then let's go to the basement—"

"Do you have a gym?" I ask.

His brows pull into a frown. "Shouldn't you know the answer to that?"

"Because I scoped out your house and its grounds?" I ask with a bitter laugh. "There was a limit to what I could see with all the doors and windows locked."

"Why do you ask?"

"I like to work through tough emotions with exercise."

Minutes later, we're walking toward a set of doors leading to a vast home gym of white walls and spongy black floors, equipped with cardiovascular machines and weight machines.

Avoiding my reflection in a mirrored section with racks of dumbbells, I peer through the glass portion of a doorway into a room filled with boxing equipment.

Gloves hang from hooks on the wall, neatly lined up by size. A punching bag hangs in one corner, but what catches my attention is the boxing ring.

"Fight me."

Cesare scoffs. "No."

I turn around. "Why not?"

"I don't fight smaller opponents," he says with a smirk.

"Especially if they're stronger."

His eyes flare. "I didn't say that, pet."

"Then why won't you spar?" I ask.

"You said fight. If you want me to help you train, that's one thing, but I don't want you getting hurt."

I tilt my head. "It's sweet that you think you could hurt me."

He walks up to me, his nostrils flaring. "Reverse psychology won't work on me, pet."

"Stop calling me that," I snap.

"If you want something to punch, then use the bag," he snarls. "I don't fight women."

I close the distance between us, so we're standing chest to chest. "You're only saying that because I beat you the first time we fought."

"I was holding back. Besides, that drug you tricked me into drinking dulled my reflexes."

"True." I slide my hands over his chest, skimming his nipples. "If you're too scared to fight me, then how about a challenge?"

"I'm listening."

I step backward until my ass hits the door. Cesare advances on me, his pupils dilating.

"Defeat me, and you can fuck me any way you want." I reach behind me, pull the door handle, and step into the boxing room. "Any position, any hole, with or without lube."

His chest resounds with a deep growl. "Rosalind."

"You can even cover me in oil, and we can wrestle."

His gaze darts to a shelf containing supplies, including several bottles of baby oil.

The pulse between my legs pounds to the beat of my heart. "Well? Are you game or are you limp?"

His eyes flicker back to mine with an intensity that makes the fine hairs on the back of my neck stand on end. "You're playing a dangerous game."

"When you lose, I get to stick my fingers up your ass and fuck your tight little hole until you squirt."

His nostrils flare. His jaw tightens. He stalks to the shelf and grabs two bottles of oil. "I'll be squirting alright, when I fill your holes with cum."

Triumph inflates my chest. I jog backward, my lips stretching into a grin. There's only one thing hotter than an enraged Cesare. That's an enraged Cesare with an erection straining through his shorts, ready to wrestle me into submission.

I ascend the steps of the boxing ring and slip between the ropes. My clit throbs in anticipation of what promises to be a game that will chase away my demons.

He unscrews one of the bottles and pours the fluid over his

chest, darkening the ink with a slippery sheen. His eyes never leave mine as he advances toward the boxing ring like a tomcat closing in on his prey.

"Strip."

I fold my arms across my chest, my gaze raking over Cesare's oil-slicked muscles, which ripple with each movement as he ascends the steps.

"Make me," I say.

His eyes gleam with a predatory excitement. "Challenge accepted."

EIGHTY-SIX

ROSALIND

Shivers skitter down my spine and arousal coils deep in my core as Cesare steps into the ring. The oil dripping from his chest catches the overhead lights, giving his body a supernatural glow.

I hold myself steady in a fighting stance. Fists clenched, shoulders square, legs braced for sudden movement. Tension crackles in the air, making my skin tingle.

He extends a slick hand. "May the best man win."

I huff a laugh. "I'm not shaking that."

His grin widens. His eyes dance with mischief. With a swift movement, he yanks down his shorts and frees his erection. "Then shake this."

My gaze drops to the piercings shining on his crown. His hand flies forward, but I sidestep.

"Focus, pet," he says.

"That was a cheap shot."

"Worked, didn't it?"

Oil drips on the canvas as we circle each other, and I almost regret not wearing my gym shoes. In a minute, the surface beneath us will become slippery, and I'm going to need every bit of traction to keep my footing.

He lunges, and I twist, using his momentum to send him skidding toward the ropes. He recovers, but not before I land a sharp elbow to his ribs.

"Nice move," he mutters before coming at me again with his arms wide.

I duck, but he crouches low, already anticipating my move. His arms encircle my shoulders, and he pulls me flush against his slippery chest. Warm oil soaks into my cropped top and into my skin.

"Got you," he growls.

"Wrong." I reach between our bodies and grab his balls. "I've got you."

His body jolts, and he makes a surprised grunt. I give his testicles a hard squeeze before freeing myself with a hard shove.

Cesare staggers backward with a laugh. "Playing dirty already?"

"Don't we always?" I wipe my oily palms on my hips. "Come on, pet. Show me what you've got."

Flashing his teeth, he charges, his feet slipping on the oily canvas. I drop low and launch myself at his legs, sending him on his back with a roar.

He hits the canvas with a laugh, and I slide my hands down his oily chest, pausing to give his cock a few pumps. When I slide my fingers beneath his balls, he grabs my wrist.

"Nice try." He flips me onto my back, pinning one hand above my head.

I wriggle beneath him, so focused on freeing my hand that the rest of the room disappears. His other hand slips beneath the waistband of my shorts and pulls them off my hips.

"Only one person here is getting filled is you, pet. Now, lift your fucking hips and let me pound that pussy."

"Get fucked." I slam a fist into his temple.

"That's the plan."

We grapple against each other on the mat, our bodies slick with oil and sweat. I wrap my legs around his waist and flip him onto his back, but he uses that opening to tear off my shorts.

"Hey," I yell.

"You're not leaving me with blue balls," he growls, his hands snapping the waistband of my panties.

I try pinning his wrists above his head, but he breaks free of that hold and grabs my breasts.

"Like my tits, do you?" I ask.

"Fuck, yeah."

I shuffle up his body until my chest is aligned with his head. He gazes up, his eyes bright, his hands encircling my waist. I jerk my shoulders from side to side, slapping his face with my breasts.

Cesare laughs. It's a rich sound that comes straight from his heart and makes my spirits soar. If I wanted, I'm sure I could climb up his body and sit on his face, but I need his strength.

I need him to overwrite all the times I've been overpowered with something pleasurable, something playful, something with my enthusiastic consent. When I'm pinned beneath his strength, all I want to feel is the weight of his affection.

He flips me onto my side, and I land on the canvas with a thud that fills my vision with stars. I kick out, but he grabs my foot and maneuvers me onto my front.

Before I know it, he's pinning the backs of my knees beneath his biceps and burying his head between my ass cheeks.

"Cesare—"

My words are cut off by a wet tongue sliding over my pucker. Shockwaves of pleasure ripple through my core. I cry out, trying to crawl out from his grip, but he holds me in place.

"If anyone's ass is going to get stuffed," he says from between my cheeks, his tongue trailing a slow circle toward the hole. "It's going to be yours."

"Fuck." I buck my hips, trying to throw him off.

Gripping my thighs, he pushes his tongue past the tight entrance, delving deeper into unknown territory. I twist backward to throw a punch at his head, but he grabs my wrist and pins it to the small of my back.

No one has ever pinned me to any surface to give me anilingus. It's more intimate than I ever imagined and oddly exhilarating. The muscles of my core flutter as his tongue moves in and out, setting every nerve on fire.

I squirm in his grip, my clit swelling, jealous with the need for attention. When I reach down toward it with my free hand,

Cesare grabs my wrist to join the other one in the small of my back.

"Hey!" I rock from side to side, trying to throw him off, but he's a dead weight. "Time out. Time out!"

His cruel laugh echoes against my asshole, his hot breath making my skin tingle. "That wasn't in the rules, pet."

"Shit."

He doubles his efforts, his tongue delving even deeper, delivering sensations so overpowering that all I can do is quiver against the canvas. Bolts of pleasure electrifying my senses. I have never felt so vulnerable, or exposed.

Releasing one of my wrists, he slides his fingers up and down my slit, making the most obscene wet sound.

"Stop teasing," I say from between clenched teeth.

"I thought you asked for a time out," he replies, his voice full of mirth.

"S-Shut up."

With a chuckle, he rubs a circle over my swollen clit. I buck and jerk against his face, needing more.

"You're so wet," he says around my asshole. "Do you like it when I toss your salad, little pet?"

"Stop calling me that," I say.

"Make me."

I yank my other hand out of his grip, slam my elbows into the surface beneath me to push upward. Cesare's tongue slips out of my asshole and grazes my clit. Sensations spark through my core, making my legs falter.

Ignoring the onslaught of pleasure, I scramble to my feet. Cesare grabs my waist, trying to pull me down, but I rush out of his grip. He slams me against the ropes, using our momentum to knock us both flying backward.

Cesare lands on the canvas first in a backward roll, holding my waist so I roll after him. He flips around, so I'm pinned with my weight on my shoulders and my ass in the air.

He positions himself between my spread legs, his face so close to my pussy that the skin there twitches against his stubble.

"Hey," I say.

"Let's see If I can make you ejaculate." He sticks two fingers past my entrance and curls them inward.

I'm so slick and wet that my pussy welcomes the intrusion. My walls flutter around his digits, and the delicious stretch sends a shiver down my spine.

He curls his fingers and strokes back and forth against my g-spot, making me tremble and twitch in his grasp.

My legs tremble, my heart beats like a wild drum.

I'm still weak and trembling from the orgasm when he drags me to the edge of the canvas and hurls me against the ropes. I fall back, my arms splaying to the side, but he entangles them within the top and middle restraints.

"Shit..." I bite down on my bottom lip to keep from moaning.

He laps at my clit, his tongue flicking back and forth in time with the movement of his fingers. My body convulses with each touch, the pleasure becoming too intense.

"Oh, fuck," I murmur.

He adjusts my position, bringing my hips toward the ceiling. Blood rushes to my head at the unusual angle. I would buck him off, but I can't resist the raw pleasure. My body convulses with each lap of that skillful tongue, bringing me dangerously close to climaxing.

"What a good little pet," he murmurs between my folds. "Holding still while I eat your sweet pussy."

"Don't stop," I say from between clenched teeth.

"Why would I when I plan on making you squirt?"

His digits continue their relentless assault, stroking back and forth against that sensitive spot that makes my core ripple.

Molten ecstasy sears my veins, and my hips buck against his mouth, seeking that delicious climax. Pressure builds, and my inner muscles tighten around his fingers.

"That's my girl," he says, still lapping at my engorged bud.

My pleasure peaks, making my body spasm and contort. Pleasure radiates from my core in convulsions so intense that I scream.

Cesare continues licking me through my euphoria, detonating every nerve like strings of dynamite. The ecstasy continues building until it explodes in a forceful release, making me squirt all over his face.

"Fuck," he groans.

I would apologize, but I'm not sorry. No one has ever made me come so hard. After holding me in position through the aftershocks, he releases me to the canvas, leaving me melting in a state of pure bliss.

As my eyes drift shut, my field of vision fills with his handsome features, framed by a chiseled jawline and tousled hair. His lips are swollen and face glistens with arousal. My heart races. This man is the embodiment of temptation, and his touch is electrifying. Every instinct says I should give in to my attraction, but there's still a part of me that wants to resist.

"Your body recognizes its master," he says. "It's only a matter of time before your mind catches up with the truth."

"Keep dreaming," I say with a groan, even though his words hold a touch of truth.

I'm still weak and trembling from the orgasm when he drags me to the edge of the canvas and hurls me against the ropes. I fall back, my arms splaying to the side, but he entangles them within the top and middle restraints.

Once he's sure I'm secured, he moves to the steps where he left the second bottle of baby oil.

Oh, shit. I can see where this is going.

EIGHTY-SEVEN

CESARE

Orgasms make Rosalind weak. Powerful ones make her especially docile. Maybe the endorphins flooding her system cloak her usual resistance, or maybe it's the sense of euphoria she can only get from me.

Whatever the reason for her current state, I have her utterly under my control.

She flops forward, trying to disentangle her arms from the ropes, but her body won't cooperate. All she can do is tremble from the aftershocks of the best climax of her life.

I grab her throat and force up her head. She pants hard through reddened lips and stares up at me through glazed eyes. My cock hardens, and my chest swells with pride at having conquered a woman so powerful.

But I'm not done with her yet.

My gaze drops to her nipples straining through her cropped top. "You're wearing too many clothes."

Without waiting for her to comment, I push up the fabric, exposing those glorious tits. Rosalind whimpers as I uncap the bottle of baby oil and pour a generous amount on my hand.

She trembles as I glide my slick hand over her breasts, coating her already glistening skin. My fingers find her hardened nipples, and I twist one followed by the other, then revel in her pretty little gasps.

My hand roams her belly, and she releases a soft sigh. Her chest rises and falls with each labored breath, and she trembles under my touch. Pouring the oil directly on her belly, I move my hand lower, caressing every inch of her bare skin, enjoying how she quivers under my touch.

I slide my fingers down to her still slick pussy. She bucks her hips and moans as I stroke her, wanting to make it purr. When she tries to close her thighs, I pull back.

"You don't get to hide my cunt."

She groans, desperate for my touch. I set down the bottle to grab her right calf and entwine it between the ropes before moving onto her left. Once she's completely restrained, her body goes limp.

Note to self. Rosalind loves bondage as long as there's a chance for her to escape.

"You're so beautiful like this." My fingers return to her pussy. "Bound and spread open like a feast."

I grab my shaft, lining up my cock head to her entrance and relishing in her helpless mewls. For a woman who claims not to like being called a pet, she's certainly playing the part.

"Eager?" I ask.

The noise she makes is an unintelligible sound of raw need. She tries to arch off the ropes to speed things along, but I take hold of her waist.

"Eyes on me, if you want me to feed your hungry little cunt."

Lashes fluttering, she raises her gaze to meet my eyes. Her pupils are blown with flames burning within those hazel orbs. A flush blooms across both cheeks, in a perfect contract to her pale skin.

Sensation surges to my cock at the sight of her vulnerability, making me lightheaded. There's only so much of this desperate display a man can withstand before something inside him breaks.

"Tell me how much you want this cock," I growl.

She cries out. "Cesare."

"Tell me, or I'll stop,"

"I want it," she says through gasping breaths.

"Now, tell me how much you want me."

She swallows hard, her throat bobbing as though I've finally pushed her too far. It was a dick move to ask while I'm edging her, but I want to hear her say the words just once.

In a voice barely above a whisper, she says, "So much... Cesare, I want you so much."

Triumph punches through my chest, breaking through the last of my restraint. With a forceful thrust, I slam into her tight heat, making her body jerk against the ropes and her eyes to fly open with shock. She inhales a choked gasp, like she's feeling my cock in the back of her throat.

"That's right, pet," I growl. "Feel me. All of me."

Tremors wrack her limbs as she strains against the ropes. Maybe a small part of her body still rebels against the bondage because her cunt tightens around my shaft with a punishing grip.

Groaning, I try not to think about how she gained this level of control over her pelvic floor muscles, and pull back, only to snap my hips and reenter her with a hard thrust.

I pick up the pace, thrusting into her with every ounce of strength I have. She makes breathy gasps as her body jerks back and forth within the ropes, the momentum deepening the penetration. It's almost like she's fucking me back.

"Fuck, Rosalind. Your greedy pussy is aching for this cock."

"Oh, god," she cries.

"I know, pet."

She squeezes extra tight, making me growl, "Good girl. Such a good little pet. You're taking it so well."

Tension coils behind my balls, but I refuse to let go. Not until she's convulsing around my cock. I clench my teeth, my mind going blank as I drive into her again and again, making sure my piercings graze her most sensitive spots.

Her eyes are feverish and wild, and her tits bounce with every shuddering breath. She's close, but I'm not sure if I can last.

"Come for me. Scream so loud that they can hear you at the gates," I growl, my hand sliding between our bodies and finding her clit. "Now."

Rosalind cries out, and her limbs thrashing within the ropes. Her pussy trembles around my shaft, pumping, squeezing, demanding more. The sight of her, open and vulnerable beneath me, pulls me deeper into her abyss.

The room spins, and my entire world disappears until it's me, my little vixen and her tight, wet heat.

I'm both invincible and exposed, feeling like I don't know if I've conquered a goddess or if she has finally conquered me. All I know is that if she ever left me, I would surely die.

Blood roars between my ears as pleasure radiates across my midsection, before concentrating on my cock. It intensifies until I reach a point of no return where I couldn't stop coming, even if Matty Galliano charged in here with a militia.

Pressure builds up, and my muscles contract. My vision turns white in the heartbeats it takes for my release to surge with unstoppable force.

Rosalind's pussy continues to contract, draining every last drop from my balls before I collapse on top of her, gasping for breath.

"Fuck, baby, you were made for me. My perfect little pet."

She makes a noise that may or may not sound like agreement. It's definitely not a protest.

Once my limbs stop trembling, I pull out of her and disentangle her limbs from the ropes. Rosalind falls into my arms like a rag doll, breathless, limp, and all mine. I gaze down into her dazed features, marveling at how I've subdued her with my cock.

Later, we soak in the hot tub, where I place her on my lap and massage feeling back into her limbs. She's everything I ever wanted in a dangerous little package, and I resolve to continue proving to her that she's going to need me in her life even after she's destroyed the Moirai.

———

When I return upstairs, there's a message from Roman, confirming that the Moirai have agreed to call off the hit in exchange for the ten hostages. They've even agreed to make the exchange on the same day as their graduation.

I drive Rosalind to Newtown Crematorium, where we meet my cousins, Aria and Elania, who are always ready to let us use their cremators. The twins are Roman's age, but they always made a beeline for me when they visited the house. I used to love how they pampered me and treated my brothers like shit. They used to be identical back then, but now it's easier to tell them apart.

People make the mistake of thinking Elania is the pushover because of her long black hair and pretty silk dresses, but I've seen her knife a man in the heart. Aria wears her hair shorter than any of my brothers and doesn't have a single feminine bone in her body. She would look like a dude if it wasn't for her delicate bone structure.

She guides us to a visitation room, where they've dressed Britt in a black pantsuit and laid her in a coffin.

Rosalind chokes a sob. "It looks like she's asleep."

Thank fuck my cousins are geniuses at making the dead appear lifelike. They've added color to the blonde's sallow features, making her look at peace.

"Do you need a moment alone with her, pet?" I ask.

"Thank you." Rosalind turns to me with a watery smile.

Pulling her to my chest, I place a kiss on the top of her head and exit the room to give her privacy.

As I walk down the marble hallway and pull out my phone, the click-clacking heels approach me from behind. Turning around, I spot Elania hurrying toward me with a scowl.

"Where's Benito?" she snaps.

My brows pull together. "Last time I saw him was a few days ago. Have you checked the casino?"

"He isn't returning my calls. That asshole owes us for two days of lost business for using up all four of our cremators."

"Have you called the house?"

"He's ghosting us," she says as though I haven't spoken.

"Take it up with Roman," I reply with a shrug.

She huffs. "That bastard owes me, too. I broke a heel at that party that turned into a gunfight and ripped the hem of my dress."

My lips quirk. "Tell Maria from Dolce Vita to put a replacement outfit on my tab."

She rocks forward on her tiptoes and gives me a kiss on both cheeks. "Next time your brothers want to use our crematorium for bulk disposal, we're going to charge you double. And demand payment in advance."

Chuckling, I watch her disappear down the hallway, and then exchange a few texts with Miranda. I let her know Rosalind has lost her best friend without giving specifics and ask her to send a message of condolences.

After that, I check my phone for messages from unknown callers. Matty Galliano has gone silent since the incident at the graveyard. Maybe Sofia shot something critical. With any luck, the bastard is dead.

Two text messages pop up from Dr. Cortese. The first says the mercury nitrovolucite is now stable enough for transportation, and the second confirms that it just arrived at the Parisii Cemetery.

I slip the phone in my pocket and exhale. Everything is going as planned. Xero's people will leave the crystals at strategic points within the Moirai HQ, and our bombs will reduce their underground hideout along with their senior management to dust.

Footsteps approach. I crack open an eye to find Rosalind hurrying toward me with her cheeks flushed.

Pushing off the wall, I walk toward her with a frown. "Are you alright, love—"

She cuts me off with a kiss.

EIGHTY-EIGHT

ROSALIND

No man has ever helped me without sinister motives. My biological father died before I was born, and my only stepfather groomed me to become a plaything. The mentor who promised to make me stronger recruited me into an organization that doesn't allow its employees to leave.

Axel, who I thought might be a suitable partner, stabbed me in the back to boost his image and take a sizable bonus for a mission he wasn't qualified to complete.

Cesare is the first man who dropped his mask and showed me the monster behind the man. He's loyal, loving, and trying hard to fix the rift between me and my daughter. Our goals might not be aligned, but he's still making every dream come true. In a few days, I'll be free from the Moirai and I can finish the job I started when I threw a rocket launcher at Matteo.

He stiffens for a second, but he joins in on the kiss, his arms wrapping around my shoulders in a possessive hug. His lips move against mine with an urgency that makes my heart pound.

This morning was exactly what I needed to soothe my grief. From the moment he pulled me out of that nightmare to arranging for Miranda to comfort to me on the loss of my best friend. I love sleeping beside Cesare. I love the way we fight just as much as I love the way we fuck.

Our personalities, backgrounds and situations in life are so different, yet everything about us makes sense. I'm water. He's fire. I'm order. He's chaos. I've felt like a pawn my entire life and he's a mafia prince.

He adores Miranda and doesn't judge me for having a child so young, and Miranda adores him. I'm starting to wonder if I'm going through the final stages of Stockholm syndrome because he's stealing my heart.

When we break apart, his pale eyes are aflame with emotions so intense that my heart flutters. He raises a hand to stroke my cheek, his touch making my skin erupt in tingles. As much as I want to lose myself in him, it's impossible to ignore his red flags.

I glance away, my breath quickening.

This is moving too fast. I'm usually so cautious with men.

"Feeling better, love?" he asks, his voice soft.

"Yeah," I reply, trying not to sound choked up. "Thanks for arranging this."

He pulls me into his chest for a comforting hug, and it takes every effort not to melt in this embrace. That doesn't stop me from resting my head on his shoulder and wrapping my arms around his waist.

It's alright to enjoy his company while I'm still in survival mode. As soon as our bargain is over, so will our relationship.

He cups my cheeks. "Xero has the delivery. Are you still okay with the plan?"

I nod. "I'm not just freeing myself, but all the students about to sign their lives over to an evil organization. Every operative at the graduation will also be set free."

He nods. "You realize the other hostages will die tomorrow?"

My throat thickens. "Yeah. Can I see them?"

———

Half an hour later, we're back in the basement. Instead of returning to the room with the five crosses, we're in an infirmary where Greta, Branson, and the other two operatives from the assassination attempt are sitting up, strapped to hospital beds.

Thick bands restrain their entire bodies, with their fingers encased in splints. Feeding tubes snake from their noses, along with IV lines delivering fluids into their veins. Catheter bags hang from the side of each cot, making me shudder.

To the left and right of them, the other six operatives lie unconscious within their beds. I recognize them all, and over the decade I've been at the Moirai, not a single one of them has shown me any respect.

"Rosalind," Greta croaks, her voice pulling me out of my musings. "How are you still alive?"

My brows rise. I almost forgot how they all colluded to throw me under the proverbial tank by telling Cesare I arranged the assassination. Hearing her voice is a reminder of the daily mockery and humiliation I faced when Gunther demoted me, and I became a scapegoat and a cautionary tale for anyone thinking of defying the firm.

Well, I'm no longer the bottom of the barrel and no longer have any reason to cringe. Ignoring her question, I ask, "Why didn't you fight with me when we were all being held at gunpoint?"

Greta glances at Branson, who bows his head.

"Branson?" I ask.

When he doesn't answer, I turn to the other two. "Well?"

"You were already marked for death," Greta spits.

"What does that mean?" I ask, already knowing part of the answer from questioning Dr. Daniel.

"Gunther said you rejected the promotion to join forces with the Montesano family, and it looks like he was right."

My nostrils flare, and I grind my teeth, not bothering to tell them I left HQ because Cesare took Miranda. Most of these people don't have connections outside the firm. Those who did sure as hell wouldn't sacrifice their lives if any of their relatives got abducted.

Recruiters at the Moirai target orphans, kids in foster homes, or those sent away to boarding schools by their families to rot. If I didn't have a child, I would be just as disconnected from the outside world.

"If Gunther doesn't kill you for being a double agent, we will," Branson adds.

"There's something you should know about your precious Gunther," I say through clenched teeth. "Every operative who gets promoted overseas is dead or has been left for dead."

"Bullshit," Greta says.

"Ask yourself how many of these lucky people have ever returned to the USA."

"You and Axel went to Zurich."

"That was a job, not a promotion," I say.

"I speak to my brother every day," Branson says.

"AI."

He flinches. "What?"

"They've recorded every communication we've made over their network since we were in the academy. Our images, voices, and mannerisms, even the way we think, are all stored in computers beneath the tenth floor."

Greta scoffs. "That's pathetic, even for you."

I turn to Branson. "When was the last time you saw your brother face-to-face? Surely, he would have used his vacation time to meet you somewhere?"

Branson's face blanches, his eyes widening. "Is this how the Montesano family got you to defect?"

"You didn't answer my question," I reply, my lips tightening. "But let me answer yours."

Silence stretches out across the infirmary, broken only by the beeping of monitors. I sweep my gaze over the four conscious operatives, my spine stiffening with their reflected disdain.

"I teamed up with the Montesano family the moment you let me fight those guards alone and left me to get beaten and shot. As I lay there in pain, I realized you were never my teammates, just another bunch of people who saw me as disposable."

"So, you're a traitor?" Greta spits, her features twisting with contempt.

"I'm finally putting myself first," I reply. "And when the four of you tried to shift the blame for the assassination onto me, I knew I'd made the right choice."

"You won't get away with this," Branson says. "Gunther will send out a rescue team."

"Gunther didn't give a shit about you until the Montesanos took six more hostages," I say.

He flinches, his lips tightening with rage. "Nothing you say will change my mind. He probably sent those six on a rescue mission, but they got captured."

It's a good thing I only came here to get closure. Even if I wanted to save their lives, they'd still want me dead. I turn on my heel and head toward the door, ignoring Greta's shouts that I'm a traitor.

They already put me in the line of fire twice, and now they've threatened my life. I'd be suicidal to ask Cesare to show them mercy.

Pausing at the door, I spare them a final glance. "Ask Gunther all about it when you see him, because they've finally agreed to call off the hit in exchange for your return."

Branson huffs. "I knew he would."

"Count your days," Greta adds. "You won't last long after I tell everyone you're a turncoat."

Nobody will live long enough to exact their revenge. Leaving that part unsaid, I walk out, ready for tomorrow's mission.

It's going to be trickier than the last time when Cesare handed the Moirai decoys. The location they've given Cesare is above the HQ, so they're going to need all the help they can get to leave the building alive.

EIGHTY-NINE

ROSALIND

I'm no stranger to explosives. We dabbled with them in the academy, and then I launched grenades into Matteo and his henchmen. Explosives are essential to getaways on large missions, but our job the next morning is different.

This is the first mission I'll be doing without Britt. Instead, Cesare will take the lead because his family won't trust me until we've ended the threat hanging over their heads.

Hours before the hostage swap, Cesare and I are in the armory with a group of his men. One of them is a skilled getaway driver named Carlo, who everyone assures me is the best.

As the other men load one truck full of explosives, we walk around another vehicle to check that all the modifications I ordered have been installed.

"What do you think?" Cesare asks, his fingers slipping into the high collar of his armor. "Does it pass inspection?"

"It should withstand the explosions if we can get out of the building in time." I run a gloved hand down the reinforced steel plating to the combat bumper we're going to use as a battering ram. "But I want everyone to wear full body armor."

Carlo scoffs. "I'm quick. I don't need it."

Cesare grabs the older man's shoulder. "When a highly

trained assassin with over a decade of experience tells you to wear armor, you follow her fucking instructions."

My chest swells with warmth. I don't remember any man I've slept with demanding that another give me respect. Cesare is the first who has even acknowledged my skills.

Carlo glances up and down my body armor, his gaze now assessing. Ignoring him, I continue to the truck's interior, making last-minute suggestions to increase our chances of leaving the Moirai HQ with our lives.

The final modification we make to the armored truck is the addition of a black box from Dr. Daniel's ambulance. This will prevent the shutters at HQ from falling, ensuring a faster escape.

When the vehicle is ready, Cesare pulls me to one side. "I want you to stay behind."

Gazing up into his pale eyes, I place a palm on his chest. His heart beats fast, echoing my own anxiety and betraying his stoic mask.

"We already talked about this," I say, my voice soft. "Who's going to help you improvise if something goes wrong?"

His jaw clenches, and his nostrils flare with frustration. "I'll put on an earpiece. You can direct us from a mile away—"

"HQ is surrounded by cell phone jammers," I say. "Their network is the only way of communicating within a half-mile radius of the building."

Scowling, he jerks his head to the side. "Don't you think you've risked enough?" In a much lower voice, he adds, "She's depending on you."

"Which is why I want to make sure we both get out of this in one piece," I murmur. "She's depending on you, too."

He turns back to me, his eyes softening. "What do you mean, love?"

"Are we ready to go?" Gil lumbers up to us, holding a chain attached to four of the shackled hostages, each shackled at their hands and feet with their heads covered in bags.

"Talk later," I say.

We board the truck we reinforced and direct Gil to seat the hostages by the double doors. The other six sit in a larger truck that contains enough explosives to reach the Moirai's middle levels. The mercury nitrovolucite Xero's people seeded around the building and the bottom floors will have to do the rest.

As we pull out of the warehouse, my phone buzzes. I reach into the pocket of my body armor to find a message from an unknown number.

Target found. St. Dismas Medical Center. Hamlet, New Jersey.

It's followed by a photo of Matteo lying in a white hospital bed, shot from outside the window.

My stomach churns at the sight of him lying there still drawing breath.

Cesare leans into my side. "What's wrong?"

I pass him the phone. "They've found him."

His nostrils flare, and his features twist with disgust. I can't blame him. Matteo brutally murdered his two exes, hoping to frame him before trying to do the same to Sofia. It's hard to imagine anyone being more despicable than him except for his brother, Tommaso, the pimp.

"Shit," he hisses. "We need to be there now, before he gets discharged."

I squeeze his hand. "We'll never get another chance to target the Moirai."

He breathes hard, his face flushing. The last time I saw him so furious was when one of his men shot me in the shoulder, and Gil had to stop him from shooting up the entire room.

"We'll handle Galliano later," I say.

He nods, too furious to form words. I also fall silent, trying to keep my mind far away from thoughts of my former stepfather.

Several minutes later, the truck stops behind the complex of buildings that make up the newly renamed Casino Montesano. From what I overheard, Roman stayed there overnight with Emberly, the woman he brought to the family dinner.

Benito won't come with us as he's only just taken back control of the business and is still weeding out people loyal to the man who framed Roman for murder.

"Put a bag over my head, so I look like the other hostages," I say to Cesare as he leaves to get his brother.

"You sure?"

I nod.

Although most operatives and support staff will be at the academy's graduation run, there will be a skeleton crew monitoring us as we approach HQ. We can't allow them to see me, sitting pretty among the Montesano brothers.

Everyone at the Moirai might act like I'm an incompetent screw up, but they'll soon remember why I was at the top of my classes and was the only graduate who was given solo missions. Everyone else had to serve at least a year as an analyst.

The bag does nothing to block my vision, but I close my eyes and focus on slowing my breath. Nothing has been left to chance, but I'm prepared in case anything goes wrong.

Several minutes later, Roman's voice cuts through my thoughts. "Can they hear us?"

"They're in sensory deprivation. All wearing earplugs and blindfolds," Cesare answers.

The brothers discuss the firms of assassins Roman has employed to track down the Galliano brothers, and I'm surprised when Cesare doesn't mention Xero's text. Roman talks about them like they're business rivals he needs to eliminate instead of a monster who married his mother.

But judging by the conversations I overheard about Tania and Allegra's murders, his family doesn't believe that Matteo would target people connected to Cesare. Outsiders think Matteo is the quieter brother, who gives the appearance of a kind uncle, while Tommaso is the raging psychopath.

Matteo probably targeted Cesare because he's the most vulnerable of the Montesano brothers. He's younger, volatile, unpredictable, and doesn't seem to command the same level of respect as Roman and Benito.

He's criminally underestimated.

Just like me.

"They know we're coming?" Roman asks.

"It's all arranged," Cesare replies.

"How do we know we're not driving into a trap?"

"It's not a trap if we're coming in with a Trojan horse."

"Explain this plan to me again," Roman says.

I tune out as Cesare tells his brother how the mercury

nitrovolucite crystals will cause a chain of chemical reactions that will increase the range of the explosives below the tenth floor.

"And Leroi's little assassin?" Roman asks.

I hold my breath.

"You mean my little assassin," Cesare snaps.

"She's leaving with the others, right?" Roman growls.

"Of course," Cesare says, sounding suspiciously calm. "She'll soon be a dead little assassin."

My jaw clenches. What the hell is he saying? I would interrupt them, but there's a bag over my head, and I'm supposed to have on earmuffs. Cesare knows I can hear him, and he knows I can break free and save myself.

My mind races through the possibilities. Is Cesare bullshitting Roman? Because after everything we've gone through together, he can't really be planning my death.

Moments later, the air changes. It's a subtle shift that's barely noticeable unless you know what to look for. Static electricity crackles against my skin, and my nostrils fill with the faintest scent of ozone. We've just crossed the first of the demarcation lines surrounding the Moirai HQ.

I've driven through this patch of road so many times I recognize every bump in the road. There's a subtle incline in the tarmac, and the vehicle slows at the entrance of the building we were told to deliver the hostages.

It's one of the decoy structures close to our official entrance, where we accept the occasional delivery. A hidden elevator shaft lies within a locked room that grants access to all except the secret levels.

We continue again into the parking lot. I don't need the use of my eyes to know it's surrounded by armed operatives. They'll remain cordial until they've retrieved their personnel, then all hell will break loose.

"Roman Montesano. Release the hostages," Gunther's disembodied voice croaks a distant speaker.

I grind my teeth. He could be anywhere, from his office several floors below, to the top of the elevator shaft. Since today is a graduation run, he should be in an observation room full of screens, watching the young people he and his colleagues groomed into a future of deadly servitude.

It doesn't matter. The mercury nitrovolucite is already in place and Xero will have told his people to evacuate. All we need to do is escape.

A door creaks open. One of the operatives drove the truck filled with explosives into the building and has already released five of his colleagues. Everything Cesare and I planned for the handover is going as planned.

Now Gunther wants the other four in our truck.

My heart pounds, even though I'm ninety-nine percent certain Cesare won't toss me out with the others. The one percent accounts for Roman's interference.

I wait while the brothers haul out a pair of hostages and toss them on the floor. As they land with two thuds, I dig in my heels.

When an unfamiliar hand grabs my arm, my stomach lurches.

It's Roman.

Shit. Shit. Shit.

I part my lips to scream, but the door slams shut, and Cesare drags me on his lap.

Bullets ricochet off the reinforced armor, and Carlo slams the truck in reverse. The rapid motion has me jerking to the side in Cesare's grip. By now, Gunther will have sealed the exits, enclosing us within the building.

I throw out a silent prayer to anyone listening that the reinforced bumper is enough. We're going to need that battering ram to work the first time to make a fast getaway.

There's a satisfying crunch of metal as the bumper plows through the barrier, and the wheels skid across the tarmac.

My heart soars, but it's too early to celebrate. If Cesare detonates the bomb too early, we're dead. Too late, and he's allowed the Moirai enough time to give chase.

The truck accelerates, the speed pushing us against our seats. My stomach lurches. What happens next will be the difference between escaping and being blown into pieces.

A slight change in atmosphere makes my ears pop, indicating we're out of the danger zone.

"Cesare," I say, my voice tense.

"Now," he yells.

A heartbeat later, a deafening explosion makes the ground rumble. The force of the blast has us lurching backward, then the wheels skid. I can't tell if we miscalculated the danger zone or Carlo lost control of the vehicle.

Cesare's grip tightens around my waist as we jerk from side to side. I no longer know where we're going. The ground is uneven, seeming to crumble beneath the wheels.

We must have collapsed an unexpected tunnel, which is why the truck won't stop floundering.

My throat closes, and I hurl my last hope toward the driver's seat, hoping Carlo can maneuver us out of the chaos. We jerk from side to side as he fights to regain control, then the wheels straighten, and the truck surges forward.

We did it. Not only did we destroy the Moirai's upper echelons, but all their data. They're gone, and I've freed myself, the academy students, and all the other operatives bound to a lifetime of servitude.

Cesare rips the sack off my head and kisses me on the mouth. He tastes of freedom, of victory, of triumph and relief. I kiss back, not caring that Roman is sitting opposite and still thinks I'm a threat.

Our next stop is ridding the world of Matteo Galliano and his scumbag brother.

NINETY

CESARE

When Rosalind kisses back, I feel like a fucking king.

Straddling my lap, she squirms against my cock and devours my mouth like I'm the only man in the entire world. She's like *Charlie's Angels*, *The A-Team*, and *Ocean's Eleven*, all wrapped up in a sexy little package.

And she's all mine.

But is she? Destroying the Moirai HQ has just bought her freedom. It's what we promised the evening she swung a metal pole at my head when she thought I molested her daughter.

Shit. Tonight, we're going to kill Matty Galliano and then go after his brother. After that, our bargain will be complete. I need to do something, say something, be someone worthy of her love before she walks out of my life.

Cursing, Carlo accelerates, reversing at breakneck speed. Rosalind pulls away from the kiss as the rumbling turns to a deafening roar.

"What's happening?" Roman asks from the seat opposite.

"Looks like the tunnels and sewers connecting HQ to the rest of the city are also collapsing," she says with a grimace. "The blast must have been stronger than I calculated."

"Thank fuck the Moirai chose such a remote location for their headquarters," Roman mutters.

I turn Rosalind's head back to mine. "Ignore my brother. He's only sore because he couldn't handle the Moirai without your help."

The truck swerves sharply to the left, jerking us sideways. Roman grunts as he slams into the wall, but Rosalind barely flinches. Her eyes are locked on mine with an intensity that makes my heart pound.

"Thank you," she murmurs.

My eyes widen. "What for?"

"For the lab, the money we needed to pay Xero, the bombs, the men, and for listening. We're finally free."

She gazes down at me, her eyes softening. The golden flecks in their hazel irises shimmering in the truck's dim light.

Cradling her cheek, I run the pad of my thumb across her cheekbone. I'm being a selfish prick. All this time, I've been thinking about what destroying the Moirai meant to me: an exciting adventure, my brothers' respect, the absence of being gunned down by assassins. Hell, I even lamented about losing Rosalind.

I'd forgotten those Moirai bastards took her in when she was no older than Miranda and wouldn't let her leave. And when she displeased her overlords, they signed her life over to a sick fuck who planned on raping her before cutting her up into pieces.

It's obvious, even to me, that I don't deserve Rosalind.

Nobody does. Not even Leroi.

"I'd do it all again," I say, my voice rough. "Anything for my girls."

She reaches around my neck, her slender fingers twining in my hair as she pulls me closer. Her lips press against mine in a soft kiss, which I return with vigor. She kisses back, this time with a fierce intensity floods my cock with sensation.

The truck jolts again, but neither of us flinches. She digs her fingernails into my skin, detonating explosions of pleasure. The world falls away, the sound of the truck engine and Carlo's curses fading into nothingness. All that matters at this moment is Rosalind.

Roman harrumphs. "Could you wait until we're not trying to escape an earthquake?"

Breaking the kiss, I mutter, "Don't like it, don't watch. Without Rosalind, we'd be running around like headless chickens. She deserves a reward."

She snorts.

Adjusting her on my lap, I press kisses on her exposed neck, and murmur into her skin, "You're wearing too many clothes."

"I swear to god, if this turns into some exhibitionism kink, I'm throwing you both out on the street," Roman mutters.

"You wouldn't dare. We owe her our fucking lives." I turn my attention back to Rosalind. "Take no notice of that asshole. He's just jealous because he can't get a sexy assassin."

Rosalind chuckles against my lips, the sound injecting my heart with endorphins. This is the second time I've ever made her laugh.

The earth stops moving, or maybe it's because I'm too absorbed in Rosalind to notice anything else. We continue kissing until Roman's hand lands on my shoulder.

"Good work," he says with a broad smile. With a nod toward Rosalind, he adds, "Family dinner tonight. It's going to be a big celebration."

"We have other plans," I reply.

Roman's smile falters a fraction, but he nods, exits the van, and disappears into the armory. I'm vaguely aware of Carlo opening the cab door and jumping out when Rosalind cups my cheek.

"Why did you reject your brother's offer?" she whispers.

"We finally have a lead on that bastard," I reply, my voice low. "There's no way in hell I want to miss out on the chance to murder him in his bed."

When her features harden with determination, my heart sinks a little with dread. Rosalind is only eager to help me kill Matty Galliano because it's bringing her one step closer to financial freedom. And freedom from me.

Matty's death will attract Tommy, if he isn't already coming to visit his brother's bedside, then Rosalind will be out of my life in less than twenty-four hours.

"Close the door," she whispers.

"Why?"

"Destroying an evil organization along with the people inside it who wanted me dead makes me horny," she replies, her eyes dancing.

"You drive a hard bargain." I rise off my seat with her still wrapped around my body like a boa constrictor, and pull the door shut. "Lucky for you, I'm equipped to handle your demands, no matter how dirty."

She giggles, the sound so sweet that it stabs me in the heart, reminding me of everything I'm about to lose.

"Let's take a look at this so-called equipment." She reaches between our bodies and unzips my bulletproof pants.

The mischief in those hazel eyes makes my breath hitch. Seeing Rosalind looking so happy is an aphrodisiac I never knew I needed.

Still straddling my hips, she wraps her fingers around my cock and eases it out from my fly, exposing it to the truck's cool air.

"Is the equipment to your satisfaction, love?" I ask.

Her bright smile is all the answer I need. She leans in, pressing her armored chest against mine, and says, "Looks like it's up for the job."

"Good, because I'm about to give you the ride of your life."

With trembling hands, I fumble with the clasps and zippers of her armored pants. Arousal courses through my veins, making me clumsy, but I refuse to give up until I expose that sweet pussy.

Her breath quickens, matching the rhythm of my heart. The pants fall away, revealing the soft curves of her ass. She reaches for the collar of her bulletproof jacket, but I grab her wrist.

"I want to fuck you just like this."

"Why?" she asks with a chuckle.

"I want to look into the eyes of the chemist who synthesized mercury nitrovolucite, the strategist who tricked the Moirai into handing us six more operatives, just so they could finally let us into their territory. I want the stone-cold assassin who planned a Trojan horse attack that reduced the Moirai to a crater. I want the genius who outsmarted a death sentence to become the queen of destruction."

Eyes darkening, she tightens her grip on my shaft, her

features morphing into a wicked grin. "What about Rosalind? Do you want to be with her?"

"I wanted you from the moment you walked into the Phoenix wearing that white dress."

"Even though I fucked your cousin?"

"It just made me want you even more."

"Because I attracted the most dangerous man in the club?" she asks with a smirk.

Huffing a laugh, I shake my head. "Because you were the most dangerous woman. There was something about you, even then, that made you stand out. If anyone other than Leroi had approached you, they would have died before they even took you in that alley."

She laughs, her eyes sparkling with mischief, and rises on her knees to position her pussy over my hard cock. "Well then, let's see if you still find me dangerous."

Then she descends, engulfing my shaft, inch by delicious inch. Placing my hands on her hips, I hold her in place, but do nothing to speed her progress. I want to fuck that boss bitch. I want her to take control.

Heat spikes through every nerve in my body as she takes my cock, making the truck echo with our mingled moans. When I'm fully sheathed, her lips crash into mine. The kiss is even more heated than before, and I've never felt so connected to another woman in my life. She's everything I never knew I needed. I never want this moment to end.

She rocks her hips, setting a rhythm that has us both gasping for air and rides my cock like she's stealing my soul. Rosalind is my deadly goddess—my queen of darkness, destruction and decadence. She unleashes a wildfire within my soul and a burning need that only she can quench.

I buck my hips, fucking into her tight heat, and reveling in the way her eyes roll to the back of her head. Her cunt tightens around my cock with a death grip, and I know she's close.

My balls tighten, threatening to spurt, but I grind my teeth. I refuse to come first.

"You look so sexy, taking control," I growl. "Using my cock for your pleasure. It's all yours, love. Ride it hard and take what you need."

"Oh fuck," she grinds out, her lips pulling back into a triumphant grin.

How the hell did I ever think I could cage this wild, dangerous woman? Or even dare try to break her unyielding spirit? I'm barely worthy enough to bask in her brilliance.

"Cesare, I'm coming," she says, her words choked.

She climaxes around my cock, her tight pussy spasming hard enough to draw the cum out of my balls. I hold back, determined to keep going until I've given her every inch of pleasure she deserves.

It's impossible to last when each thrust sends waves of ecstasy coursing through my veins, and her body feels like home. When she cries out my name and digs her nails into my neck, all my self-control erupts.

Jets and jets escape as I come in a furious rush. "Fuck," I growl as the sensations surge through my core like an electric shock. "I love you."

As I shoot what's left of my ego into her tight heat, her features flicker from arousal to alarm to awkwardness and then to something akin to pity. It's a fleeting kaleidoscope, each expression slicing through my already bleeding heart. Not a single one of them shows a hint of reciprocation.

She climbs off my rapidly softening cock, her eyes unable to meet mine, and pulls up her pants.

The weight of her rejection crushes my chest. I collapse against the seat, utterly destroyed. The only other woman I uttered those words to me walked out of my life and left me in ruins. Now, Rosalind's icy silence tears me apart more than any words of dismissal.

"Let's go to the medical center and take out the Galliano brothers," she says, her words full of ice.

My heart twists as she wrenches open the truck's doors and walks out without looking back. The thud of her boots echoes through my ears like a beat of a funeral march, each step a reminder that what we had together is dead.

Whatever made me think a woman like Rosalind could ever love me back?

NINETY-ONE

ROSALIND

My head pounds in time with the aftershocks pounding through my core. I stride through the armory on trembling legs, desperate for fresh air.

The last man who said he loved me was an abuser who got me pregnant, then told everyone the baby couldn't possibly be his because he was faithful to my mother. He got her to confine me to a room until it was time for my cesarean.

After they coerced me into signing over the adoption papers, they banished me to a boarding school where I was groomed into joining the Moirai.

Words are deceptive. Words are cheap. Words pave the road to hell. They're the red flags that remind me to guard my heart, because no good ever comes from grand declarations.

I burst through the exit, sucking in lungfuls of air. Despite the sun shining overhead, the industrial estate surrounding the armory is as bleak as my thoughts.

Why did Cesare have to ruin such a perfect moment? I loved how he was one of the few men who saw beyond my exterior and recognized my talents. I believed his compliments because they were true, but then I also thought the same about Matteo.

Matteo filled the void left by the father I never knew before the love he claimed to have for me twisted into something monstrous. It was a slow descent into darkness I didn't recognize until I was too deep to claw my way out.

And it all started with a confession of love.

He used to tell me I was beautiful, special, mature. That nobody else understood him the way I did, not even my mother. That we were soulmates.

The door opens with a thud that pulls me out of my thoughts. Cesare storms out, his eyes burning, the veins in his forehead standing out like bolts of thunder.

I turn to face him, but he pins me against the wall before I can even speak.

"What the fuck was that?" he snarls.

My jaw tightens, and my hands curl into fists. I didn't think he would follow me demanding answers. Those words of love were supposed to be a momentary lapse.

Ignoring the guilt twanging at my heartstrings, I meet his gaze. There's no doubt that he's hurt, but leaving was self-preservation.

His face looms inches from mine, every detail of those handsome features etched with fury.

"Cesare," I say with a sigh.

"No, Rosalind," he snaps. "Don't act like I'm the one who's being unreasonable when you walked out on me after I bared my soul."

My heart sinks into my stomach, bringing up a belly full of acid. I swallow it down, along with a bitter retort. "You forget we have an arrangement."

"Don't act like you feel nothing, because I know there's more to us than this truce. I love you, Rosalind—"

"Stop," I say, my breath quickening.

"Why? Because you don't want to admit to being in love with me, too?"

Pressure builds up like a tea kettle. The word love whistling through my ears. His accusation presses down on my lungs, making it impossible to breathe.

"Do you know who else used to manipulate me with that word?" I blurt.

"Your father?" he rasps.

"Stepfather," I reply.

Fury blazes in his eyes, causing them to bulge, and his face twists into a mask of venom. "You're comparing me to that disgusting pedo?"

"Does everything have to revolve around you?" I snap.

He flinches. "What does that mean?"

"I'm trying to explain to you why I had to walk away, and you're offended that I'm triggered by empty declarations of love because they remind me of him."

His nostrils flare. "They weren't empty."

Anger pulses through my veins. Sometimes, Cesare is so hard-headed I want to beat my point into him with my fists. Lashing out at him would probably only lead to another wrestling match and end up in sex.

Sucking in a deep breath, I switch tactics. "How would you expect me to respond if Dr. Daniel dropped the same words?"

His lips part with a protest, but I speak first. "Because he held me against my will, injected me with drugs, and cut off my clothes. I spent less than an hour with him, but I lost count of the weeks I was your captive."

"I never wanted you dead," he growls.

"How was I supposed to know that? I know you're sorry for what you did, but apologies can't take away the scars."

I push against his chest, but he stands in front of me like a wall. Ignoring the urge to strike out, I step out from beneath him and create a little distance.

He grabs my wrist. "Where are you going?"

"St. Dismas Medical Center. I have an assassination to complete. Are you coming?"

———

We don't exchange a single word on the journey to Hamlet, New Jersey, even though the tension is suffocating. Cesare grips the steering wheel so tightly that his knuckles turn white.

I can't even disappear into an exchange of text messages with Miranda because she's on a school trip on a remote spot within

Helsing Island's many nature reserves. Instead, I watch the scenery pass by in a blur of greens and browns and yellows.

Matteo used to say that once you've forgiven someone, you should never bring up their past mistakes. It's the type of bullshit philosophy he spewed to avoid accountability.

I hate thinking about that abuser or even acknowledging he's Miranda's father. Now that Gunther and the others are no longer breathing down my neck, I can finally finish the job I started with that grenade launcher.

The sooner he's dead, the sooner I can put the memory of him to rest. I close my eyes and try to tune out the world, but it's futile. Ignoring the presence of Cesare Montesano is like trying to ignore the sun.

At sunset, we arrive in Hamlet. It's a small town nestled in the countryside, with redbrick houses surrounded by rolling hills. I sit up in my seat as Cesare rolls up to the largest building in town.

The medical center is a modern building that looks at odds with the quaint surroundings. It's three stories high, with a mirrored façade that reflects the sunset's orange hues.

My heart thrums, and every instinct screams at me to rush in with guns blazing.

"There's a guesthouse across the road," I say to Cesare. "We could get a room, and—"

"No."

"No, you don't want to scope out a hospital that might be filled with Galliano guards? Or no, you don't want to wait and see if the brother comes in for a visit so we can make two kills instead of one?"

He turns to me, his teeth bared. "You can be insufferable sometimes, do you know that?"

"I thought you liked a woman who talks tactics."

"Bitch," he mutters under his breath, the corner of his mouth twitching.

"Don't you forget it."

"Alright, we'll check into the guest house, get a room overlooking the medical center, and watch the movement of the guards."

"Good."

"But don't go thinking I'm going to give you any cock."

Ten minutes later, he's fucking me hard and fast into the mattress, making me scream into a pillow for hurting his feelings.

NINETY-TWO

CESARE

Of all the women I could be obsessed with, why did she have to be an avoidant? Rosalind has been hurt so many times she keeps her heart in an iron safe.

The scraps of information I get from her puts together a picture of a girl whose neglectful mother exposed her to a predator. I think Britt was her only friend because it sounds like her colleagues at the Moirai treated her with contempt. Then there's Miranda, who still believes Rosalind is her sister who murdered their parents.

Each time I press for more, she retreats behind her walls or distracts me with sex. It's frustrating, but she's right about one thing: whether she forgives me or not, I'm still technically her captor.

We spend the next few days observing the hospital in shifts from the guest house window, logging the times Tommy and his men come to visit his brother.

Sofia really did shoot Matty in the stomach the morning he tried to stab her in the Parisii Cemetery. His men brought him here for an emergency exploratory laparotomy to repair the damage to his intestines and spleen.

Rosalind bribed the orderlies working in Matty's ward to keep her informed of the movements in and out of the old bastard's hospital room. According to them, there are two guards stationed inside the room to keep him company and another pair patrolling the hallway.

The guard change takes place precisely at 6:00 AM, and again at 6:00 PM. A local hooker visits after the evening change and stays in the room for an hour, and then Tommy visits at 7:00 AM and then 8:00 PM to bring a home-cooked meal.

I wake up in the late afternoon to find Rosalind stationed at the window with a pair of binoculars. Sunlight streams through the glass, turning the ends of her hair a rich shade of mahogany.

Her face, concentrated and serious, is bathed in a golden hue. I can't even bask in her beauty because I'm lovesick. It's entirely my fault for treating such a brilliant woman like a mere pet.

She's so busy sending rapid text messages she doesn't even notice that I'm awake. When she finally turns from the window and our gazes meet, her features harden.

My heart sinks at her coldness. It's confirmation that she's counting the days before she can walk out of my life. Every time I ask about the future, she changes the subject to our mission.

I pick up my phone from the bedside table and check the time, finding that it's already five. "Anything out of the ordinary happen while I was asleep?"

Her gaze darts back to the window. "They're discharging him tomorrow morning, which means we will strike tonight."

I sit up in bed, my heart pounding. "Finally."

She turns back to give me a sharp nod. "I acquired an orderly uniform and some ID. That will allow you to enter and exit the hospital without raising suspicion."

The formality in her words grates on my nerves. "And you?"

"I've canceled today's hooker so I can take her place. That gives us ample time to kill him slowly, then take out Tommy when he comes to visit."

"And afterward?"

"I already made arrangements with Xero," she replies, turning her attention back to her phone.

A burst of anger propels me out of the bed. I stalk toward her, my fists clenched, mind in utter turmoil as I grapple with rejection and confusion.

"What does that mean?" I say through clenched teeth.

Rosalind halts, her fingers pausing mid-text, and gazes at me as if I'm the lunatic. "We need a decoy to help you get past the guards. I also asked Xero to station a car at each exit with a driver. Black sedans with sequential registrations driven by men wearing black baseball caps."

"Isn't that overkill?"

"Probably, but we could get separated. That way, both of us have a surefire escape route."

It's too early to feel relief because it sounds like she's already planning our breakup. "And after that?"

She flashes me a smile. "Then we celebrate."

"And after we celebrate?"

She inhales a deep breath and sighs. "Tonight will be complicated enough. We need to take out one set of guards without alerting the other. Once we've dealt with the first brother, we only have a short window of time before it's time to take out the other."

"Alright," I say, my voice tight. "But you don't get to disappear in one of those sedans."

She closes the distance between us and places a palm on my chest. "There's no chance of that happening."

"Until you get your money," I add, trying not to sound bitter.

"Will giving you an answer help you focus better on the mission?" she asks, her voice soft.

I give her a sharp nod, the muscles of my stomach tightening in anticipation of her rejection.

"There's no such thing as love. Before you protest, I believe in filial love, platonic love, and any other kind of affection that's built up over years of sacrifices and trust. But romantic love is nothing more than an extreme chemical reaction."

"Are you comparing what we have to a drug?"

She raises a shoulder. "Maybe. Drugs fade, just like romantic love."

"Give me a chance to prove to you I'm not fickle."

Her eyes soften. "After tonight."

I nod. "Deal."

It's not the answer I was hoping for, but it's the sliver of hope

I need to get through tonight's confrontation with Matty Galliano.

I need to stay alert. Rosalind is likely to escape me the moment the Galliano brothers are dead. I'll have to move quickly before she slips away.

NINETY-THREE

ROSALIND

My heart pounds as I saunter down the stark hallway dressed in fishnets, a denim miniskirt and halter-neck top. I'm a little over-dressed compared to the women who usually visit Matteo's hospital room, but it's the most effective way to conceal weapons.

The calm I usually feel on missions is gone, replaced by a slow-burning rage that's been simmering since the moment I discovered Matteo and his brother had survived the explosion.

"Hello, sweetheart," the burly guard at Matteo's door rumbles. He's a bald mammoth of a man whose bulk could flatten a whale. "I haven't seen you around."

I flick my gaze up and down the muscles bulging out of his suit. "Maybe that's because you haven't looked hard enough."

He snickers. "Well, I'm looking now."

Wiggling my shoulders, I shoot him a flirty smile. "You gonna get hard for me later?"

He grins, his eyes dancing. "I reckon I might."

"I'll be back at Bella's Ranch in a couple of hours. Ask for Flora."

His grin fades, only for his features to morph into contempt. I don't have the mental bandwidth to wonder if that's because he expected a hooker to invite him back to her home for a freebie. "He's waiting for you inside. You got an hour."

"Thanks, sugar." I step through the door, greeted by a cacophony of beeping machines, which are muffled by the roaring of my blood.

Being in Matteo's presence is like standing on the edge of a ravine, crumbling under the sheer weight of my banked emotions. A howling wind pushes at my back, forcing me toward a watery abyss. If I don't keep a tight rein on my emotions, I'll drown.

Matteo's hospital room is more like a luxury suite with its white walls and marble linoleum floor. Vibrant floral bouquets provide bursts of color, barely concealing the scent of antiseptic. Blue armchairs arranged around a low table occupy the first few feet of the space, and a television plays a mindless sitcom with an echoing laugh track.

The only blemish on this pristine interior is the vermin sleeping in a bed against a backdrop of floor-to-ceiling windows that overlook a garden courtyard.

Matteo looks frail and small propped on a pair of pillows beneath a blue blanket. Burn scars cover his face and down his neck, reminding me of my failed attempt to send him back to hell.

The man isn't just a parasite and a predator, he's a prehistoric cockroach.

Walking toward him, I reach into the cleavage of my top and pull out a paracord, discarding the promise I made to Cesare to save him the killing blow.

Matteo means more to me than just a business rival. He's the man who robbed me of my childhood, the monster who haunts my nightmares.

My heart pounds loud enough to awaken his frail carcass, even though our positions have now reversed. I'm the predator. He's the cornered, weakened prey. Adrenaline courses through my veins, making my fingers tremble. I finally have the chance to slay my demon.

Stirring, Matteo opens his eyes and then squints as though trying to place my face. There's a moment of recognition when his features fall slack with shock before twisting into a grotesque mask of hatred.

"Rosalind," he snarls, bearing a mouthful of white dentures. "Are you here to kill me?"

Footsteps thunder toward me before I can answer. I whirl around, barely blocking the fist of one of the orderlies who sold me information. His fist connects with my arm, sending shooting pain down to my still-healing bullet wound.

"You know her, boss?" he shouts.

Matteo grimaces. "She's been on my kill list for a decade."

A second man swings a nightstick at my head, forcing me to duck. I kick out, hard and fast, my boot catching him in the knee. He stumbles forward with a pained grunt, trying to regain his balance. It's too late. I wrap the paracord around his neck and pull tight, using the momentum to throw him into the wall.

"What the fuck are you all doing? Get her," Matteo snarls.

Strong arms grab me from behind. I stamp down on my attacker's foot, but his grip tightens. He lifts me off my feet.

"How do you like this, bitch?" the man restraining me says, already sounding out of breath.

I kick out at the first orderly, but the second lands a blow into my temple. Stars explode across my vision, turning the edges of my vision black.

Oh, shit.

It's three against one.

Four if you count Matteo pointing a pistol at me from the bed.

Before I can formulate a plan, the guard from earlier crashes through the door and lands on his back. The man holding me adjusts his grip into a chokehold, while another orderly pulls out his gun.

Cesare storms inside with a gun, only for his face to fall the moment he sees the orderly point his weapon at my head.

Matteo chuckles. "Cesare, my boy. I knew you would come for me if I laid a trap."

My throat tightens as I'm forced to watch Cesare take in the full extent of my miscalculation. Those asshole orderlies selling us the information were working for Galliano all along.

Seconds later, a trio of guards burst through the door, each pointing a gun at Cesare's back and blocking our escape.

This is more than just a trap. It's an ambush.

Matteo crawls out of bed, baring his brilliant white teeth. "And you even brought me a gift. The little bitch who threw a grenade at me and my men, killing four of them and leaving me covered in third-degree burns."

He rips off his gown, revealing an incision held together with sutures and covered in transparent film dressing. Surrounding it is a network of deep, textured scars, remnants of past burns that crisscross his chest, abdomen, and upper thighs.

Any triumph I might have felt from causing him so much pain disappears under a weight of crushing dread. Cesare is about to discover the identity of Miranda's father.

"I was good to you, Rosalind, yet you threw my kindness into my face," Matteo says, his voice breaking. "Every day, I look at the mess you made of my body and think of the ways I want you to die."

Alarm rings in my ears, loud enough to block out the rest of Matteo's hateful words. This is more than just an ambush.

One glance at Cesare's shocked features says he's worked out that Matteo is my former stepfather. Cesare's chest heaves as though the air is devoid of oxygen. He stares at me, his eyes wide, his features slack with betrayal.

"Rosalind," he rasps. "Is it true?"

Matteo points his gun at Cesare. "Don't tell me the manipulative bitch got to you, too?" He cackles. "You inherited your taste for treacherous brunettes from me, son."

Son?

My breath hitches.

It's only a figure of speech. They're technically step-uncle and nephew.

Cesare lurches forward. "Let go of her."

One of the trio of guards drives the butt of a pistol into the back of his head. Before Cesare's knees hit the linoleum, Matteo fires a bullet between the guard's eyes.

The huge man crumples to the floor, his colossal bulk crashing atop Cesare. My blood turns to ice as a cold realization hits me in the gut.

"I told you all to keep your fucking hands off my son," Matteo roars, and my jaw drops.

Cesare crawls out from beneath the fallen guard. His eyes are dazed, but blazing with fury. I look beyond his attractive features, remembering how much of an outsider I once felt when he was with my daughter and finally understanding why.

Cesare is Matteo's son. They're brother and sister.

Bile rises from my throat as everything slots into place. Cesare's mercurial temperament reminds me so much of Tommaso's, as does his proclivity for violence. Then that eerie calmness he gets when he's pushed beyond his limits is all Matteo.

My lips part with a question, but I refuse to give Matteo the satisfaction of knowing I'm in shock. Instead, I slip a hand into the seam of my skirt and extract a stiletto dagger.

Matteo tears the electrodes off his chest and shuffles toward Cesare. A knot forms in my stomach as the monster of my past comes closer, but I steel myself to keep my gaze steady.

"Are you hurt, son?"

Shudders run down my spine, and I gag within the orderly's chokehold.

"I am not your son!" Cesare rises to his knees, his face a mask of disgust, and launches a punch straight into Matteo's gut.

Matteo doubles over with a strangled roar. The other guards lurch forward, but Cesare is quicker. He grabs the dead man's semi-automatic and shoots the pair by the door, then takes aim at the other two orderlies.

The one still holding me by the neck hoists me up like a shield, but I drive my dagger into his arm. He screams, loosening the grip around my throat.

I drop to my feet, whirl around, and plunge the knife into his chest. He collapses to the floor, his eyes wide, his mouth opening and closing like a fish.

"Catch!" Cesare is about to toss me a gun, but Matteo tackles Cesare to the floor.

The door slams open, and someone shoots up in the ceiling, raining plaster on our heads. "What the fuck?"

It's Tommaso Galliano, flanked by two guards, and he's furious.

He rushes forward and delivers a kick to the back of Cesare's skull. "Get off my brother before I explode your head like a watermelon."

As his guards rush forward to separate the father and son, Tommaso turns his gaze to me. Recognition flashes in his eyes, and his lips curl with contempt.

"Call the doctor and put my brother back into bed," he says to a small crowd of men at the door.

"And Montesano?" asks a guard.

"Keep him subdued."

"What should we do with the whore?" asks another.

"Take her out to Bella's Ranch and keep her there until my brother is well enough to enjoy watching her burn."

NINETY-FOUR

CESARE

Pain reverberates across my cranium, and the pulse between my ears pounds hard enough to rattle my skull. My fucked-up state has nothing to do with that brutal kick.

I'm in shock.

Not because I finally understand why Matty Galliano wears thick makeup. Not because the man has no genitals. I'm shocked at the realization that he's the man Rosalind blew up the day she took back her daughter.

Matty Galliano is the stepfather who abused Rosalind.

Matty Galliano is Miranda's father.

Which makes Miranda my little sister.

I'm running on autopilot, my ears ringing with the shattering truth. Matty flounders beneath me, filling my nostrils with the stench of his bowels.

Rough hands grab me off my feet and shove my back against the wall. At the same time, what's left of the orderlies lift Matty off the floor.

My gaze shoots across the hospital room, where a pair of Galliano guards are trying to manhandle Rosalind out of the door.

"Stop," I croak.

They ignore me.

"No," I roar.

One of them glances over my shoulder and sneers, still trying to wrestle Rosalind out of the door. I turn around and lock gazes with Tommy Galliano.

It's been a lifetime since I've seen that demon. His wavy gray hair is slicked back, revealing eyes the same shade as mine. This is the bastard who took Mom away from us and married her, only for her to perish under the blade of a plastic surgeon.

If I don't put a lid on my murderous resentment, Rosalind will go up in flames. I've seen a man burn to death, that's not a fate I want for the woman I love.

"Rosalind belongs to me," I say through clenched teeth. "You want me to join your organization, then I get to keep her."

Tommy turns to the guards, who are halfway out the door. "Manny, Gino. Bring back the girl." He turns back to me with narrowed eyes. "You're leaving your brothers to save this treacherous cunt?"

My nostrils flare. Nobody gets to call Rosalind names and keep their balls, but we're outmatched, outnumbered, outgunned.

Rosalind's gaze burns the side of my face. I never told her the reason Matty Galliano wanted to create a rift between me and my family. Instead, I let her assume all those attacks were because of a turf war.

"That's right," I reply through clenched teeth. "I won't join your family without Rosalind."

I hear her gasp over the sound of grunts and groans and the pounding of my pulse, but I can't meet her gaze. Not while knowing I share blood with the man who abused her as a child and got her pregnant.

Tommy's face stretches into the sinister grin Mom always told me to get under control. Now, I understand why. In this man's features, I see an older version of myself with a face caked in dark makeup which I can only assume hides burn scars.

Matty groans from the hospital bed on the other side of the room. "What happened to my Miriam? What did she do with my little girl?"

My gaze flicks to the creature that I can no longer deny is my father, and I shudder. Miriam must be Miranda.

"Good question," Tommy says, the corner of his eyes crinkling. He swings around to where the guards are holding Rosalind. "Where's my niece?"

Rosalind spits at him.

Tommy lurches toward her and slaps her hard across the face, which earns him a kick that he only narrowly dodges. He turns to me, his eyes dancing with madness. "I can get you better whores. Ones that aren't so belligerent, although I hear she's a tiger in bed."

Something inside me snaps.

"Keep your mouth shut!" I break free from the guards and rush at Tommy, catching him off guard. My hands wrap around his throat. I slam my head into his face before a small army of guards hoist me off my feet.

A fist lands my jaw, making my head snap to the side. Another finds its way to my gut with double the amount of force. I double over, gasping for breath, my eyes watering, my ears ringing with Tommy's manic laughter.

One day, I will cut out that bastard's tongue and stick it up his rectum.

"Tommy, stop antagonizing the kids," Matty groans.

"Look at me, boy," Tommy says, ignoring his brother.

One of the assholes at my back grabs a fistful of my hair and yanks up my head, forcing our gazes to meet.

I'm no fan of comics, but if you lighten the tan makeup to white and smear that filthy mouth with blood, Tommy Galliano would make a perfect Joker.

Jigsaw puzzles click into place somewhere in the recesses of my mind. Mom's coddling, her insistence that I go to medical school, her believing I killed my rabbit, Dr. Brunelli's pseudo psychology... They were afraid I would turn into a maniac like Tommy Galliano.

"Tell me where to find my baby niece, or I'll kill Rosalind," Tommy says, baring unnaturally white teeth.

At her pained whimper. I turn to meet her hazel eyes. Eyes that plead for me to stay quiet. Eyes that are prepared to suffer any amount of humiliation and torment to keep Miranda safe.

Eyes that glisten with tears, while her forehead breaks out in sweat.

Tommy prances across the room and holds a gun to Rosalind's temple. "It's an easy enough decision," he says, his manic smile softening to something he probably thinks is benevolent. "Save the mother's life by reuniting a lonely little girl with her daddy."

Who happens to be a pedophile.

I leave that part unspoken because Tommy Galliano is the type of man who would pull the trigger out of spite.

Rosalind's features turn blank. It's the same expression she used to make when I had her on my torture table. Chills run down my spine and the backs of my eyes burn. The only difference between this deranged psychopath and me is age, and that I don't need to hide my face behind layers of makeup.

He turns off the safety with a click.

"Come on, boy," he says, his voice coaxing. "Tell us where to find little Miri."

Blood pounds through my temples. I stare into Rosalind's eyes, noting the subtle shake of her head.

"Kill her and you may as well kill me," I snarl.

Tommy points the gun at my head. "Now."

"No," Matty croaks. "Not my boy. Not my heir."

Tommy throws his head back and releases a crowing laugh, his bent arms flapping like a rooster. This man is completely fucked in the head.

I clench my teeth, imagining him making that fucking noise on my operating table as I slice him open with a number 20 scalpel before making him eat his own entrails.

The door opens and a deep voice says, "Is this a bad time, Mr. Galliano?"

"Come in," Matty says.

"Clear some space for the good doctor," Tommy roars.

The guards step aside, leaving dead bodies still sprawled across the linoleum. A middle-aged man picks his way through the expanding pools of blood and corpses to reach Matteo.

"Someone please draw the privacy curtains?" the doctor asks, his voice urgent. One of the orderly rushes forward, pulling the curtains closed with a loud swish.

Tommy glances around the hospital room, his lips tightening with displeasure. "Clean this shit up."

Over several tense minutes, the orderlies drag out the bodies and one of them returns with a bucket and mop. I stare across the room at Rosalind, whose gaze never leaves mine.

She could never love a man like me with such tainted blood. My father is a pedophile who stabs innocent women, and my uncle is a deranged psychopath who looks capable of worse. The Galliano family is a cesspool of depravity and needs to go up in flames.

The silence continues, broken only by the beeping machinery, until the doctor steps out from behind the curtain.

"What's the verdict?" Tommy asks, his voice tense.

The doctor offers him a bright smile. "I've cleaned Mr. Galliano's wounds and replaced his dressings. He's still on track to make a full recovery."

Tommy scratches his temple with the gun's muzzle. "Get three doses of benzo and give one to my brother."

"Sir?" the doctor's features shutter.

"Benzo," Tommy barks. "Now."

Flinching, the doctor darts past the wall lined with guards and out of the room, letting the door click shut.

"You sure about this, Dad?" asks a large man with features similar to Tommy's. "We're running low—"

"Don't question me in front of the help," Tommy snaps.

The son bows his head, his shoulders tensing. I glance around the room, noting that all the other faces harden at being referred to as servants. It looks like Tommy and his brother run their organization like a fiefdom with the two of them as the lords of a manner, while we run ours like a family.

More importantly, what is benzo and why does it sound so familiar?

The doctor returns with two vials and disappears around the curtain, presumably to administer the dose to Matteo. Seconds later, there's an audible sigh, and the doctor reemerges with the second dose.

Tommy grunts his approval. "Now inject the bitch."

Alarm kicks me in the chest, and I lurch forward. "No."

The guards grab my arms and shove me back, while the ones restraining Rosalind tighten their grips.

She thrashes, but they're too strong. She kicks out at the approaching doctor, but he side-steps.

"Take her from behind," Tommy drawls, almost sounding bored. "If memory serves, my brother had to do her from behind after she put on all that weight."

His taunting words ignite a rage that burns hotter than a funeral pyre. I thrash within the guards' hold, swearing that one day, I rip off his skin.

As the doctor approaches Rosalind from behind with the syringe, I finally remember where I first heard about Benzo. It's the formula Tommy forced Dr. Cortese and her team to manufacture. The drug he would test on her son, Christian. The one Dr. Cortese said was more addictive than crack.

Fuck.

He's trying to turn Rosalind into an addict.

NINETY-FIVE

ROSALIND

Any relief I might feel from the change in subject fades the moment Tommaso orders the doctor to inject me with benzo. I scour my knowledge of drugs but can only dredge up a class of psychoactive drugs people use as sedatives.

It can't be any of the common ones that come under that category like Valium or Xanax because no hospital or mafia organization could run low on something so widely manufactured. I can only assume it's a custom formulation.

"Touch her and I'll kill every single motherfucker in this hospital," Cesare yells.

"This is for your own good, boy," Tommaso mutters.

"Get away from me," I scream, even though it's futile.

I thrash and kick against the iron grip of my captors, but one of them delivers a blow to the side of my head, filling my vision with sparks. As I struggle to regain my senses, a needle slides into my carotid artery with a cold sting, flooding my veins with a numbing coolness that makes the edges of my vision blur.

This feels like Dr. Daniel's drug, only I'm not entirely paralyzed. Euphoria spreads through my senses, drowning out the fury at yet another violation.

Tommaso's vile words echo in my ears as I struggle to remain conscious, his manic laughter slicing through my haze like shards of glass. As the drug takes hold and my body goes limp, a sense of bliss engulfs my despair.

I'm back where I started. Powerless within the grip of a Galliano. And if one of us breaks, they'll claw back the one person I would die to protect.

Tommaso's voice floats into my consciousness. "Take her to the mansion."

"Give her to me or say goodbye to our alliance," Cesare snarls.

Tommaso falls silent for several heartbeats. "Are you sure you want this one, Cesare? She's used-up. By the time my brother got tired of her, she was a no-limits whore."

My reaction is dulled by the drug, but Cesare's roar of anger penetrates my brain fog.

"The next time you insult her, I will tear out your tongue," he yells.

"Call your brothers," Tommaso snaps.

"What?" Cesare asks.

"Tell them you defect, and I'll give you the slut."

The patterns shift in my vision, accompanied by the shuffle of feet. Maybe Cesare is trying to break free from the guard's hold to get to me, but the movements make the air vibrate.

"I'll call them," Cesare hisses.

"On speaker."

My mind is a whirlpool, but I cling onto the words like a lifeline. When the call to Roman goes to voicemail, Tommaso's cackles fill the air with unpleasant shockwaves. Shit. Now, my mind is interpreting sounds into physical touch.

"Emberly left Roman tied to a bondage table. He's probably already filled the dungeon with his piss and shit."

Confusion pulses through my veins in time with my slowing heartbeat. Was that an auditory hallucination or Tommaso's idea of a joke?

My head lolls to the side, and I'm about to drift away when I hear Benito's voice.

"Where have you been?" he grinds out. "Have you seen Roman?"

Whatever Cesare is about to say is cut off as someone on the other side of the room retches. The sound feels like cockroaches skittering across my skin, their skin legs trying to invade my throat. Judging by the cacophony of concerned shouts and stampeding feet, I can only assume that Matteo is reacting badly to all the excitement.

Good. I hope he dies.

"Call the doctor," Tommaso roars.

"What about Cesare, Dad?" asks a voice.

"Take him and Rosalind to the special guest room," Tommaso says.

The men holding my shoulders shove me forward, and I fall into familiar arms.

"I've got you," Cesare murmurs into my ear, his voice carrying no judgment for all the terrible things I endured with Matteo. "No matter what, I'll keep you and Miranda safe."

My heart swells, and my conciseness gives way to an overwhelming sense of bliss. When Cesare scoops me up into his arms and lays my head against his chest, I believe he'll do everything in his power to protect Miranda and me.

I part my lips to tell him to focus on helping Miranda, but my mouth won't form the words.

The sounds of chaos blend together and fade into the background like a thunderstorm. I'm still struggling against the effect of the drug when the phone in the back of my denim skirt buzzes.

"What's that?" says a rough voice.

Large hands paw at my ass, forcing me back to awareness.

Cesare jerks to the side. "Don't touch her."

"Get real," a male voice sneers. "No one wants Uncle Matty's sloppy seconds."

If I had control over my jaw, it would clench. This must be Tommaso's son, Francesco, one of the few people who knew what his uncle was doing, but had the nerve to swear to my mother that *I* was the liar.

Jerking movements jostle me like a rag doll, even though he's clutching me to his chest. "I told you not to insult Rosalind."

"Got it!"

"Who's calling her?" Tommaso yells from the other side of the room.

"Miranda," says the snide voice.

Cesare stiffens, and my stomach drops. Matteo and Tommaso only know Miranda as Miriam, but it won't take them long to realize the caller is my daughter.

"Put it on speakerphone," Tommaso says, "And everyone shut the fuck up."

My heart sinks as the room falls silent.

"Rosalind, it's Gunther," says a slimy voice that makes my stomach churn.

Cesare tenses, his chest falling still.

"I know you didn't die in the explosion. I also know you're not a Montesano hostage. Dr. Daniel told me they're letting you run around, so I can only assume you're responsible for the crater Roman Montesano made of HQ."

Cesare's pulse quickens, resounding in my ear like a drumroll. How the hell did Gunther survive the attack? He's supposed to be dead, having watched the graduation run somewhere on the lower levels.

"Montesano's antics got me demoted. Thanks to him, I was cast out of the senior management team and sent to handle the losers who failed to graduate. With them all dead, I'm now the highest-ranking member of the Moirai." He releases a gleeful laugh.

"Who the fuck is that?" Tommaso asks.

"An incompetent bastard who needs to die," Cesare mutters.

He's missing the point. Everyone has forgotten the most important thing Gunther hasn't yet mentioned.

Why is he ringing me from my little girl's phone?

"Let me get straight to the point," he snarls. "Deliver your carcass to Warehouse 47 or I will turn Miranda into a Lolita assassin."

I inhale a shallow gasp, and the world goes black.

NINETY-SIX

CESARE

I lie naked on a mattress on the floor, spooned behind Rosalind's nude form. My body heat is the only thing keeping her from freezing to death, since they've put the air conditioning on full blast. We're in a windowless basement cell with illumination coming from chinks of light beneath the door.

Tommy's son and an entourage of lackeys bundled us into a vehicle at gunpoint then drove us to a hideout, where they forced us to undress.

That shit they injected into Rosalind made her too high to take off her clothes. I had to break one bastard's nose and another one's finger to stop him from touching her. In the end, they decided it wasn't worth trying to fight me and left me to undress her myself.

At least eighteen hours have passed since Rosalind's boss called with news that he's holding Miranda hostage. I don't know if it's bullshit, since Tommy hung up before he could even complete his demand.

Rosalind is at risk of hypothermia. Her body temperature after passing out suggests dilated blood vessels and heat loss. Now, she's unconscious in a freezing basement and her body temperature is dropping like a stone. She can't even shiver to stay warm.

All I have to offer her is the warmth of my body.

I run a hand up and down her cold forearm, trying to infuse some warmth into her frigid skin. She's almost blue in the bleak light, her soft breathing the only sign of life.

"Those fuckers will die," I snarl under my breath, pressing myself as close to Rosalind as I can. This is no place for her. No place for either of us.

Our only chance of getting out of this shit hole is Matty, who is desperate to connect with the children he fathered through rape. Rape is the only way Mom could have ever gotten pregnant by that monster. After seeing those two in person, there's no way she would have slept with either of them without being coerced.

Tucking my face into the crick of her neck, I try to breathe life into her cooling flesh. "I'm going to get you out of here," I whisper into her hair. "And we'll get Miranda."

Every primal instinct screams at me to rush to the door and wrench it open and unleash a roar to shatter those bastard's eardrums, but that shit wouldn't work in my basement dungeons. The Galliano's doors are even thicker than the ones Dad installed beneath our home and are bolted in four places.

I have a helpless woman to protect, and I'm desperate to save an innocent girl. The only way out of this mess is to use my fucking brain.

As the hours drag past, Rosalind begins to stir. Her breaths lengthen and deepen, and she shivers. Some of the tension leaves my body, and relief washes over me like a wave. She's warming up and showing signs of starting to thrive. I pull her closer into my chest, and with each passing minute, the shivers subside and her skin inches closer to my body heat.

"I've got you," I murmur into her hair. "We're going make it."

"Miranda," she croaks, her voice barely a whisper.

My heart sinks like a dead weight. I don't have the heart to tell her that Tommy wasn't interested in saving her daughter. "Focus on getting warm again, so we can save her."

She falls asleep again, this time a lot warmer than before. It's a clear sign that her body has metabolized the benzo. As I'm dozing off, the sound of bolts being drawn back makes me startle awake.

Heart pounding, I unravel my limbs from Rosalind's and rush to put myself between her and the door. The air grows colder, and I resist the urge to shiver.

It swings open, revealing Tommy Galliano, who has the nerve to wear a silky white robe with a cravat. Behind him is a wall of oversized men holding guns, because a cowardly reptile like him can't show his face without backup.

"Time to give the bitch another dose," he says, flashing his artificial teeth.

Two of the assholes shove me aside and amble toward where I left Rosalind on the mattress.

"Get the hell away from her." I lurch at them with my hands balled into fists.

"Restrain him," Tommy drawls.

Another pair of goons holds me back. Panic sets in as I struggle against their hold, desperate to break away from them and save Rosalind before it's too late. "I swear to god, if you inject that shit in her, I'll hold you down while she carves out your livers."

"Silence him," Tommy says, sounding bored.

It's no use. Another set of arms wraps around my neck in a choke hold, cutting off my air and forcing me to watch helplessly as one of the bastards inject her with fuck knows what.

Anguish burns through my veins like acid as the men back away from Rosalind, leaving her lying helpless on the mattress. As the bastards restraining me release their grip, the second pair return to flank Tommy, whose gaze flickers up and down my naked form.

"Why would you destroy your skin with tattoos?" he says, his lips tightening with disapproval.

"What did you do to her?" I yell, my heart thrashing painfully against its cage.

Tommy waves away my question. "Relax. It's just a little benzo to keep her docile."

"What's happening with Miranda?"

He puts a finger to his lips, his gaze darting toward the ceiling. "Quiet. I have a special guest upstairs. She doesn't need to know I have a Montesano in the basement."

My skin flushes with heat. "Tell me what you're doing about the bastard who took Miranda."

"I don't give a shit about that little bitch or the one you have on the mattress," he sneers. "And your only worth to me is your connection to the Montesano family." He twitches, as though he's allergic to silk.

"So, I'm a hostage," I say from between clenched teeth.

"You're going to kill your brothers and take over their empire."

His words hit me like a bullet to the chest, making my breath catch.

"You expect me to betray Roman and Benito?" I rasp.

Tommy leans forward, his fingers scratching the reddened skin beneath the silk cravat. "I'm not asking you to pull the trigger, boy. Just arrange for them to be in the right place, and I'll take care of the rest."

I glare into his dilated pupils, which should be constricted in the dim light. Heat radiates from his body, which could mean anything, considering I'm so cold, but the sweat beading on his forehead combined with the itching suggests he might be high.

My jaw tightens. I won't betray Benito and Roman, but I also won't allow Miranda to remain a hostage to this maniac. I've never heard of a Lolita assassin, but the image it conjures up is disturbing.

It's time to use my fucking brain and conjure up a plan to keep these Galliano bastards from destroying everyone I love. While Matty's weakness is his and other people's children, Tommy's is his addiction. And to a lesser extent, his younger brother.

"I have two conditions," I say.

He grins, his body twitching with triumph. "Name them."

"First, I want you to bring Miranda."

His features tighten. "Gunther won't hand her over unless I give him Rosalind, and Matteo doesn't need to be fixated on yet another young girl."

My stomach roils at the implication of his words, but I shove aside the sickening images and look Tommy straight in the eye.

"My demand still stands. We can keep Miranda at school, but I want my sister out of that creep's clutches."

Sister. The word catches in my throat, even though the idea of Miranda being my sibling fills my chest with warmth.

"Fine, whatever," Tommy mutters. "What's your second demand?"

It's time to take advantage of his biggest weakness. Keeping my features even, I say, "Better accommodation and stop injecting Rosalind with Benzo. I don't want her getting addicted. Because of you, Dr. Cortese refined her formula so her son doesn't need to take so much of it to get high."

Tommy's facade falters. His twitchy fingers stop their endless itching beneath his cravat, his eyes widen, and his mouth falls slack. "She... what?"

"Christian couldn't function until she modified the drug. I don't want the same for Rosalind."

"Give me his phone," he barks.

The bastard on his left stops pointing a gun at my chest for the minute it takes him to hand Tommy my handset.

"Call her." He shoves the phone into my hands.

"And say what?" I ask.

Tommy's breath quickens, and his body makes an excited shudder that makes my stomach churn. Someone needs to put this mad dog out of his misery. Him and his pedo brother.

"Get me some of that benzo," he snarls.

I clench my jaw, trying to contain a roar of triumph. Now isn't the time to celebrate. I need to stay calm. One wrong step could ruin everything.

Tommy clicks his fingers. "Gun."

One of the men passes him a pistol, which he presses between my eyes. The cold metal barrel pushes into my forehead, making my breath quicken. On the inside, I'm roaring with laughter, but I hold my features into a neutral mask.

"Call Isabella," he says, his voice cold. "Tell her to deliver all the benzo she's got to the St. Dismas Medical Center in Hamlet, New Jersey."

"She's more likely to deliver poison to New Jersey than Benzo," I hiss.

Tommy pulls away the gun, his jaw dropping. "Of course." He scratches his temple with the barrel. "So, where?"

"Locker 101 in Braye Airport," I say. "It won't attract suspicion because it's in New Alderney, but it's near enough to New Jersey for one of your men to pick it up without getting caught crossing Montesano turf."

"Do it on speakerphone," he says, his breath quickening.

I call Christian's burner phone and ask to speak to his mother. Fabric rushes through the speaker as he hands over the phone.

"Cesare?" she asks. "Congratulations. The explosion is all over the news."

"Thanks," I say with a weak chuckle. "This line isn't secure, but I need a favor."

She pauses. "What is it?"

"That special formula you make for Christian. How soon can you courier everything you've got to Braye?"

"An hour," she says, her voice tight. "Any particular location?"

"Airport locker 101?"

"On it." The phone goes dead.

"Courier?" Tommy says, his nostrils flaring.

I cock my head, feigning confusion. Dr. Cortese never said anything to me directly, but Roman mentioned that Tommy seemed more upset at the loss of her than the loss of the income he was getting through the meth lab. There's no fucking way I'll allow another innocent woman to fall into his scaly hands.

"How will I get back my Isabella?" he wails. "You could have at least ordered her to send Christian. He would make the perfect hostage."

My breath shallows at the reminder that I'm related to this psychopath in more than just blood. Kidnapping a child is exactly what I did to Rosalind.

"At this rate, Rosalind will die of hypothermia," I say, my voice trembling with rage. "Move us to a warmer room."

Tommy looks confused for a moment before slapping his head. "Right." He turns to one of his men. "Take the boy upstairs. I want him in the room furthest away from Emberly."

My jaw drops.
He's taken Roman's crazy balcony woman?

NINETY-SEVEN

ROSALIND

Tommaso ordered me injected with that drug because he doesn't want me warning Cesare against cooperating with the Galliano family. I've been drifting in and out of consciousness, caught in a battle between scorching heat and chilling shivers. It's as though my body can't decide whether to burn or freeze.

My fever dreams are of Miranda at the Moirai academy, suffering through grueling regimes and torture training. Gunther stands over her trembling form, offering her a friendly hand. He'll groom her the way he tried to groom me. He'll offer her a shoulder to cry on and ply her with special privileges before making her sleep with older men.

I can't allow that to happen.

"Rosalind." Cesare's voice pulls me out of my delirium. I try to open my eyes, but they're too heavy.

"Rosalind," he repeats, his voice steadier.

"Cesare?" I groan.

"That's it, love. You need to fight to stay conscious."

My chest is a raging furnace, and the air is so sweltering I can barely get oxygen in my lungs. Sweat coats my skin like a boiling shroud, searing heat into my bones.

"Too hot," I rasp.

Cesare pulls off a sheet, letting in a gust of air that cools my skin. "You were going into hypothermia earlier. I did everything I could to keep you warm."

"Miranda?"

"Tommy wants me to kill Roman and Benito," he replies with a sigh. "And I've agreed."

My eyes snap open. "What?"

We're in a dim room, illuminated by a rectangular window near the ceiling, letting in dappled light through overgrown shrubs and foliage. It's about the size of a small pantry and secured by a heavy door with keyholes at strategic points. That won't stop me from trying to kick it open or ram it with my shoulder.

I try to rise off the bed, but Cesare pushes me down. I've never seen him look so serious.

"You need to rest," he says. "They came in three hours ago and injected you with a strong sedative. If they hear you moving about, you'll get another dose."

His eyes are dark with worry, and his hair has come loose from its ponytail, framing his face with gentle waves. Stubble covers his jawline, making him appear much older than a man barely twenty-five. I've never seen him look so disturbed.

"We have to get out," I manage to croak. "Miranda..."

A sob catches in my throat.

He pulls me into his chest. "The Galliano brothers won't let anything happen to her."

"Only because they want to be the ones who hurt her," I sob.

His arms tighten around my back, but he offers no words of reassurance. Maybe Matteo came in earlier to gloat about what he planned on doing to my baby girl.

I've never felt so helpless. Not even when Cesare tied me to a cot and wrapped my body in bandages. I need to break down this drug, make sure they don't inject me with any more doses, and find where Gunther has hidden Miranda.

"Are they in contact with Gunther?" I ask.

"Tommy still has your phone."

"Then what am I still doing here? Gunther wants me. Tommaso needs to hand me over."

Cesare releases the hug and lays me on the mattress. I stare up into his shadowed eyes.

"What?" I ask.

"Tommy doesn't want Miranda in the house."

"Why not?" Realization slaps me in the face. "Because of Matteo?"

He nods.

A lump forms in my throat, and I swallow. While Gunther is a despicable human being, he didn't make a move on me until after I turned eighteen. But he threatened to turn Miranda into a Lolita assassin, which means he won't wait long before putting her to work.

"I asked Tommy to send her away to school." He squeezes his eyes shut. "There are so many things I want to tell you, but the room is probably bugged."

My eyes flutter shut, and I breathe hard and fast to increase my metabolism. Even if it only cuts short the drug's influence by a few minutes, that's a few minutes less time Miranda will spend with Gunther.

The next man to open the door will find himself incapacitated and disarmed.

"Keep breathing," Cesare says, as though reading my thoughts.

He intertwines our fingers, and I nod.

"I'm sorry."

I crack open an eye. "What for?"

"I had no idea we would be walking into a trap." He grimaces. "And if you knew the truth about why Matty was targeting me, you might have warned me not to go without backup."

"Don't." I shake my head. "I was also hiding secrets."

The click of locks turning in the door breaks our moment, and Tommaso barges in with a small entourage of goons in black suits. Beneath his leather overcoat, he wears a white turtleneck with matching gloves.

I tense, my weakened body quaking with fury and disgust. Tommaso pauses in the middle of the room, allowing the man holding a courier package to approach.

Cold panic explodes in my chest at the thought of its contents.

If Gunther has delivered Miranda's finger…

"Good news," Tommaso says. "Isabella sent us a shipment of benzo."

Dread slams in my belly like a roundhouse kick, and I flinch. There's only one reason why they brought that drug. I can't afford to spend the next few hours too high to function. My muscles tighten as I prepare to bolt.

Cesare rises off the bed and charges at the man holding the box. "You promised not to inject her with any more of that shit."

"Seize him," Tommaso says with a smirk.

Two men rush forward, grab Cesare off the mattress, and pin him against the wall.

Another walks to the man holding the box and extracts a vial and a syringe. He strides toward me, loading it with clear fluid.

Panic seizes my lungs as I hyperventilate, my eyes widening. "No," I rasp. "Not again."

Tommaso crosses the room, his teeth bared. "Be thankful you're not screaming in a funeral pyre, because that's exactly what I plan for you the moment Cesare tires of your sloppy cunt."

"Fuck you," I hiss.

He sneers down at the sheet covering my body and scoffs. "I don't pick my fucks from the gutter, unlike my nephew and brother."

"Don't come near me," I scream, my voice hoarse. Even as the words leave my lips, I know I'm wasting my breath.

"Silence the bitch," Tommaso says.

"Let go of her!" Cesare roars from across the room, but one of the men holding him back clamps a hand over his mouth.

The man with the syringe approaches the mattress, his face an impassive mask. I kick out as he bends over me, but my limbs are too weak to make any kind of impact.

He swats aside my feeble defense, takes my arm in an iron grip, and slides the needle into my vein. Cool liquid seeps into my bloodstream, sending shivers through my body as it numbs and suffocates my senses.

The euphoria from the last dose is replaced by a violent, all-consuming agony. Every muscle in my body tenses and spasms, making my eyes roll back into my head. I try to scream, but my voice is trapped in my throat with an iron fist of pain. Every inch of my body feels like it's being shredded from the inside out, and I can do nothing but endure the torture.

"Bitch sent us poison," Tommy roars.

Somewhere on the edge of my consciousness, I'm vaguely aware of something crashing against the wall. I think it's the contents of the courier box.

"Let's go," he snaps.

Footsteps thunder out of the room and the door slams shut.

Cesare rushes to my side and cradles me in his arms. "Get me some fucking water."

I can't even relax in his touch. Whatever they injected into me is so overwhelming, it feels like this is the end.

"We did it," he whispers in my ear, the sound barely audible above my noisy breaths. "Dr. Cortese sent you Christian's antidote."

NINETY-EIGHT

CESARE

I crouch beside the mattress, dabbing sweat off Rosalind's brow. It's been hours since Tommy hurled the courier package against the wall, leaving us with a large supply of antidotes. Dr. Cortese's drug has plunged Rosalind into a state of accelerated withdrawal, giving her a low-grade fever. In her brief moments of consciousness, she alternates from having convulsions to being barely responsive.

Tommy thinks she's been poisoned and has allowed us bottled water. I picked up Dr. Cortese's box and found strips of ibuprofen glued to its base, along with chewable ginger tablets to help with nausea. As soon as Rosalind was stable enough to swallow, I crushed the tablets between my teeth and fed them to her, mixed with water.

Telling myself to concentrate on helping Rosalind through her withdrawal is futile, I know there's no way I can escape a mafia stronghold with an unconscious woman. No matter how much I try to stay in the moment, my mind keeps drifting to Miranda.

My little sister.

Everything I've learned so far about life in the Moirai has been terrible, and knowing the man who made Rosalind's life hell is still alive and has taken Miranda for revenge....

It's unthinkable.

She's an innocent child.

Rosalind groans, pulling me back to the present. Her eyes flutter open, revealing dull irises set within bloodshot whites. The drugs have sapped her strength, and I've never seen her look so weakened, not even when she was my captive. She tries to push herself up on her elbows, but I ease her back down on the mattress.

"Take it easy." I run my fingers through her hair.

"Miri," she croaks. "You have to convince Tommaso to do the swap."

Even in her weakened state, she's determined to save Miranda. I grit my teeth, forcing back a surge of fury. Tommy refuses to set aside his thirst for power to save his own niece.

Leaning into Rosalind, I whisper, "I'm working on something, love. If my plan goes right, we'll restore you to health and get Miranda back ourselves."

Her pained whimper is a knife to the chest. I can't believe I once wanted to see this woman break. Now, all I want to do is protect her from any more pain.

"You're going through withdrawal, love," I whisper into her ear.

She grimaces, seeming to understand.

"I went through something similar. You'll come out of it, just like I did."

"Rehab?" she whispers back.

"Benito and Gil locked me in a room like this for a month and forced me to go cold turkey."

She shudders.

"It wasn't as bad as this," I add with a chuckle. "Sofia brought me different soups every day and Gil kept me entertained with horror movies."

My smile fades when I remember this was the time Matty Galliano first reached out with text messages, wanting to talk. He wasn't so pushy back then because his other children were still alive.

"They made us go through withdrawal at the academy, too,"

she murmurs into my chest. "Only there was no naked man on call to help me through the symptoms."

I tighten my arms around her and press a kiss into the top of her head.

She trembles. At first, I think it's another wave of withdrawal, but then hot tears spill on my chest. I cradle her closer, my fingers threading through her damp hair.

"I'm sorry," I whisper into her ear. "We'll get through it. She's a lot stronger than you think."

"You don't understand," she sobs. "Gunther is furious about what we did. What if he takes out his anger on Miranda?"

My jaw clenches. That thought has also been racing through my mind. We reduced his power base into a smoking crater. "He wouldn't dare, knowing you have powerful allies. Miranda had to grow up fast. She's a survivor."

The locks on the door click, breaking our moment.

"Don't move," I whisper.

Not waiting for her to nod, I rise off the mattress, making sure to cover her with the sheet. As far as the Galliano family knows, Rosalind is still under the influence of a tainted batch of benzo.

Matty walks in, holding Rosalind's phone, flanked on either side by a pair of armed men in black suits. He's dressed in a tan safari suit buttoned up to the neck with a white cravat identical to his brothers.

"Cesare, you look so beautiful naked."

Disgust ripples through my gut. I step back, resisting the urge to cover my junk. "What kind of fucking comment is that?"

"That Moirai bastard still has my Miriam," he says. "He could be doing anything to your sister."

A shudder runs down my spine at the chilling image, but I keep my face neutral.

"Tommy told me she wasn't of strategic importance."

Matty presses his lips together, his jaw tightening. It's the same expression he made when I told him Tommy ordered my assassination along with Benito and Roman. The more discord I can create between the brothers, the better chance Rosalind and I have to take them down.

"Tommy doesn't get to make decisions about my children," Matty snarls.

I nod. "So, we're getting her back?"

His eyes soften. "Will you help me make the handover?"

My chest squeezes at the thought of putting Rosalind in danger, but it's in line with what she wants and part of my plan to free Miranda while taking down the Gallianos. Sucking in a deep breath, I draw out the tension.

"I'll help, but we're going to need something to eat, as well as our phones and clothes."

He turns to the larger of his men. "Gio, pick her up and put her in the back of the car."

Gio swaggers toward Rosalind, but I step in his path. "Clothes first, and no one touches her but me."

An hour later, after Matty insisted that I give Rosalind another dose of Dr. Cortese's ruined batch, I'm carrying her out of the mansion and into a courtyard surrounded by low shrubs.

A full moon hangs high in the cloudless sky, illuminating the swathes of rolling hills surrounding the mansion. We're in the middle of nowhere, and the only route out of this deserted location is by car.

Matty leads the way with Gio at his side, their cowboy boots clicking on the gravel.

A bearded asshole named Nino shoves a gun at my back. "No funny business."

"How would you like me to stick that gun up your ass and fire?" I growl.

Matty's feet make an abrupt stop. He turns around, his features hardening into a mask of fury. "Cesare is my son, and you will give him his due respect."

Nino lowers his gun. "Sorry, Mr. Galliano."

Matty gives me what he thinks is a reassuring smile.

I'm too preoccupied with Rosalind to curl my lip at his attempt to create a familial bond. She's getting stronger. I can tell that much from the way she wraps her arms around my neck and how her muscles tense in preparation to attack.

She's triggered by his voice, but I can't let her react. They may not know she's an assassin, but they know she's dangerous. The only reason she isn't shackled or restrained is because they think she's reacting badly to the tampered benzo.

"The sooner we get moving, the sooner we'll save the girl," I say.

Matty's eyes soften, and the corners of his lips lift at the prospect of getting his gloved hands on a child.

He looks like a specter in the moonlight, a parasitical human clinging to existence, feeding on the lives and souls of innocent women. I'll make sure he dies before he gets the chance to lay those beady eyes on Miranda.

At the sound of tires rolling over gravel, Matty's attention switches to a black limo approaching from further down the driveway. It stops in front of us, and the driver hurries out to open the back passenger door.

"Lay her on the back seat," Matty says.

Nino steps forward to take her out of my hands, but I side-step. "Do I have to repeat myself? No one touches her but me."

He pauses, his beady eyes flickering with annoyance, but backs off to let me place her on the seat. I sit beside her, arranging her head on my lap, but another door swings open, and Gio presses a gun into the back of my head.

"You're driving," he sneers.

NINETY-NINE

Cesare balks at the suggestion of leaving me alone in the back seat with Matteo, but I give his hand a gentle squeeze. When he continues to argue with the guards, I crush his fingers to demonstrate my strength.

I was weak because of the drugs. The antidote, combined with my banked fury, has only made me stronger. Any shock at seeing Matteo again has faded into seething resentment. The last thing I plan on doing is fall apart.

He needs to trust that I can handle my former abuser and his henchmen.

"Fine," he growls, and I know he's talking to me, rather than them. "I'll drive."

He slides his hand out from beneath my head, easing it on the leather seat, and steps out of the vehicle. Silence extends as his heavy footsteps crunch on the gravel before he yanks open the driver's door and flings himself on the seat.

I peek through my lashes at the bulky figure entering the back of the limo, followed by Matteo and another goon. The trio settle onto the back seat opposite where I'm lying without a taunting word. By the time the front passenger side door opens and shuts, I've already taken stock of the situation.

Nino's gun is in a chest holster, while Gio's is tucked into the back of his waistband. Matteo appears unarmed, but that safari suit of his has multiple pockets. There's a divider separating the driver's compartment from the back seats, with an open slider window. I can only assume it's soundproof.

My heart pounds as the limo pulls out and sweat breaks out across my brow. The thought of Miranda getting hurt supersedes the terror of being trapped with Matteo and two men, but that doesn't stop my stomach from roiling.

I focus on my breathing, slow and steady, pretending to still be under the influence of drugs. Whatever happens, I need to stay alert. At least until we're far from where the men can call for backup.

"Give us some privacy," Matteo says.

Every drop of blood in my veins turns to ice. Years of training and the burning desire to protect Miranda keeps me from freezing.

Nino rises off his seat to slide the divider closed. My fingers itch to grab the gun off his chest, but I hold them still.

Not yet.

We're too close to the mansion and reinforcements.

The only sounds that follow are the rumble of the engine and the muted crunch of tires over gravel. Forcing back thoughts of what Gunther could be doing to Miranda, I focus on staying calm.

Matteo's phone rings, and he has a lengthy conversation with Tommaso, assuring his older brother that he's resting in his room. The two men talk business as the limousine navigates uneven roads before merging into the highway.

An hour passes, and I force my mind not to drift. Not when I'm so close to the creature who has haunted my nightmares for years—my primal fear brought to life. Matteo is the poison who seeped through my skin when I was at the most vulnerable, and burned through my innocence like acid.

"You look comfortable over there, Rosalind." His voice cuts through my concentration like razor blades.

I keep my eyes closed and my face impassive, even though my palms break out in a sweat. Most people think Tommaso is the dangerous brother because he's the most volatile, but Tommaso is only the predator you see coming.

It's Matteo that's the snake.

"I loved you with all my heart," he says, his voice breaking, "Yet you stole into my home, killed my wife, abducted my daughter, and left me with second and third-degree burns."

My pulse quickens. Matteo always had a way of making himself sound like a martyr.

"I was in that fucking hospital for two hundred and seventy-six days, not knowing if my sweet Miriam had survived the abduction."

Hot fury flushes through my veins. Did he think I had killed her out of spite?

"Boss," Nino says. "Take it easy. You only got discharged today."

"Yeah, don't strain yourself," Gio adds.

"You're right," Matteo says, his breaths ragged. "But you don't know how badly this ungrateful bitch hurt my family. Poor Tommaso and I are on opiates because of her explosives."

My jaw clenches. That's what happens to a man who gets a young girl pregnant, then hides her away while his wife walks around with silicone baby bumps, then forces the young girl to sign over adoption papers, before dispatching her to boarding schools haunted by different kinds of predators.

What I thought were self-defense classes were the recruitment grounds for the Moirai. Thanks to my mother and Matteo insisting that I spend the holidays at school, I became a prime candidate for a man like Gunther.

"You want us to teach her a lesson?" Nino asks, his voice breathy with excitement.

I hold my breath as Matteo falls silent.

"She belongs to my son," he mutters, as though weighing whether revenge is worth jeopardizing his newfound relationship. "Cesare doesn't want her hurt."

"How will he know when he's driving?" Nino asks.

"And she's still too high on Benzo to tell him," Gio mutters.

The lining of my stomach trembles, and my throat clogs with disgust. I've been through worse scrapes while gathering information for the Moirai, but this one comes with a heap of traumatic baggage.

"Aren't you curious, boss?" Nino asks.

Matteo scoffs. "She's no longer my type. But if you want her so much, be my guest."

Nino's lecherous snicker makes my flesh crawl, and my bloodstream surges with adrenaline. He rocks forward, rubbing his palms. His broad shoulders quake with excitement, making the light dance on his bald patch.

My gaze drops to his oversized hands and forearms, then travels over his huge bulk, which is barely restrained by his black suit. He's burly, carrying equal amounts of muscle and fat. He'll be insanely heavy and equally strong and will likely lack speed.

Every muscle attached to my bones tightens in anticipation of the fight to come, and I take another sweep of the back seat.

Gio leans back in his seat with his legs spread. The erection poking through his pants tells me he's waiting patiently for the show and will take his turn with me after Nino has completed.

Matteo sits immobile, still weakened and drugged from getting attacked by us post-surgery.

This won't be the first time I've taken out three men, so I know what to expect. Last time, I wasn't coming down from a cocktail of narcotics, but Miranda's life is on the line, as is Cesare's safety. I need to move fast, shoot true, and not give these fuckers the chance to fire.

"You just going to sit there all night with your tongue hanging out?" Gio asks from his seat.

Matteo snorts. "Don't leave bruises."

I force down a long, slow breath, and make my chest expand to crush a surge of nerves.

Nino lifts himself off the seat, his huge body blocking out the light. His meaty hand lands on my thigh, causing an explosion of nausea. My heart is beating so hard that I'm surprised he can't feel it from the vibrations of my skin.

His thick fingers slide up to my crotch, pausing at the scrap of lace, making me hold my breath. I can't react. Not until the moment is right.

"Why did you return her panties?" he asks with a chuckle. "They're in the way."

"Slide them to the side," Matteo says, his voice amused.

"Is she wet?" Gio asks.

"Gimme a minute." Nino leans closer, his hot breath invading my sinuses with a foul cocktail of stale coffee and garlic.

Not yet.

Thick fingers glide over my labia, and I suppress a shudder.

Not yet.

"Dry as a fucking desert."

Matteo chuckles. "She was never like that with me."

"Maybe I should go first," Gio says. "Get her nice and ready."

Nino grunts. "It's bad enough having you here while I'm trying to fuck. I don't need your commentating."

"Fine, fine," Gio mutters. "Just leave some for me."

Nino shoves my legs apart and reaches for his fly, leaning so close that the gun in his chest holster presses into my shoulder.

Now.

Panic squeezes my chest like a vise, crushing the breath from my lungs. I try to move my arm, but it's frozen. It's been over a decade since my last freeze response. Adrenaline surges through my veins. I command my fingers to move, but they won't twitch.

Now, Rosalind.

NOW!

ONE HUNDRED

CESARE

Gripping the steering wheel, I lean back in the driver's seat, straining to hear what's happening in the back. Rosalind could be suffocating beneath a pile of men, crying out for help, but the privacy screen is soundproofed, so all I hear beneath the pounding of my pulse is the engine's gentle hum.

Each time I glance into the rearview mirror, all I see is the fucking divider. My willpower is fraying. I want to snatch this asshole's gun, stop the car, and keep shooting until there's nothing left but blood and shattered bones.

I turn on the cruise control, already picturing how to disarm the driver before taking out our captors, but I force myself to stop.

My impulsive days are over. I'm a man in love. A big brother with a little sister in peril. Besides, Rosalind would never forgive me if I jeopardized the handover. She wants Miranda safe at all costs. So do I, but I want it to be my life on the line, not Rosalind's.

The GPS tells me to exit in a mile for Beaumont City, so I steer the limo toward the right lane. I need to trust that Rosalind can take care of herself, but my fingers won't stop twitching toward that gun.

A muffled gunshot breaks the silence. Before I can even gasp, it's followed by a second and a third. I pull out the cigarette lighter, only to find the asshole in the front passenger seat has already yanked open the divider and stuck his gun through its opening.

All three men lie sprawled in their seats with bullet wounds. Two are unmoving, but Matteo gasps for breath with blood blooming crimson across his suit.

Triumph surges through my veins.

She did it.

My little assassin took them out and saved the old bastard for last.

"Don't move," the bastard snarls into the back. "Now, get out from under him and check on the boss."

Releasing the wheel, I twist around in my seat and lurch for the asshole. With one hand, I grip his wrist and aim the gun toward the ceiling. The other shoves the lighter into his eye. His skin sizzles, bringing up the familiar scent of burned flesh.

The gun fires. Once, twice, three times before Rosalind's slender hand appears to wrench it from his grasp.

One shot later, and the side of my face is spattered with brain matter and warm blood. The bastard slumps into my shoulder, but I shove him aside and take back the wheel.

"You okay?" I ask, my voice still charged with adrenaline.

"Yeah," she replies. "But I don't know about Matteo."

"I want to stop the car and kiss you."

"Keep driving to the warehouse," she says. "If we can get there before Gunther, we can see if it's an ambush."

"I have a better plan."

She pauses. "What?"

"Our priority is Miranda, right?"

"Yes?"

"The diamond stud earrings I sent her contained trackers. If she's still wearing them, we can pinpoint her exact location without walking blindly into a possible trap."

"Cesare." She exhales a long, exasperated breath, as if she doesn't know whether to laugh or cry. "Thank you."

A pained groan echoes through the back seat as I'm about to take the exit. One glance through the rearview mirror tells me that Matty survived the shooting.

"He's alive?" I ask.

"Not for long," Rosalind says, her voice full of venom.

"Don't do this," Matty croaks.

Rosalind punches him hard across the face, knocking him unconscious. She reaches into his safari jacket and extracts my phone.

After making me disable the security, she navigates to the app. "She must have left an earring in Helsing Island. The other one is…"

"What?" I ask with a frown.

"A mile off St. Anne's Marina," she replies, her voice rising with alarm.

"So, he's keeping her on a boat."

She slams her fist into the leather. "Gunther knows I don't like water."

"Don't worry, love. You can wait onshore while I take the speedboat."

"No," she says.

I hold my silence, not wanting to remind her how water makes her weak. The only reason I captured her that first time when I was hopped up on that drug was because her body went rigid when I pushed her into the pool. When I took her to the yacht, she couldn't even bear to look out of the window.

But I shouldn't underestimate a mother's love. Rosalind will endure anything to save Miranda.

"Forward the location to the group chat and tell them we're escaping the Galliano brothers," I say, turning off the GPS.

She falls silent for a moment as she follows my instructions and then adds, "We should probably swap vehicles. If Tommaso realizes Matteo is trying to do the swap, he'll follow us with a small army."

"Let him," I snarl.

"Are you sure?"

"We crossed state borders ten minutes ago, and we're twenty minutes away from the marina. If he's dumb enough to invade New Alderney, then he'll start a war he can't win."

Matteo groans again. "Tommaso will come. He loves his brother."

Rosalind punches him in the throat. "He'd better hurry then, before I drown your bloated body in the Atlantic."

"Please," he wheezes.

Satisfaction burns through my chest at the sound of her fists landing on his flesh. I want to keep him alive so he can suffer for every innocent life he ruined. Matteo coughs, gasping for air, but remains silent for the rest of the journey.

My phone rings.

"It's Benito," Rosalind says.

"Put him on speakerphone," I reply.

"What's this about?" my brother asks, his voice tense. "Where have you been?"

"New Jersey. We got a lead on Matty Galliano's location, but it was an ambush."

"And you escaped?" Benito asks. "Are you injured?"

"Just a few cuts and bruises," I mutter, my insides twisting with dread. "Where's Roman?"

"Missing. He left the house with Emberly and hasn't returned," Benito mutters. "We also tracked Dad's Mercedes to a scrapyard."

I hoped my message would reach Gil or Roman, who act first in emergencies and ask annoying questions after the bodies have cooled. Benito won't make a move until he's nitpicked every detail and analyzed every possible outcome.

Tommy Galliano said something a few days ago in the hospital, but so much was happening that it slipped my mind. I glance at Rosalind through the rearview mirror. "Wake him up and see if he knows."

"Who are you with?" Benito asks.

I give him a sketchy outline of the situation with Rosalind's boss from the Moirai while she revives Matteo with a flurry of backhanded punches. The old bastard croaks out something about Emberly having left Roman tied to a bondage table in a BDSM hotel, leaving Benito to bark a stream of orders.

"Hey," I snap. "I'm ten minutes from the marina. What about my backup?"

"What's so urgent at the marina? Galliano belongs in the basement," Benito says.

My jaw clenches. He won't accept any bullshit answer. If I'm going to get the men I need, then I have to tell him the truth.

"The Moirai has my little sister," I say.

Benito snorts. "We don't have a sister."

"Did you ever wonder why Matty Galliano targeted me and not you or Roman?" I ask. When he doesn't answer, I continue. "When Mom deserted us to marry Tommy Galliano, she left me a note, saying that Enzo wasn't my father."

Benito's silence is suffocating, but the fear of rejection pales compared to risking Miranda's life. Every passing second feels like an eternity, each breath a struggle as I wait for him to respond.

"What are you saying?" Benito asks, his voice cold.

"Matty's been reaching out to me since his kids died in the Capello massacre."

"I thought you said the daughter died."

"His legitimate daughter's dead but he had another one with his stepdaughter. That's the one I'm trying to save from the Moirai."

"And the stepdaughter is?"

I glance at the rearview mirror, meeting Rosalind's gaze through the gap in the privacy screen. She nods, giving her permission.

"Rosalind," I rasp.

"The assassin?"

"Yes."

Silence stretches out for several tense seconds as Benito tries to make sense of my story. He's more likely to reply with something sarcastic than hang up, so I wait for him to speak.

"Tony and Gil have a small crew looking out for Roman," Benito says. "I'll come down to the marina with a few men, but if this is a diversion—"

"It isn't," I say. "And thanks."

"That went easier than I imagined," Rosalind says from the back seat, her voice wavering with uncertainty.

"He's hedging his bets and waiting to rescue Roman before he decides what to do next."

With a sigh, she stretches a hand through the divider and

grips my shoulder. Our eyes meet through the rearview mirror, and she says, "I know it wasn't easy, and appreciate the sacrifice."

"I would raze the whole world to death to protect you both. Miranda is my sister, and…" I stop myself before I say something she'll deny. "Let's just say, you've become equally precious."

By the time I turn onto the road leading to the Marina, the Bella Lucia is bobbing in the moonlit waters and there isn't a casino employee in sight.

My heart sinks. Did Benito change his mind about helping? I park the limo and step out, scanning the area for any sign of movement.

The back door opens, and Rosalind pokes out her head. "How are we getting there?"

"We don't know what we're walking into, so we're taking the speedboat on the left."

When I glance at Rosalind, her face shutters, the last thing she needs right now is to venture out into the ocean.

ONE HUNDRED ONE

ROSALIND

I step out of the limousine, and my ears fill with the roar of the crashing waves. Salty breeze hits me like a kick to the midsection, adding to my mounting dread. My eyes squeeze shut as they usually do when I'm around bodies of water. Memories of Gunther drowning me over and over rise to the forefront of my mind, making my stomach churn.

Miranda's out there, in Gunther's clutches. I can't afford to succumb to my phobia, so I force my eyes open. Moonlight casts an eerie glow on the black ocean, its reflection dancing on the waves crashing against the yacht.

My palms itch before breaking out in a sweat, and my heart beats so hard and fast that it might burst through my chest.

I clench my teeth and curl my hands into fists. Terror is irrelevant. Miranda is out there on the ocean, hurt and terrified and confused. I need to reach her before Gunther escalates.

Cesare places a hand on the small of my back, his touch soothing my fraying nerves.

"Wait here for Benito and the others, while I get a head start."

I whirl around, meeting his pale eyes. The marina lights cast harsh shadows over his face, emphasizing the sharpness of his jawline and the intensity of his scowl.

"You're not leaving me behind. Nothing you say will stop me from saving my daughter."

His lips tighten, but he has the good sense not to argue. "The keys to the speedboat are on the yacht. We can also pick up weapons, life jackets, and a medical kit."

"Let's go."

We run across the marina to the steps of the yacht, where the stewardess from before allows us to board. I follow him through the dim corridors to the infirmary, a sterile room with two cots and stainless-steel shelves filled with medical supplies.

After grabbing a medical bag, he opens a supply cabinet. "My mother used to come out to the ocean so we could swim. She loved the water."

I'm too frazzled to focus on what he's saying, especially when I spot a gun resting on the table. "Where can I get some ammunition?"

He flicks his head toward a door at the end of the infirmary. "Storage closet."

"Thanks."

I pick up the gun and hurry past the cots, fling open the door and flick on the light switch. Fluorescent bulbs buzz to life, illuminating shelves lined with boxes of medical equipment. The door swings shut, and I scan the small space, searching for any unmarked containers.

My brow furrows. "Where are the bullets?"

The click of a turning lock echoes through the tiny space, followed by another and another. Chills run down my spine, and my stomach plummets. I whirl around to the door and push it open, but it's jammed.

"Cesare, what the fuck?" I snap.

"I'm sorry, love," he says from the other side of the door. "You said it yourself. You can't function in water."

"Let me out," I yell, my voice rising with panic.

"Gunther wants you dead, and I won't let you sacrifice your life."

I pound on the door. "That's not your decision to make."

"Miranda's going to need her mother," he replies, so calm and even that the words sound rehearsed. "By the time you break out, she'll be waiting for you on the shore."

"Don't be ridiculous. Let me out. You can't handle Gunther. He might not even be alone."

"When I bring Miranda, I want you to tell her the truth. About you... and me," he says, his voice wavering.

My breath quickens, and the backs of my eyes sting with tears. I run my fingers over the seam of the door, trying to find a lock, a latch, a lever, but there's nothing.

"Why are you talking like you won't return?"

"She needs to know the truth. You're not the villain who murdered her parents. You're a mother willing to sell her soul to keep her safe."

"Cesare." My fingers curl into fists.

"I've finally found a way to make up for keeping you as a pet. And to show you how much I'm sorry. For everything."

My heart pounds so hard that it splinters. "You idiot. I already forgave you."

"It's not enough. I love you so much that I would lay down my life to keep you safe. You and my sister," he says, his voice breaking.

The words barely register through my fury. How could he do this to me after everything? How dare he lock me in a closet and go play hero? Rage sizzles through my veins, burning my heart to ashes.

"Stop it, Cesare. Open the fucking door!" My screams bounce off the walls, only to be met by silence.

Betrayal slices through my heart, letting it bleed liquid indignation. He's not coming back. The bastard imprisoned me like I'm some sort of princess in a tower.

"If Gunther doesn't kill you, I will," I snarl.

The lights blink off, encasing me in darkness. I fumble around for the light switch, too blinded by anger to think straight. He can't leave me here and go alone to snatch Miranda from Gunther's claws.

Gunther might not be a practicing assassin, but he's wily, experienced, and knows every trick in the killer's playbook. Cesare is impulsive, with no self-control.

I lean my head against the door and exhale lungfuls of frustration, needing to think past my overwhelming outrage. Cesare has more layers than his recklessness. That manic psychopath is his outer facade. Behind it is a man who is clever, calculating, and ahead of his opponents.

With a few careful words, he tricked Tommaso into ordering an antidote for the benzo, and he tricked me into walking into this brig. Cesare might be observant and know how to outsmart an opponent, but he knows nothing about Gunther.

I can't let him get out there alone.

Whirling around, I turn on the light and search through the boxes for something, anything, to help me pick the locks. I was so anxious to get those bullets I forgot to examine the other side of the door before getting myself imprisoned.

I'm slacking, letting down my guard because there's a part of me that's already dependent on Cesare to take care of my needs.

This isn't like me at all.

I rummage through cardboard boxes filled with pill bottles, bandages, gloves and syringes until I find a small box containing disposable scalpels.

Triumph flares through my chest, and I flash my teeth. I extract one of the metal instruments and slide its blade into the gap in the door. With rapid up-and-down strokes, I shim the middle lock until it finally gives way

Next, I attack the upper lock, working the scalpel until it snaps.

The high-pitched clink of metal-on-metal grates on my nerves as the stubborn lock refuses to budge. After piling some boxes to change my angle of attack, I finally make it yield.

With a muttered curse, I crouch low and work on the final lock, which is close to the floor. Sweat slickens my palms and trickles down the back of my neck. My body breaks out in chills. Heat rises off my skin, even though I'm still wearing a halter neck and a mini skirt.

What the fuck? I'm burning up with a fever. My joints throb, and my muscles pull on my bones like lead weights. There's no way I could have caught the flu.

Only it's not influenza. It's withdrawal.

Shit.

No wonder I walked into Cesare's trap. I can't even think straight.

It takes two broken scalpels and every ounce of concentration to get through the last lock, and by the time I push the door open, I'm shaking so badly I can barely stand.

The infirmary spins, and every fiber in my being screams for something to relive these maddening sensations. I can't face the ocean at night in the throes of withdrawal. Gritting my teeth, I grab hold of the edge of a cot to pull myself upright.

My gaze catches on a scrawled note along with a vial and a syringe.

Rosalind,

By the time you read this, I'll either be on my way back with Miranda or in a standoff, waiting for Benito and his crew.

Take another dose of the antidote before following.

Not sure how long the last one will hold off the withdrawal.

Love you,

Cesare

With trembling fingers, I reach for the needle and vial, drawing the clear liquid into the syringe. It would have taken that asshole ten seconds to do this for me, but he wanted to keep me in this wretched infirmary.

Nostrils flaring, I picture his huge dick caught in the yoke of a miniature guillotine with a blade bouncing off his shaft.

"This had better not be a sedative."

Sending out a silent prayer to the fates, I slide the needle into my skin, push down on the plunger, and release the liquid into my bloodstream.

"Damn it," I mutter as my veins fill with an icy chill.

I bend my head, my fingers tightening around the edge of the cot, and breathe hard. Within moments, the shivers retreat, and my limbs are restored to their usual lightness. I roll my shoulders, working through the aches until they fade.

Straightening, I rush to the infirmary door, only to find it locked.

Cesare is determined to keep me imprisoned in his yacht.

Twenty minutes of breaking through locked doors later, along with a five-minute detour to the armory, I'm rushing down the gangway, just as a line of black SUVs approaches the Marina. Black clouds cover the night sky, casting the place in an ominous gloom. I can only hope the vehicles contain Benito Montesano and his crew.

Cesare will pay for running off to save Miranda while leaving me trapped. Clutching the Uzi I found in an armory, I ready myself for anything.

We have more enemies than just Gunther and the Galliano family. Destroying the Moirai HQ has liberated all the operatives, but not all of them wanted to be free.

The vehicles park, and their doors fly open, letting out men in black suits who look more like athletes than the usual mafia lackey. I remain tense until I recognize the largest of them, wearing a three-piece suit and glasses.

It's Benito.

I walk toward the approaching men, my heart pounding. Benito might be Cesare's sibling, but the gun pointed at my chest combined with the lethal glare says he isn't ready to give me the benefit of the doubt.

"Where's my brother?" he asks.

"He locked me in the yacht and took the speedboat to confront my boss," I reply.

"How do I know this isn't a Galliano ambush?" he asks.

I'm about to reply, when an explosion sounds from behind the buildings, making everyone whirl toward the direction of the sound.

Black clouds erupt from the direction of the port warehouses, their undersides yellow with flames. My stomach plummets to the marina paving stones, and my mouth falls open with a gasp.

Benito's head whips back in my direction. "What the hell was that?"

"An ambush." My voice trembles. "That's where we were supposed to go and pick up my daughter, but Cesare put a tracker in her earring. The man holding her is on a vessel twenty nautical miles from the shore."

Fixing me with a suspicious glare, he turns his head toward two of his henchmen. "Slasher, Crusher. Get a speedboat."

The two men rush to do his bidding.

Benito rattles off more instructions, setting his men scattering in all directions. They're college-age—younger than the usual mafia brutes—athletic, tall, and move with military precision.

I breathe hard, still not entirely convinced that he's here to help Miranda or even his younger brother.

"These people aren't from around the mansion," I say.

He sniffs. "That's because I have my own organization."

But they also don't look like casino employees. I shove aside that thought and focus on Benito, who sweeps his arm toward the yacht.

"Let's go."

"What about the speedboat?" I ask.

"Your daughter could be on a battleship, a container ship, or a submarine. The yacht is equipped with enough long-range weaponry and surveillance equipment to coordinate a rescue operation."

Without waiting for an answer, Benito continues toward the gangway. I walk behind him, still holding the Uzi.

A quartet of men in black follow us, each armed with guns. I'm already thinking of ways to disarm them in case things go awry when gunshots ring out from the other side of the marina.

Benito whirls around. "What's this?"

"New Jersey plates, sir," says a man at the bottom of the procession.

Benito turns to me, his face a mask of hatred. "You ignored my question about this being a Galliano ambush. I guess now I have an answer."

ONE HUNDRED TWO

CESARE

I step off the yacht with medical supplies and more weapons strapped to my bulletproof vest than *Scarface*. The sea breeze whips through my hair that's drenched in sweat from nerves and running around.

Now that I've secured Rosalind behind a maze of locks, I can finally focus on saving Miranda.

But first, I need our father.

I jog to the limo and open the back door, finding Matty Galliano lying in the seat opposite his dead henchmen, his chest rising and falling with shallow breaths. The patch of blood from his abdominal wound covers nearly his entire safari jacket and matching pants.

His eyes flutter open. "Cesare," he rasps. "Have you come to finish me off?"

"You're not dying until we rescue my sister." I pull out a group of syringes I filled earlier. There's morphine for the pain, tranexamic acid to control the blood loss, modafinil to make him alert, diazepam to control his anxiety, and our special blend of meth to give him a boost of superhuman strength.

His eyes widen. "But I'm bleeding—"

"Save your excuses for later," I snarl and inject him with the first syringe.

Matty's eyes roll backward with a groan, but I don't give a shit. This pedo bastard only needs to stay alive long enough to confront Gunther.

After the fifth injection, I lift his carcass off the seat and drag him onto the dimly lit marina. It's deserted this time of the night, with only our steward waiting beside the yacht. My skin crawls at being so close to this piece of shit, but I sling his arm around my shoulder and walk him toward the speedboat.

He glances around, his breaths labored. "The drop off point was a warehouse. Where are we going?"

"Gunther is keeping her miles away from the mainland. Now, stop asking questions."

Matty's feet falter, but I march on with his half-dead weight, not stopping until I've reached the speed boat and thrown his carcass onto its back seat. As he grumbles something incoherent, I slam a life jacket over his head and fasten it around his chest.

He grimaces, his voice hoarse and strained. "Cesare, I'm in no shape to face an assassin."

"Stay put, don't piss on my seats, and stay quiet. The drugs will kick in by the time we arrive."

Ignoring his whimpering, I turn away from him to start the engine. Behind us, the steward unties the ropes securing the boat to the docks, and with a lurch we're accelerating past the yacht and into the pitch-black water.

The engine rumbles in sync with my frantic pulse. I stare out into the void, seeing nothing. The only light comes from the boat's dim headlamps and the moon's silver glow reflecting off the water.

By now, Rosalind should be out of the brig and have broken out of the infirmary. She might be too furious to trust that the vial I left for her containing the benzo antidote, but at least I've gotten a good head start.

I glance over my shoulder for signs of an irate little assassin, but see nothing but the fading lights of the marina. She's probably worked out by now that I've locked every door leading to the exit.

The wind roars in my ears as the speedboat cuts through the waves. I glance at my phone's GPS screen, confirming that

Miranda's position remains unchanged. With a swift adjustment of the helm, I steer the boat toward her coordinates.

This could be a trap.

I shut down the intrusive thought. Gunther doesn't want Rosalind back. He handed her over to Dr. Daniel because he wanted her dead. The warehouse is the trap, not the location at sea. Gunther is probably hiding in the middle of Rosalind's phobia because this is the last place she would look.

Movement from the corner of my eye makes me reach for the gun. Matty climbs into the front seat, now powered by the cocktail of drugs.

"I'm not a rapist," he says. "I didn't want to fuck your mother, but Tommaso said a beauty like hers would change my tastes."

My nostrils flare, and it takes every effort not to tear out his throat. "Talk about her again and I'll put a bullet through your skull."

"Well, I didn't rape Rosalind," he adds.

I grind my teeth. "No, you married a single mother so you could groom and abuse her child. That's just another form of rape."

"Like father, like son."

My grip tightens on the helm. Matty's taunts won't bait me into a brawl, not while my sister's safety hangs in the balance.

"That's pathetic, even for you," I snarl. "Every woman I've ever been with has been in their twenties. You murdered a few of them, remember?"

"What else could I do when you were ignoring my calls?" he rasps over the roar of the engine. "And don't act like you're better than me. My spy told me you took an underage girl to the Phoenix, and I bet that was the same one you had on your private jet."

My fist flies out, but I pull the punch before it lands. This asshole is either projecting or desperate for me to put him out of his misery.

"I had my sights on Rosalind for months," I say through clenched teeth. "Unlike you, I like grown women, not little kids."

He chuckles, the sound bitter. "What Rosalind and I had transcended age."

"Is that why she blew you up and turned you into a cockless wonder?" I ask.

The rest of the journey continues in blessed silence. All my thoughts are centered on saving Miranda. Not just for Rosalind, but for my redemption. I used her as a pawn to control Rosalind, but along the way, I found a sweet young girl I would die to protect.

Hell, I would rush to her rescue even if she wasn't my sister. Miranda doesn't deserve to be used as a pawn in someone else's game. My gaze darts to Matty, and I force down a burst of violent resentment. Neither did Tania, Allegra, or Sofia.

We approach a vessel floating in the distance. It's a forty-five-foot-long cruiser with a line of portholes along its hull. My chest tightens. Miranda is huddled inside one of those berths with her arms and legs bound. Only this time, it's not for a prank. The man holding her is more likely to put her to work than set her free.

If I can get Matty to approach the cabin from the back, that will give me the opening I need to sneak up on Miranda's captors from behind. I cut the engine along with the navigation lights. One final glance at the GPS confirms that I've found Miranda's location.

I guide the boat toward my target, adjusting the helm to the current's pull. Sweat beads on my brow, my heart pounds loud enough to alert Gunther, but I stay focused. The salty tang of the sea fills my senses as I draw nearer to the cruiser, and my anticipation mounts with every passing moment.

Only the quiet lap of waves against the hull breaks the silence until I swear there's a flash of light in my rear-view mirror. I glance toward the shore, finding only more of the ocean.

Matty rasps, "Is that the one?"

"Yeah."

"What's the plan, son?"

A shudder runs down my spine, and I grind my teeth. The only reason I acknowledge this monster as my biological father is because that makes Miranda my sister. I don't correct Matty because I don't expect him to survive the night.

"You're going to ask Gunther how much he wants to release Miranda."

"He wants Rosalind, not money," Matty says. "Give me a gun."

I turn the helm and laugh, the sound bitter. "So you can threaten Miranda's life?"

"She's my daughter."

"We both know what you do to your daughters."

He falls silent for several minutes. "Do you mean for me to die?"

Not bothering to dignify such an obvious statement with an answer, I maneuver the boat to the cruiser's stern. It's a platform at water level with steps leading into the vessel's interior. When we're within boarding distance, I pull out my gun.

"Get up and order Gunther to release Miranda."

He turns to look at me, his eyes blazing with a strange mix of terror and betrayal. "Come with me," he says. "Your plan to ambush Gunther won't work. Men can't scale the sides of boats. We're better off overpowering him together."

I turn off the safety with a click. "Take Gunther by surprise, just like you did with all those women you murdered."

"Everything I did was to get closer to you," he says, his voice breaking.

"That bullshit doesn't work on adults. Now, move."

Matty finally rises off the seat, leaving it covered in blood. I probably should have given him more tranexamic acid, but he only needs to last long enough to serve as a distraction.

As soon as he steps onto the cruiser, I steer the helm to starboard, guiding the speedboat into the cruiser's blind spot. My gaze sweeps up the white hull and pauses at a set of metal rails, and I calculate how to scale the vessel's side and catch Gunther by surprise.

This plot is high risk, and Gunther is almost guaranteed to shoot Matty on sight, but I only need a few seconds to create a diversion.

If this doesn't work, Rosalind will surely kick my ass.

I stand at the edge of the speedboat wanting to throw a grappling hook on the cruiser's railing and scale the hull. Swashbuckling bullshit like that will only cause a ruckus and ruin the element of surprise.

The waves lapping against both vessels barely drown out Matty's whimpering.

Contrary to his bullshit, there are plenty of hand and foot holds for me to scale the cruiser's side. "Just like rock climbing," I mutter under my breath, "except with the risk of hypothermia."

I peer into a porthole, finding the cabin inside empty and dark. Gripping the frame around it, I raise my leg to use it to anchor my foot. I stretch out an arm and grab a row of small bolts that allow me to shift my weight upward.

Adrenaline courses through my veins as I ascend the hull, balancing my weight on panels, grooves, and ledges, until I reach a cleat on the side deck.

Matty remains silent like a coward, not wanting to increase his odds of death by attracting the attention of Gunther. If he doesn't want to open negotiations, then I'll force his hand.

I climb up on the deck and crawl on my belly down the side of the cockpit, only rising to peer through its window to find a sliding door leading to a set of steps. At the end of the deck, I catch my first glimpse of the old bastard still clinging to life.

He's wringing his hands, edging to where I anchored the speedboat. Before he can think of escaping, I shoot a flare into the sky.

Bright red light illuminates the ship, accompanied by a loud bang. A rough voice from inside the cabin barks, "Who the hell are you?"

Matty's arms rise to the sky. "Please, don't shoot. I'm Matteo. Matteo Galliano. Your client. My brother, Tommaso, paid the Moirai—"

"There is no fucking Moirai," the man barks. "Not after some traitorous bitch sold us out to the Montesano family."

"It was Rosalind, right?" Matty gives him an encouraging nod.

I grind my teeth. He should be luring the man outside, not trying to find common ground. In a minute, he'll announce that there's a Montesano sneaking up behind him with a gun.

"What do you know about her?" the man asks.

"She shot me." Matty lowers his arms to gesture at his blood-soaked pants. "You see?"

When the man doesn't answer, he gulps. "She's in a limo being held by four of my men. I came out to negotiate for the release of Miranda."

My eyes narrow at the suggestion that Matty counts me as one of his lackeys, but I hold steady, ready to shoot the man the moment he shows the back of his head.

"You think you can come here and dictate terms?" the man snarls.

Matty shrinks away, making me think Gunther is on the approach. My heart soars when a large figure steps into view. He's wearing a bulletproof jacket and a helmet, so I aim for the back of his neck.

Just as I'm about to pull the trigger, Matty yells, "Cesare, now!"

The man whirls around and fires an automatic gun in my direction. The bullet whizzes over my head, and I shoot back. Matty charges at the man, pushing them both into the cabin and out of view.

"Fuck."

Fury sizzles through my veins. Is this old bastard trying to get the last of his offspring killed? I scramble to my feet, run into the cockpit and through the sliding doors.

At the bottom of the stairs, Matty wrestles the man against the wall, already having ripped off his helmet. He grinds against the other man, their bodies so entangled that I can't get a clean shot, so I fire at them both.

When they both fall limp, my insides tighten with regret. Matty wasn't supposed to die so quickly. I wanted him to save him for the basement.

I step over the bodies and into the cabin, where I find a small figure cowering in the corner. It's Miranda, her eyes wide with terror and tears streaming down her cheeks. My heart clenches at the sight of my innocent little sister.

"Please," she sobs, "Don't hurt me."

I slip my gun into my pocket. "It's me, love."

"Cesare?"

"That's right," I say with a nod. "We found you with the tracker on your earring."

Her bound hands drift toward her ear.

I rush toward her with a pen knife and cut through the zip-ties around her wrists. "Are you hurt?"

She shakes her head. As I work on the ties around her ankles, she asks, "Is Rosa here?"

"She's waiting for us in my yacht."

Miranda scrambles away from me with a panicked yelp, her eyes widening.

I turn to find what she's looking at, only to find Matty standing at the other end of the cabin, holding Gunther's gun.

"Good boy," the old bastard croaks, his sweaty face flushed, his eyes gleaming with naked desire. "Now, I'll take my pretty girl."

ONE HUNDRED THREE

ROSALIND

Vehicles advance toward the marina in a long procession. If I had to guess, Tommaso has tracked the location of his brother's limousine and wants to mount a rescue.

The yacht bobs, and the sea breeze blows through my sweat-dampened hair. I plant my feet on the gangway and force my stomach not to lurch.

Benito points his gun between my eyes. "Explain to me why I shouldn't fill you with bullets," he says in a voice so cold that my skin breaks out in goosebumps. "Because the Galliano brothers still haven't called off their hit."

I grind my teeth and inwardly kick myself for assuming Benito would be reasonable. While Cesare's anger burns hot, this bastard's fury is cold.

"Three reasons," I say. "Because Cesare won't be pleased to find you've hurt me. Because you're going to need a trained assassin to help you fight off those Galliano thugs. And I can disarm you and your doppelgängers, leaving you without a way to fight in the upcoming battle."

A bullet flies overhead, making all four of the men surrounding me turn their attention back to the cars. Men in black pile out of their vehicles, lighting up the marina with gunfire.

"Move." I shove Benito's clone aside with my Uzi and fire at Galliano's goons.

"Cover her," Benito yells over the sound of gunfire.

I hold back the I-told-you-so to focus on the immediate threat. Two of Benito's men step in front of me and flinch with the impact of bullets hitting what I assume to be kevlar vests.

Bullets scatter from the tip of my rifle. I sweep from left to right, sending Galliano's men scattering. Some fall to the ground, others dive behind vehicles for cover.

The air is thick with the sounds of screams and gunfire, but it's all muffled by the roar of blood between my ears. This is a waste of time. Cesare is out there alone, facing an unknown number of opponents, and Miranda is in peril.

I need to end this gunfight.

Now.

More members of Benito's crew join from different directions of the marina, and what's left of our enemies retreat to their parked cars.

A distant chop of helicopter blades echoes through the air, gradually getting louder. I stare up at the white aircraft, a knot forming in my gut as it approaches the marina.

"Is that the police?" I ask.

One of the men who gave me cover pulls out a pair of binoculars and peers up into the sky. "It's unmarked."

I turn to Benito. "One of yours?"

His jaw clenches. "No."

My heart races, my palms moisten, and I resist the primal urge to scream. "There was a long-range weapon in your armory. If that chopper heads out to sea…"

"Carver," Benito barks. "Go."

Carver sprints up the gangplank, leaving three of us staring at the approaching helicopter. Behind us, speedboats race out to sea in search of Cesare. My heart pounds so hard that its vibrations reach my fingertips.

If this is another Galliano attack, then Cesare and Miranda are in trouble.

"Cesare Montesano," a familiar voice says over a megaphone. "Release Matteo or I will nuke your yacht."

Two of the men snicker, but I feel sick. Not because I believe Tommaso has that kind of weaponry, but because he sounds high on drugs. That man is capable of any level of destruction.

We stand in silence, watching him approach.

One of Benito's men grabs at the Uzi. "I can take out its fuel tank."

"And earn us all a fiery death?" I shoulder him aside.

The helicopter flies over where we're standing and advances over the sea, gaining on the speedboats. Moments later, heavy footsteps hurry down the gangplank. It's a young man holding a missile launcher.

"Someone, give her a jacket," Benito says.

The four men all gape, their gazes raking over my skimpy halter neck, miniskirt, and heels.

"Now!"

Seconds later, I'm wearing a jacket and balancing the missile launcher over my shoulder, aiming its tube at the disappearing helicopter.

"This had better have heat-seeking capabilities or we're screwed," I mutter.

Benito stares down his nose at me like I've delivered the worst kind of insult. "The Stinger has a radar-guided seeker capable of tracking and intercepting airborne targets."

I pull the trigger before he completes the sentence, and the missile surges out of the launcher, trailing white smoke as it speeds toward the helicopter.

"Come on," I whisper under my breath. "Come on."

The helicopter veers to the right, but the missile slams into its tail, sending out a shower of debris and sparks. Thick smoke billows out from the helicopter before it also falls into the sea.

Exhilaration surges through my veins, flooding me with a rush of euphoria that makes my knees buckle. The relief is short-lived, replaced by a creeping dread that wraps around my chest like a noose. We might have defeated the Galliano henchmen, but I still need to overcome my phobia.

Benito turns to me, his brow raised. "So... You and my brother."

My nostrils flare. Is this an extension of his hostility from that awful family dinner? "What are you saying? That I'm good enough?"

His gaze sweeps down my hooker outfit and suppresses a grimace. "You're his perfect match. Just keep him out of trouble."

"Jet skis, sir," yells a voice.

I turn to the empty space beside the yacht, finding a pair of vessels barely larger than motorbikes bobbing on the water. Nausea hits me in the gut, and I sway on my feet. I hand the missile launcher back to one of his men and grimace.

"Problem?" Benito asks.

"Water and me don't mix," I mutter.

"That's why Cesare left behind a highly trained assassin," he says, his brows raised.

I stride toward the jet skis, terror mounting with each step, until my lungs can't take in any air. This isn't the time to freeze. If Gunther is out there with allies, then Cesare will need our help.

We reach the jet skis, where one of his men hands us both life jackets. Benito mounts one and holds out his hand. "You're with me."

"Thanks, but I can handle myself."

I slip the life jacket over my head. If I can overcome this fear, then telling Miranda the truth about our past will be easy. I might even stop denying my feelings for Cesare because what we have is more than just a truce. And he's more than just a spoiled mafia prince.

Benito revs his jet ski and speeds off without a second glance. I throw a leg over the second vehicle, my fingers gripping the handlebar for dear life.

Gazing out across the choppy, black waters, I force my breaths to slow. This is for Miranda. Cesare. For our little family. With a silent prayer, I punch the ignition, and the engine roars to life.

Blank terror clouds my vision as the jet ski lurches forward, and a cold spray rushes up to meet my face, stinging my eyes and nose. I blink away the seawater and focus on Benito's disappearing silhouette.

If I can get through this in one piece, I'll stop fussing over

Miranda's grades and worrying about what she eats. I'll stop pushing Cesare away.

Shifting my weight forward, I squeeze the throttle, making the jet ski accelerate. It bucks beneath my feet, surging forward like a wild horse. Wave after wave slams into the small vessel, but I hold steady. Within moments, I catch up with Benito and let the roar of the engine drown out my thoughts.

Up ahead, a procession of speedboats race toward a large motorboat, where a gray-haired figure stands on a swimming platform. His back is turned to us, but from the way he angles his arm, it looks like he's holding a gun.

"Is that your boss?" Benito yells over the engine's roar.

It takes a few seconds to work out that the man isn't Gunther, and my stomach plummets to the sea. "It's Matteo Galliano."

"I thought he was dead."

My jaw clenches. "So did I."

ONE HUNDRED FOUR

CESARE

Fury pounds through my chest with a touch of terror. It's even worse than how I felt when he confronted me at the airport because there's no plane to protect Miranda.

I push her toward my back and say, "Go back inside."

This time, she doesn't argue. With a whimper, she disappears back into the boat.

As soon as I'm sure she's safe, I turn back to the soon-to-be-dead bastard. He sways on his feet, his breath ragged, his eyes getting glassier by the minute.

"What are you going to do, old man?" I say through clenched teeth. "You going to shoot me?"

He lowers his gun. "Be reasonable, Cesare. You're my only son."

"Did you ever wonder how you lost your other children?"

He frowns. "They were assassinated. Why are you getting between me and my daughter?"

"You spent your entire life terrorizing innocent people. Fucking them over. They died because of you. You, your brother, and your twisted associates messed with the wrong people, and they paid the price."

His face crumples, and tears roll down his cheeks. This remorseless monster is finally putting together the consequences of his actions. "What are you saying? What's this got to do with my girl?"

"I want you to know that everything you've done has led to this moment. You losing the family you held dear and being despised by the children you have left."

His eyes widen, and his lips part with a denial. Before he can spew any more bullshit, I shoot him in the throat. The gun drops from his fingers, and he falls backward into the water.

I walk to the edge of the platform and look down at the face of Matty Galliano. The man who raped and impregnated Mom. The man who did the same to Rosalind.

Seeing him floating on his back, choking on blood gurgling from his mouth and throat gives me immense satisfaction.

His watery eyes meet mine, his features etched with betrayal and pain. He mouths my name, but the sound is lost to the crashing of the waves.

"Be grateful you're too repulsive to me to keep alive," I say. "Because I would like nothing more than to torture you for the rest of your pathetic life."

As he coughs out a mouthful of blood, I lean over his body and spit. "But don't worry. I'll make sure your last few moments of life are filled with despair."

———

Hours later, sunlight streams through the windows, landing on their beautiful faces. They sleep facing each other, looking like angels at rest. Rosalind shivered in the middle of the night from withdrawal, but she calmed when I gave her another dose of Christian's antidote.

My chest tightens at the thought of them leaving. I haven't slept a fucking wink, too preoccupied with engraving every detail of their faces to memory.

Rosalind has completed her end of the bargain. She helped me destroy the Moirai and take down the Galliano brothers. If she decides to leave, I will let her go because I love her too much to keep her captive.

Miranda knows the whole truth, now. She understands that I

used her as a pawn to get to Rosalind, that I'm no different from Gunther. The betrayal that flashed across her features when I explained what I had done broke my heart, even though she claimed to forgive my actions.

A soft knock on the door pulls me out of my funk. I go to answer it and find Gil standing in the hallway, with his head bowed.

"Roman wants to see you in the study," he says.

"Later."

"It's urgent."

With a sigh, I cast them one final glance, wondering if Rosalind will use this opening to wake Miranda and flee or if she'll at least stay to get her two million dollars.

My heart pounds as I walk through the hallways and down the stairs. They know. Know that I'm not a Montesano. Know that I'm a Galliano. Know I held this secret for years, living among my brothers like a traitor in their midst.

I pause at the study door, trying to push back a wave of dread, but the weight of my deception drags my stomach to the marble floor. Gil pushes it open, and I step inside.

Roman's desk is empty, and the portrait of him hanging above it glowers down at me, its eyes harsh with accusation. I turn to the sofas, where he and Benito await.

My oldest brother looks so disheveled and half-starved that my jaw drops. His eyes are bloodshot and rimmed with red, like he's spent the entire night crying. And the way he slumps on the sofa makes him seem like he's lost fifty pounds. Roman didn't even look this bad in prison.

"What's happened?" I ask.

Roman's jaw tightens. "How long did you know you were Matty Galliano's son?"

Flinching at the directness, I clear my throat. "I didn't know anything for sure—"

"When did you find out?" he growls.

"Mom left a letter addressed to me, saying that I wasn't Dad's son."

"Where is it?" he asks.

"I tore it and burned the pieces."

Roman and Benito exchange glances, probably detecting my bullshit. I would never destroy anything belonging to Mom, but neither of my brothers know how to break safes.

"If you're wondering about my loyalty, don't bother. Enzo Montesano is the only father I acknowledge."

Roman nods. "Considering Benito saw your girlfriend blow up Tommy Galliano's helicopter and you shot Matty, I'd say you're still loyal."

"Then why am I here?" I ask. "Is this about Rosalind?"

He waves off my question.

"Then what?"

"I got a phone call from Tommy Galliano's son, saying his father survived the helicopter crash and wants to speak to you."

My eyes widen. The Galliano brothers are as tenacious as herpes.

"He can go to hell," I spit.

Roman clasps his hands together and nods.

"What happened with Emberly?" I ask.

"She found out about Roman's scam and locked him up without his clothes or phone."

Benito's tone is filled with the familiar inflections of an 'I told you so', as though he predicted that situation with the crazy balcony woman would backfire. Roman shoots him an annoyed glower.

I don't have the mental bandwidth to look too deeply into their interactions, especially when I remember something Tommy muttered.

"The first night Tommy locked us up in his house, he mentioned having a guest. He also said you were tied to a bondage table."

Roman grimaces. "She already left them."

"Are you sure about that?" I ask.

"Tommy's son would have mentioned her if she was still at their house. Ten minutes with Tommy would let Emberly know she was in the presence of a psychopath. She's too resourceful not to take advantage of last night's chaos to escape. Trust me, she's gone."

I nod, not entirely convinced, but then I don't know Emberly.

Roman might be right. My brother already took her inheritance, so Tommy wouldn't need her for her money. If they had her, the Galliano family would use her as leverage to at least find out what happened to Matty.

Benito rubs the back of his neck and frowns like he's trying to figure out a puzzle. "Tommy can't have escaped that helicopter crash unscathed."

They continue speculating on whether Tommy's son was bullshitting about his father's survival, and where the old bastard might have crawled. None of these theories hold my interest.

The disgusting words Matty shared about my conception slither through my mind like venomous slugs, poisoning my thoughts. Would bringing up something so terrible dishonor Mom's memory, grant her a form of posthumous justice, or reopen old wounds?

"What do you want us to do with Matty's corpse?" Benito's voice breaks me out of my thoughts.

"We keep the body hostage until Tommy tells us what he did with Mom's," I reply. "He can also explain to us what exactly happened twenty-five years ago."

Roman deflates, looking like time he spent in captivity broke him more than the five years he spent on death row. "Excellent work, Cesare."

Benito nods. "Both of you."

Wow.

The first time neither of them look at me like I'm a fuck-up, and I can't even bask in their praise. I always wanted my brother's approval, but getting it now feels hollow without Miranda and Rosalind.

"If Rosalind is seeking employment, tell her we're recruiting," Roman says.

"Talent like hers is more suited to an establishment like the casino," Benito says.

A possessive rage turns the edges of my vision red. Clenching my fists, I breathe through flared nostrils, ready to claim her as mine.

But she isn't mine because our bargain is complete.

I couldn't imprison her after discovering she was Miranda's

mother and I sure as hell can't do the same, knowing that she gave birth to my sister.

"She wants to leave," I say, the words flat.

My brothers rise off the leather sofas. "Are you sure?" Roman asks. "She can't keep you from your sister."

"I already agreed to let her go if she helped with the Galliano brothers."

"Technically, she failed because Tommy isn't dead." Benito rubs his chin.

"She's more likely to cut off my balls if I try to trap her with a loophole."

The corner of Benito's mouth lifts in a smile.

"Offer a place in this family, working or not," Roman says. "And I want to meet my niece."

"Miranda is our step-sister," Benito says, not sounding sure.

"Our step-cousin, since she's our stepfather's niece."

I leave them both arguing about the technicalities of our family tree, my empty stomach roiling with dread. Emberly isn't the only one capable of escaping mafia strongholds. By the time I reach my room, Rosalind and Miranda might be gone.

ONE HUNDRED FIVE

ROSALIND

I cradle my baby in bed, something I wasn't allowed to do when she was born. Miranda smells of orange blossoms and vanilla, scents that I will cherish for the rest of my life. After nearly losing my daughter, I will never let her go.

Last night was a blur. My thoughts were already clouded with the all-consuming concern for Cesare and Miranda. I forced back my water phobia to cross the marina, only to find Matteo still standing, and it was like a punch to the heart.

Knowing he was on the same boat as Miranda sent my mind into a tailspin. Gunshots rang out before I could even scream, and Matteo fell backward into the sea. Seconds later, Cesare emerged from the boat's interior and spat on his floating body.

I couldn't even feel relief that he was finally dead until Miranda rushed to his side. It was only when Cesare pulled her into a hug and shielded her eyes that I could finally exhale.

She broke away from Cesare and cried in my arms, and the whole world disappeared. It was just me, my baby, and Cesare standing together in our little bubble.

We left Benito and the others to harpoon Matteo's corpse and drove straight back to the mansion. Miranda was too exhausted and stunned to talk about her ordeal, so we let her sleep. Now that she's stirring, she's going to want some answers.

"Are you awake, baby?" I whisper.

She pulls back from my embrace, her eyes still half-lidded. "Yeah," she says with a shudder. She swallows hard, her breath quickening as if she's reliving last night's horrors. "It feels like I've woken up from a nightmare."

My throat tightens. "Are you okay? Did he hurt you?"

She shakes her head, her eyes squeezing shut. "He was nice during the school trip. I thought he was a member of staff I hadn't met. I feel so stupid."

"It's okay, baby." I rub soothing circles on her back. "You weren't to know he was an imposter. But please tell me if he did something to you."

She exhales a shaky breath. "He just tied me up and said a lot of things about you. Are they true?"

Dread coils in my stomach and winds its way around my chest. There's no Cesare here to act as go-between or smooth over the bitterness of the truth. Every cowardly instinct screams at me to wait for his return, but Miranda gazes at me through pleading eyes.

Stop.

I've faced my worst fears—Matteo and the risk of harm coming to Miranda. It's time to stop delaying the truth.

"What did Gunther say?" I ask.

"That he recruited you when you were my age," she says, her voice flat. "And he trained you as an assassin."

"What else?" I ask, my chest squeezing so tightly that I can barely form the words.

"He says you were his best student and you murdered lots of people for money." She pauses, her huge eyes searching mine. "Is that true?"

My mouth dries, and I swallow back the lump in my throat. Her gaze burns through mine with a desperation that clutches my heart.

"Yes," I murmur. "I met him at an academy in New Jersey with Britt. We were both outsiders whose families didn't want us home for the holidays. Gunther offered me something I desperately needed at the time."

"But why would you agree to be an assassin?"

"There was someone I wanted to kill."

"Our parents?" she rasps, her head bowing.

"It's complicated."

"How?"

"How much do you remember from the time before I took you away?"

She shakes her head. "Not much."

"That woman I killed was…" I inhale, forcing down a surge of emotion. "Long before you were born, it was just me and my mother. My birth father died, and she married a very dangerous man."

Miranda's eyes widen, her lips parting. "So, we're not full sisters?"

"No." My throat thickens.

"That man was a monster. He liked…" I turn my head to the ceiling, my eyes stinging with unshed tears. "He was an abuser."

"Like a groomer?" she whispers.

"Yes," I say, my voice barely audible.

This is excruciating. I wanted to protect Miranda from my trauma. She's too young to be burdened with the gruesome reality of the past, but after last night, she deserves to know the truth.

"So, you became an assassin to kill him?" she asks, her voice trembling.

"Yes… No." I gulp. "Miri, I don't know how to say it."

"Just say the word," she says, her hands reaching to squeeze mine.

Miranda's grip on me is the only thing anchoring me to the present, but the weight of my secret pushes down on my chest like a boulder. I force in a deep breath through trembling lips.

"My mother didn't want to listen when I told her about the abuse. She had finally found a man to take care of us and wasn't going to let anything stand in her way."

"And that's why you killed her?" Miranda asks.

I squeeze my eyes shut, loosening tears that roll down my cheeks. It would be easy to end the conversation and say yes. To let Miranda believe I took out her parents on a revenge quest, but she deserves to know the truth.

"Rosa?"

"He got me pregnant," I say on an exhale. "Nobody listened to me, but when I started to show, they locked me away."

"Oh my god," she shrieks. "Did you have the baby?"

"Yes," I sob.

She throws her arms around my neck and hugs me tight. "Rosa, I'm so sorry. I wouldn't have given you such a hard time if I'd known they were so evil."

It hasn't registered. Not through her words of comfort. Not through her sympathetic tears. Not through her assurances that she'll help me find the baby.

"Miri—"

"Was it a girl or a boy?" she asks.

"Miri, stop," I rasp.

She pulls back, and stares at me though wide, tear-filled eyes. Several heartbeats pass before she says, "Rosa?"

"The baby was you, Miri."

The room falls silent, and her eyes round with shock. Color leeches from her pretty features, and her grip on my hands falls loose. She tries to speak, but all that escapes her lips are a pained moan.

"Miri?"

She breathes hard, her chest rising and falling with panicked breaths. Every fear I had of telling her the truth rises to the surface. She's too young, too delicate, too vulnerable to handle such a terrible revelation.

Her eyes dart from side to side as she backs toward the edge of the mattress, her features etched with horror.

"Please say something." My voice cracks.

"No... You can't. You're too young."

"I'm sorry, baby," I say.

"Why are you apologizing for something that wasn't even your fault?"

"Because you deserve better," I say with a sigh.

Her face crumples. "Who was my father?"

My tongue darts out to lick my lips. "His name was Matteo Galliano. The second-in-command of a large crime family."

"Okay," she says, with a nod. "He got what he deserved and died in a burst of flames."

I wince. "He survived."

"What?"

"He's the man who boarded the boat last night."

"That creepy old guy Cesare killed?"

I nod.

"Oh, god. How can you even look at me?" she cries, her delicate features contorting with pain.

"Because you're the only good thing in my life. I love you so much." I pull her into a hug. She struggles at first, but I hold her tight, wanting to convey that I don't blame her for the sins of her father.

"But you have Cesare," she wails.

"True," I murmur into her hair. "But I've had you for much, much longer. You're what gave me the strength to carry on, even at the worst of times. "When I sat in that horrible room, having you growing inside me was my only source of light."

Pulling back, she gazes at me through red-rimmed eyes. "Why didn't you ever tell me?"

"Because you were too young to know," I say with a sigh.

"Do you hate me?" she whispers.

"Never," I rasp.

She blinks away a tear. "Does Cesare know?"

I nod.

She chews on her bottom lip, her eyes growing distant. "Last night, that man called him son."

"That's right"

She blinks, her eyes sparkling. "So, you're my real mom and he's really my brother?"

A laugh bubbles up in my chest. "Yes."

"Is he angry?"

"Of course not." I cup her cheeks. "Cesare already sees you as a little sister."

"Are you sure?" she asks in a small voice.

A knock sounds on the door.

"Why don't you ask him for yourself?"

ONE HUNDRED SIX

CESARE

I charge down the hall and up the stairs, skidding past shrieking staff. Sofia stands at my bedroom door, looking like she's speaking to someone inside.

Please let it be Rosalind.

I stumble to a halt, panting like a dog, fighting the urge to shove Sofia inside and barrel into the room. She steps away from the door, staring at me with her brows raised.

"Miranda wanted some of the pastries she had last time," Sofia says. "I'm trying to work out which ones you gave her. She only remembers that they were crumbly."

My breath catches, and my legs nearly buckle with relief. They're still here? The darkest part of me thought Rosalind would take my absence as her chance to escape.

"It was something I took from the pantry," I mutter.

"Why don't I take her downstairs and she can choose what she wants for breakfast?" Sofia says with a smile.

"Thank you," I rasp.

Sofia pulls me into a hug. "I heard what you did last night. Thank you."

I hug back. "He took things too far when he went after you, but Tommy is still alive. I won't stop until the last of the assholes who broke up our family are dead."

"Let me take your sister downstairs for a few hours, to give you two time to talk," she says, her eyes bright.

My brows rise. Sofia knows everything that happens in this household.

Miranda shuffles out through the door with her shoulders hunched, her tiny frame swimming in my black silk pajamas. I've never seen her look so guarded. Not even on the day I abducted her from outside her academy.

"Hey," she says, her voice soft.

"Morning, love," I say with a smile.

She lowers her lashes. "Rosa told me."

I step forward, closing the distance until we're only a few feet apart. "Told you what?"

"Everything," she whispers, her head bowing.

My gaze darts toward the door, and it takes a millisecond for me to register what she's saying. Reaching for her narrow shoulders, I lean in close.

"Everything?"

She nods. "That man from last night was your dad... And mine."

I swallow hard, my chest tightening. "That's right, love. We're siblings."

She tilts up her head and stares up at me through teary eyes. "You're not mad?"

"Miranda," I say, my words choked. "I always wanted a little brother or sister, and I never dreamed my wish would come true."

A sob catches in her throat, and her hands rise to cover her face. The sight of her so upset pulls on my heartstrings, and I draw her in for a hug.

"Is that alright with you, love?" I ask, my heart squeezing.

She nods into my chest.

"Then why all the tears?"

"I don't know," she says.

Rocking Miranda from side to side, I revel in our closeness, already suspecting the reason for the tears. We have more than a parent in common. She just discovered she was conceived by sexual assault, something that's still a raw wound in my heart.

I want to protect this little girl with my life.

"So, Rosalind told you everything?"

"Yes," she says.

"Then you know you have a mother who loves you more than anything?"

Her body trembles. "I ruined her life."

I glance at the door, looking to Sofia for inspiration, but she's already slipped inside to give us some privacy. With a sigh, I hug Miranda closer and press my lips into her temple.

"Your mother is the strongest woman I know," I murmur into her hair. "And do you know why?"

She shakes her head.

"It's because she has you. When she's around you, her whole face lights up, like you're the sun. You didn't ruin her life, love. You saved it."

"How?"

"Because you gave her a reason to survive, even at her lowest. Want to know something else?" I ask.

"What?"

"I fell in love with her after seeing how she was with you."

"No, you didn't."

"It's true," I say. "Don't get me wrong. I was always obsessed, but seeing you together made me realize what I was missing. I wanted her to love me as much as she loved you."

Miranda finally lifts her head to gaze up at me with so much vulnerability and hope my heart melts.

"I'm so proud to have you as my little sister," I say.

She blinks away the tears. "Really?"

"Really. I finally have a little princess I can spoil. You're all mine."

Cheeks turning pink, she gives me a trembling smile. "I'm glad you're my brother, Cesare."

Her words fill my heart with a warmth I haven't felt since before Dad died. Pushing a strand of hair off her face, I tuck it behind her ear and smile. "So am I, love."

She throws her arms around my neck. "Thank you!"

I swing her around, my heart soaring. This is the best possible outcome. Two brothers who still accept me even though I'm not a Montesano and a bonus sister.

"Thank you for saving me last night," she says, her voice choked with emotion. "I used to think Rosa was exaggerating when she said the world was full of predators, but those men were the worst."

Setting her to her feet, I cup her cheek. "You'll never have to face anyone like that again. I'll kill anyone who even looks at you funny."

She blinks away tears. "Promise?"

"I swear on my life," I say, meaning every word.

Her eyes soften. "I knew you would come for me," she says, her voice breathy. "And I never realized how much Rosa loved me until now."

"She's not the only one, love."

We hug again, before Sofia emerges from behind the door and leads Miranda down the hallway for breakfast. I stare after them, my heart bursting with love. At the same time, my stomach roils with dread.

Miranda's affection for me was never in question, but Rosalind is another story. She's never wanted to discuss our future, but now there's no avoiding it.

I step into the room, my heart pounding, unsure if she'll choose to stay or leave.

ONE HUNDRED SEVEN

ROSALIND

I sit up against the bed's iron headrest, my ears straining to eavesdrop on Miranda's conversation with Cesare. Sofia stands behind the door with a smile playing on her lips, which tells me it's going well.

My little girl deserves the world.

Telling her the truth has been a burden off my chest. I now feel like we finally have a bond.

Miranda will probably still call me Rosa, but at least she knows that her mother didn't die that terrible afternoon. She knows her real mother moved heaven and earth to make sure she never had to suffer the same type of abuse.

Cesare walks in, clad in monogrammed silk pajamas that cling to his athletic frame. The morning sun shines through the loose strands in his hair, making them glow amber.

My breath catches, and my pulse quickens the way it did when I was his captive. Only this time, that desperate need for his presence isn't because of Stockholm syndrome or sensory deprivation or the result of a twisted power game.

This time, my excitement for him is fueled by emotions that have taken root deep within my heart—emotions I can no longer deny.

Knowing that he took time to speak with Miranda fills my heart until it overflows. She finally has a familial connection with another person I know can give her the love she needs and deserves.

He hesitates at the foot of the bed, his eyes searching for permission to approach. We didn't get the chance to speak much last night. I was too busy comforting Miranda, and he worked for hours with Benito and the others to make sure Gunther didn't have any more accomplices.

Based on a review of Gunther's phone, it turns out he was working with Dr. Daniel to capture me. When our Chief Medical Officer stopped responding to his messages after we captured him, Gunther left HQ to retrace his steps and missed the bombing.

I reach out a hand and beckon Cesare forward, my heart skipping a beat when his expression relaxes, and his pale eyes glimmer with hope.

"Tell me something," I say as he approaches my side.

He takes my hand and brings my knuckles to his lips. "Anything."

"What made you think I couldn't overcome my fear of water to save Miranda?"

Grimacing, he lowers himself onto the mattress, making it dip. "There was no point getting us both killed. Gunther wanted you dead. And I didn't know if we would find a dingy or a submarine filled with assassins."

"That's why you revived Matteo from the brink of death?" I ask.

"He was expendable, and I couldn't wait for Benito." His gaze drops to our intertwined hands. "I went out there, not knowing if I was coming back. At least if I slowed you down, my brother would track my location and bring you back Miranda. She needed her mother."

"And not her big brother?" I ask.

He smiles. "I always wanted a younger sibling to protect."

"You have one, now, and I don't want you risking your life."

Still smiling, he peers at me through the corner of my eye. "Why not?"

"You know why, dickhead." I try to pull my hand away, but his grip tightens.

"No, I don't."

He turns to look me full in the face, his eyes burning with more intensity than I can withstand. Now, it's my turn to lower my lashes.

"I care for you, alright?" I mutter.

"But it's more than that, isn't it, pet?"

"Don't call me pet," I mumble.

"I'll continue calling you that until you tell the truth," he replies.

My jaw tightens. Words of affirmation aren't my style, since they're so easily faked. Can't he tell I want to be with him because I haven't escaped? He can, which is why he won't stop prodding. He wants me to say the words.

"Okay, you're right."

"About what, pet?" He cups a hand behind his ear.

I bristle. "For fuck's sake, Cesare."

"You're too afraid to admit that you love me because every man in your life has been a disappointment, or worse. I've seen you at your best and worst, and I'm still obsessed. You're everything I never knew I wanted in a woman. You're deadly, beautiful, strong, and you love with all your heart. I just need to know if there's space there for me."

Tears burn my eyes, and I blink them back. I've shed enough of them over a man who was nothing but a monster, but Cesare is different. He's allowed me into his home and heart, followed through on his promises, and laid down his life so I wouldn't have to sacrifice mine.

Cesare broke through my defenses, making me crave not only his touch but his companionship. I love spending time with him, I love how he brings Miranda and me together. I love the way he makes me feel alive.

Life without Cesare would be bleak, so why can't I form the words?

"What is it?" he asks. "Is this because I'm Matty's son?"

My head snaps up, and I meet his frown. "Of course not. Miranda is Matty's daughter, and I love her more than anything."

He cocks his head. "So, this is because I'm your daughter's brother, and you think that makes me your stepson?"

I suppress a shudder. "You're more like a step-brother."

"Rosalind," he says, his voice a low command.

"What?"

"Stop overthinking things and tell me you love me."

My chest squeezes with emotions that have been building long before our truce. No man has ever made me feel the entire range of emotions. No man has ever awakened so much vulnerability and raw desire in me as Cesare.

There's a bond between us forged in hate and love and everything in between. A bond steeped in pain yet healed by his compassion. He's torn back the layers of my soul, gathered my broken pieces, and put them back together again. That's not something I can encapsulate in words.

"Maybe love is too weak to describe how I feel," I say, my voice thickening with emotion. "Anyone can say it, even the most callous, soulless creatures. But you awaken parts of me that I thought were dead. You make me feel like I'm home."

His eyes soften, and the grip on my hand tightens. "That's love."

"Is it?" I ask. "Because what I feel for you is bigger than just love."

His eyes soften. "If you can't say it, then show me."

"Not here." My gaze darts to the door. "Miranda might return with her breakfast—"

"Sofia told me she'll keep her for a few hours, so we can talk." He smirks, placing emphasis on that last word.

"Lock the door, so we can have a nice long conversation," I say, mimicking his tone.

With a grin, Cesare rises off the mattress and hurries to the door. The soft click of the latch sends a pleasant shiver down my spine that travels straight to my pussy.

He strolls back, his pale eyes blazing with desire, but I'm more fascinated by the long, thick cock straining though his silk pajama pants. The pulse between my legs thuds so hard and fast that its vibrations spread down my inner thighs.

"Better?" he asks, his deep voice curling around my senses and making every inch of my skin tingle.

"Much." I shift on the mattress, my skin already burning with anticipation. What is it about Cesare that makes me so weak? The answer is simple. I've finally met the one who makes me feel safe. A man who will never stab me in the back.

There are no hidden agendas with Cesare. He always communicates his intentions. And he's exactly my type. Sensitive but brash. Vulnerable yet strong. And an endless source of physical attraction.

But that doesn't mean I'm going to roll over. I love the way he wrestles me into submission.

He sides beside me on the mattress, his fingers reaching for the button of my pajama top. "Remember what I said about us talking?" he says as he pops the first button. "That was a lie, pet. I'm going to fuck so much love into your tight little cunt that you'll scream your feelings."

I grab his wrist with a hard yank that throws him off-balance. Before he can react, I maneuver myself to pin him onto his side, slide my hand into his open fly, and wrap my fingers around his hard cock.

"What are you doing?" he asks with a laugh.

"Starting as I mean to continue." I give his earlobe a sharp nip. "I like it when you take control, but sometimes I want to be the one who makes you squirm."

"Bad girl."

I squeeze him around his base so hard that he makes a choking sound. "Maybe I'm the one who wants to fuck love into you."

Breathing hard, he lets me stroke up and down his shaft and shivers as my fingers glide over the piercings around his crown.

"Sensitive?" I ask.

"Only around you," he says. "No one's ever done it for me from the moment you walked into the club. Now, let go of my cock, and kneel for me like a good little pet."

I slide my hand down his shaft and reach for his balls, weighing them between my fingers. "Maybe you should be the one kneeling between my spread legs."

Cesare groans as I give his balls a gentle squeeze. "Pets who misbehave don't get their pussies licked."

"What did you call me?" I squeeze harder, eliciting a moan so deep I feel it in the marrow of my bones.

He swallows hard. "Pet."

I squeeze harder, implanting my nails in his sac, and making his body jerk. "Try again."

"You're racking up the punishments," he says with a low growl that sends a thrill of excitement up my spine.

"Fine words coming from a man who's pinned on a mattress with me holding his balls hostage."

He flips us both across the mattress, so I'm the one lying on my back. I reach for his neck, but he grabs my wrist and pins it above my head. My other hand snakes between our bodies to take control of his balls again, but he captures that wrist in an iron grip.

"Hold onto the headboard," he growls, his eyes burning with lust.

I laugh. "Hell, no."

His lips pull back in a predatory grin, the same one that used to make my blood run cold. But now, my pulse races, and I'm heating up with lust. Back when I was his captive, that sinister smile signaled impending terror. Now, that grin holds the promise of a thrill.

Moving my wrists together, he holds them within one hand, and yanks the silk of my pajamas down to my hands to form a makeshift restraint.

"Hey, that's not fair," I say.

"Nothing about this is fair, but you're going to take my cock like a good girl." His voice is so smoky with desire that I almost lose track that I should be struggling.

Twisting the fabric, he loops the bulk of it around my wrist, each brush of his fingers on my skin creating electric sparks. I squeeze my thighs together, trying to stem the arousal. As he lashes the pajama top around the headboard's spokes, I buck my hips, trying to throw him off.

"You're not getting me so easily," I say, my voice breathy.

The legs straddling my rib cage clamp with enough pressure

on my lungs to make me gasp. Sensing the beginning of breath play, my pussy becomes slick.

When he knots the rope and gives it a testing tug, he finally releases the pressure around my chest. He stares down at me, his features grave. "Remember this, Rosalind. Good pets who stay in their cages get orgasms. Bad pets who escape get edged with no mercy."

"Who are you calling a pet?"

My protest is half-hearted because I know it's just a game. Cesare is one of the few men who respects me as an equal, at least outside of the bedroom.

His answer is to grab the front of my pajama top and yanks it apart, sending buttons flying across the mattress. My adrenaline surges, and a breath catches in my throat as he exposes my breasts to the cool air.

"You're mine, Rosalind," he snarls, his fingers trailing a path from my collarbone down to my belly button. "Mine to keep, mine love, mine to protect, mine to pleasure, mine to punish."

Shivers break out across my skin.

Punish?

ONE HUNDRED EIGHT

ROSALIND

Cesare's fingertips drift lower, tracing the waistband of my pajama bottoms with a tantalizing lightness that makes me squirm.

He circles the outline of my nipple with his thumb, making me arch into this touch. "Who do you belong to?"

"Myself," I say.

His dark chuckle sends shivers skittering across my skin, and he pulls his hand back toward my belly button. He lowers his head, grazing my other nipple with his lips. "Wrong answer. Let's try again."

"Rosalind."

He bites my nipple between his teeth, sending out a burst of shock that makes me jolt within my restraints. Before the pain can fully register, he soothes it with his tongue.

"Who. Do. You. Belong. To?"

"Cesare," I say through gasping breaths.

"Good girl," he croons, his fingers making their slow descent toward my pajama bottoms. "And who owns this pretty little cunt?"

"You," I say through clenched teeth, knowing good and well that he won't let me climax until I give him everything he wants.

His tongue traces a slow, tortuous path across my breast, over my ribcage, and down to my belly, punctuated by little nips and kisses that make me wriggle and writhe.

Anticipation makes every inch of my body thrum. I resist the urge to break free of the tangled pajama jacket, grab his messy hair and stick his head between my legs... at least until after my orgasm.

"Say it," he rasps, his fingers sliding beneath the waistband and pulling the silk fabric down my hips.

"My cunt belongs to Cesare," I say, my breath quickening.

"And don't you forget it."

Instead of pulling off the pajama pants, he twists the fabric around my ankles and ties several knots, leaving my legs bound. Eyes never leaving mine, he spreads my thighs wide and gazes down at my pussy.

"You're so wet for me, pet," he says, his voice thick with arousal. "And that cunt looks good enough to eat."

"Oh, fuck."

He trails his knuckles up my inner thighs, making my entire body shudder with anticipation. Then his gaze turns predatory.

"Lift your hips, pet. Show me how much you want my tongue."

His command goes straight to my libido, and I find myself obeying.

"What a good girl," he says with that same wicked smile.

"This good girl wants to come," I say.

He traces his fingers over my wet folds, his breath quickening as I shiver under his touch. "You said it yourself, pet. You belong to me, and I'll take what's mine however and whenever I want."

His fingers ghost over my aching clit, making my thighs tremble. I bite down on my bottom lip, trying to stifle a moan. He arranges his body between my spread legs, with my bound ankles resting between his shoulder blades, and his forearms hooked beneath my thighs,

When his hot breath fans over my pussy, I make a strangled gasp.

"What do you love about me?" he asks.

"I love the way you eat my pussy," I say.

His tongue flickers over my clit. "Like this?"

"Aaah... Yes. Just like that."

"What else do you love about me?"

"I love the way you lick me until I come."

He chuckles, the sound so giddy and rich I find myself laughing along. Another thing I love about Cesare is that we have so much fun.

"Pick something else," he says with another sharp lick.

"Okay, okay. I love the way your fingers stroke my g-spot."

He slips one finger into my pussy, the movement deliberate and slow. He explores my insides before stroking the spot that sends a jolt of pleasure that makes my breath hitch and my body jerk.

"Like this?"

"I said fingers, not finger," I cry out, my voice raising several octaves.

He sucks on my clit, shutting off my complaint.

Pleasure coils deep in my core as he teases that sensitive spot while lavishing my clit with gentle licks and sucks and nips. I lose track of the game we're playing and convulse, my legs shaking as he continues his sweet torture. I buck and gasp against his ministrations as my body teeters on the precipice of ecstasy.

"Greedy little pet" he murmurs against my sensitive flesh. "You can't get enough."

"Fuck, Cesare," I say between ragged breaths. "I love this so much."

His cruel chuckle makes every fine hair on the back of my neck stand on end.

My body shivers. If he stops, I'm going to die. Just to urge him along, I blurt, "I love the way you make me come."

Growling into my pussy, he adds another finger. "What else?"

"I love... Oh, God... I love the way you make me feel, I love the way you can turn me on with just your presence. I love how you've become the most important man in my life."

The truth in the words escaping my lips hits like a wrecking ball, making the room echo with a gasp. I never thought I'd hear myself baring my heart so openly to a man.

His eyes widen, and he quickens his strokes. "Tell me more."

"Cesare, I love... I love..." My breath hitches. I've only said those words to one man, who I thought I loved with all my heart. It's only fitting to say them to the man who filled his chest with bullets. "I love you."

He pauses, his eyes widening.

"Say it again."

"Please. Don't stop."

His fingers continue teasing my g-spot, sending shockwaves of pleasure through my core. It's so intense that the reverberations ripple through my body like a tsunami, making me writhe and shudder at his touch.

Waves of awareness crash over my senses as it sinks in that I just confessed my love. Before I can react, he presses harder, driving me further into oblivion.

I gasp through a whirlwind of raw emotions and sensations, my thoughts scattering across an imaginary current. Pleasure swims across every nerve ending, and my eyes roll to the back of my head, making me see a sea of sparkling stars.

"Say it again." His voice slices through my haze.

"I love you."

His fingers slide out of my pussy, and I cry out at the loss. Heartbeats later, he moves further up my body, so we're lying chest to chest with my ankles now resting on his hamstrings.

"I love the way your cock fills my pussy?" I say, my voice breathy yet still filled with hope.

"Fuck, Rosalind. Do you know how sexy it is to know the woman begging for my cock can kill me in a dozen painful ways?" he says with a groan.

"Fuck me now or I'll choke you with this pajama top."

He enters me with a hard thrust that jerks my entire body against the headboard. Intense pleasure ignites in my pleasure centers as his thick cock stretches my inner walls.

"You're perfect. Don't ever change," he says.

His bulbous crown brushes over that spot again, detonating explosions of ecstasy. Squeezing my eyes shut, I tighten the muscles of my pussy around his shaft, making us both groan.

"Open your eyes, pet, or I'll stop," he growls.

"Wait." My body still trembles through the shocks of my last orgasm. "Give me a minute."

He remains deep inside my pussy, his lips crashing down on mine. Our tongues intertwine, communicating the depth of our shared feelings with a kiss. I want this man to consume what's left of my heart and make it his own. To claim every inch of my mind, body, and soul.

Cesare has a fiery passion that's melted through my icy barriers. He burns the pain of my past and turns my doubts into dust. Like the phoenix, he's rebuilt me from the ashes into a woman ready to embrace romantic love.

"Move," I murmur against his lips. "Please."

Pulling back, he grasps my hips and pounds into me, driving that thick cock inside me again and again with forceful thrusts. The room fills with our combined moans and the sound of flesh slapping on flesh as he fucks me with no mercy or restraint. It's as though he's releasing an entire torrent of passion.

I buck against him, my pussy clamping and spasming around his thick shaft. Ecstasy radiates through my entire being as he continues his brutal assault, each delicious stroke leaving me breathless and craving more.

The bed creaks against our movements, and the room fills with the heady scent of lust. I curl my fingers into fists, resisting the urge to break through my restraints.

"Harder," I manage to choke out. "Please, don't stop."

"What else do you love about me?" he says, his voice breathy with exertion.

My mind short-circuits for a heartbeat before everything spills out. "You're complicated, strong, edgy, unpredictable, kind. I love the way you can touch me without even laying a finger. Most of all... I love the multiple orgasms."

"Then I'd better not disappoint."

He tilts my hips, changing the angle of his thrusts so each stroke hits that sweet spot over and over. The round ball of his piercing drags over my sensitive flesh, each slide inciting fresh waves of pleasure.

Cesare grabs my throat and squeezes. "Come for me, Pet. I want to hear you scream how much you love me while you come apart around my cock."

My muscles tense as he cuts off my breath, pounding into me

harder and harder as the pleasure mounts. Dark spots dance in the corners of my vision, threatening to engulf my entire being. I fight through the haze, wanting to hold on to this sensation.

His grip tightens around my throat, making blood rush through my ears. His deep voice cuts through the sound with a growl. "Say it."

My vision turns black for a few frantic heartbeats, then light pours in from a constellation of stars.

"Rosalind," he says, his voice ragged with desire. "Tell me you love me while you come."

My lungs fight for air as he buries himself deeper, my ears filling with his guttural groan. Every vein flushes with heat, while my belly dips with a delicious blend of exhalation and terror.

The sensation is all-consuming, saturating every nerve and thought. Pressure coils like a spring, tightening with anticipation of release.

"Now," he roars.

"I love you. Fuck, Cesare. I love you so much." The words release with a violent burst, sending out an orgasm more powerful than the last. My pussy convulses around his shaft, which pulses once, twice, three times before he fills me with hot cum.

Cesare releases his grip around my neck, allowing me to suck in a noisy breath. My lungs fill with precious oxygen, and I blink away the stars to stare into his handsome face.

"I love you, Rosalind," he says, his voice hoarse. "And I will never let you go." He collapses on top of me, his head resting against my cheek.

"Thank you," I whisper into his hair. "Thank you for loving me. Loving us. Thank you for setting us free."

We lie together for several moments, his cock still hard even after his climax. I wait for him to change position for another round, but he draws back and cups my cheek.

There's a warmth in his eyes I never saw before through the icy blue. It's like my declaration of love has also shattered through a barrier he held around his heart.

"Tommy's still alive," he says.

My jaw clenches. "We'll find him."

"That's not my point, love," he replies, his eyes shadowing

with regret. "I transferred two million into your account, and I have a man at the ready if you want two sets of ID. Just say the word."

My heart splinters, and I look him full in the face. His features are a mask of forced calm, but there's no mistaking the emotions behind his darting eyes. I see fear, uncertainty, and loss. He isn't asking me to go, merely opening the door to my cage. He doesn't know if I'll stay or flee.

"Do you think I would ever leave after opening my heart?" I ask.

He pulls back, but I slip my wrists out of the silk bindings and hold him in place.

"Cesare."

"You never told me you wanted to stay, love," he says, his gaze wandering toward the headboard.

He's right. That entire time we were holed up in the hotel, watching over the hospital, I refused to talk about what would happen after our bargain was complete. Even while we were fucking, I didn't mention a future that included him.

Cupping his cheek, I turn his face to meet mine. The vulnerability in his features reminds me so much of the boy in the photo album.

"I finally have somewhere I belong," I murmur, looking deep into his pale eyes. "Even if I'm halfway across the world, the only man I'll truly feel connected to is you."

"Because I broke your spirit?" he asks, the words halting.

My chest fills with so much warmth that the corners of my lips lift into a smile. "You broke something, alright, but it wasn't my spirt. You broke every expectation I had of men. I never pictured a future for myself, let alone a family, but you've given me both."

Eyes softening, he asks, "Do you really hate it when I call you pet?"

"Do you think I'm a replacement for your dead bunny?"

His eyes widen a fraction, but he hides the surprise with a shake of his head. "You're my lioness. Strong, fierce, and protective of her cub."

I laugh, feeling so giddy that I cup both his cheeks and arch up to capture his lips. "Fine, I don't mind being a lioness. I love being thought of as fierce."

"What else do you love?" he murmurs into the kiss.

"This again?"

"I never get tired of hearing it."

"I love everything about you, Cesare Montesano. The way you fight, the way you fuck, the way you love."

"So, you love me, then?"

"Don't push your luck."

He hauls me up, so I'm sitting on his lap. "You love me. Admit it."

"Fine." I give him a peck on the lips. "I love you and I'll never leave."

His breath catches and he wraps his arms so tightly around my back that it feels like he's trying to meld us into a single being. I rest my head against his, basking in our closeness.

Life couldn't be any better. I spent years being the victim, followed by the villain. Now, I'm the victor. From this point on, I'll be the heroine of my own happy ending.

EPILOGUE

ONE YEAR LATER

CESARE

Rosalind wipes a spot of blood off my cheek before smoothing down the lapels of my suit jacket. She wants me looking pristine for what will be my official first day as Tommy's replacement.

It turned out that the scaly bastard had survived the helicopter crash and spent the next six months deep in hiding until he resurfaced to abduct Emberly.

Roman shot out his kneecaps and went charging in to save his woman. While my big brother was on his knees begging Emberly for forgiveness, I transported Tommy to the dungeons.

That was three months ago. In that time, Rosalind and I took out his sons and his most loyal lieutenants, leaving us in charge of New Jersey.

"Perfect," she says with a smile.

I push open the door, letting out a gust of frigid air. This is our coldest basement room with similar atmospheric controls funeral homes use to preserve dead bodies. We both walk inside to find Tommy sitting in his bubble.

It's a six-foot-tall perspex sphere with small portholes for food and the tube that delivers warm air. As usual, he faces the wall, so he won't look at his brother's corpse.

My birth father's body rests on a rack, staring sightlessly, frozen in the stunned moment of his death. I almost wish I hadn't filled him with bullets the night we went out to save Miranda. I wanted his suffering to last longer than a few hours.

Rosalind was satisfied with his ending. She says the months he spent recovering from the explosions and the years of pain following that were enough to fulfill her need for revenge.

Our cousins, Aria and Elania, embalmed Matty's body and applied just enough makeup to cover up his pallor, but after a year, he looks more like something dredged up from an ancient tomb.

"You're looking well, Uncle," I say to Tommy's back.

He isn't. The bastard is emaciated and covered in scars and burns similar to his brother's. Some of them came from the first explosion and the rest from the helicopter crash. The vertebrae of his spine are visible through skin resembling a transparent wound dressing, making him look a cadaver.

"Did you find her?" he croaks.

"You told me she was buried under Jane Doe," I say through clenched teeth. "But the headstone said Jane Hoe."

His shoulders sag, and he dips his head. "You should know what it's like to be a former addict. I wasn't in control."

"I would never degrade an innocent woman for pleasure," I snarl. "Neither would I steal another man's wife and then force her to get implants."

Tommy releases a flurry of dry coughs. Normally, I would rush to change the humidity of his bubble to keep him alive, but not today. I've extracted everything I need to take control of the Galliano empire and he's finally released the location of where he buried Mom.

I'm ready to move on.

Tommy had been blackmailing Mom since he spiked her drink, raped her with Matty, and mailed her the polaroids. At first, all he demanded was the occasional secret meeting or dinner. When I grew up looking less like my brothers and more like a Galliano, Tommy gave her a choice. Either she worked in one of his brothels or gave him information about Dad.

Mom didn't realize Tommy was working with Frederic Capello to take down our family until it was too late. After Dad died, Capello planned on murdering Benito, Roman, and me until Tommy got Mom to agree to swap her life for ours.

Rosalind and I have taken everything from that bastard. We killed his brother and his sons, destroyed his brothels and broke up his sex trafficking rings with the help of Cousin Leroi, Seraphine, and their team of vigilantes.

The last will and testament we drew up for Tommy named me as the sole beneficiary of his estate. Miranda and I already inherited everything Matty owned, but I declined my share. Millions of dollars sit in a trust fund for when she turns twenty-one.

"Now, will you let me die?" he rasps.

"That's what we agreed," I say with a smirk.

Tommy finally turns around to meet my gaze. Without his usual thick layers of makeup, he looks like a living corpse. His skin is stretched taut over sharp cheekbones, and he stares at me through eyes sunken deep into their sockets like twin pits of despair.

He flinches at the sight of Rosalind, one of the many women he wronged. While Tommy didn't abuse her directly, he knew exactly what his brother was doing. I'm proud to say the bastard now has gynophobia.

Rosalind once beat the shit out of him and even encouraged him to fight back. Even after getting surgery to fix his kneecaps, he couldn't land a punch.

But Rosalind isn't his personal boogie woman.

Neither is Emberly, who pistol whipped him in revenge for the time he abducted her and threatened my unborn nephew.

Rosalind isn't the woman who stood over him while he went cold turkey and waited for the drug to leave his system, only to give him enough to restart his addiction. She isn't the one who spent hours subjecting Tommy to degradation, humiliation, and psychological torture.

"Kill me, then," Tommy says.

"I only came to say goodbye and to let you know that your empire is in good hands. You will die, but I promised someone else the killing blow."

His eyes widen. "Who?"

I turn to meet Rosalind's smirk.

With a nod, she walks to the door, letting in the click-clack of heels. Keeping my gaze on Tommy, I savor the way his eyes bulge, his lips tremble, and his face contorts with terror as each approaching step echoes through the room like a countdown to his tortuous demise.

Dr. Cortese stops at my side, dressed in black and holding a small toolbox. "Hello, darling. Your little puppy is here to say goodnight."

I walk to the door, where Rosalind awaits, giving my former chemistry professor her privacy. The air fills with blood-curdling screams, making my veins thrum with satisfaction.

Tommy wouldn't admit to mistreating Mom while they were married, but we knew all about how he degraded Dr. Cortese. It's only fitting that he dies slowly at the hands of one of his victims.

When I step out into the hallway, Rosalind takes my hand and pulls me into a hug. My nostrils fill with a magnolia scent that I'll only ever associate with love.

Discovering the truth about why Mom left healed my lingering sense of betrayal, but my heart will forever carry the weight of the knowledge that she suffered in silence.

"Are you alright?" she murmurs.

I huff a laugh. "Why would I give a shit about Tommy?"

She draws back, her fiery eyes meeting mine. Her brows arch as she studies my features for signs of denial. "Not about him. The funeral."

Exhale a long breath, trying to expel the impending sense of dread and guilt. A dark cloud hung over the family after Tommy told us the truth about Mom's supposed betrayal, and nobody has felt the same.

We ordered a beautiful memorial, but it was meaningless without knowing the location of her body. Tommy gave us the runaround, not remembering the location of her burial site or the name he put on the gravestone, so we only found her last week.

Our twin cousins arranged for her remains to be transferred into a beautiful casket befitting our mother.

Rosalind places a hand over her heart. "We'll honor your mom the right way. With dignity, respect and love. That's what she deserves."

"All those years I spent furious with her rejection—"

"Was for your protection. She wanted to shield you from those monsters," Rosalind says.

I nod, my throat thickening with regret. "If I'd tried harder—"

"Tommaso had her completely under his control. Anything else you might have done would have ruined her sacrifice. She wanted you to live, just like I would do the same for Miranda."

Warmth fills my chest whenever I think of our little family. We moved out of the mansion a few days after rescuing Miranda from Gunther and installed ourselves in a townhouse within a five-minute walk from her academy.

Miranda still has her dorm room for the days where we have to leave town for business, but most of the time, she stays overnight at our new home. We're now discussing options for where she wants to study when we move to New Jersey.

"You're right," I say, the ache in my chest lightening. "Let's thank her for her sacrifice."

We walk hand in hand through the basement, passing the cell that's become Dr. Daniel's permanent prison. The Moirai's Chief Medical Officer was a fountain of information that allowed us to track down the younger assassins and academy students who were displaced after the explosion.

We arranged for those who were old enough to go to college, where they reside in a co-ed fraternity house. A few of the academy students joined Xero's organization and now live in the catacombs. His medical staff also scanned Rosalind for trackers and removed all of them—including the one embedded in her C-section scar.

Most of the younger children have either returned to school or have moved into a group home that we sponsored. Xero and his people are tracking down the few members of the management team we didn't destroy in the explosion, who are now running for their lives.

After passing through the security system, we continue through the wine cellar, up the stairs, through the hallway, and exit through the front door into the sunny afternoon.

Rosalind squeezes my hand. "I can't wait for you to introduce me to your mom."

I smile. "She'll love you, just as much as I do."

She leans against my shoulder. "I love you, too."

As the black sheep and family fuck-up, I thought my life would be filled with an endless stream of failure and meaningless flings. I dreaded the day my brothers would cast me out for having Galliano blood. Now, I'm the don of the largest empire in New Jersey with the woman I love as my second-in-command.

Medical school was never for me. Neither was running away from secrets. I always felt like the black sheep because I was destined for something more than being the protected little brother.

With Rosalind at my side, I've finally reached my true potential. My heart is finally full.

END

ALSO BY GIGI STYX

Morally Black Series

Taming Seraphine

Snaring Emberly

Breaking Rosalind

Stalking Ginevra

Xero Pen Pal Duet

I Will Break You

I Will Mend You

ABOUT THE AUTHOR

Gigi lives with her husband and two cats in London. When she's not crafting twisted dark romances with feisty heroines and the morally grey villains who love them, she's cuddled up on the sofa with a cup of tea and a book.

Sign up for Gigi's updates at:
www.gigistyx.com/newsletter

www.ingramcontent.com/pod-product-compliance
Lightning Source LLC
Chambersburg PA
CBHW040849010826
48978CB00013BA/942